A
Plain and Sweet
CHRISTMAS
ROMANCE COLLECTION

Spend Christmas with 9 Historical Couples from Amish,
Mennonite, Quaker, and Amana Settlements

A
Plain and Sweet
CHRISTMAS
ROMANCE COLLECTION

Jerry Eicher, Olivia Newport,
Lauralee Bliss, Ramona K. Cecil,
Dianne Christner, Melanie Dobson,
Rachael O. Phillips, Claire Sanders, Anna Schmidt

BARBOUR BOOKS

An Imprint of Barbour Publishing, Inc.

Print ISBN 978-1-63409-781-9

eBook Editions:
Adobe Digital Edition (.epub) 978-1-63409-978-3
Kindle and MobiPocket Edition (.prc) 978-1-63409-979-0

Cover Photo: Doyle Yoder Photography, dypinc.com

Published by Barbour Books, an imprint of Barbour Publishing, Inc., P.O. Box 719, Uhrichsville, Ohio 44683, www.barbourbooks.com

Our mission is to publish and distribute inspirational products offering exceptional value and biblical encouragement to the masses.

 Member of the
Evangelical Christian
Publishers Association

Printed in Canada.

Contents

A Crossroad to Love

by Lauralee Bliss

Dedication

To my hosts, the McCormacks, who displayed the essence of hospitality while I was hiking the Appalachian Trail in New York and who furnished a computer so I could work on this idea. My thanks.

Chapter 1

1846
A crossroad near Waynesville, Ohio

Christ's cross is Christ's way to Christ's crown.
William Penn

The limp had become too pronounced to ignore any longer. Silas Jones grimaced as he dismounted, patting his mount on the muzzle even though frustration built within him. Examining the hoof, he found strange fluid oozing out, accompanied by the horse's nicker of pain. He grimaced at the ugly conclusion. They could go no farther.

"Sorry, Barzillai," he said softly to the mare. "I shouldn't have kept riding you after you threw the shoe." But he had, thinking the animal was as strong as iron, like the biblical name implied. Now he would pay the price of a lame animal, without the means to continue.

Perhaps it was for the better. Why did he feel the urgency to press this journey? He'd wanted to make it to Independence before the snows became too deep. That would set him up to join a wagon train next spring. But now that plan might be in jeopardy, all because of his hasty heart in desperate need of healing, like Barzillai's hoof. Silas knew the reason for his haste, but the poor animal shouldn't be made to suffer. He must give her time to heal. And hope the delay wouldn't be too long.

Silas looked up then and saw a rider approaching. The man was simply dressed in a plain black frock coat and hat. Silas frowned and shook his head, refusing to compare the image with his past. He was in Ohio after all. That is, until the man spoke.

"Does thee require assistance?"

Silas's hands froze. His heart jumped. "No!" The reply came out so harshly, even Silas was startled by it. He turned away, unwilling to have the man's appearance and holy nature penetrate his soul. He'd left it all behind, all the pain and more, to embrace a new future.

But looking at his wounded horse, Silas realized he did have a need. He must accept the man's help if he was to continue this journey. "Yes, I do need assistance. I'm looking for a place to stay. My horse went lame, and I need to find good care for her."

"Just up the road a bit is the home of the Hall family. They take in weary travelers. And the son there, George, is a wonder with horses. They will care for thy needs, most assuredly."

Silas nodded while avoiding the man's steady gaze. He was thankful the man

9

said nothing further but only offered a handshake farewell before continuing up the road. The methodic *clip-clop* of hooves faded into the distance.

Think nothing of the encounter, he told himself. *The appearance. The manner of speech. It's only a coincidence.* But he had to wonder if God had sent the man from Philadelphia, as ludicrous as it sounded. The past had followed him, even if he wished it hundreds of miles away where it belonged.

Silas wrapped his fingers tightly around the horse's reins and led the mare down the dirt road, hoping this place of refuge wasn't too far. His shoes had already worn thin from miles of walking to allow Barzillai needed rest. He should find a town to lay in some supplies, a good blacksmith for Barzillai's needs, and a cobbler to mend his own shoes. But at this moment, just the thought of a comfortable bed, plenty of food, and perhaps a strong drink to deaden the pain of the past sent his hopes soaring and the reminder wrought by the man in black to some distant realm.

Barzillai shook her head and neighed, limping from the wound on her hoof, until Silas arrived at a large manor house made of stone. It looked rather wealthy compared to the log cabins he had passed in his travels, and even those cabins that also welcomed travelers. The house reminded him of Philadelphia. It could have been set on a busy city street there rather than on its own small rise of ground, surrounded by brown grass long since withered from the change of season and a few hearty oak trees sporting their bare limbs. It did prove a pleasing sight to his weary and downtrodden soul, even if it held another reminder of a city he still tried desperately to forget.

A man about his age strode out of the barn and down the small hill. His face turned to a picture of a warm greeting, with a broad smile and large eyes that glinted in the sun's light. "Welcome!"

Silas removed his hat. "Sorry to bother you, but my horse is injured and—"

"I will gladly tend thy horse. I have a way with horses, or so people have told me." He held out his hand. "I'm George Hall. My father owns this place. We have many travelers come and stay, and I hope thee will decide to stay as well."

"I'm Silas Jones. Thank you for the kind offer."

George took the reins from Silas, and Barzillai ambled after the man as if they had known each other a long time. Assured his mount was in good hands, Silas headed for the main house, only to stop short when a young woman walked across the yard, carrying a woven basket of folded clothes. She wore a dark linen dress and a heavy wool cloak about her shoulders to protect her from the biting wind. Her dark bonnet hid most of her face from view until she turned to offer him a curious glance. She did not acknowledge his presence but instead opened the front door to the house and called for her father.

A short man with graying hair, dressed in dark clothes, came to the door. "Welcome to our inn!" he said with enthusiasm, much like the young man named George. "Is thee in need of a place to stay?"

"Yes, thank you. My horse went lame."

"George can help thee with thy horse. Please, come in and be comfortable."

Silas stepped inside the home. The interior held an aura of simplicity but was far richer than the rustic places he'd come to inhabit on his journey. Finely crafted wood chairs with attractive fan backs, a large drop-front desk, and a library of books met his curious gaze. There were no grandiose paintings or other fabrics of decorations but plenty of paned windows, allowing the sunlight to brighten each room. Fires burned cheerily in several fireplaces to warm the cold day. In the dining area, a long wooden table with benches on either side stood ready to receive a multitude of guests.

"There's talk of snow," the man said as Silas surveyed the warmth of the home. "Thee has surely arrived in time. God has guided thy footsteps."

Silas turned. He wondered if the family had anything to do with the Society of Friends, hearing all the thees and thys. Just like the talk he'd heard earlier on the road. Surely he didn't happen upon a village of Quakers. He dismissed it for now and took a seat in one of the fine chairs.

Mr. Hall disappeared into another room but soon returned with a steaming mug in hand. Silas licked his lips in anticipation of the mug's contents. Just what he needed—a nice mulled wine to deaden his senses and liven his situation. He took a large swallow of the contents and nearly choked, both on the hot liquid and on the realization it was apple cider in his mug. "This is not mulled wine," he sputtered. "Have you no brew at your inn? I've had the privilege of indulging many times on my journey so far."

"Brew? I don't understand."

"Liquor. Spirits, my good man."

"I'm sorry, but we don't serve spirits here. A good drink of the earth, like this apple cider, does well for one's soul. It will warm thee better than anything else. I trust thee will enjoy it."

There it was again. *Thee.* Wording he could not ignore. *They must be of the Friends' persuasion. . . .* Between the Hall family and the man he'd met earlier on the road, he must have inadvertently stumbled upon a Quaker settlement in the middle of Ohio. And just when he was looking to escape it. Was this God's way of forcing redemption when he wanted no part of it?

Silas stood, wishing now he had the means to leave this place. But he couldn't. Snow was coming. Barzillai was lame in the hoof. And his shoes were mere scraps of flapping leather with barely a nail attaching them to the soles. He sat back down with his mug of apple cider, feeling more and more like a small lad with his childhood drink. He wanted to spout his frustrations to Mr. Hall—that this was no inn, that the man had no business taking in travelers if he could not fulfill their requirement for fine spirits to warm a winter's night. And he didn't care to hear pious people uttering thees for the rest of the evening as if they reigned on some mountaintop while he lay snared in the valley's trap.

All of this weighed on Silas until he became distracted by the young woman he'd seen earlier. She now stood in the doorway, staring at him. With her dark bonnet replaced by a cap of thin white, he saw fine brown hair fixed in a bun. The color of the cap matched the creamy paleness of her skin, and her cheeks were tinted a dusty rose from being outdoors in the cold wind. But he saw a look of fire in her blue eyes and lips turned downward in distaste. Then with a rustle of her skirt, she left.

Silas folded his arms in dismay, knowing she must have witnessed the interaction with her father over the matter of spirits. But why should her reaction bother him? He certainly wasn't here to win her heart or any other, especially if this was a family of Quakers. Heaven knew he could not nor would he ever associate with such people again. He gritted his teeth. The Society of Friends in Philadelphia had purposely left the door open to evil. Evil came stalking like a predator and killed like one, too. And that, to him, was a grievous wound that nothing could heal.

Silas shook his head and drank the cider, feeling its soothing effects in his stomach, just as the proprietor had promised. And then something filled him. Not some false peace born out of liquor that fooled with men's minds. Rather, he felt comfort. Refreshment to a weary soul and spirit. A sense of spiritual peace, as strange as it seemed, when he'd experienced no such peace for many weeks.

Another woman walked in then, older, plainly dressed, with a brown kerchief about her shoulders for warmth and the simple white cap on her head. She carried a platter of biscuits. "I'm Mrs. Hall. Thee must be hungry, Mister. . ."

"Silas Jones, madam. You may call me Silas, if you wish." He took two flaky biscuits and hungrily consumed them. He hadn't tasted anything that good in a long time.

"My goodness, he is quite a hungry man, my husband," she said with a laugh to Mr. Hall as he entered the room. "I fear he would eat the platter if he could."

The husband told his wife of Silas's circumstances and Barzillai's misfortune.

Silas then lifted his foot to show them his worn shoe. "Is there a cobbler in town?"

"Oh dear. Look at his shoes! Simply dreadful. We can mend them, can't we, Husband? He cannot go like this with the snows coming. Or perhaps our neighbor, Mr. Warren, can help. He makes shoes."

The wife then pointed at her shoe, gesturing for Silas to remove his. When he did, his feet also revealed his wool socks, full of holes. Again Mrs. Hall shook her head and talked of knitting him some new socks as soon as possible. Silas sat in amazement, though he knew the Friends possessed a generosity of spirit. They cared for all people, believing God's Light lay within each. But that simple faith in humanity and a belief in equality among all also brought trouble.

Silas felt his fist clench then at a painful memory and fought to relax it for fear of observing eyes. Like those of the young woman who returned to the doorway with a look that bespoke a thousand questions on her mind. He would refuse any inquisition, even if the young woman was a beauty to behold.

He stood now and inquired about his room.

"Of course. Mary will show thee to thy room," Mrs. Hall acknowledged. "Mary?"

"Follow me, please," Mary said.

So the beauty with eyes like the deep blue skies above had a name, and a nice name, too. The name of the Savior's mother. He took his mug and followed Mary as she swiftly swept up the flight of stairs to a row of rooms on the second floor. "Thee may have the room on the far left," she directed.

"Don't you grow tired of your thees?" Silas suddenly remarked.

She faced him, centering her large blue eyes framed by arched eyebrows on him. "No, I do not."

"Why not, pray tell?"

"One man is not better than another, as scripture says. We are all equal."

"It's all foolishness. It brings you nothing. Nothing at all, you know. It only makes you appear vain and haughty. Or rather it makes *thee* appear that way." He ended with a scornful chortle.

"I'm sorry thee believes such things. Perhaps the description of vanity is better meant for those who believe they know what's best in life, though their hearts are dark with lies." She wheeled around.

Silas laughed. "Look at you. Haughty in your opinions, wouldn't you say? Maybe *thee* needs a little more humility and less pride."

"And maybe thee needs to show more respect for the household in which thee has found lodging." She strode down the hall and down the stairs.

So it appeared a black sheep resided in the flock, a sheep with eyes of blue fire and a sharp tongue to match. It left him speechless, he admitted, but also intrigued. No woman from the Society of Friends in Philadelphia held to such brazenness. They were all respectful and dignified. They wore the mark of a Friend as if it were a symbol for all to see and bear witness. A Light in a dark world, or so they believed. But this woman, Mary Hall, met his challenge face-to-face, word for word. No demureness or humility was evident on her part. Only fierce determination, and he feared what such determination could do to someone like him in the days ahead.

Silas rested in his room, thinking about his life and what the future might bring, until he heard the dinner bell. The pit of his stomach churned with thoughts of a hearty meal. He hastened down the stairs to see two other gents had arrived and stood in the hallway, eager to partake of the Hall family's evening meal and lodging. They were boisterous fellows, dressed in dusty travel garments, with conversation flowing readily from their lips. One sported a silver flask of spirits. Silas wondered what the family would think of the flask as the men made introductions.

"I'm Abe," the man with the flask said to Silas. "So how do you feel about our hosts? Strange folk, eh? But friendly." Abe laughed at his own pun, took a swallow out of the flask, and passed it to Silas.

"I had no choice. I was in need of a place to stay because my horse went lame." Silas took the flask and drank. He nearly choked as the potent liquid singed his throat. Then he thought of Mary Hall. She would be glad the liquor scorched him. She would tell him he deserved it and more. *It will never quench thy true thirst in life,* he imagined her saying.

Abe grinned and took back his flask. "We know they don't like liquor, but it will make the evening a bit warmer and friendlier, wouldn't you say?"

"Quite," Silas sputtered. "And do you know why they are called Quakers?"

Abe shook his head.

"Because they think they are so close to God that they visibly tremble in His sight." Glancing behind him, Silas saw Mary in the doorway, with her arms folded and her lips pressed tight. He waited for some rebuke from her, how he lacked good manners. He would meet her challenge with one of his own.

Instead, she rang the dinner bell once more and invited them into the dining room. Silas ignored the look on Mary's face and, laughing with the men, sauntered inside. Mrs. Hall had placed an abundance of food on the table. Already seated at the table was the son, George, and Mr. Hall, who greeted each of them. Mary and the mother hastened about, serving them. He caught sight of Mary's wide eyes traveling to the flask Abe had in his possession, its shiny metal reflecting the candlelight. She opened her mouth as if to say something and then looked to her father. Mr. Hall said nothing of the liquor in their presence but only sat at the head of the table and smiled.

Silas was enjoying this all very much. The food was good, but the spirits were even better. It wasn't long before the contents of the flask passed to him under the table had loosened his tongue. "Did I tell you about the Friends I met in Philadelphia?" he said to Abe.

"So thee once dwelt in the City of Brotherly Love?" Mr. Hall inquired.

"Brotherly love, sir? Ha! There is no such love to speak of. The city breathes evil, my good man. And the so-called Friends do nothing but speak their pious babble, which means little and does even less."

Mary gasped. George stared. Mr. Hall's smile never wavered as he lifted the platter to offer them more meat.

When little came of his remark, Silas grew silent. It was as if the wax had been stripped from his candle of discontent. Nothing remained to fuel the flame. Except Mary, who continued to stare at him with her narrow set of blue eyes, her nose slightly lifted in the air, and her arms crossed. He sensed no satisfaction over her reaction, just disappointment. Perhaps rightly so. This family had nothing to do with Philadelphia, except that they were Quakers. He should not brand them with his past.

Silas excused himself to wander out into the sitting room with the fancy wooden chairs. He no longer wanted to associate with anyone or drink of any flask. None of it brought the peace he sought. He only wished he could ride out of here in the morning. He glanced out the window to see a few flakes of snow drifting down from the skies. The storm foretold by Mr. Hall. Between his horse and the storm, God Himself had decided that Silas should remain here for now, perhaps to face what he could not. And that fact irritated him to no end.

"Oh Mr. Jones, thee has not had thy dessert!" Mrs. Hall called to him. "I made a good pumpkin pie. Come join us."

He offered her a small smile before quietly reentering the room and occupying his place once more at the long table. He made no eye contact with anyone, least of all Mary. In his heart he wanted to apologize to the Hall family for what was said. Or alluded to. But pride locked the words in his throat, where they remained.

Abe and the other gentleman, Thomas, made lighthearted comments as they feasted on thick slices of pie. Silas remained silent, eating the delicious pie, knowing that those around him likely wondered what ailed him. No matter. He would leave this place as soon as he could. Pray the snowstorm would amount to nothing and Barzillai would have a miraculous recovery. Anything, so long as he could abandon this Quaker home and be on his way, continuing a journey of the soul, with no real conclusion in sight.

Chapter 2

He's inconsiderate of our ways. He's conceited. He's like a wolf in sheep's clothing. We must send him away as soon as possible." Mary tried in vain to add a sense of urgency to her words. She could not ignore the feelings that rose each day Silas Jones remained under the roof of their home.

But Father would not hear of it no matter how much she ranted. "Mary, must I read to thee what scripture says? That like the Mary of old, thee must choose a wiser course, such as love and mercy and truth. Thee must sit at our Master's feet to hear His bidding. And take in a lost sheep like Mr. Jones. Thee should not dismiss opportunity. Only God knows the time of his departure, and I am glad he is here and told him so."

"But he's not of the brethren, Father. Opportunities are only for those in fellowship. We have taken in a wolf among us. I'm certain of it. I've seen it in his eyes. And we've seen and heard what he's said and done in our presence. Drinking spirits at dinner. Mocking our beliefs." She looked around. "And have we taken stock of our goods? The money jar? We ought to find a new place for the money."

"Come, come, Mary. Does thee truly believe Mr. Jones is here to steal from us? He is not the evil one. And who are we to judge his condition? Certainly not thee. Or myself. Or anyone. He has done nothing ill since he's been among us. He is but a lost soul in great need. His heart, I believe, is already accepting of God's mercy and light. And so we, too, should be merciful."

But Mary refused. No matter what Father said, she would not trust Silas Jones. Any man under the influence of strong drink, with contempt for others, mocking even the most sacred things, such as the trembling brought forth by the Spirit of God, should be cast out from among them. Her family could be poisoned by it. Surely the elders would agree with her.

Just the mere thought of Silas laughing at them made anger flow through her. Anger that neither Father nor the elders would approve of, she knew. But she couldn't help how she felt. If only they could see the eyes of Silas Jones that revealed the man's inner self. They were a delightful deep, dark brown, but they concealed mischief. Eyes that taunted and challenged the very fabric of her family's existence—of who and what they were.

Mary took up her basket in a huff and hurried outside. Frustration built within her. Did no one see the signs? Were they all blinded by simple trust—a trust that could turn disastrous if they were not careful? Oh, if she must remain silent for days she would, to confirm what she believed in her heart.

She spent the next hour digging in the cold, dark brown soil and the bit of snow that lay from the storm several days ago. A few vegetables still remained from the harvest many weeks back. Mother asked that the remainder of the vegetables be taken up from the ground if possible. The soil felt as hard and cold as the chunks of ice Father sometimes purchased in sawdust during the summer. *Not very different from the hardness of men's hearts,* she mused. *Like the heart of Silas Jones.*

She then considered Father's response of thankfulness for the stranger with them. Perhaps it would do well for her to think on the man's lost nature as Father did. The darkness where he hid. His wandering soul in need of God's Light to guide him back. But she could not dismiss his outright blasphemy of their ways. Or how he addressed her and the brethren's way of communicating, even going so far as to call her haughty and vain. With each aggravating thought, she dug deeper into the earth to free the potatoes before plopping them into the basket. She grabbed up the load to take back to the house.

Suddenly she felt something bump into her. Her basket sailed into the air, scattering root vegetables on the ground. She stood there, stunned, until she heard a voice exclaim an apology and saw a man's large hands gathering up the vegetables now frosted by flakes of snow.

"I didn't see you, Miss Hall. My humble apologies. I hope you aren't hurt."

She looked up then to see eyes of the deepest brown. Were they really the eyes of mischief, as she believed? Right now the eyes of Silas Jones seemed to display a look of genuine concern. Perhaps even compassion, though she had no idea why. Silas cared only for his opinions. She sucked in her breath, remembering her own words, of the wolf in sheep's clothing, prowling about, looking to devour the innocent like her family. And now this supposed sheep was trying to grab other things. Like her heart, perhaps?

She took back the basket of vegetables, brushing away the bits of snow mixed with brown grass and soil from her skirt. "Thank you, but I must go." She bit her lip, realizing she had misstepped the Friends' language. *How could that have happened?*

All at once the basket was back in his hands. His swift action surprised her. "What are you doing?" she demanded.

"At least let me carry this back to the kitchen. It's heavy."

"I can handle it quite well. I thank thee."

"Yes, I'm sure you can. Or shall I say *thee* can?" His lips turned up into a faint smile.

She grabbed the basket's woven handle. "Please, I grow tired of your mockery. I know you. I mean, I know thee. It's quite easy to see what thee is doing. But it won't work." She felt her face burn with her continued slip of the tongue. She wondered if this man was somehow causing her to stumble. What else could it be? She had never found her spirit in such disarray. Unless there was more working here to disrupt her heart than she realized.

His large hand released the basket into her possession. He took a step back. "So what is it about me you know? I thought only God could search out the depths of one's heart. Unless you all have made up your mind what ails me. And what a sinner I am in your eyes." When she didn't answer, he took a step forward. In haste she retreated. "You have no reply?"

"Only that I have seen men like thee before. Men who prefer to walk in their cloud of darkness rather than embrace God's Light. And His Light is in thee, Mr. Jones, if thee would open thy eyes and heart to it."

"I need no reminders of the Light. I have seen it. And all it has done is blind those who embrace it. And they end up seeing nothing and doing less. Not even when death takes one of their own." He turned then and strode to the door leading to the kitchen.

Gripped by his words, Mary couldn't help but follow. Now she wondered about the secret he concealed and if she could draw it out. "What do you mean? God's Light causes no such hurt. God is life and love."

He stopped abruptly, whirled, and gazed at her so intently that she felt warmth tease her cheeks and her hands tremble in response. "Please don't force me to tell you any more," he mumbled. "I won't say it. I can't." He bumped through the doorway and into the house.

Mary thought on the words uttered by a desperate voice that fought to conceal the truth. What was that truth in the heart of the man, closed over by pain? Mary wasn't certain she wanted to bear such a burden, even if the Friends taught her to do such things. Perhaps that burden was better left to others. Like Father. Or even her brother, George, whom she'd seen talking to Silas in the barn. Then again, George had taken over the task of nursing Silas's mare, and he seemed quite happy with the horse's progress. Silas might be comfortable confiding in another man his age. Or perhaps even speaking to one of the elders like Friend Daniel Gray.

Mary gathered her shawl about her shoulders and cautiously approached the kitchen. Inside she saw Mother talking with Silas. From the way they conversed, it seemed the man was also trying to win Mother's heart. She frowned in dismay. Mother seemed to respond favorably to him as she smiled and nodded. But Mary knew the truth. The man's anger toward the Quakers. The unrequited things stored in his heart.

Mary tried to scurry past the kitchen, but Mother's voice caught her short. "Mary, would you be so kind as to fetch Mr. Jones a mug of apple cider? I have some warming on the stove."

Indeed I do mind, she thought but took a clean mug from a hook on the wall. "Surely thee wishes it weren't cider," she remarked to him in a low voice, dipping out the fragrant brew teeming with spices.

He calmly took the beverage and said nothing until they entered the sitting room. "Please tell me what it is I'm eager to drink, Miss Hall, as you seem to know everything. Though I don't understand where such wisdom comes from, since I've only been here a few days."

"You would drink that poison that clouds men's judgment. How you could drink from that flask in our home…and at the table…" She didn't care that her words were directed at him without the common Friends' language. He'd disgraced their family with the drinking and the comments about their faith. He'd disgraced her.

"If I were to apologize for my conduct that first evening, would you accept it?" He took a long drink and waited for her answer. She stayed silent. "So you wouldn't."

"Why should I? You've given me no reason to believe you mean it. I mean, thee." Warmth again teased her face. She turned aside.

Silas laughed. He then approached her in a manner that sent tingles shooting through her. Only they were not tingles of concern but of some strange attraction she dared not even entertain. *He—he's an outsider. An insolent man of the world.*

"Put aside your humble speech, Mary. You trip over the words like they were stones. God isn't a respecter of persons or of the language they speak."

The words surprised her. He was not a heathen. He did know something of scripture. And using it to trap her, perhaps? Or maybe to teach her. But how could it be the latter? "I—I don't know what thee means."

"A woman of the friendly persuasion doesn't need to hide behind a bonnet or rules to be who she is. Let go and live in freedom."

"And become like thee? No, I'd rather be at peace than be miserable." She hurried away to her room to find her embroidery, anything to rid her mind of Silas Jones. How he could suggest such things went beyond her sense of reasoning. Why couldn't she convince Father of the man's disturbing ways? That Silas Jones sought to strip them of their faith. Take away all that brought them close to God by trusting in Him for everything in their lives. *I have warned them of this man's ways,* she thought in despair, even as her fingers fumbled to thread the needle. *But they won't take heed.*

She puzzled over it until she remembered Friend Daniel Gray, one of the elders. Surely he would listen to her complaint and bring the matter to Father. After all, Friend Daniel once voiced concern over her family opening this inn. While he agreed with their wish to provide hospitality to outsiders, he cautioned it would also open them to the ways of the outside world. And Silas Jones had proved him right.

◆ ◆ ◆

"Thee has come here unescorted?" Daniel Gray inquired when Mary arrived at his doorstep, chilled by the cold air. He looked beyond her as if expecting her father or George to be sitting in a wagon. She knew it was inappropriate to come alone to a man's home, but her anxiety demanded it. The sooner her family rid themselves of Silas Jones, the better she would feel.

"I'm sorry, Friend Gray. I—I had to come right away. It's very important."

"It must be." He stepped aside. "My cousins are visiting from South Carolina. We are not alone."

It was well they weren't, for Mary knew Daniel was widowed, having lost his wife in childbirth a year ago. She hadn't considered what she would do if she arrived to find him alone in his home. Now she wondered what drove her heart to do such things. Would she be rebuked? But after she greeted Daniel's cousin and his wife,

Daniel lit a few extra oil lamps in the sitting room and gestured her to a chair.

Mary wasted no time telling him about the guest in their home and how she believed him to be of ill repute in soul and spirit.

Daniel stirred. "I see. In what manner has he brought ill upon thee and thy family?"

"His words and mannerisms are like thorns. He—he mocks our ways and our beliefs."

Daniel chuckled. "And why is that so strange to us? Does thee recall the persecution of those who came before us? Friend William Penn even found himself falsely arrested and a prisoner many times. Newgate Prison twice and even the Tower itself."

"Yes, I know the stories." She had been told many times of the forbearance of William Penn, who met with grave persecutions before Friend William founded Philadelphia, Pennsylvania. The place the people call the City of Brotherly Love. And even the state of Pennsylvania was named after William Penn's father, to whom the king of England owed a great debt.

"Then thee shouldn't trouble thyself with one who doesn't know the Light of God in his heart. Rest in God's protection and His will." Daniel hesitated, looking over to the adjacent room where the cousins were. His voice lowered. "Actually, I am glad thee stopped by, Mary. I've been thinking of thee and have been meaning to come by thy father's house."

Mary caught her breath. "I—I can surely use thy prayers," she managed to say.

"Prayers, yes. But perhaps thee would consider going riding with me?"

She hadn't expected this kind of attention from a man of the Word and the Faith, looking at her with more than the simple interest of an elder to his flock. "It is kind of thee to ask."

"Actually, I blame the cousins," he said with a chuckle. "They wonder when this lonely heart of mine will seek another. And I believe it's time. I've mourned a year for Elizabeth. One must live for Christ and not the grave."

Mary paused, thinking of Silas, though she didn't know why, and said quickly, "Yes, I would like to go riding with thee."

His face erupted into a smile of pleasure. "Next Thursday, then?"

Mary nodded. They conversed a bit longer, about the short winter days, the past meetings among the Friends, and what he might speak about at First Meeting. He began to share more of his thoughts, as if he dearly wanted her to be a part of them. When she finally bid him good day, she inhaled quick breaths of cold air that sent pangs of pain fluttering in her chest. Nothing was turning out the way she'd expected. Here she had come asking for protection and prayer against an outsider and came away with a proposal of courting. Was God indeed guiding her heart? Was this what His Light did, shine in ways she never considered?

Mary mounted her horse, Whisper, and made for home, certain she would be rebuked if she did not arrive back soon to help with the daily baking. How she wished she could ride forever with the cold breeze filling her and its unseen tendrils brushing her face. If not for the unpleasant winter days, filled with cold and snow, she wouldn't mind seeing other places. Again her thoughts drifted to Silas. He talked of his desire to journey west. She shook her head, unwilling to compare his goals with her own. They were like night to day. And she could not forget how he belittled her and the family.

When Mary neared home, she saw several people gathered outside as if waiting for her arrival. Father, George, and Silas Jones of all people. "Where has thee been this day?" Father asked, his voice laced with concern.

"I. . ." She paused, glancing at Silas, who looked at her with what appeared to be equal concern. "I went to confide in Friend Daniel Gray of a matter, Father. But I have returned, as thee can see. There is no need to worry."

"Thee went to see Friend Gray? Without an escort?"

She felt her cheeks warm, even as she noticed Silas gazing at her intently. "His cousins were there." She nearly spoke of the invitation to go riding with Daniel but kept silent. Right now she must calm the rising tide of anxiety. "I'm sorry, Father. I should have told thee of my intentions."

"So thee should, taking off without a word." Father took hold of the bridle to steady Whisper. Silas was at her side, offering his hand to help her dismount. Mary wanted to ignore the gesture, but with George and Father looking on, she reluctantly gave him her hand. She refused to acknowledge his dark eyes surveying her or the warmth of his large hand around hers. She did not care to entertain any misconceptions now that she had accepted Daniel's invitation. Silas would be gone in a matter of days anyway, and that would be the end of it. Or so she thought, even as his hand tightened around hers. *Help me, dearest Lord!*

Chapter 3

Silas tried not to think about Mary's abrupt visitation to an elder of the Friends, but he couldn't help thinking she had gone on his account. After their initial encounter, he'd tried to calm the rising tide of animosity between them. He knew, of course, that an explanation for his opinions concerning the Society of Friends would set things at ease. But he was not of a mind to share that part of his life. Why he left Philadelphia so abruptly. Or why he was journeying across the country, as far away from the East as possible. Or why the Quaker mannerisms shown by the Hall family tested him beyond his ability to reason.

He did, though, find his irritation with them diminishing as the days passed. George Hall proved a wonder with Barzillai, who was making a rapid recovery from the injured hoof. Mr. Hall had shown him the workings of the inn, and his acceptance of Silas comforted him. And Mrs. Hall slipped him freshly baked desserts, bread, or biscuits hot from the hearth. Despite his irritating ways when he first arrived, the family had been forgiving and patient. All but Mary, who viewed him as a thorn in their heel. Or as she had once said, some predator out to destroy the family. The connotation proved unsettling, and he vowed to somehow change her opinion.

But this day, Mary seemed in another world. She walked around humming a joyful tune. Her face appeared sunny like the bright day as she went about her chores. He wondered what spawned such happiness. Certainly he had nothing to do with it. He took up the ax to split firewood over Mr. Hall's protest. Silas preferred work and not idleness while waiting for Barzillai to make a full recovery. After roaming about the house, bored with the library of books that espoused the works of George Fox and other notable Friends, he decided physical labor would do his mind well.

Silas brought the ax to bear, neatly splitting the log into quarters that were then thrown into the ever-increasing woodpile. He glanced over to where Mary stood in the yard, and suddenly she rose up on tiptoe, clutching her raven-black bonnet. He heard the nicker of horses. A buggy rolled up the dirt road, driven by a man in a black hat and dark coat.

"Good day," said the man. "Thee is the visitor from the City of Brotherly Love?"

Silas blinked and heaved the ax into another waiting log. And how would a stranger know that? "I have been there," he admitted cautiously.

"Friend Mary told me of thy sojourn here at her family's inn. I'm Daniel Gray, an elder of the Friends in Waynesville." He offered his hand, a common act of greeting with the Quakers. Silas reluctantly shook it. "I'm here to take Mary for a ride."

"I'm sure she will enjoy it." Silas hefted the ax and drove the blade deep into another log. Now he knew why Mary was so happy. She had a suitor. And a fine gent he appeared, outfitted in humble clothing, conveying the mannerism of a pious Friend and an elder at that. A perfect man for her, without a spot or wrinkle. The ax flew into the wood, sending a spray of wood chips into the air.

"How long does thee plan to stay among us?" Daniel asked.

"Not much longer. I hope to be in Independence before the snow gets deep. That is, if my horse is well enough to make the journey. I won't go without her. As it is, I walked part of the way and wore my shoes through."

Daniel Gray smiled then turned his attention to the fair Mary, who ventured forward in her cloak and dark bonnet, the smile ever broadening on her pale face. Silas tried to ignore the scene but couldn't help watching her take the man's hand and climb into the buggy. She smiled warmly in the man's direction and settled in, tucking the corners of the lap robe around her. Silas thought then how he would like to take her in his rig and drive her around, that is, if he had a rig. And if he weren't plagued, too, by nagging thoughts of their previous conversation. He and Mary were more akin to iron sharpening iron than feeling any love and devotion like this couple who shared smiles and warm conversation. He grimaced, wishing he and Mary had been introduced differently when he arrived. Wishing, too, he hadn't allowed the past to infect the present or the future. But what was his future? And where? California, perhaps? Certainly not with the Quakers.

He couldn't help his conflicting emotions at hearing the laughter on the wind as the buggy containing Mary and this Friend Daniel rolled down the road. No doubt they were speaking in humble language while espousing the Light shining within. Silas considered God's Light. Grandfather had spoken of it when Silas was a mere lad and still a stranger to its principles. The older man spoke of his affections for the writings of George Fox, the founder of Quakerism, and William Penn, the founder of Philadelphia, whom he esteemed a great man of wisdom despite his rough beginnings.

"Thee is much like Friend William Penn, young Silas," Grandfather told him as they fished in the river near Philadelphia.

"How is that?" young Silas wanted to know.

"Like thyself, William struggled with his newfound faith. He desired to find justice among the unjust. And like thee, he found it difficult submitting to God's will in such matters. He wanted to take justice into his own hands."

It was as if Grandfather had a foretelling of future events. The very thing he'd spoken of had come to pass. Silas had confronted the pain of injustice: that terrible struggle to right the wrong and his inability to do it.

"It will not go away either," he said, squeezing his eyes shut to ward off the images. Of his beaten and bloodied grandfather lying on a cobblestone street. The man's labored breathing as he struggled to live. The glazed eyes and silent heartbeat that followed. The criminals who had taken away a man's life but still roamed the streets of the City of Brotherly Love without paying for their crimes.

"I will not accept it!" he shouted aloud and then turned about, wondering if anyone had overheard. He hoped God Himself had. If He had ears to hear, that is. If He cared at all to act on Silas's behalf.

"Silas?"

A soft voice spoke like one eager to reach him, though he wanted to turn a deaf ear. George had emerged from the barn. "Is thee well?"

Silas shook his head, his complaint lodged in his throat.

"What troubles thee?"

"I—I was thinking of the past. And seeing how it affects my future."

"Like how it affects my sister? Thee does have affections for her, right?"

Silas's mouth dropped in stunned amazement. He thought for a moment but decided not to pursue his actual pain-filled memory of Philadelphia. "Even if I did, I am not of the Friends' persuasion. Certainly not like the elder who is escorting her."

George shrugged. "Mary has little difficulty making up her mind. But I wanted to tell thee, also, that if thee still wishes to leave on thy journey, thy horse is nearly healed."

Silas straightened. "Really? She's well?"

"A fine animal with a strong heart. I can see thee has cared for her."

Silas relished the comment as he followed the young man into the barn. Barzillai greeted him with a soft whinny. "Why, she does look well enough to ride. You've done a splendid job." And he meant it. As much as the Quaker family had irritated him at the outset, far be it from him not to give noteworthy praise. And plenty of well-deserved coins, too. But really, he owed more than he could pay for the tender care given, not only to his animal but also to himself.

"A fine horse," George acknowledged, stroking the horse's muzzle. He found a carrot and fed Barzillai, who munched it with pleasure. "A horse is one of God's great creatures, to help a man in his pursuits. I'm certain this horse has done much for thee, bringing thee here from so far."

"Yes. She was a gift from my grandfather. That's why when she took lame, I wanted. . ." He paused. "I wanted her made well. If she continues on, a part of my grandfather does as well."

"He no longer lives?"

Silas shook his head and slowly retreated inside himself where no one could see, or so he thought. Into a realm of anger and injustice and an overwhelming desire to right the wrongs committed. He looked up then to see George staring at him. Silas flinched.

"It's hard to see death come to those we care about. I'm not without understanding, Friend Silas. A good friend of mine drowned last year in the Ohio while carrying supplies on his bateau. I asked God the reason why. It seemed senseless to me."

"Did you get an answer?" Silas couldn't help the eagerness in his voice.

"Friend Gray, the elder of our meeting, told me that God knows best. That He sees beyond our mortal minds. And we must have faith in His providence. With God there is more than this life. Those departed are with Him in eternity. We're here for a moment. Like the grass that fades or the flower that withers and dies. We must do what we can now for His glory. And leave eternity and its timing to God."

Silas said nothing more as he watched George feed Barzillai another carrot. While the words seemed good and true, they brought him little satisfaction. Nor a calming of the torrid waters stirring him. There would be no peace until justice was served.

◆　◆　◆

"Thee has said little on this trip," Daniel observed. "Aren't thee well?"

"Oh, I'm fine. Just enjoying the lovely day. There is so much to see." Mary didn't realize how silent she'd been, with her sights set on the beautiful Ohio countryside. On this cold December day, the land appeared ready to receive whatever the winter planned to bring, though they had already seen some snow. Along the way they passed several farmhouses of families that were outsiders, preparing for the Christmas holiday. Pine boughs decorated porches, and fruited arrangements hung above the doors. Mary remembered several guests who had stayed at their inn last year and asked her family what they did to celebrate the holiday. Father announced privately to the family that they would have a day of remembrance while the outsiders in their midst celebrated the Christmas holiday. And Father honored his guests by having a special meal prepared for them and allowing them to exchange gifts at the table.

Now Mary wondered what this season would bring as she sat huddled beneath the blanket. Then she thought of Silas Jones. Why, she didn't know, even as Daniel cast her another glance.

"Actually, I'm also thinking," she added.

"About what? The outsider staying at thy father's place? This Silas Jones?"

Mary straightened, hoping Daniel didn't notice the flush of her cheeks as a positive answer to his inquiry. Why would he say such a thing? Unless he perceived that she and Silas had shared words earlier that day. God could whisper such things to an elder like Daniel. But now was not the time to bring out the secrets of the heart. Besides, she felt right in her dealings with Silas and his ill regard for their faith.

Now she'd rather change the subject. "I—I only wonder who we may have during this Christmas season. I'm certain Silas Jones will not be there. He plans to leave for Independence as soon as his horse has recovered."

Daniel nodded. "It's strange that people feel they must have a special day to remember our Lord's birth. We know that every day is a day of remembrance. But I know, too, we must show understanding. And the Lord's love and Light."

"Last year we exchanged gifts. Father thought it proper but then told everyone at the table that each day is a gift from God, that we only did it in our guests' honor to remember the occasion they celebrate."

"As is right. For thee knows one occasion isn't better than another. Each day is a gift to be shared." He took Mary's hand, covered in the warmth of a mitten, and held it in his hand. "Just as thee is also a gift."

"Friend Daniel, it—it's kind of thee to say." But she didn't feel much like a gift these past few days, especially during the confrontations with Silas Jones. Why the man bothered her, she didn't know. Or she feared knowing. She must instead focus her thoughts on this fine man before her. Daniel Gray was an honorable man and a gift in his own right. An elder and a man Father would be proud to have court his only daughter. If it was the right thing to do. But now she remained uncertain.

Daniel guided the buggy down another road leading toward home. She was glad he'd taken a more country route and not one through the town of Waynesville. Quaint as it was, and even with the Friends' meetinghouse there, she instead felt closer to God among the great fields and forest He'd created. And they also avoided the curious eyes of the townsfolk.

When they arrived back, Silas was in the yard with his horse, looking as if he were about ready to take his leave.

"Thank thee, Friend Daniel," Mary said swiftly, her gaze falling on Silas. "I enjoyed the ride very much."

Before departing, Daniel offered his hand once more to Silas, who shook it. Then Daniel left. Mary stood in her place, uncertain what to say or what might unfold between them.

"Barzillai is much better," Silas finally said. "Your brother did a fine job caring for her."

"I'm glad. George is a wonder with animals. God has given him a great gift of healing." She paused. "So thee is leaving?"

"Yes. I'm certain things will be better here if I do. I know you're unhappy with me."

Mary inhaled a sharp breath, recalling Daniel's words that she was a gift to others. She had hardly represented herself as a gift to Silas in her words and thoughts. Nor did she allow for God's Light to pierce the darkness in his heart through her. "Silas Jones, I beg forgiveness if my tone with thee these past days has not been pleasant. I felt I needed to come to the defense of my brethren. But I should remember that God is our defender."

"I admire someone who stands for justice."

His words took her by surprise. "But surely it is the Lord who justifies and who brings forth fruit from what is sown. It is not for me to judge. And I did judge thee severely."

Silas was silent for a minute. "I accept your apology, but I do have reasons for what I say. Even if I'm at fault for having harsh opinions."

"A man is right in his own eyes until he is corrected."

"True. All I've had the last few weeks on my journey is a lame horse to tell me right from wrong until I came here. A horse doesn't speak too well to one's condition."

Mary couldn't help but chuckle, which brought a smile to Silas's face.

"But Barzillai's limp did speak in other ways," he continued. "It told me to stop and take notice. To not let my ideas affect everything I see and do. And so I think I will stay through Christmas, which is not far away, and then leave."

"We don't celebrate Christmas. . . ," she began then caught herself. "Rather, we have different ways of celebrating among the Friends. We believe every day is a celebration of our Lord and His coming."

"I know. I'm Quaker also."

Mary stepped back, stunned by the revelation. "You're a Friend? But I thought. . ." She knew her mouth had dropped open, but she could barely close it. "I—I don't understand. After all that's been said between us and. . ."

Silas turned away. "Now I see I've said too much." He led his horse back into the barn, as Mary stood fast in place, unable to believe what she'd heard. *Silas is a Friend?* The man who had mocked their language and their manner of keeping? What was it, then, that had turned him from the Light? What had sent him into darkness? Curiosity overwhelmed her. She hoped and prayed the man would not take his leave until all had been revealed. Even with that, she wasn't sure how she would react or what she would say.

But right now it looked as if Silas didn't wish to reveal anything more. "Lord, I pray Thee will keep him here until his heart's condition lays open," she whispered. "Do not let him leave with a troubled heart and a wandering soul. Keep him in Thy tender care. And our care, too, until he finds healing for his soul." With that prayer, Mary found her thoughts about Silas changing. A heart of compassion began to emerge, to help one in need. Silas Jones was in desperate need, whether he believed it or not.

Chapter 4

Silas chastised himself for allowing part of the past to slip out. Why he told Mary he was once a Quaker was beyond him. He'd wanted to avoid it. Disown the mere fact out of his choosing. But since his arrival here at the Hall home—watching the tender care given to his horse and the warmth of a true Quaker family who helped each other and greeted strangers with kindness and smiles of joy—his heart had softened. If only that warmth could change what had happened. But even with the Halls' displays of kindness and generosity, nothing could take away a past that still left a deep wound in his spirit.

Now with the revelation of his ties to the Friends, Mary looked at him oddly for the remainder of the day. That evening over a fine meal of chicken and dumplings in savory gravy, he noted Mary's fiery blue eyes observing him as if desiring to know why he'd left the Society of Friends. What led him away from the Light? Why had he run from Philadelphia? But the questions remained unspoken, and for that he was grateful.

After a dessert of delicious molasses cake, Silas cleared his throat and looked around the table. "I wanted to thank you very much for your kindness. I've decided to leave tomorrow."

The cups of evening tea were set down on the table. Every member of the Hall family gazed at him, except for the two guests in for the night.

"But I thought thee was staying until. . . ," Mary began.

"I'm sorry to hear this," Mr. Hall said. "We do thank thee for gracing our home with thy presence and for helping chop wood. We enjoy having others come and stay, but we also know the road beckons to thee. May thee find a satisfactory ending to thy wanderings."

Silas was both happy and unhappy. Thankful Barzillai was well and he could continue his journey westward. But sad, too, that he would leave a family who appeared ready to have him be on his way, despite their friendly attentions. Did Mary feel the same? he wondered. He cast a glance at her, but she said nothing. It was fitting. Elder Daniel stood poised to court her. They would enjoy many a fine sleigh ride when the winter snows piled high. She would have a fine Quaker gentleman who did not suffer like he did. Oh, but he did wish he no longer suffered in his soul. It would be good to have lasting joy and peace in embracing the Light of God.

If only he could.

After dinner Silas returned to his room to begin packing his satchel of meager belongings. He heard a rustling in the hallway and looked out of his room to see Mary standing there, clutching a small cloth bag. She looked lovelier than he'd ever seen her. Maybe it was her hair, which had loosened and fallen around her shoulders, though she still wore the modest white cap atop her head. Or maybe it was the innocent look on her face.

"There were a few biscuits left over from the meal. I—I thought thee might want them for thy journey."

"Thank you." He took them, and when he did, their hands brushed. And for an instant he had the overwhelming desire to take her lovely form in his arms. He inhaled a quick breath. She would feel so good in his arms, too. Warm and soft and sweet. The fragrant scents from the day's baking still lingered on her. He would slowly take off her white cap and let his fingers drift through her luxurious brown hair. Her blue eyes would look up into his, so trusting, seeking his protection and his love. . . .

Silas gulped and turned away, feeling a bit too warm by these thoughts. He expected her to leave. But when he looked back, she was still standing there.

"Are you really a Quaker, Silas?" Mary caught herself. "I mean, are thee. . ."

"Yes, I was. I may still be. I don't know who I am. Or really, where I stand with God."

Mary took a step forward. "There is no need to leave now. Friend Daniel Gray can help," she added, the eagerness lacing her voice. "He can show thee thy condition, show God's Light within thee and. . ."

"Mary, I know you want to help, but no one can. What I suffer goes too deep for any kind of understanding."

"Nothing is too deep that God is not in it." She drew even closer, and her warmth filled him. They stood but two feet apart. Her blue eyes held no fire as they had in the past but a measure of questioning and even compassion. Her lips appeared moist and inviting. Silas took hold of her arm and led her gently into his embrace. She did not resist. He enjoyed the taste of her fair lips until finally she struggled out of his grasp, her breathing rapid.

"Please. . . ," she managed to say, her face flushed like a strawberry. "I—I was trying to help."

"Yes, you were. And I was letting you know that you're a beautiful woman. Did you ever stop to consider there might be better plans for your life than just the small life you live here as a servant in your inn? That we may have been brought together for a reason?"

She grew rigid, and the compassion that had softened her features rapidly changed to a fire of indignation. "I'm glad to be here. There is nowhere else I wish to be. And. . .perhaps it is better thee is going away after all." She began to retreat.

"As you wish." He stood his ground, only to see her turn and scurry away. Yet the warmth of the encounter remained, especially the touch of her lips on his. But he must force it away and ready himself for the journey, now marred by another haunting memory.

❖ ❖ ❖

Oh, why did I ever allow myself to be kissed by him?

Mary thought about what had happened in the upper hallway, wishing she'd had enough strength to ward off temptation. But Silas Jones crept in when she was most vulnerable to the hurt in his heart. And worst of all, she'd allowed him! She shuddered, wondering if she should confess to the elders her troubled state and ask for their prayer. But if she did, Daniel would know she had kissed another man, and a fallen one of the brethren at that. What would he say? After all, she knew Daniel's intent was to court her. He would suffer hurt, and he'd already endured so much hurt after the loss of his wife. She couldn't bring that kind of pain upon him.

But why was my heart so quick to respond to Silas? Did she find him that appealing, out of all the men God had put in her path? Silas had mocked them. Abandoned the Friends. Then he used the moment when she wanted to help to trap her. The wolf in sheep's clothing, as she once described him, had swooped down with stolen kisses, looking to take full residence in the confines of her heart. She felt weak in spirit, as if suffering the ravages of a fever. Without direction. Thoughts trapped in a fog. Her only hope was that he'd be gone by dawn, and she could wait upon God to cleanse her and make her whole in mind and emotion. But did she want to be cleansed? Did she really want Silas to be gone forever?

Mary hurried outside to find her brother handling his new acquisition to the herd—a fine stallion in desperate need of breaking. He looked at her as she approached. "Mary? Why so downcast?"

Was it that apparent in her features? Mary tried to smile then, but it felt forced. "Oh, it's nothing, George. Nothing at all." Nothing that hasty abandonment couldn't cure. But her lips still tingled from his kiss, and her arms still remembered the warmth of his strong embrace. *Dearest Lord, help my feelings.*

"There *is* something wrong. I can see it." He strode over to the fence and leaned against it. "Is it Silas?"

"I . . ." She hesitated.

"I know he has feelings for thee. He told me as much."

"I—I'm glad he's leaving," she blurted. "It will be better for all of us. He's done little but stir trouble among us. And did thee realize he was once of the Friends' persuasion but abandoned the Light?"

George's eyes widened. "No, I didn't. But I knew something had happened with regards to the Friends. If only he could find his burden lifted. Perhaps a meeting with Friend Daniel would help."

Mary felt her face heat at the suggestion. "No, no, that will never do. The only choice is for him to find the Light for himself. I've heard his words." *And felt his lips on mine. And the strength of his arms.* She shivered at the memory. "He—he really must go."

George looked at her with a strange expression, almost as if he knew what had transpired in the house. She turned quickly, lest her expressions give away anything. George returned to training the young horse with a short pole, giving commands.

She thought of the Friends, the beliefs they held to, the ways in which she was to guard her heart and her thoughts, focusing them solely on the one who loved her and held her in His hands. Of the full devotion she must give. Until she saw it all thrust in a whirlwind by the man with deep-set brown eyes and an overpowering will to take hold of her when she least expected it.

Suddenly she caught sight of a tall figure exiting the house. Silas, carrying a satchel as he walked toward the corral, stopped short when he saw her. He opened his mouth as if to speak but instead went to the door of the barn. Mary edged closer so she could hear the conversation.

"So thee is truly going," George remarked to him.

"Yes, I need to go before the snows get too deep. I want to be settled in Independence, maybe by Christmas if all goes well."

"Thee has a long way to travel. Why not stay until spring? Father could use the extra help, I'm sure."

Silas glanced in the direction of the house. "I can't, George. But thank you for inviting me. Your father does have an excellent place. Even if. . ." He hesitated. "Even if I was not appreciative of it when I first arrived."

George smiled. "Thee has seen the Light, Friend Silas."

"I don't think so. But maybe I will once I find out where I'm supposed to go." He entered the barn. Mary waited, watching until Silas returned, leading Barzillai by her bridle. She inhaled a sharp breath as his tall, sturdy figure mounted the mare with his large hands gripping the reins.

"I pray God will keep thee in thy journey, Friend Silas," George said, offering a handshake of farewell.

Silas shook her brother's hand. He looked at Mary then tipped his hat to her. He appeared strong and commanding on his mount, ready to face whatever the world gave. At that moment it brought him little but disappointment, as he had conveyed to her. But that was not for her or the family to heal. Only Silas could find the healing he needed, through God's mercy and guidance.

Just then Mary heard a loud neigh then a thump, followed by a groan. She whirled to find George a crumpled heap on the ground. The horse he had been training nosed him with its muzzle. "George! George, are you all right?" She ran and knelt before him, shaking him. His eyes were closed, his breathing ragged. One look at his contorted lower leg and bloodied trousers told her something terrible had happened. "Oh dearest God!" she cried, the tears burning in her eyes. She looked around to see the dust of Silas's departure. Or rather a cloud of dust stirring as someone came galloping up in a frenzy.

"What happened?" It was Silas. Mary had never felt more relieved to see him. He dismounted and hurried to her side, kneeling next to George.

"I—I don't know. I was. . ." *I was looking at you, wondering why you were leaving.* . . . She paused. "I didn't see what happened until I heard a loud noise." She pointed with a trembling finger. "Look at his leg. It looks terrible!"

"I'll go for the doctor. Where is your village?"

Mary gave him directions to the doctor's residence with a wavering voice. Then she felt a strong hand take hers and give a gentle squeeze. "It's going to be all right," he said.

Mary wiped away the tears so she could see better and composed herself with a few quick breaths. George began to stir then and moan in pain as his hand fumbled for his leg. "Just lie still, George. Silas is going for the doctor. You have broken your leg."

"It hurts," he moaned. "It hurts badly. Oh Mary. Pray. . .pray for me. Please. Oh."

"Yes, yes, I will labor with thee, dear brother. Thee knows I will, with all my heart." And she did, for many long minutes, thankful to see George calming under the prayerful words.

Father and Mother came rushing out when they heard the commotion. Even the two visitors who had been inside the house followed. Mary told them all what happened and that Silas had gone for the doctor.

"We can't leave George lying in the dirt," Mother said. "And we have trusted his well-being to some outsider? What if he doesn't return? He was leaving, after all."

"George shouldn't be moved, Mother. And Silas will return with the doctor. He said he would," Mary added in confidence.

Father agreed, and together they tried to make George as comfortable as possible. But the leg wound was grievous, with the white of bone protruding. Mary knew he would be bedridden a long time. The elders and Friends would help in their time of need. They would be all right, she felt certain. If only she didn't feel so helpless.

George moaned again and struggled to sit up. He saw his leg, groaned, and looked to heaven. "Why? Why did this happen?"

Why indeed? Mary thought. No one was more faithful and protective; no one was a better man than her brother. Mary could only stay by his side with the others and wait.

At last they heard the sounds of horses. Silas arrived, bringing the doctor and, to her surprise, Friend Daniel. Mary wasn't about to ask how Daniel discovered their misfortune—if Silas had gone to fetch him also. She laid aside her questions with the physician here to tend to George, and Daniel here to give spiritual guidance.

The men gathered to hoist George up on a litter made from a blanket and take him into the house. They placed him on the bed, where the doctor examined the extent of the injury.

"Thank thee so much for fetching the doctor," Mary said softly to Silas, who stood by her side, watching as the doctor cut away the pant leg to expose the open wound. George groaned and shook violently. Mary trembled and turned away. Silas winced also. They looked at each other rather than at what the doctor was doing. Finally Silas stepped outside the room, and Mary followed.

"This is terrible," she said, and suddenly the tears came fast and furious.

"I'm sorry, Mary. Truly I am. George is a fine man. He cared for my horse, and he cares about others. He doesn't deserve this. I don't understand the ways of God or why good men must suffer so."

She wiped her eyes. "Sometimes it isn't for us to understand. We have to trust and believe in God's goodness, no matter what happens." But little did he know that she, too, struggled with the reason why. And with the terrible pain her brother endured as the doctor worked to fix the leg.

Mother rushed out then, her face pale. "The doctor says he must try to straighten the leg." She wrung her hands in despair. "He. . .he needs men to help hold George down. Silas, will thee help?"

Silas immediately went inside the room. Mary took Mother into the kitchen area at the back of the house, but even there they could still hear the awful screams. A fresh round of tears came forth as they held each other and murmured prayers. When it was over, they returned to find the doctor had splinted the leg and wrapped it in heavy linen. George lay still, having fainted from the pain and the effects of the laudanum the doctor had given him to ease his suffering.

The doctor gestured the family to the sitting room. "I will not lie to you. It is a bad break. With an open wound, fever is likely and could be severe. Even if he survives the fever, he could very well be crippled."

If he survives? Mary gasped. It was as if the heavens had fallen. She might have collapsed in despair if not for Silas supporting her.

Chapter 5

For the next week a cloud of somberness hung over the Hall home. While Mr. Hall insisted they keep the inn running despite George's accident, the family found themselves further and further behind in their work. Mary and Mrs. Hall ran ragged trying to keep the inn's guests entertained and well-fed while caring for George. Mr. Hall was away on the supply runs that George normally did and struggled with the upkeep of the house and grounds.

Silas could hardly turn his back on a family so in need, especially when they had helped both him and Barzillai. He did what he could to help, but he maintained his distance from Mary. Since the kiss, he'd decided to stay away, not wishing to cause her further discomfort. But still, a yearning rose within him to be with her, to hold her, to offer comfort for the trials she was facing, like he had when George was first injured.

Silas was busy hitching the horses to the supply wagon when Mary came around the side of the house, toting the usual basket filled with the weekly wash. He offered a smile, which she returned.

"How's George today?" he asked.

A frown appeared, and likewise his good cheer disappeared. The news must not be good. "He still has a fever. I don't know what else to do for him but bear his burden in prayer and give him tea made from herbs."

"The fever will break soon," Silas tried to reassure her, though he didn't know the future. He'd seen a loved one injured beyond the ability of medicine and even beyond God's ability to heal, it seemed. He prayed that would not be George's lot.

"Where is thee off to today?" she asked.

He waved a piece of paper. "I have a list of supplies from your father that I need to buy from the store in town."

To his surprise, Mary hastily put down the basket of clothes and came forward, her face bright with excitement. "I would very much like to go to town." She gazed back at the house. "Thee will go and return quickly? I shouldn't be gone long."

"Yes, but doesn't thee think thee should ask?" He waited, hoping she would notice his use of the Friends' language.

The response was not what he expected. "There is no need." She climbed into the wagon beside him without asking for help or even inquiring if she might go along. Her boldness surprised him. "I need this trip, and I'm quite able to decide for myself if it's reasonable. There are no new guests in for the night. George is resting.

All that can be done has been done." She settled herself on the wagon seat, with her hands folded in her lap and her gaze focused directly ahead.

Silas said nothing further, only flicked the reins and guided the wagon to the rutted dirt road. He'd been careful to keep his distance from the attractive Mary, but all determination to do so melted away with her close proximity and her aroma reminiscent of spring wildflowers. Her bright face and blue eyes reflected the clear sky above. He nearly reached for her hand but kept a firm grip on the reins instead.

"Ah, such a lovely day for a ride," she said with a sigh.

"I'm sure thee had a nice ride with Friend Daniel that one day." He cringed then, wishing he hadn't brought up the subject. Now the talk would steer Mary into thinking about the fine Quaker gent.

"He is kind and wise. But. . ." She paused. "I would only be in conflict with a memory if we were to court."

"I don't understand."

"His wife died in childbirth a year ago. I don't want to be compared to her in matters of marriage. Who she was. What they did together." Her hands trembled, and she looked off into the distance to the farmlands surrounding their travel. "I'm sorry. I've said too much about this. It isn't proper."

"Thee has shared thy heart, Mary. If one can't do that, what good are the brethren? Or the cause of helping one another in times of need?" Despite the joy he felt over her reservations concerning Daniel, Silas was uncertain her words proved the man held no interest in her eyes. Or that a door now lay open to him. She'd shown little interest in him except in his past. They had shared the one kiss, but it might as well have been a kiss farewell, as he'd planned to leave before George's injury. But things were changing day by day. Could this conversation mean that she did hold some affection for him?

He inhaled a quick breath, hoping it were so, as the wagon approached the outskirts of town. Dropping Mary off at the general store, Silas went to see about a shovel and to have the ax head sharpened. Several people asked about George, having heard about the accident. Silas told them what he knew and what the future might hold.

"Very sad," several said.

"He trained my horse," said another.

Silas, too, felt remorse for the situation. He would do what he could to help while he remained there. Later he'd decide what would become of his journey westward or if Almighty God had other plans.

He stopped the wagon before the general store to await Mary's return. She soon came out of the shop carrying several parcels. She never looked prettier, even if her clothing was a bit drab with the black skirt and matching cape, and the black bonnet concealing her fine hair. He helped her with the packages, which included a pie, and put them in the wagon bed. He offered her a hand up. "The townsfolk shared their condolences over George's accident," he told her.

"Several of the Friends asked about him, too. And one gave me the pie. The brethren are so sweet and giving."

Silas didn't comment, though his thoughts buzzed as they headed out of town. While his opinion of the Quakers had changed since coming here to Ohio, he still couldn't rid himself of what had happened in Philadelphia. How a roving gang of rogues came upon his grandfather on the road and beat him. The Friends who warned Silas not to take matters into his own hands. Then they forgave his grandfather's murderers, allowing them to go unpunished, while he was cast off from among the Friends for harboring thoughts of revenge.

"Thee is quiet all of a sudden," Mary observed.

Silas wanted to confess the inner workings of his heart, as she had done concerning Daniel Gray. But her advice would be like that of all the Friends. Treat everyone with respect, even the murderers. Do not give evil for evil. Allow God to deal in judgment.

But Silas could not accept it right now. Instead, he made small talk, inquiring about the work that still needed to be done and what they would do about the holidays should any travelers arrive.

"Mother will make her famous molasses cake she made the other night, I'm sure," Mary said. "Last year Father allowed us to give gifts to each other. We had a nice dinner for those who came. And Father lit candles in the windows for each person present to symbolize God's Light in all of us." She paused. "I'm certain in Philadelphia thee did not celebrate Christmas."

"A few friends I know did. Not 'Friends' as in the Quakers," he added, "but friends among strangers. I was invited to one such gathering over my father's objections. It was a grand time. They had a feast, a Yule log, warm cider, and even a tree."

"A tree inside the house?"

"They cut down a small tree in the woods, brought it inside, and decorated it with candles and paper trimmings. I had never seen anything like that before."

Mary shook her head. "Such grave idolatry. Worshipping a tree as if it could grant one Light. How foolish."

"They didn't worship it. It was only a decoration, and many liked it. It was as if a bit of creation was brought inside. They said the candles on the branches bore witness to God's Light in each of us. Which the Friends themselves believe of course."

Mary paused and dropped her head, folding her hands tightly in her lap. "I'm sorry. I shouldn't be so judgmental."

Silas couldn't help but chuckle. "Thee has a mind of thy own. And a mind God can surely use. He used it well with me." Out of the corner of his eye he saw Mary smile. And again his heart leaped in hope. If only the past didn't hover over them like a storm cloud.

◆　◆　◆

Silas sensed nervousness when he was called into Mr. Hall's study one afternoon. The man sat in one of his fine chairs, his Bible spread open in his lap. He glanced up through wire-rimmed spectacles, which he slowly removed and folded. "Please come in."

Silas slipped inside the room and into a chair opposite the fatherly figure, wondering why he had been summoned. Had he been improper with Mary since the day of George's accident? True, he did try to comfort her. He'd held her hand a few times. Whispered soothing words. And took her to town on an errand. But surely those incidents shouldn't bring about a rebuke.

"I wanted to thank thee for all thy help these many days," said Mr. Hall.

"I'm happy to do whatever I can."

"I wish, especially with the approaching season, to keep my establishment open to all who travel," Mr. Hall continued. "But I fear without George's help, I will be unable to do so. I know it isn't right to ask thee to remain any longer, as I know thee has other plans. . . ." The man hesitated and looked down at the Bible. "I wonder if thee might consider staying on to help."

Silas sat still, absorbing this.

"I would pay thee fairly. And we expect more visitors wishing to celebrate Christmas, as I'm sure thee does."

"I do not celebrate it, Mr. Hall."

"Oh? I would have thought a man of the world would." He hesitated. "Not that God doesn't abide in all of us, for He surely does. But anyway, I would be most happy to have thy presence at the inn. Please consider it."

"I will. Thank you." Silas shook the man's hand, stood, and wandered out. He saw the open door leading to the bedroom where George had been since the accident. He walked over and peeked in. George lay in bed, staring up at the ceiling, his wounded leg a mass of bandages and resting on a feather pillow.

George's gaze fell on him. "Silas." He tried to shift in bed and grimaced.

"Please, don't move on my account. How does thee feel?"

"In pain. And frustrated. The horse I was training will falter if the training isn't continued. Father wanted to shoot the horse for attacking me." His face twisted at the thought. "I told him no. The horse didn't know any better. It was an accident."

"I'm sorry thee is hurt." Silas was glad to use the Friends' language. A wounded Friend lay before him, one who struggled with a terrible injury, who might even be crippled. Using the wording was wholly fitting and honoring of the man and his beliefs, the one who had tried his best to help him and Barzillai.

"Thanks. I don't know how long I must stay in bed. No one will tell me." He tried once more to sit up and muttered in pain. "Has thee heard any news?"

"Only that it's a severe break. And how sick thee has been with the wound where the leg bone pierced through."

George winced. "I may never be the same, will I, Silas?"

The voice of desperation tugged at the core of Silas. "I—I don't know, George. I will pray." And he meant it. Pray he must, but restoring fellowship with God he must do first. If he could reconcile the past.

He walked out, his head down, scuffing along the wooden floor, when he noticed a pair of leather shoes before him and a brown skirt. He looked up to see Mary, carrying a pitcher. "Did thee see George?" she asked. "His fever has broken. I'm so thankful."

"He looks much better. And he's asking questions about his condition. How long he might be in bed. He fears being crippled."

Mary's hands trembled at the words, and for a moment Silas thought she might drop the pitcher. He thrust out his hand to steady the vessel, which she placed on a nearby table. "The doctor comes again today. I fear what he will say. But we must remain hopeful in God."

"I told him I would pray."

Mary stared at Silas in appreciation when he said these words, as if they had unlocked another door between them. During the past week he'd already sensed a door opening. The other day she'd thanked him for helping her father with the chores around the house. What would she say now if she learned that her father wanted to hire him? Would she welcome it? Or would she wish him gone, as she did before the accident and after the kiss they'd shared?

Silas decided not to say anything just yet. Instead, he went to the woodpile to make certain the woodbox was filled. He then walked to the corral and George's precious herd of horses, including the rambunctious stallion that had been the cause of the young man's misfortune. He knew a little about training horses from helping with Barzillai. What a surprise it would be for George if he could train the animal not to rear up and kick. It was a small price to pay for the way the young man had nursed Barzillai back to health.

Silas picked up the pole George had used with the animal and began gently rubbing the tail. At first the horse neighed and backed away. Ever so slowly Silas worked with the animal. A gentle prod there. A poke here. And then he was able to lead the horse to one side of the corral. Excitement built within him, even more so when he noticed Mary coming over to the corral to watch.

"Wherever did thee learn to do that?"

"My grandfather. Barzillai was actually his horse. He gave her to me." Silas allowed the horse to rest and met Mary where she stood by the fence. "I thought it might be a nice surprise for George if I could continue at least some of the training."

"It's kind of thee."

He stared at the horse as it gathered grass from a hay bale.

"So does thee plan to stay here?"

Silas glanced at their fine home and then at Mary. "Does thee want me to stay?"

She looked at him in surprise. "It's not for me to decide. I know Father asked if thee might be able to help him. He needs an extra hand, what with all the work that must be done." She paused. "I would be grateful if thee did stay."

"Then I will stay, Mary, if thee wants me to." He saw her face brighten and even the teasing of a smile form on her delicate lips. Inwardly his heart sang. Not for their circumstances, but that those circumstances could be used in good ways. Like being with Mary.

Mary turned and made for the house. Then he heard the rumble of a wagon from the road. Friend Daniel Gray. Silas blew out a sigh. The pious Quaker had come for a visit and maybe more. So much for his good intentions where Mary was concerned. He feared he would be forever lost in the elder Friend's holy shadow.

Chapter 6

Mary sat still in her chair, her hands folded demurely, her gaze focused on the wooden flooring beneath her shoes as Friend Daniel sat opposite her. He had come to pay a call, first to check on George's progress and then to be with her. She'd heard the elder and Father conversing in the sitting room and wished she were a mouse scurrying about so she could overhear their words. But afterward Daniel came out, his thin lips curved into a crooked smile, and inquired if she would like to sit with him. She knew then the result of the meeting. He'd asked Father's permission for visits between them in their home, and Father had agreed.

But now her gaze drifted to the window and Silas outside in the front yard, hard at work splitting wood. From the swiftness of his work with the ax, she wondered if he wrestled with some internal struggle. He turned back to the house with his face contorted in a grimace. Her cheeks felt warm at the sight. What might he be thinking? Was he dismayed over Friend Daniel's visit? Did he have a desire to be inside talking to her rather than her conversing with the elder?

She heard Daniel clear his throat, and her gaze turned to him. He stared at her. "Once again thee appears preoccupied during our visit. Is thee upset to be with me?"

"Of course not. I'm glad thee is here. George is thankful to have an elder come bear his burden. Thee brings the joy of God's Light into our home." She hoped she didn't sound too zealous, even as her sights once more drifted to the window and Silas attacking the logs as though the chunks were some enemy he wished to conquer. She considered the last few days. George's accident and how Silas had rushed to help. The trip into town. His decision to stay and help Father. She spoke up then. "Does thee know that Friend Silas is staying to help us?"

"I did ask thy father if he required help, and he said that Silas Jones agreed to stay and assist. I was very glad to hear it." He paused. "I was wondering—would thee consider accompanying me to Meeting this Friday?"

"Go to Meeting with you?" Her mind was a blank.

"We are having a special gathering. I thought thee might want to attend with me."

"I. . ." She found herself twisting her fingers. "Oh, I do love Meetings, Friend Daniel. It's just. . ." She paused. "George may still need help. If we have guests also, Father and Mother need help serving them."

Daniel looked at her rather somberly. "Why do I feel as if thee is avoiding me?

40

Have I done something wrong?"

Mary straightened and looked into his dark blue eyes that displayed his concern, along with the rigid lines crisscrossing his face. "Oh no, certainly not. It's just. . ." Mary didn't even know why she stumbled over such an important invitation. Surely it couldn't be the man behind the ax outside their window. She felt strange even considering it. There was, too, the other reason she had confessed to Silas during their journey to town. "I know that with thy loss of thy wife, Elizabeth. . . ," she began.

"Is that what this is about? Mary, please don't think that my previous affection for Elizabeth means I cannot love and care for another woman. It has been over a year since her passage to glory. She is in a better place. God is the healer of our wounds and the giver of life and love."

Her gaze fell once more to the window. To her startled surprise, Silas was staring straight at the window at the same moment, as if they shared some secret communication of the heart and soul. She wondered if God would heal Silas's wounds and be the giver of life and love in their circumstances. *Oh dear, what am I thinking?*

She stirred in her seat, again feeling the warm flush in her cheeks. Then she sensed Daniel's stark perusal, as if he could read every thought and feeling passing through her. She stood quickly. The wrap around her shoulders fell to the floor. "Let me fetch us some tea, Friend Daniel. Please excuse me." She grabbed the shawl off the floor and hurried into the kitchen, thankful for the respite. "Dearest God, what am I going to do?" she said aloud, looking for the kettle. "I don't know what to do."

"Is something wrong, Mary?" Mother entered the kitchen, clad in her apron dusted white with flour from the morning's baking.

"I—I was only praying, Mother."

"A good thing to do, dear one." Mother gave her a kiss on the cheek. "But thee does seem troubled these days. I must say I'm not sure why. George is feeling stronger every day. I believe we will soon see a miracle with his leg."

Mary sighed, thankful Mother didn't realize her inner turmoil had nothing to do with George, though she did care for him. It had everything to do with the two men outside the walls of the kitchen, each playing with her heart in different ways. "Mother, did thee always know Father would be thy intended?"

"Of course. Our parents agreed to it. And so did the eldership. There was no mistaking it."

"I don't want to make a mistake either."

"Oh dear one." Mother reached out to take Mary's hand in hers. "Is it Friend Gray? I know he has asked to court you."

"He is a nice man. A good man of God. But. . ." She hesitated. "I don't know if he's the man for me. I fear thee and Father will both agree that he is, and then my heart will be forever troubled, wondering if it was truly God's will."

"Mary, thee must trust God in these things. He guides us in matters of the heart. He will guide thee and help thee see His will with regards to the perfect man and husband." The kettle began to steam, and Mary fetched a cup. Mother poured hot water over the tea leaves. "I believe thee will be happy and content with God's choice."

Mary nodded and carried the tea to Friend Daniel who, to her surprise, stood with his back to her, staring out the window to witness Silas in his labor. He whirled as she entered. "Thank thee," he said quietly as she set the cup on a table. "Is this outsider, Mr. Jones, still affecting thee?"

"Affecting me? I don't understand."

He picked up the teacup. "I know thee was deeply troubled by his difficult mannerisms when thee came to see me awhile ago."

Mary remembered it well and now wished she had never made the visit. Perhaps if she had given her fears over to God and allowed Him to correct them as He saw fit, she wouldn't be in this predicament of the heart. "He did apologize."

Daniel grimaced. "Does thee realize the man was once a Quaker and then disowned by the Friends in Philadelphia?"

Mary stared wide-eyed. "Silas told me he was a Friend. But I. . .I didn't know he was disowned. What did he do so wrong among the brethren?"

"Awhile ago I met with a visiting Friend in Waynesville who was once associated with the Friends in Philadelphia. It seems Silas Jones had a grandfather who was mistreated by outsiders. The man eventually died from his wounds. Instead of embracing the Light in this grave situation, Silas wanted revenge. That, of course, is not the Friends' way. When he became disorderly, looking to take matters into his own hands, he was asked to leave."

Mary continued to stare at Daniel until she realized what she was doing and shifted her gaze to the floorboards. "I didn't know this. I knew he was troubled by some matter. I knew he'd suffered loss."

"He didn't just lose a loved one, but I fear he has also lost his soul and spirit. Thee would do well to allow others to deal with his condition, Mary. Thee isn't meant to have this brought upon thyself, nor is thee meant to correct it. He must bear witness to the truth."

Mary listened to the elder's advice. Instead of yielding, she yearned to help Silas even more now that she understood why he reacted the way he did. She realized how the previous disagreements they had were spurred by events in his life. Loss can sometimes cause one to do things one wouldn't normally do. Driven by grief, in deep mourning, some must act out their feelings. She recalled his struggle with injustice. How the Friends had seemingly turned a deaf ear to the things that weighed him down. The shattered glass of life could be mended still. All was not lost.

Friend Daniel placed his hat on his head. "I hope thee understands that we must release Friend Jones to the elders and to God. And thee must take care to keep separate from this situation."

Mary struggled with this pronouncement as she watched Daniel stride toward the door. Of course she wanted to humble herself and agree with the elder. Instead, she returned to the window to see that Silas had just finished his task at the wood-pile. Outside, Friend Daniel stopped before him to offer his hand, which Silas shook. They exchanged words that Mary could not hear but wished she could. Then Daniel left in his wagon.

At dinner that night Mary couldn't help but watch Silas eat as he sat opposite her. He'd said little at the table, which didn't matter since the three guests who had arrived made plenty of conversation for them all. But his stark silence weighed heavily on her. What thoughts were roaming about in his mind? Torturous thoughts, no doubt. Thoughts of grave loss and then chastisement for being human when he needed a loving touch and firm guidance. All the things the Friends normally did in times of trouble. But he did not receive such love, only chastisement. No wonder he disliked the brethren and was eager to find a new life elsewhere. A new life in a new place seemed much more appealing, but it would not heal what he'd left behind. The past would continue to haunt him until he made peace with it.

After the dishes were done, Mary wandered into the library to find Silas reading a book. To her surprise, it was an older work by Friend William Penn. He seemed so engaged; he never even glanced up until she sat down in a nearby chair and cleared her throat.

"Mary." In an instant he put down the book.

"Friend Silas. I'm surprised thee has chosen to read a work by a Quaker."

Silas shrugged. "Grandfather once told me how the man suffered injustice and wanted retribution. But he found the strength of God to stay his hand and his spirit."

"He suffered like thee."

His eyebrows drew together. "And how would thee know what I feel?"

"Oh, come now, Silas. It wasn't hard to see that thee was troubled the moment thee came to find rest in our home. How thee scorned the Friends when thee first came here. And then thee talked of trouble in Philadelphia, which was confirmed by Friend Daniel on his visit."

Silas blinked, silent for a moment before he straightened. "I don't understand. How does your Daniel know anything about me or what happened in Philadelphia? Is he so enraptured by the Light that God came and spoke to him in a vision?"

Mary felt her cheeks warm, and she turned aside to gaze at the lone flame flickering within the lamp on the table. "I shouldn't have brought it up."

"Yes, you should. You know things. Things about me. Things you obviously don't understand."

"Yes, there are things I do know. How your, I mean, thy grandfather was mistreated in the streets by outsiders and died from his wounds. And yet the Friends would not oblige thee by making retribution but sought forgiveness instead. And when thee found thyself unable to bridle the passion that demanded an eye for an eye, thee was forced out of fellowship." She watched his fingers tighten around the book he held.

"So you know now I didn't leave Philadelphia peaceably. What they did was wrong. My grandfather loved the brethren with all his heart and soul. They punished me and showed mercy to those who murdered him."

"Oh dearest Silas." Mary looked at him and extended her hand. "If thee could only know God's true heart. His understanding. His compassion for those in His Light and for those who only look in. And His justice."

In an instant her words drove him to his feet. "I saw no such compassion or justice. My grandfather is still dead and my name tarnished when I have done nothing to deserve it."

"It isn't tarnished here. You are accepted. In fact, I will show thee. Come to Meeting with me." She paused. "There is one this Friday."

Silas shook his head. "I can't."

"Why? Thee is not banished from us. Or from our home. Or from me."

Silas sat back down, his gaze never leaving her. Mary realized now the strength found in the words she spoke bordered on a commitment to him in her heart. What was it about Silas Jones that drew her? She wasn't sure, yet during the past week she had seen the true essence of the man buried beneath the wound. The Light shone quite brightly, even if it was sometimes covered by a basket of disappointment. He was a man who helped in their time of great need. A man of commitment. A man who could love with great depth. And a man whose heart needed only to receive the healing balm of God to make him whole. But Silas must choose whether to embrace God's love and the care of others, like herself. Or live life in misery.

She saw then his internal struggle with the way he shifted about, his fingers clenching and unclenching. He stood once more and began to pace, until they heard a shuffle in the nearby hall. George struggled into the library, limping along on the pair of wooden crutches Silas and Father had made for him.

"George! Why is thee out of bed?" Mary cried, racing to his side.

His pinched, drawn face revealed his pain, yet he looked at Silas with unmistakable compassion. "I couldn't help but hear. And Mary is right, Silas. In thy heart thee must know she speaks the truth."

Silas looked at him but said nothing. Mary saw his taut face begin to relax, as if George's opinion meant something to him. Especially now, watching him teeter on a pair of crutches with a fractured leg. How similar to a wounded soul, crippled by the heartrending things that happen in life. But George came forward in determination to walk through his suffering. She wondered if Silas could see it and be encouraged.

"Mary told me about Meeting this Friday," Silas began.

"I hope to go," George said. "I already missed First Day Meeting. And I hope thee will be able to help me. I need a strong arm to support me. As we all do, I should say."

"Of course I will help in any way I can. But I don't agree to attend the meeting itself, thee understands."

Mary couldn't help but smile, seeing George wink. A clever man, her brother. *Thank Thee, O Lord. Thou has made the way for Silas to seek the help he needs. How I pray he will see Thy glorious Light where he might find rest for his soul.* She inhaled a nervous breath, and her heart began to flutter furiously. *And maybe a path of Light for us both, Lord, if it be Thy will.*

Chapter 7

Silas didn't know what guided his footsteps as he helped George from the wagon that carried them all to the white brick meetinghouse. If he didn't know better, he'd think that George had purposely injured himself so Silas would need to help the man attend Meeting. Of course that wasn't so, but Silas could see the scripture coming to pass that speaks of all things working together for good.

After he'd guided George to the steps of the building, where the Friends warmly greeted each other, he decided to find a seat in the rear of the humble building. He didn't care that Mary was at the front of the gathering with Friend Daniel sitting across the aisle from her. Instead, his heart and soul were on the words shared and the sense of belonging that replaced the abandonment he'd once felt.

Silas could picture his grandfather then. The man's sturdy frame and shining blue eyes. His strong faith that refused to surrender even in the midst of persecution and death. A faith that surpassed it all to stand in eternal glory. Silas felt his soul stir. Perhaps he'd disappointed Grandfather. He hadn't allowed Christ to triumph over his enemies but met the enemy with anger, an enemy that eventually became one of Silas's own making. Everything Grandfather had taught him would be for naught if Silas allowed his anger to continue.

At the conclusion of the meeting Silas still sat in his place on the bench, not even hearing his name until he looked up to see Friend Daniel Gray standing above him. "I'm pleased to see thee here, Friend Silas. And what did thee think of Meeting? Has thee seen a change in thy condition?"

Silas waited, listening. Then his gaze caught Mary's as she walked up the center of the meetinghouse, her lips forming a faint smile, her cheeks flushed with excitement—a pure vision of holy beauty in his eyes. "Yes, a change, Friend Daniel. I will let the darkness out."

"Praise be." The man patted him on the shoulder. "I'm very glad to hear this."

"Really? I should think with thy heart on a certain young lady, it would be difficult."

Friend Daniel flushed and looked around as if expecting someone to be eavesdropping on their conversation. "It is not proper to. . ." He paused. "I will allow our gracious Lord to deal with the matters of the heart, Friend Silas. But thee has no fear. I understand that both thee and Mary have affection for each other. Thy name was on her lips today as she announced that thee was coming to Meeting. So be of good cheer." He smiled.

Silas sat in amazement as the elder left. His name had been on Mary's lips? She had been speaking about him to others? And then suddenly she stood before him, the radiant beauty of God's true Light burning inside her heart and beaming from her soft features. She had physical beauty, to be sure, but spiritual beauty as well. He came to his feet and faced her.

"Is something wrong?" she asked. "Thee is looking at me strangely."

"Nothing is wrong. Everything is good. More than good, I must say. There is peace once again in my heart."

"Oh, I'm so glad, Silas." She threw her arms around him as several Friends gasped and stared. She withdrew, looking sheepishly about as if expecting a rebuke for such an outward display. But smiles were on the faces of the brethren as well as their own as they left the meetinghouse together.

George waited for them, having already been helped to the wagon by some other Friends. He reclined in the wagon bed on some blankets, observing Silas and Mary with interest as they walked over. "I see it was a prosperous Meeting, Friend Silas. In more than just the Light? Perhaps also in love?"

"Yes, it was indeed prosperous." Silas said it with such passion that it drew a gleeful chuckle from Mary. "I only fear, Friend George, that thee had wished this injury upon thyself just to drag a lowly one like me to Meeting."

George shook his head. "I'm not *that* fond of thee! If God had another way, I'd much prefer it, but I trust in His wisdom. And I'm grateful that everything does work together for good, according to the blessed scripture. If the suffering of one can bring healing to others, then it's good suffering to bear."

Silas marveled at his words. How could suffering ever be good? But looking at Mary, so fair and lovely at his side—if his own personal suffering came about just so he could meet her, then it was well for his soul, too. He could find the same measure of peace in it as George had.

On the ride home they said little, but the unspoken words conveyed much. With no one observing, Silas's fingers found Mary's hand beneath the woolen lap robe and gave a squeeze of reassurance, and he prayed a symbol of his affection. To his delight, she returned the favor. So she was thinking of him, too. He also thought about other things. What it would be like to marry a true Friend of the faith. Though he did hope on occasion they could dispense with the Quakers' formal language. He would love to simply say—*"You have the most wonderful smile, my love. And your lips are like clover honey that I would very much like to consume."*

"Thee hasn't heard a word spoken," Mary murmured, poking him playfully in the arm. "What is thee thinking?"

He saw her scrutinize him. "If I told thee, thee would blush."

She blushed anyway. "So did thee hear George's question? He asked if thee will be leaving anytime soon."

Silas glanced at her and then to the wagon bed to consider the young man who had been a help to him in more ways than he could say. "No matter how many times I wanted to leave, God has kept me here. And for very good reasons."

"And not because of my injury," George reminded him.

"Because He knows our hearts. He knew I wouldn't leave all of thee in thy time of need."

Mary snuggled beside him. "Does thee see his heart, George?"

"I always knew Silas had a heart full of God's Light. But he didn't, and maybe neither did others. Everyone was mistaken."

Silas hoped he did have a proper heart, even though he'd made mistakes. If he could be even a fraction of what Grandfather had been to so many in Philadelphia, he would thankfully carry the Jones' name. He settled on doing all that he could to help here in this place. Any thought of removing himself to go west lay as a forgotten dream while he embraced a hopeful future.

◆ ◆ ◆

A few days later, several visitors arrived to share in the Christmas holiday. While the Halls did not celebrate themselves, they prepared to host their guests with a celebration that included a fine meal, prayers, and lighting candles. Mrs. Hall baked her famous molasses cake, which was greatly enjoyed. But one of the visitors at the table, a young man, stared at Silas in a way that made him feel uncomfortable. He tried to place the man, with his medium frame and sandy-colored hair, but could not.

After the meal, the man motioned to Silas to come join him in the sitting room. "What can I do for thee?" Silas asked, taking a seat opposite him.

The man sighed numerous times, wiping his hands together as his feet thumped the floor. "I–I'm not sure how to say this...," he began. "But I needed to come here. If it weren't for that Quaker in Waynesville..."

Silas stared. "I don't understand. Have we met?"

"No, not really. You see, I come from Philadelphia."

Silas straightened. His muscles tightened, but he forced himself to relax when he saw Mary standing in the open doorway of the room. He hoped she was praying for him. He feared what was about to happen, and he would need all the strength he could muster to face it. "Oh?" he managed to say.

"I found out where you were staying from the letter sent by the Quaker in Waynesville to the Quakers in Philadelphia. I—I came as soon as I heard of your whereabouts."

Silas wondered if something had happened in his family. To his father. Or his brother, though he had never mentioned them to Mary or anyone else. He felt convicted.

"I went and talked to your father about what happened." He paused. "He has forgiven me. He showed me the letter and said I should see you as soon as possible."

Silas sensed the heat filling his ears. He wasn't sure he had the strength for this. "Forgiven thee for what?"

"For what I did to the old man. I—I didn't know he was your grandfather. No one did. We—we thought he was just a crazy old man no one cared about. I wasn't the one that injured him. Th–that was Paul. But I know..." He hesitated. Silas saw him begin to tremble, and he tried his best not to tremble, too. "But I helped hold the old man along with others while Paul beat him. Please, I have nightmares about it. What we did in the street. And. . .and I know he didn't live. I am so sorry. I live with the guilt of it every day. I realized from your father how much the man meant to you. How what we had done drove you away. When I learned where you were, I had to come beg for your forgiveness."

The news shook Silas to the core. He looked over to where Mary once stood. The spot was vacant, but she was undoubtedly close enough to overhear the confession. And she would look at him with her clear blue eyes, accompanied by her soothing voice. *"Oh dearest Silas. Thee must forgive and let it go. Thy grandfather is at peace with God. And so must thee be."*

Silas heard himself say to the man, "Grandfather is at peace. But I know thee is not. The only way thee can find true peace is through the Prince of Peace, who thee celebrates this Christmas Day. He must dwell in thee to make thee whole." Silas hesitated. "It's true I was angry about what happened. I lost someone I dearly loved. I wanted to see thee hurt because I was hurt. But I see now what it has done to me, thee, and others. That true forgiveness is the only path to peace."

The young man's eyes glistened with tears. "I could not go through Christmas with this in my heart. That's why I came as quickly as I could. I prayed you would still be here. Rumors were you were headed west to California."

"I've found my place and purpose here. And thee must find thy place." Silas saw the man's face quiver.

"I don't know. There is no peace for me on this earth."

"Yes, there is. While forgiveness can take time, I trust in my God that He will supply this free gift and supply thy need as well."

"That is all I can hope for. Now I can leave."

Silas held out his hand. "There is no need. Stay as long as thee wishes."

He waved to Mary, who had ducked into the doorway once more. "Please say hello to my new friend here, not of the Society, but a friend in need and of the kind we will not turn away. No matter what hurt has been caused."

With those words, Silas found what he had been longing for. Peace at last with Grandfather's passing. And perhaps even an affirmation the older man would have given had he been alive. *"Yes indeed, grandson. Thee has truly seen and felt the Light! Just as our elder William Penn once said: 'Christ's cross is Christ's way to Christ's crown.'"*

◆　◆　◆

That evening Silas sat in front of the fireplace, looking at the flames dancing before him. Everyone else had already gone to their rooms for the night, but he couldn't sleep after what happened. He marveled at God's hand that could take a situation many miles away and arrange for healing to occur even in a remote place in the middle of Ohio, and at an inn of all things.

He heard a sigh then and saw Mary approach. He stood to his feet, watching the golden firelight cast a holy aura across her face. She came forward without hesitation. "God indeed worked miracles this night," she said softly, smiling. "With the guest."

"Yes," he agreed. "Who would have thought?"

"God cares about our pain and our healing. But most of all, He cares that we draw close to Him in our time of need. Just as we also need each other."

"I care for thee," Silas said quickly. "I care what happens to thee. How you feel. Or how thee feels, that is. I hope thee has need of me."

"More than just a need, Friend Silas. I wonder if thee might be in a dream for my life."

"I do dream of you," he said, drawing her gently to him. She submitted, and they shared a sweet kiss before the snapping of the fire as the flames consumed the wood.

"Dream no longer," she said softly.

"I have no need, if I can ask thy father to court thee."

"He already suspects."

Silas stepped back. "But how can he? I haven't spoken of it, and—"

She laughed. "Father doesn't live on the roof. He knows quite well what is happening in his household. He will be most glad to have thee as my suitor. And I must say, I'm glad as well."

Silas took her in his arms, with a peace that surpassed all his understanding, thankful for these precious gifts from God above.

Mrs. Hall's Molasses Cake

1 cup molasses
¼ cup butter, cut in pieces
½ tablespoon cinnamon
2 small eggs, beaten
1¾ cups flour
½ teaspoon baking soda, dissolved in small amount of warm water

Grease 9x9-inch pan. Stir molasses and butter in saucepan over very low heat until butter is soft enough to mix together easily. Then add cinnamon, the beaten eggs slowly, and sifted flour. Stir until lumps are out then add dissolved baking soda. Bake at 350 degrees for 35 to 40 minutes. Test with toothpick for doneness.

May be served with sweetened whipped cream or a cream cheese frosting like this one:

1 (8 ounce) package cream cheese
1 tablespoon milk
¾ cup powdered sugar
Dash cinnamon

Mix all ingredients, adding more sugar if needed to desired consistency and sweetness. Spread on cooled cake.

Lauralee Bliss has always liked to dream big dreams. Part of that dream was writing, and after several years of hard work, her dream of publishing was realized in 1997 with the publication of her first romance novel, *Mountaintop*, through Barbour Publishing. Since then she's had twenty books published, both historical and contemporary. Lauralee is also an avid hiker, completing the entire length of the Appalachian Trail both north and south. Lauralee makes her home in Virginia in the foothills of the Blue Ridge Mountains with her family. Visit her website at www.lauraleebliss.com and find her on Twitter and Facebook Readers of Author Lauralee Bliss.

Simple Gifts

by Ramona K. Cecil

Chapter 1

S hoo!"

Lucinda Hughes gently nudged the Rhode Island Red hen off its straw-filled nest.

Puck, puck, puck, puckaaw! The plump bird angled its rust-colored head and gave Lucinda an amber-eyed glare. But the hen moved away from the nest and, with a flurry of wings that sent dust flying in the dim chicken coop, jumped to the dirt floor.

Coughing, Lucinda wrinkled her nose and fought the urge to sneeze. "Well, thank thee, Miss Red. Thee took long enough." The fowl strutted into the next room as if proud of what she'd accomplished. A giggle bubbled from Lucinda's throat. The sound surprised her. Her laugh faded as she reached into the indention in the moldy straw and wrapped her fingers around the warm, brown egg.

When had she regained the ability to laugh? Not so long ago she'd thought she would never laugh again.

She and Alan used to laugh all the time. She remembered how they'd laughed that day last March when he brought home the crate of pullets and young roosters. He might have brought her a crate of gold, for the jubilation it evoked.

She tucked the egg into the basket along with the eight she'd already gathered—fruits of the now-mature hens.

Alan had caught her up in his strong arms, lifting her feet off the ground as he'd loved to do. "Thee is a Quaker farmwife now," he'd said. "Thee should have thy own chickens."

Old Mercy Cox said love didn't just happen. That real love grew slowly over time. But Lucinda had known she loved Alan from that first moment sixteen months ago, when she first saw him at a Gurneyite Quaker revival meeting in Kentucky. Could all that had happened since been stuffed into the short span of sixteen months?

Blinking back hot tears, she passed through the roosting area of the coop where several of the chickens already clung to the stair-stepped sapling poles, their eyelids drooping. She emitted a small groan as she bent over her expanded middle to exit the coop's low doorway.

Outside, a cool gust of November wind dried the wetness on her cheeks and sent a shiver through her. Gripping the handle of her egg basket, she gazed at the two-story cabin that sat on the rise in front of her. How proud Alan had been that day last December when he brought her, a new bride, to the hewn-log cabin his grandfather had built sixty years before.

Her gaze drifted to the back of the cabin where a small frame structure jutted out from the old log building. A bittersweet feeling twanged in her chest. Alan had completed half of their new kitchen by the middle of June, when the explosion happened at the grain mill where he worked. So great was the blast that even from a mile away, the cabin had shaken, sending a stoneware pitcher flying from the mantel above the fireplace.

She remembered wondering if the loud boom and shaking was an earth tremor and then grieving over the loss of the pitcher, a wedding present from Mercy. She would soon learn that she'd suffered a far greater loss than any keepsake. For the same instant the pitcher smashed against the puncheon floor, the explosion had killed Alan, shattering Lucinda's life.

The babe within her kicked, as if flailing against the injustice of never knowing his father.

She'd never felt as alone as she did the day of Alan's funeral when she walked away from the little Quaker graveyard, leaving her young husband beneath the mound of dirt. Only the thought of her coming child had saved her mind and spirit from crushing despair.

The congregation of Serenity Friends Meeting had gathered around her, seeing to her immediate needs. The men had even worked together to finish the kitchen. But when Lucinda stopped attending Meeting, the helping hands had become fewer. Only Mercy Cox and Will Davis came regularly now.

At the thought of her late husband's best friend, warmth filled Lucinda. Since the accident, not a week passed without Will stopping by to bring her milk and groceries, take care of some chore, or make a repair to the cabin.

Her face turned unbidden toward the dirt road running past the front of her property. Earlier, when she'd stepped out of the cabin to head for the chicken coop, the mill's whistle had sounded, signaling the end of the workday. Will's mule and wagon would appear soon if he planned to stop by on his way home.

Squinting against the setting sun's bright rays, she gazed through the nearly barren branches of the old poplar tree that partially obscured her view of the road. But the only movement on the dirt thoroughfare was a shower of brown and yellow leaves caught up by a gust of wind.

Though she had no need for provisions or Will's assistance, a feeling akin to disappointment pushed a sigh from her lips and dragged down her shoulders. When had she started looking forward to Will's visits?

She brushed aside the unexpected pang of melancholy along with a strand of hair that had blown across her face. Tucking the errant lock back under her bonnet, she started for the cabin. Maybe Mercy was right when she warned that spending too much time alone in the cabin would shrivel Lucinda's mind and spirit.

The *clip-clop* of hooves and the rumble of a conveyance drew her attention to the road. For a moment her heart quickened but then slowed at the sight of a one-horse shay in the distance instead of a mule-drawn wagon.

When the buggy turned into the lane that wound up to her cabin, she groaned in dismay and immediately felt guilty. Mercy had hinted during her visit yesterday that Levi Braddock and his wife, Charity, might stop by this week. Though Lucinda knew the elder and his wife meant well, she'd begun to dread their calls. Lately, their visits focused less on inquiring about her welfare and more on encouraging her to attend Meeting. But she refused to sit in Meeting and pretend to pray to a God with whom she no longer felt a connection.

The buggy rounded the curve in the lane, and Lucinda saw that it carried only one person. A man. He lifted his head, and she recognized not Levi Braddock's but Will Davis's face beneath the wide-brimmed black hat.

Her heart began to prance like the young black horse pulling the buggy.

It's just because I'm glad it's not the Braddocks wanting to pressure me into attending Meeting tonight.

Then why had her thumping heart not slowed its pace? She ignored the troublesome thought and stepped toward the buggy.

"Lucinda." Smiling, Will raised his hand in greeting and reined the horse to a stop. In one continuous motion, he wrapped the reins around the brake's handle and stepped to the ground. His lanky frame moved with grace as he came around to the horse's head to pet the skittish animal and murmur reassurances.

"Is there somethin' the matter with Bob?" She nodded at the young horse.

"Naw, the mule's in fine fettle." He ambled toward her, giving her that shy, little-boy smile that seemed somehow odd on a grown man. "Simeon just bought this two-year-old colt." He glanced over his shoulder. "He asked me to get him used to the buggy before Naomi takes it out."

Lucinda nodded, her smile fading. Cold and sharp-tongued, Will's sister-in-law, Naomi, was not one of her favorite members at Serenity Friends Meeting.

Will took the egg basket from Lucinda's hands and headed toward the cabin. "I just came from visiting Mercy Cox."

Lucinda fell in step beside him, and it struck her how, without being asked, he was always doing little kindnesses. "I pray Mercy is well."

He nodded and gave her a reassuring smile. "Yes, she is well and holds thee in the Light."

Lucinda loved the Quaker expression for keeping someone in one's thoughts and prayers.

When they reached the kitchen door, he stopped and glanced upward. "Mercy mentioned that thy kitchen roof is leaking."

"Yes. It is just a small drip, but when it rained the day before yesterday, I had to put a pan under it to keep the floor dry." Had Will visited Mercy this evening in hopes of finding a reason to stop by here on his way home? Shame filled Lucinda for both the thought and the spark of joy Will's visit ignited inside her.

He held the egg basket out to her. She took it, and their hands touched, sending a pleasant ripple of warmth up her arm. "It will be winter soon. And a hole that will let in rain will let in cold air. I would be happy to fix it if I wouldn't be a bother."

"Yes—I mean no." Heat flooded Lucinda's face. She must look like a ninny with her words tripping over her tongue. Her laugh, the second one today, came out in a nervous-sounding warble, sending another burst of heat to her face. "Yes, I would like the roof fixed. And no, of course thee is not a bother." That was a flat-out lie. Will's presence bothered her greatly. She wrapped her arms around the egg basket to calm her discomposure. "I'm afraid I'm the bother."

For an instant, a shadow passed across his face before turning serious. She could almost feel the warm caress of his gray eyes on her face. "Thee is not a bother to me, Lucinda."

Somehow Lucinda managed to escape his gaze and stumble into the kitchen on legs that felt like they'd turned to jelly. With unsteady hands, she set the basket on the table then slumped to a chair. Will was like an older brother to Alan. Of course he wanted to help her. Just like all the other times he'd helped her since June.

He only meant that doing God's work is not a bother.

Yet she didn't believe a word of it. She'd heard Will's voice and seen his face. The look in his eyes snatched the breath right out of her lungs.

But Will was Alan's best friend!

That fact, however, didn't calm the tumult in her chest. Her heart beat like the wings of a gaggle of geese about to take flight. Something had changed between her and Will. And that change both excited and terrified her.

Chapter 2

Perched high on the ladder, Will slipped the top edge of a new red cedar shingle beneath the bottom edge of the weathered one above it. The wood's rich scent filled his nostrils and whisked him back to last spring when he had helped Alan cut the shingles for the new kitchen's roof.

He paused to gaze over the roof. As always, thoughts of his late friend sent tentacles of guilt throughout his chest—guilt that gnarled painfully around his heart. The feeling had become a constant companion.

Alan should be doing this. Alan should be here. . . .

But he wasn't here. And the blame for that lay squarely on Will's shoulders. Over the past five months, the weight of that blame had become a ponderous mantle that grew heavier each day.

If only he had refused Alan's request to switch jobs that day at the mill. *If only. . .*

Balancing on the ladder's rung, he shoved his hand into his trouser pocket and pulled out a nail. Two sharp blows of his hammer drove it deep into the shingle. The aggressive movement relieved a measure of pent-up emotion building inside him, and he quickly added two more nails to the shingle.

He reached for a fourth nail but let it fall back into his pocket with a clink against its fellows. The job was done. And no amount of hammering would expel the anger and regret that dwelled inside him. Sometimes he wished Quakers were not so peace loving. Once in a while, it would feel good to plow his fist into. . .something.

"Cease from anger, and forsake wrath." The words from Psalm 37:8 convicted him. He would need to spend much time in prayer at Meeting this evening.

But anger was the least of his sins. He breathed out a ragged breath and began to back down the ladder. All day he'd tried without success to think of a reason—any reason—to stop by Lucinda's cabin. So this afternoon when Mercy told him about the leak in Lucinda's roof, his heart had leaped inside his chest.

Another wave of shame and guilt washed through him. When had his vow to see to the needs of Alan's widow become more than a simple act of Christian charity?

He remembered the first time he saw Lucinda sitting beside Mercy Cox, with whom she'd resided, at Meeting nearly a year and a half ago. A group from the congregation had just returned from a revival trip to Kentucky where the preaching of Friend John Henry Douglas had convinced many, including Lucinda, to join the Quakers. For a brief time, he had even considered courting her. Then he learned that she and Alan—his best friend and foster brother—had become attached to one another. After that, he'd thought of her only as a sister. Until now.

He hoisted the ladder onto his shoulder and headed to the toolshed. When he opened the door, its rusty hinges creaked in protest. Perhaps he should oil them.

"Tomorrow," he promised the dim interior of the shed as he slid the ladder along the floor lengthwise and leaned it against the wall. Yes, tomorrow would be a good day to see to the hinges.

His heart quickened as he strode through the lengthening shadows toward the cabin. Only an amber wedge of waning sunlight caressed the west side of the log building. Through the poplar tree's skeletal fingers he could make out streaks of pink and gold smeared across the slate gray sky.

A cold gust of wind lifted a pile of dried leaves in front of him. Despite his wide-brimmed hat and canvas coat, the wind sent a chill through him. The light from the kitchen window beckoned. How easy to imagine walking into the warm embrace of the cabin. *And that of the woman inside it.*

But those things could never be his. Even if by some miracle God blessed him with Lucinda's affection—affection beyond that of a sister—his abiding guilt surely would throw up a barrier thicker than the log walls of the old cabin to separate them.

He knocked at the kitchen door, his heartbeats matching the quick tempo of his raps. At his summons the door opened, drenching him in a comforting rush of warmth. The tempting scents of sassafras and cinnamon met him, teasing his nose. Lucinda stood framed in the doorway. Her black bonnet was gone now. A few wisps of her hair had pulled loose from the bun at the back of her head and curled appealingly against her temples. The sun's dying rays caught them, burnishing the locks to the rich color of clover honey. He had seen her at least once a week over the past year and a half, but he couldn't remember her looking lovelier than she did at this moment.

His throat went dry. He cleared it. Twice. "Thee only lost one shingle. Probably during that storm last week." Needing to shift his gaze from her face, he looked up at the roof. How stupid she must think him. His face turned back to hers as if pulled by a magnet. "There were extra in the shed, so I replaced it."

"Thank thee, Will. Now I can keep the dishpan in the sink instead of on the floor." Smiling, she glanced down almost shyly. "Good night to thee," she murmured then turned and started to close the door.

"Lucinda." Desperate for one last glimpse of her, he blurted her name without thinking.

She turned back at his summons. Her light brown eyes, which always reminded him of sassafras wood, grew rounder, questioning.

"Meeting is tonight, thee knows." Every week he asked, and every week she turned him down. But he had to try. Without regular Christian fellowship, he feared her young faith might wither. And besides, when her babe came, she would need the support of the congregation even more. "With Christmas coming, the women are planning food baskets for the needy. Mercy may have told thee. I'd be happy to take—"

Dismay filled her features. "No." The word felt like a slap. She blew out a ragged sigh. "Please don't ask me anymore, Will. I just can't go."

"But why?" His breath exploded in a huff of exasperation. "Thee needs to be in Meeting among those of thy faith, hearing God's Word preached and listening for God's voice." In light of her condition and the shock of Alan's death, the elders as well as the congregation in general had exercised unusual restraint and leniency concerning Lucinda's long absence from Meeting. But after five months, Will had begun to notice signs of fraying patience among the elders of Serenity Friends Meeting.

The frown drawing her delicate brows together didn't bode hopeful. "If God cares to speak to me, He can surely speak to me in my own home."

Will heaved a sigh of surrender. "Of course He can, but. . ." How could he get through to her the importance of gathering with those of like faith without sounding judgmental?

Within the cabin, a teakettle sent up a shrill whistle.

"Oh, I forgot I left the kettle on." She whirled toward the sound. As she turned, the rag rug beneath her feet slipped, and she tilted sideways with a gasp.

At the last instant, Will reached out and grasped her around the waist, saving her from the fall. For one blissful moment he stood holding her, safe and warm against him.

"Ahem!"

At the sound of a voice, Will's head jerked around, and he found himself staring into the shocked faces of Levi and Charity Braddock.

Chapter 3

"Thank thee for savin' me from fallin', Will." Heat filled Lucinda's face as she quickly stepped out of Will's embrace. "This rug is always slippin'." Hopefully, the Braddocks would attribute any redness in her face to her near accident. She only wished she didn't sound so breathless.

Levi and Charity Braddock's stunned expressions quickly turned to looks of concern.

"Thee should tack down that rug, Lucinda," Charity said in hushed tones that held a definite reproach. "A fall at this time could be very dangerous for thee and the baby."

"Yes, Charity, thee is right. I will do that." Lucinda pressed her hand against her chest as if to muffle the sound of her pounding heart.

Charity looked at Will, and tiny lines of disapproval etched the corners of her tightly pursed lips. Lucinda knew that Will's ruddy complexion had little to do with the chilly air. "It was truly a blessing that thee was here to prevent such an accident, Will." Despite her complimentary words, Charity's voice held a disapproving tone.

Will's hand fisted at his side, and the muscles moved in his jaw. "We should all be thankful that Mercy Cox sent me here to see about a leak in Lucinda's roof." The cold tone of his voice broached no further conjecture about anything the Braddocks might have witnessed.

Remembering her manners, Lucinda forced a bright smile.

"Please come in, Charity, Levi. I was about to brew some tea."

"Thank thee, but we cannot stay." Charity clasped her hand on Lucinda's. "Levi and I are on our way to Meeting and felt led to stop by and offer thee a ride this evening."

Lucinda wished she didn't recoil inside every time someone mentioned attending Meeting. In truth, it was becoming increasingly difficult to come up with both credible and at least partially true reasons to avoid Meeting. But if she blurted out the real reason—that she and God were no longer on speaking terms—she'd invite a sermon from Levi right here on her doorstep. "I—I don't know. I don't feel—"

"I'm sure thee will understand that Lucinda needs to rest after her fright." Will stepped between Lucinda and Charity. "I'm of a mind to fetch Mercy Cox to stay with her this evening."

"Of course," Levi and Charity Braddock said in near chorus. "We will hold thee in the Light, Lucinda." Levi's smile held genuine kindness, twisting the thread of guilt wriggling in Lucinda's chest.

Lucinda watched Levi guide his wife toward the front of the cabin, hating the thought of appearing frail to the Braddocks. Lucinda knew she was fully capable of hitching her horse, Star, to the buggy and driving the three miles to the meeting-house in Serenity. After the couple had gone, Will hammered a tack in each corner of the offending rag rug.

"There. That should give thee no more trouble," he said as he stood.

"Thank thee, Will. For. . .everything." Gratitude filled Lucinda. He had come to her rescue twice today.

"I meant what I said. I shall fetch Mercy if thee thinks—"

"No." Although she would enjoy Mercy's company, Lucinda needed time alone to sort through the tangle of disquieting feelings she was experiencing regarding Will. Besides, she wouldn't deny Mercy the opportunity of attending midweek Meeting unnecessarily. She managed a smile. "As thee told Levi and Charity, I just need some rest."

Will nodded, but he continued to study her face as if reluctant to leave until reassured that she meant her words.

"Rest well, Lucinda," he finally said in a near whisper. For a long moment, his gaze caressed her face. Then in a sudden movement he turned and, taking long-legged strides, headed toward the front of the cabin.

Five days later, swathed in her wool shawl, Lucinda ambled along the dirt road toward Mercy's house. She still struggled to make sense of her unexpected reaction to Will the previous week. Her mind flew back to the moment when she'd slipped on the rug and he'd caught her in his arms and held her warmly against him. Despite the chilly wind that buffeted her bonnet and snatched at her shawl, a rush of heat rolled through her. A part of her felt relieved that he had not stopped by again, while another part nursed a niggling disappointment that he had not.

Mercy was right. Loneliness did strange things to a person's mind. And Mercy should know. Though widowed five years ago, the older woman scarcely spent a full day alone between selling her rag rugs and tending to the needy. If Lucinda followed her friend's example and became more sociable and less dependent upon Will, surely these unsettling feelings and thoughts about him would go away. And once again she would view him as she had before Alan's death—a dear friend and nothing more.

She looked down at the basket full of woolen strips sewn together and wound into balls that bounced against her hip. Since she'd first known Mercy, the older woman had pestered Lucinda to let her instruct her in the skill of rug weaving. Today, she would accept Mercy's offer.

Lucinda couldn't expect to live off the charity of her neighbors for the rest of her life. She would need a way to provide for herself and her child. Many times, Mercy had commented on how thankful she was for her loom, how rug weaving provided her with an enjoyable occupation, as well as a comfortable living since the death of her husband. Lucinda saw no reason why it shouldn't do the same for her. And as Mercy seemed to always have more work than she could keep up with, Lucinda wouldn't be taking anything away from her teacher. But perhaps most importantly, weaving lessons would give Lucinda a reason to spend afternoons away from her cabin, lessening the chance of another unsettling incident with Will.

She rounded the bend in the road, and Mercy's pale yellow house came into view. Always an inviting sight, the building, with its sunny color and white-railed porch, looked especially warm and welcoming on this raw autumn day. She cast an upward glance at the pewter-colored sky. Hopefully, any snow would hold off until tonight. The thought of walking the mile home in a snowstorm didn't appeal.

Quickening her steps, she made her way up to the front porch. She'd scarcely rapped twice at the door when Mercy opened it.

"Child, come in." Stepping back, the older woman ushered Lucinda into the front room. When she turned from closing the door, Mercy's smile faded and she eyed Lucinda, worry lines etching her forehead. "Is anything the matter?"

"No, I am very well." Lucinda gave her friend a reassuring smile.

"I praise the Lord for that." Her smile back in place, Mercy took Lucinda's wool shawl and hung it on a peg by the door.

Inside, Lucinda scanned the familiar space that smelled of cotton, vanilla, and cinnamon. Before her marriage to Alan, she'd spent many enjoyable hours here as Mercy's houseguest. With its white-painted walls, large denim rag rug that centered the floor, and black potbellied stove tucked in one corner, the room was at once inviting and functional. But the object that dominated the room and drew her eye was the giant floor loom situated near the south window.

"It looks like thee has brought me more work." Linking her fingers over her apron-clad middle, Mercy glanced at the basket of woolen balls on Lucinda's arm.

"I've actually brought *me* some work." Lucinda walked to the loom and set the basket down beside it. "That is, if thee will teach me to weave."

"Of course I will teach thee." Mercy's round face practically glowed. Yet her smile didn't show the least hint of smugness at having finally coaxed Lucinda to the loom. She cocked her head, and her delicate gray brows rose. "Thee was never interested in learnin' before. Why now?"

Fleeing Mercy's studying look, Lucinda's gaze slid to the loom. "I—I don't have the book learnin' to be a teacher, and I'll need a way to make a livin' for me and my young'un." She preferred to keep the part about avoiding Will to herself.

Mercy motioned for Lucinda to sit on the bench in front of the loom then pulled up a ladder-back chair and sat next to her. Fixing Lucinda with an intent gaze, she crossed her arms over her chest. "Which brings us to what I've been harpin' on since the accident that took Alan."

Lucinda stifled a groan. She hadn't come here to argue with Mercy about moving back into this house. She blew out a weary sigh. "I would love to stay here with thee, Mercy. But thee knows how it pleased Alan to think that his child would be born in the cabin his grandpa built. I have to stay in the cabin. It's what Alan wanted."

Mercy reached over and gripped Lucinda's hand. "Child, thee knows Alan would want what is best for thee and the babe." She sat back and gave her head an emphatic nod. "But if thee won't come here, then after Christmas, when my rug weavin' slacks off, I'll go stay with thee. The babe could come any time durin' the last month, and we can't risk thee bein' alone."

"Thank thee, Mercy." At the thought of having Mercy near during her last weeks of confinement, relief washed through Lucinda. But despite the older woman's comment about less work after Christmas, guilt pricked. It bothered Lucinda to think she'd be taking Mercy away from her home and loom. "Is thee sure thee can afford to be away from thy loom for a month?"

Mercy's grin widened. "With thee helpin' me, I should be more than a month ahead in my orders." She patted Lucinda's hand. "God is the master weaver. See how He weaves everything together for good for them who love Him?"

Lucinda didn't answer. Once, she'd believed that. When there seemed no escape from Pa's drunken cruelty, she'd believed that God had sent the Quakers with their revival tent to the town near her family's tenant farm to save her. Coming to Serenity, finding a second mother in Mercy and a loving husband in Alan, had all seemed like miracles to Lucinda. But when Alan died, her belief in miracles dimmed along with God's Light within her.

Mercy stood. "Since I already have the warp threads strung, we shall begin a rug, usin' thy material." She glanced down at Lucinda's basketful of woolen balls. "I'd say thee has the makin's of a nice-sized rug, maybe two feet wide and three feet long."

Though she had watched Mercy weave rugs for hours on end, Lucinda was surprised at how much she'd absorbed and how quickly she picked up the steps. And aside from her protruding abdomen impeding her reach for the beater beam, she actually enjoyed the work.

When Lucinda had woven two lines of woolen weft, Mercy plucked at the material, checking the tightness of the weave. "Oh, thee is doing well, Lucinda." With a critical eye, she appraised the beginnings of the brown, green, and blue rug and smiled her approval. "At this pace, thee will have a new rug in no time. Where does thee plan to put it?"

Lucinda paused as she stepped on the treadle to raise the harness for the next row. She hadn't considered what she might do with the rug. "Christmas is coming, so maybe I'll give it away." People were always helping her. She liked the idea of doing something for someone else for a change. "Does thee know of someone who could use a rug?"

Mercy reached up and ran her fingers through warp threads that, to Lucinda, didn't look tangled. "Perhaps thee could give it to Will Davis." Mercy's voice held a touch of hesitancy, as if she were testing the air with her words. "I've never known a kinder, more giving person than Will, and he has done much for thee."

At Will's name, warmth flooded Lucinda's face. Keeping her head down to hide any telltale redness, she focused on her work. "Yes, Will has been very kind to me. Maybe I should give him the rug," she murmured, hoping to put an end to the subject.

Mercy stood at Lucinda's side and instructed while Lucinda wove a couple dozen rows. Then, pronouncing the work excellent, she headed to the kitchen to start supper.

Gradually Lucinda's motions became smooth and rhythmic, her speed at the loom growing with her confidence. When she finally looked up at the clock on the mantel, two more hours had passed. Two more rows and she would have a three-foot-long finished rug. As she again passed the shuttle through the space between the warp threads, which Mercy had called the "shed," three quick knocks sounded at the front door.

Lucinda rose to answer it.

"Prob'ly somebody wantin' a rug made." Mercy strode into the front room, drying her hands on a dish towel.

Lucinda reached the door first and opened it to find Will Davis standing in the blue-gray gloaming amid a swirl of snowflakes. Her heart jumped then raced like a scared rabbit. "Will." His name came out in a breathless puff of air, snatched away by a gust of wind that whistled past the porch.

"Lucinda." Only a slight widening of his gray eyes hinted at his surprise. She thought she detected his face reddening beneath his hat's wide brim. But more likely, the cold wind had simply whipped extra color into his features. After a long moment, his gaze shifted from Lucinda to Mercy. "I just stopped by to add some wood to the rick on thy porch, Mercy. Does thee need any brought into the house?"

"Yes. Thank thee, Will." Mercy's scrutinizing gaze bounced between Will and Lucinda. "I could use more beside the heat stove and some willow or birch, if thee has it, for the kitchen stove."

"Yes, I have some nice pieces of willow." His smiling gaze drifted from Mercy to Lucinda before he turned and headed back to his wagon.

Her heart pounding, Lucinda returned to the loom. She picked up the wood shuttle and tried to pass it through the shed, but her hand trembled so that the shuttle kept getting caught in the warp strings. She'd thought her odd reaction to Will last Wednesday was nothing more than a symptom of her loneliness. But if so, then why should his presence still affect her in the same jarring way after she'd spent an afternoon with Mercy? Whatever the cause of her strange malady, she remained resolute as to the cure. Until this disquieting feeling went away, she must try her best to avoid him.

Mercy came up behind Lucinda and put her hand on her shoulder. "For a beginner weaver, thy work is excellent, Lucinda." She ran her hand over the woven rug wound on the cloth beam. "I'd say thy rug is at least three feet long."

Basking in her teacher's praise, Lucinda gave a little laugh. "Thank thee, Mercy. I'm blessed to have such a good teacher."

Using a pair of scissors, Mercy showed Lucinda how to cut the rug from the loom and knot the ends of the warp threads to finish it.

"Does thee want to leave the rug here and finish knotting the fringe tomorrow, or take it home and finish it there?" Mercy asked as she rolled up the rug.

"I think I'd better leave it here," Lucinda said. The thought of lugging the bulky bundle a mile through wind and snow didn't appeal. "I'm not sure I could carry it all the way home."

Mercy pressed her hand to her chest and chuckled. "Oh child, I'd never allow thee to carry this home." At that moment the front door opened, and Will entered with a bundle of kindling in his arms. Smiling, Mercy glanced at him. "Will has agreed to stay and have supper with us. Then he will take thee and thy rug home."

Chapter 4

Will strode to his wagon and bounded to the seat, his foot barely touching the wagon tongue. Frustration surged through him, firing every nerve. Grabbing the reins, he slapped them down on the mule's back with a sharper-than-intended snap. The normally placid animal jumped, sending a wave of guilt through Will. "Sorry there, Bob. Didn't mean to whack thee so hard."

For the third evening in a row, he had stopped at Mercy's only to learn that Lucinda had headed home on foot an hour earlier. It hurt to think that she was avoiding him on purpose. But things certainly looked that way, especially considering her oddly reticent attitude when he drove her home from Mercy's last Monday.

A queasy feeling welled up in the pit of his stomach. Could Lucinda have somehow learned the details of what had transpired between Alan and him the day of the accident? He dismissed the thought the second it formed in his mind. Even if she had found out—though he couldn't imagine how—Lucinda was not one to brood. She doubtless would have confronted him with what she'd learned.

But regardless of why she'd chosen to leave Mercy's each day before he could take her home in his wagon, his concern for her health and safety remained. The thought of her making the mile trek twice a day through inclement winter weather filled him with dread. And despite their best efforts to do so, both Mercy and he had failed to convince Lucinda to either move back in with Mercy or give up rug weaving until spring.

Will blew out a long sigh. "Lord, just help me find a way to keep her safe." *Why did women have to be so hardheaded?* With that thought, his sister-in-law's stern visage flashed in his mind. He groaned, remembering that Naomi had asked him to stop by the mercantile and purchase a tin of baking powder on his way home from work. With the mercantile a block down from the grain mill where he worked, such errands often fell to Will.

Sending up a prayer for patience, he clicked his tongue, turned the mule around, and headed back to town.

Inside the mercantile, Will continued his silent petition for patience as he waited his turn in line behind several other customers. Spying a *Farm Journal* magazine on an up-ended crate, he picked it up and began to thumb through it to pass the time.

Suddenly a black-and-white image on a page caught his eye, and he flipped back to it. Beneath the picture of a home rug loom, the manufacturer promised that for the price of twenty dollars, their product could provide a handsome living for any industrious soul.

Of course! If Lucinda had her own loom, she wouldn't have to walk to and from Mercy's house each day.

When it was finally Will's turn at the counter, he asked for the baking powder and then held up the magazine. "How much for this magazine, Zeke?"

Zeke Reeves scratched his head, mussing the thin strands of gray hair he'd combed over his balding pate. "Aw, I reckon you can have it at no charge." He shrugged. "It's last month's issue. I should get a new one in another day or two."

"Thank thee, Zeke." Will plopped a quarter on the counter to pay for the baking powder and then hurried out of the store with the powder and the magazine in hand. Whispering a prayer of thanks for God's direction, he could hardly wait to get home and write out an order for the loom.

A half hour later, he'd just sat down at Simeon's desk in the living room when he felt a hand on his shoulder.

"I hope thee does not plan to be long at the desk, little brother." The mingled scents of sweat, chalk, and Simeon's shaving soap filled Will's nostrils as his brother hunched over the desk. "I have a satchel full of test papers to grade this evening."

"No, I won't be long." Will stiffened beneath Simeon's touch, rankling at the absurd term his brother insisted on using to address him. Though seven years Will's senior, Simeon stood a good six inches shorter.

"What has thee here?" Simeon craned his neck, poking his head farther over Will's shoulder as if checking the work of one of his students.

Shrugging away from his brother's hand, Will slid his arm over the magazine's cover. Though Simeon didn't lack in Christian charity, he, like his wife, possessed a strong frugal streak. Will wasn't at all sure how his brother might react to Will spending the substantial sum of twenty dollars on a gift.

"I found something in the magazine I thought might be useful and wanted to read more about it." Will hoped his evasive answer didn't stray too far from the truth.

Grinning, Simeon stood and backed away with his palms held forward. "Thee need say no more, little brother. My students are constantly reminding me that with Christmas only weeks away, this is the season for secrets." With that he retreated to the sofa and picked up the newspaper, leaving Will alone to write the order for the loom.

When he finished, Will stuffed the letter into the envelope and tucked it into the magazine. Thankfully, for the past several months, he'd been setting aside money to buy a new saddle. Tomorrow he would use some of his savings to purchase a money order at the post office to pay for the loom.

"Simeon. Will. Thy supper is on the table." Naomi stepped into the living room, smoothing back her jet-black hair that looked to Will as prim as ever.

Smiling, Simeon set the paper aside and rose from the sofa. "Thank thee, my dear. Sausages and cabbage, if my nose tells me right."

"And fried potatoes," Naomi added, turning her attention to Will. "Has thee washed up?" She trained her green eyes on his hands.

Will forced a stiff smile. "Thee knows I would not bring dirty hands to thy table, sister." Still childless after five years of marriage, Naomi tended to treat Will more as an errant child than a brother.

After they gathered round the table and Simeon said grace, Naomi passed Will the fried potatoes. "At least thee is on time for supper this evening. I never know whether to cook for two or three." She lifted her chin a smidgen, and the shadows cast by the kerosene lamplight accentuated her sharp features.

Will dished out a portion of potatoes, ignoring the censure in Naomi's voice. "I am sorry, sister. But thee knows I often stop to do chores for our widowed friends, Lucinda and Mercy."

"Of course thee should help Mercy." Naomi's voice lowered to a near whisper. "But does thee think it is wise to spend so much time alone with Lucinda?"

Will gritted his teeth as he slid his knife through the link of sausage on his plate. "I am only doing as the scripture commands—to see to the widows in their affliction."

Naomi fixed Will with a green glare. "'But the younger widows refuse: for when they have begun to wax wanton against Christ, they will marry.' First Timothy, chapter five, verse eleven."

Will dropped his knife and fork to his plate with a clatter. It took every ounce of his strength to stay in his chair. How dare Naomi use the scriptures to scold him for helping Lucinda. "I know the passage as well as thee does, sister." He fought to keep the anger from his voice. "In that same chapter, Paul preaches that widows of a congregation should first be cared for by family. Alan was like a brother to me. I'm the closest thing to family Lucinda has here."

"Brother. Wife." Simeon's voice held a weary plea. He breathed a heavy sigh. "I spend all day settling arguments between my students. Is a peaceful meal at home too much for a man to ask?"

At Simeon's words, regret drove the anger out of Will. The last thing he wanted was to cause discord in his family. "I'm sorry, Simeon, Naomi. I meant no disrespect."

For the next few minutes everyone ate in silence, which was only disturbed by the clinking of utensils against plates.

At length, Naomi took a sip of water and then delicately cleared her throat. When she spoke, her measured voice held the barest hint of contrition. "Please forgive me, Will, if I spoke too harshly. But as thy elder sister, I feel it is my place to guide thee." She took another sip of water. "I must admit it pains me to see my dear husband shoulder more of the work here at home because of thy absence." She reached over and placed her hand on Simeon's arm. His mouth full, Simeon answered her wifely concern with a grateful smile and a pat on her hand.

As if emboldened by Simeon's support, Naomi's voice grew stronger. "I worry that thy well-meaning acts of charity might be. . .misconstrued." On the last word, she lowered her voice to a near whisper and then gained strength again. "Lucinda has not attended Meeting for almost six months now. I am concerned that she did not experience true sanctification. Levi and Charity Braddock have attempted to labor with her and bring her back into the Light, but she refuses to hear them. So unless she shows in some way that her sanctification was genuine—"

Struggling to keep his voice even, Will pushed back from the table, scraping the chair's legs against the wood floor, and stood. "If thee both will excuse me, there is something I need to work on in the woodshop before it gets too late." He had quietly listened to Naomi's admonishment of his conduct. But to hear her casually suggest that Lucinda had not experienced true sanctification was more than he could bear in silence. If he stayed another moment, he'd be putting himself in danger of sinning by saying something he would regret.

Will looked at Naomi but couldn't force his lips into even the semblance of a smile. "I thank thee for the fine supper, sister," he mumbled and fled the kitchen. As he passed through the living room, he snatched the *Farm Journal* off the desk and took it to his bedroom where he slid it under his pillow and then headed to the barn.

Five minutes later, he stood in a corner of the barn he'd avoided since Alan's death. Here, years earlier, he and Alan had built a small woodworking shop.

He picked up a rasp from the dusty workbench and hefted it in his hands. The words he'd said to Alan when he first handed him the tool nearly eight years ago echoed in his ears. *"We are brothers now. Everything that is mine is thine, too."*

At nineteen, Will had simply tried to make the sixteen-year-old orphaned Alan feel welcome after he'd come to live with Will's family. And indeed for the better part of seven years—with the exception of clothes that rarely fit both Will's tall, lanky frame and Alan's shorter, stockier build—the two had shared most everything.

A shared love of tools and carpentry had cemented their relationship and helped them become closer than many natural brothers. Certainly Alan had been more like a brother to Will than bookish Simeon.

Even after Alan's marriage to Lucinda, he'd continued to stop by often and work on one project or another in the woodshop. But it was the project Alan had left unfinished that brought Will back to this place he himself had neglected for so long.

Will blew out a long breath, creating a misty cloud in the chilly evening air. The memory of the words he'd spoken to Alan so long ago returned to haunt him. Did that road run both ways? Had Will inherited what Alan had left undone?

The piece of cherry wood still fixed in the vise where Alan had left it said that he did. Alan had meant to finish the project for Lucinda's birthday last August.

Shame filled Will. He should have finished Alan's gift then and given it to her as Alan had wanted. But Christmas was coming.

He ran a piece of sandpaper along the rough edge of the plank, smoothing it. After checking for any missed splinters, he took the plank from the vise, set it aside, and replaced it with another rough-cut piece.

Alan had done much of the work. So if Will devoted an hour each day to this project, he should have it done long before Christmas.

"Will." Will turned toward Simeon's voice behind him. In the dim lantern light, Simeon's hard features looked as if they were chiseled from stone, a sight eerily

71

reminiscent of Will and Simeon's dead father. "My wife's intent was not to anger thee. But she is right. It is unseemly for thee to spend so much time alone in the company of Lucinda Hughes. If thee cares naught about thy own reputation, at least think of thy sister's. I will speak with the other elders of the Meeting, and we shall see to it that Alan Hughes's widow is provided for." His voice took on a no-nonsense tone Will could imagine him using with an unruly student. "But as Naomi's husband and thy elder brother, I must insist that thee refrain from visiting Lucinda Hughes further."

Chapter 5

Lucinda waddled along the leaf-strewn brick walkway that led to Mercy's porch as quickly as her unwieldy figure allowed. How wonderful it would be when she could walk with ease again and carry her sweet child in her arms instead of in her belly. Thankfully, the weather had remained mild enough for her to continue making the daily trek. And because of that, her skill at the loom had markedly improved in the two weeks since she wove her first rug.

Thoughts of that day brought with it thoughts of Will. At the memory of their ride together on his wagon through the snowy twilight, warmth flooded her cheeks. She could still feel his hands, strong and secure, lifting her to the wagon's seat. How carefully he'd tucked a woolen blanket around her. Several times, he'd inquired of her comfort and had used his tall frame as a barrier to protect her from icy gusts of wind. And when they finally reached the cabin, he'd eased her down to the ground as if she weighed no more than a feather.

Remembering that moment, and how close she'd come to leaning her head against his chest and inviting his embrace, a blast of shame shot through her. What kind of woman entertained such feelings about a man—even a good man like Will—less than six months after she'd buried her husband? The husband whose child she would bear in little more than a month.

Knowing she couldn't allow another such moment to happen, she'd kept a more diligent eye on Mercy's mantel clock while working at the loom. Each day, she made sure she headed home a good hour before the grain mill's whistle blew, signaling the end of Will's workday.

She let herself in the front door as Mercy had instructed her to do. Inside, she was met by the welcoming scent of gingerbread. Not finding Mercy at the loom, she hung her shawl and bonnet beside the door and then followed her nose to the kitchen and the source of the delectable, spicy aromas.

"There thee is." Smiling, Mercy turned from rolling fragrant brown dough at the kitchen table. Her round cheeks glowed pink from the oven's heat, and her sleeves were rolled up at the elbows. Flour covered the tabletop as well as Mercy's hands, which gripped the worn rolling pin.

"Since thee has helped me get caught up on my rug orders, I thought this would be a good afternoon to do some Christmas baking." Mercy pressed the rolling pin against the shapeless piece of dough and angled a grin at Lucinda. "I was lookin' through my cookie recipes and ran across my mother's old gingerbread recipe. I thought maybe thee would like to help me make gingerbread men for the children at the orphanage."

Joy filled Lucinda's heart as she rolled up her own sleeves. "Oh yes. I'd love to." Though Christmases at home growing up were sparse, somehow Ma always managed to scrape together enough ingredients to make at least one batch of cookies with the help of Lucinda and her older sisters, Esther and Lydia. Those memories, among the few happy ones of Lucinda's childhood, brought unexpected tears to her eyes.

If Mercy noticed, she kept it to herself. She snatched an apron from a peg on the wall beside the stove and handed it to Lucinda along with a cookie cutter shaped like a little man. "Thee can begin cutting out the cookies while I start a new batch of dough."

Lucinda tied on the apron and then pressed the sharp edges of the tin form into the rolled-out dough, repeating the process until she had a dozen faceless, chubby, little men-like figures.

A sad smile graced Mercy's face as she poured a cup of sugar into a crockery bowl. "My, but this takes me back to when Jedidiah used to help me make these cookies. That is, before he got old enough to consider such things woman's work." She gave a little chuckle, but Lucinda thought she noticed tears glistening in the older woman's eyes. Mercy rarely mentioned her only son, who had worked as a brakeman on the Ohio & Indiana Railroad and died years ago in a train crash.

Struck by life's unfairness, something akin to anger flared in Lucinda's chest. Mercy didn't deserve to lose her son, and later, her husband, any more than Lucinda deserved to lose Alan. Yet God had allowed their loved ones to die. Still here she and Mercy stood, making Christmas cookies to celebrate God's love in the person of the Christ child. Did Lucinda even believe in God's love anymore? That was a question she wasn't prepared to explore. So she was glad when Mercy's bright voice intruded on her dark musings.

"Did I ever tell thee about my mother?" Mercy plopped the sticky blob of gingerbread dough onto the floured tabletop.

Lucinda shook her head. "No, I don't think so." She only remembered Mercy mentioning that she had been raised in Illinois and later came to Indiana with her husband, Ezra, whom she'd met at a Quaker yearly meeting.

"Well," Mercy said as she rolled out the dough, "Mama was quite a character. The black sheep of the family, thee might say. Papa always said she was as spicy as her gingerbread." She grinned. "Some say I take after her."

"Then she must have been a good cook, too." Using a spatula, Lucinda carefully lifted a dough man from the table and laid it on a waiting greased and floured jellyroll pan.

Mercy chuckled. "Oh no. Mama was a terrible cook. In fact, this cookie recipe was one of the few things she could cook really well. And what was worse, her family didn't even want her to make it. . .at least, not as any celebration of Christmas."

At Lucinda's puzzled look, Mercy explained that her mother had belonged to a sect of Quakers that did not observe religious festivals such as Christmas.

As she talked, Mercy reached into the flour sack for a handful of the white powdery stuff and gave the table, dough, and rolling pin all a generous dusting. "As a young woman, Mama craved anything exciting and interesting. And though her family refrained from sharing in the Christmas traditions of their non-Quaker neighbors, Mama was drawn to them. Like this recipe for gingerbread men, she collected anything associated with Christmas celebrations." She shook her head. "Well," she said with a huff as she began to roll out the dough, "as thee might imagine, that didn't set well at all with her folks. And then when Mama's appetite for excitement plopped her smack dab in the middle of Papa's family of river pirates—"

"River pirates?" At Mercy's stunning revelation about her family's history Lucinda's eyes popped, and she stopped in her work of decorating the cookies with pieces of raisins.

Mercy laughed out loud, and her blue eyes twinkled. "Don't gape, child! I will tell thee all about it later. But the upshot is that Mama learned that our lives don't always go as we think they will. No matter what happens, God still has a plan for each of us." She paused in rolling out the dough and cocked her head. Her forehead scrunched in a thoughtful expression. "I reckon thee could say He has a recipe for our lives."

Last year, Lucinda could clearly see God's plan for her life. But when Alan died, that plan, that recipe had become smudged and unreadable. She pressed raisin eyes into the round face of a gingerbread man. "But what if we can't read all of God's recipe for us?" She blinked back tears. "What if parts are missing?"

Mercy came around the table and took Lucinda's hands in her flour-covered ones. "Dear one, God is the only one who can see the full recipe." She sighed. "When I put this dough together, I did it one step, one ingredient at a time. We must take each step in faith. Just be open to God's direction." She smiled. "Sometimes God surprises us, so don't reject His instructions just because they are not what thee expects."

"But how can I tell if it's God's direction, or just something I want?" Oddly, the image of Will's face flashed in Lucinda's mind.

"Thee should know by now that thee will only find discernment through prayer." An imploring look came into Mercy's eyes, and she gave Lucinda's hands a gentle squeeze. "Thee needs to come back to Meeting, Lucinda. The longer thee stays away, the dimmer the Light within thee becomes."

Lucinda slipped her hands from Mercy's grasp and turned back to her work at the table. She lacked the courage to tell the woman that she wasn't even sure if she'd uttered a single prayer since Alan's funeral. "Maybe after the baby comes," she murmured, forcing a weak smile. "Maybe I'll be ready then."

Mercy heaved a deep sigh and took the finished pan of cookies and put it in the oven. When she straightened up again, she fixed Lucinda with a somber gaze. "If thee wants to know if something is from God, just remember that God gives only good gifts. If something is good, it's from God."

Though Lucinda was tempted to say that God may give but He also takes, she bit back the retort. She would rather their cookie making not be marred by more sermons about her need to return to Meeting. So she nodded silently and went back to cutting out and decorating gingerbread men. As she and Mercy worked together, Mercy kept Lucinda enthralled with stories of her parents' daring exploits as young people in southern Illinois on the banks of the Ohio River.

Before Lucinda realized it, the afternoon had slipped away. She had just put the last pan of cookies in the oven when a knock sounded at the front door. Her heart jumped. Could it be Will coming to take her home? She hadn't heard the living room clock chime five o'clock, but she might have missed it.

Mercy turned from where she stood washing up the mixing bowls and utensils. "Would thee see who is at the door, Lucinda? I'm up to my elbows in soap suds."

"Yes." Hoping her voice didn't register her dismay, she headed to the living room. When she opened the door, a measure of relief washed over her. She couldn't think of a time when she was happier to see Naomi Davis.

"Good afternoon, Lucinda." Mild surprise edged Naomi's voice. "Is Mercy home?"

"Yes." She glanced toward the back of the house and the kitchen. "We were just making gingerbread cookies for the orphanage. Please, do come in." Remembering her manners, Lucinda backed away from the door, allowing Naomi to enter with a rather sizeable basket on her arm.

"That is very commendable of thee." Naomi's voice held little warmth. Her green-eyed gaze avoided Lucinda's and instead flitted about the room like an insect searching for a place to land. It finally rested on Mercy's loom.

At that moment, Mercy, with tea towel in hand, bustled into the living room. "Good afternoon, Naomi. How nice of thee to visit. Please come in and sit down." She motioned toward the bench against the north wall.

"Thank thee, but I can't stay." Naomi held out the basket. "I know it is late notice, but I've brought rag strips for a rug I'd like to have made before Christmas."

Smiling, Mercy took the basket full of balled cotton strips in hues of browns and greens and set it beside the loom. "We should get this done before the end of the week, shouldn't we, Lucinda?"

"Oh." The word came out of Naomi's mouth more like a gasp, and her wide-eyed gaze bounced between Mercy and Lucinda. She fidgeted, and her complexion reddened. "I—I didn't know that Lucinda wove rugs," she said as if Lucinda wasn't present.

"Yes." Beaming, Mercy glanced at Lucinda. "She just took it up a couple weeks ago, but she's already doin' an excellent job."

"I'm sure." Naomi's voice sounded weak. Her tortured smile looked more like a grimace. "As I plan to give the rug as a Christmas gift, I would really prefer that thee made it thyself, Mercy."

"Of course." Mercy's smile didn't waver, but Lucinda thought the lines around her mouth tightened. Suddenly Mercy's eyes flew wide open, and she gasped. "Oh, I almost forgot that last pan of cookies in the oven! If thee will excuse me..." Without waiting for an answer, she bustled off toward the kitchen.

Naomi cast a worried look at her basket of rags as if having second thoughts about leaving them. Then, looking down her pinched nose, she ran a chilly gaze over Lucinda's form. "It's good to see thee looking so...well. Since I hadn't seen thee at Meeting for months, I supposed thee might have taken to thy bed. But I see that is not the case."

Lucinda managed a stiff smile. Though she would not question the woman's honesty, Lucinda found it hard to believe that Naomi wasn't aware of her general health. "I thank thee for thy concern, Naomi, but I am well."

Naomi's voice turned hard, dropping any pretense of friendliness. "Then I shall expect to see thee at Meeting this Sunday. For if thee is well enough to walk two miles every day to weave rugs, thee is well enough to attend Meeting." Her critical gaze sharpened to an outright glare. "I will tell thee plainly, Lucinda Hughes, Simeon and some of the other elders have begun to question if thee ever truly experienced sanctification and if thy name should remain on the membership rolls of Serenity Friends Meeting."

Chapter 6

*W*e buried Pa last Tuesday."

Lucinda stared in disbelief at the words on the page of her sister's letter. Despite the roaring fire in the belly of the coal stove a few inches away, she sat as if frozen to the bench along the wall of the mercantile that doubled as a post office.

She'd read Esther's announcement three times and still felt only numbness. Surely there must have been some scrap of tenderness between herself and Pa—something to evoke a smidgen of emotion. But nothing came. Not sadness. Not even relief. Nothing.

One image of Pa muscled out all others in Lucinda's mind. Her most vivid memory of him was the day she told him she'd be leaving their tenant farm and going to Indiana with the Quakers. She could still see him towering over her in a drunken rage. His slurred voice still echoed in her ears. *"You leave this place with them black-hatted Bible thumpers and you'll be dead to me, girl. You want to leave, then leave. But don't you ever come back, or I'll put you in the ground. I swear it!"* After that he'd seared the air with obscenities, the memory of which still blistered her ears.

She shivered. If not for the half-dozen Quakers standing in the yard behind her, Lucinda had no doubt that Pa, in his fury, would have swung his raised fist and struck her down where she stood.

She blinked, willing the frightening image to disappear. When she focused again on her sister's letter, she found Esther's next revelation nearly as jarring as the news of Pa's death.

> *I'm fixing to have another young one next summer. Me and Lonny would like for you to come back down and live with us. You wouldn't know Lonny. He done found religion. He quit drinking and has started taking me and the children to church on Sundays.*

Esther's words filled Lucinda with happiness for her sister as well as her little niece and nephew. But she found it hard to picture Lonny Ray Malloy as a teetotal churchgoer. In part, Lucinda's desire to escape the fate of her two older sisters had convinced her to leave home. Both Esther and Lydia had married men cut from the same whiskey-soaked cloth as their father—demanding when sober and cruel when drunk. Though she was glad for Esther, the notion of returning to the grim life of a tenant farmer held little appeal.

Still, as she read on, her sister's description of Esther, Lonny, and the kids searching the woods along Raccoon Creek for the perfect Christmas tree strummed a compelling melody across Lucinda's heartstrings. She liked imagining her child growing up alongside his cousins.

"I hope all is well with your family in Kentucky." The voice of Beulah Reeves, the storekeeper's wife, brought Lucinda's face upward.

"Yes." It was not a lie. Whether or not her siblings grieved Pa's passing, Lucinda knew his absence removed a constant danger. Feeling the need to digest all she'd learned before sharing it with anyone, she stuffed the letter back into its envelope and tucked it into her skirt pocket.

Beulah struck an expectant stance, her head cocked to one side and her arms akimbo as if waiting for Lucinda to divulge more of the correspondence. But when she failed to oblige, Beulah gave her a lukewarm smile. "Well, I have your groceries all boxed up. So unless you can think of something else you might need, I'll have my boy, Henry, carry the box to your buggy."

Lucinda rose from her perch on the bench. "Thank thee, Beulah. That will be all." She'd almost forgotten why she'd driven into Serenity in the first place.

Fifteen minutes later as she drove home, Esther's words still dominated her thoughts: *"Me and Lonny would like for you to come back down and live with us."*

After Pa's hateful warning nearly two years ago, Lucinda had put all thoughts of ever returning to Kentucky out of her mind. But now, for the sake of her child, she must at least consider it.

Through a flurry of snowflakes, she guided Star along the dirt road toward home. *Home.* Was this place even her home anymore? Maybe Naomi was right and Lucinda had never experienced true sanctification, despite how real it had felt that night at the tent meeting.

Sniffing back a wad of hot tears, she flicked the reins against the horse's rump, urging the mare to a trot. If, as Naomi Davis believed, Lucinda was not a true Quaker and didn't belong with the Serenity Friends Meeting, then what was there to hold her here?

The image of Will's face drifted unbidden before her mind's eye, setting her heart trotting faster than Star's feet. She sighed. So far, no amount of rug weaving or visiting Mercy had managed to diminish her uncomfortable reaction to Will. And he hadn't helped, insisting on stopping by the cabin every few days to inquire about her health and comfort. Indeed, she'd made the trip to the store for groceries so he'd have one less reason to stop by her house.

Aside from her own disquieting feelings about Will, even more troublesome was her growing sense that he felt the same about her. And what *if* they should make a match? Her child would need a father. But Naomi and Simeon would doubtless stand squarely against Will marrying outside the faith. Will, too, would expect Lucinda to attend Meeting. And Lucinda would not sit in Meeting and falsely pretend a connection with God she no longer felt.

As she came to the spot where her lane converged with the road, Star turned unprompted onto the narrow path that led up to the cabin. "No." Lucinda surprised herself by speaking aloud. It would be better for both her and Will if she simply accepted Esther's offer and moved back to Kentucky.

The mare whinnied and bobbed her head as they rounded the curve in the lane that led to the front of the cabin. When the house came into view, Lucinda's heart turned a somersault. Will's mule, Bob, stood hitched to a flatbed wagon. But more remarkably, the cabin's front door stood wide open.

Lucinda reined Star to a stop behind the wagon. What could Will be up to that required the door to be open? And why would he go into her house without her there? Eager to learn the answers to the questions burning in her mind, she scrambled down from the buggy and headed to the front porch.

At the open door, she stopped, stunned. Will stood in her front room with a wrench in his hand, constructing something that looked suspiciously like a loom.

◆ ◆ ◆

At a sound near the open doorway, Will looked up and his heart catapulted into his throat. Lucinda stood as if frozen in place, her eyes growing to the size of silver dollar pieces. This was not the way he had envisioned presenting her with her new loom.

"I hope thee doesn't mind me letting myself in." Could he have thought of anything more stupid to say? Of course she minded. Otherwise, she wouldn't still be standing there with her jaw practically scraping the floor. He wouldn't blame her if she turned tail and headed to Serenity to get Sheriff Brewster.

"What—what is that?" She finally stepped into the room, but her unblinking eyes never left the loom.

"It's a rug loom. See?" In what seemed even to him a ridiculous demonstration, he swung one of the moving parts of the contraption. After two hours of work, he prayed he had the thing put together correctly.

"For me? Thee got this for me?" Lucinda, who'd given the loom a wide berth as if afraid it might come to life and pounce on her, inched closer.

"Yes." Despite a chill breeze blowing through the open door, sweat broke out on Will's forehead. How could he explain why he had let himself into her house and built a loom in her front room without sounding overbearing, crazy, or both? "I thought thee might like to weave here instead of walking to Mercy's. I mean, in case it snows and thee can't. . ."

She reached out and touched a timber as if to assure herself that the thing was real. Then she turned and looked at him. Straight at him. Tears welled in her eyes, and panic grabbed Will's chest like an iron fist. She hated it.

"Please, do not be distressed. If thee does not want it, I promise I will have it gone within the hour." He moved to begin loosening the closest bolt. "It was wrong of me to—"

"Oh no!" She reached out her arms toward the loom in a protective motion. "I do want it. But I cannot accept such a gift. It is too dear. And I—I cannot pay thee for it." Her voice wilted, and Will's heart seized.

"Thee owes me nothing." He dropped the wrench into his toolbox with a clatter. "I am repaid by knowing that this loom will keep thee home safe and out of the weather."

At that her lips pressed into a straight line, and he knew he'd said too much. He groaned inwardly. He should have heeded Proverbs 13:3. *"He that keepeth his mouth keepeth his life: but he that openeth wide his lips shall have destruction."*

"So thee bought this to keep me home." There wasn't so much as a hint of question in her flat tone. Staring at the loom, she pressed her fingertips against her lips, hiding her expression.

"I'm sorry. It was wrong of me." Befuddled, he gathered up his remaining tools scattered around the floor. He needed to leave before he angered her any further.

A sputtering sound escaped from between her fingers then a full-blown giggle burst free. "Poor Will." Grinning, she gave him a piteous look. "Thee does not know me as well as thee thinks."

Will fought the urge to take her into his arms and declare that he would like to learn to know her better. But that could never be.

The mirth left her face, replaced by a smile so sad and sweet it made his chest ache. Then she stepped toward him, and his heart pounded like a bass drum. "Thank thee, Will." She placed her hand on his forearm, sending tingles dancing up to his shoulder. "The first rug I make on this shall be for thee."

Abandoning all caution, he took her hands into his and gazed into her cinnamon-colored eyes. "Lucinda."

"Will!"

At the harsh male voice, they both turned toward the open doorway to face a nearly purple-faced Simeon.

Chapter 7

Will touched his fingertip to the wood to check if the varnish had dried. When he felt no tackiness, he reached for the can of varnish on the shelf above the workbench and then drew his hand back with a sigh. Another coat of varnish would not improve it. Nor would varnish improve his mood.

Though pleased with the finished project, he almost hated seeing it come to an end. As long as he had something to keep him busy, to concentrate on, he managed to keep his anger in check. So he wasn't particularly pleased when Amos closed the mill at noon to make needed repairs, sending Will and the other workers home early.

At the memory of Simeon's actions last week, Will's simmering rage boiled again in his belly as if his insides were a cauldron. He'd been but an instant away from declaring his affection for Lucinda when Simeon had appeared at her door. Determined to protect her from any embarrassment, Will had insisted that he and Simeon take their conversation, which eventually escalated to a heated argument, outside away from the cabin and, he'd hoped, beyond earshot.

Though pride was sinful, Will couldn't help feeling more than a tinge of it. In the face of Simeon's demands that Will leave Lucinda's home immediately, he had stood his ground. Simeon had left in a huff, while Will stayed to carry in Lucinda's groceries and put her horse and buggy away in the barn.

But the worried look Will had seen on Lucinda's face after Simeon's departure told him she had indeed heard the argument, including Simeon's complaint about the money Will had spent on the loom.

Guilt lashed at his heart. The last thing he had wanted was for her to feel that she was to blame for the contention between his brother and him. He also hated that she might feel indebted to him or his family in any way.

The anger pulsating through him exploded, and he kicked the empty metal bucket near his feet clear to the other side of the barn. It smacked against the mule's stall with a clatter, causing the animal to jump and bray in protest.

A small measure of his frustration eased, Will blew out a long breath. "Sorry, Bob," he muttered and then looked up at the cobweb-covered rafters. "I know, Lord, I know. Proverbs, chapter nineteen, verse eleven. 'The discretion of a man deferreth his anger; and it is his glory to pass over a transgression.'"

With that thought, part of another scripture—Luke 6:37—came to mind. *"Forgive, and ye shall be forgiven."*

Turning back to the piece of furniture he'd just finished, Will's heart throbbed painfully. In truth, no one, including Simeon, stood more in need of Lucinda's forgiveness than Will did. But she couldn't forgive him without knowing what he had done.

He picked up the ragged length of quilt he'd used to cover the object since beginning work on it and carefully swathed the varnished wood. Next week was Christmas. The moment he gave her this might be the perfect time to confess fully his transgression. At the thought, an icy chill slithered down his spine. Did he have the courage to face losing what small measure of affection Lucinda felt for him?

Leaving the barn, he stepped toward the house and groaned. He'd sooner stay out in the frigid December air than enter the chilly atmosphere that now held sway inside his home. Simeon and Naomi hardly spoke to him anymore. And when they did, their words held little warmth.

He looked back at the barn. The need to converse with a compassionate soul gripped him hard. His mind instantly flew to Mercy Cox. Aside from his own sainted mother, he could think of no one else who possessed more maternal wisdom and caring than Mercy. And at this time of day, she should be home and most probably alone since Lucinda was doubtless safely inside her cabin, weaving at her new loom.

With resolute steps, he walked to Bob's stall.

The mule lifted his nose from the manger and paused in chewing a mouthful of fragrant timothy hay.

Will rubbed the animal's velvety muzzle. "Don't get too comfortable with that hay, Bob. We have somewhere to go."

◆　　◆　　◆

Lucinda walked to the jelly cupboard and pulled open one of the cabinet's twin drawers. Had it been a week since she found Will in her front room constructing the loom?

Remembering the moment he took her hands in his and gazed into her eyes, her heart throbbed with a sweet ache. For that one instant, the two of them had seemed to teeter on the brink of something special. . .until Simeon yanked them back to reality. What had Will been about to say before his brother interrupted? Part of her longed to know, while another part of her was glad she didn't.

But whatever affection she and Will might share, it didn't matter. Witnessing the argument between Will and Simeon had convinced her to accept Esther's offer and move back to Kentucky.

Glancing toward the living room, she smiled. Whether here in Serenity or down in Kentucky, Will's loom would continue to provide a living for her and her child. She was eager to try it out and make that first promised rug for Will. But until she could get thread for warp and material for weft, the loom would have to sit idle.

She rifled through the drawer in search of paper on which to pen a letter to Esther. "Where is that writing paper?" But all she found were her recipe books, some canning lids, and sundry kitchen gadgets.

She sighed. The sooner she could get a letter to Esther, the sooner her sister and brother-in-law could begin making plans to fetch her and the baby down to Kentucky in the spring.

Abandoning the first drawer, she tried the second but still found no paper. Suddenly she remembered the last time she'd written a letter to her sister. Mercy had provided her with the writing paper and envelope.

She glanced out the kitchen window where large snowflakes filled the air. The thought of leaving the warm cabin and going out into the snowy day made her shiver. Also, the winding lane with its steep downgrade in places could become slick and treacherous when snow covered. On the other hand, the wind appeared light, and she'd walked the mile to Mercy's house through snow showers many times. And if Mercy could spare the warp thread, Lucinda could weave a rug for her in exchange for the paper and envelope.

After tying on her black wool bonnet and wrapping her warmest shawl around her shoulders, she picked up her market basket from beside the kitchen door and left. Outside, she pulled her shawl closer around her and grinned, thinking how Will would scold her if he knew she was out in the snow.

So far, the snow had hardly made a dusting on the frozen, packed dirt lane. Using extra care, she made it down the lane and to the road without any problem. She had gone only a few yards when she heard the rumbling sound of a horse and wagon in the distance behind her.

Moving to the edge of the road, she looked over her shoulder to see who was coming. Her heart jumped. Even at the distance of a quarter mile, Will's mule, Bob, with his lop-ears and loping gait, was unmistakable.

Lucinda turned back and resumed walking. Hopefully, he would just give her a friendly wave and continue on down the road. But as the sound of the wagon and mule became louder, the clopping of the mule's hooves slowed.

"Lucinda." Will's voice held no censure, only mild surprise as the wagon and mule came to a stop. "If thee is going to Mercy's, I would be happy to take thee."

Lucinda's mind raced, trying to think of a credible reason to decline his offer. "I would not want to cause thee more trouble with thy brother." She wished her silly heart would cease its jubilant hopping. At least he would likely attribute any redness in her cheeks to the cold temperature.

His face turned as cloudy as the gray sky behind him. "Simeon is my brother, not my master." With that, he climbed to the ground and helped her up to the seat with the greatest of care.

"I was on my way to Mercy's myself," he said as he settled beside her and flicked the reins down on Bob's rump. He shot her a sideways grin from beneath the wide brim of his hat. "Thee was right. It was silly of me to think a loom would keep thee home. I hope I constructed it properly and it works well."

Lucinda turned her head away so her bonnet would hide her smile. "I don't know. I'm hopin' to get some warp thread and rags from Mercy so I can begin a rug."

"I'm sorry. I never thought. . .I reckon I should have brought thee some with the loom."

His penitent tone squeezed Lucinda's heart. How could he imagine he owed her anything more after gifting her with such an expensive item as a loom? She placed her hand on his forearm. "I didn't expect thee to bring me thread. Thee has done far too much already."

Will became quiet, and his pensive look filled her with regret. Was he thinking of Simeon's warning? They traveled the rest of the way in silence except for the clopping of Bob's feet on the frozen road.

Lucinda knew she should tell Will of her plans to move back to Kentucky in the spring. But they'd arrived at Mercy's house, and this was not the proper moment to blurt out her news. Will deserved a full explanation as to why she had made such a decision, and she needed time to give him one.

Will climbed down first and then helped her down. Would she ever again feel as safe as she did in Will's hands?

When they reached the front door, Will knocked twice. When several seconds passed and no answer came, he knocked twice again.

Still no answer.

"She's probably in the kitchen." Lucinda opened the door. "Mercy is always telling me that if she doesn't answer the door and it's unlocked, to just come in." She walked into the front room, but Mercy was nowhere in sight. "Mercy."

Only the crackling of the fire in the belly of the stove in the corner answered her call.

A sick feeling began to grow in the pit of Lucinda's stomach. She hurried to the kitchen with Will at her heels but found no sign of Mercy. Lucinda checked Mercy's bedroom on the first floor. It was empty as well. Will bounded up the stairs to check the two rooms there and then came down an instant later.

"She's not up there," he said, shrugging his shoulders.

The wad of worry balling in Lucinda's stomach grew. "I don't understand it. Where could she be?"

"She's probably just gone into town or to visit someone," Will said. Though his tone was light, Lucinda saw concern in his gray eyes.

Lucinda shook her head. "I've never known her to leave the front door unlocked when she leaves home."

Will smiled and put his hand on her shoulder. "Don't worry. I'm sure she just forgot to lock the door. Stay here in the warmth. I'll go check the barn to see if her horse and buggy are gone."

Lucinda nodded, but unable to stay still, she headed for the kitchen the moment he closed the front door behind him. Something compelled her to open the back door and step out on the porch. "Mercy," she called.

This time a soft moan sounded just beyond the far end of the porch. Lucinda hurried to the spot, and terror leaped into her chest. Mercy lay in the snow, her bleeding head leaning against the house's stone foundation.

Chapter 8

The best I can tell, the bones are intact." Dr. Jennings finished tying the bandage he'd wrapped around Mercy's head. "But I fear thy head may be slightly concussed, and thee has badly sprained thy wrist and ankle."

At the doctor's diagnosis, Lucinda sniffed back tears and clutched Mercy's uninjured hand. She couldn't bear to think what might have happened if she and Will had not come by.

"Oh, don't fret thyself, Lucinda." Wincing, Mercy raised her head from the pillow and then sank back with a groan. "I'm just a little banged up. Nothin' Dr. Jennings can't fix."

"But thee could have died." Fresh tears rolled down Lucinda's cheeks, and Will slid a comforting arm around her shoulder. The doctor eyed the move with a critical glance, and Lucinda experienced a flash of concern that Dr. Jennings, an elder at Serenity Friends Meeting, might mention what he saw to Will's brother.

Mercy slipped her good hand from Lucinda's fingers and touched her bandaged head. "Reckon I deserved it for chasing that raccoon off my back porch with the broom, but the critter eats the scraps I put out for the barn cats." She gave another low moan. "I must have hit a patch of ice, because the next thing I knew I went flyin'."

"Well." The doctor snapped his black leather bag shut. "The raccoon is safe for a while. Thee won't be going out there again anytime soon. Actually," he said as he rose from the chair beside Mercy's bed, "I suggest thee have someone come here and stay with thee until that ankle heals, which will probably take two or three weeks."

"No." Mercy rolled her head on the pillow.

"Mercy." Will bent nearer to the woman's bedside. "I know thee is used to taking care of thyself, but now thee needs—"

"I know I will need help for a while, but I don't want to stay here." Mercy looked at Lucinda. "I might as well go to thy place now. I'd planned to stay with thee after the first of the year anyway." She grinned, and her gaze slid to Will. "And when my hand gets well enough, I want to try out that fine loom thee bought Lucinda." Now she turned her attention to Dr. Jennings. "Can thee get me in thy buggy?"

The doctor scowled and grasped his chin between his thumb and forefinger. He bounced a narrow-eyed glance between Lucinda and Will. "Although I would normally recommend that thee stay put, in this case it might be best if thee did go to stay with Lucinda. I think with Will's help, and so long as thee doesn't put any weight on thy injured foot, we should be able to manage moving thee."

Lucinda bundled Mercy in a warm shawl and tied her black wool bonnet beneath her chin. At Mercy's instructions, Will gathered up spools of warp thread and bags of rug rags so Lucinda could make promised rugs in Mercy's stead. Then with Will and Dr. Jennings supporting her, Mercy hopped out to the doctor's buggy. The four headed to Lucinda's cabin with the buggy in the lead and Will and Lucinda following in the wagon.

A few minutes later, in Lucinda's front room, Will and Dr. Jennings ensconced Mercy in the big horsehair-upholstered chair that had once belonged to Alan's father. Under doctor's orders to keep her injured ankle elevated, Will brought a chair from the kitchen, and Lucinda placed a feather pillow on the seat.

Dr. Jennings eased Mercy's stocking-clad foot onto the pillow. Then taking a step back, he crossed his arms over his chest. After giving Lucinda a skeptical glance, he eyed Mercy. "Is thee sure thee wouldn't like for me to send another one of the ladies from Meeting to see to thee? I'm sure any number would be happy to—"

"Lucinda is quite capable, I'm sure." Giving her a confident smile, Mercy settled back in the chair.

Dr. Jennings dropped his double chin to his chest and gave a muted *harrumph*. "Of course." With that, he reiterated his instructions and took his leave.

Will lingered. "I will come by soon to check on thy firewood and see to thy outside chores." Though he spared Mercy a glance, his gaze rested gently on Lucinda's face.

The big chair creaked softly as Mercy sat forward. She looked first at Will and then at Lucinda. A hint of a smile touched her lips. And though it might have been but the reflection of the fireplace flames, Lucinda thought she caught sight of a knowing glint in the older woman's eyes. "I praise God that thee came by my house this afternoon, Will, but thee never said for what reason thee came."

Will's gaze dropped to the scuffed toes of his black boots as if pondering his reply. Finally he raised his face, and with a glance at Lucinda, he looked at Mercy and smiled. "I believe God sent me."

Two days later, Will's words still rang in Lucinda's ears as she sat weaving at the loom. Had God sent Will. . .not only to Mercy but to Lucinda as well? It didn't matter. In the spring she and her child would be moving back to Kentucky. But so far, she hadn't found the words to tell Mercy of her decision.

She looked over at Mercy, who sat reading her Bible by the sunlight spilling through the front window over her shoulder. Lucinda couldn't remember the last time she'd even picked up the Bible, let alone read it. If she'd ever had any faith—any Light in the first place—it had obviously gone out. And it was high time she told Mercy.

After beating down a line of woven weft she paused, shuttle in her hand. "I'm moving back to Kentucky in the spring," she blurted.

Mercy looked up from the pages of her Bible, concern pinching her features. "But thy father warned thee not to come back. Thee must think of thy child. It may not be safe."

"Pa is dead." Lucinda turned back to the loom and her weaving. "I got a letter from my sister Esther. She told me that Pa had died and that she wanted me to come back and live with her and her man, Lonny. That's why I went to your house two days ago—to get some sheets of writing paper so I could write and tell her to come and get me in the spring."

"Thee has stopped using the plain speech. Has thee turned from the faith, then?" Mercy's voice was tinged with sorrow.

Sighing, Lucinda faced Mercy. "I'm not even sure I ever had any faith. And no, I'm not a Quaker anymore." She swallowed down the wad of tears that had gathered in her throat. "Naomi Davis says I'm an impostor, that I was never sanctified. And she and Simeon don't like Will comin' here." She didn't even try to mask the bitterness in her voice as she recounted to Mercy what had transpired between Will and Simeon the day he brought her loom.

Anger flashed in Mercy's blue eyes. "Thy sanctification is not for Simeon and Naomi to judge, and I'd advise them to heed Christ's warnin' about doin' so." The anger lines left her brow, and she breathed a soft sigh. "Child." Her tone held patient kindness. "I saw thy convincement. I know it was real. But I fear thy faith was too new, too young and tender to withstand the gale of grief that assailed thee. Thee needs to nurture thy faith, not turn thy back on it."

New tears sprang in Lucinda's eyes, and she blinked them away. "And why should I have faith in a God who abandoned me?"

"Dear one." Mercy leaned forward in her chair. "God has not abandoned thee. He says in His Word that He will never abandon us." The pages of the Bible whispered as she thumbed through them. "'Be content with such things as ye have: for he hath said, I will never leave thee, nor forsake thee,'" she read.

She laced her fingers together and rested her hands on the open pages. "God's plan for our lives is like a road. For a stretch it may go in a straight line. But sometimes when we don't expect it, there is a fork in the road, and if we don't seek God's direction, we can get lost."

Lucinda stepped on the treadle and slid the shuttle through the open threads. "But. . .but when we come to a fork, how do we know what direction to go?"

Mercy tapped the Bible. "It's all in here. Next week is Christmas, and Christmas is all about God sending His Son to find the lost and show them the way they should go." She grinned. "I think God has been giving thee signs all along as to what direction He wants thy life to go. Thee is just ignoring them." She paused. "Like Will, bringing thee this loom."

At Mercy's mention of Will, Lucinda froze and nearly dropped the shuttle. Recovering, she focused again on her work. "So what do you think God is trying to tell me?" She couldn't help the bitter tone that crept into her voice.

"I think," Mercy said, "that God is telling thee to continue thy weaving." Then cocking her head in a thoughtful pose, she gave Lucinda a knowing smile. "And maybe something more."

Chapter 9

Conflict swirled through Lucinda's heart like the gusting wind that swept showers of fine snow from the porch roof.

Would Will stop by on his way to the mill this morning? Did she even want him to?

In the days since Mercy's accident, many members of Serenity Friends Meeting had come by to offer their good wishes, prayers, and help. But Will had not been back. After Simeon's warning to Will and Dr. Jennings's critical looks, Lucinda couldn't blame Will for staying away. Still, it hurt to think that he had bowed to Simeon's wishes, especially since Mercy was here now to chaperone.

Hugging her wool shawl tighter around her shoulders, she took careful steps toward the diminishing woodpile next to the front door. Her hope gusted with the wind. Still, he *might* stop. He rarely allowed her supply of wood to dwindle lower than half a rick.

She lifted her face to the December wind that snatched at her hair. With a crooked finger, she caught an errant lock that had escaped its pinned moorings and tucked it behind her ear. Squinting, she peered beyond the snowy field across the road to the Davis family woods. The bare trees appeared sketched with charcoal onto the pristine whiteness of last night's snowfall.

Will always replenished her firewood from the cords of cut wood he kept stacked near this entrance to his family's woods. If he had driven his wagon into the woods this morning, she should see some evidence in the new-fallen snow.

Yes, she could see tracks now, where the snow blushed beneath the kiss of the morning sun. Her heart quickened at the sight of the muddy gouges that disfigured the otherwise unblemished blanket of snow. The tracks made by a wagon's wheels disappeared into the shadows between the two large barren oaks that stood sentry on either side of the forest path. But her next thought reined in her galloping heart. The indentions might not have been made by Will's wagon at all, since he and Simeon allowed several of their neighbors to use the woods as well.

Lucinda breathed a deep, ragged sigh and rubbed her arms against the biting wind. Staring wouldn't cause Will's wagon and mule to materialize.

She emitted a small groan as she bent over her expanded waistline to lift three pieces of firewood into her arms.

Inside, she laid the largest—a chunk of maple—on the stone hearth that jutted out from the large fireplace.

From her perch on the horsehair chair, Mercy glanced up from sewing together strips of faded calico that Lucinda would soon weave into a new rug. "How much snow did we get last night?" Since their conversation three days ago, neither woman had spoken again of Lucinda's plans to return to Kentucky in the spring.

Lucinda cradled the two small pieces of willow wood meant for the cookstove in the crook of her arm. "Looks like about four inches."

"Thee should have waited to bring in the wood, Lucinda. If the pile of wood on the porch is as low as thee says, Will probably will stop by on his way to the mill to bring us more."

Fearing her face might reflect her hope that Mercy was right, Lucinda turned toward the kitchen. "Maybe. But that won't help me keep the fire going in the cookstove now."

"Thee should make biscuits, I think," Mercy called after her. "I would like some biscuits, and I'm sure Will would, too, if he should stop by."

Lucinda didn't reply but carried the two pieces of wood into the little kitchen.

Warmth radiated from the cookstove in which she'd earlier built a fire with corncobs soaked in kerosene.

Using a piece of quilted flannel, she pushed down the hot lever on the door covering the stove's firebox, swung the door open, and pitched in the two pieces of willow wood. The cold, wet wood sizzled and popped as she fed it into the hot stove, sending orange sparks flying.

Two pieces should be enough to bake biscuits. Mercy was right. If Will did stop by to bring them wood, he would appreciate hot biscuits.

As she reached for the flour sack on the shelf beside the cupboard, guilt nibbled at her conscience. If, as she suspected, Will did harbor a special affection for her, was it fair of her to encourage his affection when she planned to leave both Indiana and the Quaker faith?

Minutes later, her heart fluttered at the sound of a wagon rattling to a stop in front of the cabin.

"I think thee has company, Lucinda." Mercy's voice held a noticeable smugness as she called from the front room.

Using a dish towel to protect her fingers, Lucinda reached into the oven and grasped the hot pan full of fragrant, golden-brown biscuits. She plunked the pan of freshly baked bread onto the stove top and started for the front room.

Opening the door, she found Will peering around a pile of split maple wood in his arms.

"I see thee needs more wood. I have brought plenty for both the fireplace and the cookstove." He stamped on the porch boards, knocking snow from his boots.

"Thank thee, Will. I was hoping thee would come." The words leaped from Lucinda's mouth before she thought. Not only did they express her true feelings, but she realized that she had lapsed back into the plain Quaker speech. Just as well. Will didn't need to know that she had all but abandoned the Quaker faith. She moved aside, inviting him to come in, and admonished her racing heart, which refused to behave at his smile.

"Good morning, Mercy." Will stepped into the front room and turned his smiling attention to the older woman. "I pray thee is feeling better."

Dropping her work back to her lap, Mercy returned his smile. "I am. Thank thee, Will." She gingerly touched her fingers to the dark scab forming on her bruised forehead. "My cut is nearly healed." Then she lifted the forked stick she now kept beside her chair. "Lucinda found this outside beneath the big old poplar tree in the yard." She grinned. "Just sitting in this chair gets powerful tiring, so with this I can manage to hobble around some." Half turning in her chair, she glanced over her shoulder toward the front window. "Does thee think it will snow again tonight?"

"Think so." He shifted the load of wood in his arms. "The wind has picked up, and it is coming from the north now." He shot a worried look at the lonely piece of wood lying on the hearth. "Are thee both staying warm enough?"

"Plenty warm," Lucinda chimed in. "In fact"—she grinned at her houseguest—"Mercy more often complains about being too warm."

He left three more pieces of split wood on the hearth and then headed to the kitchen, Lucinda following behind him. "But we would freeze for sure if it wasn't for the wood thee brings," she said as he stacked six pieces of willow wood by the cookstove.

"I'll bring in as much as I can pile up by the hearth then I'll finish the rick on the porch." A worried look etched a V between his pale brows. "But thee must be careful when thee goes out on the porch to fetch it. And do not carry too much at once." He glanced at her distended middle. Immediately, his face turned bright red, and his gaze skittered quickly away.

His sweet concern touched her deeply, bringing a knot of hot tears to her throat. She swallowed them down and forced a light tone to her voice. "Thee will stay for biscuits and coffee, won't thee?" She turned her back to him and began transferring the hot bread to a stoneware plate. If her eyes held hope, she'd rather he not see it.

His voice behind her smiled. "I was hoping thee would ask when I first walked in and smelled them. I would not want to miss *thy* biscuits, Lucinda."

When she turned back to place the plate of biscuits on the table, he leaned his face close to hers, sending her heart skipping. He lowered his voice to a whisper. "Thy biscuits are better even than Mercy's," he said with a glance toward the front room, "though thee must not tell her I said so."

At his nearness, Lucinda's breath left her lungs. Grasping the table's edge to support her suddenly weak knees, she caught only a glance of his grin as he turned and headed toward the front room.

◆　◆　◆

Will's heart pounded as he stood at the back of his wagon and loaded his arms with wood. Guilt had smote him at finding such a small amount of firewood on Lucinda's porch. He should have come two days ago. But before seeing her again, he had needed to spend much time in prayer.

After the first of the year, Simeon and the other elders would likely meet with

Lucinda and question the state of her faith. And if, as Simeon believed, she had turned away from the faith, Will might be forced to choose between her and his brother.

Last night as Will lay in bed, praying for God to give him the answer, one came. Not heralded by trumpet or an angelic choir but a still, small voice that spoke directly to his heart. The words he heard were simple. *"Love is to give."*

He needed to keep doing what he had been doing all along—taking care of Lucinda. And as long as she allowed him to, that was what he would do.

He turned toward the cabin, and his gaze flitted over its weathered porch posts. The porch would need painting in the spring. Hefting the firewood in his arms, he prayed he'd be the one doing the work. But when he shared with her the burden he'd carried for six months, Simeon's opposition to Will seeing Lucinda would likely be rendered irrelevant

Sometime soon he would have to tell her. But not today. This morning he wanted only her smiles. Today he needed to go to the mill still believing that in the spring he would paint Lucinda's porch.

After building up the stack of wood on the porch and bringing in all that the hearth could hold, Will walked to the kitchen.

There Lucinda stood pouring steaming cups of coffee, while Mercy sat buttering biscuits.

"Sit down, Will." From the end of the table, Mercy motioned him toward the chair across from the one in which Lucinda had taken a seat.

He dragged off his hat and ran his hand over his hair in an attempt to smooth it down, aware that it must look like so much straw. After hanging his hat on the knob of the chair Mercy had indicated, Will sat down.

Mercy looked over at him. "Will, would thee say the blessing, please?" Although it was Lucinda's home, the older woman seemed to have assumed the role of host, as befit her age.

Will bowed his head over his plate of buttered biscuits and cup of black coffee. "Lord, we thank Thee for this food and all Thy blessings and the opportunity to commune with Thee and dear ones of like precious faith. In Jesus' name, amen."

When he raised his head, he looked across the table, directly into Lucinda's eyes. He hadn't seen her bow her head, but he might have missed it.

Her glance flickered from his face to the lone plate of biscuits. "I'm sorry I have no eggs to serve thee. The chickens have slowed down on their layin', but I haven't checked this mornin', so there might be some out there."

"Too cold." Mercy shook her head. "The cold weather always slows them down."

"Thee has no business traipsing out to the chicken house through this snow." Concern roughed his tone. Every time he thought he'd done all he could to keep Lucinda safe, another worry cropped up. "I'll feed and water the chickens and check for eggs before I leave."

A hint of a smile touched Lucinda's lips. "If thee finds some, maybe I could make a Christmas cake, if thee would care to share it with Mercy and me." Her cinnamon-colored eyes looked almost childlike in their hopefulness.

All morning, he'd tried to think of how best to invite her to the midweek Meeting on Christmas Eve, two days away. So her unexpected mention of the coming holiday seemed to present the perfect opportunity. *Thank Thee, Lord.*

Aloud, he said, "I would love to share thy Christmas cake. If thee would like, I'd be glad to take thee to Meeting on Christmas Eve." He fixed his gaze on his plate. In the past six months, she'd turned down every invitation to attend Meeting. But it was Christmas. He needed to try.

She paused and then exhaled a long sigh that frayed at the edges. "Yes, I think I'd like that. Thank thee."

It took him a couple of seconds to accept what he'd heard. "I'd best come by about six thirty, then. Meeting is at seven." He tried hard to keep the surprise from his voice as his ridiculous heart sang.

His joy immediately withered.

I'll tell her then. I'll have to tell her then.

He couldn't allow it to go on. She had to know. And if telling Lucinda the truth killed all hope of winning her love, then so be it. Maybe he deserved that. Maybe that would be fit penance. The burden had grown too heavy. On Christmas Eve he would lay it down.

Chapter 10

Six o'clock Christmas Eve, Lucinda frowned at her reflection in the oval dresser mirror. Tugging at her best black bombazine dress, she wished it fit better. She'd been able to let out enough pleats to accommodate her swollen belly, but it seemed to hang all wrong. Hopefully, her black wool shawl would hide a lot.

Had she made a mistake in agreeing to this? How would the congregation she had so long shunned receive her? Worst of all, would God view her as a hypocrite? Well, it was too late to change her mind now. She'd promised Will and couldn't bear the thought of disappointing him.

Chiding herself for her case of nerves, she slipped another pin into the coil of hair she'd twisted into a bun at the back of her head.

Outside, the jangling sound of a wagon sent her to the front room, her heart racing with her feet.

"Will is here," Mercy called unnecessarily from her chair in the front room.

When Lucinda answered the knock at the door, her focus shifted from Will's face to the long, narrow parcel wrapped in brown butcher paper that he held in his hand.

"Good evening, Lucinda, Mercy." He knocked the snow off his boots and stepped into the front room.

"What has thee brought?" Curious, Lucinda followed him as he stepped to where Mercy sat.

"Merry Christmas, Mercy." He held the package out to her.

Mercy accepted it with a puzzled grin. "What could thee have brought me?"

"Open it up and find out," he said, his smile stretching his face wide.

"Yes, Mercy, open it up!" Leaning forward, Lucinda clasped her hands together, trying to guess what Will's gift to Mercy might be.

Mercy tore away the paper to reveal a wooden stick. But the gift was more than a stick. It was a lovely, varnished cane of dark wood. Lucinda guessed black walnut. The end was crooked like a shepherd's staff and padded with black cotton material.

"I thought this might work better for thee than the forked poplar branch."

"Oh, thank thee, Will! It is perfect. Exactly what I need." Mercy's eyes filled with wonder and tears. She immediately used her new gift to stand and give Will a hug.

Lucinda's heart swelled at his sweet gesture. Was there ever a kinder, more thoughtful man? She didn't want to contemplate how empty and sad her life would be without him.

Oddly, without saying a word, he went out the door again. A few seconds later, he returned holding a large object wrapped in a crazy quilt. "This is for thee," he said to Lucinda.

Her mind whirling, Lucinda stepped back to allow Will and his mysterious burden into the front room. Her curious gaze followed the quilt-wrapped gift as he set it down in front of her. "But thee already got me the loom. Thee didn't need to—"

"I'm really just delivering this," he broke in, his tone almost apologetic. "Alan started it," he said, stealing away her breath. "I only finished it."

◆　◆　◆

Will held his breath as he lifted the quilt from the cherry wood cradle. How would she react?

Still no words.

Mercy emitted a soft gasp.

Lucinda's trembling fingers ran tenderly, almost reverently over the varnished red-gold wood, her large eyes questioning, unbelieving, helpless. At last she turned them to him—huge brown eyes glistening with tears.

The silence lengthened until he could no longer bear it. He had to fill it.

"He'd started working on it right after he learned about the baby. He'd planned it to be a birthday gift for thee last August." Will squirmed, his nervous hands crushing his good black hat.

Her tears escaped their beautiful confines and slipped silently down her cheeks.

"I hope it does not offend thee that I finished it. I thought he would want. . ." Will felt lost now. Floundering. Unsure.

"Yes. Yes, that's exactly what he would have wanted." Her voice quivered, but he marveled at her courage and how her words had hastened to his rescue. "Thank thee for finishing it and bringing it to me." Her words lent the impression that she'd sensed his discomfort and wanted to console *him*!

His heart writhed. If only he could put his arms around her. But that wouldn't do, especially with Mercy looking on.

But Mercy's glistening eyes were fixed on the cradle. "It is a beautiful cradle, Will. I can see the love shining from it."

"Thank thee," Will mumbled and then cleared his dry throat.

◆　◆　◆

An hour later, in the midst of the midweek Meeting, a peace Lucinda had not felt for many months settled over her heart. The Prince of Peace. Moments ago, she'd sung those words in a carol along with the rest of the congregation.

Entering the meetinghouse, she'd expected snubs and even outright hostility. Instead, she'd been met with smiles and welcoming hugs. Even Naomi and Simeon Davis had greeted her with smiles, albeit a tinge stiff.

In the congregation's loving embrace, Lucinda realized the truth in Mercy's words. God had not abandoned her nor had the congregation of Serenity Friends Meeting. Lucinda was the one who had left them. She had let her anger at God separate her from His comfort, His peace, and His Light.

When they left the meetinghouse, Will tucked Lucinda's arm securely around his and helped her across the snowy ground to the wagon. As they walked, she glanced up at the quiet figure of the man beside her. God had not left her alone. Whenever she needed something, Will had been there. He never gave up on her. As he was doing now, he'd quietly provided caring support. Patiently and lovingly, he'd nudged her back to God's guiding Light. And with that Light shining brightly within her once more, she could now see clearly God's direction for her life. And that direction was not back to Kentucky, but right here in Serenity with the man to whose arm she clung.

As Will ensconced her on the wagon seat, wrapping her in a quilt, Lucinda returned his smile. She no longer needed nor wanted to deny what her heart felt for him. At last she could unflinchingly call it by name—love. Yes, love.

Her heart twirled with joy at the admission. Oh, love hadn't come with the sudden loud clatter of a summer thunderstorm as it had with Alan. This time, love had crept slowly, quietly, like a winter snowfall, covering her heart like a soft, warm, comforting blanket.

◆ ◆ ◆

Will's fingers tensed around the reins as the mule pulled the wagon away from the meetinghouse. When would he tell her? How would he begin?

The wagon had come up even with the cemetery's wrought iron fence when she pressed her hand against his arm. "Will, stop for a little."

"Is thee warm enough?" Concerned, he reached to snug the lap quilt around her.

"Yes, I am warm." Her sweet smile relaxed his worried frown.

The time to tell her had come.

"Lucinda. . ." Praying for courage, he hesitated.

She waited quietly for him to continue. Their gazes drifted to the cemetery, which looked serenely beautiful in the moonlight. The new snow covered all the reality, white fluffy caps softening the headstones.

Will cleared his throat and began again. "There is something I need to tell thee. Something I should have told thee before." He took a deep breath and then allowed the words he'd harbored so long to escape in a rush. "It should have been me, not Alan." There, he'd said it.

"No, Will. Thee mustn't say that."

She didn't understand. He would have to finish it. His courage nearly deserted him. He kept his gaze directed toward the vicinity of his friend's grave. If he looked into her beautiful brown eyes, he'd be lost.

"Amos had asked Alan to make the trip to the railroad depot with the wagon that day, but he wasn't in the notion, so I went instead. If I had just refused to make that trip, Alan would not have been at the mill when the explosion happened. I will understand if thee never wants to see my face again."

◆ ◆ ◆

Lucinda watched Will's Adam's apple bob with a hard swallow, his gaze firmly fastened on the cemetery. Her heart ached for him. How quietly he had carried the burden all these months. How needlessly he had suffered.

She gently covered his large hand with hers, praying for words that might lift the undeserved burden from this sweet man's heart. "I know. Amos told me at the funeral. Will, I lost one man I loved. I don't think I could bear to lose another."

His face swung toward hers, his gray eyes growing wide with wonder. When their gazes locked, a sweet understanding swept away all uncertainty. For a moment, his eyes glistened in the moonlight before closing, and he lowered his lips to hers.

Lucinda's heart sang as she welcomed his kiss. She'd found where she wanted to be—where she needed to be. After a long moment, she dropped her gaze to her lap, feeling oddly shy. "I'm sorry I don't have a Christmas gift for thee after thee gave me the loom and then the cradle. Just a Christmas cake. Maybe the cake..."

"Sweetheart." Will gently took her face into his hands and tipped it up to his. "Thee has given me better gifts than I could have ever hoped for. They are the same gifts the Christ child brought to the world that first Christmas—the gifts of love and forgiveness." His calloused thumb prickled against her skin as he brushed a tear from her cheek before tenderly kissing her lips again.

"Take me home, Will." She barely breathed the words, allowing her gaze to melt into his.

His smile nearly split his face as he snapped the reins against the mule's back. "Come on, Bob!"

Along the road, they passed a group of young people caroling outside a farmhouse. The words wafted through the frigid night air and wrapped tenderly around Lucinda's heart.

"'How silently, how silently, the wondrous gift is given; so God imparts to human hearts the blessings of His heaven.'"

Snuggled in the warm circle of Will's arm, Lucinda knew that God had indeed blessed her.

Resting her hands on the mound beneath her heart, she felt a tiny kick and thought of the cradle. Quietly, but clearly, God's voice spoke to her heart. The life that she and Alan had begun, she and Will would finish.

She'd learned something else this extraordinary Christmas Eve. The best gifts were the ones wrapped in pure love, exchanged silently from one heart to another. She and Will had exchanged such gifts. Gifts they would share for the rest of their lives.

June's Molasses Crisps

From *The James Whitcomb Riley Cookbook* by Dorothy June Williams (curator, Riley Home, Greenfield, Indiana) and Diana Williams Hansen (Food Editor and Consultant), 2001.

This old-fashioned recipe is a Greenfield, Indiana, original, perfected by Dorothy June Williams when her six children were small. Unlike most households, ours had rolled and decorated cookies frequently as the children grew up, and one of "the Williams girls" won a sweepstakes ribbon at the Indiana State Fair with these cookies. Besides various fancy decorated cookies, you can make good gingerbread men with this recipe.

    1 cup mild molasses (or honey)
    1 cup sugar
    ½ cup butter
    ½ cup lard or solid white shortening
    5 cups sifted all-purpose flour, divided
    2 eggs, beaten
    ½ teaspoon baking soda
    ½ teaspoon salt
    ½ teaspoon ground ginger
    ½ teaspoon ground cinnamon
    ½ teaspoon ground cloves

In saucepan, while stirring over medium heat, bring to simmering the molasses, sugar, butter, and lard or shortening. When simmering, remove from heat. In large mixing bowl, place 2 cups of the flour. Carefully pour the hot molasses mixture over the flour and beat the mixture until it is smooth and well mixed. Cool. When mixture is no longer hot to the touch, stir in the additional 3 cups flour which has been mixed with the soda, salt, ginger, cinnamon, and cloves. "Work" the dough until it is well mixed, then refrigerate, covered, until chilled. To bake, remove from refrigerator and cut off small pieces of dough (dough becomes very firm and hard). Roll out thin on floured surface, using floured rolling pin. Cut into shapes with cookie cutter. Bake the cookies in preheated 375-degree oven for 8 to 10 minutes, until set and cookies look just dry. Remove to wire racks to cool. When cold, frost as desired with colored confectioner's-sugar icing, nuts, and decorative sprinkles. Makes about 6 dozen cookies. Store cookies in tightly covered container.

Ramona K. Cecil is a wife, mother, grandmother, freelance poet, and award-winning inspirational romance writer. Now empty nesters, she and her husband make their home in Indiana. A member of American Christian Fiction Writers and American Christian Fiction Writers Indiana Chapter, her work has won awards in a number of inspirational writing contests. Over eighty of her inspirational verses have been published on a wide array of items for the Christian gift market. She enjoys a speaking ministry, sharing her journey to publication while encouraging aspiring writers. When not writing, her hobbies include reading, gardening, and visiting places of historical interest.

A Christmas Prayer

by Dianne Christner

Chapter 1

Mountain Lake, Minnesota, 1881

The ground, air, and trees were cloaked in a world of white. Harsh white. With her back hunched against the frigid cold, Hanna Friesen saw the schoolhouse's dim silhouette. The sky had dumped so much snow so fast, she'd lost hope of making it to her destination. Falling so quickly upon the heels of a warm front, it caught most of the Russian immigrant village unawares. Dmitri Friesen had a keen sense for the weather and had sent his eighteen-year-old daughter to the school early to fetch her brothers home.

But struggling through the storm brought back vivid memories of two winters past, when she'd gotten frostbitten feet and even lost some toes, resulting in a slight limp and ongoing pain, especially in cold weather. Although the school was now within sight, she didn't know if her brothers were safe inside or if she had passed them along the way.

As the snow swirled and blanketed everything in its grasp, she'd kept vigilant watch, her heart thumping with dread that they could have started home and gotten lost without the advantage of snowshoes or sled. It wouldn't take much to harm her middle brother who was by nature frail. Breathing in the cold could either make you feel alive or take the life from you. And Miss Katia Kroeker, the schoolteacher, was unpredictable. Surely she hadn't released them to venture out into the storm alone?

Hanna was heartened in the schoolyard to catch the faint musical notes of children singing. But Katia had allowed the door to get blocked with snow. Fortunately, Hanna carried a tiny shovel strapped to her sled. Quickly she went to work to dig the snow away from the door. As she did so, the wind increased, diminishing her vision, and she was grateful to God for allowing her to reach safety. When her shovel finally scraped against wood, the singing halted and Katia called from inside the schoolhouse. "Who's there?"

"Hanna Friesen."

"Thank God! I hope you've brought help along."

And what am I? Hanna mumbled to herself, then asked, "Are my brothers inside?"

"Yes, they're here."

Relief flooded over her. "Good!"

Within several minutes, she'd cleared the snow away from the doorway. Nearly overcome with fatigue, she managed to pull her sled inside before the wind blew the door closed. As Katia fussed over her, the teacher frowned at the messy sled.

However, Hanna maintained it was a necessary precaution.

While she fervently scanned the room for her brothers, Katia pulled her to the warmth of the stove, saying, "See, children. All is well. Your family will come for you."

"Hanna!" Viktor, a blond ten-year-old who was sturdy enough to do a man's work, ran to embrace her, nearly toppling them both to the floor. "I was worried about you. How are your feet?"

"I'm fine," she replied.

"Warm up by the stove," he insisted, pulling her closer.

Skinny eight-year-old Stefan and six-year-old Yury, who resembled his oldest brother in stamina and countenance, wrapped their arms around her waist. Gratitude flooded her to be able to hold them in the flesh and confirm their safety, but she quickly noticed that only a remnant of the students remained. As soon as she could distance herself from the children and the stove's warmth, she questioned Katia and listened to the other woman's distraught accounting. Though kind and excellent in her teaching abilities, the woman bore a nervous countenance, and Hanna hated to think what might have occurred if another adult hadn't shown up to lend support.

"The children who lived closest to the school set out for home hours earlier," Katia explained. But she had kept the rest at Mountain Lake, Minnesota's, one-room Mennonite school, fearing they'd be frozen or lost if she released them. Keeping her voice low so as not to distress the children, she explained, "I should've brought more wood in, but I thought it more important to get the children started home and then to occupy the remaining ones until their families arrived. I never dreamed the storm would arrive in such a fury, burying us inside. Do you think anyone else will come? We need more wood." She glanced nervously at the windows, which shook and groaned from the wind, but nothing was visible through the white haze.

"Then we should get it now before the door is blocked again," Hanna replied, wondering where she would garner the strength to carry out her proclamation.

Nodding, Katia continued, "I'm so worried about the children who left. I don't know if I did the right thing."

Hanna touched Katia's arm. "You did your best, and they're in God's hands. Now we must consider the children who remain in our care. We can burn a few desks, if need be."

"Oh no. I hope that's not necessary. The town has put this all in my care. The children, too."

"Would we be more comfortable at your house?" Anna referred to the teacher's small lodging behind the school. "It would be better to be someplace with food if we get snowed in."

"Surely you're not suggesting we move the children in this blizzard? I fear I've waited too long for that."

"I suppose you're right." She suddenly remembered a trick her dad often used during blizzards to reach the barn. "If I had a rope, I could use my sled to get to your house and bring back some supplies."

Katia considered the request. "The only rope I have is attached to the school bell outside. It wouldn't reach that far. But it has some extra length looped against the post. I always wondered why the townsmen left it that way. Now I know."

Hanna nodded thoughtfully. "It might reach the school's woodpile." She rushed to the stove where the children were gathered. "Viktor, come with me."

The blond lad was eager to obey. His ten-year-old voice cautious. "What is it?"

"May I borrow your knife?"

Katia crooked an eyebrow at her pupil, for such implements were supposed to be left at home.

With a sheepish grin, he dug in his pocket and handed it to Hanna.

"Thanks. Will you help us?"

"Sure," he nodded enthusiastically.

"If the three of us make a human chain, I can reach the rope."

Choosing one of Viktor's friends to help, they opened the door. With an eerie howl, snow swirled into the classroom. Moving quickly so she didn't lose heart and change her mind, Hanna ducked her head and hunched into the assault. The storm had worsened since she'd been inside the schoolhouse, but she found the rope and cut it as high as she could reach. Then it took the four of them to tug it loose from its bed of frozen snow. Back inside, they pushed the door shut against the snow's fury. Hanna's heart beat rapidly from the exertion. Next they dragged Katia's desk close to the door and secured one end of the rope. The other, Viktor fastened around Hanna's waist.

"I should be doing this, not you," Katia insisted.

"Nonsense. You need to remain with the children."

"I'll do it," Viktor tensed his jaw. "You know I'm in charge of the wood at home."

"Not this time," Katia replied sternly. "Not under my care."

"Your teacher is right." Hanna placed additional layers of clothing over her woolen shawl and donned her snowshoes. She secured the ties on the dark hooded bonnet worn by the Russian Mennonite women. Then armed with shovel and sled, she headed back into the storm trying to ignore the constant pain throbbing through her feet as she inched her way around the side of the building to the woodpile. But all she could see was a blinding swirl of snow. She knew it was their only chance to get the firewood needed for survival. Feeling helpless, she almost turned back. But suddenly she heard singing. The children sounded like angels, their voices so faint against the wind's howl, it could have been her imagination. But it gave her the determination she needed to proceed.

Now Hanna's mom, Sonya Friesen, was a woman of deep faith who'd taught Hanna to pray by utilizing scripture in her prayers. As part of her child rearing, her mom had required each of them to memorize an entire book of the Bible of their own choosing. Hanna had chosen Proverbs. So her mind involuntarily sought for a verse to cover her present situation. Proverbs 31:21 came to mind. *"She is not afraid of the snow for her household: for all her household are clothed with scarlet."* A smile tugged her nearly frozen lips. She dressed plainly as all her Mennonite Brethren sisters—Mennonite Brethren was the official name for the branch of Mennonites of the Russian immigrants. Scarlet wouldn't have been her color of choice, but she recited the verse into the frigid air, where it became a frozen swirl. But as the woman in the scripture, she was prepared with winter clothing and sled. She'd survived frostbite once. She would overcome this time, too. If the Proverbs woman hadn't feared the snow, she mustn't either. *Lord, I know You can protect Your little ones who need this wood. I ask for them. Please help me find it and get enough to last through the storm.*

After that, she thrust the shovel in three times and hit gold. *Thank You, Lord!* Excited, she worked feverishly to heap as much wood as her sled could hold. She tugged the rope as she worked her way back to the door, and the others helped pull until the sled was safely inside. Gasping, she slumped onto the floor as the children scurried to help Katia unload the wet wood and get it near the fire to dry.

"Come to the fire," Viktor urged, drawing her to her feet.

Thank You, Lord. Willing herself to move, Hanna obeyed. Her hands stung as they began to warm, and her feet throbbed. The wood she'd recovered would get them through the night, but after that she didn't know how they would survive. While they could always burn desks, she didn't think the children would be too happy to have them served for lunch.

◆　◆　◆

Martin Penner turned to his father one last time before he and his brother Filipp boarded the Sioux City & St. Paul train. "I hope you make it home before the storm."

Filipp nudged him playfully. "Don't worry so much."

"Grow up," Martin retorted.

"I'm older than you."

"Exactly." Martin rolled his gaze heavenward. It was an old argument, but given the new responsibility they'd been given, couldn't Filipp at least act as if he was taking their mission seriously? At least until Dad was out of sight.

Their father furrowed his brow. Ignoring the upcoming storm, he warned, "I'm trusting you'll quit squabbling and work together. I'm sending you both because of your different perspectives that will help us decide if it's the right move to make for the family. Act like a team, for once."

For the family. . .which included his five younger brothers and sisters. Ever since their immigration from Russia when he was small, the family had struggled. Now they were settled in Iowa, but working at a meat packing facility, not farming. Scraping by, not prospering. They still felt like outsiders in their community. But they had heard that in Winnipeg there was a Russian community where they could worship with other Mennonite Brethren. Land was available. It seemed too good to be true. Which was why they were about to board the train.

"Godspeed. I'll be praying. Now go before I change my mind."

Martin embraced his father and boarded the train. He found his seat and stared out the window at a gray sky, trying to recover from a sudden flood of emotions. Sadness—for he'd never left the family before. Gratitude—he was allowed to travel with his older brother and not have to remain behind. Then there was the weight of his responsibility pressing down, especially since he believed he was more responsible than Filipp. And even though he would never admit it to his brother, excitement also coursed through his veins. All in all, he wasn't ready to look at Filipp when he felt him slide into the seat next to him.

"Go ahead and worry. Cry if you need to, while I dream about pretty faces and Canadian prairies."

He clenched his jaw and met Filipp's eyes. "It's no secret you have big dreams and a way with the women." Not that Filipp was better looking. The brothers shared the same brown wavy hair, strong high cheekbones, bright blue eyes, and straight noses. Handsome features in every way and features able to turn a woman's eye, but Martin disapproved of Filipp's way of sweet-talking people. He preferred to be blunt and serious. He favored action over charm. "I may not get the girls, but I also have dreams. I don't see this as some grand adventure where I might get lucky. Whatever good happens will be the result of choices and hard work."

Filipp stretched out his legs and pulled his hat over his eyes. "If that's how it's going to be, then I'd better take a nap. Sounds exhausting."

"Sleep, then," Martin replied sarcastically.

But sleep was far from Martin's grasp. For an unexplainable almost painful yearning rose up in his belly, and it wasn't hunger. He was too unsettled to even think about sleep. His mind wouldn't rest. Even as the railcar rocked and Filipp snored, Martin continued to watch out the window until, as he'd predicted earlier, the snow flurries began. This opportunity was a once-in-a-lifetime occasion. Everything depended upon what would happen after they made their connection in St. Paul, boarded the Canadian Pacific, and stepped out of the train onto Canadian soil.

Chapter 2

In Mountain Lake, Minnesota, the next morning, the blizzard ended and some nearby townsmen dug out the schoolhouse. A note was posted on the door and the children were moved to the teacher's home where they would wait for their families. At that time, Hanna departed with her brothers. However, along the way, the reprieve ended and snow began to fall again. Wet and steady but no longer blinding, allowing them to arrive home safely. Dad hurried from the barn, relieved to see them. But Hanna could tell something was wrong.

"Your mom's sick. Go to her so she can rest. She's been worried over your safety. Viktor, warm up and then come help. This storm is not over yet. There's much to do."

"Yes, Dad," Viktor replied.

Their mom wept with relief over them. She asked about all the other children, and Hanna shared as much as she knew. Then Hanna shooed the boys from the room. "Go warm up by the fire." When they were gone, she examined her mom with growing concern. "You're feverish. What happened?"

"Too long in the snow, I guess. Helping your dad. I just need rest. I spent the night praying. Now that I know you are safe, sleep will come and I'll be good as new. There's so much to do. Especially in this season. Only ten days until Christmas with so much to do," she repeated.

Hanna nodded. "Don't fret." She lifted a cup to her mother's mouth. "Drink something." Then she pulled the covers up around her neck and kissed her forehead. "Get better."

Next she cut thick slices of bread and spread it with apple butter for her brothers. As they ate, she stoked the fire and instructed Viktor, "Bring some meat from the smokehouse before you help Dad."

Viktor took that as his cue to get busy. She handed Stefan a broom and instructed Yury to put away coats, line up the boots, and dry the floors with a rag. Soon she had a stew cooking on the stove. She felt fortunate for their comfortable home, a far cry from the crude soddy they used to reside in, which still remained tucked into a hill on their property and used as storage.

Her mother was right to be concerned about the fast approach of Christmas. While the Mennonite Brethren didn't celebrate with trees or wrapped gifts, they offered gifts of service, especially to those in need. At Christmas, her mom always delivered peppernut cookies and quilts to the Immigration Depot, which housed new Russian settlers until they could procure land and a home. It was a free service, set up by the railroad company and run by the community. In Mountain Lake, they'd all been through similar circumstances, and most of the residents were eager to help newcomers who would eventually become part of their church and community. Hanna determined to nurse her mother back to health in time to keep up her beloved traditions.

But several days passed, and Sonya hadn't improved. She maintained a low fever and developed a cough. With her illness added to the storm, the joy had departed from the house. Dad was grim and overworked. Stefan and Yury were irritable from being cooped inside. Even Viktor had lost his sense of humor. And Hanna was worried. She peeled potatoes and watched the relentless snowfall. Would it never cease? And why wasn't God healing her mother? Didn't Proverbs 3:7–9 say, *"Fear the Lord, and depart from evil. It shall be health to thy navel, and marrow to thy bones. Honour the Lord with thy substance"?* Mother did all that and more. She did so much good for the community. *Lord, please restore health and joy to our home*—Hanna didn't usually add stipulations to her prayers, but this time she felt impelled to do so—*in time for Christmas.*

As she released her Christmas prayer, Dad bounded out of the bedroom, his voice gruff. "You must go for the doctor." As was his custom, he reasoned aloud, "I'd go, but it's too hard for you to remain and take care of the animals. But you're deft in the snow, and I know I can depend on you to fetch your mother the help she needs." However, he didn't say what they both were thinking. *Deft in the snow because she'd learned the hard way—from her mistakes—how to survive.* "And take some food along for the Immigration House. She would want you to do that."

"Is she worse?" Hanna panicked.

"That's for the doctor to tell."

"I'll go right away."

The journey wasn't far, but given the snow accumulation, it was midmorning by the time she arrived at the village. She stopped directly at the Immigration House to deliver food. The building swarmed with people but not Russian immigrants. So unusually cramped, she could barely maneuver through the mishmash of bed pallets strewn across the floor. Pressing through the crowd, she went directly to the kitchen to find a flustered administrator helping the cook. He rushed to accept the food, gushing thanks. "Tell everyone you meet that we need volunteers to house people. And we need more food. The train's snowed in, and all these passengers have no place to go. It will take days before they can get the track cleared. If it quits snowing."

Hanna gulped at the dire situation. Though their own house was more than sufficient for her family, it contained no extra beds. But evaluating the situation before her, the floor space in front of their hearth would be better accommodations than the depot provided for the stranded. If her mom weren't sick, she'd find a way to help. Then it hit her. *The soddy!* "Mom's sick and I'm going for the doctor, but our soddy is available. I'll swing back by and see if anyone is interested. If so, they can return with me."

"Bless you, Hanna. I'm sure you'll have some guests."

"I can take two on my sled, and I'll spread the word about the need. I'll have the doctor do the same."

"Godspeed. Go and get the doctor. Bless you."

◆　◆　◆

Martin Penner slapped snow off his gloves. "The engineer thinks we'll be stranded at least a week. Says they can't even start to clear the tracks until it stops snowing and conditions will worsen the farther north we go. Says we might as well settle in. But I don't like it. Don't like being idle."

Filipp agreed. "But there's nothing we can do until it quits snowing. Wait. I saw a woman bring food to the cook. They were speaking *Plaudietsch*—the low German of the Mennonite Brethren. Intrigued, I got close enough to overhear part of the conversation. Her family is offering an empty soddy. It'd be better than this."

Martin scanned the room, feeling claustrophobic. "Sounds good. But shouldn't we allow a family with children to take it?"

"I heard her say she only has room for two on her sled. I'll go see what I can do."

Within the hour, a pretty girl entered the building and drew Martin's attention. She had blond hair and wide-set, large, slightly slanted eyes. Her countenance was serious and determined. She definitely wasn't from the train, or he would've noticed her earlier. At least Filipp would've noticed her.

He did now. "There she is! Let's go."

Martin scrambled to his feet, amazed Filipp hadn't mentioned her beauty.

Filipp made quick introductions. "We understand you're offering a soddy?"

Hanna replied, "Yes, you're welcome to stay in it. But my mother is ill, and I need to return at once. Can we talk along the way?"

Martin snatched up his belongings even as Hanna led them outside. When his brother noticed her marked limp, he touched her arm. "Are you all right."

She jerked it away, her chin jutting upward. "I'm fine."

It gave Filipp enough pause that Martin found himself standing next to a sled, which was equipped with steerage that allowed its passengers to stand but appeared too small for their use. He voiced his concern. "This holds three?"

"All the time. My brothers are a bit smaller though." Her blue eyes twinkled as she looked at Martin. "You'll have to hold my waist. Filipp can hold yours. And you can both help push."

Filipp grinned at him and nudged him to get on first. He tried to resist, not wanting to be the one so tightly sandwiched.

She gave the hint of a smile, her eyelashes glistening with snow. "I won't bite, Martin. We're fully bundled in clothing, so I won't even feel your touch. And I'm not making more than one trip."

"I'll drive," Martin replied.

"No thanks. I wouldn't even be able to see over your back. You don't know the way, and it's my sled."

He appreciated her logic if not the fact she'd singled him out to be the one sandwiched. Seeing no other option to get to the soddy, he stepped onto the sled and felt

Filipp embark behind him.

Hanna pushed off. "It's like rowing a boat if we work in sync."

It took awhile to get the hang of it. They made good time going downhill, but when they went uphill, someone had to get off and pull. Since Filipp was on the back and the strongest of the trio, he did most of the pulling, which gave Martin breathing room as well as a chance to get to know Hanna better.

She explained how she came to be in town that day, and Martin hoped her father would be agreeable to her spontaneous offer. "The soddy will need some work. We use it for storage. But it has a stove and a few old furnishings."

"We're en route to Canada and may find ourselves living in a soddy for a while, so it will be good practice."

"Why are you traveling in winter?"

"We're scouting for our family. Dad has a job he couldn't leave, and if all goes well, the family will join us in the spring."

"Sounds like you have it all planned out. It appears God is providing for you. You're obviously Russian. You've probably noticed this is a Russian Mennonite Brethren settlement. It may be His way of showing you He is caring for you and favoring you on this venture."

"I know." What were the chances of getting stranded with other Mennonites? "It does seem to be a God sign." And it didn't hurt that his hostess was fetching and strong, appealing traits in a female. No matter what shape the soddy was in, this was more interesting than being cramped at the Immigration House.

◆　◆　◆

Martin's story intrigued Hanna. And although she'd claimed she wouldn't feel his touch, she did. Very much so. As when they went downhill, he leaned heavily against her. Though she normally was one with the sled—and, as Dad claimed, quite agile—Martin's presence affected her attentiveness. Quite belatedly, she noticed a newly fallen log blocking the road. "Jump!" she shouted.

She leaped, and everything else went blurry until she opened her eyes and found herself sitting in a snowbank. The brothers scrambled to their feet from the opposite side of the road and hurried to her aid. Filipp reached her first. "Are you all right?"

"Are those the only words you know?" she retorted tartly.

"This time, I was referring to your eyesight."

They glared at each other a moment.

The way Martin's lip twitched, he enjoyed his brother's discomfort. He silently held out a hand to her. While both men were strangers to her, from the start she'd been inclined toward Martin. For some reason, she allowed him to help her. She brushed off. "I just hope the sled's not damaged."

Filipp had already retrieved it and was pulling it around the log back onto the snowy road on the other side. "Looks fine," he said. "Maybe I should drive?"

"Does the soddy still seem appealing?" she asked.

"It does to me," Martin replied.

"Then both of you, on the back."

"Quit distracting her," Filipp warned. "I can't see a thing back here."

Biting back a grin, she shoved off and laughed when she caught both men off guard. But she quickly chastised herself. Her family remained at home working hard with Mom sick while she flirted with two strangers, one whose touch sent electricity through her body.

"Filipp's right," she said. "Let me concentrate on driving. It's not far now."

She felt Martin's hand rest briefly on her shoulder. "I didn't mean to rattle you." She tried to ignore his touch, remaining quiet, brooding, and watchful.

When they reached home, Dad and Viktor were shoveling snow, digging out the barn door—which had become a routine chore and one which appeared to be a losing battle against the snow.

Dad set down his shovel and seemed inquisitive, but it was Hanna who broke the silence. "How is Mom?"

"The doctor saw her and left already."

"I'm surprised we didn't meet him on the way."

"He's checking on some neighbors before he heads back to the village. He said all the schoolchildren made it home safe."

"Thank God," Hanna replied. "And Mom?"

"He gave us something for her cough and will try to come back in a few days if he can make it through the snow." He turned his attention to the brothers. "He mentioned the trouble with the train. Are you passengers?"

Filipp introduced themselves. "And Hanna offered us your soddy. I hope you've no qualms. We can take over your shoveling."

"Good thinking, Hanna." Dmitri paused to consider the offer. "Maybe later. For now, go and get settled so that you can have a fire and bed tonight. Tomorrow I'll find something for you to do."

"Thanks. We appreciate the hospitality."

Viktor, who'd been curiously silent until now, asked, "Did the train run off the tracks?"

"No. But it was slow going, and we were fortunate to make it to the station."

Hanna felt relieved of her family's acceptance. Though she'd never doubted her decision, she'd been feeling guilty for entertaining her handsome guests. She shook away her thoughts and motioned. "Grab shovels and follow me. Let's go open up the soddy."

Chapter 3

Martin followed the path Hanna made with her snowshoes, each step sinking to his thigh. If he didn't know better, it would seem she was leading them into a frozen wilderness. But suddenly a dome shape materialized within a small thicket of trees. Upon reaching it, he could see some mud bricks peaking through the snow. Most of the soddy, however, was buried in the white hillside.

"Here we are." She shrugged apologetically.

It was easy to see the first order of business was digging out the door.

"I'd help, but I must check on Mom and prepare supper."

Martin quickly replied, "You've already gone out of your way for us. And this doesn't look so bad, the way it's sheltered."

"It was once a good home for us." She smiled. "Come to the house for firewood."

"We'll earn our keep."

"I've no doubts. But we've plenty to share."

He wondered what it would be like to have ample and enough to share. His family barely scraped by feeding their nine mouths. "Thanks. For everything."

She nodded and turned to go. As soon as she was out of earshot, Filipp laughed. Tossing a shovelful of snow to the side, Martin bristled. "What's so funny?"

"Watching you watch her. You aren't immune to women after all."

"If you want to sleep warm tonight, then put your energy into your work and not your mouth."

After that, they worked in silence to dig out the door, which also needed to be unboarded. When they burst inside, rodents scattered, but Martin was pleased to see wood flooring and a stove. "This is better than I'd imagined."

Filipp examined some pallets stacked in a corner and a swarm of dust filled the air. He coughed then waved his hand in front of his face with a grin. "Rats under there. But the soddy seems dry. Ready to take possession?"

Grabbing his shovel and opening the door with a grin, Martin nodded. "Ready."

Filipp kicked the pallets, and rodents scattered everywhere. A battle pursued. Martin mostly missed. Filipp proved to be quicker with the shovel. But Martin found his talent in shooing them out of the soddy. When at last they couldn't scare up another living thing, he leaned on his shovel. "Want to sweep or go after firewood?"

"Far be it from me to hinder love. You go."

"There's nothing to it. We aren't staying here. So there can't be."

"Oh, there's something to it. Just enjoy it while you can, little brother."

Feigning disgust, Martin started toward the house, thankful that in spite of the snow, a path of sorts was taking shape and making the task easier. Filipp was more practiced with women, and he was right about the matter. Even if they were on a Canadian mission, he couldn't resist the draw that Hanna had immediately held over him. And he was thankful Filipp was behaving and not pursuing her for himself. For Filipp would steal kisses and leave her brokenhearted, but Martin would withhold his pleasures so that she need not get hopeful over a relationship that could never be and get hurt when the day came for them to leave. But secretly, he hoped the snow would continue to fall for a few more days so he could bask in her beauty and make a few more memories to last him through the cold winter nights.

At the Friesens' main house, he stepped onto a small porch and knocked at the door.

Hanna opened it, looking domestic with a kerchief on her head and rubbing her hands on an apron. She wore a modest dark dress with black stockings peeking out beneath. It comforted him to be among his own people.

"The soddy is good."

She laughed. "The depot was really bad, wasn't it?"

"Not so many rats though."

"I could hear you waging war all the way up here."

He found her easier to talk to than most women and fun to tease. "Now, Hanna, you know we don't believe in war."

"What do you believe?"

"That our elders are right when they say it is important to love thy neighbor. And we are neighbors now."

Hanna blushed. "Well, who am I to argue with the elders?" Martin laughed. "I assume you came for the firewood?"

"If the offer remains?"

"Along the note of loving thy neighbors, the offer remains." She tilted her head and studied him. "But you may need to make it up to Viktor."

"What has Viktor to do with love?" He watched her blush again.

"He chops our firewood."

"Oh, we were talking about firewood?"

"Firewood is all that will keep you warm this night. Well, that and your brother."

"I hope you have plenty of wood, then. And I'll keep Viktor in mind. But there's still one other thing."

"Oh?"

"You'll dig us out if we get snowed in?"

Hanna's eyes widened. "I didn't even think about that. For sure, take extra wood. And food just in case."

He touched her arm. "I was just teasing."

"Even so, when you come back for supper, I'll have a box of food ready, and some other items you may need."

❖ ❖ ❖

Hanna stoked the fire while stealing glances out the window where Martin was stacking wood onto a sled. His dark figure, clad in the somber color and conservative cut of the Mennonites, made a sharp contrast to the bleak white winter surroundings. She couldn't explain why his presence made her heart quicken or even why it preferred him over his equally handsome brother. They looked similar with brown wavy hair worn in the Mennonite cookie cutter hairstyles. Of course Filipp had instantly looked down his nose at her when he noticed her limp. She supposed she'd subconsciously held it against him from the start. While she'd seen no pity in Martin's clear blue eyes.

Ever since the frostbite incident, she'd fought hard to be strong and capable and not a weakling who was useless or unmarriageable. The incident had put up an instant barrier between herself and other young men who once sought her attention. And now she wondered if anyone would ever see her as desirable again.

Mom claimed it was a blessing because it would weed out the unworthy husband candidates. She'd clung to that statement as a positive element in her life, one that would bring her the right man at the right time. So of course, she'd discarded Filipp because it was the first thing he seemed to notice about her. But Martin. . .

He gave a playful wave. *Caught!* She jerked the curtain closed, her heart beating like a train careening off its tracks. Well, she'd show him she wasn't weak. She'd make something from their homeland for supper, the traditional *Varenikje*, cottage cheese dumplings with ham gravy. And she wouldn't succumb to pride. She needed sunlight to work. She opened the curtain again. His black, broad-brimmed hat was now a mere black dot bobbing in an endless white expanse. But she still felt the thrill of his wave and the warmth of his presence so that she hoped it didn't trickle over into the dough and cause a flop.

As she dumped ingredients together and worked her fingers through the smooth damp mixture, she reminded the Lord of her Christmas prayer: *Please restore health and joy to our home.* Martin had brought a bit of joy into her life. It was evidence God was in control and Mom would also recover. She was sleeping now, but with the doctor's medicine, Hanna had every hope Mom would be better for Christmas.

❖ ❖ ❖

When the snow broke that afternoon, Hanna used the opportunity to get dry bedding to the soddy. She invited her younger brothers, "Want to go with me to take supplies to our guests?" With a joyous shout, Stefan and Yury scrambled to put away their marbles and don their boots and coats. As she pulled the sled, the boys whooped and threw snowballs, letting out long-suppressed energy. Only when she was struck on the back of her black bonnet did she intervene. "*Ach* now! Not at me! You'll get the bedding wet. Behave yourselves."

"But you are the biggest and easiest target," Yury argued.

"*Jah*, it's not fair that Yury's my target. He's the smallest," Stefan reasoned.

Before she could give her opinion on the matter, they'd spotted the brothers, who were working outside the soddy, and darted off ahead. She watched them run and tumble and felt sorry she'd kept them inside so long. When she reached the others, Yury exclaimed, "Martin and Filipp built a fort in front of the soddy. Can we play in it?" She grinned. It had only taken seconds for them to be on a first-name basis.

Her gaze ran over the makeshift porch created from natural cover and dead wood.

Martin shrugged. "So you don't have to dig us out tomorrow."

"Brings back childhood memories. Dad did something similar when we lived here."

"Can we play?" Yury repeated.

"Only while I put the supplies inside. Stay close," she warned.

As the men unloaded the food supplies, she carefully placed bedding on the pallets, allowing her mother's quilts to add the finishing touch.

"Those look new," Filipp protested.

"They are. Every Christmas, Mother takes some quilts and blankets to the depot. But when I told her about you, she asked me to use them here instead. She'd like to keep the soddy stocked from now on. She's trusting the Lord to direct travelers to us who will need a haven."

"I'm jealous already of your future guests," Martin said.

"And I'm going outside to play in the fort. More fun than being a third wheel." Filipp smirked.

Martin's gaze followed his brother until he was outside. "Such tact."

Hanna laughed. "Do you flirt with all the women you've met on your trip?"

"Usually Filipp does. But this trip is doing strange things to us."

She tilted her head. "Such as?"

"He's usually all fun and games. Joking and nonchalance."

"While you're the conscientious one?"

"Jah. But he's showing his resourceful side. The porch was his idea. And regarding you. . ."

"Jah?"

"Like I said, he's usually the one who pursues the women. But. . ."

Her gaze dropped to the freshly swept floor. "But he isn't interested in me because of my deformity."

"That's not what I meant at all."

She met his gaze and quirked her lip. "It's my limp."

"Why would that matter?"

She appreciated Martin's sincere though somewhat blunt nature. His eyes held no hint of deceit. "Because it's repulsive. In case you're wondering, it's the result of frostbite." *Which left my deformity even more unsightly.* "I had a suitor once. But he spurned me afterward."

"Frostbite? No wonder, living in this frigid place!" Martin remarked angrily. "And I imagine Canada will be no better!" His anger quickly subsided. His eyes softened. "I don't see why someone would treat you that way. It only endears you to me."

With surprise, she realized, *His anger is protective.* "Why?" she urged.

"Because I admire the strength I see in you."

Her heart burgeoned to discover he was one of the good ones her mom had depicted. "The Lord blesses me as He sees fit."

"I've seen how the Lord's blessed your family. This community."

"Then maybe you should consider Mountain Lake for your future home. Perhaps it's your destiny." Her heart beat rapidly as she waited for his response.

"I fear not."

A heavy shroud of disappointment fell over her, and she wished she hadn't been so bold.

"You don't understand. I'm not the head of the family or even the eldest. I have five younger siblings. My dad has his heart set on Winnipeg. He's depending on us, and we can't let him down. I must do my duty for the family."

"I understand. I don't like to let my parents down either." Yet her heart wasn't ready to give in to his rebuff. "But maybe God will change his heart."

Martin sighed and stepped close. She stilled when he cupped her face with a gentle touch. "I wish it were so. It's amazing this attraction I've felt from the start. I've known you less than a day, but I can't stop thinking about you."

A shiver shot through her body, and it wasn't from the weather. "I feel it, too."

"I know. But we can't act on it. I don't want you to get hurt. When the train leaves, Filipp and I will be on it."

Her hopes deflated. She nodded. "I understand."

He withdrew his hand, and she turned away until he stopped her. "Tell your mother thanks for the beautiful quilts. I hope I get a chance to meet her."

"I hope so, too." She hesitated then added, "I can't explain it, but I believe you're part of God's answer to my prayer."

"Oh?"

"To restore health and joy to our home for Christmas."

"That's a sweet thought. I wonder where we will be at Christmas. Wherever it is, I'll have this warm memory."

"Then let's make it a good one. Come for supper around dark."

"We'll be there."

Chapter 4

At supper Dad seemed even more despondent. When he prayed over the meal, he added, "Lord, we ask You to stop the snow so we don't lose the animals. And keep our neighbors safe and those at the Immigration House fed."

Remembering their earlier conversation about loving thy neighbors, Hanna exchanged a meaningful glance with Martin. Then she said, "The Lord will provide, Dad."

After the meal, he went to spend time with her mom, and Yury convinced Martin and Filipp to play marbles. Hanna listened to the whoops and laughter as she cleaned up the kitchen. When she was finished, she went to her mom's rocker and began to knot a half-finished comforter. It would be faster to finish than a quilt, and she'd determined to have something to offer the Immigration Depot at Christmas. Soaking in every bit of joy and warmth, she was sorry when Dad shooed the younger boys off to bed.

As Filipp and Martin prepared to go back to the soddy, she went after the extra food she'd prepared. "There's zwieback and borscht. Just heat up the soup."

Martin nodded. "Our Dad says hunger is closely linked to despair. That during the hard times, the family in the homeland always claimed 'where there's zwieback, there's proof of a living God.'"

Hanna glanced at the double-decked buns and laughed. "That's a good saying. And I guess it's another sign that He's alive and watching out for you now."

Martin glanced at his brother. "We should be writing down all these signs to show Father."

Filipp tapped his head. "They're all in here."

"As I was saying, we should write them down."

From the bedroom, a harsh coughing was heard—as it had been all through the meal and evening.

Martin touched her arm. "God be with you."

Once they were gone, Hanna leaned against the door in wonderment.

◆ ◆ ◆

In the morning Hanna went to her mom's bedside. "Rough night?"

"I had to sit up to breathe. Is it still snowing?"

Hanna pulled back the curtains. "It's quit. But it snowed throughout the night.

The barn door was buried so deep that Dad propped a ladder and used the hayloft opening to access the barn. Says he's going to try to exercise the animals inside today."

"He's good with them. Should've been a rancher instead of a farmer. What's happening with our guests?"

"They wanted to help Dad, but he sent them to the village to see if the railroad needed assistance in digging out the tracks. I sent some food with them to take to the Immigration House."

"Good. It was nice to hear the laughter in the house last night."

"I like them. I wish they could stay. Not with us, of course."

"Tell me their story." By the time Hanna finished, her mom said, "It sounds like one of them has caught your eye."

With surprise over her mom's intuition, she replied, "Jah, but he's not staying."

"Miracles happen. Which reminds me. You will have to make and deliver the peppernut cookies for me. Can you do that?"

With less than a week until Christmas now, Hanna realized she needed to face the truth. Even if Mom recovered, it wouldn't be in time to perform her traditions. Hanna needed to take everything on herself. She would need to cook, bake, and make the extra trip to the village.

"Hanna?"

"Jah. I can do it. And I'm working on a comforter, too."

"Bring me the other one I started. Maybe I'll get something done on it."

"I will as soon as you finish your borscht."

Mom stared at the soup as if it had grown horns. "Ach! I'm tired of soup. But I'll do it for Christmas."

"That's the spirit."

◆　◆　◆

In town, Martin and Filipp delivered the Friesens' food to the Immigration House. He was encouraged to see that half the occupants were gone. The cook explained, "They've found temporary homes among the villagers. But this food is still much needed. Give the Friesens our appreciation."

The train depot was an arctic anthill of activity. "It's hard to believe so many townsmen would turn out to help," Martin remarked.

Filipp replied, "It's our people sticking together. This is what Father described when he told us about Winnipeg's Mennonite Brethren community. It will be good to be a part of something like this." Martin let the words sink in, but what he really wanted was to be a part of this particular community.

They were putting men on push and crank handcars, crowding four to a car, and sending them down the rails to dig out the tracks. Martin and Filipp were paired with a father and son who owned the village blacksmith shop. The muscular pair competitively provoked them to work, pushing beyond their comfort. Once Martin found out Kir was Hanna's previous suitor, he pushed even harder. But it really wasn't a contest, for he couldn't keep up with the blacksmiths. When Martin brought up the topic of the Friesens' hospitality, he burned with jealousy over Kir's remark, "Hanna, she's a lovely one."

"Are you interested in her?"

"I once was. I thought she was the one. But after her injury, she pushed me away. Everything I said and did offended her. Women are hard enough to figure out, but with the barrier she's put up and how busy Dad keeps me, I don't have the time to work through it."

Martin didn't relish the idea of anyone pursuing Hanna besides himself, yet he knew he would soon be on a train and never see her again. He remembered her Christmas prayer: *"To restore healing and bring joy"*. If he could leave her with a gift, joy would be it. Might even be the reason he was stranded in Mountain Lake, given the way God seemed to favor her family. Being around them was strengthening his own faith.

Martin ventured, "I can tell you it's only because she thinks everyone feels repulsed by her deformity. She doesn't even realize she's the one who pushes others away. She thinks it's her limp. And she doesn't know she's beautiful. Now that she's had time to adjust, you could probably win her back. If you just talked honestly about the matter."

"How do you know all this?" Kir asked with agitation.

"While we were snowed in, she told me."

Kir eyed him warily. Finally he said, "Maybe come spring, I'll try again."

Martin slapped the other man on the back. "Good luck to you." Grimly, he thought. It would be all he could think about. . .come spring.

By the time they returned to the Immigration House, he and Filipp were exhausted and had yet to make the trek back to the soddy. Bone weary, when they finally arrived at the Friesen farm, they were heartened to see smoke coming from the soddy's chimney. Martin motioned, "Go on and I'll tell them we're back."

His legs ached as he climbed the steps to the porch, but he was grateful when Hanna was the one who came to the door.

Her eyes widened. "You look tired."

"It's that obvious? We shared a hand car with Kir and his dad."

"The blacksmith?" She burst into laughter. "No wonder."

He could be even more gallant and tell her how the blacksmith felt, but he was too weary to make such a grand gesture. "It's amazing how the town turned out to clear the tracks."

"Will you be leaving soon?"

"Not yet. Not until they can push all the way through."

"I'm glad."

He liked her candor, but he shouldn't encourage her. Especially now that he'd met Kir. "I can't even think about tomorrow. All I can think about right now is sleep."

"I took stew to the soddy. You'd better hurry, or Filipp will eat it all."

Chapter 5

The next morning Hanna heard a rap at the door and Martin stood on the porch. "We're about ready to head to the train depot to help with the tracks. I just wanted to see if you have any chores for us first."

"I fear not." Hanna blushed. Her verbal outbursts that reflected her wishes of detaining them were becoming humiliating. Yet she couldn't discipline her tongue. Stressing the *we*, she said, "We missed you and Filipp yesterday, but now that Dad is using the hayloft to enter the barn and since it quit snowing, there's nothing to keep you from doing your duty. But you've made your mark here, and it will be lonely when you leave Mountain Lake. The boys were restless last night."

"My duty," he repeated. "You just described how I feel. This trip, which once seemed like a grand adventure, now feels like a begrudged duty. And digging out the tracks seems duplicitous. I like it here."

"Then don't leave."

"We've been through all that. You know Filipp and I must fulfill Dad's instructions."

She couldn't keep a man who didn't wish to stay. Yet she strove for something to ease the tension and delay him a few moments more. "You seem rested. Will you be teamed with Kir again today?"

Martin's expression sobered. "There's something I should tell you about him."

"Jah?"

"I guess it's best to be blunt. It's my nature."

Her smile widened. "So I've noticed."

Martin heaved a great sigh and said, "He has feelings for you and plans to court you, come spring."

Startled and somewhat confused, she asked, "How do you know? Did he warn you away?"

"No, nothing like that. But we talked."

Her voice raised an octave. "About me?"

Martin nodded. "He said you pushed him away. He lost confidence. But I encouraged him to deal honestly with you." Shrugging, he said, "Just thought you should know."

Hanna's face warmed with anger. "You've no right to get involved in my personal life. To trifle with my future. How dare you? And the things I shared with you were not to be spread around the village like gossip."

Martin's expression filled with shock. "I wasn't gossiping. I was only thinking about your Christmas prayer and wanting to bring you the joy you deserve."

"And so now you are replacing God?" She huffed. "For He isn't able to answer my prayers?"

Martin's eyes narrowed and darkened. "Don't be ridiculous. I just wanted to leave knowing you would be cared for and that your dreams would come true."

She arched a judgmental brow. "How big of you. But I don't need your pity or anyone else's. I see things clearly now. I misjudged you. You don't need to push me away by recommending Kir." She shook her head. "Godspeed on your journey, and I hope it occurs speedily."

"I can see how you pushed Kir away. Just like you're doing to me now."

She retorted hotly, "Isn't that what you want?"

"It's not what I want. I'd rather stay. Surely you know that."

Her lips thinned. "If you did, you would."

His expression became pleading. "It's not that simple."

"Isn't it?"

Filipp stepped onto the porch. "Is this the way you show our appreciation, brother? By riling our hostess? I'm sorry if he's offended you. Martin doesn't have any soft edges."

"I'm fine," she said bitterly.

"Jah, I've heard that one before." Filipp grinned sheepishly.

She felt sorely reprimanded. "I'm sorry."

He winked and turned to Martin. "Dmitri doesn't need us, so whenever you're ready."

Martin gave her a hot, piercing look then wheeled and left. She hurried inside and bent over the sink, her heart tight with misery. Was he right? Did she push everyone away? Was she so prideful that she couldn't accept any words of concern without spitting out, *I'm fine*. She bit her bottom lip until she tasted blood. With the pain came the truth. Her real wretchedness came from the fact that Martin didn't return her feelings, at least not enough to stay in Mountain Lake. And compared to what she felt for him in such a short time, she knew she didn't love Kir. *Lord, this isn't joy, but 'tis anguish I feel.*

◆ ◆ ◆

As they started to the village depot, Martin festered over Hanna's angry rebuff.

"What was all that about?" Filipp pressed.

"Women!"

"What'd you say to her?"

"I told her Kir was going to court her in the spring."

Filipp shuddered from the cold and pulled his coat tighter around his neck. "Why would you do a crazy thing like that?"

"I care about her. Want her to find happiness."

"Can't you see she cares for you? Telling her that would feel like a slap in the face."

As the frigid trees sped past, Martin considered his error. "And after that I accused her of pushing men away."

"What a hole you've dug for yourself."

"Why does it matter? You know we aren't staying."

Pulling his sled up a hill, Filipp panted, "Have you considered returning to her someday? After you fulfilled your obligations to our family."

"No." Martin fibbed, unable to admit his brother was practically reading his mind. Stubbornly, he refuted, "I've been spending all my energy guarding my heart against her."

"And has that worked?"

Martin jumped back on his sled. "No. I'm miserable."

Ducking to avoid a low-hanging branch and brushing snow off his shoulder, Filipp replied, "At least you need to make things right with her so you leave on good terms. Then after a season, if you can't forget about her, it will be easier to come back and win her over."

Martin was beginning to catch Filipp's vision. "I'm a fool. The way it stands, I've probably pushed her into Kir's arms, come spring."

"It's a fine fix you're in, but I know what will make amends."

Filipp sounded so sure of himself that Martin glanced sideways, but his brother was looking straight ahead at the snowy road. A long silence continued. Finally he asked, "And you're going to make me beg you for this information?"

Grinning, Filipp goaded, "You'll do my soddy chores for the rest of our stay?"

"I'll haul the wood and water, but that's all."

Filipp shrugged. "Kiss her."

Amused, Martin shouted, "Oh, that's your fine advice?"

"Have you tried it?

Martin shot him a hot look.

"Kiss her and speak honestly and tenderly. Tell her you've been a fool. She'll forgive you."

Martin shook his head. "I've no intentions of breaking the girl's heart."

"You already have. Don't crush her dreams, too. Leave her with some dignity."

Martin's opinion of his brother changed all in a moment. Filipp possessed a great deal of insight and soul. And he'd proven he could be counted on when troubles assailed. Surely Father had known it all along. Could his own opinion have been tainted by jealousy over Filipp's natural charm and easygoing personality? Had he been coveting his position as the eldest? Martin suddenly realized that if he let down his guard, there was a lot he could learn from Filipp. "And what would you do, if you'd met the woman of your dreams here in Mountain Lake?"

"And you'll do the dishes, too?" Filipp teased.

◆　◆　◆

The sun shone brightly through the kitchen window, warming Hanna's cheek, but she hardly gave it notice as she continued to stare at the tracks in the snow made by Martin's recent departure.

"You look troubled."

Hanna wheeled. "Mom! What are you doing out here?"

Sonya was a tall, large-boned woman whose words normally carried authority. But given the pallor from her illness and the way she presented herself, in nightdress with her long braid resting prettily down the front of her shoulder, she appeared almost vulnerable. "I'm finished with the sickroom." Her voice rusty from disuse, her declaration came across more feeble than persuasive.

"Are you sure?"

"Jah. Now you didn't answer my question. What has you looking so forlorn?"

"Oh"—Hanna shrugged—"I was just watching the brothers leave. They're going back to the village again. To dig out the railroad tracks."

"And you don't want to see them go?"

Hanna glanced at her mom then dropped her gaze to the floor.

"So much has happened since I've been sick. It's time I met them. I'm tired of not knowing what's happening under my own roof. I hope you invited them for supper."

"Hardly." Hanna raised her gaze and met her mother's eyes with a sheepish grin. "I told Martin the sooner he left us, the happier I would be."

"Now that's an unusual tactic. Will it work, you think?"

"I spoke out of anger. He worked with Kir yesterday, and they had a discussion about me. He persuaded Kir to court me in the spring." She saw the surprise in her mom's eyes. "I don't know if Martin pities me or really cares about me. Of course, I jumped to the conclusion that he pities me."

"I can see your confusion. And understand your disappointment." Sonya clutched a chair to steady herself.

"Mom! Please sit until you have more strength. And don't worry yourself about my affairs."

"Very well. I'll sit a spell before I get dressed. And I'll think the matter over. I'm sure it's not comforting to hear, but love does have a way of working itself out. But sometimes the process is painful."

Hanna sighed.

"Meanwhile, let's take inventory to see if we have everything we need for peppernut cookies. Oh. But first bring me my comforter to work on. We've no time to lose."

Happy for the distraction, Hanna replied, "Jah, I'll go get it." She paused in her parents' room long enough to make the bed and glance at herself in her mother's looking glass. Her appearance was tidy and her face prettier than most in the village, but her expression was guarded, stoically not reflecting the matters at war within her heart. She didn't want to be a person who couldn't display any emotion except anger. It was time she softened her guard. She would begin to try at once. When she returned to the kitchen and plopped the comforter in her mom's lap, she meant it wholeheartedly when she exclaimed, "It's so good to have you back."

Chapter 6

"Hanna! Come quick!" Viktor exclaimed. "Dad fell."

"Oh no." Sonya jumped to her feet, her comforter slipping to the floor.

"Hurry!" Viktor grabbed Hanna's cloak from the peg by the door and tossed it to her.

"Stay here, Mom! We don't need you to get sick again," Hanna demanded.

She watched her mother waver then sink back into her chair. "Go to him, child. Hurry."

Shrugging into her cloak, she ran as fast as she could, given her limp, following Viktor to the barn. The ladder that had been used to access the hayloft was toppled to the snowy ground, and Dad was crumpled on his side next to it. Dropping to her knees, she touched his cheek as she slid her gaze over his body to assess his injuries. It was hard to see through his coat and boots, but there wasn't visible blood in the snow, and his limbs didn't appear to be twisted grotesquely like she'd conjured up in her imagination as she'd fled from the house. "Can you move?"

He groaned. "Jah, but it's my leg."

Hanna looked helplessly about her, knowing her mom remained worrying inside. "We need to get you to the house."

Viktor clenched his fists. "But the brothers took our sleds."

"I've got an idea. Get a hammer from the tool chest. You need to pry some boards off the corral. The animals aren't using it anyway. Long boards."

With understanding, Viktor nodded and ran for the hammer.

As Hanna knelt in the snow, her legs burned through her stockings and her feet throbbed, but she ignored her own needs and examined her father closely. It was frightening to see the once powerful man's face pinched in pain. "Once we get you inside, I'll go for the doctor."

"Thank goodness the soft snow broke my fall. If only I hadn't hit the ladder. It's my own fault. I should have dug out the barn door by now. Quit using that ladder. I knew it was icy."

"Of course, it's not your fault. It was an accident." She watched Viktor break free some wood slats from the fencing then drag them near.

"But I don't have time for an injury. It's been hard enough with your mother sick."

Hanna was glad Dad always spoke whatever was going through his mind. It helped her to comfort him now. "Mom is up! She's left the sickroom."

She watched his eyes light up then darken when Viktor kneeled beside them and touched his leg.

"We're going to move you onto the boards now."

◆　　◆　　◆

Hanna hurried as fast as she could on foot. It was clear and sunny, but the cold air stung her airways with every inhalation. Thankfully, she was able to catch a ride with a neighbor within a mile and a half from home and made it swiftly into the village.

"Thanks, Mr. Bergmann," she called with a wave as her neighbor dropped her off in front of the blacksmith's shop, where he had business to arrange. She'd not gone far until she heard her name called. Wheeling, she waited for Kir's approach.

"I heard the news. How can I help?"

Instantly all that Martin had told her about his recent conversation with the blacksmith came to mind. And almost as instantly, her pride rose rebelliously against his aid. "We'll manage."

"How do you know that? From what I heard, your barn isn't even accessible yet."

She sighed. "That's true, but what about your work? Surely the town needs you."

Kir shook his head. "I'm not too busy to help you, Hanna. In fact, we have some spare time lately."

She glanced down the street. "I need to fetch the doctor."

"Then I'll hitch up the sled and pick you up there. Wait for me?"

She knew the doctor would be taking his horse, and she didn't relish the idea of walking home. Reluctantly, she nodded and watched Kir's husky form as he hurried away.

Moments later she was disappointed to discover the physician was out making calls. Fortunately, he'd left his itinerary on his desk. It looked like she could catch him at the Epps' farm and was glad she hadn't refused Kir's help.

As soon as Kir returned for her, she said as much, explaining her new plan.

"I guess it's fate," he said. With a determined nod of his blond head, they were on their way.

"The Lord is our helper. Not fate," she replied. Then she laughed at herself. "That sounded sanctimonious, didn't it?" A sideways glance at the burly man beside her caught his smile, and she felt glad for his capable assistance. Being with him again brought back a flood of pleasant memories, and she knew he would do everything in his power to help her family.

As they left the outskirts of the village, the horses found their gait and easily pulled the sleigh. Even beneath his coat, she could see Kir's bulging muscles relaxing as he loosened his grip on the reins. "It's good to see you smile again."

"Have I been that bad?"

He shrugged. "No, but you've withdrawn since your accident. At least with me."

The ease she had once felt with him returned, and she regretted having hurt him. "Sometimes healing is a slow process."

"I'm a patient man."

"I know you are, but what if it isn't fate?"

He furrowed his brows. "You talking about us?" She fingered her shawl and started to speak, but he touched her cheek. "No. Don't answer that yet. For today, just let me help."

The gesture reminded her of his gentle ways and the respect he'd always shown her when they were courting. She knew he was an honest, capable, and dependable man. Many would feel fortunate to take such a man as their husband. Once, when she was sixteen and he was twenty, she'd thought they were headed in that direction. Now, two years later, she didn't want to lead him on. But if he was willing to give her time to sort out her feelings, then she would accept his gift. She'd only known Martin for a short time, and he seemed determined to push her away. Rash decisions were not always the best ones. What was it Mom had just told her? Love had a way of working itself out. With God's help, of course. For she didn't believe in fate at all. She believed in prayer.

"Thank you for understanding," she replied.

He smiled and turned his attention back to their surroundings. They were nearing the Epps' farm. "Look!" He pointed. "The doctor's horse."

Relief flooded her being.

◆ ◆ ◆

As Kir and Viktor climbed the ladder back into the barn to milk the cow and take care of the Friesens' two horses, cow, and flock of chickens, Hanna prayed and prepared a meal for the doctor, who was attending her dad. When he came out of the bedroom, she motioned him to the table and placed a platter of eggs and ham in front of him.

"This smells good."

"How is he?"

The doctor's face sagged with fatigue. "A very fortunate man. It's a clean break. The trick will be keeping him off his feet. Of course, he'll sleep now that I've given him medicine."

Hanna knew they would need help and she would have to swallow her pride to accept it. Mom was still weak, and she didn't want her taking over the housework yet. Hanna wasn't as good with the animals as Viktor. But school would reopen soon. And surely Kir would have to get back to the blacksmith shop. If only Martin and Filipp would be willing to stay, now that there was a need. But it would be weeks before Dad could take over the chores again. And hadn't she just told Martin she'd be happy to see him leave? The sooner the better? Upon his return, she would apologize. Whether or not he helped with the chores, she owed him a heartfelt apology. She hoped he would stop by the house and not go straight to the soddy. Anxiety welled up within her. Christmas was only five days away, and it was not turning out at all as she had envisioned.

◆ ◆ ◆

As they pushed forward, sledding over the snowy rolling hills toward the Friesen farm, Martin thought about the day's work. Once again, many of the townsmen had volunteered their services to help clear the tracks. They'd even invited him to church services. But as they neared their destination, his heart sped up over the conversation he'd had that morning with Filipp. *"Kiss her"*. Those two small words had wormed their way into his brain, and as the day progressed, he'd entertained many scenarios about how he might make it happen. He knew his time with her was short, and the sooner amends were made, the more time he had to make sure they were in a good place when he boarded the train.

Given her anger, he didn't think she'd invite him to supper but would probably have something ready for them in the soddy. So after he ate and cleaned up, he'd go to the house and return the dishes. Then he'd apologize and hopefully get the chance to take that kiss.

Around dusk the farm came into sight. Instantly Martin noticed a sleigh unhitched and parked near the barn. He pointed. "Someone's here. And the barn door's open." They hurried and were perplexed to find Kir inside straddling a stool and milking the Friesens' cow. A quick glance told him that everything was in order. "What's going on? Is everything all right?"

"No, Dmitri fell off the ladder this morning and broke his leg."

A scenario flashed through Martin's mind of Hanna trudging to the village and going to Kir for help. With it came a pang of remorse and jealousy. It appeared the blacksmith had capably put everything in order, if not better than it was before. "Kind of you to help. But it's almost dark. We can take over here, if you want to head back to town."

"I'll finish the job. I'm almost done. Anyway, Hanna invited me to supper."

Watching the blacksmith reclaim his territory made the hairs on Martin's neck bristle. But he knew he'd left Hanna angry and now had lost even more ground where she was concerned. He glanced at Filipp. His brother came to his aid. "There's no need for you to come back tomorrow. We can handle the chores."

"You won't be leaving?"

"Not yet."

Kir opened his mouth to object but closed it again as Viktor bounded into the barn. "Hi, Martin, Filipp. Hanna says supper's ready and there's plenty for everybody."

"We'll be right in. Ten minutes more," Kir replied.

After cleaning up, they all went inside the small house. Before Martin could get a private word with Hanna, she'd ushered them to the table and was serving ham and eggs. He studied her face for any signs of remaining anger, but all he saw was strain and fatigue. He regretted his harsh words of earlier. The poor woman had enough to deal with, without his judgmental comments. He would be apologizing even if Filipp hadn't recommended it. But now, everything had changed. Now it would be a contest with the blacksmith to see who would stay the longest to get a private word with Hanna. And everything he'd planned to say was no longer appropriate.

The door to the bedroom creaked, and a woman who could only be Hanna's mother came into the room. Quickly, Martin and Filipp stood and scooted back their chairs. Following their lead, the blacksmith also stood. She crossed the room and placed a steadying hand on the wall. Filipp made the introductions. But Martin didn't miss that she gave him the most scrutiny.

"I'm sorry I haven't been much of a hostess," she apologized. "Please, sit down and enjoy your meal."

"How's Mr. Friesen?" Martin asked.

"The pain lessens with the medicine the doctor left. He's fretting about his work. Worried about the animals freezing."

"I won't let that happen," Kir assured her.

Martin jutted his chin. "As long as we're here, we can handle the chores."

"Any idea when you'll be leaving?" Kir asked.

Straightening his shoulders, Martin met the other man's steady gaze. "No."

Kir nodded and looked at Sonya. "I'll check in at the train depot. After they leave, I'll make sure your chores are taken care of, whether it's me or someone else."

Hanna, who'd been refilling their drinks, paused behind Kir's chair and placed her hand on his shoulder. "That's kind of you. I don't know what we would've done without your help today."

Jealousy burned like fire in Martin's chest.

Sonya Friesen swiped tears from her eyes. "It's humbling to accept help when everyone has their own work and hardships to consider, but I know the good people of Mountain Lake will take care of us. This is a good place to live." She turned to Martin. "We'd welcome your family if they'd choose to come here instead of continuing on to Winnipeg."

Filipp cleared his throat. "We've met a lot of good people, but I don't think Father would want us to abandon his plan at the first bump in the road."

"Is that all this is?" Sonya asked. "A bump in the road?"

The woman was even more direct than her daughter. Dessert was served, and when Martin saw how heavy Hanna's eyes grew, he knew it wasn't fair to drag the evening on any longer. It was obvious Kir had no intentions of leaving first. Martin stood and carried his plate to the sink. "We'll check on the animals on the way out. Then be up early and go straight to the barn. You can find us there if you need anything."

"No need," Kir said. "I've got to get my horse from the barn tonight. Best I get going, too." Yet he lingered, so Martin and Filipp snatched their hats and coats and left the house.

As soon as they were in the soddy, Filipp started the fire. "Things changed in the blink of an eye. Maybe it's time we reconsider this situation."

Chapter 7

The next day Hanna washed a breakfast plate and placed it on a towel next to the kitchen's dry sink. Sunlight glinted off the copper, drawing her attention to the window where her brothers hovered around Martin. A pang of longing pierced her heart. How would God answer her Christmas prayer to restore health and joy to their family when every day brought more complications?

"You're going to stare a hole in that window."

"I'm watching Stefan and Yury. It's good to have them out from underfoot."

Her mother stepped up behind her and placed a hand on her shoulder. "It looks as though they are pestering Martin as he mends the fence. Maybe you should go and rescue him. I can finish here."

"Martin's mad at me."

"At supper he came across protective. Jealous of Kir, even."

Hanna disagreed. "He thinks we're a good match." But the rivalry between the men couldn't be denied. The air had been so tense, she wouldn't have been surprised if it had ignited.

"He said that?"

"Practically."

"Kir made his intentions pretty clear. I don't think he's waiting until spring to court you."

"Helping Dad is not courting," Hanna continued to protest even though she harbored the same suspicions.

"No, but it will put him in your dad's good graces and give him the opportunity to make his intentions known."

Hanna sighed. "Jah, you are right about Kir. Yesterday he broached the subject but warned me not to give him my opinion on the matter until I'd had more time to consider it. Being with him causes some old feelings to return. I know he's a good man who makes me feel safe and secure. I suppose we could have a good life together. And until I met Martin, that would've been good enough. But not now." She folded her rag and placed it over the rim of the sink. "I don't know. Maybe this attraction to Martin isn't even love. Maybe it will diminish, and. . ." Her voice softened. "It really doesn't matter; he's not staying in Mountain Lake. I wish he'd never come."

"Poor thing. It will work out. You'll see. But it wouldn't hurt to go out and see if Martin has anything he intends to say about the matter."

Smiling, Hanna replied, "I do owe him an apology. But it's hard to face."

"Your dad wants to talk to the brothers about the farm. If you don't want to go, then I'll do it."

"I'll go." Hanna donned her dark bonnet and pulled her shawl tight against her long blue dress as she headed toward the corral where Martin was working. From a distance, she saw that he knew how to handle a hammer, and his lean physique possessed a rugged strength she found more appealing than Kir's hard, bulging muscles. "I'm glad you found the breach before you brought the animals out."

Martin flinched, lay aside the hammer, and turned. "Viktor told me. Clever on your part. I'm sorry we'd taken the sleds. That we weren't here to help."

She gazed into his shuttered blue eyes. Yet she plunged ahead. "I'm the one who's sorry. I said things yesterday I regret. It was a rough day. I scarcely remember what I spouted off about." She dropped her gaze. "Foolishness on my part."

"I understand your frustration. You've been honest with your feelings, and I've been holding back. Under the guise of not hurting you, but maybe for my own protection. Only, I'm discovering that holding back doesn't change how I feel."

She nodded. He was right. Hearing that he cared about her didn't change the fact that once the tracks reopened, he must ride out of her life.

He pushed up the brim of his black hat. "Maybe it's not in my place to say it, and I'll probably make you mad again, but I think Kir is using your father's accident to worm back into your life. Say the word, and I'll warn him to stay away."

Hanna raised her chin. "And why would I do that?"

He stepped so close it was hard for her to think. His eyes mirrored his desire, nearly buckling her legs. He tilted his head, and she held her breath as his lips brushed hers. When she opened her eyes, he smiled, dropping his hands to her waist. Her pulse quickened as he drew her closer, and she readied herself for another kiss.

Instead, he jerked and released her when a snowball smacked the back of his head. A fine showering of snow burned her cheeks.

"Yuck!" shouted Yury.

Martin's shoulders sagged with regret as he turned to face the two giggling intruders. The boys continued in their sport, pummeling Martin with snowballs. Hanna laughed and ducked behind a fence post to scoop up a handful of snow.

"Loser has to play marbles with Stefan," Yury goaded.

Hanna got a few good shots in, but her cloak was white by the time she and Martin were able to properly defend themselves and drive back their attackers.

"You lost," Yury shouted before he and Stefan ran for shelter behind the barn.

"That was a setup." Martin grinned. "And couldn't have been more ill-timed. Where were we?"

Having her good sense return in realizing they were visible from the kitchen window and her brothers could return at any moment, she shook her head. "I was sent to tell you that Dad would like to talk to you and Filipp about some farm matters."

She was almost disappointed when he let the matter drop. "All right. Tell him I'll soon be done with the fence. Then I'll fetch Filipp and be in."

She nodded and started to leave.

"Hanna."

Turning, she asked, "Jah?"

He stood with legs askance and arms crossed, sporting a wicked grin. "I'll probably send Kir away with or without your permission."

Saucily she replied, "Be sure to include that information in your conversation with Dad." Then she wheeled and headed for the house, her heart feeling lighter than it had in days even though Martin had no intentions of staying. Right now knowing that he shared her feelings was enough. She paused on the porch and whispered a prayer.

◆　◆　◆

"The cow's still milking?"

"Jah. All the animals pulled through."

"Good." Dmitri sighed, resituating himself on one elbow. "This is a fine fix I've gotten myself into. I knew better than taking a shortcut."

"You did the right thing. You didn't want to keep the animals waiting, digging out the barn door every day. That's probably why they're still doing good."

"I'm fortunate I should be back on my feet before plowing and planting. But with such a harsh winter, my worries aren't over. I know the townspeople will pitch in, but I can't expect them to make it to our farmstead through a blizzard. If that happens, it could wipe us out. Or the women will try to do the work."

"God will provide, dear," Mrs. Friesen interrupted, setting a pitcher of water by his bedside. "I'm sure it's His provision that we have these good brothers here to help us. See? Anyway, we women aren't as frail as we appear."

Dmitri laughed. "Says the girl who's just recovering. It's true He takes care of us, but the snow's caused everyone a lot of problems."

"Mountain Lake is a good stopover for the passengers. These were not all Christian people, and they've experienced the love of God here. I believe it was all a part of a bigger plan."

"Jah. You're right."

She patted his shoulder and left the room.

"I like to let her think that," he teased after she was gone.

"Good thinking," Filipp replied. "It's a trick our dad uses, too. While we are talking, do you have any special instructions for us? Martin finished repairing the fence, and we're planning to exercise the animals outside to give them some fresh air."

"Jah, that's what I'd do. Just keep water and wood and care for the animals. As you know, Viktor knows what needs to be done. But when you leave the farm, would you close up the soddy and stop in at the blacksmith's on your way to the train depot? Tell Kir the situation. I'm confident he'll keep his word and figure something out for us. He knows everyone in town, and he's a good man." He chuckled. "I'll probably have him for a son-in-law someday. If Hanna ever comes to her senses."

Martin cringed.

"I hate to impose, but you look to be sturdy lads. Help me get out of the bedroom?"

"Sure," Martin replied.

Dmitri started to throw back the covers then hesitated. "Better yet, have Sonya come and get me dressed. If it's not too much trouble."

"We'll be back."

"Thanks. Sonya's right. You're a blessing."

"Just returning your good deeds. For lending us the soddy."

Outside, Martin mumbled, "He favors Kir and soon there'll be nothing to stand in the way of him pursuing Hanna. I can't believe I encouraged him in the first place."

"Don't fret so. Tomorrow I'll go into the village and get us some answers," Filipp replied. "You know what's at stake for our family. I know it's hard, but be careful around Hanna."

Chapter 8

The next day Hanna found Martin alone in the barn. "I suppose you know Filipp checked to see if we needed supplies and then headed to the village?"

"Jah." His voice sounded rusty, gruff even.

She toed the snow with her boots. "And I suppose he's checking on the train? You must be anxious to be on your way again."

Martin dropped the pitchfork and stepped close. "Surely by now you know that's not so." His gaze was piercing, demanding. "But you must be anxious for us to leave so that Kir can return. You once told me you hoped we'd leave soon."

She touched the sleeve of his coat. "And I apologized for that angry outburst. But I'm not going to keep embarrassing myself by begging you to stay. Anyway, Kir has nothing to do with the matter."

"Doesn't he?" He slipped his arm around her waist possessively. "We would get along so good, you and I. We're both blunt and honest. There wouldn't be any secrets between us, would there?"

She laughed, touched his cheek with her glove. Maybe not if they were allowed to pursue a relationship, but for now, she wasn't going to blurt out all her feelings about him or Kir. But his nearness caused her heart to race. He sensed it and pulled her into an embrace. She didn't resist. She didn't want to hinder what might be the most thrilling moment of her life. This time he kissed her tenderly, taking his time.

When she drew back, heart thudding with desire, it was all she could do to put some sane distance between them. Breathless, she admitted, "You do strange things to me. I don't deny it. But this is not why I came to the barn."

"You sure? You knew we'd be here alone."

"I was checking on the cow." She went and gave the Holstein a soft swat on its black-and-white hindquarters. "We're old milking buddies. She must miss my soft touch."

"I can attest to that."

Feeling her face heat, she said, "Dad's ready to be moved out of the bedroom, if you don't mind helping him."

"Hanna."

"Jah?"

Martin's conflicted emotions flittered across his face. "I wish I could tell you"— he shrugged. "Let's not keep him waiting."

So much for not keeping secrets, she thought.

◆　◆　◆

The next day dark snow clouds accumulated in a graying sky. With only two days until Christmas, Hanna planned to take their gifts to the Immigration House before the weather prevented her from delivering their offerings. The two comforters had been finished and wrapped in paper the night before. Enticing aromas filled the air as Hanna and her mother sang the German version, "*Stille Nacht, Heilige Nacht,*" of "Silent Night" and finished the last batch of peppernut cookies.

"When you take these into the village, why don't you invite one of the brothers to go along? They've been working hard and may enjoy the experience of Christmas giving since they're away from their family. And with the weather so unpredictable, it's best not to go alone."

"I've gone to the village many times alone." *Too often for the doctor,* she thought.

"But it always worries me. And you don't want to spoil Christmas for me."

Hanna was reminded of her prayer and knew she must acquiesce for her mom's sake. "Fine. I'll ask Martin."

"Ask me what?" Martin peeked inside, while keeping his snowy boots planted on the porch.

Hanna's hand clasped her bosom. "You scared me. How long have you been standing there?"

Laughing, he replied. "Just now. The smell drew me in. My mom makes those cookies."

"Then come in," Sonya insisted. "And close the door, or you'll mess up this batch. We've got the temperature just right."

Quickly cleaning his shoes, he stepped into the female domain and seated himself at the table across from Stefan and Yury, who were already enjoying fresh milk and cookies. "Can you play marbles tonight?" Yury mumbled with his mouth full.

"I hope so." Martin bit into the small round delight. "Mmm, delicious. Ask me what?"

"I'm going into the village and Mom doesn't like the way the sky looks."

"Me either. I'll go along."

◆　◆　◆

Later on the journey to the village, the temperature dropped drastically and the clouds became even more menacing. Hanna and Martin concentrated solely on making it to the village in good time. When they jumped off their sleds, she was breathless and her feet throbbed from the bitter cold. Taking the lead, she limped straight for the Immigration House. Entering, she longed for the warmth emanating from the hearth but turned instead to the kitchen with her cookies.

"Peppernuts!" the cook exclaimed. "I didn't know if you'd come through this year with all your troubles."

"Mom practically crawled out of her sickbed to make it happen."

"What a treat. We still have a full house, but the townsfolk are helping to make their stay comfortable. We're even going to have special Christmas services. The Mennonite preacher's coming here and is going to preach in English. It's been hard not meeting since the storm. And regular services won't be until next week. Can you come?"

"I'm sure it will be wonderful. But with Mom still recovering and Dad's situation, we won't make it."

"I understand. Thanks for the cookies. Merry Christmas and God bless."

Hanna hugged the cook and asked to see the manager.

"He's in the supply room."

Martin followed her carrying the bundle of blankets, which were also accepted with gushes of gratitude. "You'll be happy to know that the train is expected to get back on schedule day after Christmas."

Three days, Hanna calculated, exchanging a regretful glance with Martin.

"Thanks for the news." As Martin gave the other man a firm handshake, Hanna turned her gaze away.

Feigning a smile, she choked out, "Merry Christmas," then headed into the main area to, at last, warm up by the hearth. "This feels heavenly."

"I'm sure all these occupants appreciate the shelter."

Glancing around, she noticed how families were clustered together. A teenager was entertaining a group of children with an animated story. Many of the men were absent, probably doing business or seeking employment, working toward their future in becoming a part of the community. She couldn't know for sure, but from snatches of English conversation, a high percentage of the group consisted of stranded passengers.

"Jah. This is a good place to be stranded."

"But not as good as your soddy."

A sullenness fell over them, and they warmed in silence for several minutes. The heat caused Hanna's eyes to grow heavy, but she knew she couldn't give in to such a comfort. "We should be on our way." Slipping her gloves on, she stood and started toward the door.

Catching up to her, Martin informed, "I'd like to stop by the blacksmith's before we start home."

Startled, she nodded. Of course, he'd promised her dad to make arrangements with Kir before he left Mountain Lake. In the few minutes they spent by the hearth, he must have been making plans that didn't include her. So much for his threat to run Kir away. That had been his heart talking, not his head. She straightened her shoulders and worked hard to keep pace as they dragged their empty hand-sleds behind them. It hurt that God would take him away the day after Christmas.

At the blacksmith's, Kir looked up from his forge, sweat beading his forehead. He worked coatless, his shirt strained beneath his muscular form. He lay aside his tongs and motioned them forward. Hanna hovered near the fire.

"How is your father?"

"He's healing and his spirits are high."

"Good." He turned to Martin. "And the farm?"

Martin replied, "Everything's in order. But Filipp and I have some matters to attend to tomorrow. Would you be able to find someone to take on the morning chores? We should be back by evening."

"Sure. I can do it."

Martin tightened his mouth, and Hanna could see it irked him to accept her suitor's help. But not enough to change his mind and stay in Mountain Lake. Once he stepped onto Canadian soil, he'd probably forget all about her. She watched the two men, saw the challenge in their eyes, and wondered for a moment if Martin was going to object after all. Normally, Mennonite men didn't resort to fighting, but the occasional skirmish was known to happen. And Kir would have the upper hand when it came to brute strength. But Martin was stronger than he looked. She caught her breath and held it as they bristled their male feathers, but finally Martin relented. "Mr. Friesen will be grateful."

It angered her that circumstances were not going her way, and she felt like punishing Martin. "I'm grateful, Kir," she said. "I won't forget your kindness." She didn't dare look at Martin but could feel his hot gaze. Let him hurt now, for she was sure she would feel the pain of his loss for months after his departure.

But when Kir's eyes brightened and he replied, "I'll see you tomorrow," she felt sorry to have raised his hopes.

With a quick nod, she turned toward Martin and saw giant snowflakes filling the air behind him. "It's snowing. We'd better go now."

In silence they started home. The snow feathered Hanna's lashes and peppered her cheeks with icy taps. But soon the sensations dulled as her mind worked in circles, going over the village conversations. *The train is leaving after Christmas. Martin and Filipp are making arrangements for their departure. Kir will be underfoot for weeks to come.*

"Hanna!"

With irritation, she glanced sideways. "What?"

"Let's rest a bit."

She slowed to a stop beside a rocky outcropping, sure he wasn't actually needing a physical rest if she wasn't. "We shouldn't stop."

"Just for a moment." He motioned her toward a stone ledge where they could take temporary shelter from the wind and snow. "This is a cozy spot. Don't you think?"

She rolled a frustrated gaze to the stone overhead. "What do you want? We need to get home before dark."

"To explain." Feeling her resolve weaken, she rolled her bottom lip between her teeth. He moved so close she could feel his frosty breath. "I can tell you're angry with me. Can you just trust that I'm doing what is best for both of us? And keep in mind, things are not always as they seem."

She studied him, releasing her lip. "I admit I'm disappointed. And frustrated with God."

"Better to trust Him, too."

"I know. I'm usually the one telling that to everybody else." She smiled. "I'll try."

He placed his arm around her shoulder and dipped his head close. "Are you warm enough?"

Was he going to kiss her again? Was she going to allow him the privilege? But he hugged her and drew away. "Don't be alarmed, but I noticed large cat tracks behind you. And you're right that it'll soon get dark. We'd better go." And taking her hand, he drew her back to the safety of the road.

Chapter 9

It quit snowing sometime during the night. The brothers left before Hanna awakened, and when she went to the kitchen to help her mother prepare breakfast, Kir tapped on the door. He carried a pail of milk in one hand and water in the other.

"Thought you might need this."

Hanna smiled. "Thanks. Coffee's ready."

Her mom wiped her hands on her apron. "Would you mind helping Dmitri to the table?"

"Sure." Kir nodded.

But it took them a long while to return to the kitchen. "Was Dad dressed?" Hanna finally asked her mom impatiently.

"Jah. They're probably just talking."

This sent a foreboding up Hanna's spine that trembled her hands and spilled the coffee. She quickly moved to clean up the spot. Mom shot her an inquiring look.

When the two men appeared, they both sported smiles. Kir thanked them for the coffee and left the house, shooting Hanna a parting grin over his shoulder. Hanna pushed coffee toward her dad, once again splashing it over the rim. "I don't know what's wrong with me this morning."

"Perhaps love is in the air," Dad suggested.

"Not in the way you're thinking," Hanna replied sharply, mopping up her mess for the second time.

"Oh, no? Kir just asked me if he could court you, and I gave him my permission."

Hanna twisted the rag in front of her. "What? But I'm not ready."

"Why not?"

She looked at her mom, who nodded.

"Because my feelings are for Martin."

"What?" Dad thundered, grabbing the edge of the table with both hands. "Has he made his intentions known? Why haven't I heard about this?"

"No. Because he has no intentions. He's leaving in two days when the train resumes its schedule."

"Surely you're not going with him?" Dad demanded, looking aghast.

Her mom looked suddenly alarmed, too.

"No," Hanna assured them. "He didn't ask. But I'm not interested in Kir."

"Ach. So it's just bad timing. Just a flirtation." Her dad relaxed his shoulders but still carried a grudge. "I wish I'd known he was tampering with your feelings. Getting cozy in our soddy and disrespecting our hospitality. You need to get him out of your mind and think about Kir. He's a man who can provide a good life for you here. He's forthright about his intentions and his feelings for you."

"I know. But I'm not ready for that right now." Didn't know if she'd ever be.

Dad narrowed his eyes. "He's patient, but take care you don't turn him away. You've already done that once. He's older than you, and he's ready to settle down."

"I know you like him, but don't you see why I can't make any promises right now?"

Her dad pointed at his wife. "You talk to her."

"Your coffee's getting cold," Sonya replied.

Frosty looks exchanged between the parents, and thankfully, the topic was dropped.

But that afternoon when Hanna returned the pails to the barn, Kir asked if he could show her something. A little leery but hoping it had something to do with the farm, she allowed him to lead her around the corner of the barn. He grinned and pointed toward an ice sculpture. "For you."

Her jaw dropped when she saw the amazing piece of artwork, which gave her an intimate peek into the man's soul and what it would be like to be cherished by him. "It's beautiful."

"Jah. The curlicue reminded me of flowers, so I thought I'd make you an ice bouquet."

She swallowed, taking in the branches with icicles he'd arranged and potted in a snowbank, which he had carved to look like a curved vase. She placed her hands on her hips and tried not to let him see how the gesture had touched her. "I guess there's not enough chores to keep you busy," she teased.

"When I'm working here, I can only think about you. About us. It's a long time until spring, and real flowers and courting. So I improvised." He looked so proud it broke her heart.

"It's a beautiful gesture. But I shouldn't have encouraged you yesterday."

"At the smithy, I work the forge. Embers sometimes burn so low they seem cold. It doesn't take much to fan them back to life." He stepped close and took her hand. "Though I'm ready to make a commitment, I won't rush you. Trust me to handle your embers with care."

Kir was too dear a person to string along, with all his talk about fire and love. He deserved better than she had to give him. "I'm sorry. But you're wrong about me. Those embers are cold. They aren't going to come back to life again."

She saw the pain in his eyes and refused to look away until he met her gaze with understanding. "Then I'll wait until spring. Everything comes alive in the spring."

"No. Not everything. Because I love someone else."

His gaze hardened. "Penner," he spat, dropping her hands.

She knew she needed to finish it now, for his sake as well as her own. "It's not his fault. And he warned me that he's not staying in Mountain Lake." Once she started explaining, everything spilled out, "But now I know that I wasn't in love with you.

And you deserve someone better than what I'd have to offer you."

He bent, picked up a nearby rock, and crushed the icicle bouquet. "Happy?"

She gasped, stepping backward, slightly frightened at the brute strength he possessed and the sudden fury she read in his eyes.

"I talked to your dad."

"I know. I'm sorry. But he'll release you from all your promises. About everything. . .and the farm."

"Then after today, I won't be burdening you with my presence. I'll find someone else to take care of your farm."

"I'm sorry," she replied. But his eyes remained cold, so she turned and fled for the house. Tears froze her cheeks as she paused on the porch to get control of her emotions. She knew she'd done the right thing, but she felt ashamed and distraught. Getting through the next few days would be hard. *Lord, please help Kir to heal, and give me the strength I need to tell Dad and say good-bye to Martin. Lord, everything's so messed up. I need You.*

◆　◆　◆

Meanwhile, Martin stood spellbound as he gazed at a frozen plot of land situated in a small valley with a large ice crusted creek cutting through its western border. It was farther from the village than the Friesen farm, but it was a perfect property for farming and raising animals. The trees grew in clumps along the creek, but the majority of the land was ready to cultivate and develop.

Martin pointed to the east. "See that slope? We could build a soddy there like the Friesens'."

He felt the pressure of Filipp's grip upon his shoulder. "I'm partial to the openness, not having to remove so many trees. There's plenty of lumber for building. I'm not sure we could have found such a perfect parcel in Canada. I hear the land there is thick with trees and brush. And you know how lazy I am." He grinned. "And the journey won't be as long and hard for the children."

Martin felt responsible for the daring switch they were considering. "You think Dad will be disappointed in us? Mad?"

"Nah. He'll be proud of us. He'll get over Canada. It was the only option he'd heard of, and we understand why he chose it. Mountain Lake fulfills all those requirements of being able to worship and live among our own people. But we just have to make sure we're making a good investment. Buying the right piece of land. That's what concerns me."

Martin replied, "The price is right. But with this parcel, we'd have to be self-sufficient in the winter, so far from the village."

Filipp nodded. "But at least we would have neighbors."

The land agent, a robust, thick-chested man with thick black eyebrows, was listening and jumped into the conversation. "Folks in this area take the creek until they get to the main road. This is a tributary off the Watonwan River. It's a bit farther than taking the road but more navigable in winter."

Suddenly skeptical and feeling the weight of responsibility their dad had placed on them, Martin asked, "Does the property flood?"

The agent rubbed his black stubbly chin. "Not here. Closer to the main river it would, but this is a solid property, or I wouldn't have brought you here. I was a German immigrant once myself. Even lived in Russia for a while. When the railroad set up the Immigration House, I knew I wanted to be a part of helping newcomers and got hired on in the land office."

"We trust you. That's why we're considering staying in Mountain Lake—the good people we've met. But our dad's life savings are at stake. So we'll take a look at the maps when we get back to your office."

The land agent replied, "Sure. But first, I'll take you to another area that's open now. It's closer to the village, but this was my favorite. By the way, this property also has more land patents available, even adjoining, if you boys want to buy your own land someday soon. In fact, the railroad's put financial aid in place if you want to buy it now while it's available."

Martin exchanged a meaningful look with Filipp. This settled his choice, before he'd even seen the other parcel. His heart thundered with excitement. He knew his perception was clouded by his desire for Hanna and crazy dreams about their future. But on the other hand, there were many good reasons they were making the right choice. For instance, they would have to start this process all over again in Canada, and it would be harder because they wouldn't know a soul.

◆ ◆ ◆

Martin and Filipp returned their horses to the livery, and Martin waited outside as Filipp paid the liveryman. Martin was considering the advantages of purchasing a horse when suddenly he felt a painful clamp upon his shoulder, which spun him completely around.

"What—" he gasped. Then he saw the glaring eyes of the hulky blacksmith from across the street. He tried to shrug out of the determined man's grip. "Let me go."

But Kir held tight and clutched the front of his coat with his other hand. "You told me you'd be back to do the evening chores. You lied. Just like you have about everything."

Martin choked, "We'll get them done."

"You're a phony. Filling Hanna with your romantic ideas."

Getting angrier by the minute, Martin lashed out with both arms trying to free himself, and when he was suddenly released, he stumbled. As he found his footing, a hard fist met his jaw, knocking him to the ground. Blood warming his mouth, he jumped up and rammed the blacksmith in the chest with both hands.

"Stop!" Filipp shouted, jumping between them to keep Martin from charging again. At the same time, the liveryman clutched Kir's arm, reasoning with him.

Kir easily shook free and pointed a thick finger in Martin's face. "You get to the farm and take care of your responsibility. And stay away from Hanna. Then come Monday, you'd better be on that train."

"You need to butt—" Martin started, but Filipp pulled him away, shaking his head.

"Let him cool off."

As they dragged their sleds to the edge of the village, Martin touched his jaw, blotted the blood from his mouth. Then he grinned. "Just when I thought I had everything worked out. Think there's another blacksmith in town? We're going to need a blacksmith, aren't we?"

Filipp laughed. "And you thought I was the rascal who would mess up our mission. Who would've thought I'd be the one trying to keep you straight?"

"He started it."

"This whole detour has been your undoing, not mine."

"I guess you're right about that. But we need to quit talking and get to the farm. It appears we've still got chores to do." He hoped that Hanna and her mother hadn't taken up the slack. And when they reached the Friesen farm, sure enough the chores were finished and everything was in order. Thus, he went to sleep on Christmas Eve feeling uneasy. He hoped it wouldn't mar the surprise he had intended for Hanna and her family.

Chapter 10

The next morning Martin mucked out the stables, looking startled when Viktor entered the barn. "I told Dad you'd be back chorin' this morning." The lad stopped in his tracks. His mouth gaped. "What happened to you?"

"Nothing much. Met up with something bigger than me."

"Huh?"

Martin tried to dismiss his injuries, though he was aware that his jaw was swollen and one eye was turning shades of blue. "Guess the animals couldn't wait? I'm sorry our business in the village took longer than we'd hoped."

Viktor's jaw clenched. "I could handle it alone if Dad would give me a chance."

"But school will soon be starting."

"You sound just like him."

"So you did all the chores yourself last night?" Martin fished.

"Nope." The boy seemed frustrated. "Hanna helped me."

Martin cringed.

"Then she had to stay up late, preparing special things for today." Viktor's gaze softened. "She's already busy helping Mom cook up a real Christmas meal. We're having roasted duck and Cherry Moos." Martin's mouth watered, especially over the dessert dumplings. Viktor's burst of enthusiasm waned, and he lowered his head and toed the ground. "She said it would be your last meal with us, the train leaving tomorrow an' all."

"You're right about the train." Martin wished he could confide in Viktor with his real plans, but it was too early. Yet while he had the lad's ear, it wouldn't hurt to ask a few questions. "The blacksmith showed up yesterday morning, didn't he?"

"Oh jah. Dad was real excited about that. He asked him if he could court Hanna, and of course, Dad gave his permission. Dad and him are real thick. When I helped Kir chore, he was grinning and singing. He's got a terrible voice. He's got it bad for Hanna. He even made her some kind of ice sculpture flower bouquet. Then there was some kind of—" But Viktor didn't get to finish because he heard his mother calling his name. "Gotta go. Oh! When you get done, come to the house early. Dad's gonna read the Christmas story, and Yury says you owe them a marble game."

As soon as the lad disappeared, Martin pitched his pitchfork in the straw and hurried over to Filipp, who was brushing one of the horses in a nearby stall. "Did you hear that?"

"Jah, marbles. Sounds fun."

Clenching his fist and wanting to hit the nearest stall post, he snapped, "You know what I mean."

"Calm down."

"No wonder Kir was so riled last night. Do you think he came to some kind of understanding with Hanna?" He started to pace the floor. "She really encouraged him when we went to the smithy together. I thought she was doing it to get even with me because she thought I was making plans to leave. But maybe I was just a distraction and she's been inclined toward him all along." He let out a long sigh and hung his head. "I'm too late. It's good we didn't put our money down on the property yet."

"Martin." Feeling his brother's grip on his shoulder, he looked up. "All's not lost yet. You'll get your opportunity to present your case today. Then it's up to Hanna to decide."

"And her dad."

"He doesn't know your intentions. He only knows Kir's. Let's get the chores done so you can spruce up before the meal. Use the time to think about what you'll say to Hanna and her dad."

Martin nodded, but he was feeling jittery inside. "Better pray for me."

Filipp laughed. "I have been, brother."

"It isn't funny."

Shrugging, Filipp replied, "It is from my view. Glad I'm participating from the spectator's seat. I just never thought you'd beat me to the altar. It's humbling."

Martin shook his head. "Just keep prayin'."

"I will, but you gotta do your part, too."

Martin took off his hat and slapped it against a stall wall then raked his hands through his hair. "And what's that?"

"Gotta have faith. You know what Mom always says. Faith is being sure of what we hope for and what we don't see. That without faith we can't please God, but we must believe He exists and rewards those who earnestly seek Him. That He wants to give us good gifts. I think Hanna is one of those good gifts."

Martin nodded, remembering how their mom often referred to the book of Hebrews in the New Testament as it was one of her favorites. "I'll try." Thinking of his mom helped. She'd like Hanna, and if she knew what was transpiring, she'd be supporting him.

◆　◆　◆

Early afternoon, Martin and Filipp headed to the main house. Martin hoped he'd get a chance to talk to Dmitri first, but everyone was already congregated in the main room sitting around the hearth. When he and Filipp stepped inside, they were accosted with delicious smells. Yury ran up to them. "Come play with us?"

"Sure," Filipp replied. "Just let us hang up our hats and coats."

"Boys, give them room to breathe," Sonya laughed.

But Stefan looked up at Martin. "What happened to your face? The cow kick you?"

He wished. He felt everyone's gaze and saw Hanna's eyes widen. "That story can wait a bit. When the timing's right."

Stefan shrugged. "All right. Must be a good one."

Hanna hopped up and served them eggnog.

As the boys led them to the center of the room, Filipp made their apologies. "I'm sorry we missed last night's chores. We got held up in the village."

"Must've been a misunderstanding," Dmitri remarked. "Usually Kir keeps good to his word. I expected him to take care of it. But he must've had work at the smithy."

"I sent him home," Hanna said, blushing slightly.

"You did?" Martin blurted. Hanna nodded, and it gave him hope that all was not lost. He stole a quick glance at Filipp and saw his subtle nod. "About that, I'd like to tell you about our trip to the village."

"Is it about your face?" Yury asked.

"Partly."

"Can it wait till after marbles?"

"Yury!" Sonya said. "Let go of Martin's clothes and let him finish his story." Reluctantly, Yury sank to the floor beside his brother. "Please have a seat Martin." She motioned to a chair beside Filipp.

"Thanks, but I need to stand for this." He set his eggnog on the table and took a few strides toward Dmitri. "Since we've been in Mountain Lake, everyone's been accommodating." He touched his jaw and gave a sheepish smile. "Well, most everyone, and we see the way the community comes together in a crisis. Your village is exactly what our father sent us out to find. What I'm trying to say is we don't think we need to go all the way to Canada. Yesterday Filipp and I spent the day with the land agent and found a couple parcels that suit our needs."

He glanced at Hanna, who was seated, eyes wide and wondrous, hands wringing in her lap. At his sudden declaration, her cheeks had reddened significantly. "You're staying?"

"Under one condition." He turned back to Dmitri. "If you'll let me court Hanna."

"Bah!" Dmitri's face turned red as his daughter's. "You're too late. The blacksmith aims to court her."

Hanna jumped to her feet. "No he doesn't. I sent him away. I turned him down."

Sweat trickled down the back of Martin's neck. Now he really understood why the blacksmith had tackled and threatened him. "Mr. Friesen, my family and I are coming here as immigrants without much to our name except the land we will buy. But I intend to get some land right away, too. I'm not sure how soon I'll be able to work it, but I want you to know I love your daughter and will do my best to take care of her. But I'm getting ahead of myself. I'm just asking if I can court her."

Dmitri's face twisted in a scowl. "How can you say you love her when you've only just arrived? We hardly know anything about you or your family."

"Dmitri, he's only asking to court her," Sonya reasoned.

"Humph." Dmitri tilted his head, scrutinizing Martin. "So what happened to your face? Was it Kir?"

"Jah. That's the short of it."

The older man's expression remained stoic. "You know we don't believe in violence or fighting. It's not our way."

"Tell that to Kir."

Slowly Dmitri's scowl softened until his face creased in a smile. "Don't know why I'm so slow to know what's goin' on right under my nose. What have you to say about the matter, Hanna?"

She crossed the room and gave her dad a hug. "Jah. I love Martin, too."

"Yuck." Yury made a face. "Now can we play marbles?"

Martin raised a brow, waiting for Dmitri's answer.

"I give my consent. We can talk about your plans later. One game, and then we're doing the Christmas story."

◆　　◆　　◆

Everything changed so rapidly, Hanna felt as though she'd been swept up into a wonderful dream. As delightful as it was, she longed for time alone with Martin. To hear words of the affirmation of his love again. When after the Christmas meal he rose from the table with intentions of looking after the animals, she grabbed her shawl and hurried after him, ignoring the family's grins.

They stood together on the porch, and he encased her gloved hands between his own as if he cherished her. His eyes, so filled with untold promises, pleaded for her understanding. "I wanted to tell you the day we took the peppernuts to the village, but Filipp asked me to wait. He wanted to look at land prices before I raised your hopes. Then this morning, I thought I'd lost you to Kir."

"Never."

He raised her hands to his lips then lowered them with a grin. "What I really need to know. . . Does Mountain Lake have more than one smithy?"

She laughed. "No, but he'll come around. He's just a bit of a hothead."

"You were right from the beginning, when you said God was showing us His favor by stranding us in a Russian Mennonite village. And I must add, sending us to your particular soddy. It just took me awhile to realize that the best-laid plans can be changed."

"Have you told your dad?"

"Not yet. But Filipp thinks it was the right thing to do, too. God's will." He glanced toward the soddy. "The family won't come until spring. Guess we should move to the Immigration House."

"Stay at the soddy as long as you like. It would be pointless to live at the Immigration House and come here to chore every day. Dad'll come around as long as you mind your manners."

"I will. We'll take it slow and get to know each other, though it will be hard to do." He glanced up at a row of icicles that edged the roof. "I can't make ice sculptures or do many things right. I'll probably bumble my way along for a while. But I promise, I'm yours and I want to make you happy."

She touched his cheek. "You're God's gift. The answer to my Christmas prayer."

"Jah, I guess I am."

She tugged his sleeve. "Don't look so smug about it."

He pulled her close. "You'd better get used to this look. This is the look of a man in love."

Peppernut Cookies (Pfeffernüsse)

Recipe by Elizabeth Warkentin, Mountain Lake, Minnesota. From *Mennonite Community Cookbook*, by Mary Emma Showalter (Herald Press, 1978).

⅓ cup shortening
1 cup sugar
1 cup sweet cream
1 teaspoon peppermint extract
6 cups flour (approximately)
3 teaspoons baking powder
½ teaspoon salt
1 cup milk

Cream shortening and sugar together. Add flavoring and sweet cream; beat until fluffy. Sift flour, add baking powder and salt, and sift again. To creamed mixture, add sifted dry ingredients alternately with milk. Beat until a medium-soft, smooth dough is formed. Chill dough in refrigerator for several hours.

When thoroughly chilled, divide dough into 5 or 6 parts. Remove one portion from fridge at a time and turn out on lightly floured board. Cut off small portions and form into fingerlike sticks, rolling with the flat part of the hand. Lay sticks in parallel rows and cut across, making pieces the size of a small marble. Place pieces close together on a greased baking sheet. Bake at 425 degrees until they begin to turn a light, golden brown.

These are popular at Christmastime in many Mennonite homes.

Dianne Christner lives in New River, Arizona, where life sizzles in the summer when temperatures soar above 100 degrees as she writes from her air-conditioned home office. She enjoys the desert life, where her home is nestled in the mountains and she can watch quail and the occasional deer, bobcat, or roadrunner.

Dianne was raised Mennonite and works hard to bring authenticity to Mennonite fiction. She now worships at a community church. She's written over a dozen novels, most of which are historical fiction. She gets caught up in research having to set her alarm to remember to switch the laundry or start dinner. But her husband of forty-plus years is a good sport. They have two married children, Mike and Rachel, and five grandchildren, Makaila, Elijah, Vanson, Ethan, and Chloe.

She welcomes you to visit her website at www.diannechristner.net.

Treasure of the Heart

by Melanie Dobson

Behold the work of the old. Let your heritage not be lost,
but bequeath it as a memory, treasure, and blessing.
CHRISTIAN METZ, AMANA SOCIETY LEADER AND PIONEER, 1846

Chapter 1

*H*_{ome.} The simple word, laden with sweet memories, slipped into Sophie Keller's mind as their black carriage rolled into the village of Amana. Meredith—her thirteen-year-old daughter—didn't look up from the book in her lap, but Sophie's tense shoulders began to relax as she scanned the row of sandstone and brick homes beside them, wood smoke curling out of their chimneys and up into the pristine blue sky.

She'd been longing to visit the Amana Colonies for years, but Conrad had been too busy with his law practice in Des Moines to return. And she—she'd just been busy.

At the moment, she couldn't remember exactly what had kept her so occupied. Some days she felt like one of those cyclones that touched down on Iowa's plains each spring. She would whirl through her daily tasks in the city, her head and hands in constant motion, but she really wasn't doing anything to help others. Not like she had done as a young woman working in these colonies.

The scenery here hadn't changed much since she and Conrad left thirteen years ago, but the people had. Both her mother and Conrad's father, an elder in the Amanas, went home to be with the Lord before the end of the century. Hilga, Conrad's mother, followed her husband into glory two years later, and then Conrad—

Meredith didn't remember coming to the Amana Colonies as a child, nor did she remember her grandfather, Niklas Keller, or even Sophie's mother. She did remember Conrad's mother because Hilga had taken the train to Des Moines twice for a visit. With every visit, Hilga had brought a little taste of the Amanas with her in the form of pastries and wheat beer.

Now Sophie wasn't just coming home. She was running away from the busyness of the city to contemplate John Hoffman's proposal in peace. By the new year, she had to sort out whether or not she would become the senator's wife.

A canal flowed beside the village, the water powering the woolen mill on the east side. Snow dusted the roofs of the houses and shops, clung to the white clapboard fencing around each lawn. The white garland reminded her of childhood Christmases gone by when she'd stood at the window of her family's rooms, her nose pressed against the glass pane as she'd looked out at the lofty *Glockenhaus* and the dairy cows tromping through the white-laced field, grazing the remaining brown cornstalks before the deep winter snow buried them all.

The cows were grazing today at the outskirts of town, just like they had been doing when she and Conrad left in 1894. Women bustled in and out of the kitchen houses as they prepared their midday dinner meal for the Amana community. Men drove wagons along the cobblestone road, canvas tarpaulins covering the goods they transported to and from the woolen mill.

"It's just like I remembered," Sophie whispered.

Meredith glanced up. "I don't remember it at all."

"The last time we were here you were two."

Meredith squinted out the window, watching the women with their heavy shawls wrapped tightly around the shoulders of their plain calico dresses. Each woman's long hair was parted in the middle and pulled back into a neat bun. "Why are they dressed funny?"

"They don't think it's funny here," she tried to explain. "Just practical."

Meredith's silky black hair was plaited in one braid with a copper-colored silk bow tied on the end. Her long braid rested on the back of her traveling dress, the wool material trimmed with black on the sleeves, collar, and ruffled hem.

As Meredith's gaze returned to the pictures in *The Wonderful Wizard of Oz*, Sophie leaned her head back against the leather seat. Her daughter had been looking at the same image of Dorothy and the Cowardly Lion for the past hour.

Their carriage journey from Des Moines had taken more than two days, and Meredith spent most of their trip sitting rigidly on the opposite seat, her arms crossed as she looked at this book. She'd wanted to ride the train to the Amanas, but Sophie refused to ever get on a train again.

Sophie reached out to take her daughter's gloved hand. "You're going to like it here."

Meredith pulled her hand away. "I want to go home."

Her heart twisted. What was once home to her was a strange land to her daughter. Home for her daughter was the lofty house high up on Sherman Hill in Des Moines.

The carriage slowed as they neared the hotel.

There were seven villages in the Amana Colonies, all of them circled together on a large plot of prairie land their ancestors bought in eastern Iowa. Liesel, her childhood friend, had invited them to spend Christmas with her and her family here in this main village.

The carriage stopped by the hotel built mainly for the men who came to do business with Amana's woolen mill. It would be their residence for the rest of the month.

As they waited for the coachman to open the door, Sophie glanced back down at Meredith's lap. Same yellow lion on the page. Same tears rolling off his cheeks.

It was two weeks before Christmas, and Sophie had promised Liesel that she'd stay in Amana until the new year. But Meredith didn't want to be here—she didn't seem to want to be anywhere except lost in the pages of a book.

She desperately hoped that her daughter would find healing here, but if she didn't improve, perhaps they would go back to Des Moines the day after Christmas.

John had invited her and Meredith over for Christmas Day, but returning to the city meant so much more than just having dinner with John's family. It meant flitting among the city's festive balls for the entire week and attending dinners with Iowa's governor and city leaders. It meant pasting on a smile when everyone asked how she was doing, pretending that she was fine, pretending that she didn't miss her husband and that even though there were thousands of people in Des Moines, she'd never felt lonelier in her entire life.

Their grand house on Sherman Hill felt like a tomb to her, and she suspected it felt the same to Meredith. Ever since Conrad's death, it seemed that both she and her daughter had been wandering around in isolation. Meredith couldn't seem to focus on her schoolwork nor was she interested in spending time with other girls her age. It was almost as if she felt guilty for having fun.

Sophie understood. She missed Conrad desperately. Every day. Sometimes all she wanted to do was slip back under the black cloak of mourning and stay there forever, but Conrad would say there was still a lot of life to be had for both her and Meredith.

John certainly thought a year was long enough for her to mourn. After Thanksgiving dinner—in front of his two daughters and Meredith—he'd asked her to become his wife. She'd promised him an answer before the end of the year. Then she'd left Des Moines while he was in the District of Columbia, leaving behind only a note that she would see him in January. It was a cowardly move, but she needed to think more about their future before she gave him a decision. And she couldn't seem to think at all in the city.

John hadn't swept her off her feet like Conrad had so long ago, but his wife passed away six months ago. He was a senator in Iowa, and he needed a hostess for his beautiful home, a mother for his two daughters. And a devoted wife to help him campaign for the next election.

She wasn't quite sure what she needed and had taken no offense to his matter-of-fact proposal. The practicalities of a respectable marriage were much more important than any romantic notions either of them might have entertained in their youth.

John needed a wife, and she was desperate for a father for Meredith, even more than a husband for herself. With Conrad's successful law practice and good stewardship, he had left her and Meredith with a regular income from his investments. They would have to sell their beautiful home, move into something much smaller, but they would make do with the money they had.

The spendthrift practices from her childhood lingered with her. She had learned how to manage a kitchen house when she was eighteen, bustling around to feed three meals a day to forty men and women, and if she continued to manage their money well, she and Meredith would be in need of nothing in the material realm.

Yet it felt as if they were in need of everything.

The coachman opened the door, and Sophie climbed out, the cold breeze ruffling her long dress. The air smelled like baked apples, chimney smoke, and dried grass. Pine trees, hot coffee, and bread fresh from a brick oven.

Meredith closed the cover to her book and tucked it at her side, but she didn't move.

"Come inside," Sophie said, offering Meredith her hand. "We'll unpack and eat."

Meredith glanced at her hand, but she didn't take it. Instead, she stepped out of the carriage on her own, onto the icy walkway.

Sighing, Sophie pointed her daughter toward the door of the small hotel.

Even though she was back in the place she'd once called home, her heart still felt homeless.

Chapter 2

S ophie!" Liesel Hirsch called, her long skirt lifted up to her knees as she rushed down the sidewalk masked with mud and snow, an hour after Sophie and Meredith's carriage arrived in Amana.

Sophie leaned against a hitching post, smiling at the sight of her dear friend hurrying toward her, the strings on her prayer cap trailing behind. None of her friends in Des Moines would ever shout her name in the street like that. And they would most certainly never hoist their skirts like a dance hall girl and burrow their way through the slush.

The chill in Sophie's arms warmed as Liesel wrapped both arms around her shoulders and then stepped back to study Sophie's mossy-green velvet dress, the fur-lined neck and matching stole that kept her warm. "You look beautiful," Liesel proclaimed.

"So do you," Sophie said. The simplicity of her calico dress and woolen shawl was a welcome sight compared to all the feathers, ribbons, and bows found on women aspiring to be fashionable in the city. Liesel's pale blond hair was tucked under her elegant cap, the black tatting on the edges a perfect frame around her heart-shaped face.

Liesel glanced up and down the walkway. "Where's Meredith?"

"Back at the hotel," she replied. "Since she turned thirteen, she seems to be tired all the time."

Liesel smiled. "So does my Peter."

Sophie clutched her hands together. "I can't wait to see him and Cassie."

"They are looking forward to seeing you, too, but are most excited about seeing Meredith."

"Of course they are," Sophie said with a laugh.

"They've been writing down their many questions to ask her about Des Moines."

Liesel had married an outsider named Jacob Hirsch, a man from Chicago who'd stumbled into their colony the same year Sophie married Conrad. Jacob already had a daughter named Cassie, and the moment Liesel met him and Cassie, she'd fallen in love with them both. Jacob eventually joined the Amana Society, and he and Conrad worked together dredging the millrace until Conrad left to attend law school.

She and Liesel had dreamed of raising their children together in the colonies, but in order for Conrad to achieve his dream, she'd had to sacrifice hers. It had been worth it, giving up her dreams to marry Conrad, but sometimes she wondered what would have happened if Conrad had decided to continue working on the millrace instead of becoming an attorney. He would probably still be here for their daughter.

"Are you hungry?" Liesel asked, nodding toward the brick kitchen house at the end of the block.

"Yes, but we'll eat our dinner at the hotel."

Liesel looked offended. "Our food is much better than anything you'd order there."

"I can't argue with that." Sophie waved her gloved hand in front of her. "But we can't impose."

"*Pfui,*" Liesel exclaimed in German. "It's not an imposition. I'm the kitchen boss now, and I want you to eat with us."

Sophie sighed. "Not everyone will feel the same."

This time it was Liesel who waved her hand, reassuring her. "They'll be fine."

Sophie smelled the baked apples again in the air. Sausage and sauerkraut. "I'll have Meredith with me," she said, one last excuse to avoid the community of people she once thought she'd never leave.

"I hope so," Liesel replied, smiling. "Cassie will be disappointed if she doesn't come."

The two girls would be so different, Sophie thought. Cassie, confident and strong, raised by a community with the benefits of hard work and a strong faith. Her sweet Meredith, reared by a loving family up on Sherman Hill who loved God, too, but lacked the kinship of their neighbors.

Even though she was loved, her daughter had begun slipping away in the months before Conrad's death. After he died, Meredith had plunged inside herself so deeply that Sophie only caught glimpses of the young woman who'd once been confident as well.

Sophie didn't know what to do about her daughter's insecurity, the self-doubts. Growing up in Amana, any self-doubt of hers was quickly drowned in the abundance of opportunities for the youth here to thrive.

Liesel glanced into the window of the general store, toward the clock on the wall. "I have to get back to work," she said. "Dinner is at eleven thirty."

Sophie nodded. "We'd love to join you."

Sophie returned to the hotel and climbed the narrow steps up to the third floor. Meredith didn't stir as Sophie sat on the narrow bed beside her.

Her daughter had unbraided her hair, and the dark tresses splashed over her shoulders like the rolls of an ocean's stormy waves. While she was sleeping, Sophie gently took Meredith's hand. It seemed gaunt to her. Frail. Meredith had been losing weight since Conrad died, and if she lost any more, Sophie feared that she might slip through the cracks of the wooden floor.

Sophie rubbed the top of her daughter's hand. "Sweetheart, it's time to wake up."

Meredith groaned.

"We're going to eat dinner at Liesel's kitchen house."

"I don't want to go," Meredith said, shifting to her other side. But not before Sophie saw her red-rimmed eyes. The tears that stained her cheeks.

"They're having sausage and apple pie," she continued, desperate to ignite any sort of spark inside her daughter. Desperate for any emotion at all.

Meredith pulled her hand away one more time.

Standing, Sophie quietly donned her coat again and backed toward the door. Meredith would be safer here in this hotel than she'd ever been in Des Moines, even with the household staff bustling around. Sophie would be back in less than an hour, and then she would try and coax Meredith to eat a meal downstairs.

Her shoulders slumped as she reached for the doorknob.

Perhaps in Amana, her daughter would find healing for her heart as well.

◆　◆　◆

Will Kephart stomped his boots on the rug outside the brick communal kitchen—called Hirsch Kitchen House—and the snow he'd picked up on his walk from the mill scattered across the entry. The *Speisesaal*—dining hall—didn't open for ten more minutes, but there wasn't any harm in arriving early. He needed a few extra minutes to clear his head anyway.

Work at the woolen mill had fallen behind this winter, and no matter what he did, he couldn't seem to inspire his crew to work any faster. Already they worked long days, trying to meet the demand for the blankets and fabric they'd become known for, but they needed to increase their production right away.

Already they produced three thousand yards of woolen goods every day, but they needed another five hundred yards daily between now and January 15th to supply the largest order they'd ever received—a shipment of black wool for Sears, Roebuck & Co. No matter how he configured the workers and space, he couldn't find a way to make up those extra five hundred yards. Fifteen thousand total in the next month.

Most of his thirty-four years had been spent working on Amana's farmland, cultivating their crops with a crew of men who enjoyed being outside, getting their hands dirty. His grandfather, Matthias Roemig, managed the mill, but his health was beginning to fail. Matthias had pulled Will inside earlier this year to help, saying he needed someone who could inspire a group of people to work well together and complete a large task.

Still they were behind, and Will needed to find a way to increase their production, or they would have to cancel this order.

No one in their society had ever canceled a woolen order before—and he had no desire to become the first—but what else could he do?

Men and women began lining up on the walkway behind him, most of them wearing long black coats made from the mill's wool. Each of them had a specific job to perform in the Amanas. Some of them cooked in one of the colony's kitchen houses; others washed laundry, painted walls, repaired machines as a millwright, laid bricks for their new buildings, cared for the animals and gardens, or wove the mill's wool. Several women cared for the younger *kinder* in the kindergarten, and each village had a teacher to instruct the school-age children in the mornings. In the afternoons, the older youth labored alongside the adults.

Work and their daily prayer meetings kept all of them grounded as a society and deepened their faith in God and His Spirit as He continued to meet their needs.

As he waited, Will prayed silently that God would also help him meet the community's needs through his work at the mill. None of them made money for themselves, but the sales of their wool provided the food the community couldn't grow, paid their taxes to Iowa, and purchased any supplies they couldn't make for themselves.

In the corner of his eye, Will saw the flash of a green dress, one worn by a worldly woman walking down the sidewalk. Visitors often came to the Amana Colonies in the summer, some to buy wool, some for refreshment. Others just wanted to gawk at the unique way of living. It was strange for them to have visitors in the winter though, especially in the weeks before Christmas.

Perhaps this woman was here to purchase woolen goods. If so, he would ask her to come back in the summer. Hopefully, the mill would be on track by then, and he would be back out in the fields with his crew of men.

The woman's black-ribboned hat tilted slightly, covering the side of her face. He didn't want to stare, but he watched curiously as she stepped into the line for the kitchen house. With her brightly colored dress, flaring out from her waist, and black ribbons, she looked like a peacock, fanning her plumage over a flock of plain birds.

Did she think this was a restaurant? Outsiders were often confused about their way of living, especially when they realized that the Amana people ate together in a communal kitchen instead of cooking in the rooms they occupied in the large houses around town. He, for one, had never understood why women outside the colonies preferred to make meals in their own home—but then again he'd never understood much about women.

Here in Amana, they could be much more productive by having only a small group make their meals while the remaining members worked for the community six days a week before resting on the Sabbath. None of them concerned themselves with tasks outside their assigned duties, but his assigned job seemed overwhelming right now.

Two younger women chuckled behind him, and he turned back toward the door.

Jacob Hirsch, his friend and co-manager during the summer months, stopped along the sidewalk nearby and called out to him. "I didn't think you were allowed to eat anymore."

Will pretended to hush him. "No one knows I'm here."

Jacob thumbed over his shoulder. "You need to get your men out on the field."

"We don't have time to play baseball," Will replied. These days they hardly had time to attend the evening prayer meetings. The elders would never agree to let them play a sport for the afternoon.

"Baseball might be exactly what you need." Jacob glanced at the unmarried women behind Will. "That and a wife."

The women giggled again, and Will wished he was on the diamond, bat in hand. Ready to sprint around the bases.

Just because Jacob—once an outsider himself—had enjoyed his marriage to Liesel for well over a decade, didn't mean that Will needed to marry as well.

As Jacob moved toward the end of the line, Will didn't continue their conversation. If he turned again, he would need to exchange pleasantries with the women behind him, and he didn't want either of them to think he was interested in anything beyond cordiality. Neither woman had ever tried to speak with him, but they stared at him across the aisle at church and at the prayer meetings. It was terribly distracting, but he was relieved, at least, by their reservations to converse.

While some of the older women had hinted in years past about him marrying one of their daughters, no one had openly tried to push him into marriage. Most people in their society seemed to understand that he resented being pushed into anything, including being forced into this management position at the mill.

The door to the kitchen house opened, and he moved inside quickly, forty people flooding into the dining hall behind him.

The Amana men and women sat on benches around separate trestle tables—the women eating at the long table on the left, the men on the right. Both tables were covered by a white oilcloth and topped with tureens of barley soup and platters filled with sausages. There was a kettle with hot coffee on each table, pitchers of fresh milk, and serving bowls with cabbage slaw.

Each man and woman silently thanked God for the meal then began filling their bowls with soup, their plates with the food. The meals in the colonies were hearty, but the mealtimes didn't last long because each person needed to return to his or her job.

Will took a long sip of coffee and then glanced back over at the women's table. The woman in the green dress was sitting among the Amana ladies, quietly spooning soup into her mouth.

He stopped suddenly, coffee dripping onto his plate.

This woman wasn't just any visitor from the outside. It was Sophie Henson Keller sitting across the dining hall from him, all dressed up like a city girl.

He turned back toward his food, ducking his head slightly. He'd heard rumors about her returning to Amana after she and Conrad married, but he hadn't seen her since she'd left the colonies. And he certainly didn't want to see her today.

He studied the sausage and cabbage on his plate but didn't feel hungry anymore. Glancing down the narrow table, he saw Emil Hahn studying Sophie, too. Did he recognize her from when they all used to play as children? They'd all attended the same *Lehrschule* with Conrad, too. Learned the same songs together. How to write and do arithmetic and knit.

Then they'd all grown up.

Emil met his gaze. Neither man spoke in the silence, but when his friend's eyebrows slid up into a question, Will knew that he recognized her.

Will glanced toward Jacob near the end of the table. Jacob's wife and Sophie had once been the best of friends. Did Jacob know that Sophie was visiting? He probably did, but he didn't know how utterly lovestruck Will had been with her in their youth.

Both Conrad and Emil knew how much Will cared about Sophie. Once, when he was nineteen, he'd tried to tell Sophie about his growing, almost overwhelming, affection for her, but she had laughed at his attempt, thinking that he was teasing her like he'd done when they were children.

He'd never gotten another opportunity to express his sentiments. Conrad, with his courage and confidence, had beaten him to it. A year later his friend and Sophie were married.

Pining.

That's what Emil used to call his bouts of despondency, even after Conrad and Sophie married. But Will didn't pine anymore. He'd grieved when the terrible news arrived in Amana last year that Conrad had died in a train accident between Council Bluffs and Des Moines. He'd prayed for Sophie and her daughter, of course, but it had been a detached type of prayer. Not from his heart.

He didn't want Sophie to have any part of his heart again.

After he set down his fork, he filled his tin with coffee again.

Why had she returned to the colonies?

And the most important question of all—when would she go back to Des Moines?

Chapter 3

"M eredith Keller," Liesel exclaimed as she burst through the door. "You are just as beautiful as your mother."

Liesel quickly crossed the room, a blue kettle of coffee swinging from one hand, a bulging basket of food in the other. "I'm told you're as smart as her, too."

Sophie closed the book in her lap, her eyes almost as big as her daughter's as Meredith tried to figure out what this sprightly woman was doing, rushing into their hotel room a few minutes after noon.

Meredith elbowed her way up on the sea of pillows, her mouth drooping open as Liesel rounded the walnut posts on the bed and pushed back the gingham curtains until sunlight soaked every corner of their small room.

"It is a spectacular day outside," Liesel explained. "Sunny and warm enough to melt most of the snow and warm us all up in the process."

Liesel grinned down at Meredith, wide and welcoming. Sophie knew her daughter wished she could fold herself back up into the blue flannel sheets and wine-colored comforter, sink deep into the feather tick, losing herself again.

Meredith hadn't left their hotel room since they arrived in Amana on Monday. Three days past. She'd slept, stared at *The Wonderful Wizard of Oz* pictures, watched the snow that fell most of yesterday. Sophie had brought her meals from the hotel dining room, but Meredith only wanted to drink the milk. At Sophie's insistence, she'd taken a bite of food at each meal, but it wasn't enough to sustain her.

Early this morning, after she ate breakfast at the kitchen house, Sophie had told Liesel about her growing fears for her daughter. It seemed like Meredith no longer cared about the realities of life.

Or perhaps she cared too much and the burden of it all confined her to bed.

Either way, Sophie had spent most of her hours since they'd arrived reading quietly as she watched over her daughter.

Liesel had agreed with her—something must be done to rouse Meredith from this stupor.

"I have a job for you," Liesel told Meredith as if she were offering her the greatest gift in the world.

Meredith stared at Liesel, her wide eyes beginning to narrow again. Sophie knew her daughter thought Liesel was crazy, but her friend wasn't deterred. Reaching into her basket, she began laying out pastries, watermelon pickles, bratwurst, *Süsskäse*—a soft white cheese—and a small loaf of bread on the stand beside the bed.

As she worked, she continued to talk.

"Before you start working, you must eat," Liesel said as if Meredith had already agreed to her proposition.

Then again, Liesel hadn't given her an opportunity to agree or disagree.

"My Cassie comes every afternoon after school to help at the kitchen," she explained as she sliced the sausage with a knife. "Today we need your help, too."

Meredith shook her head, her gaze focused on the pastries. "I don't know anything about working in a kitchen."

"Cassie is so excited to see you," Liesel continued. "She'll show you exactly what to do."

Meredith glanced over at Sophie, her eyes pleading for help, but this time Sophie decided an afternoon in the kitchen house might be the best way to help her.

Liesel studied Meredith's nightdress. "You can't wear that in the kitchen."

Standing, Sophie crossed the room to the large wardrobe near the door. Folded inside were six different dresses for Meredith, all of them waiting to be worn. Sophie lifted up the plainest one her daughter owned, a pale rose dress with lace around the collar and waist. She'd still stand out in the village but less so than if she was wearing ruffles, ribbons, or pleats.

Liesel took the dress from Sophie's hands. "This is lovely," she said before smoothing it out on the bed. "I have an apron for you to wear over it in the kitchen."

"But—" Meredith started to protest again.

Liesel pointed at the array of food. "Eat up," she said. "You'll need your strength to work."

Sophie wrung her hands together. She'd been idle for too long as well. "Can I help, too?"

A shadow crossed Liesel's face. It disappeared quickly, the easy smile returning, but Sophie knew there were others in the community who didn't trust her. She'd left the Amanas to be with her husband, but in their minds, she'd abandoned the entire community.

In the Amana Colonies, work was a privilege, so different from the elite in Des Moines who viewed work with disdain. Here you had to earn your right to work.

Sophie glanced out at the sunshine. "Actually, I think I will take a walk on this lovely afternoon so Meredith and Cassie can enjoy their time together."

Liesel nodded and then looked back at Meredith. "I'll need you in the next half hour."

With that, her friend turned, winked at Sophie, and then breezed out the door as quickly as she'd arrived.

Sophie broke off a small piece of the iced pastry, filled with blackberry preserves, as she prepared herself for a fight. When Meredith refused to go work, she would have to decide whether or not to make her leave their room.

Conrad was always the strong one when it came to confronting their equally strong daughter. And their daughter always respected his strength.

Meredith leaned back against the headboard. "Do they really need me?" she asked.

Sophie almost choked on the pastry. "I suppose they do."

Meredith looked down at the bedcovers then up at the window before her gaze landed again on the spread of food.

Sophie wanted to tell her daughter she needed to eat, like she'd been doing since they'd arrived. She wanted to tell her daughter to get out of bed, dress herself, and go down the street to work at the kitchen. But something stopped her. It was that same quiet voice she used to hear during the silent prayer meetings in the *Saal*.

"*Wait.*"

The word was as clear to her as the word *home* had been when they arrived.

Instead of urging Meredith to leave, Sophie decided not to say anything at all.

Quietly she took her coat from the hook by the door and buttoned the front. Then she kissed Meredith's forehead. "I'll meet you at the kitchen house for supper."

"You're leaving?"

She nodded. "I'm going to take a walk while it's warm."

Meredith crossed her arms. "I don't know how to cook a meal."

Sophie had tried to protect her daughter from working too hard in her childhood, wanting her to enjoy her youth instead by reading the books she loved, attending school, and spending time with her friends. But perhaps she had robbed Meredith in the process.

Sophie had labored hard when she was younger. She remembered being bone-tired at night, but she never remembered being unhappy. "Liesel will teach you exactly what you need," she said.

With that, Sophie turned and walked out the door.

She didn't go far though. Standing across the street, she waited beside the Glockenhaus, her back against the stone wall, praying that Meredith would emerge on her own.

Next to her, snow clung to the eaves on the house where she and Conrad had lived when they first married. She'd admired Conrad since they were both nine years old, learning how to knit scarfs together in elementary school. He was never harsh, but he was confident in his ideas, even when they clashed with the elders in their community.

In those early days of their youth, Conrad had loved to debate. He could present an argument about anything from the type of yarn to use for their socks to whether or not the Amana men should be permitted to fight in their country's wars or even play baseball. Sophie didn't enjoy verbal volleying like her husband, but he'd always valued her opinion.

Back in 1894, the Amana elders had wanted Conrad to continue his work dredging the millrace instead of becoming an attorney, but Conrad hated the drudgery of manual labor. When Meredith was a newborn baby, Sophie and Conrad had left the Amana village and the people they loved so he could pursue his dream of practicing law. The work satisfied him, but they both missed the simplicity and community of their childhood.

Conrad didn't miss the communal living in Amana enough to give up his career, so they carved out a new life for their little family in Des Moines. Sophie had learned quickly about Gibson girl fashion, how to style her hair into a soft pompadour, how to step into her new role as a hostess in a large home. Instead of helping manage a kitchen alongside her friends, she managed paid servants to cook and clean for her family. They were respectful to her, but she wouldn't consider them to be friends.

She missed those hours in the kitchen, working alongside her Amana friends. Liesel had truly given Meredith a gift by inviting her to join them in their work. As she waited, she prayed again that her daughter would accept it.

After a half hour had passed, she feared that Meredith had gone back to sleep, but then the door of the hotel opened, and she watched her daughter glance both ways before stepping onto the wooden sidewalk.

Meredith didn't see Sophie hiding between the tower and house, but Sophie could see her. After an Amana woman pointed Meredith to the kitchen house, Sophie stepped out onto the sidewalk and watched her daughter stroll slowly down the sidewalk until she reached the kitchen house. Meredith stopped again, hesitating at the front door, then went inside.

With a loud sigh, Sophie released the air she'd been holding in her lungs. Finally Meredith was out of the hotel, and Sophie hadn't had to force her to leave.

She prayed silently that her daughter would enjoy her time with Cassie. That she would find healing among her work with the Amana women.

Sophie moved back up the hotel steps, into their room. The tray that once towered with food was empty. There weren't even crumbs from the pastry left behind on the tray.

Smiling, Sophie turned back around to take a walk following the path along the millrace that led outside town.

◆　◆　◆

Will punched his leather mitt as Jacob pitched the ball to the opposing team. Mud coated the boots of all the players, making it hard to run, but no one seemed to care. The sun was shining, and they were all outside instead of stuck in the mill.

"Strike!" George Beyer yelled from behind the base.

Their team was winning, three to two. Not that he was keeping score.

The elders had begun letting the Amana men play baseball just a year ago—as long as they kept the competition friendly and it didn't distract from their work—but a group of them had been playing for more than a decade without permission. When they played during the summers, at this field along the millrace, a small group always gathered to watch, but it was too cold this afternoon for a crowd.

They shouldn't be playing baseball now, even with the sunshine, but two of the mill's carding machines had stopped working this morning. He figured the machinery was just as tired as all the workers right now. While the millwright was fixing them—and the sun was shining—he decided to take Jacob up on his proposition to play ball.

"Strike two," George shouted as Emil tapped the bat on home base.

Will punched his mitt again. On one side of the field was the canal built for the mill. On the other was a *Schulwalder*—a pine grove planted by the children when he, Sophie, Liesel, and Conrad were in school. Their winter green color reminded him of the dress Sophie had worn to the kitchen house on Monday. He'd tried to press the image of her out of his mind—and he'd been eating at another kitchen house for the past two days—but he couldn't seem to escape it.

Was Sophie still in Amana, or had she returned to Des Moines?

He could ask Liesel after prayer meeting tonight, but if he mentioned Sophie, Liesel would start asking questions that he didn't want to answer.

The crack of the wooden bat echoed through his thoughts, but he failed to react in time. The ball flew right over his head.

"Kephart!" Jacob cried.

"Got it," he shouted back.

Growling at himself, he turned and sprinted toward the grove of trees. He should have been focusing on the game. Not on Sophie and her dress.

The ball dropped into the forest, and he quickly thrashed through the cone-studded arms of pine to retrieve it.

On the other side of the tree was a woman, dressed in a navy blue overcoat and white scarf. He blinked, his eyes widening as if he were seeing a ghost. Sophie was here in the forest, just like she'd been in days gone by, watching them play ball.

She held out the leather baseball, dripping with mud, and he took it from her.

"What are you doing out here?" he demanded, words clipped.

"I'm staying in Amana for a few weeks," she said, her blue eyes sparkling in the sunlight. "And I needed a walk."

Her gaze traveled out toward the field behind him. In the distance he heard shouting, the men screaming, but he didn't move.

When she looked back at him, her eyes widened. "Will?"

He squeezed the ball in his mitt, nodded his head. "All grown up."

"William Kephart." She drew out his full name as if she couldn't believe it either. "It's been years."

"Fourteen."

"Kephart!" Jacob shouted his name again in the background.

Sophie pointed her soiled glove back at the field. "You'd better hurry."

He held up the mitt. "Thanks for the ball."

He turned, but his feet were weighted down by the mud.

Emil rounded third base, but as he pushed toward home plate, he slipped in the mire. As Emil struggled to stand, Will threw the ball to Jacob, who tossed it in to home.

George's arms flew wide. "Out!" he cried.

When Will finally jogged back onto the field, Jacob clapped him on the back, but Will didn't feel the enthusiasm. Nor did he dare a glance back at the pine trees.

These colonies were his home, and yet for a moment he wished he could run far away. Like Conrad and Sophie had done long ago.

Chapter 4

*W*ill Kephart.

The name of her old friend tumbled around in Sophie's mind as she walked toward the kitchen house, along with the image of his handsome brown eyes looking back at her, swollen with surprise when he'd found her hiding in the pines.

She'd seen the same questioning in some of the women's eyes when she'd taken her meals at Liesel's kitchen house. The wondering why she had returned after all these years.

She hadn't thought about Will in a long time, but the memories of their friendship began to return. The way he used to tease her when they were kids and make her laugh. How he'd brought her wildflowers when they'd grown older and sometimes candies like the pink and white marshmallows obtained with the coupons they used to procure things at the general store.

He'd always been a good friend to her until Conrad stole her heart. Once Conrad announced their plans to marry, Will seemed to disappear.

Fifteen years had passed since they'd laughed together. So many changes.

Who had stolen Will's heart?

Hopefully, he'd married a woman who enjoyed laughter as much as he did. They would be living now in an apartment in one of these sandstone homes around her. After a long day of work, they probably read and laughed together in their rooms, not worrying one whit about social engagements or finding a place to belong.

She tried to fight back the tangling vines of envy that tightened around her heart.

In the years before his death, Conrad had rarely spent the evenings with her and Meredith at home. At the time, she understood his need to work and the importance of attending a host of society events alongside his clients, but looking back, she wished they'd had more time together as a family. If they'd only known what the future held. . .

But they hadn't known. And slogging through the past wasn't helpful at all. She needed to focus on her future—their future—for Meredith's sake.

Reaching into her pocket, she felt the piece of paper with a message from John Hoffman. He'd telephoned this afternoon while she was on a walk, asking her to return his call tonight.

Since John had been working in the District of Columbia when she left Des

Moines, she'd written him a letter explaining that she and Meredith were going to spend Christmas in Amana. Now that he had returned to Des Moines, the telephone message said he wanted them to come back home for the holidays instead.

But Des Moines didn't feel at all like home.

She wouldn't stay in Amana much longer if Meredith was miserable here. And the truth was, she was getting edgy herself. Part of what she missed about the Amana Colonies was working with others, and she hadn't done a lick of work this week. At least back in Des Moines, she could lose herself again in the busyness of the season.

Her heart felt as if it were tearing into two pieces between her past and her future. Somewhere between the two was a murky present she didn't quite understand, and it terrified her. At times it felt as if she were drowning, the waves crashing over her head. Perhaps she should grab on to John's outstretched hand and let him pull her out of it.

When she reached the side door of Liesel's kitchen, she scraped the mud off her shoes and stepped into the room filled with Amana men and women eating their supper. The sound of forks clanking against glass plates echoed between the light blue walls. After her long walk, she was late for the meal, but she was more concerned with checking on her daughter than eating anyway, worried that Meredith might be sitting in a corner of the kitchen, anxious and alone.

When she peeked over the swinging doors into the kitchen, she saw Liesel standing over a parade of copper boilers bubbling on the long stove, directing the eight or so women around her in their tasks. When Liesel looked toward the doors, she smiled.

"Go eat," Liesel said, waving her back toward the Speisesaal.

"Where's Meredith?" Sophie asked, scanning the room.

"In the back room, peeling potatoes."

Sophie pressed her fingers into the top of the painted doors. "Is she okay?"

"She's been a tremendous help this afternoon."

She searched her friend's eyes for the truth but didn't see anything except sincerity in them. Meredith would be angry at Sophie, but the work was good for her. Good for both of them.

Stepping back into the dining hall, Sophie glanced over at the men's table, inadvertently searching for Will, but she didn't see him. In fact, there seemed to be quite a few empty spaces compared to days past. Perhaps the men had forgone their meal for a few more innings.

She sat down at the end of the women's table and dished up a helping of the German dumplings, soaked in a brown butter sauce. Scanning the women's faces, she wondered which one—if any of them—was Will's wife. While she recognized several of these ladies from her childhood, she couldn't remember everyone's name. Some of them had probably come over to work from one of the nearby Amana villages, just as some of the men and women in Amana had moved to another village in the last decade, depending on where they were needed to work.

Much had changed since she'd left for the outside, but when standing in the pine grove this afternoon, across from Will, she felt for the briefest moment as if she were sixteen again, alive with the fire of youth.

Her face warmed at the thought, and she looked quickly down at the pool of dumplings on her plate. Thankfully, none of these ladies could read her thoughts.

She tried to redirect her thoughts toward the man who wanted to marry her in Des Moines. The one waiting for an answer to his proposal.

She'd never love the senator like she had Conrad, but she and Meredith would have a home for the rest of their lives with him. A family. John had made his fortune from the coal mines near Des Moines. He respected her and had agreed to welcome Meredith as one of his daughters.

But before she married again, she wanted more time with the man about to become her husband. Even if they didn't have years spent getting to know one another—like she and Conrad had—she wished she could know more about his heart instead of just his perfectly polished facade.

It seemed that she didn't know John nearly as well as she should to accept his proposal of marriage, but then again, she didn't know when she would get to know him much better. John spent months working in the District of Columbia. She would never travel with him on the train, so they would only spend his vacations as husband and wife until he returned for good to Iowa.

She sighed. If only the idea of spending a lifetime with John thrilled her.

As she took another bite of her dumplings, she glanced toward the kitchen on her left. Occasionally, one of the younger women would bring out a refilled platter, but she still didn't see her daughter.

Minutes later, the benches cleared as everyone except Sophie filed out for their evening prayer service. She slipped into the kitchen and found Meredith sitting on a stool in the back room, a potato peeler in her hand.

Sophie had expected tears or anger, but her daughter was grinning as she picked up another potato from the basket beside her.

Liesel stepped up beside Sophie. "She's worked hard," her friend whispered.

Meredith lifted her head, met Sophie's gaze. Then her smile slipped away as she swiped the sweat off her forehead with her sleeve. "Cassie and I had to peel fifty potatoes," she complained.

Cassie was in the kitchen now, scrubbing one of the kettles at the wooden sink.

Sophie pointed back at the door. "Let's go rest for the evening."

Meredith considered her words for a moment and then shook her head. "Liesel asked me to soak the oats for tomorrow and then grind coffee beans."

"You don't have to. . . ," Sophie started, afraid to exhaust her daughter.

"But they need me," Meredith said, pleading.

"I can walk her home in an hour," Liesel said. "We couldn't have finished supper on time without her."

A smile lit Meredith's sweat-caked face again, and Sophie knew that look. She was basking in her usefulness.

As Sophie left the kitchen, she heard Cassie and Meredith's laughter, and it reminded her of the afternoons that she and Liesel had spent giggling after school as they cracked eggs, rolled out dough, and peeled potatoes. She hadn't realized at the time how blessed she was to have such a sweet friendship and the satisfaction from working hard with her hands. And the promise of a good night's sleep after the community prayed and sang together in the Saal.

Loneliness settled over her again as she strolled back among the houses. A German worship song drifted out of the long stone building across the street, the voices blending together in a beautiful a cappella. They didn't use instruments in the Amana Colonies. Didn't need them.

Threads of twilight wove above the roof of the Saal and draped over the building like a pink curtain flowing down on both sides. Wind rustled the tree branches around her, but she didn't rush to the hotel. Instead, she leaned back against an iron railing and listened to the worship.

What would happen if she slipped into the rear of the Saal?

She wouldn't disrupt the worship and prayer, but for a few minutes, perhaps she could feel as if she were part of the community again. That she belonged.

But when she stepped into the street, the music started to fade.

Perhaps the Amana people would sing again, but they may spend the rest of their half hour in silence, listening to the voice of God. And if she opened the door now, she would disrupt their prayers.

She folded her arms across her chest as she walked toward the hotel, craving the community she once had. The sweet friendships built from working alongside others who wanted to serve God and worship together.

How she missed this kinship with people who prayed every night for their brothers and sisters, who cared for each other in their need.

The Amana community began to sing again in German, and she stopped to listen, basking in their song about the love in which they were bound and anchored, love in which they would never part. An enduring, persistent love that overcame their stubborn and wayward hearts.

◆　◆　◆

"We need someone else to help manage the mill's production," Matthias told Will, his crippled hand trembling on the edge of his desk.

The carding machines, revived to their working power, clicked and whirled on the floor above them. About half of their 125 workers were sorting, washing, dyeing, carding, and spinning the wool this morning, but they still weren't working fast enough to meet the deadline for Sears, Roebuck & Co.

Will crossed his arms as he leaned forward in his chair toward his grandfather on the other side of the desk. "Do you want me to return to managing the farms?"

Matthias shook his head. "No, I want to find someone to work alongside you."

"There's no one else—" he started. Everyone else with management experience was engaged in his or her own assigned tasks.

Matthias tapped one hand on the desk. "I've learned that Sophie Keller has returned to Amana."

Will swallowed hard. "For good?"

"For a season," Matthias said. "I'm hoping to convince her to stay through the new year."

"We don't need her help," Will insisted.

Matthias's gray eyebrows climbed. "We need someone's help."

"Call it pride if you must." Will tried to calm the frustration in his voice. "But I'd rather have someone else help us."

"I think this is about more than your pride, Will."

He shook his head. "I don't know what you mean."

Matthias cleared his throat but didn't say anything, his gaze focused on the edge of his worn desk.

His grandfather's silence was worse than a thousand words of rebuke. His grandparents had been married more than fifty years now, and both Matthias and Amalie had conspired over the years to help Will find a wife, as if he couldn't find one on his own.

Was this part of their conspiracy?

Matthias finally spoke. "Sophie was an excellent manager when she worked at the kitchen house."

"Too many cooks spoil the broth," Will retorted.

Matthias laughed. "We aren't making any broth here."

"You know what I mean—"

"You can't do everything, Will, and I'm too old to be walking the floor," he said, the tone of his voice marking the end of their debate. "I'll have you both manage different areas."

Will drummed his fingers on his flannel sleeve. "She won't agree to it."

Matthias's voice turned serious again. "Let's both pray that she will. If not, I'll have to cancel our order with Sears."

And the whole community would suffer as a result.

Matthias rapped his knuckles on the edge of his chair. "You'll have to convince her to join us."

Will fell back against his seat. "Me?"

"Amalie said the two of you used to be friends in school."

"A very long time ago."

"Aah," Matthias said as he dipped his pen into the inkwell. "'Iron sharpeneth iron,'" he quoted from Proverbs. "'So a man sharpeneth the countenance of his friend.'"

Will wasn't certain he wanted to be sharpened anymore by his friendship with Sophie.

"Talk to her first thing in the morning," Matthias said, looking up again. "And do it kindly, please."

Will nodded his head, but kindly or not, he didn't want to ever speak with Sophie again.

Chapter 5

Meredith whispered good-bye in the candlelight, closing the door of the hotel room long before the sun made an appearance outside their window. Sophie glanced at the clock. It was only five, but she wouldn't be able to fall back asleep. Rising slowly from her bed, she poured cold water into the basin and splashed it on her face.

Her daughter's transformation this past week was astonishing. Meredith arose early each morning, rushing off to help Liesel and Cassie in the kitchen before Cassie went to school. Then she helped Liesel scrub dishes and prepare dinner while Cassie was gone. When Cassie returned, she stayed to help Liesel in the afternoons, too.

Meredith no longer complained about the work, even when all she seemed to do was peel and peel the endless baskets of potatoes.

Bells on the baker's wagon chimed outside the window, making its morning run to the kitchen houses. Sophie looked out the window and watched the horses, glowing in the baker's lantern light as they pulled the wagon down the street.

If only there was something she could do to help here in Amana as well.

Her mind wandered back to the streets of Des Moines, to the morning that she and Meredith had left. The street below Sherman Hill had been packed with unemployed coal miners who'd protested their company's dangerous policies as part of a new union, asking residents on Sherman Hill instead for a day's work.

She didn't know which mining company they worked for—and she was afraid to inquire. John was the co-owner of a coal mine in Des Moines. Even though he wanted to do right for the citizens of Iowa, she feared he had been blinded by his own enterprise.

Conrad had been one of the attorneys who fought to help the coal miners organize and ask for safer conditions inside the mines, but it seemed the company had still let them go.

She'd seen despair in the miners' faces as she and Meredith had left town, and now she understood it even more. The men couldn't support their families, and the idleness of wasting another day when they desperately needed the income was probably eroding their self-respect.

She pressed her fingers together, wishing she had work for them. And work for herself as well.

John had called two more times this week. Left two more messages with the hotel clerk. Today she would call him back and decline his invitation for Christmas dinner again. He would be irritated at her for not returning to Des Moines, but when she told him how Meredith was thriving here, he would understand.

She dressed in a warm black gown, twisted her long hair into a chignon, and then sat back down by the window, waiting for breakfast to begin at seven.

Minutes later, someone knocked at her door, and she eyed the clock. It was ten minutes after six now.

Who would be at her door this early? Most people in Amana were just waking up.

Then her heart lurched, and she jumped to her feet, rushing toward the door. What if something had happened to Meredith?

Standing in the gas lamplight, on the other side of the door, was Will Kephart, dressed in a brown chambray shirt and dungarees. She glanced up and down the dim corridor. "Is something wrong?"

"I need to speak with you," he said, unsmiling.

She persisted. "Is this about Meredith?"

When he shook his head, her breath resumed its normal pace. "What do you need to say?"

He pointed toward the staircase. "Let's discuss it in the parlor."

She nodded. "I'll be down in ten minutes."

Retreating back into her room, she leaned back against the doorpost. Had the elders sent Will to ask her to leave the colonies? The thought of going back to the city now, before the holidays, saddened her more than she could have imagined. Meredith was finally climbing out of this fog. They couldn't leave quite yet.

She prayed the elders would let her stay for another week, at least through Christmas. Perhaps a little more time would help Meredith retain the hope she'd found here.

Breathing deeply, she tied her high-top boots and unhooked her coat from the peg on the wall. And prayed for strength.

Will was standing in the parlor when she arrived, his broad back facing the braided cover on the sofa, his arms crossed.

Had he been this handsome when they were younger? She couldn't seem to remember with him staring down at her, his dark brown eyes flickering with what looked like disdain.

What had she done to make him think so poorly of her?

"We will return to Des Moines the day after Christmas," she said simply, fidgeting with her gloves.

Surprise replaced the disdain in his gaze.

"Liesel has invited us to spend Christmas Eve and Christmas with her family, but I know we don't belong—"

He stopped her with a sweep of his hand. "The elders don't want you to leave," he replied. "In fact, quite the contrary."

She tilted her head, the gloves resting at her side. "What do you mean?"

"They would like you to stay another month and help manage the woolen mill."

She stepped back, shocked. "What?"

"Matthias and I have been trying to manage it together, but we're behind on production."

She shook her head. "I've never managed a mill—"

"According to my grandmother, you did a stellar job managing the kitchen house."

Fourteen years ago.

And the production in a mill was nothing like producing a meal.

"The hours are long," he said, his fist knocking against the rolltop desk beside the sofa.

She lifted her chin. "I'm not afraid of hard work."

"And you'd be the only woman."

His offer terrified her, yet it ignited something within her as well. For a few weeks, at least, she could be useful, helping like Meredith was in the kitchen. She could be a part of the Amana community one last time.

She nodded slowly. "I will consider it."

A shadow crossed over his face, and she wondered at it. He'd asked for her help at the mill, yet it seemed he really hadn't expected her to accept this task.

Or perhaps he really didn't want her to do the job.

"When will you make a decision?" he asked.

She glanced at the white curtains around the window, probably made from the mill's calico. At the simple furnishings in the small room.

What did she have to consider before making her decision? There was no one to ask except Meredith, and after the last couple of days, she was almost certain her daughter would agree to the plan. She should probably ask John, but he would try and talk her out of it. Not only could she be useful here in Amana, it would buy her more time before she gave him a decision.

"I'll visit the mill after breakfast," she said.

"Matthias will give you a tour." He shoved his hat back on his head before turning to leave.

She sat on the sofa and watched him walk past the window.

Had she done something to upset Will before she left the Colonies? Perhaps he was simply uncomfortable talking to her after Conrad was gone.

People had responded to her in all sorts of odd ways since her husband had died. Some ignored her; others were awkward and kept talking long after they'd run out of meaningful things to say. Still others seemed angry with her, as if they blamed her in some way for Conrad's death.

Removing her gloves from the pockets of her coat, she ran her hands over the soft doeskin.

She didn't know the first thing about making woolen materials, but she had enjoyed managing the kitchen long ago. If Meredith approved, she would meet with

Matthias today to see if he was serious.

And then she would start working right away.

◆ ◆ ◆

Sophie slowly followed Will around the second floor of the mill. The male workers didn't look hostile as much as they looked perplexed, probably wondering why an outsider and a woman was touring their floor. Part of her wondered as well why she had agreed to do this. Like she'd tried to explain to Will and then Matthias, a woolen mill was nothing like a kitchen house, but Matthias said he was confident that she could do this job.

She wished she felt confident as well.

After the picking machine removed dirt and debris from the wool, Will explained, the workers washed it in the mill and spread it out on long wooden frames to dry overnight. The wool was dyed and fed through the giant rollers on the carding machines on the floor above them. Then it was either spun into yarn or woven into flannel on the looms in the nearby weaving building.

She brushed her fingers over the wet wool as she watched the men work at the carding machines, the wooden floor trembling under her boots.

How could she possibly help when she knew nothing about turning wool into yarn or flannel?

A bell rang, and the workers dried their hands on their overalls as they stepped away from the frames.

"Where are they going?" she asked Will.

He nodded toward a table at the center of the room. "They're stopping for a coffee break."

"How long do they work?" she asked.

"Nine hours a day. The same as everyone else."

"Except the kitchen workers," she said with a wry smile. "They are in the kitchen from five until midnight sometimes."

He sighed, clearly exasperated at her. "They work in shifts."

When she met his gaze, he looked quickly away. Like she'd seared him with her glance. "Have I done something to offend you?" she asked.

He crossed his arms. "You don't have any power over me, Sophie."

"I—" She hesitated, not quite knowing how to respond. "I'm sorry if I did something to anger you."

"You don't need to apologize for anything."

His lips pressed together in a hard line, and she wondered where that easy smile had gone. The one that used to make her laugh.

"Why did you ask me to work at the mill?"

"Matthias thinks we need your help."

"What do you think?" she asked.

"I think we need a miracle." He turned abruptly away from her toward the table. "Do you want coffee?"

She hesitated, uncertain if he was talking to her or someone else. When he didn't turn back, she followed him into another room.

After breakfast this morning, she'd asked Meredith about staying in Amana for a few weeks longer. Not only did Meredith approve of the plan, she'd hugged Sophie.

She couldn't remember the last time her daughter had hugged her.

Meredith had also asked if she could go to school with Cassie in the mornings after the holiday. Sophie asked Matthias about schooling when they met, and he'd readily agreed to the plan. The community, he'd said, would provide for Meredith and Sophie alike until they returned to Des Moines.

She studied the workers huddled around a table, some of them drinking beer from bottles, others sipping black coffee from tins. They all held bread in their hands as they laughed together with their colleagues and friends.

It reminded her of her years in the kitchen house. Of the friendships that she'd taken for granted back then.

As she watched them eat, an idea began to form in her mind.

She smiled when Will handed her a tin with the coffee.

Perhaps she could help them after all.

Chapter 6

This is ludicrous," Will declared, leaning against the desk in his grandfather's office, his mind racing at Sophie's proposal.

It was unheard of in the Amana Colonies.

Matthias, however, pressed his fingers together in an arch over his desk, seeming to consider Sophie's idea. "How much would it cost?" he asked.

Sophie slid a piece of paper with numbers across his desk, and Matthias slowly reviewed them. When he looked up again, Will saw the admiration in his eyes. "This is good, Sophie," he said. "Very good."

Will groaned, shaking his head. It wasn't good at all. "The elders will never approve this."

Finally Matthias looked over at him. "If you have a better idea, I want to hear it."

That was the problem. He didn't have a better idea nor would he. Sophie's idea was unconventional but solid and completely workable if the elders approved. They'd never done anything like it before, but it didn't mean they shouldn't try.

He admired her creativity—and honestly admired her for much more. But that didn't mean he wanted to work alongside her to implement this plan.

"When can we begin?" Matthias asked.

Sophie tapped her pencil on the desk. "Depending on the elders' approval, we could start by the end of the week."

Will shook his head. "We have to find outsiders to employ first."

Turning, she smiled at him. "I know exactly where to find them."

With her smile, he caught a glimpse of what this plan could mean for them. For him. If they switched to two shifts, like the kitchen house workers, they could potentially double their production.

While they didn't have enough workers in Amana for two shifts, Sophie proposed that they hire outside workers for a short season, a couple of months at the most, to complete their order for Sears and then catch up on their other work. If they could fulfill all their current orders by March, perhaps he could return to managing the fields in the spring. No longer would he have to be cooped up in the mill.

He uncrossed his arms, glancing back at his grandfather. "When can you talk to the elders about it?"

Matthias leaned back in his chair. "Tonight. After the prayer meeting."

Perhaps he would pray they'd approve her idea.

◆ ◆ ◆

Machines stalled inside the mill as workers flooded toward the second-story window. Sophie stepped up to the window beside them and looked down at a black Stanley Steamer as it parked beside the front door.

Who had come to Amana in such a fancy automobile?

There were more automobiles in Des Moines these days, but clearly it was a rare sight here as the men admired the vehicle from their perch above the street.

Thankfully, no snow covered the road into town—and the sky was clear—but who would be driving an automobile so far away from a city, during the winter? The driver could easily get stranded in one of Iowa's snowstorms.

Sophie started to move away from the window when the car door opened, and she saw the flash of a bowler hat. Then a man with a wool overcoat stepped out of the vehicle. When he turned his head up toward the second floor, her heart seemed to collapse.

Senator John Hoffman was in Amana.

She braced herself on the windowsill, her mind swirling as she stepped to the side, moving toward a chair. What was John doing here?

She'd left him a telephone message a few days ago explaining that she wouldn't be returning to Des Moines until the end of January. She hadn't received a reply back, and she'd been much too busy at the mill to think any more about it.

Eyeing the door to the staircase, she thought about running again, this time away from Amana, but there was no place for her to run from here.

All the workers drifted away from the windows, back to the machinery. The work resumed around her at a steady pace, but her heart drummed a different beat of its own. Not one of anticipation or delight. It was the erratic, pounding beat of dread.

In that moment, she wished that Will was here with her.

The thought startled her and then slowly settled into her mind. Will had changed from the jovial man of their youth, but his animosity toward her began to chill after the elders approved her idea. She admired his strength and leadership and—after fighting her initially—his willingness to change his mind and try something new.

John would be in the downstairs office by now, but she didn't move from her chair. Ironically, the same day she'd left a message with his housekeeper, Will had boarded a train in the nearby village of Homestead and traveled to Des Moines to ask thirty or so unemployed coal miners if they'd like temporary work.

According to Matthias, it had taken an hour to persuade the elders to invite outsider workers into the mill, in order to double their production, but eventually everyone agreed that they needed to attempt this for the good of their community.

The carding machine clicked behind her; the floor vibrated under her boots. And she felt comfort in this steady rhythm of work.

Just like Matthias had convinced the elders, she would need to make John understand how important it was for her and Meredith to remain in Amana for another month. Surely he would be pleased that Meredith was beginning to engage in life again and that Sophie was helping at the mill.

When she returned to Des Moines, she would give John an answer about marriage. These four weeks would give them both some extra time to evaluate their future together.

The door to the staircase opened, and Matthias stepped into the carding room. Reluctantly she rose and walked across the floor to greet him.

"You have a visitor downstairs," he said.

She nodded. "The entire crew watched him drive up in his automobile."

One of his gray eyebrows slid up. "Yet you are still up here."

"John won't be very happy with me."

"He doesn't seem to be happy at anyone."

"He's—" She hesitated, wondering how much to tell the man in front of her. And she wondered why she felt the need to defend the man downstairs. "He's a very important person in Des Moines."

"I see." Matthias moved back toward the door. "Much too important to spend his day motoring over to our colonies."

"He wants me to spend Christmas in Des Moines."

"What do you want?" Matthias asked.

She rubbed her hands together. "I want to stay here."

Matthias reached for the latch on the door to reopen it. "Then it seems that you've already made up your mind."

She straightened her shoulders. She knew what she wanted, but what if her decision induced John to change his mind about their marriage? What if Meredith had to spend the rest of her life without a father to help care for her?

Matthias quietly descended the stairs in front of her, and when they reached the bottom floor, she could see John through the office window, pacing the floor. He was twisting his stiff bowler hat in his hands, clearly not pleased.

Matthias motioned to the door, and she took a deep breath before walking inside.

"Hello, John," she said simply.

He turned abruptly toward her, but instead of greeting her, he pointed toward Matthias in the doorway. "We need to talk in private."

Matthias nodded his head. "I will wait in the next room."

Sophie turned back to John. His face was flushed, and for the first time it seemed, she really looked at him. At the ribbon of extra flesh that bulged around his starched collar. At the dark green eyes that flashed with anger. He was the same height as her, but with his bravado, he'd always seemed much taller. Larger than life.

What did she really know about the man before her?

"Matthias is a good man," she said, scolding him like she might have done with Meredith when she was younger. "You didn't have to be so harsh."

John shook his head. "He has no right to make you work here."

"No one is making me do anything," she tried to explain. "I'm helping them with their production."

His laughter grated on her skin.

"Why is that funny?" she demanded, her fists balled up at her sides.

"You are a beautiful woman, Sophie, and a delightful hostess, but how are you supposed to help with the production at a woolen mill?"

She cringed. There was so much that he didn't know about her. So much that he would never appreciate about her years growing up in the Amanas. Until this past week, she hadn't even realized that she'd lost part of herself when she and Conrad moved away.

Here she wasn't prided on her own work though. In Amana she was part of a team.

"They need me here through the new year."

"I need you, Sophie," John said. "In Des Moines."

She pointed to the window. "Did you buy a new automobile?" she asked, attempting to calm his frustration.

He placed his hat on the cluttered desk. "I was going to surprise you."

Unlike a train, she would ride in an automobile, but she still wasn't fond of them. "I liked the green one you had."

"This one's not for me," he said. "I bought it for you, as a Christmas present."

She nodded slowly, her gaze focused on the window glass. He was waiting for her to express her gratitude, but she couldn't seem to muster her thanksgiving for a gift she didn't want.

"I thought you'd be excited about it."

"It's still hard for me to be excited about anything, John."

"Conrad has been gone for a year," he replied, his voice bland. His wife had only been gone for six months now, and somehow he'd had the strength to move on.

Back in Des Moines, she'd felt as if she were stuck in a whirlpool of grief, but in Amana, she'd felt glimpses of joy returning to her heart. She'd delighted in the treasure of God's priceless gifts—the snow on the fence posts, the scent of pine in the breeze, the stillness of the night, the peace in her heart after a hard day of work.

God's gifts were good. Pure. Given without expectation because she could never give such beauty back to Him.

This gift from John was much different. He gave it because he wanted something in return. Something she didn't know if she could give.

And she knew in that moment, she wasn't ready to marry him. Nor was she ready to return to Des Moines before or in the days after Christmas. She had to stay in Amana a little longer, for herself and Meredith.

The words slowly formed in her mind, but she never got to speak them.

"What is that—" John muttered.

Following his gaze out the window, she watched as three covered hacks, their benches filled with workingmen, pulled up beside the Stanley Steamer.

Will had returned. And it appeared he'd brought an entire force with him.

She forgot John as she watched Will hop down from the wagon's bench, rounding the wagon to speak with the men.

And she prayed her idea wasn't ludicrous after all.

Chapter 7

As he stepped around the wagon, Will eyed the fancy automobile parked outside the mill. Had a representative from Sears come to check on their order? They could have telephoned from Chicago, but perhaps they were getting nervous about fulfilling their catalog orders in time.

Surely Matthias had assured them that they were moving quickly forward with production, though Will didn't know how well it would bode for a customer to watch an entire crew of new workers arrive at the mill.

It was too late to worry about that now, he supposed.

He'd found the coal miners near the base of Sherman Hill, exactly where Sophie said they would be. And they were as anxious for work as she'd thought.

It had been a sloppy hiring process, but he'd taken the men who seemed the most desperate for work. Then he'd paid each man ten dollars in advance pay to give their families before buying them a ticket on the train, eastward bound to Homestead.

He hesitated beside the sideboard, scanning the windows on the second floor of the mill as the coal miners stepped out of the wagon.

Was Sophie working up there this morning? While part of him was anxious to see her again, the honest part of him knew it would be heart wrenching.

When he was in Des Moines, he'd traveled up the hill to find the house Conrad had built for his family. It was a three-story home, painted yellow and white, with a fancy turret enclosed by windows. A front lawn sloped up to the house, and Will imagined it blooming with flowers each spring.

Standing on that hill, he wondered about Sophie's life there. And he realized that no matter how hard he tried, he would never have been able to build Sophie a home as grand as that one. He might have loved her, cared for her needs, but wealth would have eluded them. All his needs were met here in Amana—and he received a few luxuries as well—but he never would have succeeded like Conrad on the outside.

Sophie wouldn't be here in the colonies much longer. This time together, the stolen weeks working together, would end very soon.

He sighed.

No matter how much he pined, it was much too late for him and Sophie. She'd crossed over into a different world now while he had both feet solidly set in the Amanas.

Distraction wasn't an option in the next month. Nor was failure. As much as he'd protested her idea to recruit a second shift of workers, he hoped the plan would work. With almost three-dozen men in these wagons, committed to learning the woolen trade, perhaps they really could finish this order in time.

The front door of the mill opened, and he shaded his eyes, looking for Sophie, but a man rushed out of the mill instead—an outsider he didn't recognize—and marched straight toward the second wagon.

"Henry?" the man asked.

Henry, one of the former managers at Saylorville Coal Company, lowered his head. "Hello, Senator Hoffman."

"Why aren't you at the mine?" The senator demanded before he addressed the entire group. "Why aren't all of you at the mine?"

Will read a copy of *The Cedar Rapids Gazette* almost every week. He knew all about Senator Hoffman and his opposition to the new labor unions for coal mine workers. But why was Senator Hoffman here?

Perhaps he wanted to stop the Amana people from hiring his miners.

Will hurried toward the back of the wagon, holding out his hand to introduce himself to the man, but Senator Hoffman didn't shake it. "Why are you carting my men all the way from Des Moines?"

Will forced a smile. "Actually, we took the train."

"They are supposed to be at the mine."

"Not today—" Will tried to explain. "They've decided to work in our mill for a decent month's wage."

Senator Hoffman looked back at Henry. "How long have you been working in my coal mine?"

"Ten years."

"And the wages are suddenly too low?"

"I have four children, Senator," Henry said, slipping his hands into the pockets of his overalls. "And they all eat."

"They will eat more if you keep working."

"Mr. Keller used to say that we miners have to protest together before we get paid fair wages."

"Blast, Conrad," Mr. Hoffman muttered.

Will heard Sophie slide up beside him. "Conrad didn't do anything wrong."

The three men turned to look at Sophie. Her arms were folded into the sleeves of her coat, and her blue eyes flashed with a determination that Will hadn't seen since they were children.

Will turned back to the senator, wondering how he knew Conrad.

"I didn't mean to dishonor Mr. Keller's memory," the senator said. "But his rhetoric continues to stir up discontent among my miners."

Sophie's eyes flashed again. "Conrad fought for anyone who was being mistreated."

"These men are paid a fair wage for their work, Sophie."

Will cringed when the man addressed Sophie in such a familiar way.

"I'm sorry, we haven't officially met," Will said, not bothering to extend his hand again. "I'm Will Kephart, the manager of this mill and Sophie's friend."

"John Hoffman," the man across from him replied curtly. "I'm a US Senator and Sophie's fiancé."

When Sophie didn't say a word to deny or acknowledge John Hoffman's words, Will curled his fingers into fists, praying for self-control. He could pummel this guy in a second, send him right back to Des Moines, but in Amana, they didn't solve their problems by fighting.

Nor did they allow themselves to daydream about another man's future wife.

Perhaps he should pummel himself for his renewed pining.

John glanced over at her then looked back up at Will. "Are you married?"

Will wanted to tell him it was none of his business, but there was no reason to hide anything from him. "No," he said slowly. "I've never been married."

Out of the corner of his eye, he could see Sophie staring at him, but he didn't dare return her gaze. She might guess at his feelings, at the reason he never married. And by all accounts, the reason he probably never would.

John took a step closer to him. "As Sophie's friend, I hope you will come to our wedding."

"I don't leave Amana very often."

The man's eyes narrowed again. "Except to round up my employees."

"It seems to me that you haven't been taking very good care of those in your employ."

When John lurched forward, Sophie stepped in between them. "Why don't we finish this discussion inside?" she said, her voice soft but strong. Like a spider's silk.

When John moved back, Sophie motioned to the men in the wagons. "Let's get you settled in your rooms before we show you the mill."

As Will watched her walk away, he wondered how she could consider marrying such a proud, spiteful man.

He hadn't wanted her to marry Conrad more than a decade ago, but at least Conrad was a good man. He'd taken care of Sophie and their daughter.

The familiar ache clenched inside him. The frustration at himself for his lack of courage. Perhaps Sophie would have considered returning to the colonies for good, but once again he was too late—Sophie already belonged to someone else.

The new workers trailed Sophie toward the basement of the Saal, which had been converted into a bunkhouse for the thirty men. They would be working nights inside the mill and then sleeping at the bunkhouse during the day. Liesel and the other kitchen bosses had already arranged to provide extra food as long as the men were here. In fact, it seemed the entire community was rallying together to help the mill succeed.

Will nodded toward the front door of the woolen mill. "Do you want to continue our discussion inside?"

John shook his head. "I have nothing left to say to you," he said before he turned, following Sophie as well.

❖   ❖   ❖

Sophie walked briskly down the street by herself. Her heart raced, but it wasn't from the exercise. It was from the startling revelation that Will Kephart had never taken a wife.

Over the past week and a half, she'd assumed that he was married, like most of the men in Amana, but here in the colonies it was often hard to tell who was married to whom since men and women sat separately at both mealtimes and in church. And no one treated either men or women who chose not to marry with scorn.

She'd often wondered if any of the women at her table was Will's wife. Several times she'd almost asked Liesel directly about Will's family, but it didn't seem appropriate to inquire. But then today, when John decided to announce to all the men that he and Sophie were to wed, Will had looked devastated by the news.

Ever since he'd found her in the pine trees, watching their baseball game, he'd been cold to her. Distant. So very different from their youth.

Was it possible that Will once cared about her as more than a friend? Could he still be angry at her for marrying Conrad? In hindsight, perhaps he did love her, but in her youth, she hadn't recognized it.

Long ago, when they were about nineteen, Will had brought a bouquet of freshly picked daisies to the kitchen house. When he handed her the flowers, he'd said that one day he wanted to marry her.

She'd thought he was teasing her, waiting to see how she would react to the joke, so she'd laughed like she always did at his teasing, said she would enjoy the flowers even if he was being insincere.

She had few memories of Will after the flower incident. When Conrad came to visit her a few weeks later, he held no flowers in his hand, but he had a head full of dreams about their future together. At the time, neither of them realized that his dream to become a lawyer would take them away from Amana, but it wouldn't have mattered. She wanted to spend her life with him.

Was it possible that, after all these years, Will might still care for her?

Her heart somersaulted at the thought.

After stepping into the kitchen house, she stood at the doorway to the kitchen and watched her daughter and Cassie laughing as they rolled out dough for a pie. She and Liesel used to laugh like that, before they grew up. Full of joy and life.

Then she heard Liesel laugh nearby and realized that she was the one who had lost the laughter.

"Mama!" Meredith exclaimed, running toward her. Sophie relished her hug. "I thought you were at the mill."

"Something has come up."

Fear darkened Meredith's eyes. "What happened?"

Sophie took her hand, and Meredith clung to it. "Nothing bad, sweetheart," she said, trying to reassure her. "Senator Hoffman has come to visit us."

"That's not good," Meredith said, her hand trembling.

"It will be fine."

Meredith glanced toward the doorway. "Where is he?"

"At the hotel."

Meredith shook away her hand. "He's come to take us back to Des Moines, hasn't he?"

"He would like us to spend Christmas with his family," Sophie tried to explain.

Tears formed in Meredith's eyes, the first of her tears that Sophie had seen since Conrad's funeral.

"I don't want to spend Christmas with his family," Meredith said, stepping back toward the kitchen. "I want to spend Christmas right here."

"You want to work on Christmas Day?"

Meredith nodded slowly.

"What about spending time with Rose and Clara?" John's two older girls.

"They think I'm strange."

"No, they don—"

Meredith stopped her. "You don't know what they say when you're in the next room. How they look at me."

She wanted to tell her daughter that she was imagining things—that the girls would learn to love her like Cassie did—but she'd seen John's daughters snickering together at dinner. She'd thought them silly, but perhaps it was more. Perhaps they were mocking Meredith.

Her stomach rolled.

"You go back to Des Moines," Meredith continued. "Liesel will let me stay with her family for the winter."

Sophie's heart felt as if it might split into two. She couldn't bear to leave her daughter behind while she was in Des Moines. The only reason she'd ever agree to a marriage with John was so Meredith would have a respectable man for a father. A man she could admire.

But looking back on the afternoon at the mill, at the way John treated the miners, she didn't know if she would ever be able to respect him again. How could she ask her daughter to respect a man that she herself no longer admired?

Meredith wiped her sleeve over her eyes. "Cassie needs me to finish the crusts for the pies."

"Of course."

"I want to stay here, Mama," Meredith said. "And I want you to stay here with me."

With those words, Sophie felt the warmth of healing well inside her, as if her heart were being stitched back together. "I won't leave without you," she promised.

Back outside, her warm coat buttoned high on her neck, Sophie leaned back against a fence post. What if she and Meredith stayed here in Amana longer than January? What if they stayed for months? Or even stayed for good?

In order to return, she would have to give up everything Conrad had worked so hard to secure for them. Her fine dresses. The chinaware. Their carriage. What remained of their household staff after she found a smaller house for her and Meredith.

She missed having a sense of purpose in her life, a community who cared for each other, a faith in God more than the reliance on things that money could buy.

Was it too late to gain back all she'd lost when they left?

Here she and Meredith were both beginning to find peace. Perhaps they could savor the gift of joy as well.

If she didn't accept John's proposal, he'd probably find someone else to marry soon. He needed a wife—and she happened to be available—but she wasn't the only widow in Des Moines.

Turning away from the kitchen house, she rushed toward the hotel, up to the third floor where John had secured a room for the night.

When she knocked, he opened the door, a tight smile straining his lips. "I've been anxious to talk with you," he said.

She stood tall beside the doorpost. "I wish you had been kinder to the people at the mill."

"I don't have to be kind," he said flippantly. "No one in Amana votes."

His rudeness made her cringe at first then spurred her on. "Meredith and I aren't going back to Des Moines for Christmas."

The smile faded from his face. "What do you mean?"

"I mean Meredith and I are staying here through January," she said. "And perhaps longer."

He crossed his arms. "You may have grown up in these colonies, Sophie, but you don't belong here anymore."

His words stung her. She'd begun to feel as if she might still belong in Amana even after all of these years. "I don't belong in Des Moines either."

"That's not true," he said. "You belong with me."

A picture flashed into her mind, of her and John twenty years from now, after their three daughters were married. The years when John was no longer the esteemed senator from Iowa, traveling for months at a time. It would be just the two of them, living in his massive stone mansion built and maintained with the money from his coal mine. There would be no home. No peace. No laughter between them. If Meredith didn't feel welcome in their house, she might not even return for a visit in her adult years.

The thought of it was more than she could bear.

"I'm sorry, John," she said. "I can't marry you."

His mouth gaped open at first, and then his lips pressed together in another hard line. When he finally opened them again, his voice was harsh. "You'll regret that decision, Sophie."

"You need a wife who loves you, John. Who will make a home right beside you for the rest of your life. Now that Conrad is gone, my heart doesn't know where it belongs."

He glanced at the clock by the door. "I don't think I will spend the night here after all."

She stepped back into the corridor.

"I'm going to start driving toward Des Moines tonight," he said, turning to close his valise on the bed. "I'll spend the night at an inn along the way."

She nodded as he carried his bag out into the corridor. Then she followed him down the stairs.

Standing at the parlor window below, she watched him drive away in her Christmas present. And she didn't feel a single regret when he was finally gone.

Chapter 8

Sophie wiped the sweat off her forehead and glanced toward the frosty windows of the woolen mill. It might be freezing outside, but the interior of the mill was quite warm this evening. Snow caked the bottom of the glass, and in the lamplight she could see it piling up below, covering the ground in a soft layer of down.

Thankfully, she didn't have far to walk tonight. Matthias had arranged for her and Meredith to live in a room across the street while they worked in Amana, on the floor above the Hirsch family. Meredith had gone to pray with Liesel and Cassie at the Saal while Sophie worked at the mill. Once Will returned from the evening prayer service, she would join Meredith and the Hirsch family in the rooms on the second floor.

The carding machines drummed a new rhythm in the background, rattling the floor as the new workers began the night shift. The Saylorville miners had learned the woolen trade quickly, and they had increased the mill's production by more than a thousand yards a day. The elders were thrilled that they were back on track to fulfill their Sears order along with another ten orders they needed to ship out before the end of January.

"Happy Christmas Eve."

She jumped at the sound of Will's voice, spinning around on her heels. "I thought you were at the Saal."

He cleared his throat, stared down at the toes of his boots. Ever since John had announced that he and Sophie were to marry, Will seemed to be avoiding her. He worked nights, overseeing the new workers, while she assisted Matthias during the day. She'd wanted to tell Will that she wouldn't be marrying John, but there had been no opportune time to deliver this news. And she wasn't certain that Will even cared whether or not she married again.

"The meeting ended early," he said. "I thought you might want an escort home."

She glanced over at the machines. "One of us should stay here."

Will nodded toward the door by the steps. "My grandfather said he would take the night shift."

Turning, she watched Matthias emerge through the doorway. "Go on," he said, shooing them. "Celebrate for a few hours tonight."

"I'm only going to walk her home," Will replied.

"Jacob and Liesel have invited you over for Christmas Eve," Matthias said as he sat down on a chair. "You've both done a fine job with the mill. Go enjoy your friends."

Downstairs, Will helped Sophie into her coat, and she wrapped her new blue scarf, made from Amana's wool, around her neck. The winter night was cold, and yet beside Will she felt strangely warm. Even though things were awkward between them, she hoped he would stay tonight and celebrate with the Hirsch family.

As they started their walk across the street, the heel of her boot slipped on the ice, and she almost fell. Will reached out, catching her before she landed in the snow.

"Are you all right?" he asked, helping to steady her.

"I'm fine," she said, though all her limbs were shaking.

He gently tucked her hand in the crook of his arm, and they proceeded again toward the warm lights in the house ahead.

"What do you usually do on Christmas Eve?" she asked, trying to calm the tremor that had traveled to her voice. "When you're not at the mill—"

"I attend the service in West Amana with my parents and sister's family," he said. "Then I help fill the children's shoes with gifts from *Sankt Nikolaus.*"

"Meredith says she has outgrown visits from Saint Nicholas."

He laughed. "I don't think anyone's ever too old for his gifts."

She joined in his laughter, like they were children again. Snow fell on her scarf, clotted in her hair, and she wondered at the beauty and simplicity of this Christmas Eve with Will at her side.

If only they could don ice skates and head out to Lily Pond, skate alongside each other instead of slowly slipping across this street. If only they could steal away for an hour or two by themselves, reminiscing perhaps about the days gone by.

Will opened the heavy front door, and they entered the large house. A small choir of voices, singing "*Stille Nacht, Heilige Nacht,*" drifted down the staircase. Together she and Will climbed the gas-lit steps, but instead of knocking on the Hirsch's door, Will lingered in the corridor on the second floor.

"Before we go inside," he started. "I wanted to speak with you."

She smiled. "I was hoping to talk to you, too."

He leaned back against the whitewashed wall. "A long time ago, I asked you to marry me," he said quietly. "Instead of answering, you laughed."

She swallowed hard, trying to fight back the butterflies winging their way around her stomach. "I thought you were teasing me."

"I wasn't."

She rubbed her hands together, wishing for a moment that she could slip back fifteen years and be honest with him. Tell him that he was the best of friends but that her heart belonged to Conrad. Tell him that he would find an amazing woman who would laugh with him one day—when he was trying to be funny.

"I'm so sorry, Will."

He stepped closer to her. "I was young and stupid," he said. "When I realized that I loved you as much more than a friend, that I didn't think I'd ever be able to live without you, I had to speak with you right away. But I should have asked you properly."

"You've done quite well without me."

He didn't seem to hear her. "I'm standing at a crossroads again, Sophie, but this time, I don't want to walk away."

Her voice softened. "Walk away from what?"

"Don't marry John Hoffman," he said, pleading with her now. "Whether or not you and I have a future together, I don't want you to ruin your life committed to a man like him."

"Oh Will," she said, feeling light-headed in his shadow. Much had changed since his first raw attempt at a proposal. "I'm not going to marry John."

He leaned back against the wall again. "What?"

"I turned down his proposal."

Will stared at her for a moment, seemingly stunned by her words. Then he took another step forward. "Sophie," he said, his voice low as he reached for her hand.

Before he continued, the door beside them opened suddenly, and she moved away from him. Peter—Jacob and Liesel's twelve-year-old son—glanced back and forth between them before shouting over his shoulder. "They're here."

Liesel bounded out into the corridor. "I'm so glad you've arrived," she said, clasping her hands in front of her chest. "I was getting worried."

Sophie glanced back at Will, and he shrugged his shoulders. But he was smiling again at her, and she reveled in it.

Inside the family room, the coffee table was filled with plates of Christmas cookies baked earlier this month at the kitchen house—peppernut, cinnamon, black walnut, molded *springerli*, and honey cookies shaped as bells, trees, and Christmas wreaths. Beside the table was a traditional white wooden pyramid that stood higher than Sophie's waist. The pyramid was layered with round tiers, each one topped with wooden or glass figures of shepherds, sheep, and magi. When Jacob lit the candles, the tiers slowly began to rotate, colorful lights flickering across the ceiling and wall.

Meredith and Cassie were playing a board game on the braided rug that covered the wooden floor. Peter was arranging the shoes in front of the coal stove for Saint Nicholas's gifts while Jacob and Liesel sat on their black sofa, laughing with each other.

"It's magical," Sophie whispered to Will.

"Indeed."

Inside her raged a new longing. Instead of just standing near her, she wished Will would wrap his arms around her, hold her tight. He knew her so well, both the good and the bad, and yet he still seemed to love her. No pretense. No facade.

Sophie looked up at Will. "Why didn't you ever leave the colonies?"

"Because everything I ever wanted and needed was right here," he said, his eyes on her face. "Until now."

The butterfly wings fluttered again. "I don't know what to say, Will."

"Promise me something," he whispered.

She glanced nervously at everyone across the room, but no one seemed to be paying attention to them. "What is it?"

"Promise me that you won't accept another man's proposal until I'm able to say what's on my mind." His gaze swept the room. "Without an audience."

She hesitated only a moment before smiling. "I promise."

Meredith hopped up from the floor, moving toward them. Instead of talking to Sophie though, she spoke to Will. "Will you play a game with us?"

Will winked at Sophie before swiping a cookie off the table. Then he sat down on the rug.

A year ago, she never would have imagined that she would be spending Christmas Eve back in Amana, celebrating the birth of their Savior with her dear friends, but here she was. Meredith was happy, and now it seemed that Will might still want a future alongside her.

The butterflies stopped moving as she sat between Will and Meredith.

For the first time in a long time, her heart felt content.

Chapter 9

Hoarfrost clung to pinecones and branches as Will steered the horse-drawn sleigh through the snowy forest. The frost glistened in the sunlight, and Sophie felt as if they were gliding through the grand halls of a crystal palace. Everything sparkled around them—the snow, the trees, the pond emerging in front of them.

"It's beautiful," she said.

He pulled on the reins, and the horses stopped near the edge of Lily Pond.

It was January 16th. The train from Homestead left yesterday morning filled with one hundred thousand yards of wool, headed straight for the Sears, Roebuck & Co. warehouse in Chicago. Some of their miners had returned to Des Moines on the westward-bound train while others had called for their families to join them in Amana while they finished fulfilling the other orders.

She glanced across the frozen pond. "What are we doing here?"

"I wanted to give you a belated Christmas present," he said, smiling. "From Saint Nicholas."

She pressed her gloved hands together. "What is it?"

Will reached under a blanket in the backseat and pulled out a pair of brown ice skates. "Oh—" She gasped. She'd left her pair behind when she moved from Amana.

"Allow me." As she sat in the sled, he stood in front of her and unlaced her boots. Then he laced up the new skates.

It was just like old times.

"They're a perfect fit," she said. So different from the gift of a Stanley Steamer—and so much better. It was exactly what she wanted.

After he put on his skates, he held out his hand. "Do you remember how to ice-skate?"

"I'm afraid I don't know."

"I'll help you," he said.

They moved slowly at first around the edge of the pond, her shaky legs trying to recall the art of balance. Then they flowed into a gentle rhythm as they glided around the pond, under a sky that glittered blue.

She imagined herself at one of the balls in Des Moines, dressed in an exquisite gown, the shimmering color of frost. But this time she was happy, her heart overflowing with joy. This time Will was making her smile.

"I have another gift," he said, steering her back toward the sleigh.

As she waited, he drew out a dried bouquet made of cattails and milkweed, bound together with red and white ribbons. "I wish it was daisies," he said with a lopsided grin.

She clutched the winter bouquet to her chest. "It's perfect, Will."

His eyes met her gaze, steady and strong. "There are some things I would never tease about," he said.

She trembled, the familiar wings fluttering again inside her.

"One of those is my love for you, Sophie," he said. "I've tried and tried over the years to move on, but my heart won't let me. I want to keep loving you, for the rest of our lives."

Her mind spun again, as it had since he'd asked her on Christmas Eve to wait, trying to figure out how she could marry Will when they both lived in such different worlds.

For a moment, she imagined Will returning to Des Moines with her and Meredith, living in their house on Sherman Hill. "Would you ever leave Amana?" she asked.

He reached for her hand. "I don't want the treasures of this world, Sophie," he said. "All I want is the treasure of your heart."

With his words, the butterflies in her stomach calmed, the ice coated around her heart thawing. "I have to talk to Meredith."

When his face flushed, she pulled her hand away from him and placed it on her hip, feigning irritation. "You already talked to her?"

"I knew you'd want her blessing."

Her head tilted. "And?"

"She said I better hurry before either of us changed our minds."

Laughter bubbled up from deep inside her, spilling out on this winter day. She and Meredith both loved being in Amana. And they both loved being with Will.

Was it possible that they could really stay here for good?

His fingers entangled hers again, and then he gently took off her glove, pulled her hand to his lips. The tenderness from his kiss warmed her entire body.

"What will the elders say?" she asked.

"They will welcome you back—if you really want to come home."

"Home," she said, repeating his word. "It's exactly what I want."

"Will you marry me, Sophie?" he asked, kneeling down in the snow.

This time she didn't laugh. This time she told him that she wanted nothing more than to become his wife.

Amana Honey Cookies

4 cups honey
2⅓ cups brown sugar
½ teaspoon cinnamon
3 teaspoons baking soda
¼ cup whiskey
4 eggs
9½ cups unbleached flour
Vanilla frosting (optional)

Warm honey on stove top. Stir in brown sugar. When lukewarm, add cinnamon. Dissolve baking soda in whiskey. Combine honey and baking soda mixtures in a large bowl. Stir in eggs and flour. Cover and chill overnight.

Preheat oven to 325 degrees. Knead dough until it is springy. Roll dough into 1- to 2-inch thick ropes. Cut ropes into approximately 2-inch long pieces and place on greased baking sheet. Bake for 10 minutes until cookies are golden brown. After they cool, ice with frosting if desired. Makes about 11 dozen cookies.

Note: With fifty-five kitchen houses in the Amana Colonies, there are many different versions of this cookie recipe. This recipe was based on one featured in Emilie Hoppe's *Seasons of Plenty* (Iowa City: University of Iowa Press, 1998).

Author's Note

This novella is the continuation of a story started in *Love Finds You in Amana, Iowa* and *Love Finds You in Homestead, Iowa.*

The Amana Colonies are a cluster of seven quaint villages tucked into Iowa's beautiful rolling hills. For eighty years, the Amana Society provided food, housing, medical care, and schooling for each member and their children. While the Amana people no longer live and work in a communal society, they share a profound spiritual heritage that continues today as they worship and work together.

Thank you for joining me on this journey. For more information about my Amana novels and other books, please visit my website at www.melaniedobson.com.

Three-time Carol Award winner and bestselling author of fifteen novels, **Melanie Dobson** is the former corporate publicity manager at Focus on the Family and owner of Dobson Media Group. Because of her husband's work in the film industry, their family has lived in multiple states as well as Germany, but the Dobson family is settled for now in a small town near Portland, Oregon. Melanie loves connecting with readers via her website at www.melaniedobson.com.

Love Is Forever

by Jerry Eicher

Chapter 1

September 7, 1941

Mattie Beiler stole a quick glance out of the kitchen window of her parent's old Lancaster County farmhouse. The trees in the yard were still green. Their fall rush of yellow and gold had yet to come, but before too many weeks passed, all of Lancaster County would be one glorious display of the Lord's handiwork. A smile crept across Mattie's face. Nature was full of the Lord's beauty as was her heart. For a long time the Lord had blessed her with a *wunderbaar* love for a young man.

Mattie's smile dimmed at the thought—a long time. *Jah*, Mervin Yoder wasn't exactly young anymore, and neither was she. They should have been wed last year, but she was not going to think about that at the moment. This year's wedding season approached, and Mervin would wed her in November. He would have to. He had purchased a farm last month, and they could discuss their plans in detail after supper tonight.

Mattie hadn't told Mervin this when she gave him the invitation, "Just a special evening for the two of us."

Mervin hadn't hesitated long, so surely his mind was made up about their fall wedding and his doubts banished forever. Hadn't the Lord led them this far? Jah, He had. Right through last year when Mervin postponed their wedding. She had to believe now.

Mervin's buggy would appear soon. He'd drive over from his parents' place farther west toward Lancaster. His face would be aglow with the prospect of the evening spent with her. She would also let her joy show, even if the future was anything but certain.

"Be with us, Lord." Mattie breathed the quick prayer as she turned back to the stove.

She couldn't blame Mervin exactly. There were reasons. Mervin hesitated this year because of what might happen to the community's young men when the horrible *English* war in Europe came to America. *Daed* had even begun to buy a newspaper when he came through town to keep up on the news.

"You must trust the Lord, Lamar," *Mamm* chided him often, but Daed still brought the paper home and pored over the pages while he sat in his rocker in the evenings.

From the lines of concern written on his face, the news was not *gut*. Daed made sure he took the papers with him into the bedroom and shoved them under the bed, but Mattie cleaned the house on Saturdays and scanned the paragraphs while Mamm was occupied elsewhere in the house. The names of the cities and political parties meant little to her, but she could understand enough to know that this was war, an awful war. All of the news seemed related to this madman Hitler, who had stormed over Europe with his armies and tanks. The community believed in peace, and they trusted the Lord. None of them could ever take up arms in the defense of anything. So if the United States joined the war and the community's young men were called to serve in the army, they would refuse. This would not sit well with the government authorities or with their English neighbors.

Already Mrs. Falks, who lived a mile down the road and stopped in for vegetables from the Beilers' garden, had begun to speak of what might lie ahead. "If it comes to war," Mrs. Falks had said, "my grandson Eugene will be signing up to fight. That Hitler's doing awful things over there, and someone must stop him. Right now our government is of another mind, but madmen can't be ignored."

Mrs. Falks had jerked her head for emphasis. Her look of fierceness lingered even after she left with her vegetables. Likely the old woman knew that none of the community's young men would fight and wanted to make clear where she stood on the matter. Dark times lay ahead, indeed.

But Mervin was on the way. And Mervin loved her, and Mattie loved him. They would enjoy Sunday supper with Daed and Mamm tonight. The food wasn't plentiful in these difficult economic times, but she had an offering of potatoes and gravy with corn and beans simmering on the stove.

Money wasn't plentiful in the Beilers' household or, for that matter, in any of the community's homes. The Depression had taken its toll, as it had on their English neighbors. Mamm shopped in Lancaster or Guys Mills for what they didn't have but needed. The rest they grew on the farm. Thankfully, no one had gone hungry.

And love continued even with all the troubles in the world.

"Maybe the next wedding season we can marry," Mervin had told her after his purchase of a farm had fallen through last year.

They had never set the date exactly. Mervin always avoided the subject, but their love shouldn't have had to wait this long. She should have been Mervin's *frau* for many months now. If the Lord had so willed, she could have born Mervin a little one late this summer. Instead, she held empty arms and life moved on with only hope in her heart.

Mattie lifted the lid on the gravy and took a long breath. Perfect, but she had best taste the final product. Mamm always warned, "Better safe than sorry." With the spoon, Mattie extracted a sample and blew vigorously. She tasted it, and the gravy melted on her tongue. Perfect! The scarce salt had been enough, and Mervin was worth every expense.

"About right?" Mamm's voice teased from the kitchen doorway.

Mattie smiled. "It's about as right as right can be—not unlike Mervin himself."

"So he's coming tonight?"

"Of course! It's time we discuss our wedding plans."

Mamm busied herself with setting the table.

Mattie turned to face her. "You don't object, do you? I. . .Mamm, we can't wait again. I could have *kinner* by now—Mervin's and mine. This is not right that we're still unwed."

"Calm yourself," Mamm told her. "The years roll past soon enough, and this trouble will be over before long."

"I—I—we—" Mattie sputtered. The heat from the stove flamed her face. "Surely you're not suggesting that—"

"I'm not saying anything," Mamm interrupted, "because I don't know anything. No one does. That's the worst of it. Though Deacon Joe did ask Daed at the last Sunday services how things were going between you and Mervin. I guess the ministry is concerned with our young couples and the choices they make in these difficult times."

"He knows how things are going!" Mattie exploded. "Mervin bought a farm last month, and Deacon Joe knows this. Surely he has no objection to our marriage this wedding season."

"Jah, the deacon knows." Mamm tried to calm her. "And the purchase of the farm was a wise choice, but we must take council easily, Mattie. Remember that. It's the way of the community."

"And so is love and marriage and kinner!" The words burst out.

"Mervin's here," Mamm said. "Control yourself, and don't sound like that in front of Mervin. He might think he's getting a forward woman for a frau."

"Mervin loves me, and I love him," Mattie muttered. "We're getting married this fall."

Mamm gave Mattie a sharp look and headed for the front door.

"Gut evening, Mervin," Mamm's voice sang.

Mattie fanned herself with one hand while she transferred the mashed potatoes to the table with the other. Mamm should have taken over the supper preparation, and she should have gone to welcome Mervin, but Mamm still schemed how best she could impress her youngest daughter's suitor. In Mamm's opinion, a woman busy in the kitchen ought to warm any man's heart, and to Mamm's credit her techniques had worked well for eight daughters—and the ninth one would have been married last wedding season if things had gone as planned.

Mattie had things under control, ever since she had noticed the handsome young Mervin Yoder many years ago. At first Mervin had ignored her and pretended he didn't have similar feelings. But eventually, Mervin had taken her home from the Sunday evening hymn singing and asked her, out of all the girls in Lancaster County, if she would be his future frau. So why shouldn't things work out?

Mattie pasted on her brightest smile as Mamm appeared in the kitchen doorway with Mervin in tow.

He held his hat in his hand and smiled at Mattie. "I didn't see your daed in the barn," he said, "so I came on in."

"That's perfectly all right," Mamm gushed. "Lamar is still in the back fields with the team. I'll ring the supper bell, and he'll be up in a jiffy." Mamm hurried toward the washroom door and cast a quick glance over her shoulder at Mattie. At least Mamm approved of her love—delayed love, jah, but still love.

Mattie gave Mervin another smile. "Sit yourself. I almost have things ready."

"At the table?" Mervin's hat went around in circles in his hand.

"I'm sorry. I'm not minding my manners." Mattie made a wry face. "I'm almost done with the food. Throw your hat behind the stove and you can wash up out there." She motioned with her chin toward the washroom door, where the loud clanging of the bell sounded.

Mervin gave his hat a whirl, and it landed perfectly in the corner of the wall away from the worst heat of the stove. Mattie gave him an appreciative look, and Mervin winked.

"You don't have to impress me," she told him. "You already have that deal sealed."

Mervin came close enough to lay his hand on her arm.

"Not now," Mattie whispered. "I'm busy, and Mamm might come back in."

"The bell's still clanging." Mervin stated the obvious.

"Okay, a quick kiss, then." Mattie set the hot bowl of corn back on the stove. The heat flamed into her face as she grabbed his shoulders and pulled him close.

"I thought you said. . ." Mervin drew back a few inches.

"Forget that." She lifted her face to his again.

Mervin gently broke away and whispered, "The bell has stopped."

Mattie grabbed the handle of the bowl even as the washroom doorknob rattled. Mamm glanced at both of them when she entered but said nothing. Mamm had to notice Mervin's triumphant look.

"Got to go wash up," Mervin said and disappeared.

"Were you. . ." Mamm studied Mattie's face. "Right here in the kitchen. Well, I guess you claim you are getting married this wedding season."

"Thank you." Mattie said and transferred the bowl of corn. "That's much better."

Mamm muttered something that Mattie couldn't hear and seated herself at the table to wait for Daed's arrival. The water splashed in the washroom bowl on the other side of the wall. Mamm smiled up at Mervin when he reappeared, his face red from his scrubbing.

"You can sit," Mattie told him again.

He complied with a chuckle. "I guess I'm clean enough now."

"You're perfect," Mattie told him, and Mervin glowed.

"Ahem!" Mamm cleared her throat. "How's the farm work going, Mervin?"

Mervin turned reluctantly in Mamm's direction. "I got most of the fall plowing done this week and bought another Belgian at the auction that looks. . ."

Their voices drifted into Mattie's subconscious, while Mervin's face lingered in front of her. He hadn't shaved this week yet. Most of their kisses were shared on Sunday evenings when Mervin had cleaned up the day before. The bristles had added to his manliness tonight. There was no question about that. Once Mervin said the wedding vows with her, he'd begin to grow his beard, which would be even—

Mattie focused and gave Mamm and Mervin a quick glance. Mervin was busy answering another of Mamm's questions about his farm. She hadn't heard the question, but she didn't need to. The point was that Mervin had completed the purchase of the farm and should have no further excuses not to marry her this fall. There was the English war, of course, but that was so uncertain. She had lived in the land of questions long enough. What she wanted was a husband of her own, in her own house, all week, all day, and all the time—a man who lived with her, who saw her in everyday dresses, and who loved her with all of his heart. Dating Mervin on the weekends was wunderbaar, but she was ready to enjoy life with Mervin as his frau.

The outside washroom door rattled, and the water splashed again. Daed appeared with water droplets on his beard and a big grin on his face. "Well, if it isn't Mervin himself come for supper. I guess we'll get something to eat tonight."

They all laughed as Daed seated himself. Mattie took the chair beside Mervin.

"Let us pray and give thanks," Daed said, and they bowed their heads.

Mattie stole a look at Mervin's face while Daed led out in prayer. He noticed and smiled at her. They were awful, Mattie told herself. They shouldn't sneak glances at each other through prayer time as if they were teenagers, but they couldn't help themselves. If the Lord didn't allow her to marry Mervin this wedding season, she was going to explode. Her heart would break. There was no question about that.

But Mervin was here tonight, and there was food on the table, which was more than some people in the country could say. Maybe if she gave thanks more often for what she did have, the Lord would give her what she didn't have.

"Amen." Daed finished the prayer, and Mamm hurried to pass the first bowl of food.

"Corn and beans and potatoes and gravy," Mervin intoned. "This is a feast."

"Like I said." Daed grinned. "When you come, we finally get to eat."

"Mattie made all of this herself," Mamm added, as if that needed to be said. Mervin knew that she could cook.

Mervin grinned. "I'll be getting a gut frau, a really gut one. I know that."

"Oh, that's sweet." Mattie cooed. She could have kissed him again, right at the kitchen table, but that would not have been decent.

"This is gut food," Daed said, and the moment passed. "We can be very thankful."

"Jah, I know," Mattie agreed. "I have so much I can be thankful for."

The light conversation continued until supper was completed and another prayer of thanks offered.

"You want to help with the dishes?" Mattie teased.

Mervin shook his head. "I think I'd best be going. But thanks so much for the supper. I still have some chores at home that must be done tonight."

"Oh." She let her face fall and followed him to the front door. "I wanted to speak with you about—"

He touched her cheek with his hand and smiled. "I love you, dear. We can talk some other time. Don't you think?"

"Can we—"

Mervin gave her a gentle smile before she got any further. "Maybe later, Mattie. I need to get back home. I do have chores to finish, and I have a full day's work in the fields tomorrow. But thanks again for supper." Then he was gone.

"Don't fall too deep in the dumps," Mamm warned when Mattie came back to the kitchen. "Mervin knows what he's doing."

Mattie pressed her lips together and said nothing. Mervin knew how to get out of conversations about their wedding plans. That much was clear.

Chapter 2

On Saturday morning, almost three weeks later, Mattie drove Bell, the Beilers' driving horse, east toward Mervin's small farm a mile outside of Whitehorse. Tucked under the buggy seat was the latest copy of the English newspaper that Daed had brought home last night. Daed had hidden the paper under his bed, as usual, but she had found it this morning. She had scanned the pages in the bedroom, but she would read the words further in a moment.

"The war is close," Mervin had claimed on Sunday evening when she tried to bring their wedding plans up again.

Mervin had clamped his mouth shut and refused to give her details. He had kept her occupied with light chatter and sweet smiles for the rest of the evening. There was, jah, a kiss at their parting, but what gut were kisses without a wedding in their future? All she had managed to accomplish was to secure plans for a visit to his farm today. That Mervin hadn't objected to.

Well, she would read for herself and talk to Mervin afterward. He couldn't ignore her if she had firsthand information from the English newspaper. Perhaps even the news that things were not as bad as everyone thought. She could intelligently converse with him if she had facts in hand. Mervin had his doubts, but there were bigger reasons that canceled those.

Wasn't love worth sacrifices, even a thousand sacrifices? Certainly love was greater than fear and the decision to marry shouldn't be based on what the English world did. She could tell Mervin those reasons before she read the newspaper, and had tried to, but he wouldn't listen. Facts were better. A man thought differently from a woman. If only she could show him that all of this was likely the English hyping the news of the war.

"Whoa," Mattie called out to Bell. She pulled into a small roadside stand and parked at the far end. No one would disturb her here with the constant traffic in and out. She could read in peace.

Mattie pulled the newspaper out from under the buggy seat and unfolded the pages. The front page headline caught her attention: HITLER CONSOLIDATES HIS HOLD ON EUROPE.

Mattie read on:

Resistance has faded in the occupied countries held under Germany's boot. Paris is silent this fall, spared from destruction. Its usual exuberant spirit in the face of the approaching winter is not on display. When snow falls on the Eiffel Tower, marching beneath will be the boot prints of Hitler's storm troopers. Southern France has been declared a free zone. Little, though, is free in Hitler's world. He is a barbarian, a man whose word cannot be trusted. The whole world knows this well by now. Hitler knows one language, that of brute strength. England is still under siege and barely survives after Hitler's brutal bombing campaign last year. Few dare hope they will ever find the strength to crush this tyrant. The new year will bring worse, many fear, as the armies settle in for winter. President Roosevelt speaks of peace and not of war. He is caught between a populace that hates the thought of another European entanglement and the American spirit that has no sympathy for dictators and thugs installed at the head of political parties.

Mattie's gaze moved on, and the pages rustled. This was not helpful. Another article caught her attention: "What Would Peace Look Like?" She read quickly:

It is the business of any editorial page to have an opinion. With this in mind, we have searched our hearts on the subject of peace in Europe. What would peace look like? Can subjection to a foreign power be considered peace? Can Europe make peace with Hitler and, God forbid, his eventual replacement years from now? Do we as Americans have a right to spell out this peace? Can we deny Europe their choice if they desire to live with the present status quo? Either way, it seems to us that answer will fall to America.

If we do nothing, Europe will not have the strength to throw off the German yoke. To think that England can achieve such power in this generation is a fantasy, and France will not even try. Remember that the Great War was not won with British and French troops. It took America's might. Of course, Russia is the wild card in this equation, brought into play with Hitler's ill-conceived invasion of that country. At present, President Roosevelt seems to think the answer lies in that direction.

We do not know if the president is right or not, and no one may know, but the president believes in the cause sufficiently to commit the materials of war. Many are asking the question: Is the evidential, and distant, and perhaps impossible victory over Germany worth the long, drawn-out struggle? If failure remains a real possibility, would not the best choice be an allocation of what is now expended in war on efforts toward peace?

Would the world not be better served with peace than war? The question turns to America for an answer. Are we up to the task? Many, including this editorial board, wonder whether we are. But the answer doesn't matter if destiny has placed the task in our hands. We pray that God would give us the wisdom to know what is right and the strength to execute the choice we make. Neither will be easy. The cost of peace is high, whether we fight or seek to live with a German-occupied Europe.

◆ ◆ ◆

Mattie sighed and stuffed the newspaper back under the buggy seat. There were no answers here, only more questions. She had best not show any of this to Mervin.

"Get up," Mattie called to Bell, and the buggy moved onto Route 340 again.

Mattie jiggled the reins and Bell increased her speed. She had found no answers in the newspaper, but her desire to see Mervin on his farm was still there. She would have to resort to the answers she already knew. Wasn't love its own answer? She would try to persuade Mervin. He would have to listen to her. She would make him listen.

Mattie pulled back on the reins when Mervin's farm came into view. The small white house was set back off the road a few hundred feet, with an equally small barn farther back. The sixty or so acres didn't constitute a large farm, but it was enough to begin farming and enough to need a frau to tend the house. That was another argument she could use. Surely Mervin didn't want to live here alone for another year.

But she could hear Mervin say it now, "If the English war brings about America's involvement, I won't be here next year."

A pang ran through Mattie as she brought Bell to a stop by the hitching rail. If war came, Mervin would have to respond to the government's call and serve somewhere. He wouldn't fight, but he would have to put in his time. There was no choice in that matter.

She pasted on a smile when Mervin appeared in the barn door.

"Gut morning," she called to him.

"Gut morning," he responded. "So you did come?"

"Of course," Mattie scolded. "I had to see you, and—"

Mervin wrapped Mattie in his arms for a quick hug then held her at arm's length. "How gut to see your face, dear." He gave Mattie a quick peck on the cheek.

She wanted more, but now was not the time.

"You keep everything so clean around the place," she told him.

Mervin chuckled. "What did you expect? A trashy bachelor? You know that means a trashy husband."

"You'd never be trashy," she told him. "You're too sweet for that."

Mervin laughed. "I see I've pulled the wool over your eyes quite easily."

Mattie faked a glare. "Tie up Bell, and I'm going to check the house. That will tell me the truth."

Mervin continued his chuckling while he tied Bell to the hitching rail. "Come," he said. He took Mattie's hand and led the way toward the house. He opened the front door and waved his hand inward. "Welcome to my bachelor quarters, and see for yourself."

She peered inside. "This looks gut, but the bachelor bit isn't my fault, you know. I would have—"

Mervin silenced her with a touch on her lips. "Come. Shall we sit on the front porch, or do you want to see the kitchen yet?"

She tilted her head and smiled up at him. "I know you're a gut housekeeper, but let's be serious, Mervin. You've been avoiding the subject, and we have to discuss our wedding plans. November is coming quickly, and Mamm and I. . ."

He sighed. "Let's sit, then. I don't have a swing yet, but I have chairs in the basement. Wait here and I'll get some."

Mattie nodded, and Mervin hurried down the porch steps and over to the outside basement entrance. He came back quickly with a wooden chair in each arm. They didn't look too comfortable, but she didn't need comfort at the moment. A fixed wedding date would be comfort enough.

"There," he said and helped her sit. "Comfortable as can be!"

She met his gaze and pled, "We can't go on like this, Mervin. We must be wed this fall. We—"

"Jah," he interrupted. "I feel the same way. You should have been my frau for almost a year now, but the Lord willed it otherwise. All the advice we got back then pointed—"

Mattie stopped him. "I know the advice. But surely you're not having doubts again. It's almost the first week in October, and we don't have much time."

His smile was thin. "I would want nothing more than to have you as my frau this wedding season, Mattie. You don't know how I long for that hour. The house is empty here all by myself." Mervin glanced over his shoulder at the living room window. "Your presence in our home would be heaven on earth. Maybe that's why the Lord keeps putting things in our path."

"But we love each other!" she scolded. "You know that, Mervin. How could marriage be wrong? It's time. . ." Mattie looked away. "Marry me this fall, Mervin. I don't know if my heart can go on living if I have to wait another year."

His gaze was fixed on the horizon.

"Mervin," she finally said.

His face was grim. "Surely you know what the problem is, Mattie. We are not talking about waiting another year. If America becomes involved in this war, the struggle will be long and difficult. I will be drafted and will have to serve somewhere as a conscientious objector. None of us will be home until peace returns. Not those who fight. Not those who work for peace. Everyone will have to stay at their posts until the war ends. I'm not complaining, Mattie. I'm speaking the truth. We should be willing to sacrifice for our faith. Our witness for the Lord should cost us what is precious. Many of our English neighbors will give their lives for what they believe. They—"

"Years!" Mattie cut in. "Is that what you said?"

"Jah." Mervin didn't look at her.

"This cannot be," she wailed. "Marry me tomorrow, Mervin. If this must happen, give me a few months as your frau. I could by then be carrying your—" She stopped. What plain speaking this trouble had driven them to.

Thankfully, Mervin didn't look strangely at her. His face had fallen into sadness. "Didn't you hear what I said, Mattie? The war may come, and your reasons don't help. A child is yet another point why we shouldn't wed. I cannot leave you behind with kinner while I am gone for many years. Who would support you? There will be enough of those situations already with the young couples who married last year. We need not add to the burden the community must carry. That is tempting the Lord."

"Tempting the Lord!" Mattie cried. "Forbidding our marriage is tempting the Lord. That's the truth. Leaving me with kinner on my hands is the exact problem our faith believes the Lord can handle. I will have a small farm here. I can grow a garden, perhaps a big one. We will have potatoes and carrots and vegetables. Daed will give me seeds if things come to that. We will not starve, Mervin."

Sadness still filled his face. "You will not have the farm, Mattie. My daed will have to take care of things, and there will be hardly enough money to pay for his time and the mortgage. He will have to rent out the place. Our marriage cannot be, Mattie. That's why I have been avoiding the subject. I'm sorry."

"But you must wed me, Mervin!" The wail hung in the air.

This was what she was down to, the cry of her heart.

"I love you, Mattie." Mervin reached for her hand. "Our love will still be alive when I return."

"Maybe there will be no war," Mattie whispered. She had to control herself. "I read the newspaper this morning, and—"

"Maybe," Mervin allowed. "But let us speak no more about this today. I have work on the farm, and I'm sure you have work at home."

Mattie stood, but her legs trembled. Once more her wedding had been postponed, and she was helpless to change the situation.

Chapter 3

Early Wednesday morning, Mervin spread the last of the straw over the floor of the horse stall. A dozen feet away, his driving horse, Windy, neighed at him from the open barn door.

"Jah, it's about done," Mervin told him. "But you should stay outside for a while yet."

Windy shook his head as if he understood. Mervin set his fork against the wall and walked over to stroke Windy's neck. The horse neighed again and pranced into the barnyard to join the team of Belgians. Mervin watched the three horses nuzzle each other before they took halfhearted steps toward the gate and the pasture beyond. The horses were lonesome, Mervin told himself. But how could that be? Three horses could keep each other company just fine. He was the lonely one. In hindsight, his decision to move onto the farm by himself had not been a gut idea. He should live with his parents and drive over each day to tend the place. But that plan would have been impractical. They all knew that.

"You can't farm right if you're not there," Daed had told him.

Which begged the question, how would Daed farm his acres once he left when the war broke out? Maybe he shouldn't have purchased the place with the government's draft hanging over all of their heads.

Mervin sighed and retreated into the barn. The truth was he couldn't resist the purchase of the farm—not after his inability to buy a place last year. What a disaster that had been. His wedding with Mattie had been planned and the date set. He had a farm to the west of the Yoders' home place picked out and the contract at the lawyer's office. That was when things had begun to go wrong. He needed a down payment, the last of which was to come from his share of the crops Daed gave him for his work on the home place. Then the summer rains had set in and continued for days, and after that for weeks. Fields had flooded, and the cornstalks began to tilt in the wet ground. The fall harvest had been tackled with wagons that sank deep in the mud. Before they were finished, an early October snowstorm blanketed Maryland and Delaware and reached well into Lancaster County. The devastated countryside appeared smitten by the Lord's hand. There had been a much-reduced harvest, and Daed had barely survived the year. They made silage out of the damaged crops once the ground had frozen, which was gut cow feed, but he had needed the cash.

On the Saturday after he called off the purchase of the farm, he had driven Windy over to Mattie's home. Mattie came running out to meet him with a bright smile on her face. "Couldn't help coming over to see me this morning," Mattie had teased.

He had cleared his throat and leaned out of the buggy door.

"What's wrong, Mervin?" Her joy had faded.

"The farm," he had told her. "I couldn't buy it. There's not the money, but maybe next year."

"Next year!" She had stared. "But the wedding?"

"Mattie, please." He had climbed down from the buggy to take her in his arms.

"You're calling off the wedding?" Her shoulders had shaken for a long time.

He didn't let go until she quieted down, but she kept her eyes downcast. "Perhaps I'd best go in the house, then."

"Mattie, please." He had begged again.

"It's not decent to cry too much on your boyfriend's shoulders"—she gave him a quick glance—"and since you're not going to be my husband anytime soon."

"It's not my fault that we can't wed, Mattie. The country is in a depression, things are a mess, and Europe's threatening war."

"You love me, don't you?" The words were more accusation than question.

Of course he loved her. Did Mattie think the decision had been easy for him? Mervin leaned against the stall wall and hung his head.

Nearly a year had passed since then, a year in which he could have had his own farm and a frau in the house. Did Mattie think he didn't want that? Of course he did, although the way she had questioned him a week and a half ago made him wonder if she didn't really understand how committed he was to marrying her. That was why he had pressed ahead and purchased the farm this year, but now his nerve had failed him.

Mattie wanted a wedding date set, and they should have one by now. But the purchase of the farm had taken all the resolve he could muster. He had taken a risk that involved only money, not lives. With a wedding, their hearts would be at stake. He had spoken the truth to Mattie. If they wed, Mattie could be left to face the birth of their child alone. That was not right, even if he knew that things should not be easy for conscientious objectors. His child must not grow up without his daed. He couldn't live with that. Not when he knew they could have waited.

On the other hand, this war might never involve the United States. Doubtless this was why many of the dating couples moved on with their wedding plans.

"We are taking the plunge, and so should you," Willis Stoll had told him at the last Sunday service. "Mary and I plan to keep our date. We think we have to trust the Lord."

That's easy to say, Mervin had almost replied. He had nodded instead. "Jah, I know. These are difficult decisions made in difficult times."

"But the times are always difficult," Willis insisted.

"Will Bishop Martin marry you?" Mervin asked him.

Willis laughed. "When the day comes, how will the bishop not marry us?"

Which wasn't exactly the question. The question was, did Bishop Martin approve of weddings this year? Neither of them wished to press the bishop for an answer. One thing was certain: Love could be irresponsible. He didn't want to blame Willis of such a transgression, but Willis and Mary were younger, and this was their first planned wedding date. Surely Willis had given the subject serious thought and had simply come up with a different answer than he had. Willis planned to live in the spare bedroom upstairs at the home of Mary's parents. Even with a more prosperous year, Willis couldn't afford a farm.

Mervin, on the other hand, couldn't imagine that this was the right way to treat a wunderbaar woman like Mattie. He wanted a place of his own. Mattie deserved the best. He didn't exactly have the best, but he had a decent farm with a decent house on the place. Why would the Lord take him away from all that with this war? Which was a useless question. The draft was very possible, and his faith and resolve would be tested to the fullest. He might not return for ten years.

When he looked back from that perspective, would he wish he had married Mattie this wedding season and allowed the future to take care of itself? What if he did marry Mattie and came back in ten years to a child in the fourth grade who didn't know his daed? Mattie would have raised the child by herself. Would Mattie's love for him survive such a thing? Did he have the right to ask this of her? Or allow Mattie to think she could carry such a load on her tender shoulders?

Willis must have asked these same questions and decided that Mary could handle things. Did Willis know something he didn't? Willis and Mary did have a freshness about their love. But didn't Mattie and he have the same thing? They had been through the fire last year with their postponed marriage. Perhaps that gave them a maturity the others didn't have.

Mervin closed the stall door and gazed across the pasture to where his horses held their heads high in the air. The air held the promise of a storm, which explained his restless animals. They found a resolution of their rumpled spirits with a race across the fields. He couldn't do that with the approaching war or with Mattie's insistence that they wed this year. He needed council, a man to speak to about the matter. This had become too much of a confusion for him to sort out, and Deacon Joe was the one to approach. Why not make the trip over to Deacon Joe's place this morning? The deacon lived only a few miles up Route 340 toward Lancaster.

Mervin whistled, and Windy, at the far end of the pasture, jerked up his head.

"Come here." Mervin waved his hand, and Windy trotted toward the barn. When Windy arrived, he stroked the horse's neck and led him inside, where he tossed on the harness.

Windy neighed, as if he were in full agreement with this trip.

"I thought you wanted to stay inside the barn a moment ago?" Mervin teased.

Windy tossed his head.

"Maybe I should take lessons from you and get excited about adventure." Mervin fastened the last strap and led the horse out of the barn. A soft stir of wind greeted him. Windy neighed again.

"Storms coming," Mervin agreed and rubbed the horse's neck until Windy calmed down.

He held up the shafts of the buggy, and Windy swung himself into place without much prompting. Mervin fastened the tugs and hopped into the buggy. He jiggled the reins, and Windy trotted out the lane.

The traffic was light on State Route 340, and Mervin waved at the few buggies that passed. An English automobile approached him just before the turn toward Deacon Joe's place. Mervin slowed and held the reins tightly. Windy wasn't a skittish horse, but he didn't take any chances. Everything had him on edge this morning. The driver of the Plymouth waved as he passed, and Mervin returned the greeting. He stared after the sleek lining of the automobile's frame. How strange the English world was compared to the simple buggies and lifestyles of the Amish. Each year saw more changes in the English world and further pressures on his people, who wanted only to live their lives in peace. Now the English had brought the threat of their war to the Lancaster County districts.

Mervin turned his thoughts away from the fancy English automobile. They were almost at Deacon Joe's driveway.

"Whoa there," Mervin called out to Windy.

The horse slowed but still took the turn at a fast trot. With a whirl they pulled up to Deacon Joe's barn door. The deacon appeared with a grin on his face. "Gut morning there, Mervin. What's the rush?"

Mervin smiled and climbed down from the buggy. "Looks like a storm's on the way."

"Jah." The deacon glanced toward the west.

"Ahh. . ." Mervin cleared his throat.

"Jah." The deacon waited.

Mervin stared at the ground for a few seconds. "I've been thinking and wrestling with something, and I thought it was time to ask for council."

"Your wedding to Mattie this fall?"

"Jah, is it that plain to see?"

Deacon Joe grinned. "That's an important step in life, Mervin. Of course you're thinking about it." The deacon's gaze drifted back to the western horizon. "There are lots of reasons to think about it."

"Willis Stoll says he's going ahead with his plans."

The deacon's grin faded. "That's what it looks like, and so are some of the others."

"You don't approve, then?"

"Mervin, please don't put me in that place. Marriage is a sacred thing in the eyes of the Lord, and only the hearts involved know when the time has come." Deacon Joe paused. "We pray, jah, and we are concerned as a ministry, but we can't make those decisions."

"I guess not," Mervin allowed.

Deacon Joe met Mervin's gaze. "We will support whatever decisions our young people make during this time. That's what Bishop Martin has decided. Only Bishop

Amos in the south district is openly encouraging his dating couples to place their marriage plans on hold."

"There is plenty of reason." Mervin stared at his shoes.

"I agree, but reasons are not always the right choice. You should know that, Mervin."

Mervin forced a chuckle. "Can I use that excuse for breaking the *ordnung*?"

Deacon Joe joined in the laughter for a moment. "I wouldn't try it if I was you, but we both know this is a matter of the heart."

Mervin nodded. "That's what has me worried."

"You are a wise man." Deacon Joe smiled. "I highly respected your decision last year to place your wedding plans on hold. Some would have rushed in and let the sticks fall where they would, but you chose caution. We could use more young men like you in the district. I'm sure the Lord will reward you for your faithfulness."

Mervin fixed his gaze on the deacon. "Then we should wait? Is that what you're saying?"

Deacon Joe laughed. "You are a tenacious one, Mervin, but I wouldn't be the one to second-guess the bishop. That's all I'm saying."

Mervin ran his fingers over Windy's bridle. "Mattie wants to take the chance. She wants our wedding date set this season in a bad way. Should I let her council influence me?"

Deacon Joe patted Mervin on the shoulder. "Sorry, son. I'm not going there. That's even more dangerous than disagreeing with the bishop. Make the choice that you can live with, and Mattie will follow. If she doesn't, you'd best be finding that out now than later. No one in the district wants a frau who can't submit herself to her husband's lead."

"She is quite submissive," Mervin protested. "But the heart must always speak. I wouldn't take that from her."

"And neither would I," Deacon Joe assured him. "But you must make the decision in the end."

"I know," Mervin said. "Well, I won't be keeping you. I should batten things down at the place before the storm arrives."

Deacon Joe nodded. "Seek the Lord's will, son, and everything will be okay."

"Thank you," Mervin muttered.

He climbed back in the buggy and waved good-bye as he turned the buggy around and drove down the deacon's lane. At least Deacon Joe was confident that things would turn out well—if the heart was submitted to the Lord's will. He could share in that confidence. But the burden seemed a heavy one to carry. One choice was no lighter than the other. Maybe he should do what he wanted and take Mattie as his frau this wedding season. Maybe the Lord would understand. Could duty and desire both be right? He seemed forced to choose between them.

Mervin jiggled the reins, and Windy headed back toward the town of White-horse at a fast trot. Dark clouds hung on the horizon and a blast of wind whipped across Route 340.

Chapter 4

Mattie climbed down from Daed's buggy and squinted her eyes in the bright morning sunlight. Of course Cousin Mary would be given a beautiful day for her wedding. The bitter thought spun in Mattie's mind. This is what came from taking gut chances and doing the right thing. Willis and Mary had shown everyone the way. The young couple had opened the district's fall wedding season. They had done so with the storm clouds of war on the horizon. Tonight Mary would be with her loved one as his frau. Wasn't that worth whatever risk was needed? Mervin didn't think so, but she did. This should have been her wedding date, instead of Cousin Mary's.

Mattie waited while Mamm climbed down from the buggy behind her.

"It's a fine morning for a wedding," Mamm said with a bright smile.

Mattie remained silent. Anything she could say would only reveal her own unhappiness. She had managed to smile at the proper places all morning, but her resolve melted away when they had driven up her cousin's driveway.

Mamm stopped and turned around. "Your turn will come, dear. Don't worry."

Mattie forced another smile. "Mervin loves me. I know that."

"Of course he does," Mamm said and led the way toward the house. "And he always will," Mamm tossed over her shoulder.

At least she could think about Mervin's love, Mattie comforted herself. She would be with Mervin all day. As Mary's cousin, she had been asked to serve as a table waiter. Mattie paused to glance toward the barn. There was no sign of Mervin, but his buggy sat near the barn, tucked in the long line. That must mean Mervin was in the house. But what did she expect? Mervin wouldn't be late unless there was a perfectly gut excuse, and she didn't want to think what that might be. Perhaps trouble at his farm or some such disaster. Mervin placed duty and fear of the Lord first in his life. She loved the man for his devotion, but she should also be by his side tonight as Mervin's frau. Instead, she would leave the hymn singing this evening as his girlfriend.

Mattie pulled her thoughts away from Mervin and the wedding that wasn't. Ahead of her, the front porch was filled with women, and a chorus of gut mornings greeted them.

"Gut morning," Mattie responded along with Mamm.

Mamm began to shake hands, while Mattie slipped past her through the open front door. She wanted to find Mervin. If she couldn't be his frau, she would enjoy being his girlfriend for the day. Girlfriends had privileges. She could snuggle up to him and hold his hand—discreetly of course. Tonight after dark, she might steal a kiss from Mervin. He wouldn't object to a long kiss on Mary's wedding day.

Mattie pressed through the crowd gathered inside Mary's living room. Most of them were either family members or cooks. Their chatter as they caught up on news filled the house with a low hum.

"The table waiters are in the kitchen," one of the cooks spoke in Mattie's ear.

"Thank you," Mattie told her and pressed on.

Mervin was in the corner by the woodstove, along with several of the other male table waiters. He caught her eye at once and grinned.

"I love you," he mouthed across the room, followed by a louder, "I thought you'd be here soon."

Mattie slipped between the group of young girls and came to a stop beside him.

"No smooching beside me," Cousin Henry teased. "That's for Mary. It's her wedding day."

Mattie almost stuck her tongue out at him but stifled the impulse. Instead, she said, "You don't have to add salt to the wound."

"Oww! We are sore." Henry gave Mervin a quick look. "What's wrong? At last check you two were old enough."

Just hush it, Mattie wanted to say, but she should have kept her mouth shut earlier. Mervin's smile was gone, replaced by a somber look. She would get nowhere if she shamed him in public.

"We have our reasons," Mervin told Henry.

"We?" Henry sent a pointed look Mattie's way.

"Jah, we." Mattie retorted. That wasn't a lie, because she did want to support Mervin in his decision. At the same time she wanted to change his mind. What a bundle of contradictions she was, but frustrations could drive a woman to extremes. Everyone knew that.

Henry apparently agreed. "Take my advice and get married," he said. "Let the future take care of itself."

"That's not what the older people are thinking or Deacon Joe," Mervin replied. "They are much wiser than we young people are."

Henry shrugged. "Mary's getting married today. Heaven forbid that I should throw any cold water on her wedding." *And you shouldn't either,* his look said plainly.

"Agreed." Mervin nodded. "To a great wedding day and to a happy bride."

"I'm in on that," Henry seconded. "Now shouldn't we get busy?"

"Show me the way," Mervin told him.

"Hold your horses." Mattie held up her hand. "This is the kitchen and the women's domain. You two stand there and look handsome while I help with the food. You're not needed until after the service."

"Is she always that bossy?" Henry asked Mervin.

"Only in the kitchen," Mervin shot back. "She has me holding the dishcloth when I visit."

You'd be the boss if you'd marry me, Mattie almost replied. She bit off the words and smiled instead. "Don't look too handsome, Mervin. Not for anyone but me."

"She does have you firmly in hand," Henry declared.

Mattie left them to the sound of hearty laughter. Before she had taken two steps, Mary appeared in the kitchen doorway in her wedding dress. A hush fell over the kitchen. Mary looked stunning, her face aglow. Mattie stole a look at Mervin. Maybe if Mervin saw how joyful Mary was and how well the wedding went today, he—

"Howdy, everyone," Mary sang out. "I know I'm not supposed to be about yet, but I couldn't resist coming down."

"You're looking mighty gut," Henry shouted from the back wall.

Mary blew him a kiss and beamed brightly. The three of them were cousins, or Henry wouldn't dare offer such plain talk. Mattie peeked at Mervin's face again. He wore a smile, so he had noticed Mary's beauty and appeared pleased. Surely he would make the connection. She wanted to reach over and plant the thought in his head: *If I like Mattie now, how much more wunderbaar would she be after we've said the marriage vows.*

Marriage was of the Lord. How could the Lord want anything less than for her wedding to happen this season? Couldn't Mervin see that the community was far removed from the world the newspapers reported on? She should have seen this earlier and told Mervin. But maybe her silence was better. Mervin would come to the same conclusion today, and their wedding plans could begin in earnest. They could marry by the end of November, and she could be on the farm well before Christmas. What a way to celebrate the birth of the Christ child. They could comfort each other with faith and hope in the future. Had not Jesus come to bring peace and good will to all men?

Mattie glanced at the kitchen doorway, but Mary had disappeared. The chatter began again and enveloped her like a cocoon. On the wall, the clock inched toward nine o'clock, when the service would begin.

"Can I help with something?" Mattie touched her sister Edna's arm to gain her attention.

"No dear, we're fine," Edna replied. "It's time for you table waiters to get out to the barn though."

"It's a little early," Mattie protested.

"Just go. We're falling over each other here." Edna waved her hands about.

Mattie laughed and slipped through the crowd to pull on Mervin's hand. He followed, and the others lined up behind them. Apparently, Edna had been right, because the people in the living room had begun to move outside, where they sorted themselves out by age. The older women led the way down the sidewalks and up the slight incline toward the barn loft.

Mervin said nothing on their walk. They went first since they were the oldest couple among the table waiters. She didn't mind if she was the oldest today if Mervin was with her. Wasn't this another sign that she was ready to marry? Everything was made right when Mervin was by her side. She was more than ready to say the wedding vows with him.

Mattie almost whispered the point into Mervin's ear, but she remembered in time. Mervin didn't want to wed this year, because he couldn't stay by her side.

Mattie stifled her objections and leaned against Mervin's arm. How confused everything was. Her best arguments were turned against her. She had best stick to her hopes that Willis and Mary's joy today would make the point for her. Wasn't Willis a gut friend of Mervin? That ought to keep Mervin's heart open to what the Lord was so clearly speaking.

Mattie looked up at Mervin's face and smiled as they entered the large barn loft. The empty benches prepared for the table waiters stretched out in front of her, and Mervin led the way to the end of the front one.

Mattie settled in, and the songs began. Bishop Martin stood to lead the line of ministers back to the house. Willis and Mary followed for their last instructions before their wedded life began. Would the ministers speak to them of coming troubles and separations? The subject seemed far removed on this sunny, late-October day. There hadn't been a cloud in the sky on their short walk in from the house. No doubt the ministers would be inspired to speak of the sweet things that Willis and Mary would share in their married life. Things like kinner and a home together.

True, that life would begin in an upstairs bedroom where Mary had been born. But what was wrong with that? Mattie would gladly have lived in her parents' house for the last year with Mervin. She could have driven to Mary's wedding this morning in Mervin's buggy, as Mervin's frau.

Life would have been okay. Look how the Lord had worked things out after the disappointment Mervin had suffered last year. The rich silage the cows ate from the storm damage had produced extra milk, which hadn't brought in the funds like the lost corn would have, but it was enough for Mervin to be able to purchase another farm. How foolish Mervin's fears had been. She had suffered through life as a single woman this last year for nothing.

Mattie took a quick look up at Mervin's face. He wore a slight smile and seemed to share none of her bitter thoughts. Why couldn't she be serene and peaceful? Mervin kept his composure through thick or thin. Maybe that was the lesson the Lord wished her to learn. Mattie pasted on a smile and stilled her thoughts as another song began. She focused on the words: "Great Redeemer, our Creator, blessed be Your holy name."

The words had been written by a man who languished in prison years for his faith. Now they were gathered all this time later and singing the man's words at a wedding. The tune rose and fell; the sounds were rapturous. How could a man locked away from the world write such glorious music? She couldn't be happy if she was deprived of her wedding date this year. All while she still had Mervin and his love. Mattie reached over to hold Mervin's hand when Willis and Mary walked in from their wedding instructions. Everyone had their eyes on the happy couple and didn't notice the public attentions she gave Mervin.

Willis and Mary took their seats, their gazes fixed on each other and bright smiles shining on their faces. The ministers returned ten minutes later and the preaching began. At eleven o'clock, Bishop Martin began the concluding sermon. "Greetings, dear brothers and sisters, on this wunderbaar wedding day. We must not forget the instructions the Lord has given us on how men and women should live together," the bishop said. "They are to respect each other and walk in the different roles the Lord has given the man and the woman. No matter how much the world changes, the Word of God does not change."

Mattie listened and nodded. She had no problem with Bishop Martin's words. Thankfully, the bishop said nothing about the war that loomed on the horizon. Maybe he thought the danger over? She could almost imagine that scenario as Bishop Martin concluded his sermon and looked down on Willis and Mary to say, "Now if our brother and sister still wish to exchange wedding vows, let them please stand to their feet."

Willis stood first, followed by Mary. The glow on Mary's face had spread. How beautiful a bride appeared when she was in love. This was among the Lord's most precious gifts to humanity. Mattie knew this because of the glow in her own heart. Outside of the Lord Himself, nothing was as wunderbaar as her love for Mervin.

The last jah was soon spoken by Willis and Mary in answer to Bishop Martin's questions, and the service was dismissed. The line of table waiters stood and filed behind the curtained-off area of the barn loft. Long lines of tables stretched along the back wall, filled with food dishes. The cooks must have worked nonstop to bring all the kettles up the steep barn steps while the service had been in progress.

"Mmm," Mervin said and bent low over a bowl of chicken for a deep breath.

Since everyone was equally occupied, Mattie brushed Mervin's cheek with hers. This would have to suffice as her first kiss of the day. Mervin grinned, the food forgotten as he gazed into her eyes.

"Our wedding day could be soon," she whispered.

"Maybe," he allowed.

Mattie stilled the pounding of her heart and busied herself with organizing the food dishes they would carry out. Had Mervin just said what she thought he had? She glanced at him. He had!

Chapter 5

The next Sunday evening, Mattie opened the front door of the Beilers' home with one hand, while she held on to Mervin's arm with the other. He stepped across the threshold, and Mattie let go to close the door behind them. Mervin flopped himself down on the couch while she came closer and beamed a bright smile down on him. "Want something to eat?"

Mervin laughed. "You know the answer to that."

"Jah, I do," Mattie agreed. "Oh Mervin." She could go no further. "I'll be right back with chocolate chip cookies and milk."

"Sounds great to me." He folded his arms and looked up at her with contentment.

Mattie hurried into the kitchen and opened the cupboard to set a plate on the counter. She transferred the cookies from the canister, five of them. Mervin would be hungry, but she couldn't hold down a bite.

Not one! Not with their wedding plans scheduled for discussion tonight. Mattie hugged herself and took deep breaths. Mervin might feel pushed if she came across too strong this evening. She didn't want to rush him. She was too thrilled that Mervin had agreed to a wedding date.

Willis and Mary's wedding had convinced him. She had waited with all the patience she could muster these last few days until Mervin was ready to discuss details. Mattie did a little jig on the kitchen floor, her soft-soled shoes soundless on the vinyl floor. Even if Mervin heard, he would think that she bustled about the kitchen.

Mattie calmed herself and filled two glasses with milk, one to the brim and the other a quarter full. She would manage a sip or two, but that was all. She had to hold something in her hands. Mervin wouldn't want her to sit there with nothing while he ate. Mattie took the plate in one hand and the full glass in the other. Mervin had Daed's newspaper raised high in front of his face when she walked back into the living room.

"Oh no," Mattie cried, and the glass slipped from her hand. With a crash, it hit the hardwood floor, and a thousand slivers skidded in all directions, driven by the waves of white milk.

"Mattie!" Mervin looked up with concern. He laid the newspaper down and stood up.

"Where did you...? I thought...that thing...I had it hidden," Mattie sputtered. She pointed at the paper with her empty hand.

"It was on your daed's rocker." Mervin appeared puzzled. "Does he buy one often?"

"Only when… Oh Mervin" Mattie wailed. "I didn't want you to see that tonight."

"Why not? I was checking on the weather." Mervin glanced at the floor. "But shouldn't you clean this up?"

"The weather?" Mattie stared. "You…"

Mervin shrugged. "The English do know some things that we farmers don't." A smile crept across his face. "But who can really know what the weather will do?"

"Of course." Mattie forced herself to focus. "How clumsy of me. I slipped when I saw… Oh Mervin, I can't even carry a glass of milk from the kitchen to the living room. What has become of me?"

His smile grew. "Maybe the excitement of the evening overcame you? I did hear noises in the kitchen a moment ago."

"I was dancing a jig," Mattie confessed. "I was thinking about you."

That tidbit was better than the truth about the newspaper. Maybe the Saturday paper said nothing about the war. She hadn't wanted to look, but she had taken no chances and hidden the thing under the couch. Obviously, Daed had figured that out and undid her precautions.

Mervin motioned toward the floor with his head. "Maybe we should clean this up before the evening gets too old. I think we had some things to discuss." His smile was soft.

She could have hugged him, but he was on the other side of the slivers of glass.

"Jah, of course." Mattie almost threw Mervin the plate of cookies and dashed back into the kitchen to return with a broom and dustpan. The wastebasket in the corner was almost empty. She dumped the few papers in the corner and began to sweep the debris into the dustpan. Her first try at the wastebasket with the dustpan tilted sideways resulted in a spill.

"Here, I'll do that," Mervin told her. "You can fix a bucket of water and soap. Milk makes an awful stink if it's not cleaned properly. We wouldn't want your parents thinking badly of me all week, all because unpleasant odors waft through the house."

Mattie forced a laugh and handed Mervin the broom and dustpan. "They wouldn't think badly of you. I'll tell Mamm it was my fault."

"While we made wedding plans?" Mervin raised his eyebrows. "If possible, we had best keep this between us."

Mattie opened her mouth to protest when the bedroom door opened and Mamm appeared in her long nightgown. "What happened?" Mamm asked. "I thought I heard a crash."

Mattie stood in front of the mess. "It was just an accident, Mamm. Go back to bed."

Mamm peered around Mattie. "You dropped a glass of milk on the floor. The smell—"

"Jah, I know," Mattie broke in. "I'll clean it. We'll clean it up."

Mamm seemed to notice Mervin for the first time. "You spilt milk in front of. . . This is not gut, Mattie."

"Mamm, please," Mattie begged. "I feel bad enough already, and we'll scrub things well."

"We will," Mervin joined in.

"Okay." Mamm took a step back. "I'll leave, then. But be sure and get soap into the cracks—plenty of soap—and sop the water up well."

Mattie nodded. Mamm had a right to her concerns, and she had dropped the glass of milk.

"We'll do a gut job," Mervin assured Mamm.

Mamm smiled and retreated down the hall.

Mattie covered her face with both hands once the bedroom door clicked shut. "I'm so embarrassed."

Mervin's hand slipped around Mattie's waist, and he pulled her close. "It'll be okay. Accidents happen to the best of us."

Mattie rested her head on Mervin's shoulder for a second. When she looked up, the newspaper lying beside the couch caught her eye. The offending object was to blame for all this. She almost kicked it out of sight, but that would only draw attention to the wrong thing. Mervin hadn't read anything about the war, and she didn't want him to. Enough had gone wrong for one evening.

Mattie stepped away from Mervin to retreat into the kitchen, where she rinsed the slop bucket and filled it with warm water from the teakettle. She added a stream of dishwashing soap when the bucket was full. Back in the living room, with a firm grip on the wire handle, Mattie found Mervin on his hands and knees. He picked away at the glass between the cracks of the hardwood floor, his gaze intent.

Mattie joined him, and when they finished, she scrubbed away with the wet cloth.

"Let me have that one," Mervin ordered. "You can get another one."

Mattie handed over the washcloth. She got up and returned to the kitchen for another rag. When she came back, Mervin gave her a smile from the floor.

"I feel awful." Mattie groaned. "What a mess, and you're so nice about it."

Mervin smiled and scrubbed away. "There's nothing to worry about if we get this clean."

Mattie went on her knees to join him, and they worked silently until Mervin declared, "There! No smell tomorrow, I think."

"Maybe I should pour soap directly on the floor," Mattie suggested.

"Maybe," Mervin allowed.

Mattie hurried back to the kitchen and grabbed the soap bottle. She returned and placed droplets all over the affected area. Mervin scrubbed again, and she joined him.

"Satisfied?" Mervin finally asked.

"I guess so." Mattie got slowly to her feet. Her face was flushed, and the time was late. Why did nothing ever work out the way she had planned? Did the Lord wish to take her wedding away from her again? The evening so far had shed little light on the future.

Mervin pushed the slop bucket out of the way and flopped down on the couch. "So when should we have this wedding, dear."

Mattie joined him before she answered. "Before Christmas. That's all I know. Unless you object?" She peered up at his face.

"I'm trying to trust the Lord," Mervin muttered. "But Willis and Mary did set such a gut example."

"And there's another wedding this week." Mattie told him. "In fact, two of them in our district. We can't be doing the wrong thing."

Mervin smiled. "Then when is our date? Sometime before Christmas, you say. What about the second Thursday in December?"

Mattie took a long breath. Did she dare? She should at least try. "Maybe the first Thursday in December, right after Thanksgiving?"

Mervin looked down at her with tenderness written on his face. "You'll need all the time you can get to prepare, Mattie. The second Thursday in December is soon enough for our wedding."

"Okay." Mattie gave in. This was already more than she had once hoped for. "Just think," she whispered. "I'll be your frau before too long."

Mervin cleared his throat. "Don't we have other plans to make?"

"That was the big one," she said, and begged, "Can I please? Just one kiss? I have waited a long time for this moment."

Mervin nodded, and Mattie grasped his shoulders with both hands and pulled him close. She reached upward to where the bristles on his chin began and higher. He was as sweet as he always had been, strong and gentle, a well that filled her heart with great joy.

"Satisfied?" Mervin held her at arm's length.

Another one, she almost said but let her eyes speak. He lowered his head and held her close for a long time. She eased her lips away from his and rested her cheek against his.

Mervin stroked Mattie's hair away from her face. "The plans," he whispered. "We have to make plans."

"Jah," Mattie murmured into his chest. All she wanted right now was to hold Mervin tight and never let go. But of course, that couldn't be. She sat upright and focused. "We'll need table waiters of course. Maybe a dozen."

Mervin laughed. "A big wedding, then."

"Of course!" Mattie declared. "I've waited long enough for this."

"We should have a small one," he said. "We are both older."

Which isn't my fault. The retort died in Mattie's throat. She moved closer to lean against his shoulder. "Whatever you want is fine with me." She gazed up at his face. "That you're marrying me is all I need on my wedding day. Oh, this is so wunderbaar, Mervin. I can't say how much I love you. This is so right, and the Lord must be pleased. Did He not give us plenty of direction at Willis and Mary's wedding?"

"Jah, it appears so." A cloud passed over Mervin's face. "But there will always be trouble, Mattie, and this war is still a possibility. Are you sure you want to run the risk?"

"We're not talking about that tonight," she told him.

He stroked her face, his calluses tender on her skin, his dark thoughts apparently forgotten.

"Just think," she told him. "I'll be your frau regardless of whether we have a big wedding or a small one."

He nodded. "I love you, Mattie, and the Lord does seem to have given direction, so that's gut enough for me. The second Thursday in December it will be."

"The second Thursday," she echoed.

"And a small wedding," he added.

"Only a few guests," she agreed. "Our immediate family and a few others."

His chuckle filled the living room. "You know that's not a small wedding. The cousins will all want to come."

Mattie hid her smile. "That sounds small to me."

Mervin shook with laugher. "You are a wise one, you know."

"Is that why you love me?"

"Among other things," he said. "But never mind. We still haven't picked out the table waiters."

"Let's see," Mattie mused. "There are your two brothers, Emery and John, from your side of the family, unless you want one of them for a witness?"

"I think we should go with gut friends for that role," he said. "Especially since all your siblings are married."

"You don't have to exclude your brothers because of me," Mattie protested.

"Emery, then," he said with a smile. "I like that."

"I'll think about who I want later," she told him. "Right now I just want to enjoy this moment."

"I thought you wanted to plan things?"

"We have planned things," she said. "We're getting married."

He wrapped his arm around her shoulder for a quick squeeze. "That we are, and I'm going home. It's getting late."

Mattie followed him to the door and stepped out onto the porch to watch his buggy lights leave. She could have used one more kiss, but she could also wait. She had her wedding date. Was that not gut enough?

"Thank You, dear Lord," she whispered up into the heavens. The stars twinkled back as if they had joined her dance of joy.

Chapter 6

On the Monday before Thanksgiving, Mervin whistled a merry tune as he hitched his team of Belgians to the wagon. Overhead a few stars still twinkled with the sunrise on the eastern horizon. This was an early start of the day, but they needed an early one if Willis planned to complete the job of filling his daed's smaller silo. Herman helped the young couple gain a financial start with a portion of the farm's production while the two lived at Mary's former home. The last of Willis's share of corn was out of the fields, and the stalks would be put up today as feed for the cattle. Last year this time, most of Lancaster's corn had been destroyed by the mid-October snowstorm, and all hope of a decent crop was lost. Mervin's tune faltered at the dark memory. He straightened his back and stood upright. He would not think of troubled times today. His time spent with Mattie yesterday had been too wunderbaar. Their wedding plans continued, and he would not change his mind.

His whistle began again. Mattie was right about the wedding, and he had been wrong. Willis and Mary's happy married life showed that plainly enough. Willis's face shone with love for Mary every time Mervin saw them together. Clearly, the two were filled with happiness, even while they lived in her parents' upstairs bedroom.

Mervin fastened the last trace and hopped on the wagon. His whistle stopped again. If Willis and Mary were happy, that must mean he had wasted the last year of his life while he could have lived with Mattie in marital bliss.

"That's a bummer," Mervin muttered into the morning air. Why had he let his fears get the best of him? Mervin jiggled the reins, and the Belgians dashed out of the lane at a brisk trot and down Route 340, away from the town of Whitehorse. Several other wagons soon joined his, headed in the same direction. He waved to them but focused on his faltering spirits. The past was the past and could not be changed, and no one was the same. He shouldn't compare himself with Willis and Mary. Mattie wasn't Mary, and he wasn't Willis. They had learned from the young couple's example, but they were different people. He might not have been happy with life in the upstairs bedroom of the Beilers' home. Mattie thought she would have been, but living a thing was different from thinking a thing.

Mervin's whistle began again, and a smile was spread over his face by the time he pulled into the Stolls' place.

Willis stood beside the barn and waved his arms toward the barnyard gate. "On back, boys, on back," Willis hollered.

Mervin thundered past Willis with his team of Belgians. The sun had burst over the horizon and illuminated the stubble of a beard Willis's face had begun to show since the wedding.

"Gut morning," Mervin hollered over his shoulder, but the sound was lost in the rattle of steel wagon wheels behind him.

Willis's daed, Herman, stepped out of the cornfield in front of him and directed Mervin where to turn. He was the first one here, which was quite an accomplishment. But he was single and had no frau or kinner to distract him. With Mattie in the house, he might have lingered over his breakfast and stolen one last kiss before he headed out to the barn.

"Howdy there," Herman greeted Mervin. He had the corn binder ready to go. His team of four horses hungrily pulled fresh stalks into their mouths and chewed the best they could with their bridles on.

"A little different than things were last year," Mervin commented.

"Jah." Herman's cheerful look vanished. "That was some snow, but the Lord had mercy on us this year."

"Jah, this is true," Mervin agreed. "But sorry, I shouldn't have mentioned anything."

Herman managed to smile. "You suffered, too, if I remember right. You had a wedding planned."

Mervin nodded.

"Anything this year?" Herman had a twinkle in his eye.

Mervin chuckled and didn't answer.

Herman grinned. "Can't let the cat out of the bag, I see."

"Got to keep the strings tight." Mervin grinned.

They laughed together, and Mervin positioned his wagon on the side of the corn picker as Herman clucked to his horses. The extra man on the wagon behind Mervin, young Peter Miller, joined him to hold the reins. Mervin greeted him with a smile and a nod of his head.

"Nice morning," Peter said as he kept Mervin's team in time with the corn picker. "How are you doing?"

"Couldn't be any better," Mervin told him and threw the first bundle of cornstalks toward the back of the wagon. They came fast and thick, and Mervin scurried back and forth. Peter soon switched places with him, and they paced each other until the load became top-heavy.

Mervin hollered down to Herman. "We're full."

Herman nodded and pulled back on the reins. Mervin hollered to his team, and they lurched forward so the wagon behind them could take their place. At a fast walk, they moved toward the barn and the thunder of the silage filler. An old steam engine powered the contraption. The English farmers had begun to use corn choppers in the fields, but little changed in the community. Mervin positioned his wagon near the whirl of the blades and tied the reins to the front rack. With Peter's help, he began to toss in the bundles of corn. The racket filled their ears, while an extra roar sounded each time a sheaf of corn hit the blades.

"You know to be careful," Mervin mouthed the words in Peter's direction.

Peter nodded and made sure he had solid footing before he tossed the next bundle. Mervin did the same, and the wagon was soon empty. By midmorning they had repeated the routine half-a-dozen times. On their next time up, Mary appeared with a pitcher of lemonade and began to serve the men. Mervin and Peter emptied their wagon, and Mervin pulled his team aside to jump to the ground, with Peter behind him.

"Gut morning," Mary greeted them, her face aglow with happiness. "Thanks so very much for coming over to help Willis today."

"I'm more than glad to help," Mervin assured her, and Peter nodded.

Mary handed each of them a full glass of lemonade. "Any wedding bells this year for you and Mattie?" Mary teased.

"I didn't hear that," Mervin said, and Peter held his ear shut with his free hand while they all laughed.

"You can't go wrong—that's all I can say," Mary told him.

"How can I not go wrong?" Peter quipped.

The laugher rose and fell again.

"You have to take a girl home first," Mary chided. "But isn't it about time, Peter?"

Peter reddened. "I have to find a girl first."

Mary made a face at him. "You're not fooling me, Peter. There's any number of girls willing to go home with a handsome young fellow like you."

Peter's color increased, but he shook his head.

"Jah, there is," Mary insisted. "I saw young Lydia making eyes at you on Sunday. Just buckle up your nerve and ask her home."

"Maybe I don't want to," Peter muttered.

Mary reached over to tickle his chin. "Who are you fooling, young man? You couldn't keep your eyes off of Lydia."

Peter pretended to withdraw in horror.

"He'll get his courage up someday," Mervin spoke up with his glass of lemonade almost empty. "It might be best to hold off on things anyway, with. . ." He stopped. Why spoil a perfect moment on a perfect day?

Mary fell silent and stared at the ground. "Do you think it will be bad, Mervin? The men. . ."

"If there is war, war is always bad," he said.

"Maybe the president will keep the country out of this thing." Mary had hope in her eyes.

"Maybe," Mervin allowed. "But thanks for the lemonade, Mary. That was very gut."

Mary took a deep breath with some of the glow back on her face. "There was just a touch of salt to bring out the flavor. Thanks again for helping us out today. We hope to have our own place by this time next year."

"To a splendid little farm, then." Mervin smiled and turned to go. Peter was close behind him.

"What's marriage like?" Peter mused when they had climbed back on the wagon.

"Don't ask me," Mervin retorted.

"But you have kissed Mattie, haven't you?" Peter's face was intense.

"It's a beautiful thing." Mervin patted him on the shoulder. "Just take your time, and seek the Lord's will."

"Do you think I should ask Lydia home before this war begins? Daed says we could all be gone for years. Lydia might not love me by the time I get back, or someone else might have taken her."

Mervin attempted a laugh. "Who would be left to take her?"

"We are a little young," Peter agreed, as if that had been the question. "But I don't want to lose the girl. Lydia's a jewel."

"Then at least let her know how you feel. Take her home for a few dates." Mervin loosened the reins and clucked to his horses. The two men on the wagon behind them had hopped off, and Mary held out brimming glasses of lemonade to them. Mary's smile filled her whole face.

They rattled back in line behind the corn binder. "So are you and Mattie taking the plunge this year?" Peter asked.

Mervin glanced at him. The man seemed to want encouragement, but he had struggled with the question himself for the longest time. "Each must arrive at the conclusion on their own," Mervin told him. "You know weddings are a great secret. I can't say." Mervin attempted a grin.

Peter didn't answer, his gaze fixed back on the silage filler. "Something's wrong up there," he said.

Mervin turned sideways for a better view. Several of the men near the steam engine scurried about. That was strange behavior, but. . . "The blades might have gotten jammed," he said. "If that's the case, we'll get set back for thirty minutes or so."

"It's something else." Peter continued to stare. "We had best go see."

"We can't drive up there with the wagon," Mervin protested.

"I'll run up." Peter leaped from the wagon to race across the field.

Mervin kept his gaze fixed on the site. The men still scurried about the corn chopper, which didn't make sense if the blades were jammed. They'd be busy at work on the machine. As Mervin continued to watch, a figure detached itself from the small group and tore up the lane toward Route 340. He hadn't seen a man run so fast in a long time. Mervin tied the reins to the rack and leaped from the wagon. He ran up to the corn binder and waved his arms about. Herman jerked his head up and brought the contraption to a halt with a puzzled look on his face.

"There's something seriously wrong at the steam engine," Mervin hollered.

"What's wrong?" Herman asked the obvious.

"I don't know," Mervin replied. "But Peter went up to look."

Herman appeared ready to cluck to his horses and continue when one of the men high on the wagonload of cornstalks hollered down. "We best go find out what's going on, Herman."

Herman shrugged. "It can't be anything serious, but I guess the horses can use the rest. Can one of you run and check?"

"I'll go," both men said together and slid down the side of the wagon. They hurried across the cut corn, where Peter's figure met them midfield. A short conversation ensued, with the two men running on toward the steam engine. Peter made slower progress back toward the corn picker. He didn't speak until he was a dozen feet away from the wagon. "We'd best unhitch and go on up. There won't be any more silo filling today."

"Can't they fix the machine?" Herman asked.

"It's not the..." Peter studied the ground.

"What's wrong, then?" Herman demanded.

"I'd rather not say," Peter said.

Herman's face twitched, and he leaped down from the corn binder. "Here! Can you men take care of the team?"

"Jah, of course." Mervin didn't hesitate. Herman had already set out across the field at a steady run. Peter climbed up on the seat of the corn binder and secured a firm grip on the reins.

"Can you tell me what happened?" Mervin asked him.

Peter hesitated. "Willis fell in," he finally said. "They think he was waving at Mary and not paying attention. He's dead."

"Willis?" Mervin gripped the edge of the wagon with both hands.

"Jah, Willis," Peter said.

Mervin shook his head. His ears buzzed, and he heard thunder in the distance instead of words. He shook his head again. "We had best go up, then," he said.

"You don't really want to see it," Peter intoned. "He fell in the blades. There's only..."

"Did Mary see him?" Mervin asked.

Peter nodded, and a siren wailed in the direction of Whitehorse. Mervin made sure the reins were secure before he unhitched the four-horse team from the corn binder. Peter came down from the seat to help with hands that trembled.

"Can you drive them up?" Mervin asked when they finished.

Peter nodded and clutched the reins. Mervin watched him go, the young man's feet almost lifted off the ground at times. Mervin hesitated. He didn't want to return to the silo-filling area. He didn't want to think about what this meant for his future, but it couldn't be avoided. Mary was a widow, and Mattie and he had their wedding date set. His face was grim as Mervin climbed back on his wagon.

Chapter 7

On the morning after Thanksgiving, Mattie sat beside Mary with her arm around her cousin's slender shoulders. The casket that contained the body of Willis was set up on a plywood platform in front of them. Mary's mamm, Lois, was on the other side of Mary, with family members seated on either side of them. Mattie normally wouldn't have been by Mary's side for the funeral, but Mary had requested her presence.

Mary's shoulders shook as the line of ministers filed in to begin the service. Bishop Martin took his place at the head of the bench with a bowed head and deep pain written on his face.

Tears trickled down Mattie's cheeks. How any of them had any tears left was beyond her. There had been little but tears since Monday and the horrible accident. The casket would be closed today, so awful had been the damage to Willis's body, and Mary had been there to see it all. Mattie's arm twitched at the thought.

She could not imagine the horror Mary must have felt. One moment Mary had been lost in rapture, waving to her husband perched high above her on the wagon of corn sheaves. With her other hand, Mary had held the glass of lemonade she had anticipated Willis would soon drink. Then death had come. Awful and sudden, an evil that stole away the wunderbaar love the Lord had given Willis and Mary. The whole community had been in shock, and the English authorities suspicious.

"Was there a feud among the three men on the wagon?" the chief of police asked Willis's daed, Herman.

"Of course not!" Herman had declared. "Our men live in peace with each other."

"This was a young married couple, right?" the chief of police continued undeterred. "Any jilted rivals on that wagon?"

That had led to many more unspeakable questions. When Ezra Miller, one of the unmarried men on the wagon, who had made a desperate dive after Willis when the fall began, admitted that he had once taken Mary home for a few dates, the questions had become worse. Willis should have been buried on Wednesday in peace. Instead, the district had spent Thanksgiving Day in prayer and fasting for the situation. It was the awful European war that had everyone on edge, but the thought was a small comfort. Thankfully, the English authorities had backed down, influenced no doubt by the district's intercession before the throne of the Lord.

Mattie hadn't spoken with Mervin since the Sunday evening before the accident. She shouldn't think of herself on the day of Willis's funeral, but she couldn't help it. Would Mervin still marry her? Their wedding date was the second week of December, not many days away. Willis and Mary had been their example. The two were why Mervin had found faith and accepted the risk, but now Willis was dead.

Mattie choked back a sob as Bishop Martin rose to his feet and began to speak. "Dearly beloved, we are gathered here today with hearts broken and torn. We have searched our hearts for answers, but answers are not often found when the Lord chooses to move with His hand in these ways. There are times when the Lord covers His face with a deep cloud, as He did with Moses and as He did in the whirlwind with Job. This has been an awful tragedy to visit our community, all in the midst of so much uncertainty in the world. Yet we have been warned that in the world we would have troubles. The Lord has told us this truth, but we didn't imagine how painful those troubles would be, or how deep the cut. Our brother Willis has been called from us, and from the arms of his young and greatly beloved frau, Mary."

Bishop Martin paused to turn his bowed head toward the casket. Mary placed both of her hands over her face, and muffled cries filled the room. Mattie hung on to her cousin as Mary bent forward in her agony.

"Let us not sorrow as the world sorrows," Bishop Martin continued. "We must not think ourselves above the worse troubles others suffer. The world is in great pain, and the children of God must not think that they can be spared. We would wish to cry for special favors from the Lord, but that is not His will. Instead, we must ask for grace, for endurance to bear the trial, for faith that does not grow dim. We must be secure in the Lord's love and in our love for each other."

Was Mervin listening? The bishop couldn't possibly be thinking of their situation at the moment. But might this be a message from the Lord? They must not falter in their determination to walk on, regardless of the tragedies that occurred along their path. But she must think about Mary and not herself. Mattie pulled Mary closer and helped her sit upright again.

Help Mary bear this, Lord Jesus. Mattie sent up the silent prayer. She couldn't help adding, *And help us, too.*

Which might mean bearing the trial of Mervin calling off the wedding again, as Mary was now bearing her sorrow. Mattie flinched. Had she just doomed herself?

Oh Lord Jesus, please not, Mattie prayed again, but the words seemed to bounce off the ceiling. What right had she to ask for blessings while Willis's casket sat in front of her?

"The Lord will be with us," Bishop Martin continued, "even as the trials of this life increase. None of us know what lies ahead or what dark hours await our community or the world. Satan has gone forth in our time as a roaring lion seeking whom he may devour. War is an evil that has gripped the nations. We may ask and pray for peace, but our request may not come, even as our request at Willis and Mary's wedding for a long life lived together in peace was not answered. We wished them the Lord's blessing on that blessed day, and here we are with what we cannot understand or explain. Only our faith will carry us through, along with the Lord's mercy. I know that these words I speak carry little hope on this day of sorrow, but in the future the Lord may recall them to our minds and give us comfort and strength to walk on in this life."

Bishop Martin sat down, and another minister from a neighboring district rose to his feet. He began to speak, but Mattie didn't hear him. Only Mary's soft sobs registered. The hands on the clock above the casket slowly moved. Mattie tried to keep her gaze away from both the time and box that contained Willis's body, but she couldn't. She wanted this behind them. Mary would soon pass out from exhaustion if her cries continued unabated. More tears could flow in the days ahead, but it was better for Mary to collapse at home with her mamm than in public view.

The sermon finally ended, and a line formed beside the closed casket. Each person paused briefly, and a few touched the wood before they moved on. The line continued for what seemed like hours, but the clock on the wall claimed otherwise. Thirty minutes later, once the ministers had filed past, Mattie helped Mary to her feet with Lois on the other side. Together they moved Mary toward the casket, where Mary collapsed over the top. Everyone waited as Mary whispered words they couldn't hear. Mary would be saying what she could no longer whisper in Willis's ear as his frau. Mattie finally glanced over at Lois, who nodded. It was time to move on. Mattie prepared herself to pull up on Mary's arm, but Mary stood by herself and tottered toward the door. They stayed beside the young widow and helped her into the backseat of the buggy. In front of them sat the open spring wagon that would carry the casket to the graveyard.

"You stay with her," Lois whispered, and Mattie climbed up to sit beside her cousin. Lois climbed in the front and was soon joined by Mary's daed, Ben. He held the reins as they waited. The casket was soon brought out and loaded onto the spring wagon, and the procession of buggies began to move down 340 toward the town of Whitehorse.

"He's dead," Mary said. "He's really dead."

Mattie grasped Mary's arm and said nothing.

"He was such a wunderbaar husband." Mary stared out of the open buggy door. "But he's with the angels now. I must tell myself this truth often. Willis wouldn't want to come back to this troubled world."

"He loved you," Mattie assured Mary. "You don't have to forget that."

Fresh tears formed in Mary's eyes. "Jah, I know, but. . ."

"I'm so sorry for you," Mattie whispered.

"Thank you for being with me today." Mary tried to smile through her tears. "You don't know how great a comfort that's been."

"I didn't. . . ," Mattie protested then stopped. "I'm glad it helped," she added.

Silence filled the buggy until they turned down the side road and into the graveyard.

"You will stay with me for the rest of this?" Mary asked through a blur of tears.

"Jah, of course." Mattie climbed down the buggy steps and offered Mary a hand. Lois joined them, and together they approached the open grave to wait while the casket was brought over.

Mattie caught a glimpse of Mervin in the crowd. Surely Mervin would approach her once the graveside service was complete. She had to speak with him today. If the worst must be said, it must be said, but she wanted to hear the words from his mouth. Perhaps if she gazed into Mervin's eyes while he said them, the pain would be lessened.

Mattie forced herself to focus as Bishop Martin appeared in front of them and began to pray: "Now unto our most gracious heavenly Father, we commit these remains of our brother until that day when our Lord returns with a shout and with the voice of the archangel and with a trumpet sound, to gather us home to a land where we shall forever be with the Lord through all eternity. Be with us, Lord, in the days ahead. Be also with our nation as we continue this journey through these dark hours. You have told us in Your Word that we are to pray for our leaders and all those who are in authority over us. We ask that You would give them wisdom in the choices they must make. We know these are hard choices, difficult decisions that will affect the lives of so many. Death will come again. We ask that You would receive into glory all those whose faith is fixed on You, as our brother Willis's faith was set. Amen."

All heads were raised, and a soft shuffle passed through the crowd. The casket was lowered, and a line of young men formed and began to shovel dirt. Mervin came up to help, but he didn't look at her. This was right, Mattie comforted herself. She had already spent way too much time today in thoughts about herself instead of comforting Mary. She would not be offended. Mervin loved her. He did his duty in the fear of the Lord.

Mattie gave Mary one final hug as the last of the dirt was thrown on the mound. Lois took her daughter's hand, and they moved toward the buggy.

Mattie stayed rooted to the ground for a long time. She couldn't stop her thoughts about Mervin and what the future would hold for them. Her mind whirled. Their wedding date was less than two weeks away. Maybe if she said nothing, Mervin would pick her up for their regular date on Sunday evening and life would be unchanged. Maybe that was the best course of action. Mattie stared at the fresh mound of dirt heaped high in front of her. She jumped when a soft touch came on her arm, and whirled about to see Mervin's sober face above her. She wanted to wrap her arms around him, but this was a public place, and they had just buried Willis.

"Mattie," he said, his hand still on her arm, "this has been a very sad day. I was glad to see you comfort Mary the way you did."

Mattie nodded, unable to speak.

"Are you thinking what I'm thinking?" Mervin asked.

Mattie held still. She didn't dare speak, but Mervin could be referring only to one thing. She knew him well enough to know that.

Please help me, Lord. Mattie moved her lips in a silent plea.

"We had best rethink our wedding plans," Mervin finally said. "Don't you think so?"

"No!" Mattie almost wailed. A few heads turned in their direction, but this was a sorrowful day and people would think she still mourned for Mary. How selfish and self-centered she was, and how right Mervin must be. Yet how could she lose her wedding date?

"The Lord has spoken pretty clearly, I'm thinking," Mervin said. "We should listen."

"Don't do this to me." Mattie turned and grasped the front of Mervin's shirt with both hands. "Give me at least what Mary had, a few weeks with you before you have to leave." Her mind raced. "And you don't have to leave yet, and you may not have to leave. You can't call off the wedding, Mervin."

Reproof was written on his face. "We must bear our sorrows, Mattie, not grab things from the Lord's hand. But come." He took her hand. "We will walk through this together, but I think the wedding should be called off."

She would collapse today in public instead of Mary, Mattie thought, as Mervin led her toward Daed's buggy and helped her climb in. But she was still conscious when Mervin told her, "I'll see you on Sunday evening," and then he was gone.

There was hope, Mattie told herself. Somewhere there was always hope. Now if she could just find it. But where?

Chapter 8

Mattie threw the quilt off her bed and swung her feet out on the floor. The early morning chill crept up through the soles of her feet as she walked over to the bedroom window. She pushed the drapes aside to look up at the starry heavens. A three-quarter moon hung overhead and dimmed the stars. The sun would be up soon, but no joy sprang up inside of her at the thought. This was Sunday morning and the Lord's Day, and her wedding had been planned for this week. Only it would not happen. She had barely slept nights since Mervin had Bishop Martin make the announcement after the services last Sunday.

One, the guests needed time to change their plans. Two, they couldn't go on with the wedding after Willis's death. These were reasons Mervin had given for his decision, but none of them healed her heart. She would have held the wedding by herself this Thursday, but one couldn't get married that way.

"I love you," Mervin had told her last Sunday evening by the front door.

She had tried to smile and murmur the words back to him, but nothing had come out.

"We'll make this together," he had added.

This was how their relationship had been conducted since Willis's death. Reassurances given of what once had been, and was supposed to be, but there would be no wedding this week.

Mattie gazed up at the heavens. She should be thankful for what she had. Someday Mervin would wed her—maybe sometime before her hair grew old and gray. And she would see him today. She just wouldn't get her wish for a wedding before Christmas.

The reality was a load like lead upon her shoulders, and the months stretched out in front of her like years. Of course, that was a light load compared to the one Mary bore. Willis would never come back to her.

Mattie closed the drapes and walked back to the bed. Her head throbbed, and she should get another hour of sleep before dawn, but she couldn't. Too much raced through her mind. There had been no kiss with Mervin last Sunday, not even a good-bye kiss by the front door, only a soft brush of his hand on her shoulder. They had both changed. There was no question about that. They might act like they could go on unscathed by the trouble around them, but that wasn't true.

By next year's wedding season, something would be lost, maybe their freshness, their trust in each other, their nearness of heart, or the tremble of their hands when they clasped them together. They might be joined as husband and wife, but their innocence would be gone. Too much had happened. Their love would never be the same. Something would die inside of her when Thursday morning arrived and her wedding dress hung in the closet untouched.

Mattie dressed but left her hair undone to make her way down the stairs with a kerosene lamp in one hand. No one was in the kitchen. Stillness hung over the house like a blanket, and wild thoughts continued to race through Mattie's mind. Maybe she could still persuade Mervin to have the wedding on Thursday. She should ride over to his house this morning and place one last plea. She could get down on her knees and beg. She could make promises. But what promises? What would impress Mervin?

Maybe they could be married without any guests this Thursday. All that was needed was the bishop. Surely Bishop Martin would make an exception in their case. The announcement could be made right after the services today.

Or if Mervin wanted something else, she would agree. This could still happen. The time was short, but whoever could attend the wedding would come. Mamm had the food in the house for the meal, and her sisters would lend a hand. They understood the desperate times everyone lived in.

Mattie shook her head and pulled out a kitchen chair. She sat down and held her head in her hands. None of that was possible. Mervin would not change his mind. Monday morning would dawn and the week would be set in concrete.

Mattie looked up as Mamm appeared in the kitchen doorway. "You're up early."

"Jah." Mattie pushed her hair back out of her face.

"You should get ready for the day," Mamm chided. "And put your *kapp* on."

"I'm going to crawl back in bed and not get out forever," Mattie muttered.

Mamm clucked her tongue but said nothing. They both knew she would not hide out in bed today or any day.

"I have to try one more time to persuade Mervin," Mattie said, but she made no attempt to get up from the chair.

"I wouldn't try," Mamm said. "I don't think Mervin's one to change his mind, and we don't have the food prepared anyway. Nor do we have a way of getting so much done so quickly. You already gave me too little time the way things were set up."

"I want to be married on Thursday," Mattie said, as if that settled the matter. "We have to get married on Thursday."

Mamm gave Mattie a sharp glance. "You know that's not true, so get a hold of yourself. At least you don't have Mary's heartache."

The protest died on Mattie's lips as lights from a buggy came into the Beilers' driveway.

"Who would be coming this early in the morning?" Mamm asked.

Mattie rose to her feet, but Mamm sat her down with another sharp look. "You're not going to the door looking like that. I told you to put up your hair."

Mamm hurried off, and a moment later Mattie stood to peek out of the kitchen window. She caught her breath at the sight of Mervin's buggy. Had her hopes been answered? Her head pounded. Why else would Mervin make the trip over to see her on a Sunday morning?

Mervin's voice came from the direction of the front door, and Mattie rushed over to peer around the corner of the kitchen doorway. Neither Mamm or Mervin were visible, but she could hear them outside on the porch.

"Mamm," Mattie hollered. "I'm getting ready. I'll be right there."

She made a dash for the stairs. Halfway up, Mattie tripped on the stair step and caught herself with both hands. Her knee still crashed against the wood, and the pain shot all the way up her leg. Mattie got up and managed to hobble into the bedroom before anyone could look into the stairwell. Both Mamm and Mervin must have heard that loud noise.

Mattie flopped down on the bed and rocked with her knee in both hands until the pain subsided. What a fool she was. She couldn't do anything right. Mervin surprised her with a Sunday morning visit, and all she could do was try to break her leg.

Mattie moaned and flexed the offended member. Everything seemed to work. A few sharp pangs ran through her knee, but she couldn't change that. She tested the foot and it worked. With a hop she moved in front of the mirror and did her hair. The pins slipped into her kapp. One step at a time she made her way down the steps. Mervin met her when she limped out of the stairwell.

"Are you hurt?" he asked. "We heard an awful noise."

"What happened?" Mamm called from the kitchen before Mattie could answer.

"I just slipped," she muttered. "It's nothing serious."

Mervin didn't appear convinced. He came over and went down on his knees in front of her. "Where?"

She pointed to her right knee.

His hands caressed the joint. "Nothing's broken," he said. "But I'm not a doctor."

"I wouldn't be walking if it was broken." Mattie forced a laugh.

"You'd better baby that leg all day," he said.

Mattie winced and placed pressure on the leg again.

"I can use help in the kitchen," Mamm called out.

"Looks like no babying today," Mattie told him.

He made a face. "I didn't intend to be a burden this morning."

"You're never a burden," Mattie assured him. "Are you. . ." She stopped. Of course Mervin wasn't here to change the cancellation of their wedding date. He was here to comfort her, to coddle her for the day, and she had just given him the perfect excuse.

"I love you," he mouthed the words.

Mattie squeezed his shoulder before she took cautious steps toward the kitchen. The tears sprung to her eyes, and Mervin noticed. She couldn't help that anymore than she could help the slip on the stairs. So much of life was out of control right now.

Mattie worked in silence beside Mamm, while murmured voices rose in the living room behind them. Daed must be up. The front door slammed, and the men's voices faded away. Mattie fried the eggs while Mamm did the bacon. Pancakes came after that, all without instruction or plans between the two of them. They seemed of the same mind this morning.

"It's awful nice of him to come over this morning," Mamm finally said.

Mattie nodded but didn't reply.

The food steamed on the table when the men came in from their chores.

"Sit," Mamm said, words were at a minimum this morning.

Daed and Mervin ate in silence, as if they had talked themselves out in the barn. Mervin's plan wasn't working too well. She felt worse now than before he had arrived.

After the prayer of thanksgiving, Mattie began to clear the table, and Mervin joined her. Mamm vanished into the living room without a protest.

"I'm sorry about all this," Mervin ventured, the dish towel draped across his arm.

"We could—" Mattie choked on the words.

Mervin wiped away at the wet dishes. "The Lord is still with us," he said. "Even if this week won't be quite like we had planned."

"Quite like we had planned!" The words exploded, and Mattie rushed on. "I won't be your frau. That's more than 'not quite like we had planned.'"

"I didn't mean it that way," Mervin told her. "My heart also hurts, and my hopes have also been dashed. I want you as my frau, Mattie. I want that in the worst way."

"Then why aren't we marrying this Thursday?" Mattie wailed.

"Mattie!" Mamm's sharp rebuke came from the living room. "Control yourself."

"That's not a decent attitude to have," Daed added.

Mattie ignored them.

Mervin's face was pained. "My love for you has not changed, Mattie. I want only what is right."

"And love is not right?" Mattie managed to keep her voice lowered this time.

"Love is always right," Mervin said. "The time is just not right."

Mattie sighed and continued to wash the dishes. They would get nowhere with this argument, and she wanted to enjoy her limited time with Mervin.

"I guess it was nice for you to come over this morning." She gave him a crooked smile.

His pained look didn't fade. "If I could see my way through to have the wedding this Thursday, believe me, Mattie, I would marry you this week. But—"

"Jah, I know," she interrupted him. "Mamm already told me what the problems are with that arrangement, so let's not speak of it anymore. Did you bring along your Sunday clothing?"

A slight grin filled his face. "You don't think I'd venture forth on a Sunday morning without the proper clothing in my buggy."

Mattie gave him a bright smile. "I know you wouldn't. You're decent and orderly, and you always do the right thing, which I don't."

Mervin sobered. "I don't know about that, but I do know that you are sweet, and—"

"Stop it," Mattie ordered. "I can only take so much."

Mervin seemed to understand as they finished the dishes in silence. Daed led out in devotions afterward, and everyone changed clothing in preparation of the services. True to Mervin's statement, he produced a paper bag from his buggy that contained his Sunday shoes and clothing, all neatly folded.

"You look quite handsome," Mattie told him, once he had changed upstairs while she waited for him in the living room.

He only smiled and led the way out to his buggy. Mattie tried to keep up a light chatter and not think about what could have been as they traveled to Bishop Martin's home.

"See you," Mervin said when he dropped her off at the end of the sidewalks.

Mattie gave him a little wave and limped into the washroom. She left her shawl there to greet the women lined up in the kitchen.

The services began right at nice o'clock and ended at five after twelve. The men spilled out on the front porch while the tables were set up for lunch. Mattie helped serve but didn't eat until the last table was laid out. She felt no hunger, just a numbness that filled her whole body.

By three o'clock, all the tables were cleared, and the men had seated themselves out in the yard on the sunny side of the house. Mattie went in search of Lois but paused by the front window when an English automobile pulled in Bishop Martin's driveway. Their neighbor Mr. Falks climbed out and approached the group of men. He began to speak with exaggerated hand motions.

Mattie stepped out on the porch to listen. She could hear his words clearly all the way across the yard.

"The Japanese bombed our fleet at Pearl Harbor this morning. That's what I'm saying. In Hawaii! Our boats! Our ships! Our soldiers! The entire Pacific Fleet. It is war, men. War!" Mr. Falks's voice rose even higher. "I'll be expecting you people to do your part!"

"We will pray," Bishop Martin said. "We will call a time of prayer and fasting tonight for your people and for ours."

Mr. Falks waved his arms about again, but Mattie could no longer hear him. Her legs buckled under her, and she slid to the floor of the porch to lean against the house. There would be no wedding now. Not for years and years. The worst had come, and she was not married.

Chapter 9

Mervin harnessed Windy to the buggy on Monday morning and drove toward the town of Whitehorse. His face was grim. He had been up since well before dawn and hadn't eaten after the Sunday noon meal yesterday. Bishop Martin had declared a district-wide fast last night. He could have made breakfast for himself, but he hadn't.

Mervin jiggled the reins, and Windy increased his speed. He would see for himself what all this was about. He had never purchased newspapers before. He had no interest in newspapers or in the news they carried. He wanted only peace and a life lived in the fear of the Lord on his farm with Mattie—a wish that obviously wouldn't happen for years now. Not with the surprise attack on Pearl Harbor. He knew that, but he had to look fear in the eye, the same fear that had been on Mr. Falks's face yesterday.

He had known only the sheltered life of the community. He knew nothing of war, or of bombs, or of guns that tore men's lives away from this world. He had always made his decisions with the community's strength around him, like a barn that gave shelter in the fiercest storm. All while the people in the English world were caught in a fight that could snatch their lives away at any moment. They faced death, while he didn't. He didn't fear death. He tried to fear the Lord and choose the right path, a path that had become rocky and steep to climb. He should have gone over to see Mattie last evening, to comfort her in this troubled time, but he hadn't.

The thought troubled him all night. He had fallen asleep only to awaken again with a start. He could see Mattie's face, her simplicity, her desire that they wed, and her fearlessness. Mattie hadn't wanted to call off their wedding last year, and she had wanted to wed him before Christmas. He had told her the way was too difficult and the cost too high. He had pointed to Willis Stoll's death and to his frau, Mary, left to walk the world without her husband. It would have been better if Willis and Mary had waited. Willis might still be alive.

But how did he know that? That's what Mattie had asked. Willis would have been happy to see Mary that morning of the accident whether he was married to her or not. Willis's fall could still have happened, and Mary wouldn't have been Willis's frau for the few weeks of time she had shared with him. Mattie would have reminded him of similar things last night, which was why he hadn't visited. He had feared Mattie's words.

So he was on his way to Whitehorse for an English newspaper. He had faced fears before, and he could face his own. Mattie wouldn't marry anyone else while he was gone. That was not his fear.

He was afraid of himself. He feared his ability to handle the future with Mattie. That was why he repeatedly called off his wedding. If there had been only himself to worry about, he could handle that, but not with Mattie along for the journey. He had tried to override his fear with the joy that Mattie gave him. He had imagined the happiness he would feel when he held Mattie in his arms after they said the wedding vows. But how could that be right with such uncertainty in his heart? How could he accept pleasure while the years of sorrow stretched out in front of them?

Mattie had no answer for those questions. She spoke of love, and how love was enough, and how love was the answer, and how love could not be wrong. But how could love be right in the face of danger, especially when he wanted that love so badly? That was the question.

Mervin pulled back on the reins as he approached the small town. He pulled into the gas station and stopped by the picket fence in the back and let the reins hang. The young attendant looked up when he walked in. "Can I help you?"

Mervin pushed back his straw hat and pulled out his billfold. "Just the morning's newspaper, please."

The attendant motioned toward the front of the counter. "Help yourself. Are the Amish into the war, too?"

Mervin ignored the question. He didn't want to explain himself.

The attendant shrugged. "That's an awful thing that happened over there. We'll never be the same again, I suppose. The country, I mean. You people. . ."

Mervin paid for the newspaper with a nickel.

"I suppose you won't be signing up." The attendant glanced at him as he gave Mervin two pennies back.

"We believe in peace and in the Lord's strength," Mervin told him.

The attendant squinted. "Seems like the rest of us do, too, and we still have to fight. Doesn't seem right, does it? You people sitting things out comfortably on your farms while the rest of us rush off to die for the country."

"Things won't be easy for us," Mervin said. "I. . ." He stopped. Nothing he had to say would compare to what this young man might face. "I'm sorry," he said instead. "Will you have to leave to fight?"

The nod was curt. "I'm signing up tomorrow. The country needs me."

"I hope the Lord protects you," Mervin said. "Are you leaving behind someone?"

A soft smile crept across the young attendant's face. "We'll be marrying before I go. I haven't asked her yet, but I think she'll say yes. I wouldn't want to leave her unspoken for, you know. If I don't come back, we'll at least have been married. I think I'd rather go like that than to always wonder what could have been."

"I hope she says yes." Mervin held out his empty hand. "My name's Mervin, and yours?"

"Wheelie." He shook Mervin's hand. "Thanks for asking."

"And hers?" Mervin still hadn't let go.

"Anthelia. Isn't that a sweet name?"

Mervin smiled. "I'm sure she's sweet, too. The best to you." He turned to go.

"And how about you?" Wheelie's voice stopped him.

"I'm not married," Mervin said, as if that had been the question.

"Surely you have someone," Wheelie insisted. "You're handsome, and the Amish marry. . ."

"Thanks for the newspaper." Mervin forced a laugh, and Wheelie joined in. He hurried out of the station without a glance back. Wheelie would think he was bashful instead of rude. Wheelie didn't know that he was embarrassed. His explanation of why he didn't plan to marry Mattie sounded empty and trite in the face of what Wheelie had told him. The man faced death and a girl who hadn't expressed her willingness to wed him and might not accept the offer.

Mervin climbed back into his buggy and turned Windy around to head east on Route 340. He laid the newspaper on the seat. He didn't look at it until he had pulled in the driveway of his small farm and parked beside the barn.

Mervin scanned the headlines: US ENTERS THE WAR. 1,500 DEAD. CONGRESS REACTS AT ONCE. ONLY ONE MEMBER OF CONGRESS VOTES AGAINST THE WAR. TOKYO CLAIMS VICTORY IN THE PACIFIC.

Mervin looked away. He didn't need to read the details. This was a world he knew little about, but he could understand the words and hear the violence. War was where some men died and where other men were wounded and maimed and came home broken in heart and spirit. This victory would be won with blood and lives. With young men like Wheelie at the gas station, who loved even when that love was uncertain. Wheelie believed in things greater than himself. He had courage in the face of great danger. Wheelie had hope in the future, when death was the likely outcome. If Wheelie came home from the war, he would be forever changed, yet Wheelie wanted to leave a married man.

Mervin hung his head and turned the buggy around. He was shamed. There was no question about that. Windy shook his head in protest but sped up to a fast trot when Mervin jiggled the reins.

The familiar distance rolled under the buggy wheels, and Mervin kept a tight grip on the reins. His whole body was tense. He knew what he would say to Mattie, but he could never fully explain to her what he had felt at the gas station. Maybe he wouldn't have to. Mattie was that kind of a woman. Her arms seemed always open to him even when she expected his usual cautiousness, his long waits, and his spoken fears. Mattie would expect nothing different with what had happened yesterday and with his absence from her home last night.

Windy neighed when Mervin pulled into the Beilers' driveway. He stopped at the hitching post and jumped down with the tie rope in his hand. Mattie's daed came out of the barn door while he tied up.

"Gut morning," Lamar greeted him.

Mervin nodded.

"Mattie's in the house," Lamar said.

"I may be awhile," Mervin told him. "I've come to the conclusion that I. . . Do you think it wise if. . ." Mervin took a deep breath. "I've not been the man I should have been, Lamar. I'm sorry."

Lamar smiled. "I think you should wed my daughter, Mervin. The girl has been crying all night. You two should face the future together, as man and wife, even with the shocking news we received yesterday."

Mervin hung his head. "I've not always made the best choices."

Lamar gave Mervin a quick pat on the back. "You did what you thought was right. I don't fault you, son. But things are serious now. It's time you married the girl."

Mervin tried to smile. "I'll be speaking with Mattie."

Lamar turned to go, and Mervin made his way to the front door. Mattie's mamm, Esther, opened at his knock. She appeared surprised.

"Can I speak with Mattie?" Mervin asked.

Esther motioned toward the stair door. "She's in her room. You can go up."

Mervin took the stairs one at a time. He knocked on the familiar bedroom door.

"Come in," Mattie called out.

She was seated on her bed when he opened. A smile twitched on her face and wrinkled the obvious tear stains. "It's you."

Mervin came closer and took her hand. He seated himself on the quilt beside her.

"I'll be okay," she whispered. "Sorry you caught me like this."

He tried to speak, but his words didn't come.

"You don't have to apologize," she said. "I've been wrestling with the Lord, and I've found peace. We can wait, Mervin, for whatever time it takes, until this wicked war is over and you come home. I might be an old woman by then." Mattie choked back the tears. "But it'll be okay. Our love will last that long. It'll be there for whatever years are left to us." The tears streamed freely down her face. "I'll always love you, Mervin. Always and always and even when you're not here, and when you come back, and—"

"Hush, dear," he interrupted to take her in his arms.

"I'll never hush." She pulled away to peer up at his face. "I love, I love you, I love, and I'll say that even if you don't want to hear it."

"Dear heart." He stilled her with his fingers on her lips. "Let me get a word in please."

Tears brimmed in her eyes again. "I don't want to hear what you have to say. Reasons and excuses and—" Her voice broke. "I've already accepted it, okay? Just hold me, and hold me, and never let go."

He pulled her close, and she sobbed on his chest, with great choking sounds that tore at him.

"Mattie," he tried again. "I'll marry you. Listen to me. I didn't come to explain things but to say that we can wed."

"We can wed." The sobs ceased. Her tear-stained face lifted to his. "Like when you come back, like in—"

"Now," he said. "This month. Before Christmas, if you can get ready by then."

"Before Christmas." She stared at him. She yelled, "Before Christmas!"

"Jah!" He held her face with both hands. "That's what I'm sorry about. That we aren't already wed."

"You are sorry? That we aren't wed?" She leaped to her feet and danced a jig on the floor in front of him, her hands aflutter.

"Of course." He forced a laugh. "I've always been, Mattie." He gathered her in his arms again. "We can marry whenever you are ready."

"When we are ready." Her voice was muffled on his chest. "I'm ready right now."

"Well." He held her at arm's length. "Not now, but as soon as it's decent. With the bishop here, of course, and the wedding guests."

"Mervin, are you okay?" She touched his forehead with one finger. "Are you well?"

He laughed out loud. "I'm not ill. I can explain. This morning—"

She stopped him with an uplifted hand. "Just say it again. What you said earlier about this month."

He took a deep breath. "I'll marry you before Christmas, Mattie Beiler, if you can get ready."

"Get ready!" she screamed. With a leap she was on her feet again and twirled about the room. "Go, go, go. Out of the room." She waved both of her hands at him. "No, no, Mamm has to hear this. She'll never believe it. Come! Come! Come!"

Mattie seized his hand and bustled him down the stairs. Esther appeared at the kitchen doorway, and Mattie parked Mervin in front of her. "Say it," she commanded.

Mervin grinned. "I will marry your daughter as soon as you can get the wedding ready."

"There!" Mattie pronounced. "Now go." She jerked on his hand, and almost threw him out of the front door.

"What?" He stopped on the front porch.

"I have work to do," she declared, her face a beam of happiness in the front door. "We have to get ready for the wedding."

Chapter 10

It was Christmas Eve, and Mattie held Mervin's hand under the table. The number for the last song of the evening hymn singing had just been given out. She already knew what the words would be. She wished another parting song had been chosen, but all parting songs had a note of sadness in them. Even so, she wouldn't let sadness creep into her wedding day. She was now Mervin's frau, and nothing could change that.

She stole a quick glance at Mervin as the song began, "God be with you till we meet again, by His counsel's guide uphold you, with His sheep securely fold you..."

Mervin smiled and mouthed the familiar words, "I love you."

Mattie looked away and gave his hand another tight squeeze. His smile grew as they began the chorus, "Till we meet, till we meet, till we meet at Jesus' feet..."

Mattie joined in the soaring voices of the young people. Outside tonight lay all the troubles of the world, but inside this little gathering there was joy and happiness. Christmas was tomorrow, and hope had been born that day—and promise. How fitting that she had made her promises to Mervin today and that he had made his to her. Bishop Martin had held their hands and declared them man and wife right after twelve o'clock. They were forever together in heart while they lived on this earth.

"My frau," Mervin leaned over to whisper, as if he knew her thoughts.

"My husband," she whispered back and gazed into his eyes.

The sound of the singing faded away, and she saw only Mervin and the love that shone back at her. He had been so sweet these last weeks, so tender with her, as if he wanted to make up for all the time they had lost when their love had been denied and they'd had to wait. But she was his now, and he was hers.

Mervin cleared his throat and pulled his gaze away to focus on the songbook. She didn't have to look to sing the words. She could only see Mervin's face, anyway. She wanted to reach up and touch him as she had done so many times in the past, but that would have to wait.

The song ended, and the guests began to file past to wish them congratulations for the last time. Mervin stood, and Mattie took her place beside him. Her eight sisters with their husbands made a line of their own. Mervin and Mattie shook each hand and thanked everyone that had come. The crowd lingered even after the last relative and friend had passed by them. Mattie sat down again, and Mervin did likewise. It would be awhile before everyone left, but she had Mervin with her. Little else seemed to matter at the moment.

"Thank you for helping out today." Mervin leaned over to speak with his brother Emery and the girl Emery had asked to sit with him for the day, Millie Troyer.

Millie turned all sorts of colors and giggled. "It's been so great, that's all I can say. I have enjoyed myself immensely sitting up here on the day that you said your wedding vows."

"We are glad to have you," Mervin told her. "And I'm sure Emery is, too."

"Yep," Emery chirped. He gave Millie a quick glance, and they smiled at each other.

Emery would ask Millie home on a date before long, if Mattie didn't miss her guess. Unless Emery was also called up for the draft. Mattie pushed the horrible thought away and turned to Mary, who was seated beside her. "And thank you, dear, for consenting to be my witness. I know it was hard, but you have been a jewel today."

Mary wiped away a quick tear. "We share in each other's joys and sorrows. I wouldn't have missed your joy for the world, and on Christmas Eve."

"Thank you," Mattie whispered and gave Mary a quick hug. She leaned farther out to say to Mervin's younger brother, "And thank you, John, for sitting with Mary. That was kind of you."

John gulped and nodded. There had been no sly smiles or glances exchanged between John and Mary all day, which was how it should have been. She had asked Mary to choose her partner, and Mary had chosen John. The funeral had been too recent for Mary to entertain any romantic thoughts, and John fit the bill exactly. He was handsome, but he would never ask Mary home on a date. That privilege would belong to some older man, a widower perhaps, once this awful war was over. But Mattie wouldn't think of the future tonight. She would think of Mervin, who was finally her husband.

Mattie turned her head when Bishop Martin waved his hand about. Silence settled over the building.

"I think it fitting that we have one final prayer before we all part for the evening," Bishop Martin proclaimed. "So let us pray."

Every head bowed, and Bishop Martin led with the words, "Our Father which art in heaven, hallowed by Thy name, Thy kingdom come. . ."

The amen came, and Mattie took Mervin's hand again. She held him tight while the guests filed out. When some of them still chatted on the front porch, she pulled on Mervin's hand, and they slipped out by way of the washroom door and down the dark side of the house. Daed must have anticipated her move, because he had Mervin's horse Windy hitched to the buggy and ready to go.

"Here we are," Daed said with a smile. "And a special blessing to my daughter and my new son-in-law."

"And to you," Mervin told him. "Thank you for raising such a wunderbaar woman."

Daed chuckled, and the newlyweds climbed into the buggy to dash up the lane and down Route 340 toward Whitehorse. A light snow lay on the ground. The moon had set, and the stars overhead blinked in all their brilliance. The only lights on the road were the bright flashes from the Christmas decorations in the English homes.

"It's Christmas tomorrow," Mattie whispered, her head on Mervin's shoulder, "and I'm married to you."

He smiled. "Jah, it is, and we made it through, no thanks to me."

She sat up straight. "It's all thanks to you, so don't say that. But tell me, what made you change your mind."

"You didn't want to know before," he replied.

"Well, I do now," she said and leaned against his shoulder.

Mervin took a moment before he answered. "An English boy shamed me with his bravery and courage."

"An English boy?" Mattie sat up again. "You'll have to give me more details than that."

"Maybe I don't want to."

"You're my husband, and we will have no secrets."

Mervin laughed. "I hope not."

"Tell me." She peered up into his face.

"I went to Whitehorse for a newspaper that morning," Mervin began, and he continued the story in bits and pieces.

"Mmm!" Mattie proclaimed when he finished. "I never thought things would happen that way. But you're my husband, so it doesn't matter how the Lord moved."

"We must pray for all those who must fight in this war," Mervin said, as he pulled into the driveway.

A dim kerosene lamp burned in the kitchen window. Mervin brought the buggy to a stop, and Mattie climbed down. "Did you leave a light on?" Mattie asked.

Mervin shook his head. "Mamm stopped in on her way home. I wanted a light in the window when we arrived."

"You did." Mattie clasped her hands together. "I'm home. I'm really home."

They climbed down from the buggy. Mervin led Windy forward after they unhitched, and Mattie held the shafts for him. Mervin tossed a smile over his shoulder and took off with Windy toward the barn. Mattie lingered near the buggy, the glow of the stars bright on the snow. Tears threatened as she gazed toward the house and the light in the window.

"Come," she told Mervin when he came back from the barn. "Let's sit on the front porch for a moment. The moon is down, but the stars are so bright."

"Anything you want," he agreed and followed with his hand in hers.

The soft glow of the kitchen light crept out of the living room window, and the swing creaked as they sat down.

"I always want to remember this day when I said my wedding vows." Mattie drew close to him, and Mervin wrapped his arm around her shoulders.

"So do I," he agreed. "I will think of you all the time after I have to leave."

She touched his face. "Shhh. . .it was right what we did today. We will never regret it, not if troubles come, not if the road is long, not if the time never seems to end, and not if I'm old and withered when you come back. I will have loved you. For that, I will never have regrets."

"You are the sweetest thing, you know?" He brushed her hair back from her face. "Where did you come from? Did the angels drop you off somewhere between heaven and earth?"

She giggled. "You wish."

He laughed, and she leaned against him. The silence fell around them, the twinkle of the Christmas lights bright in the distance.

"Will our men die in the camps where you are going?" Mattie asked.

"This won't be World War I," he replied. "The government will have more compassion, but how do you know these things?"

"I asked Daed," she said. "And you are going, aren't you? Why shouldn't I know?"

"Sometimes it's best not to know."

She shook her head. "You would think so, but that's not true. To know is to share, and to share is to lessen the pain. You must always tell me what you go through."

"I doubt if I can write the details," he said. "At least not from the camps. It's wartime, and everyone will be on edge."

"You must tell me when you come back, then."

"Jah," he said. "When I come back."

Mattie stared at the distant Christmas lights. "Many of them won't come back. Daed's newspaper is already full of deaths. The world will suffer more than any of us can imagine."

"Jah, I know."

"Is it right, do you think?" She looked up into his face. "That we don't die with them?"

"We died once for our faith all those years ago, when the others didn't," he said. "But these things are in the Lord's hand. It is not for us to decide."

"But we can cry with them, can we not? I do at night after I've read Daed's paper. They are just like us, Mervin. They hurt, even if they are brave."

"They are afraid like us, I think."

"Is that not what bravery is?"

"Then we are very brave." He stroked her hair again.

"Oh Mervin." She clung to him. "How am I going to let you go?"

"I don't know," he said. "But the English do, and we will also find the strength."

She nestled against him, her shawl wrapped around her shoulders, until the distant Christmas lights blinked out and only the glow of the stars remained.

Amish Christmas Cookies

12 eggs
2 pounds brown sugar
4 cups sugar
1 tablespoon vanilla
1 tablespoon corn syrup
8 tablespoons baking soda
1 pound butter, melted
6 cups peanut butter
1 pound chocolate chips
1 pound red and green M&M's candies
18 cups quick oats

Preheat oven to 350 degrees. Mix ingredients in order given. Drop by spoonfuls onto ungreased cookie sheet. Place in oven and bake for 9 to 11 minutes. Do not overbake.

Note: Recipe can be halved.

Jerry S. Eicher's seven Amish fiction series include The Land of Promise, The Beiler Sisters, and The Emma Raber's Daughter series. He wrote of his experience growing up Amish in his memoir, *My Amish Childhoo*d, and taught for two terms in Amish and Mennonite schools in Ohio and Illinois. Jerry has been involved in church renewal and preaching and has taught at Elnora Bible Institute. He lives with his wife, Tina, in Virginia.

Love's Pure Light

by Olivia Newport

Chapter 1

G lory Grabill!"

Still adjusting to her married name of seven weeks and standing among the chickens, Gloria let the scrap pail dangle from one hand and turned toward the caller. Lyddie, her husband's youngest sister, waved an envelope in the nipping December air. Sun on rolling hills of white spun a dense glare. As Lyddie approached Gloria, she came into focus.

"You got a letter," Lyddie said.

Lyddie moved toward the side of the yard where the chickens gathered around Glory's feet anticipating the contents of the pail. Glory's mother was always protective of her chickens in the winter, but her mother-in-law advocated that chickens were heartier than most people gave them credit for and made sure at least a small portion of the yard was cleared for them after a snow.

"Do you want the letter now, or shall I put it in the house?" Lyddie said.

"Now, please." Glory upended the remains of the household's midday meal and took three swift steps back from the mass of chickens that hustled toward the instant buffet.

"It has always been Marianne's job to feed the chickens," Lyddie said.

Having spared her only pair of winter gloves the mess of handling the slop bucket, Glory reached under her cloak and used her apron to wipe clean one icy hand. "I like to be helpful while I am here." She flicked her eyes toward the letter.

"From your *mamm*," Lyddie said. "I recognize the writing from the others."

Though she lived only fifteen miles away, Gloria's mother wrote nearly every day and managed a couple of times a week to find someone with reason to go by the Grabill farm. Other letters came through the mail. She remembered what it was like to move into the home of brand-new in-laws, she had said in her first letter to Gloria after the wedding.

Glory smiled at Lyddie and took the letter. Growing up in the same church district, she had known Marlin's family all her life. But they were not *her* family, and her mother's letters were a lifeline to all that made her feel certain of herself.

Lyddie lurked.

"Thank you," Glory said. She did not dare open the letter, or Lyddie would be looking over her shoulder. Instead, she tucked it under her cloak, savoring a moment of warmth for her fingers as well. "Are you working in the henhouse today?"

Lyddie glanced toward the structure, where the usual after-school chores awaited the fourteen-year-old. "I guess so."

Gloria waited another minute, watching Lyddie scuffle toward the henhouse, before she loosened the envelope's flap and slipped out the single half sheet of white paper. Although her mother's handwriting always looked as if she was in too much of a rush to let the point of the pen do more than scratch across the paper in light, angular strokes, each letter swirled the fragrance of love.

Gloria blinked, focused on the date—today, December 21, 1910—and read the brief lines again.

There was no encouraging phrase from the Bible, no sweet memory of her mother's own newlywed days, no chitchat of familiar household routines.

"We have decided we must move," the letter said. *"Your brother will look after the farm and take in the animals since we do not know when we will return. We were to see you on Old Christmas, but that seems impossible now. I am sorry not to be able to kiss your cheek before we go, but your Aenti Beth is failing quickly. I fear she is not long for this world, and someone will have to look after her little ones. Perhaps we will return by the spring planting or know by then what the call is on our future. Pray for Gottes wille. Daed is already waiting in the buggy for me to catch the first train. Curly Jake promised he would get this letter to you. Love from your mamm."*

Her parents were gone. They were not fifteen miles away across the Lancaster district, where she would see them at church services and spend all of Old Christmas with them on January 6, when her brothers and sisters—all older and married— would gather on the family farm. They were hours away on a hurtling train.

Gone. Her parents were gone.

Glory spun, trying to think where Marlin had said he would be.

◆　◆　◆

"It is not a competition." Marlin winked at his three brothers. "Making *putz* should help us worship the Christ child."

Leroy and Josef, his older brothers, scoffed immediately. John, younger and the only unmarried brother, shook his head in disbelief.

"Your mouth says the right words," Leroy said, "but your eyes have something else in them."

Marlin paced across Josef's small barn. God willing, a year from now he would be in his own barn tending the animals he and Glory would use to begin their own stock.

"We have only three days until Christmas Eve," Marlin said. "We all have work to do. There is no time for competitiveness."

"But you will work on something new," Josef said. "You do not have a newborn keeping you up half the night."

"You do not have to make something new," Marlin said, patting the rump of one cow. Leroy had already promised Marlin this cow's spring calf. "Daed will want me to use some of his pieces in the Nativity."

"So you claim the Nativity?" John said. "I am the unmarried son. I should do the Nativity while you start a tradition with Glory."

"Now who is being competitive?" Marlin grinned. "If you want the Nativity, you shall have it. I will do the Angels."

"That leaves the Annunciation and the Shepherds." Josef glanced at Leroy. "Your choice."

"Joannah will want me to do the Shepherds," Josef said.

"Sadie likes news of a woman with child," Leroy said, "so the Annunciation will suit her. Everyone please remember that we are not trying to win a prize. It is a family tradition for all to share, not an opportunity to make ourselves stand out."

"That is just what I would expect the oldest brother to say," Marlin said.

"Do you disagree?"

"Of course not. But the Bible tells us to do everything as unto the Lord, and does that not mean that we should offer Him our best effort?"

John kicked up straw. "This is the first year that you do not want to work together with me."

"I am married now," Marlin said. "This will be my last Christmas living with Mamm and Daed."

"You are only a year older than I am," John said. "I will be gone soon as well."

Leroy planted his pitchfork in a bale of hay. "Are you making an announcement of your own, John?"

The youngest brother blushed and turned to the wall of tack.

"I suggest you enlist Marianne and Lyddie," Marlin said. "They both like to make putz."

"You mean they are both as competitive as you are," John muttered, his face still toward the wall.

"It is not a competition," Marlin repeated.

Again, his brothers laughed with little effort to mitigate their response.

The barn door opened, heralding a blast of December air. Marlin looked up.

"Glory! What are you doing here?"

◆　◆　◆

Glory flinched as she shoved the barn door closed behind her. She had not traversed three-and-a-half miles over the crunch of six inches of frozen snow in search of her husband only to be greeted with surprise that superseded welcome. The temperature inside Leroy's barn was above the twenty degrees outside, though perhaps not by much. The brothers were supposed to be working on insulating the structure more efficiently, but it seemed to Gloria that the gathering had been more ruse for the Grabill boys to spend the afternoon together.

She shivered under her cloak and moved closer to the cow sharing its warmth with Marlin, probing his face for signs of his attention. While he touched her elbow, his eyes panned between his brothers.

"We were about to start work on filling in the cracks," Leroy said.

One corner of Glory's mouth twitched. The Grabill brothers were notorious for procrastination when they were together, but at least they had a conscience. They would eventually rope in a sense of purpose and accomplish the necessary work.

"Your husband is determined to make the best putz in the entire church district," Josef said.

"All of Lancaster County," John said.

"All of Pennsylvania," Leroy said.

Marlin waved them all off. "*Ummieglich*. You are an impossible bunch."

"Does your family make putz?" John asked.

"We never have," Glory said. "We sometimes rode to neighbor farms to see what families had done, but we never made our own." Her parents were a well-matched quiet pair, sincere in their faith and loving in their sacrificial ways. But other than a few homemade gifts that came out of hiding on Christmas morning, the season changed little of the family's routine. Certainly her brothers would not have isolated themselves in a barn where they seemed to be doing nothing.

"You are a Grabill now," Leroy said. "You will have to learn our ways, because your husband does not let go of tradition easily."

Josef laughed. "That is a well-spoken way of saying Marlin likes to be the best."

"*Demut,*" Marlin said. Humility.

Gloria had never known Marlin to be proud or self-centered in ambition. But she had never spent a holiday with him, never seen him in his own family as she had over the last seven weeks. Moving in with the groom's family was common for the first year of marriage, or visiting a few weeks at a time among other family and relatives while the new couple readied themselves for their own farm. Glory had always known this, yet living this tradition brought surprises every day—not all of them welcome.

"We should get to work," Leroy said. "If we do not make some progress, Sadie will give me a peculiar look over supper."

The brothers laughed. Marlin pecked Glory's cheek. "Thanks for coming to say hello."

Glory kept her voice low. "Could we talk for a moment?"

Chapter 2

Marlin did not often hear this tone from his bright, compassionate bride.

"Maybe outside," Glory said.

Marlin glanced past his brothers to the door and nodded.

"I will just be a minute," he said as he led the way outside.

Outside, frigid air bit his cheeks, and for the first time he saw the chapped redness his wife's journey had inflicted on her face.

"Why did you not come in a buggy?" he asked.

"You had ours," she said simply, the warmth of her breath hovering before dissipating as if it had never been.

"But we have plenty of buggies on the farm," Marlin said.

"I did not want to presume."

"It is no presumption, Glory. You are part of the family. You can use a buggy if one is available."

"Maybe next time." She shivered.

"It is freezing out here." Given the distance, Glory must have already spent close to ninety minutes in the piercing cold. "Did you tell anyone you were coming?"

"I just said I wanted some fresh air," Glory said.

If she had stumbled or been injured, would anyone have known to look for her? Or would he have found her heaped on frozen ground on his way home? Marlin choked on the image in his mind.

"I had a letter from my mamm," she said.

Marlin fixed his eyes on her. Letters from her mother cheered Gloria, but she looked far from pleased now. She had not ventured all this way to tell him of her mother's latest advice.

"What is it?" he said.

Her features rolled in distress. "They've gone away."

"For Christmas?"

"Probably a long time. At least until spring but perhaps much longer."

Marlin tilted his head to listen as Gloria read her mother's letter aloud.

"The *English* doctors said Aenti Beth has cancer," Gloria said. "But I did not know she might go so quickly. They live all the way in Holmes County, Ohio. Her husband's parents are gone. He will need help for a long time."

"Perhaps he will just need time to sort things out," Marlin said. "Your parents will be back before you know it, and your mamm will keep sending letters."

"It is not the same."

Marlin took Gloria's hands. "Where are your gloves?"

"I forgot them."

He blew warm air on her fingers and put his own oversize gloves on her hands. "You are not alone. Your brother is just a few farms over, and I am here. My whole family is here. You are a Grabill now, and Grabills are never alone."

"If only God had granted us Old Christmas together before this happened." Gloria looked down at Marlin's fingers wrapped around hers.

"God's timing is best," he said.

The barn door opened. John stood in the opening.

"Are you two conniving on the putz?"

"I must take Gloria home," Marlin said.

She shook her head. "I will walk."

"At least take the buggy," he said. "You have been out in the cold too long already."

"I have two cloaks on."

"Please take the buggy. John and I can walk, or Leroy can drive us."

Marlin paced off to hitch the team.

◆　◆　◆

Every night at supper in the Grabill home, Glory wondered how the family generated as much sound as it did. Leroy and Josef were on their own farms with their wives and babies. But there were still six Grabills—parents David and Magdalena and their children Marlin, John, Marianne, and Lyddie. Although Glory was a seventh person in the home, she did not make up one-seventh of the noise at suppertime.

Most of the Amish families Glory knew were efficient about preparing a simple evening meal at the end of a long day of labor, and they ate in subdued gratitude. Her own family had been this way, even when all her older siblings lived at home. For a fleeting moment, Glory wondered whether her parents had waited for her to be married before moving away. If she had not married Marlin a few weeks ago, would they still be on the family farm fifteen miles away having a quiet supper and praying for Aenti Beth's family from a distance?

But she had married Marlin, and her mealtimes—at least for the first year of her marriage—were wholly unfamiliar. The sisters teased each other during food preparation, their mother's amused voice cackled above the din, and the men's voices boomed in analysis of what had been accomplished during the day and what must be done tomorrow.

Glory did not fit.

"You are a Grabill now, and Grabills are never alone," Marlin had said that afternoon. No doubt he meant it as encouragement, but to Gloria it was a descriptive statement of her new life—but not entirely accurate. Her last name was Grabill, and there were always people around. Yet she felt alone.

She passed the bread basket to Marlin before he asked for it. At least one person at the supper table was someone she knew well enough to anticipate.

Every other Sunday for all of her life the church district had gathered for worship and a communal meal that followed the service. It was not that she had never prepared food or eaten alongside anyone from the Grabill family before marrying into the household. But it was not the same. Everyone at church had on their "company manners," as her English school friends used to call them. Glory could enjoy the dishes, make polite inquiries about people's welfare, laugh at humorous stories, nod at somber prayer requests—and then go home.

Home. Where she fit. Where she belonged. Where she was known and understood. Where life felt organized. Where she knew what to do, what to say.

Glory passed the bread basket in the other direction now. She might not know if anyone other than Marlin wanted more bread, but it could not hurt to offer. If she could not keep up with the rapid inundation of table conversation, she could resist being sucked into its eddy by simple gestures of what families did for each other.

◆　◆　◆

In their bedroom three hours later, Marlin put a hand on his wife's back as she let down her braids.

"Are you feeling any better?"

He expected her to lean her head back into his chest, a gesture of the intimacy that had grown between them in their short weeks as husband and wife. Instead, she pulled another pin from her hair and dropped it in a small white porcelain bowl on the chest of drawers without speaking.

"Glory," he said, "it will be all right."

She nodded, still without words.

Another pin dropped into the bowl, the only sound in the room.

Footfalls in the hall approached their closed door, and Marlin reflexively turned toward the noise, braced for a knock. Sometimes he envied the privacy that couples with their own farms enjoyed—or at least he thought that Glory envied it and he wished he could give it to her.

The knock did not come. The steps did not pause. It was probably just one of his sisters coming in from a last trip to the outhouse on another ice-bound evening. The temperature at night had not been above freezing for at least a month. Though the hour was not yet late, the farmhouse was drafty, and even inside the temperature was dropping. Soon everyone would find warmth under layers of quilts even if bedside lamps burned for a while longer.

"Do you need anything else tonight?" Marlin asked. Water? A book from downstairs? Another quilt? More oil for the lamp? Whatever Glory needed, he would give if only he knew what it was. He had not imagined being a husband would be so befuddling.

She shook her head and picked up her hairbrush. When her shawl slipped off one shoulder, he was tempted to slide it off the other as well. Instead, he adjusted it to keep her warm while she pulled the brush through thick, rich brown locks that reached her waist.

"I could read to you," he said, reaching for the Bible that had been one of their wedding gifts. Gloria was partial to the book of Proverbs for its practical wisdom, and Marlin had come to appreciate familiar words afresh.

Glory hesitated and then said, "Not tonight."

"You seem extra tired."

She nodded.

Her mother's letter had taken the wind out of her that afternoon. They had not sold their farm; her brother would run it and it would be there when they were ready to come home. Glory understood the circumstances of their departure and even agreed that it was right they should go. Yet their leaving had widened a bereft chasm within her. Marlin did not know how to reach across it.

"You need some sleep," he said. "I will go downstairs and do a bit of carving while you settle in."

"You do not have to do that." Glory spoke at last.

"Would you rather I stay?" *"Two are better than one,"* Ecclesiastes said.

"I am just saying you do not have to leave. But if you want to. . ."

He hated to leave her, but he was not ready to sleep, and his tossing and turning would only keep Glory from slumber. The pale exhaustion of her face made up his mind.

"You need to rest. I will only be a few minutes, and I will be careful not to wake you."

Chapter 3

Occasionally Glory wondered what it would be like to have curtains on an upstairs bedroom window sufficient to resist the light of dawn. An old English classmate made sure the entire one-room school knew that she had new bedroom curtains every two years in her house in town. Glory pressed the thought out of her mind. The girl had never been anything other than an uppity aggravation, and Glory had been grateful to leave school after the eighth grade if for no other reason than to be free of Minnie Handelman. But one of Minnie's cast-off curtains would come in handy just now. Glory rolled away from the dawn, knowing that most of the household was already up and her mother-in-law was frying bacon and mixing biscuits to go with dippy eggs.

Marlin's movement in the room chastised her. He would never scold her—at least, she did not think he would—but when he sat on the side of the bed to wriggle his feet into work boots, guilt spread its tentacles. She pushed up on one elbow.

"I did not even hear you come to bed last night," she said.

"I was only gone thirty minutes, but you were sound asleep."

Glory fell back against the pillow, her limbs leaden and her mind a thick fog.

Marlin leaned over and laid a hand against her cheek. "*Wie geht's?*" Are you all right? "Still tired?"

Any word Glory could think of, whether in English or Pennsylvania Dutch, was wholly insufficient to describe the unfamiliar physical sensation that overwhelmed her.

"You can write to your mamm," Marlin said, "and she will write to you. You will have more information after Christmas."

She exhaled a shallow breath. "I know."

"Glory, what can I do for you?"

He was sweet to want to do something, but Glory was the only person who could make her feet swing to the floor and push her frame upright.

Except even she could not manage it. Her eyes drooped closed.

"Glory? You will miss breakfast."

Behind closed eyelids was the peculiar sensation of light insisting its way through her resistance, but Glory could no more lift her eyelids than her feet.

"I am not hungry," she murmured. "A few more minutes."

"If you are unwell, I will explain to the family."

Unwell? Not precisely. Glory did not often fall ill, but illness had never felt like this. Even before her mother's letter arrived the previous day, something was amiss. But if she told Marlin that it was because she did not fit in his family, she would wound him.

"Perhaps I am unwell," she said, prying her eyes open to look into his. "If I could rest awhile longer. . ."

"Take your time," he said. "We have plenty of help for the chores."

She knew that well. For seven weeks she had foundered for needfulness.

"I promised I would return to help Leroy again," Marlin said, "but I do not have to go."

"Yes. You should go. He will wonder what became of you."

Marlin hesitated, his black felt hat in his hand. "I will ask someone to check on you."

"No need. I will be up before anyone has to be concerned."

She thought he would lean in to kiss her. Cheek, lips, forehead—it would be his parting affection.

But Marlin pushed up off the bed and shuffled across the wood floor out of the room.

◆　◆　◆

"Balmy," Marlin said. "Must be right up there close to freezing."

"Hush," Leroy said. "Just find the holes and jam some plaster in them."

Marlin heard the anxiety in his brother's voice. He dragged a trowel through a tray of plaster, transferred the muck to a wall, and spread it strategically. Admittedly, Leroy's barn did not have long sections where daylight was visible within direct line of sight, and the temperature inside the barn was warmer than outside. Yet at moments wind gusted like a knife to the lung, whistling through the turns that brought the outside in. Leroy, four years older than Marlin and three years married, was running his farm with limited capital. He managed essential repairs on the house and barn, which doubled as a stable, when a particular need became urgent. It may already be too cold for plaster to dry properly, but if they waited until January, they might as well wait until spring to find and fill the gaps. Marlin would not point out any of this. He had his eye on a farm not too far from here, but the value of the barn was questionable. Soon enough he would be relying on the generosity of his brothers.

"Angels," Marlin said, threatening to swipe plaster in the arc of an angel's wings.

"Sadie was quite pleased with the putz selection," Leroy said.

Marlin jiggled the water bucket. So far it had not frozen. This was a good sign.

"I suppose Sadie has some ideas," Marlin said.

"She might." Tight-lipped, Leroy eyeballed another hole.

"Will she send the little ones out to help you?"

"She might."

"Maybe the *boppli* are too young. Awfully cold for them anyway."

"Might be."

"But the wife might add a few suggestions."

"Might."

"Might be something I could do to help," Marlin said. "If I knew what you had in mind, that is."

"Doubtful." Leroy scraped his trowel on the side of a tray.

"Seems to me you do not have much to say," Marlin said.

"Seems to me you ask a lot of nosy questions."

"Just trying to be helpful."

"You are angling for a little more than that, but you will not find it here."

Marlin feigned indignation. "You doubt my motives?"

"You will see the putz on Christmas Eve, same as everybody else."

"Only two days," Marlin said. "Not much time."

"Then you should go home and get busy."

"Are we finished here?" Marlin scanned the most vulnerable barn wall.

"Looks that way to me." Leroy dropped his trowel in the water bucket. "I am sure Glory would like to have you home. I remember what it was like to be newly wed."

Marlin turned his back and scooped up work rags. He was less sure than Leroy of his wife's welcome. Was she ill, or did she simply not want his company? He had been gone most of the day. If Glory was ill, he hoped she had let someone care for her.

◆　◆　◆

The soup was cold, and the bread untouched. Glory had thanked Mrs. Grabill—Magdalena, her mother-in-law insisted she call her now—for going to the trouble of preparing soup for Glory when she must have made a full midday meal for her husband, David, and John and Marianne. Glory was grateful for the kindness, but she had not awakened when Magdalena carried the tray in. Why had no one warned her that adjusting to living in a new household could be so exhausting? Or that one disappointing letter would so strain her ability to cope?

But she could not lie in bed another day, nor for the rest of this one. Glory pushed herself upright in the bed, leaned against the headboard, and reached for the glass of well water Magdalena had included on the undisturbed tray. Draining the liquid, she turned her thoughts toward dressing for an overdue trip to the outhouse. Once she and Marlin were in their own home, she could simply pull a cloak over her nightdress, but seven weeks among the Grabills had not yet provided the necessary ease for a quick dash. One way or another there would be a smile on her face when she went down the stairs and out the back door.

She had just dropped a dress over her head and put her arms into the sleeves when a sharp rap on the door was followed swiftly by a turning doorknob.

"Oh good, you are up." Home from school, Lyddie entered the room. "You have not even put your hair up."

"I have been under the weather."

Glory had not been as forward as Lyddie when she was fourteen. Surely she never would be. Their temperaments were nothing alike. She picked up her hairbrush and began arranging her thick tresses.

"How was school?" Glory asked. It was either make conversation or ask Lyddie to leave.

Lyddie rolled her eyes. "I suppose it is sinful to look forward to a school break simply to get away from one of your classmates."

Glory knew well the sensation. Minnie Handelman.

"What is her name?" Glory asked.

Lyddie's dark eyes widened. "I should not have said that."

"It is all right. You can tell me."

Lyddie's hesitation vanished. "Madeleine Madison. She thinks she is the star of the Christmas program."

Glory pinned up one braid. "When I was in school, everyone had a part in the program."

"It is still that way. Poems, readings, songs. But every day when we rehearse, Madeleine Madison has at least three suggestions for how to change things. I am not sure how much more Miss Draper can take."

"She will manage," Glory said. "Teachers always do."

"Will you come to the program?"

Glory flushed with the realization that she had not considered the question before this. All the families with children in the school attended. She had not been since her own eighth-grade year, but she was a Grabill now. Marlin's sister was her sister.

At least it ought to feel that way.

Chapter 4

Marlin stamped snow off his boots in the sparse entryway off the Grabill kitchen and then wiped them dry on the mat. Inside, a hearty beef aroma wafted from a pot on the stove set over a simmering heat. Marlin paused long enough to fill his lungs with the fragrance but resisted the temptation to lift the lid and peek at the supper menu. Instead, he took the back stairs two at a time in long lunges. The door to his bedroom was open, and sounds of a woman's light movements buoyed his expectations. Whatever had kept Glory in bed that morning had passed.

He made a one-quarter pivot on his left foot to enter the room.

"Lyddie," he said.

"Hello, Marlin."

Lyddie looked into a small dull mirror not much good for anything other than confirming that facial features were in their proper positions. Glory had never complained. Her nimble fingers could braid and roll her hair under a prayer *kapp* without confirmation from a piece of glass.

"Where is Glory?" Marlin asked.

"She will be right back." Lyddie winked and returned her attention to the mirror, trying out a practiced smile and then a somber pinch in her cheeks.

Marlin surrendered. "What are you doing, Lyddie?"

"I have a solo in the Christmas program," Lyddie said, her tone chastising Marlin for being duller than the mirror. "Glory promised to listen to me practice when she gets back."

Marlin looked past his sister to the rumpled bed. Glory cannot have been up for very long. From the first day of their marriage she insisted the bed be made promptly. Underneath a flour sack dish towel that his mother had cross-stitched a few cheery flowers on, the contents of a tray on the bedside table remained in a careful arrangement that was his mother's handiwork as well. John used to call it the "sickly tray," but the Grabill children had to be good and sick to warrant a sickly tray. Marlin's stomach lurched.

"Maybe Glory could listen to your song another time," Marlin said.

"But she promised."

"She does not feel well today."

"She said she was fine." Lyddie squared her shoulders and folded her hands at her waist. "It is my last Christmas program, and finally I have a part that is

267

not complete twaddle."

Complete twaddle? Where had Lyddie learned to say something like that? It was a good thing she was leaving school in a few months.

"Maybe everyone would like to hear you sing after supper," Marlin said. When Glory returned, he wanted a few minutes alone. Their bedroom should be a sanctuary for privacy, not a music practice hall.

"I do not mind singing again later," Lyddie said.

Marlin sighed. Glory must have given in to similar duress.

◆　◆　◆

Glory knew that the ninth step creaked, and even in the middle of the day when the noise would disturb no one, she did not like to provoke it. Having shed her wet boots in the mudroom, she moved with only the sound of thick socks sliding against polished wood, which was almost no sound at all.

At the top of the staircase she turned left, her eyes already on the third door on the right. The door was open, as she had left it, but Lyddie was not merely talking to herself. Marlin's murmuring tones answered Lyddie's higher pitch. Glory could not make out his words. Though he could laugh with abandon at even slight amusement, Marlin was not one to raise his voice simply to be heard more clearly—and certainly not to be heard from down the hall.

Glory paused outside the door, leaning against the wall out of sight. She had promised Lyddie she would be right back, but if in her absence Magdalena had called for her youngest child's attention, Glory would not have been disappointed to return to an empty room.

"You have been practicing for weeks," Marlin said softly.

"Months!" Lyddie's exclamatory correction was swift. "Miss Draper started planning the program almost as soon as school started in September."

"Then it is sure to be a success," Marlin said, "and you will do well."

"My English friends who go to the German Lutheran Church say that sometimes they have solos in their service."

"Is that what you want?" Marlin asked. "To sing a solo in church?" Music in their church was limited to congregational hymns with no accompanying instruments.

"Not exactly," Lyddie said. "I just wonder what it would be like."

"Many families in our church have children in the school. They will be there to hear you sing."

"I know. And I will be ready."

Glory inhaled and exhaled with intention. Then she pushed off of the wall and stood in the doorframe.

Marlin's head turned, and his eyebrows lifted. Glory loved his face and all its expressiveness. Even the scruffy beard, filling in far more slowly than Marlin would have liked since becoming a married man and finally being allowed to let it grow, was adorable. Perhaps one day it would be long and white and soft the way her own father's beard was.

"You are not going back to *bett*, are you?" Lyddie asked.

Glory shifted her eyes from Marlin to the bed. Truth be told, she would not mind crawling back into it. Going downstairs, across the yard, and back again had sapped her energy, which had been feeble to begin with.

"No, of course not," Glory said. "I was just about to straighten the quilts."

◆ ◆ ◆

Marlin adjusted his weight to one side and caught Glory's eye. She was no more rested than when he left her hours ago. While she might indeed make up the bed, she would still want to stretch out on it.

He should not have left her last night, even for thirty minutes, and he should not have gone to Leroy's farm two days in a row. He was home now. He would be a husband.

"Lyddie," Marlin said, "Glory needs to rest."

"This will only take three minutes," Lyddie said.

Lyddie was fourteen, but when she made up her mind about something, it was as if she was seven all over again.

"Maybe later," Marlin said, his eyes on his bride. Had she been so pale this morning? Or last night?

"That is what Mamm used to say when we were little," Lyddie countered, "and later never came."

"Lyddie," Marlin said, his voice growing less conciliatory.

"It is all right," Glory said. "I will be fine."

Marlin was not persuaded. "Just one stanza."

"Fine," Lyddie said. "One stanza. One minute."

"If you do not mind, I will sit in the reading chair to listen," Glory said. "You will have my full attention."

Marlin followed Glory across the room and stood behind the chair, one hand on her shoulder. Lyddie straightened her shoulders, held still, and created a dramatic moment of anticipation. Even if the teacher had not been coaching her, Lyddie, of all the Grabills, would have come to this technique on her own.

The lyric, pure tone flowing from the perfect O of his sister's mouth stunned Marlin.

How did he not know she could produce such beauty?

"Silent night!" she sang. "Holy night! All is calm, all is bright."

Glory's fingers patted Marlin's hand on her shoulder.

"'Round yon virgin, mother and child, holy infant, so tender and mild, sleep in heavenly peace. Sleep in heavenly peace."

She stopped, reminding Marlin that she had agreed to his condition of just one stanza. Somehow, when Marlin was not paying attention, Lyddie had become a young woman and exchanged a child's sweet voice for a startling soprano. She had a habit of humming during her chores, but no one else in the family sang outside of church or the young people's Singings. Lyddie was too young for Singings that Marlin and Glory attended until they married, and Marlin had crossed the aisle to sit with his father among the men during church services before Lyddie was born and had never heard her sing during worship.

Though Lyddie stood still and silent now, the room burst with the beauty of her gift.

Glory spoke. "That is lovely, Lyddie. Lovely."

Marlin stumbled toward his sister. "I confess, I had no idea."

"I can still practice," Lyddie said. "I can do better. I want to give God my best."

"There is no need," Glory said. "As long as you know the words, the music will be gorgeous."

"Perfect," Marlin said, "it's perfect, as every Christmas carol should be."

He glanced at Glory, whose eyes glistened. Tears? The streaming afternoon light catching her eyes for a split second? A plea for. . . Marlin could not finish the thought.

Chapter 5

T hank you." Glory stood. Beneath her dress, her knees wobbled, and she did not let go of the chair until she found her balance. One glass of water all day was not sufficient nourishment. She would make herself eat the bread on the tray.

Lyddie took a long step sideways. "Mamm will be looking for me. Work on a farm never stops."

Glory's stomach soured, putting her off the notion of eating the bread. What must her mother-in-law think of her? The English would call it lollygagging. Dawdling. Malingering. And maybe they were right.

Lyddie shuffled out of the room, and Marlin closed the door behind her.

"Are you all right?" he said.

She neither nodded nor shook her head.

"Glory, what's wrong?"

"If I knew, I would tell you."

"Something *is* wrong, then." Marlin approached her.

"Just a passing gloom." Surely even Marlin had despondent moments. "I will be all right. Just give me a minute."

"You should go back to bed."

"But—"

Marlin shook a finger. "It is still three hours until supper. You may as well rest until then."

"I should help with the vegetables, or at least set the table."

"My sisters will do that," Marlin said. "Someday you will be the mamm, but right now you are a bride, and the household will run as it always has."

Without me. Glory understood the compassion in Marlin's words, but their truth stung. The Grabill household did not need her. No one would miss her even if she did not go down to supper, missing the third meal of the day as she had the first two.

"I insist," Marlin said. He straightened the disarrayed evidence of a bed that had not been made that day. "Just lie down on top of the bed, as if you are taking a nap."

"Will you stay with me?" Grateful, Glory stepped to the bed.

When Marlin patted the bed, Glory sat down. She swung her feet up while Marlin plumped a pillow and, as she sank into it, spread a quilt over her. He had not yet answered her question about staying with her.

"I never thought of myself as a nervous person," she said, forcing her eyes to stay open long enough to look into Marlin's.

"You are not a nervous person," he said. "If you are sick, we will send for the English doctor."

Not *sick*. That seemed an incomplete word for what she could not describe.

"I am sure you have things to do," she said, eyes drooping. Although she had no place in the household, Marlin did. Even in the winter months there was work to do on a farm, especially one that kept livestock.

"I will be back to check on you," Marlin said. "You and your appetite can come down for supper. The nourishment will strengthen you."

Her eyes were closed before Marlin crept out of the room. Her fingers found a line of stitching in the quilt she had made three years ago for her hope chest, long before Marlin began catching her eye. She knew the Jacob's Ladder pattern well. The stitches took careful counting to yield the same number on each side of every seam. Counting forward and backward, she had checked and rechecked her work.

Counting. Backward. Counting again.

Glory's eyes flipped open and her hand went to her belly. Perhaps it was not nerves after all.

◆　◆　◆

He should have stayed with her. He should have encouraged her to eat now, rather than wait three hours for supper.

When Marlin first brought Gloria home to live on the Grabill farm for much of their first year, she was happy. At least she gave that impression. After Old Christmas, they would visit other relatives, both in their church district and others, to receive well wishes and gifts that would give them a good start on their own home. They would be guests together—helpful guests, but guests. The Grabill farm should be different. It was home. It would always feel like home, even when he and Gloria found the land that would be their future.

Christmas was less than three days away, a time of rejoicing in the Savior's birth, of gifts that recalled the gifts of the kings from the east, of gratitude for family. The putz was meant for all of this. Glory would see that.

Two days. In two days Marlin had to be ready, not only for the Angels putz he taunted his brothers with but the gift that would reassure Glory.

Marlin left the house and hustled down the shoveled path to the barn. The snow on either side of the path was several inches deep but also several days old, awaiting a stretch of warmer temperatures and sun so the moisture could melt into earth to serve the roots of next spring's crops and garden vegetables. One cleared path led to the outhouse, another to the barn, another to the stable, another to the henhouse. It was an efficient layout and one that Marlin could imagine using again on his own farm.

He heaved a reluctant barn door open just far enough to slip in and closed it against the bracing air. The family dairy cows and the livestock they raised for butchering or taking to market were outside. It was John's task to round them up at the end of the day so they could be milked or inspected for signs that the winter exposure affected their health. Marlin breathed relief that he found himself alone in the barn and made his way to an unused stall where an old horse blanket covered a small mound in the corner. He flipped back the coarse covering, sat on the half bale of hay, pulled his knife from its base, and lifted his work for examination.

Marlin had goaded John into speaking up for the traditional Nativity putz. The Angels had been Marlin's choice weeks ago, even before he was married. He had carved two angels from a single block of white pine wood. He did not possess the smaller carving knives that would have allowed more detail work, but the ragged style that resulted was not unattractive. It would please him to polish it to a sheen that would catch the lamplight of those who came to see it, but otherwise it was complete. The step that remained was deciding how to create the appearance of black night sky dotted with a host of glittering angels.

Glory's gift was the greater challenge with only two days remaining.

◆　◆　◆

In seven weeks in the Grabill household Glory had not yet discerned the pattern for when, apart from Sunday suppers, Marlin's married brothers would turn up to share the meal that closed out the day. Rarely did both families come on the same evening, but usually Glory had not heard anyone was coming. Extra plates on the table were the first sign, and then the sounds of horses rattling a buggy behind them. On this evening, Glory welcomed Leroy, Sadie, and their two small children. While the parents went through the motions of trying to teach the *kinner* quiet, polite table manners, David and Magdalena's eyes would light up at the presence of boppli, and Marlin's sisters would manufacture excuses to tend the children.

As she hoped, the meal had a focus other than everyone wondering why she had remained in bed the entire day. Glory nibbled at the beef *yamasetti* and vegetables canned from Magdalena's garden with sufficient consistency to satisfy Marlin's glances.

Lyddie and Marianne were clearing dishes when Leroy's wife turned to Glory.

"Come and help me in the barn," Sadie said. "I would be glad for your company."

"Of course," Glory said. "Is there milking to do?"

Why would Sadie be concerned with barn chores at her in-laws'? If there was extra work, Glory would gladly do it.

"Sadie is a marvel with aloin," Magdalena said, setting a stack of plates in the sink. "We have a cow that we may need to keep in the barn for a few days until we are certain she is ready to be out in the winter."

"So you are going to give aloin to the cow?" Glory said.

Sadie nodded and then scooted back her chair to hand her youngest child to her husband.

Glory's daed always looked after the livestock. Among the Grabills, though, the women seemed to know as much as the men. She swallowed, supposing that they intended to make a Grabill of her after all.

Sadie and Glory bundled into heavy cloaks and boots and took a lantern from the mudroom. In the barn, Sadie hung the light on a hook protruding from the side of the stall where the suspect cow turned to stare at Glory.

"She likes you already," Sadie said.

Glory had drawn a different conclusion.

"Do you want to try?" Sadie said.

Glory's fingers went to her chest. "Me? Give the aloin capsule?"

"Anyone can learn," Sadie said as she prepared the capsule of aloin and ginger in the capsule gun. "All you need is one spot along the jawline where you feel an opening."

Glory was not skittish about farm animals. No Amish child would be allowed to grow to adulthood without knowing where and where not to touch an animal or how to recognize basic signs of peculiar behavior that might mean illness. But so far she had never had to stick her finger in a cow's mouth.

"I will show you," Sadie said. She ran her finger along the cow's jaw a few inches, backtracked, and settled. "There. Put your finger where mine is and you will feel it."

Glory obeyed, moving her finger in both directions to detect the resistance around the opening. Sadie readied the capsule gun in one hand.

"Now push your finger through and wiggle it to rub the roof of her mouth," Sadie said. "I will do the rest."

Glory moved her finger gently.

"Harder," Sadie said. "We want her to be irritated enough to open her mouth."

Glory increased pressure. The cow complied. Sadie shot the capsule in and swiftly wedged the animal's mouth under one arm.

"We have to be sure she swallows it," Sadie said. "It might take a couple of minutes."

Finally Sadie released her hold. "There. Finished. Next time you can try the capsule gun."

Next time. There would be a next time. And another and another. Glory was a married woman with a husband aspiring to his own farm as soon as they could manage it. She looked at the finger that had been inside the cow's mouth, and her stomach revolted.

"You look a little green." Sadie took the lantern off its hook and adjusted it for a good look at Glory. "Do not worry. It gets better in a few weeks."

Chapter 6

Wake up, sleepyhead."

Marlin opened one eye to find his bride dressed and standing beside the bed to look down at him.

"What time is it?" he said, glancing toward the window.

"Early still but late enough," Glory said.

"That does sound like just the right time to get up." Marlin sat up and reached for his trousers at the foot of the bed. "You feel better, *ja?*"

Glory shrugged one shoulder, which was not a persuasive response. She was up and moving, but her spirit did not shine through her face in the way that had made him fall in love with her long before she ever knew. Marlin's bare feet hit the bare wood floor and he winced at the chill of the collision. With yet another resolution to learn the virtues of slippers at this time of year, he stepped to the chest of drawers and pulled clean socks out of the top drawer before snatching his shirt off a hook.

Glory's gaze snapped toward the door. In the hall, footsteps pounded toward their room. Marlin shoved his arms into sleeves just as the banging on the door started.

Glory opened the door. "What is wrong?"

"John needs Marlin," Lyddie said, breathless. "He said right now, please."

"But what is wrong?" Glory said again.

"Marlin will know what to do," Lyddie said.

"Do about what?" Glory opened the door wider.

Lyddie looked past Glory to Marlin. "Just come. I promised John. Right now. In the stable."

Lyddie's steps retreated down the hallways as insistently as they had approached.

"What do you think it is?" Glory said.

Marlin thrust his feet into work boots, squelching the wish that he had new footwear. "I guess I will not know if I do not go."

It was early in the day for an emergency. The time was still well before breakfast, but it was hard to say what John might have encountered on the early round of chores. John, though, had a penchant for being dramatic. So did Lyddie. Perhaps it was nothing requiring such haste.

But perhaps it was.

Marlin took a thick sweater from another hook. Whatever he was about to encounter, the stable would be frigid. "It must be one of the horses. Gone lame, maybe."

Marlin looked out the window, frosted at the edges. The way the snow glistened was enough to tell him that the night's plummeting temperatures had glazed everything afresh, even the pathways branching out from the house. The English would put an image like this one on a postcard or a Christmas card and pin it up on a wall to enjoy. Marlin would simply savor the sight in his mind.

And he would dress warmly for stepping into it.

He glanced at Glory, who returned his smile. Was that hesitation at the corner of her mouth?

"Go," she said. "I will see you at breakfast."

◆　◆　◆

Glory was grateful that the family seating plan at the broad kitchen table put her at her husband's side. Occasionally under the table his fingers would graze hers. It had been that way since the first morning she woke under the Grabill roof. At breakfast, she made sure to find reason to put a hand in her lap every couple of minutes.

But the grazing never came, and she wondered if he had tired of the gesture already. She was a Grabill now, he had said. Did he also think she should not need reassurance any longer?

Glory ate a slice of bacon and one of the biscuits ubiquitous in the Grabill home. Glory made tasty biscuits—but no one would know, because it seemed that Magdalena or one of her daughters had always just pulled another batch out of the oven.

"There is Sadie," Lyddie said.

Glory caught the blur of Sadie's cloak as it passed the kitchen window on its way to the back door. John jumped up and opened the door, and Sadie burst into the kitchen, shivering.

"I thought I would check on the cow," Sadie said, clapping gloved hands together.

"You could have waited," Magdalena said. "No need to come all the way over here before the sun has warmed the morning."

"It is not so far," Sadie said. "But I will not stay long. I left the kinner with Leroy, but all he has on his mind is the putz of the Annunciation, and they are too little to help him."

John tapped the table twice. "But the putz is supposed to bring the family together. He should let them help."

Sadie gave her easy laugh, a quality Glory admired about her new sister-in-law.

"That is easy for you to say," Sadie said. "You have the capable assistance of Lyddie and Marianne. Our two can barely stand in the snow without tumbling. They would hardly give Leroy the same advantage."

"Perhaps," Marlin said, "Leroy should focus on essentials and not be competitive."

Sadie laughed again. "I have been a Grabill long enough that you cannot fool me."

Glory glanced at the indisputable twinkle in Marlin's eye.

"Thank you for helping to insulate the barn," Sadie said. "Your help is what gives Leroy the time for this greater task. The result will be remarkable, I am sure."

"No doubt." Marlin broke another biscuit in two and put half in his mouth.

"Next year," Sadie said, "decide sooner than three days before Christmas what to make. You have all done this enough times to know better."

"Is that your way of saying Leroy feels pressure?" Marlin said, holding the smile back from his mouth. He pointed a finger at John. "And you, my little *bruder*, do not again cause my heart anxiety with an early morning emergency about your putz. You asked to be able to do the Nativity."

"You are helping each other?" Sadie feigned shock. "That hardly seems fair."

"I did not succumb to his sorry shenanigans," Marlin said.

"You are my big bruder," John said. "I ought to be able to seek your advice on many issues of life."

There was Sadie's laugh again.

Glory's eyes bounced from one Grabill to another. Her family was quietly fond of each other, but they did not tease in this manner—especially not during the somber days before Christmas. She hoped she would still see her siblings on Old Christmas, even though her parents were gone. A letter would remind her nearest brother how much she looked forward to the day. His farm was just far enough away to belong to a different district, so she did not hope to see him on Christmas Day. The others lived farther still.

"Glory, come with me, please," Sadie said. "If we need to do anything else for the cow, we can do it together."

Glory glanced out the window and nodded. She could hardly complain about not feeling included in the family if she turned down the opportunity to share in their work. Sadie had come all this way.

They bustled along the outdoor path, knowing the barn would be warmed by the animals that had not yet been led to snowy pastures.

"Have you told Marlin yet?" Sadie said.

"Told him what?" Glory said, watching her breath swirl ahead of her.

"About the babe of course."

Glory's heart lodged in her throat. That was what Sadie meant. *"Do not worry. It gets better in a few weeks."*

Sadie yanked open the barn door. "It is all right. I will not mention it to Leroy if you do not wish me to."

"I have barely even told myself," Gloria said. The thought that someone might guess had not crossed her mind in the fifteen hours since she had counted backward and counted again before coming to her suspicion.

"I know the feeling."

"I am sure you do, with two little ones."

"No, I mean I know the feeling now."

Gloria's heart quickened. No wonder Sadie saw the early signs.

Sadie grinned. "Sisters having boppli together. Such fun it will be!"

◆ ◆ ◆

"We know how to set up the house for church, Mamm," Marlin said. The Grabills had hosted at least one church service each year for his entire life—and more often two. He and his siblings knew how the furniture would be moved and what check-list of tasks their mother carried in her head.

"It is different this time," his mother said. "Our turn to host falls on Christmas Day. I cannot imagine such an opportunity will come to us again."

"Of course," Marlin said. Even when Christmas fell on a Sunday again in a few years, it might not be on one of the two church Sundays each month. If it were, it would likely be another family's turn to host. Perhaps someday he and Glory would have the privilege.

His sisters listened attentively to the list of items their mother wanted them to bring from the cellar for the Christmas pies. Marlin and John watched as she pointed around the wide front rooms of the house designating how to relocate the furniture to make room for the church benches already waiting in a wagon pulled up alongside the house and covered with tarps. The floors would be spotless. Every windowsill would have a Christmas candle. A bit of greenery on the mantel from one of their own trees would not be sinful as long as they did not add ornamentation. Marlin and his siblings nodded at every stage. He would gladly do whatever made his mother feel more prepared about the day after tomorrow.

Two days. Today and tomorrow. Glory's gift was nearly ready, and perhaps he could coax her into helping him with the Angels putz—they were a family now and should do it together. Perhaps she would not find the tradition so odd if she saw it from the inside.

Christmas would soon be here, and he wanted happy memories of their first Christmas together.

Chapter 7

The cow was fine, and Glory's secret was safe with Sadie. After a quick cup of *kaffi* to warm up, Sadie was off to her own home. Glory wandered into the front room, which opened onto a large dining room. She had been to church services in the Grabill home before, so she could easily imagine how the benches would be arranged. With his father and brother, Marlin was moving furniture to the perimeter of the rooms. The floor space was barely cleared before Marianne attacked it with a broom. A bucket and rags stood as sentinels, awaiting their orders.

"Shall I help you?" Glory asked. There would be another broom in the kitchen.

Marianne looked up and smiled. "No need. We mopped day before yesterday, so I will only need to scrub the worst spots."

"I can do that."

"No need." Marianne jabbed the broom into a corner and whisked out the lurking dirt.

I must not be very good at offering help. Glory stepped out of Marianne's way.

Marlin brushed his hands together. "Come on, John. We should put some fresh straw down in the stable."

"I can help," Glory said.

"With the straw?" John asked, blinking.

"Why not? I used to help my daed with barn work."

The brothers looked at each other.

"We have a system," John said.

A system that worked with two people. That is what John meant. Glory searched Marlin's face but found no encouragement. But he did come close to her.

"You should take care," he said.

Take care to what?

"I could at least keep you company," Glory said.

Marlin shook his head, and the gesture stabbed her.

"You do not want me to come," she said.

"It is not that," Marlin said. "You were ill yesterday. Take care to recover."

The door from the kitchen swung open, and Magdalena emerged.

"Good," she said. "You are all still here. Remember Lyddie's program at three o'clock. Do not be late."

"No, Mamm, we will not forget," John said, nudging his brother's elbow. "Let's go."

Marianne was on her knees, scrubbing furiously and efficiently along a length of floor where the family's feet often fell on the way to the front stairwell. Glory's eyes went from Marianne to the front window. The pair of brothers sped toward the stable at a pace Glory could not have kept up with, but from the angle of Marlin's head Glory knew he was laughing heartily. Were they still teasing about putz, or did they have another favorite topic Glory knew nothing about?

"Gloria," Magdalena said.

Glory turned.

"I suppose all your life people have told you that you have the perfect name for Christmas."

Glory nodded. "I was named for my father's grandmother, who was born on Christmas Day."

"Come with me," Magdalena said, turning back toward the kitchen.

Glory followed.

"You and I are going to bake cookies," Magdalena said.

Glory's heart lifted. She was adept at baked goods.

"Not just any cookies," Magdalena said. "Glory Divine cookies."

"I have never heard of them." Was her mother-in-law making up a cookie name to make Glory feel better? It was not necessary. She did not seek pity.

Magdalena took a large mixing bowl from a shelf. "I do not have a written recipe. You will have to pay close attention."

"Are they really called Glory Divine?"

"I guess we can call them whatever we like. I think it is the extra butter that goes into them. My aenti used to make them and said it was like biting into glory divine."

Glory laughed.

"I used to surprise my children with them on Christmas morning, but I have never shown the *maedel* how to make them. Would you like to be the first to learn?"

Glory sucked in air. "Are you sure?" What would the girls think when they discovered Magdalena had taught Glory first?

"When Marlin said he wanted to marry you, I knew I had been keeping this secret for this moment."

Glory's throat thickened.

"Let's begin," Magdalena said. "Four cups of flour."

◆　◆　◆

"We should have come earlier," Marianne said as Marlin guided the buggy toward the white, square schoolhouse that afternoon.

"They would not have let us in if we had," John said. "They only set up for the Christmas program after the lessons are finished."

Marlin remembered. It was as if each teacher left an instruction sheet for the one who followed. The last school day before Christmas must have its share of genuine teaching—even exams—before welcoming families for the program. He parked the buggy and set the brake. John, on the bench beside him, jumped down and offered a hand to their mamm and then to Marianne. When Daed had emerged, Marlin waited for Glory to fold the lap quilt that warmed her on the brief journey, and cradled her elbow while she climbed out from the back of the buggy.

"Are you feeling well?" he murmured.

"Well enough, considering," she said.

"Considering what?"

But Glory gave no answer. Instead, Marianne called to them. "*Kumme.* Let's not stand out in the cold longer than we have to."

"Take my arm," Marlin said to Glory. "Just in case." If she felt as wobbly as she did yesterday, an ice patch was sure to get the best of her.

Inside, the schoolhouse looked much as it did every year. This was Lyddie's last year in school. The next time Marlin attended a Christmas program might be several years from now, perhaps when Leroy's eldest had begun school. In addition to the desks, folding chairs offered seating, though many more people would cram into the school than the number of chairs could accommodate. The teacher's desk was pushed out of the way to create a stage area. Decorations were more elaborate than any of the Amish families would put up, but more than half the scholars in the school were English children accustomed to trees and greenery and ornaments and red and gold ribbons and brightly colored gift packages.

"Where is Lyddie?" Magdalena asked.

"There." Marlin pointed to a far corner.

"What is she bothered about?"

Marlin fixed on his sister's face. His mamm was right. Lyddie, in conversation with another girl, had clamped her lips and puffed her cheeks.

"That must be Madeleine Madison," Glory said.

"How did you know?" Marlin said. Glory had never met Madeleine.

Glory said, "You should go to her."

Marlin wove through the growing assembly toward his sister, who grew redder by the moment.

"You only got the solo because the teacher feels sorry for you because you have to leave school." Madeleine flipped wavy dark hair over a shoulder.

"You do not know what you are talking about," Lyddie countered. "You are jealous because you did not earn the solo."

Madeleine rolled her eyes. "You really have no idea how much she pities you."

"Girls," Marlin said, a hand on each girl's shoulder. "That is enough."

"Now you need your brother to rescue you," Madeleine said.

Marlin squeezed Lyddie's shoulder harder. "Madeleine, you might want to say hello to your own parents before the program begins."

Madeleine huffed, but she left.

"She has no idea of all the things I thought but did not say," Lyddie said.

"Take a deep breath," Marlin said. "'All is calm, all is bright.' Remember?"

◆　◆　◆

Glory watched her husband calm his sister, an ability that would bode well for their own children. Soothing tones. Gentle touches.

If Glory mentioned Minnie Handelman, Marlin would remember her. In a one-room schoolhouse, all the scholars knew each other regardless of grade differences. And if he thought about Minnie, he would understand how she recognized Madeleine. Wherever Minnie was now—perhaps married and living in the city she always thought she deserved—Glory was glad she was nowhere near the Grabill farm.

Finally Marlin made his way back to her.

"We should have made sure you got a seat," he said.

"I will be fine." Glory spoke with more confidence than her knees felt after being on her feet baking most of the day, harboring her own secret while conspiring with her mother-in-law. She had the wall to lean on, and Marlin to reach for if needed.

The form of the program was recognizable as well. Scholars took turns reciting portions of the story of Christ's birth as given in the book of Luke. At times Glory's lips moved silently with the familiar words. *"She brought forth her firstborn son. . .the glory of the Lord shone round about them. . .good tidings of great joy. . .and they came with haste."*

"The best gift you can give is simply called love," one of the youngest scholars announced. Students recited poems, sang songs, invited the audience to join in singing "O Little Town of Bethlehem" and "Joy to the World." Several older girls, decked in aprons and holding mixing bowls, presented a recipe for gratitude for the greatest gift of all, Christ Himself.

Twelve children, each holding a tall red candle aflame, spoke lines of thankfulness that pointed to the Christ child as one by one they lined themselves up across the front of the room, leaving a space in the center.

Into that space, Lyddie stepped, hands clasped in front of her as they had been when she rehearsed. Two parents assisted the teacher to turn down the lamps around the room until the candles glowed in darkness.

Glory was holding her breath. The entire audience anticipated the dramatic climax to the program.

When Lyddie's mouth opened and the pristine, transparent, lyrical timbre lit the darkness, even restless babes in arms stilled to worship the Christ child.

Chapter 8

S upper was boisterous, as it always was. Marlin loved a loud, crowded meal. He had friends whose families ate in somber silence, as if food was all that mattered when the family came to the table. Marlin cared less about whether the biscuits were overcooked than about the joy that swelled when the Grabills were under one roof. When Josef and Leroy came with their wives and children, the kitchen table was crowded, but sitting shoulder to shoulder was a small price to pay for being drenched in family bonds.

"Lyddie was the best part," Marianne insisted.

"All the children did well," Mamm reminded her.

"But Lyddie!" Marianne insisted. "All the practice brought reward."

"It is our Lord we want to honor," Daed said.

But Marlin saw the glow in his parents' faces. It bordered on pride, which no one around the table that night would confess but was true nonetheless. Lyddie's solo had been perfection, three lustrous stanzas of "Silent Night, Holy Night" that would shine through memory at future school programs.

Slice by slice the roast disappeared. Leroy took the last potato and Josef the final biscuit just before Mamm shifted a chocolate cake from the counter to the table and Marianne exchanged dinner plates for cake plates. Every snippet of conversation strummed strings of joy in Marlin, resounding the program's theme of gratitude.

"Girls," Mamm said at last, "I will leave you with the dishes while Daed and I take care of a few things."

Marlin grinned at his brothers. "I suspect we all have things we need to take care of tonight."

"I might just have to wander out to the barn." Leroy winked.

"And I am sure Leroy requires my assistance," Josef said.

"You will stay out of my barn." Marlin glared across the table.

"He will not even let me in," John muttered. "Makes me work in the stable."

"The stable seems appropriate for the one working on the Nativity." Marlin stood and pushed his chair under the table. "Tomorrow night all will be revealed."

He paced into the living room, where his parents were making final adjustments to the rearrangement of household furnishings. The floor gleamed with Marianne's effort as he knew it would. Marlin was nearly to the top of the stairs when he realized someone followed. He turned.

"Glory. I did not realize you were coming upstairs."

"I have a surprise for you," she said, catching up to him.

In their bedroom, while Marlin collected a carving knife he reserved for the more delicate cuts though it was not as nimble as he wished, Glory opened a drawer and removed a dish towel.

"Here," she said, offering the bundle to him.

"It is not Christmas yet," he said.

"Just open it."

Marlin unfolded the towel to find a plate of cookies. "Glory Divine!"

Glory grinned.

"How did you get these cookies before Christmas?"

"I made them!"

"But it is a secret recipe. Mamm never lets anyone watch when she bakes them."

"Until now."

"My sisters will be stunned." Marlin admired the confectionary perfection. Precise circles. Superb rising. Even the weight in his hand was consummate. Now his wife would be able to continue the tradition of Glory Divine. He began to wrap the cookies again.

"Are you not going to have one?" Glory asked.

"The tradition is to eat them on Christmas morning," he said.

Her face fell.

He put the bundle on top of the chest of drawers and turned to take her hand. "Come with me. Work on the putz with me."

"Another of your family traditions."

He nodded, confused. What had made her unhappy?

"It will not take long," he said. "A few final touches."

"You have spent a lot of time in the barn in the last few days."

"Tomorrow is Christmas Eve," he said. "All must be finished by dark."

"You were right this morning," Glory said, turning toward the bed. "I have been tired all day."

"I would enjoy your company. Mamm used to help Daed."

She shook her head. "Not tonight."

"Then I will stay in as well." If he could find just one extra hour tomorrow, he could still be ready in time.

"You should go," Glory said. "It is what you want to do."

"I will not be long." When Marlin withdrew from the room, his wife's back was to him.

◆　◆　◆

The knock on the door came softly. Glory, still dressed but stretched out on the bed, sat up quickly.

"Yes?"

The knob turned, and Magdalena entered just as Glory had pulled herself erect.

"I wonder if you would enjoy setting the candles in the windowsills," Magdalena said. "We like to put them in every room, both upstairs and downstairs."

Another tradition. Something else Glory must learn to do if she hoped to please her husband.

"I left a basket in the hall with everything you need," Magdalena said. "Feel free to begin with the upstairs bedrooms. Just arrange a bit of greenery at the base of the glass and make sure the candle is snug in its holder."

Glory nodded. "Of course."

"No need to light them. We save that for Christmas Eve."

And we must not alter tradition.

"Fine." Glory forced a smile. "I will practice by starting in here."

"I am sure you will manage nicely."

Glory stood in the hall to pick through the basket of thick red candles, the base holders, and the glasses that would go over them. The greenery must have been left over from the branches Magdalena had used on the mantel downstairs. There was only enough for a sprig or two around each candle. No one could accuse the Grabills of adopting English manners of ornamentation.

Voices rose up through the stairwell. Glad voices. Laughing voices. Teasing voices. Would she ever feel that at ease with Marlin's family? Glory moved from one bedroom to another. She had not yet been in any bedroom but the one she shared with Marlin, but they distinguished themselves easily. David and Magdalena's had a wide bed. Dresses and aprons hung from the hooks in the room Marianne and Lyddie shared. John's room had an empty narrow bed in addition to the one he used.

Marlin's old bed, Glory realized. She could nearly feel him in this room. The shelf where he must have kept his personal things. The window where he looked out on the barn. The corner where he would have kicked off his boots in the haphazard way of boys.

Glory quickly set the candle and withdrew. There was so much she did not know about this man she had married.

Downstairs, the kitchen had two windows. While Glory arranged candles, Marianne pulled a pair of cakes out of the oven. Lyddie gushed in noisy relief that her solo had gone well. Sadie and Joannah were bundling their little ones to brace the cold and joking about which of them would be first to call for her husband. All four brothers were missing, no doubt together despite their admonitions to stay away.

"Come on, Marianne," Lyddie said, reaching for a cloak on a hook near the door. "Let's find John."

"He is sure to be in over his head without us," Marianne said.

Two sisters, and two sisters-in-law, exited in a single rush of cold air through the back door. Silence in the kitchen provoked an odd sensation for Glory. She had never been alone in the Grabill kitchen before—and had not supposed anyone ever was.

Glory worked with deliberation on the downstairs windowsills. Her task was not complicated, but Marlin had said he would not be gone long, and he might be heartened to come in and find her at her task.

The girls came in, checked on the cooling cakes, said good night, and went upstairs.

John came in, sighing in a manner which Glory could not interpret, said good night, and went upstairs.

David and Magdalena turned down the gas lamps that lit their home, separated the logs in the fireplace, said good night, and went upstairs.

Finally, having checked and adjusted every windowsill on the ground floor three times, Glory went upstairs.

Where was Marlin?

◆　◆　◆

Marlin tripped as he entered the dark room. Glory turned over in the bed.

"Sorry," he whispered.

She said nothing.

"Are you awake?" he said.

She rolled over again, and Marlin knew she was. He felt his way to the foot of the bed.

"Are you warm enough?" he asked.

"Yes." Finally she spoke.

"I am sorry if I woke you."

"You did not wake me."

"You said you were tired."

Silence.

"Glory?"

Sniffles. "Where were you, Marlin?"

"In the barn. I told you."

"You said you would not be gone long."

"I. . .discovered some work I needed to do."

More silence. Marlin's heart clenched. He did not want to quarrel.

"I was embarrassed," Gloria said. "I felt silly acting as if I was waiting for you to come in while everyone went to bed, but you never came."

"I am sorry. I did not think."

Silence.

Marlin undressed and slid under the quilts. "Let's not go to sleep angry," he said. "We promised that to each other."

Glory rolled toward him and gave him her hand, but to Marlin it felt limp.

Chapter 9

The waking day heralded Christmas Eve. Marlin still held Glory's hand when she woke. She squeezed it and got out of bed. He did the same. But they spoke little as they dressed and prepared to join the family for breakfast.

"May I have another biscuit?"

"Please pass the salt."

"The kaffi is especially good today."

Marlin's contribution to breakfast conversation was slight. Glory spoke only if someone addressed a question to her.

When David spoke the *Aemen* of the family devotions, Marlin and Glory looked at each other. In this daily pause between devotions and labor, they had become accustomed to walking to the back door together, Marlin full of plans for the day and Glory foundering aloud for where she should offer to help. Today Glory followed him to the door and formed a smile, but Marlin said only that he would see her at the midday meal. By this time, Magdalena and her daughters swarmed the kitchen.

Marlin stepped outside.

"The benches," his mother called after him.

Marlin gave no wave of the hand or turn of the head to indicate he had heard Magdalena.

"What is wrong with Marlin?" Lyddie asked.

"He has many things on his mind," Magdalena said. "He did not hear me."

Glory began pumping water in the sink. She could do the washing up and put things away. Her stay at the Grabill house had been long enough that she knew her way around the kitchen.

Stay. Were they staying with or living with Marlin's family?

Glory startled with a new thought. Marlin knew she was unhappy, and perhaps he was unhappy as well and regretted their marriage. Glory's hand traced across her flat belly. She thought they had made up after last night's spat. Perhaps Marlin did not see it the same way. She should never have chastised him.

"Thank you, Glory," Magdalena said, "for jumping in with the washing. Marianne and Lyddie, you know where the serving dishes are in the hutch. We are going to want all of the platters, and bring the large spoons as well."

Glory scrubbed, rinsed, and dried the breakfast dishes. Lyddie was lining the counter with dishes for the meal after church the next day.

"Here comes Sarah," Lyddie said, looking out a window.

Glory looked up. Sarah was several years younger—Marianne's age—and sang with gusto at the Singings.

Lyddie opened the back door.

Sarah pulled a scarf off her head. "I am here to help. I know getting ready to host church can be a lot of work."

Magdalena smiled. "We can always use an extra hand."

Marianne leaned toward Glory to whisper. "Sarah is sweet on John. She is waiting for him to notice."

Sarah hung her cloak on a hook, as if she had done it dozens of times, and said, "I see we have cakes to frost."

We.

Glory wished that word came to her lips more often.

"You know what to do," Magdalena said.

Marianne pushed up her sleeves, grabbed a mixing bowl, and followed Sarah to the sugar bin. Their heads bent toward each other as they measured and mixed.

If John did notice that Sarah was sweet on him, and if they did wed, Sarah would not wonder how to fit into the Grabill household.

Glory put the last of the breakfast plates on the shelf. She was—probably—having a baby. Her own parents had moved away indefinitely. If there was ever a time to feel the *we* of being a Grabill, it had come.

◆　◆　◆

Marlin shoved a bench through the front door. John should have grabbed the other end by now, but Marlin leaned into the weight of the bench to push in on his own. Winter air blasted in behind him. Once he had the bench—and himself—inside, he latched the door. A wagon full of benches awaited transference into the house, and he had enough sense to minimize the outside air that entered with them.

"John?"

No response?

"Daed?"

No answer.

His father and brother had entered ahead of him, leaving Marlin to wrestle the first bench from the porch into the house. It was not that he was unable to manage on his own, but it would take twice as long and he would be twice as tired. He opened the door, hurtled through, and yanked it closed behind him. If he discovered that John had snuck out the back door to work on his putz, leaving Marlin with the benches, John would suffer rebuke once Marlin tracked him down. And if John laughed while he told the story later to Leroy and Josef, he would suffer rebuke again. In two years it might be amusing, but today it was not.

At the base of the steps off the front porch, Marlin hefted himself into the open wagon and slid another bench to the edge. Then he dropped to the ground and prepared to grip its weight. If all he did was get a few benches to the ground, he would not have wasted his time waiting for his dawdling brother.

When the front door opened, Marlin looked up the steps, prepared with a glare only a brother would comprehend.

Glory stood on the porch with both hands clutching a shawl around her shoulders.

"Marlin?" she said.

"Not now, Gloria." He set a bench as close to the bottom step as he could manage.

"I—"

He jumped back into the wagon. "I cannot talk right now. And please do not stand there with the door open."

She had left only a crack of space, but that was enough to send a draft shivering up the stairwell.

Glory withdrew.

Regret washed over Marlin. He had not even listened to what she wanted.

"I may not be married," John said from behind Marlin, "but I know that is not the way to speak to a wife."

"Where have you been?" Marlin snapped.

"Mamm asked Daed and me to carry potatoes from the cellar. It only took a minute."

Marlin exhaled. "You are right, and I am sorry."

"Do not apologize to me," John said, crouching to pick up one end of a bench. "It is Glory's head you just snapped off."

Marlin picked up his end of the bench and clomped backward up the steps. He would not blame Glory if she disappeared for the rest of the day. All he wanted was for his new wife to love the family's traditions as much as he did. Somehow it had all gone wrong.

◆　　◆　　◆

Glory returned to the kitchen.

"Is everything all right?" Magdalena asked as she dropped a knife against the butcher block and split a potato.

Glory blanched. What had her mother-in-law heard? "I thought I might like a moment of fresh air, but it is too cold."

The icy wind from her husband's spirit had frozen Glory's resolution to speak to him. There was never any sign of trouble between them while they were courting. And now this. And she might be with child. The time for regrets was past.

"You look pale," Magdalena said. "Are you well?"

"Not entirely." Glory picked up a tray of glazed pastries, Marianne's specialty.

Lyddie came in from the back porch and stamped snow off her boots. "I am pleased to announce that the cow is as ornery as ever."

Magdalena laughed. "In other words, she is fine."

A bench thudded to the floor in the front room, and Marlin's voice rose in chastisement.

"Maybe Sadie should give Marlin an aloin capsule," Lyddie said.

"Hush," Magdalena said.

Marlin's voice rose another notch.

The tray clattered out of Glory's hands, spilling the pastries meant for a special treat for the family after supper.

"*Est dutt mir leed.*" Glory knelt to scoop the mess back onto the tray before the mess worsened. "Sorry. I am sorry."

"Lyddie," Magdalena said. "Get the mop before anyone tracks through."

"I cannot believe I did that," Glory said. "How will I make it up to Marianne?"

"You need to rest, Gloria," Magdalena said. "Clean your hands, and then go up the back stairs."

Glory nodded for lack of a better response.

"I will have a word with Marlin. He is expecting too much of himself and everyone else."

Lyddie handed Glory a damp towel and then went for the mop.

Is that all it was? Marlin was expecting too much? Glory wiped glaze off her fingers, certain that she was chief among his disappointments.

Chapter 10

Benches filled the front room, which was ready now to welcome the church tomorrow. Marlin stopped snapping at people he loved and found a moment to kneel in the barn and confess his failure to love God with all his heart and to love his neighbor as himself. But he had not wanted to wake his napping wife, and now the hour had come when a moment alone with Glory would be difficult to manage.

Darkness had descended. Marlin arranged two lanterns on stools on one side of the house so that their gleam would light his Angels carving. It was not an exquisite piece of work—nothing like what his grandfather used to do. But he was a young man with many years ahead to master the craft. For now, the simplicity of his Angels would remind those who saw it of the humble birth of the Savior. Around the carving, Marlin rolled and shaped leaves of tin foil and stood them upright in mounds of snow to catch the lantern light as a multitude of heavenly hosts.

With only the span of the wide front porch to divide them, Marlin heard John fussing over his Nativity, which would be the pinnacle of the family's pilgrimage to see each putz display. Marianne and Lyddie's harmonious voices suggested adjustments. Even Daed's murmur rose in admiration of John's fresh arrangement of traditional family pieces. Leroy and Josef had their wives and children, Marvin supposed, bundled against the cold night and having one last look at their creations.

Marlin stood alone.

This was not what he wanted. Glory should have been helping to roll tin foil angels. Glory should be bundled against the night with him. Glory should be standing beside him on their first Christmas Eve. He took a few steps back and lifted his eyes from the angels to his bedroom window.

"She is awake," Lyddie said.

Marlin found her form in the shadows of the front porch.

"All she wanted to tell you was how tired she was," Lyddie said. "Mamm told her three times she should have a rest so she would not miss Christmas Eve."

Marlin cleared the lump from his throat. "It must be almost time to go."

"It is. Mamm says we should all squeeze into one buggy. It will help keep us warm."

"Good idea."

"Glory can sit between Marianne and me, and we will make sure she does not catch a chill."

"Thank you." Marlin could keep his ailing wife warm, but he could not blame her if she preferred to be with his sisters.

"Come," Lyddie said. "The Angel Gabriel is waiting."

◆　◆　◆

"Josef," Marianne said. "Josef will have done the most."

"More than Marlin?" Lyddie was skeptical.

Wedged between her sisters-in-law, with a heavy buggy quilt spread across their laps and hanging over their knees, Glory let their speculations fade from her hearing. Her mind was on her husband, seated beside his father on the driver's bench. All Glory could see was the back of Marlin's head, with his hat pulled down as far as possible for warmth and his coat collar turned up to cover his neck. Despite his layers of clothing, the slope of his shoulders told her his mood.

He was quiet, on this night when they would see the putz he had been talking about all week. Thinking—or perhaps praying. He cast no teasing tones over his shoulders at the bait his sisters dangled. And he had said nothing to Glory other than to offer assistance into the buggy.

Marlin was out of her reach on this holy night.

The buggy turned onto Leroy's farm. In the summer they could have walked the three-and-a-half miles. The buggy ride took only a few minutes, barely enough time to feel cold even if she were not wrapped in Grabills.

I am a Grabill.

"There are Josef and Joannah," Lyddie said. "I hoped we would get here first."

The buggy emptied. The only thing Glory could think to do was walk beside Marlin, bringing up the end of the straggling line tramping through the snow toward the Annunciation and forming a semicircle to view. Leroy had not carved, as Marlin had. Although Glory had not yet seen her husband's workmanship, she had noticed the care he took with the few knives he owned and supposed he had been putting them to use.

"It is papier-mâché " Glory said in surprise.

Leroy laughed. "Those school projects we used to have to do for history lessons have finally proved useful."

In school they had all made miniature papier-mâché scenes that fit within small crates they brought from home. Leroy's figures were the size of children and painted in bright colors. The Virgin Mary kneeled, her arms upstretched toward a white-robed angel. Between Mary and the angel, a brightly lit lantern bathed them both in holy light.

Beneath her heavy cloak, Glory's hand went to her belly. What wonder Mary must have felt at the angel's words, a thousand times greater than what Glory felt when she imagined herself as a mother.

Marlin stepped closer. "You have outdone yourself, Leroy. I am not sure I have ever seen such a beautiful putz, yet you give all the glory to God."

Glory watched her husband's face. Gone was the teasing twinkle that had been in his eye all week when he spoke of the putz. Gone was the playful competition.

Instead, marvel glowed. For the first time, Glory glimpsed why he was so eager for this night. She took another step forward as well and leaned against his arm to slide her gloved hand into his.

◆　◆　◆

"'And the angel came in unto her, and said, Hail, thou that art highly favoured,'" Leroy said. "'The Lord is with thee: blessed are thou among women.'"

"'Fear not.'" Josef picked up the story from Luke 1. "'For thou hast found favour with God.'"

"'And, behold,'" Marlin said, "'thou shalt conceive in thy womb, and bring forth a son, and shalt call his name Jesus.'"

The familiar verses echoed around him as family members passed the good news from one voice to another.

The angel's news. Mary's wonder. The angel's explanation. Mary's response.

Marlin picked up the final thread. "'And Mary said, Behold the handmaid of the Lord; be it unto me according to thy word.'"

They stood in silence, all the Grabills gathered in one moment of awe. This was what Marlin loved about the putz. Hearing the ancient story flowing from the mouths of those who knew him best.

"We should go on to find the Shepherds," Lyddie said finally, and they crunched back to the waiting buggies, where horses' breath broke the night. As he helped Glory into the buggy, he squeezed her hand and did not turn away from the tears that gleamed in her eyes. His words of apology would wait for a private moment.

Josef had used his lanterns to cast heavenly glitter across a hillside of flat shepherd and sheep figures cut from packing boxes, painted, and propped up with braces in the back. Startled shepherd faces were turned upward to the night sky, and Marlin could not resist looking up into infinite darkness expecting to discover what they might have seen that night outside of Bethlehem.

"While by our sheep we watched at night," Lyddie began to sing.

In the same manner in which the church congregation joined a hymn begun by one member, the family took up Lyddie's melody.

"Glad tidings brought an angel bright. How great our joy! Great our joy! Joy, joy joy! Praise we the Lord in heav'n on high!"

"We must go see Marlin's Angels," Leroy said, "now that we have already begun to sing of them."

Marlin kept close to Glory on the way back to the buggy and would have sat beside her if it had not meant that another member of the family would have to bear the cold in the front seat.

He had set his Angels to be visible as soon as the buggies turned into the lane. The closer they got to the house, the more the angels took shape and the tin multitude glimmered. When the gasps behind him began, he could pick out Glory's drawn breath.

He jumped down before his father had set the buggy brake.

"Marlin!" Glory said as she pushed to be next to put her feet on the ground and quicken her pace for a closer view.

Marlin had restrained his own breath from fullness for hours, and now he released it. Side by side, they stood before his carved angels.

Behind them, Lyddie began another carol. "Angels we have heard on high, sweetly singing o'er the plain. And the mountains in reply echo back their joyous strain."

"Gloria in excelsis Deo," the family sang.

"It is so beautiful," Glory whispered in his ear. "All of it. I did not know."

"Gloria in excelsis Deo!" The family trekked to the other side of the house to see John's Nativity.

Marlin smiled at the pieces John had selected from two dozen available in the barn's loft. There had been other putz pieces over the twenty-five years of his parents' marriage, but these were the ones that survived the weather and six children poking at them. Now the oldest grandchild, Leroy's boppli, tested a finger against the nativity stall fashioned from potter's clay. It had been Marlin's first independent putz creation half a lifetime ago. It was not symmetrical, and the front trim crumbled more every year, but John had chosen this piece to shelter the Christ child that their sisters had stitched and stuffed from rags.

"O Little Town of Bethlehem, how still we see thee lie," Lyddie sang.

Marlin did not sing this time, instead savoring the weight of his wife's head on his shoulder.

Chapter 11

The aromas of Magdalena's evening meal tantalized Glory from the moment she stepped from the crisp air outside into the cozy warmth of the Grabill kitchen. Supper was usually the simpler meal, compared to the midday dinner, but tonight with all the family gathered for Christmas Eve, Magdalena had managed to have pork, potatoes, and vegetables roasting in the oven. She opened the stove for the briefest inspection before declaring the feast would be ready in twenty minutes.

"Glory," Magdalena said, "would you and Marlin mind lighting the candles in all the windows?"

"Of course." Glory turned toward Marlin's nod. Magdalena handed her a box of matches. The other rooms would not be as warm and welcoming as the kitchen until David and John stirred up the coals in the fireplace, but Glory anticipated satisfaction in lighting the candles she had arranged the evening before. This time her husband would be at her side.

Marlin picked up a slender starter candle from the counter and struck a match. Glory chose a second loose candle to tip into Marlin's and transfer the flame to the window candles without disturbing the arrangements.

"We can start right here in the kitchen," Glory said. At the first window Marlin held his candle low enough for Glory to easily catch the flame and light the candle on the sill. She moved carefully to the window's twin. With both lights burning bright against the darkness outside, sighs sounded around the kitchen. Magdalena and Marianne stilled their food preparations. Joannah turned the baby in her arms around and his fussing eased.

"The candles are sure to be beautiful inside and out," Sadie said. "My favorite tradition."

"What is your favorite tradition, Glory?" Lyddie asked.

The question caught Glory off balance. She raised both shoulders toward her ears. "Simple moments like this one."

Magdalena smiled, nodded, and turned back to the stove.

Marlin and Glory went to the main rooms next, with their rank of windows across the front of the house. The benches were set up for church in the morning, so the family would not enjoy these rooms tonight, but as they passed through them or paused to stand and warm themselves at the fireplace, they could still catch a glimpse of the burning flames. Upstairs Glory went first to John's room, then to the girls', then to her in-laws', and finally walked beside Marlin to their room to light the last candle.

"Look," Glory said. "Buggies."

They had not been there a few minutes ago, but now two buggies had drawn up in front of the Nativity and another approached Marlin's Angels.

"I have not been around to see putz in years," she said. "Until tonight, I mean."

"I hope you will not want to wait so long before doing it again," Marlin said.

"No, I do not suppose I will." She leaned her forehead against the glass, careful of the candle. "Do they always come?"

"Every year for as long as I can remember," Marlin said. "We are quite well-known."

"We never drove this far across the district when I was little. My mamm simply wanted to have us all home together on Christmas Eve." Another buggy rolled down the lane. People seemed to know which direction to circle around to avoid knotting the flow of rigs. "I hope they enjoy the candles."

"They will."

Glory pictured the symmetry of the view from outside—a putz off each corner of the front porch, glowing candles centered in an even number of windows on the front of the house, four downstairs and two upstairs forming well-measured triangles of light. As one of the buggies departed, an English wagon arrived, and children leaned out of the back pointing in delight. Glory let her weight fall against Marlin's chest.

"How long will this go on?" she asked.

"A couple of hours, or as long as we leave the candles and lanterns burning," he said. "And I am sorry for my burning spirit earlier. Please forgive me."

The rap on the open door startled both of them. Light from the hall framed Lyddie's contented expression.

"Mamm said to find you for supper."

◆ ◆ ◆

Marlin ached to recover the quiet moment of listening to the wonder in Glory's breath and feeling her near.

Supper was, as always, where conversation exploded as soon as Daed pronounced the Aemen on the silent prayer that opened the gathering. The brothers were free now to talk about how they had accomplished their putz, where they kept them hidden from prying eyes—mostly Marlin's, the others agreed. His brothers' wives, his own sisters, and his mother shot bits of information toward each other that lacked context to other listeners, but gradually Marlin pieced together that they were talking about tomorrow's church dinner after the worship service. Eventually he discovered that Glory had deviled four dozen eggs for the occasion.

Now the kitchen was cleared, and Magdalena had alerted her family that breakfast the next day would be simple and prompt. They would want the counters and table clear for the dishes arriving with worshippers. Leroy and Josef had collected their sleepy children, bundled them in buggies, and taken them home. In the post-meal commotion, Marlin had lost track of Glory, and now he wandered into the front rooms.

Glory stood before the one candle that had not yet been snuffed for the night.

"Glory," Marlin said softly.

She turned, her face shifting from the candle's glow into the shadows of the large room.

"Your mamm asked me to tend the candles," she said.

"Bedtime," Marlin said.

Glory nodded. "A busy day ahead."

"Christmas."

"And church." Glory turned back to the window. "The putz lanterns are still on."

"Let's go turn them off together," Marlin said. "I will get your cloak."

"All right."

He retrieved their outerwear and a rarely used lantern from the mudroom with particular swiftness. He did not want to give Glory time to change her mind and say she would go upstairs instead. As he spread her cloak over her shoulders, she leaned toward the window and extinguished the final flame. Marlin adjusted the lantern he carried so they could safely see their way through the maze of church benches and displaced furniture and down the steps off the front porch.

The yard was clear of buggies. By now many of the English would be on their way to a late-evening Christmas Eve service, and the nearby Amish who had admired the putz would have turned their minds to checking on animals and being ready for the shared worship and feast tomorrow. But in this moment, Marlin could be alone with his wife.

They went first to the Nativity.

"Did you really make that clay stable?" Glory asked.

Marlin smiled. "I had to glue it together in a few places. I do not suppose I will ever be much of a sculptor."

"I love the idea of looking at something you made as a child." Her voice drifted in a gust of wind. "I do not have many things like that. My daed did not want us to be vain or attached to worldly goods."

"Your daed wanted you to learn the way of eternity," Marlin said. "Fathers see eternity in different ways, I suppose."

She went silent. Marlin reached into the display for the lantern, turned it off, and picked it up. They moved to the opposite corner and stood before the Angels.

"You may not be a sculptor," Glory said, "but you are a carver."

Marlin shook his head. "I am only beginning to learn what the craft requires."

"But you will learn."

"I hope to learn many things in the next forty or fifty years."

Glory was quiet again. Marlin waited, leaving the lantern on the ground. Her face was turned toward the Angels, but her gaze was unfixed.

"Marlin," she said.

"Yes?"

"Your family's traditions are very different than mine."

"My eyes have seen that this week."

"You love the way your family is."

"And you love your family's ways."

She nodded. He should have paid more attention when her mother's letter arrived three days ago. Glory had taken to her bed for an entire day and had not been herself since.

Or perhaps Marlin did not understand her as well as he thought he did.

"Marlin."

"Yes?" The tremble that had overtaken her voice alarmed him.

"Do you regret that we married?"

◆　◆　◆

Having spoken the words, she could not snatch them back. The question had tangled itself into Glory's spirit for three days. Marlin's love was certain. But were they suited to be husband and wife? Could they be happy? Could they spend a lifetime together? Glory stared at the Angels and the lanterns that lit them. If Marlin extinguished the flames now, they would be standing in blackness save only for the dimness of the old mudroom lantern no one liked to use because it did not work well. Perhaps full darkness would have been better. She did not want to see his face as he inhaled.

Marlin leaned his head toward Glory and brushed her cheek with his chin.

"It is not so scruffy anymore," he said.

Glory nodded. Marlin's beard had been slow to come in after they married, its uneven patches giving him the look of a newlywed longer than many new husbands.

"It is a proper married beard now and will only get better," Marlin said. He stood behind her and brushed his beard across the back of her neck, first in one direction and then the other. "I intend to be doing that for at least fifty years."

"Marlin, I want to be the best *frau*," Glory said. "I am just not sure. . .these last few days. . .your family."

"*Our* family," Marlin corrected, putting his arms around her from behind. "Everyone loves you already. Do not worry about being the best wife. Just be the best you, and all will be well."

Glory gulped.

Marlin began to sing softly in her ear. "Silent night! Holy night! All is calm, all is bright 'round yon virgin mother and child, holy infant so tender and mild, sleep in heavenly peace, sleep in heavenly peace."

He stopped, but Glory did not want the song to end.

"Silent night! Holy night!" she sang. "Shepherds quake at the sight, glories stream from heaven afar, heav'nly hosts sing alleluia; Christ, the Savior, is born! Christ, the Savior, is born!"

"This carol is my favorite of them all," Marlin said.

He nuzzled the back of her neck again. Some of her friends complained about their husbands' scratchy beards on their more delicate skin. Glory never would.

Marlin could brush the back of her neck as often as he wanted if it made her feel as safe and loved as it did in that moment.

"It is my favorite as well," Glory said. "Let's finish."

They started together. "Silent night! Holy night! Son of God, love's pure light, radiant beams from Thy holy face, with the dawn of redeeming grace, Jesus, Lord, at Thy birth, Jesus, Lord, at Thy birth."

Marlin let go of her long enough to snuff the Angels lanterns and set them beside the others at their feet. He turned the mudroom lantern down even further.

"Look up," he said.

The night was not a perfect cloudless velvet bed of glittering diamonds, a description Glory once read in a book during her school years. It was an ordinary slightly overcast winter night, but enough starlight sparkled for her to know what Marlin intended.

"Love's pure light," she said. "Right from the heart of God."

"'And the light shineth in darkness; and the darkness comprehended it not.'"

"From John 1," Glory murmured. "It would be lovely if that were the passage for church tomorrow."

"Practically today," Marlin said. In one hand, he gathered the handles of the lanterns. In the other, he grasped Glory's fingers and led her back into the house.

Glory had forgotten to be cold or doubtful or anxious. She hummed the notes of *love's pure light*, and Marlin picked up the tune as they climbed the stairs together.

Chapter 12

Marlin's mother kept her word about Christmas breakfast being simple and prompt. As Lyddie removed his coffee cup from his hand before he had finished with it, he raised his eyebrows toward Glory. They had agreed to exchange gifts after breakfast, before church. Glory nodded and started up the back stairs. Marlin followed.

"It is not fancy wrapping," Glory said, kneeling to pull a package from under the bed.

He took it from her hands. Oddly shaped, firm, with lumps.

"Open it," Glory urged.

Marlin untied the green string that held the butcher paper in its irregular form and folded back the flaps. Then he opened a leather pouch. "Carving knives!"

Glory's head bobbed. "My grandfather's. I know they are old, but he collected them over many years and always kept the blades sharp and the handles sanded smooth."

"Last night I had three not very good knives," he said, "and now I have twelve that belonged to a craftsman. I will have no excuse not to become a much better carver."

"You do not mind that they have been used by someone else?"

"They were your grandfather's. They are a tradition." He folded the pouch closed and set it on the chest of drawers. Glory's bundle of cookies still lay there. He grinned and took out one of the Glory Divine cookies and popped it in his mouth. "It's Christmas morning. Another tradition fulfilled. Did you write down the recipe?"

She tapped her temple. "No need for a pencil."

Marlin took Glory's hand and tugged her toward the door. "We have to go to the barn for your gift."

"You are not giving me a cow, are you?"

"Just come."

They still had a few minutes before church families would start to arrive. Marlin pushed open the barn door and led Glory to the empty stall where he had been working for weeks. His effort was no longer hidden behind a half bale of hay.

"Move the covering," he said.

Glory picked up one corner of the horse blanket and carefully rolled it back. Marlin watched her face. Confusion. Astonishment. Elation. Gratitude.

"You made all the parts of the putz!" Glory said.

"Just the main pieces." Marlin tapped a shepherd on the head while Glory knelt before Mary holding her child. "What do you notice is missing?"

"The angels," Glory said quickly. "But I know where we can get some."

Marlin laughed. "One day we will have our own home, and we can begin our own traditions. We can add to this every year—sheep, barn animals, more shepherds, a manger, magi, a star to hang above it all. Your grandfather's knives will be perfect."

"I hope you will not mind if a child is underfoot," Glory said.

"Of course not. That will be part of the tradition."

"We are barely used to living with each other," Glory said, "and now we will be three before next year's first snow."

Marlin's hand began to shake and he could not stop it.

◆　◆　◆

Glory unfolded her knees and glanced around the barn, relieved to see no prying human eyes. There was nothing to stop Marlin's kiss.

His arms were around her before she had found her full height, lifting her off the ground and swinging her in a circle before settling his mouth on hers with exuberance. He had not kissed her properly all week, and Glory eagerly received his enthusiasm now. Even through the bulk of their coats his arms swarmed to hold her close. When his hat dropped off his head, neither of them tried to catch it.

"Happy Christmas," Marlin murmured.

"Happy Christmas," Glory said, taking a breath before finding his lips again. The moment was bliss.

And then the morning's reality broke in. The *clip-clop* of horses approached, and voices called across the farmyard. Glory would have to go inside the house, welcome guests, collect coats, and carry food to the kitchen. Marlin would guide rigs to safe parking, and he and his brothers would assist any church members who preferred to unhitch their buggies and shelter their horses in the stable or another of the outbuildings.

They walked, arms around each other, to the barn door, where Glory had to let go of her husband so he could open it. Several buggies were in the lane now. Church would not begin for another hour, but it might take that long for everyone to arrive and the horses to be settled and food situated to heat during worship. Church on Christmas Day was unusual, and Glory had wondered if some families would prefer to stay home and enjoy their own traditions, but one after another the buggies came. The Grabill house would be full that morning, warmed both by the fire in the hearth and faithful hearts.

When she was settled in her seat between Lyddie and Marianne and the bishop was announcing Christmas greetings, Glory looked across the aisle to where Marlin sat among the men. His married status now meant that he sat farther forward than the unmarried men, and he was shoulder to shoulder with Leroy and Josef. Her eyes moved to John, a few rows back, the last of the Grabill men waiting for the blessing of marriage. His gaze ought to have been forward, but like Glory's it wandered at a subtle angle. He had found Sarah, and she had found him. Perhaps next year would be their wedding season.

Glory pulled her attention to the bishop's words.

"Our brother David Grabill has made a wise recommendation," the bishop said. "His son, Marlin, has suggested that our reading for this Christmas Day should come from the Gospel of John. As the Holy Ghost has also given me this passage for our reflection this morning, we celebrate the agreement of our hearts with God as we listen to these words. I invite Marlin Grabill to come forward and read for us."

Glory looked at Lyddie and then Marianne. This was unusual. Marlin was not a minister—at least not yet. But he stood, moved to the preacher's table set up in front of the fire, and began to read. Glory closed her eyes and gave herself to the exultant passage.

"'In the beginning was the Word,'" Marlin said, "'and the Word was with God, and the Word was God. The same was in the beginning with God. All things were made by him; and without him was not any thing made that was made. In him was life; and the life was the light of men. And the light shineth in darkness; and the darkness comprehended it not. There was a man sent from God, whose name was John. The same came for a witness, to bear witness of the Light, that all men through him might believe. He was not that Light, but was sent to bear witness of that Light. That was the true Light, which lighteth every man that cometh into the world. He was in the world, and the world was made by him, and the world knew him not. He came unto his own, and his own received him not. But as many as received him, to them gave he power to become the sons of God, even to them that believe on his name. Which were born, not of blood, nor of the will of the flesh, nor of the will of man, but of God. And the Word was made flesh, and dwelt among us, (and we beheld his glory, the glory as of the only begotten of the Father,) full of grace and truth.'"

The sermons, the hymns, the prayers—the richness of worship on Christmas Day filled Glory's heart, choking away all thought of uncertainty, of anxiety, of doubt, of insecurity. She had grown up under the tutelage of faithful parents—so faithful that they would abandon the convenience of their own livelihood to care for Aenti Beth and her husband and small children. Glory murmured a prayer for Beth, who might already be in the presence of the Lord on this Christmas morning. And Glory's family had belonged to this church family. She had not married into another district, where she would have to meet new people and make new friends. These young women sitting on either side of her were her sisters now. Sadie and Joannah were her sisters. Leroy, Josef, and John were her brothers. The babe in her womb—she glanced at Sadie, who also carried a babe—would both remind her of where she had come from and lead her to the future God planned for her with Marlin. Whether her parents remained in Holmes County, Ohio, for four weeks, four months, or four years, Glory was loved. She would find her way.

Marlin found her after the service, in the tiny space before the men would begin to transform the benches to tables and the women, in the crowded Grabill kitchen, would undertake their familiar ministrations of presenting food for the congregation.

"You read beautifully," Glory said to her husband. Later, without onlookers, she would tell him again with an embrace.

"It was the disciple John who wrote beautifully," Marlin said, "and the Christ child who beautifully became the Word made flesh."

Glory swallowed. How could she have ever doubted the blessing of marriage to this man?

"The Christ child is the best gift of all of course," Marlin said. "But next to that, *we* are the best gift we give each other."

We.

"Yes, *we*," Glory said. The tiny word tasted less foreign on her tongue and was more tethered within her mind. She would notice it more carefully, speak it more frequently, understand it more fully. For was this not what Christ Himself had done—become *we* when He took on flesh?

Glory made no effort to wipe the tears that filled her eyes. "Happy Christmas. Happy Christmas."

For more of Marlin and Gloria's story—including what became of Minnie Handelman—look for Hope in the Land, *a full-length Amish Turns of Time story by Olivia Newport.*

Amish Frosted Buttermilk Cookies

½ cup butter, softened
1 cup sugar
1 egg
1 teaspoon vanilla
2½ cups flour
½ teaspoon baking soda
½ teaspoon salt
½ cup buttermilk

Frosting:
3 tablespoons butter, softened
3½ cups powdered sugar
¼ cup milk
1 teaspoon vanilla

Cream butter and sugar, and then beat in egg and vanilla. Combine flour, soda, and salt. Alternate adding dry ingredients and buttermilk to creamed mixture and stir well. Drop by rounded tablespoons onto greased cookie sheets, leaving two inches in between. Bake at 375 degrees for 10 to 12 minutes. Set aside to cool.

For frosting, combine butter, sugar, milk, and vanilla and beat until smooth.

Olivia Newport's novels twist through time to find where faith and passions meet. Her husband and two twentysomething children provide welcome distraction from the people stomping through her head on their way into her books. She chases joy in stunning Colorado at the foot of the Rockies, where daylilies grow as tall as she is.

Pirate of My Heart

by Rachael O. Phillips

Chapter 1

Rock and Cave, Illinois
September 1825

Mama said the red shawl was of the devil, but Keturah begged to differ. Its luxurious warmth around her shoulders made this blustery September morn even more special.

"Where did you get it? How did you leave the house with it?" her friend Delilah whispered after Papa's wagon rumbled down the dusty road to the village stable.

Keturah chuckled softly as they walked away from Scott's General Store, owned by Delilah's father. Caleb, Keturah's older brother, trailed after them with his usual gangling, unhurried gait.

"The shawl came from my aunt Rachel in Pennsylvania. She sent barrels of castoffs in answer to Mama's appeal for the poor here in Illinois."

"Surely she knew your mother would not allow this shawl in her house." Delilah's shoe-button eyes twinkled.

"Surely she did." Keturah kept her expression demure, though she longed to laugh aloud. "Aunt Rachel is her sister. She also knew Mama would no more give this shawl to the poor than she would steal alms."

"Quite convenient for Keturah that our rich aunt should be read out of Meeting for marrying a Methodist," Caleb drawled. "Perhaps in the next barrel, thee will find geegaws fit for the Christmas thy soul craves." He grinned. "Or thee could marry a Methodist, too."

Caleb often teased Delilah, who was a Methodist. Keturah tolerated his frequent reminders that she, at twenty, was past the usual age of marriage. But his poking fun at Christmas ruffled her. Why did Mama consider it wrong? Even Papa and other Friends discounted it. *Should we not celebrate the birth of the Son of God, the Light of the World?*

Keturah decided not to waste her breath on Caleb. With a winsome smile, she said, "How fortunate for our parents their son's affections dwell safely within the Friends' fold."

His face turned pink. "Thee art mistaken."

"Perhaps." Keturah glanced down Rock and Cave's main road. "Still, Priscilla Norris doubtless would welcome a greeting." She steered him toward the gray-caped blond girl carrying a large basket. Keturah hoped to keep her giggles inside until she and Delilah managed to lose their chaperone. "Good day, Priscilla."

"Good day. And to thee, too, Delilah and Caleb." Priscilla's childlike voice feigned innocence, but her knowing blue eyes searched Keturah's.

Delilah echoed the greeting, but Caleb turned red as Keturah's shawl, as if Priscilla had said something bold.

"Would thee join us for a walk?" Keturah edged Caleb toward Priscilla.

"I would, but I feel ill." Priscilla sighed. "My basket is heavy—"

"I will take it." Caleb moved faster than Keturah thought possible. He clasped the handle. "Perhaps thee should rest under that oak."

"Carry it to her house," Keturah urged him.

Caleb hesitated. "But Pa—"

"Papa would want thee to help a lady in need." The firmness in her voice sounded so much like Mama's, it startled her. "We shall not wander far."

Caleb opened his mouth for a token protest, but Priscilla captured him. "I am thankful for thy help, Caleb. God Himself must have sent thee my way."

"God smiled on us all," Delilah whispered as Caleb trailed after Priscilla, unblinking as if under a spell.

Laughter bubbled in Keturah, but she and Delilah held their peace until the couple disappeared around the corner. They laughed at poor, lovesick Caleb as they headed toward the Ohio River shore.

"I'm so glad your father does business in Rock and Cave rather than taking Ford's Ferry across to Kentucky." Delilah almost skipped along.

"So am I." Keturah squeezed her arm. Otherwise how would they, years out of school, see each other? "Papa questions Mr. Ford's honesty."

"Nor should he trust many who run Rock and Cave." Delilah never hesitated to voice her opinions. "They say river pirate days are gone, but I don't believe it."

The gleeful wind pulled at Keturah's shawl, and Delilah, fingering its silky fringe, forgot about pirates and corruption. "You did not tell me how you escaped wearing this."

"I slipped it out of the rubbish bin and washed it while Mama rested. Then I hid it in the washhouse." Keturah hugged herself. "When I brought it today, dear Papa tried to object. But he said, 'That is the color of the cardinals outside our window,' and I knew he would not forbid me to wear it."

"It is red as holly berries at Christmas." Delilah's dark eyes widened with longing. "I would save it to wear to the Christmas dance."

"Thee knows I cannot join in such revelry." Keturah sighed and then straightened. "But I intend to celebrate Christmas this year any way I can."

"Perhaps I can teach you carols and customs we keep," Delilah offered.

Keturah squeezed her arm gratefully. "I'll be asking thee as Christmas nears."

The girls sorted through bits of ripe news and gossip like persimmons in a basket. Half Keturah's mind grasped every sight, sound, and smell of the village— even the stench of animal skins drying behind the tanner's—framing them like portraits to be viewed later without limit. Although Papa's farm was only three miles from the village of Rock and Cave and the Ohio River, she rarely joined him on a trip to town. Only Papa's gentle maneuvering—and Mama's dislike of poetry—had freed Keturah from the usual drudgery of housekeeping.

"Did you recite Shakespeare aloud to your mama?" Unlike her biblical name-sake, Delilah had a heart of gold—but her wicked smile suggested at least a small kinship.

Keturah nodded. "Shakespeare, Burns, and Blake!"

"'Tis small wonder she relented. You should read her poetry every day."

Keturah giggled, but a voice in her head waged an indignant protest. *Why must I scheme like a naughty child to spend a few hours away from the farm? And from Caleb?*

The vast green-and-gray Ohio River absorbed the road, reminding her that Mama feared it like a monster serpent coiling among forests and farms.

Keturah shook herself. The day was too precious to waste. Thin crimson threads embroidering the green maples along the shore reminded her of the skeins she'd bought earlier with her birthday money, thread she would work into a special Christmas sampler.

The wind's gusts died. The sun ceased its coy hide-and-seek among the clouds and shone warm on her back. She loosened the shawl and let it hang from her shoulders. She and Delilah gloried in the giant river's beauty, watching muscled boatmen keel and steer boats, some eighty feet long, around snags and other perils. The friends exclaimed as a majestic steamboat appeared, trailing a train of black smoke as if to say "the queen has come to Illinois." Men wearing top hats and elegant ladies strolled down its tiered decks.

Yearning caught in Keturah's throat like a fishbone. During the past decade, steamboats had become a common sight. But she never had stepped foot on even a keelboat. *If only I could go, too.*

"Would you ladies be needin' a ride to McFarlan's Ferry?" A leathery-faced man offered them a near-toothless grin from the village's wooden dock. He held out a clawlike hand. Other boatmen stared at them with hungry eyes.

"No, thank you." Keturah grabbed Delilah's arm and hurried away. She longed to escape to McFarlan's Ferry Golconda, even down the Mississippi to New Orleans! But not on that boat.

Her shawl suddenly left her shoulders as if the man had grabbed it. Fingers of terror stole down her back. But when she turned, only the impish wind dangled it, swirling it—and her life, it seemed—toward the water.

"No!" She chased the shawl, skirts clogging her steps. Delilah darted beside her, but they could not outpace the wind. Guffaws from the keelboat met Keturah's ears, but she ignored them and dashed down the pier.

If only she could grab—

Splash.

She dropped into a cold, green underworld, ramming against the rock-strewn river bottom. She lay stunned and bruised, undulating skirts binding her like bandages. Gold strands of light writhed in the water, water that filled her eyes, her mouth, her throat. She retched, only to swallow more. Mama had never allowed her to swim.

Something gripped her shoulder. A mental picture of Jonah and the big fish in

Papa's Bible filled her with fresh terror. She kicked and tore at the thing with her nails. Ironlike bands pinned her arms to her sides. She felt as if her eyes would burst.

Dear Lord Jesus. I am going to die.

Suddenly she broke the surface. Coughing and shivering, she shook her sodden hair from her eyes and realized a stranger held her in his arms.

◆　◆　◆

From the boat he saw her fall and go under, her friend screaming from the dock. He leaped into the river.

Now, standing in the water and holding her as she coughed and spit on him, he shared her stupidity. Catcalls from other boatmen greeted them—the silly girl who ran off a pier, nearly drowning in only five feet of water, and the soaking-wet fool who jumped in to rescue her. He would never hear the end of this. Still, her eyes, greener than the water, locked him in a vise. He trembled—but not because of cold.

"Keturah! Are you all right?" The girl's friend stretched out a hand.

"You that hard up, Henry?" Old Sol cackled from the deck. "I know where you can find a woman that will hug ya up good without drownin' ya dead!"

"Not as pretty as that 'un though."

The boatman's tone wrenched Henry's eyes away from the girl's. He hated the look the man gave her. Turning away, he waded ashore, still carrying the girl who lay limp in his arms, her eyes like green stars. "Sol. You got a blanket?"

The old codger pulled one from his poke, jumped from boat to pier, and brought it to him. The girl's friend scurried close behind.

Keturah. What a pretty name.

Sol shook the tattered brown blanket out. "Wrap her up good, boy."

The girl wriggled to free herself. His arms did not want to release her, but he set her on the grassy shore and covered her. Her friend hugged her.

"I—I thank thee." The girl avoided his eyes now and looked to the older man. "And I thank thee for the blanket, Friend Sol, is it?"

"Yes, ma'am. Hope you're feelin' better." The man turned back to Henry. "We got to go. You comin' with us to McFarlan?"

He needed the work. He did not need to waste an afternoon with a girl who didn't have the sense to swim when she fell in. And she, hearing Sol's words, said nothing. She did not need him.

But he could not bring himself to leave.

Sol chuckled. "I see. You're gonna stick with this here damsel in distress. Just be sure you bring my blanket back."

Sol returned to the keelboat. With a final round of catcalls, the boatmen guided it out of the dock.

The girl searched behind Henry as if for something lost. But she addressed him in a polite voice. "I am sorry for the way I behaved. I thought—"

"People who think they are drowning do strange things." He stared at the ground.

"I—I cannot swim."

"You should learn. Then a few feet of water will not scare you." He stole a glance, hoping to regain the communion of those wonderful eyes. But they still darted behind him, scanning the river. "You lose something?"

"My red shawl." She struggled to rise, her soggy clothing weighing her down. "The wind blew it into the river. I chased it and fell in."

"Shawl?" He felt like tossing her back.

"I must find it." She struggled free of the blanket, rose, and stepped toward the shore.

Her friend grabbed her arm. "Keturah, you'll catch your death of a cold."

When Keturah's steps grew more determined, her friend picked up a long, gnarly stick from nearby underbrush. "If you insist, perhaps we can fish it out."

Henry retrieved Sol's blanket. "Wait. This is bound to be dryer than a shawl fresh from the river. Better wrap up. Please, or you'll get sick." Why did he feel compelled to accompany her?

"I thank thee." Though dripping hair clung to her cheeks like river weeds to white stone, her smile outshone her eyes. "I am Keturah Wilkes. My father owns a farm outside Rock and Cave. This is Delilah Scott."

Why had he not seen her before? He bobbed his head as steamboat gentlemen did. "I am Henry Mangun. I work on the boats." He did more than that, but she need not know.

"We had better hurry." She turned toward the river, brandishing her stick like a child. "My brother, Caleb, will return shortly."

At his name, Delilah rolled her eyes. "How will you explain—"

"Let's not think about it." Keturah swished the stick in the now dark gray water.

As they searched the shallows, clouds bullied the sun into hiding. No one had given Henry a blanket to ward off the sharp breeze rising from the west. Not a pinch of fat to keep him warm, as Ma said. And his cold, wet leggings and coarse blue linsey woolsey shirt rubbed him raw.

"This is useless." Keturah threw the stick into the river.

Delilah gave a sigh of relief. He almost followed suit—except he feared Keturah would disappear, leaving him empty as an upset bucket. Still he must end this futile search. "A red shawl would stand out in the water. It must have been swept into the drop-off."

Keturah tossed the blanket aside, kneeled, and removed her still-soppy moccasins.

"Keturah Wilkes, whatever are you doing?" Delilah squealed.

"I'm going to find my shawl." Her chin rose.

"You want to jump into the river again?" He *had* rescued a crazy woman.

"No. But I must." Her trembling cheek looked lily-petal soft. His hand ached to touch it.

He heard himself say, "I will look for the shawl."

All his life he had doubted the sanity of the people around him. Now he wondered if she had driven him to madness. He plunged into the chilly water.

Like a catfish, he slid along the river bottom. When he found nothing, Henry gulped fresh mouthfuls of air and swam well past the pier's mossy posts. Nothing. Popping through the river surface, he opened his mouth to tell her he was done. Finished.

She was yelling for him to try that spot. He already had searched near the drop-off twice. He might have told her to find another madman for her task, except with the wind sloshing waves up his nose it was simply easier to drop back down into the water and look. Perhaps. His open eyes, braving the silt, burned.

There, caught among the weeds. He grasped the shawl, wadded it into a shapeless mass, and held it close to his body with one hand as he made for shore. Planting his feet in the muck, he held up his trophy.

At the joy on her face, his irritation evaporated. She splashed in, and he handed her the muddy, slimy shawl. Clasping the blanket around her with one hand, she hugged the shawl. He wished he could take its place. But she did hold out a hand, and though he did not feel worthy of its whiteness, he clasped it as if he were the one drowning.

"Keturah Wilkes."

The bass voice sounded more powerful because the man did not raise it. Keturah, clinging to her filthy bundle, dropped Henry's hand as if it contained hot coals. She turned slowly around. The birdlike friend on shore gave a funny little chirp.

Henry did not want to look up. But he lifted his chin and looked squarely into the rocklike gaze of a big man with Keturah's eyes.

Chapter 2

"Perhaps thee would like to explain?" Papa's tone, though controlled, spoke more words than his dictionary.

"My shawl blew into the river." Keturah knew only the truth would set her free. "I fell in, trying to retrieve it. This person witnessed my misfortune and helped me to shore."

She dared not look into Henry's odd, yet wondrous, golden-hazel eyes again, eyes that had imprisoned her when he pulled her out.

"That does indeed relieve my mind." Her father's probing gaze did not soften. "I thought perchance thee had grown too warm in thy lovely shawl and decided to take a cooling bath in the mud." He gestured toward the village. "Perhaps thee knows Caleb's whereabouts?"

"He carried Mistress Norris's heavy basket to her house," Delilah chimed in. "She was ill."

"Of course." Papa nodded sagely. "The air fairly reeks with charity today. Would thee be so kind, Delilah, to go ask Caleb to meet us at the edge of town?"

With a wave, Delilah skittered away. Keturah, wading ashore, looked after her in despair. After this escapade, who knew when she would come to town again?

Papa turned to Henry, still standing in water. "I would be far remiss if I did not thank thee for helping my daughter. What is thy name?"

"Henry Mangun."

"God bless thee, Friend Mangun." Papa pointed to the blanket wrapped around her. "This belongs to—"

"Sol. I work with him."

Keturah tried not to shiver as she handed it to Henry. "I will use Papa's horse blanket on our ride home." She wrinkled her nose at the thought of the smell.

"That will no doubt complete thy elegant toilette." A tiny smile escaped Papa's mouth.

Perhaps there was hope after all. And thanks to Henry, she still had her shawl. "I cannot thank thee enough."

He smiled for the first time, a slow light that filled his tanned face like a sunrise. Almost before she realized it, he had disappeared into the nearby forest.

Caleb, his mouth hanging open like a sheep's, joined them in the near-silent ride home. Wrapped in the scratchy horse blanket, Keturah held her nose. She checked the wet red and green crewel in her pocket. Hopefully, her unexpected bath had not

315

affected the bright colors. She anticipated no further remarks from Papa. He would say little to Caleb—usually the dutiful son—about leaving his sister unescorted in town. Papa would assume both had learned from their misadventures and would adjust their ways accordingly.

But Mama? She, Caleb, and Papa had left the mighty Ohio behind, but Keturah knew they all were preparing for the flood of reproaches that surely would sweep them away.

◆　◆　◆

Henry stuck his fingers in his ears and tried to invite sleep back into his dark, musty loft. He liked fiddle music and sang a good ditty. Though he tended to watch more than participate, he liked parties. But not this kind, especially after several hard days of loading and keeling boats.

Ma's hee-haw laugh scared away any lingering dreams. He flipped off his corn husk tick, crawled to the ladder opening, and stuck his head into the room below.

"Ma, you trying to wake the dead?"

She laughed uproariously. "Boy, when things is good, I gotta dance."

Several people clapped as his red-haired mother, hands on ample hips, never missed a step in her jig to someone's wild fiddling. Her feet blurred, she danced so fast. He couldn't help grinning. Nobody could outdance Ma.

"Henry, you missed the best loot ever." Charlie, his brother, raised a gourd filled with wine. "Rich farmer on his way home from New Orleans. But we were kind. Left him his underdrawers."

The room rocked with huzzahs and toasts. Charlie's eyes glittered with a look Henry had come to dread.

He pulled back and flopped on his tick. As children he and Charlie had been the best pickpockets at the docks. Now Henry only stole when he or his family were hungry. But Charlie wanted to get rich. Someday he would trespass on James Ford's territory one time too many. Or worse, join Ford in his schemes to lure travelers to Potts' Inn and rob and kill them.

I'll never touch Ford or Potts, no matter how poor we get.

He lay sleepless until they grew too drunk to notice his leaving. He grabbed his poke and climbed down the ladder, navigating dancers and snoring bodies on the dirt floor. He unlatched the door, welcoming the forest's fresh, chilly air as he escaped to the limestone bluffs along the river, honeycombed with caves he'd explored since a child. Not that he would go to the big pirate cave. He would never go there again. Ever.

Henry, using the silent walk his Shawnee Indian father had taught him, meandered through the forest to his secret cave. Even Charlie didn't know this favorite spot, big enough for him to build a fire and lie down for a rocky but peaceable night.

◆　◆　◆

Tea-kettle-tea-kettle-chee-chee-chee! One Carolina wren woke Henry. Soon several chattered outside. He dragged his aching body to a sitting position. Sly sunbeams peeked through a small opening in the cave's roof, teasing him to come outside. Henry, swathed in the blanket he kept in the cave, munched a piece of hardtack from his poke. He did not work on Sunday—a welcome rest from his usual back-breaking labor. Beyond that, Sundays had always seemed special. For the life of him, he could not imagine why. After Saturday nights, his home looked like a pigsty. He would not return there today. The peaceful village streets drew him, but churchgoers wearing their Sunday best eyed him. Their faces told him ragged half-breeds did not belong.

Henry pulled a small worn book from his poke and opened it under the sun-beams. Ma hadn't given a fig whether he went to school as a child. But he went because he liked the teacher and wanted to read.

As a teen, he stole a Bible because he'd always wanted one. He read it off and on, trying to sound out the hard words. Now he scratched his head, deciphering a New Testament verse: "'Therefore if any man be in Christ, he is a new creature: old things are passed away; behold, all things are become new.'"

What did it mean? At twenty-five he felt old and hard as the cave. "Any man," it said. How could any man—especially him—become new, like a baby?

The memory of Keturah, her softness and sparkling eyes, invaded his thoughts as they had many times the past week. Despite the cave's chill, his face heated like an iron skillet. He should not think of scripture and Keturah in the same moment. Yet he felt they were linked. She and her father were obviously Quakers, saying "thee" and "thou." Keturah and her pa sounded as if they had stepped out of the Bible.

But other things about them intrigued him. Keturah told her pa the truth about her "swim." She could have made up a story, even blamed him for dumping her into the water. But she didn't.

Her pa's patience surprised him, too. Men swore and struck their families when they annoyed them. Henry had never seen an angry man show such calmness. He had called Henry, a river rat, *friend* and blessed him.

Keturah and her pa must know God. Something inside him leaped. But was it the girl or her God that excited him more?

He would have to think on it. Clutching the Bible, Henry shouldered his poke and headed for the river. He hunkered down on top of a cliff overlooking the water sparkling in the sunshine as if God had just made it. Humming a scrap of a hymn he'd learned at school, he opened the Bible again.

◆　◆　◆

Keturah tied on her First Day bonnet. Mama gave the kettle of beans baking in the fireplace's coals a final stir. They joined Caleb and Papa, who had driven the wagon to the door of their cabin.

"Thee is ready for Meeting?"

Papa's words meant more than finishing chores and donning their best clothes. Keturah nodded. Although sitting in silence strained her ready tongue, she genu-inely loved First Day, when a few area Quaker families gathered in the tiny cabin that served as a meetinghouse. Sharing God's Light and listening for His wisdom, rather than scrubbing and cooking, seemed an excellent use of time to Keturah. Did Mama like sitting still? She hid a grin.

Keturah enjoyed the meetinghouse more during summer, when the wide-open wooden shutters let in the forest's fresh scents. But the candles Mama brought for the table at the front glowed like the Light within. Sitting beside her on the women's side of the room, Keturah pondered the scriptures Papa had read at breakfast, all about becoming a new creature in Christ. At times her thoughts and actions had nothing to do with Christ's Light. As one Friend spoke of God's refining fire, and another rose to praise God, Keturah asked Him to make her the woman He wanted her to be.

Yet she could not believe God had designed her like Mama or most Quaker women, who married at sixteen or seventeen, kept house, raised children. Her heart longed for adventure, for learning, for newness of life she had not yet tasted.

Keturah felt an odd sense of someone watching. To be sure, she had felt boys' covert stares at Meeting throughout the years. Now, the group's marriageable young men had all found wives. She rejoiced in their happiness—and her own respite. Why this uneasiness?

She turned her head, coughed into her handkerchief, and cast a glance behind. Large golden eyes met hers. A tall, thin figure sat on a bench at the back. Henry Mangun. Why had he joined them? How had he slipped in without anyone hearing?

Henry blinked and then stared at the floor. She shifted back to the front, surprised to find herself blushing as Meeting ended.

"Friend Mangun?" Papa strode to the door.

Papa remembered his name, too. Henry looked as if he wanted to escape. But as Papa talked, he asked hesitant questions, then more. With the buzz of the women's after-Meeting conversation, Keturah heard little. But they appeared to discuss the scriptures read. Henry said nothing to her before disappearing into the forest as he had done after rescuing her.

She knew all—including Mama—were bursting with curiosity, but they would keep their post-Meeting discussions to spiritual and family matters. As she expected, Henry's attendance came up at dinner.

"Who was that boy?" Mama ladled beans onto their plates. "Is he from Rock and Cave?"

She frequently sent food and clothing for the village poor with Papa, but she had not set foot there in years.

"Henry Mangun. Lives downriver." Papa drank his cider, taking care not to look at Keturah.

"Why would he come? How could he know where we meet?" Mama sputtered.

"Perhaps—" Papa put his cup down. "Perhaps he is looking for God."

Chapter 3

Two weeks later, Mama's small hands pounded bread dough on the big oak table in their cabin's main room. "Thee *shall* see the man."

"Mayhap thee might tell me before inviting a gentleman to keep company." Keturah pounded hers harder. "I am not a child."

Mama stoked the big stone fireplace. "Perhaps thee knows another grown woman who swims in the river wearing her best dress?"

Keturah gritted her teeth. Mama would display this unfortunate incident like a prize ribbon until Keturah turned eighty. At least she did not know about the shawl.

The set of Mama's mouth told Keturah further argument would be a waste. In silence they formed the loaves of white bread they ate only on First Day or when visitors came. Keturah's kneading almost matched her mother's. But that did not guarantee baking success. Often Mama hid Keturah's bread from company—especially male company.

"Bring in a ham." Mama chopped apples for pies as if wielding a battle-ax.

Keturah welcomed an escape to the smokehouse. The brisk October air cooled her hot cheeks as she detoured into the drafty washhouse. Keturah pulled the red shawl from its hiding place behind pokes of rags Mama kept to make rugs. She threw it around her shoulders, parading past big wooden tubs, imagining she wore it openly today. Especially on Christmas Day. Every day if she chose.

If she chose. The words rattled in her mind, useless and noisy as stones in a bucket. She wished she dared shout from the rooftops that she harbored no interest whatsoever in Thaddeus Squibb, son of wealthy Friends from northern Illinois.

Keturah could not recall Thaddeus, though Mama said they met at the last yearly Meeting. Keturah enjoyed those rare gatherings of Friends from across the state. But this was not the first time a man only Mama remembered had appeared afterward at their door, eager, suitable, and impossibly dull. She considered appearing at dinner wearing the shawl. Friend Squibb, seeing her in all her scarlet glory, would disappear like a bad dream.

She giggled but then felt a little ashamed. People prone to rash judgments annoyed her. Should she not keep an open mind, too? She had not told her parents a deep part of her longed for a strong man's love. He had not yet appeared. If God chose to bring him with Mama's help, who was she to reject him without so much as laying eyes on him?

Remembering the river episode, Keturah realized her mother was right about her occasional lack of common sense. Reluctantly, she restored the shawl to its hiding place. She dashed to the smokehouse and cut down a large ham. Carrying her greasy bundle, Keturah hurried into the cabin and managed to slice it for frying without wounding herself. She raised cloths covering the rising bread to check its progress and sighed. Mama's loaves looked perfect. Hers were lopsided.

As a final peace offering to Mama and Friend Squibb, she made gingerbread cookies using Grandmama's recipe, the only dish she never ruined. As she rolled and cut the rich brown dough into circles, she recalled that, long ago, her Methodist aunt Rachel had told Keturah her Quaker grandmamma secretly called them Christmas cookies. Keturah had followed that example. Now the cake-like treats added their aroma to the cabin's mouthwatering aura.

Keturah tidied up and set the table with Mama's white tablecloth and dark blue-and-white crockery, brought precariously downriver from Pennsylvania. The room with its scrubbed wooden floor, cozy rag rugs, and polished pewter would smile a welcome to Friend Squibb.

Keturah washed up then clambered up narrow stairs to her bedroom. She brushed her hair until it glowed like summer wheat, and donned her best dress—without the red shawl.

◆　◆　◆

Friend Squibb did not appear nervous, if one judged by appetite. He ate as much as Keturah's father and brother combined. Had he devoured a whole pie? But he also was making Keturah's Christmas cookies disappear. Between bites, he declared he had not eaten such a feast since his dear Sally departed this life.

Keturah choked on her pie. One glance told her Mama had known. *No wonder I did not remember him. He has to be at least fifteen years older than I.*

Still, he was handsome, an enormous tanned, blond-haired man. She brushed away a biblical reference to the giant Anakites of Canaan from her mind and tried to smile. She did not have to make conversation, for Friend Squibb devoted his whole attention to eating. Due to a full mouth, he rarely answered. At least not so she could understand. Keturah tried not to panic when Papa and Caleb left to do chores after dinner without inviting their visitor to join them. Her mother accepted Keturah's fervent offer to help with dishes but went to fetch heated water from the washhouse.

She hoped Friend Squibb's heavy meal would make him drift off. Instead, his alert blue eyes surveyed her with a pleased air. Keturah gulped.

"Thee has been well?" Friend Squibb gave her a huge, toothy smile.

"Very well, indeed." She could not tell him his manners nauseated her.

"Thou art tall and strong, not frail and fussy, like so many young women." He cocked his head to one side. "Thee likes children?"

"Yes." She began to regale him with tales of their neighbor girls, when the words died on her lips. "Dost thou have children?"

"Seven sons." He chomped more cookies. "But my quiver is not yet full. I would have seven more to work my farm and a lovely girl or two—like thee—to care for and civilize the household."

"Civilize," Keturah said faintly. A vision rose before her of a gargantuan table surrounded by wide-mouthed blond Anakites with her and two skinny, pitiful girls shoveling food like hay. She broke out in a cold sweat.

Friend Squibb gave her a gooey smile, and her gorge rose. With a stammered apology, she ran out the door toward the barn.

Papa's hands held her head as she retched. After she washed her face, he seated Keturah in the empty but still-warm washhouse. "I will inform Friend Squibb of thy illness."

But Mama, returning from the house, already had done so. "When I said thee was feeling delicate, he expressed thanks for the meal but said perhaps he should leave thee in the tender care of thy mother and father."

Keturah twisted her apron.

Her mother's fine eyebrows drew together in a straight black line. "What did he say to thee? What did he do?"

"Nothing dishonorable," Keturah assured her. "He complimented my good health. He wishes to marry and have seven more sons—"

"Seven!" Caleb appeared out of nowhere, as usual. "Seven who eat like him?"

"Seven *more* to help run his farm." Keturah shuddered.

She knew Papa was searching for something positive to say. "Friend Squibb appeared a very. . .hearty man."

Keturah bowed her head. "I—I did try to like him, Mama."

"I am glad thee did not. He would work thee like a slave." Mama sniffed. "I had not seen him at table. His god is his stomach."

She laid a rough hand on Keturah's cheek. It felt good. Her mother hastened inside to scrub Friend Squibb's presence from her table.

Papa's glance followed his wife fondly and then wrapped Keturah in a gentle embrace that quieted her heart, mind, and insides.

Perhaps Mama would think twice before finding her more suitors.

Chapter 4

Henry dropped his lunch poke. Beautiful Keturah looked straight at him. Standing near Scott's store beside her brother, Keturah did not blink. Henry avoided her at Meeting each week, but now he could not escape that jeweled green gaze. His legs teetered, but his feet refused to move.

"Henry."

Keturah's smile devoured his breath. He looked away, trying to inhale.

"Henry?"

Was there a note of hurt in her voice? He rose from his seat on the ground, flattening his voice into politeness. "Miss Keturah, how are you? And you, Mr. Wilkes?"

Caleb nodded.

She giggled. "By now thee should know we Friends do not give each other titles."

Last month she had played the fool, falling into the river. Today he was doing everything wrong.

"Do not worry thyself." Keturah read his uneasiness. "Call me miss if thee wishes."

"I—I don't want to be too familiar."

"Thee rescued me, and now thee knows my name. I know thine, as does Caleb. We worship together. Are we not friends?"

He let himself smile. "We are."

"Would thee like Christmas cookies?" She eyed the leathery dried fish in his hand.

He puzzled at this, since it was only October. But his stomach growled at the sight of plump brown gingerbread cookies. "I would not eat your vittles."

"We have eaten plenty." She held them under his nose. "Even Caleb has had enough."

Caleb nodded, his gaze wandering.

Henry took two. *Mmm.* Sweet and spicy. Like Keturah. She must be a wonderful cook.

Caleb's stare fastened on a blond girl down the way. "Keturah, may I assume thee will not swim?"

She shot him an annoyed look. "I promise."

"Remember what Mama said. Stay within my sight."

Watching Caleb amble off, Henry laughed. "If you do fall in, I will teach you to swim. At least I will not have to seek your shawl."

Her smile faded. "I do not trouble Mama further by wearing it in public today.

She does not think bright colors proper." Keturah set her jaw. "But I wear it often alone, especially when I stitch my Christmas sampler."

"Why does she dislike color?" He was being too bold but could not restrain his curiosity. "At Meeting, all wear gray or dark clothes."

"Friends prefer to keep their lives simple and free from pride. I see their wisdom." She raised her chin. "But surely the God who created cardinals, dandelions, and pumpkins, who paints the sunrise each day, does not forbid the joy of color to His people."

He nodded. Looking into her emerald eyes, he knew their Creator must take even more pleasure in them than he.

"I want to open my life to beauty." Keturah cupped her hand over her eyes to scan the Ohio. "I was born here yet know the river so little because of my mother's fears."

"Why is she afraid of the river?"

"Her sister drowned one spring."

No wonder. He'd seen the river flood, changing overnight into a roaring monster that swept dead people and animals downstream before his very eyes.

"That was years ago." Impatience tinged her voice. "Tell me what thee has seen."

He didn't want to frighten her. "I see it sparkle in the sun's light and hear its voice in the dark. I've keeled many boats, even past where the Ohio meets the Mississippi."

"Thee has ridden a steamboat?"

He basked in her smile of admiration. "Occasionally." Twice, actually.

"Thee has met travelers. How exciting." She gestured to the east. "And has thee explored the big cave?"

Henry nodded, but uneasiness chilled him. Pa knew the big cave too well.

"Thee must have many stories to tell." Like a little girl, Keturah hugged herself. "I would see the cave, but Papa forbade it. I heard pirates once lived there, preying on passing boats. Some say they still stop boats—even steamships—and demand money. Did thee ever meet up with pirates?"

His soul dropped like an anchor. Finally he wet his lips and said, "Yes. A time or two."

◆　◆　◆

How glad Keturah was that Mama, regretting Friend Squibb, allowed her to go to town now. She wanted to know Henry better. Once past his first shyness, he seemed almost lighthearted with a boyish smile that warmed his feline eyes. As they talked, she felt more comfortable with him than with her own brother. But now his face stiffened. He said little as she chattered. Still, she was disappointed when Caleb and Priscilla walked toward them.

"I must go." She sighed. Back to the farm where adventure consisted of runaway livestock. "I will see thee at Meeting?"

"I would not go elsewhere."

The hunger in his voice startled her. She had gone to Meeting every week since a babe and never encountered such fervor.

"Come, then, and feast," she said impetuously.

His face lit up.

"Till then. Good-bye."

Henry nodded and faded into the forest. She blinked and turned to her brother. "How does he vanish like that?"

"Because he looks like a walking sapling." Caleb waved farewell to Priscilla. "Except for the black hair."

"The sapling calls the sapling thin." Keturah crossed her arms.

"He is much thinner than I."

She was about to say, *He does not eat as many cookies.* Instead, she said softly, "He does not eat as often as we."

Caleb nodded, his eyes suddenly serious. He said no more as they walked back to Papa's wagon.

"What, thou art not late? Nor soaked?" Papa gave them a quizzical look. "To what do we owe this strange state of affairs?"

Keturah impulsively held his hand against her cheek. "Sometimes Caleb and I forget to be thankful for all we have."

Papa looked pleased but more puzzled than ever when Caleb did not add a retort. As he urged Sam on home, Keturah thought perhaps the farm with its snug four-room cabin, full table, cellar, and smokehouse was not a bad prospect after all.

◆　◆　◆

"Where you goin' so early?"

Hand on the door latch, Henry felt Ma's words hit him between the shoulder blades like birdshot. "I can't sleep."

"You're goin' to see that Quaker girl."

Ma knew. How? He dropped his head.

"I saw you talking to her in town. Pretty. You have an eye for the ladies. Like your Pa."

Pa was dead, shot in Kentucky when vigilantes hunted down his pirate gang. Why couldn't Ma let him die? He wanted to run but faced her. "I'm going to Meeting."

Ma's face and hair had absorbed the gray morning light. Her weary mouth twisted in a chuckle. "Henry, I'm your ma. You may present a fine front to others, but don't try it on me. Meeting? You, a Quaker?"

"Don't know if I'll be a Quaker. But I find peace there." He took a deep breath. "I find God."

"And that girl has nothin' to do with your gettin' religion?"

He knew his face was turning red. He threw the door open. *Today I'll do it. I'll run and run and never come back.*

"Henry!" Her tone dropped to almost a whisper, a thin chain that pulled him. "This foolish dream can't come true. She and her thee-and-thou family will never think of you as anything but dirt. She doesn't know you—"

"You don't know me, Ma!" The cry ripped from his chest as if she had opened it with a knife. "You never have!"

He ran for the meetinghouse as if his life depended on it.

◆　◆　◆

"Therefore if any man be in Christ, he is a new creature: old things are passed away; behold, all things are become new."

Papa had read this scripture weeks ago. The words sprouted in her daily thoughts, and now, sitting before the crackling fire on a gloomy October afternoon, she stitched them onto the sampler she had marked herself.

"I am glad to see thee so industrious." Mama, trimming candles they had made, smiled approval, but her voice held a note of amazement.

Keturah did not wonder; she had cared little for samplers—until now. "This scripture comes to me during Meeting. I think on it almost every day."

The verse was not among other familiar passages women sewed. Keturah feared Mama would remark on the bright red crewel, which had not faded during her unplanned bath in the river. She soon saw, however, that Mama was not about to discourage this combined spiritual and needlework miracle.

Nor did Papa as he brought in more wood. "An excellent verse." He beamed. "Friend Henry questioned me about it. I loaned him my pamphlet on the Corinthian epistles. That boy asks good questions."

"*Humph.*" Mama sniffed.

Keturah feared her mellow mood had departed with Papa. Mama eyed the decoration Keturah had marked on the sampler. "Roses? Such large roses."

"Yes, Mama. One above the scripture, one below." Green pine needles and holly would give it a Christmas air, but she wouldn't point that out.

"Lilies would match the verse's meaning better."

"The rose does symbolize love." Keturah knew what Mama feared: Romantic overtones would feed local gossip. "But Christ's love makes us new. What better flower for my sampler?"

Mama nodded. Though she lived her faith and her love, her mother did not speak easily of either. Mama bustled upstairs to battle imaginary dust.

Keturah chuckled then hummed "While Shepherds Watched," a carol her friend Delilah had taught her. Her awkward fingers gained speed, stitching the wondrous words and Christmas roses in bright red.

◆　◆　◆

"Henry!" She waved from the bench outside Scott's store and readied her Christmas cookies. Sharing them had become almost a ceremony, though she now added thick bread-and-butter sandwiches and apples to her food packets.

He joined her, his face rosy with the brisk October day. While he munched, she read poetry, including a Robert Burns poem, sung in Scotland on Christmas and New Year's Day.

"'Should auld acquaintance be forgot, and never brought to mind? Should auld acquaintance be forgot, and days o' auld lang syne.'"

He grinned. "I doubt that would be read at a Friends' Meeting."

"Mama likes Christmas songs no more than she likes red." Keturah rolled her eyes. "But I have decided this year to celebrate Christ's birth with poems and carols."

"My grandmother sang carols in French every Christmas." His eyes glistened a little. "Sometimes Ma sings them."

"Is thy papa French, too?"

"He was a Shawnee." Henry's eyes hardened to sandstone.

"Thee has not yet eaten thy cookies." Although itching with curiosity, Keturah changed the subject. "I shall finish mine. When Caleb returns, he may try to steal them as he only ate a dozen before we left home."

The strained lines around Henry's mouth relaxed.

Until a teasing voice broke in. "You could share one with your hungry little brother."

Turning, Keturah nearly dropped her treasured book of poetry into the mud.

Wide, dark eyes fastened on hers. Rich black waves of hair curled on his bronzed forehead and neck. The most handsome man she ever imagined gave a slight bow. He took her limp hand in his and kissed it.

Chapter 5

Y ou going to introduce me, Henry?"

"Guess you've done that yourself." Heat and ice fought in Henry's stomach. He tried to steady his tone. "Keturah, this is my brother, Charlie. Miss Keturah Wilkes."

Charlie did not drop her hand. "So glad to make your acquaintance."

Of that Henry was sure. "Thought you were headed downriver today."

"Ma asked me to change my plans." Charlie sounded like an obedient choirboy.

"Of course she did." If Ma couldn't shipwreck his friendship with the "Quaker girl," she would do it through Charlie the Lady-killer.

Keturah gave Charlie the same smile Henry remembered when she spoke of her red shawl. "If thee is hungry, I'll gladly share my cookies." She handed all three to Charlie.

"I would not think of it." He returned them, looking hopefully at Henry.

He clutched his Christmas cookies like a greedy five-year-old. But he offered his brother two.

Charlie ate them slowly, telling Keturah how delicious they were. She forgot to eat while he told stories of fascinating ladies and gentlemen who traveled on the river—neglecting to mention he often picked their pockets.

You do it, too, Henry's conscience prodded him. Faces of their thievery peered around the corners of his mind, shrinking away in terror. As Charlie continued the I'm-so-wonderful script Henry knew well, he sat mute.

When Caleb returned from his rendezvous with Priscilla, he raised his eyebrows at Keturah, who did not notice. Henry wanted to escape, but he would not leave Keturah and Caleb alone with Charlie. Finally Friend Wilkes drove up. Henry watched Charlie assess Keturah's father. A Quaker, but a big one with a shrewd eye, not to mention an adult son and a hunting rifle beside him. For now the Wilkeses were safe.

As they drove away, Keturah turned and waved. "See you at Meeting!"

He marveled that the frost on the ground did not melt from her smile's warmth.

But did she smile at him? Or at Charlie?

◆　◆　◆

Henry and his brother had left town, yet Charlie still wore his choirboy face. "You could have given me more than two cookies."

"Or I could have knocked you down." Henry held his fist under Charlie's nose. "Thinking of robbing them? Don't try it."

Charlie threw him a scornful look. But at Henry's intensity, he stepped back. "What's gotten into you? We were the best together, even as boys."

"You mean the worst."

Charlie laughed. "And proud of it. Until you started reading too much." He rolled his eyes heavenward. "Why did you have to steal that Bible?"

Henry felt the familiar flood of shame but glared at Charlie. "It wasn't my idea to rob a circuit preacher."

"I figured on Monday he'd be carryin' a fat offering." Charlie snorted. "His wallet was skinnier than he was."

"What made us think we knew anything about preachers?" Henry shook his head.

"You're gettin' along good with them now."

"Quakers don't have preachers. They believe God has put His Light in all His followers."

"That would be you, right, Henry? And Keturah." Charlie cast sly eyes at him. "She makes you feel downright holy, don't she?"

Henry ached to beat his brother into the mud. He could do it, despite Charlie's muscles.

Charlie knew it, too. He took off like a deer, and Henry darted after him. They wound through the forest, panting, sweating, running all four miles. How many times had he chased Charlie home? He had lost count.

Henry ran most of his fury off. Drawing near their cabin, he wondered if he had overreacted. Still Ma might try anything to keep him away from the Quakers. And he wouldn't put anything past Charlie, especially when it came to a pretty girl.

He was breathing down his brother's neck as Charlie burst through the cabin door. "Hoping Ma will protect you?"

Charlie turned with his infuriating smile. "She always does."

A snore fairly shook the cabin walls. Ma, her mouth as open as the big cave's, lay on her corn husk tick. They knew better than to awaken her.

Charlie rummaged an old wooden box they called the cupboard. "No hardtack."

"Any cornmeal?" Henry rummaged another. Nothing like food concerns to unite enemies.

Charlie shook his head then headed for the loft ladder. "Oh well. Got to catch a few winks."

"Business tonight?" Henry glared. "Make sure it's not with Keturah's family."

"I got better things to do." Charlie climbed the ladder, yawning.

Likely thieving and drinking. One minute he wanted to kill Charlie. The next, he worried his brother was getting in over his head.

Henry's near-empty stomach growled. If he wanted to eat, he'd better get moving. Henry picked up his gun and headed into the forest again.

◆　◆　◆

"*Mmmm.*" Keturah, stitching a rose in her sampler, inhaled the fragrance of the sweet buns Delilah took from her dutch oven. "Those smell almost as good as Christmas gingerbread."

"Like all excellent cooks, we must make sure our food tastes good." Delilah laughed as she poured hot cider. They "tasted" two buns apiece.

"It is almost time to walk to the river." Keturah loved fun times at Delilah's house, but she had waited all day for this moment. She donned her red shawl. "At Meeting last week, Henry told me he had a surprise for me."

Delilah put her hands on her nonexistent hips. "You've been meeting Henry for weeks. Do you think this friendship is wise?"

"Henry is a good friend, but a friend only," Keturah stammered. She did not dare mention Charlie. Her cheeks felt as if she faced the fireplace.

"Do tell." Delilah gave Keturah a schoolmarm look.

"You will come with me, Delilah, will you not?" Papa would never accept her going alone!

"Of course. I must ensure my best friend's well-being." She grinned. "And I must see this surprise."

As they walked Rock and Cave's main road, Keturah thought of Mama fussing because Caleb, gone on business for Papa, could not accompany them. Mama need not worry. Delilah would keep her sharp eyes on Keturah.

Would Charlie come today, too? Her pace and heartbeat increased.

Sure enough, in the usual meeting place, Charlie's broad-shouldered figure stood beside Henry's tall, thin one.

Henry greeted them, a rare ear-to-ear smile on his face. Surely his shining eyes were the color a crown must hold. Charlie stooped to kiss her hand. When he also kissed Delilah's, her friend's mouth froze into a large O.

"Would you like a keelboat ride?" Henry pointed toward the river. Sol, who had lent Keturah the blanket after her "bath," waved cheerfully from a small boat beside the dock.

Delight filled her. "Have you always owned a keelboat?"

Charlie laughed. "Did he tell you that?"

"I told her no such tale," Henry said stiffly. "We do not own a boat. Sol found a small one we could use for an hour."

"I—I would like nothing more. I have long dreamed of this moment." The Ohio, borrowing blue satin finery from the calm sky, beckoned. She longed to ride through its quiet ripples. Even on this chilly day, she wanted to leave the shore, the solidness that had bound all her life. But desire was a futile dream.

"I am sorry, Henry. I cannot without telling Papa, and he will not return until later."

To her amazement, his grin widened. "I spoke to him after Meeting last week.

He agreed, if we take only a short ride."

She did not know which startled her more, Henry's audacity or Papa's permission. Obviously, he had not discussed this with Mama.

"Let's take the boat down to McFarlan's Ferry." Charlie struck a dramatic pose. "I will show the lady sights she has never imagined—"

"Too far." Henry sounded almost like Caleb.

She felt annoyed then remembered Henry planned this lovely surprise. She restored his smile with her own. "Of course it is too far. We will go only a short distance. May Delilah join us?"

Henry nodded. His mouth still curved upward, but his face had lost its glow.

This boat ride has become complicated. She turned to Delilah. "Do you think your father will agree?"

"Yes, since yours does. Keturah, will you come with me to ask him?" Delilah's words came a little slowly, like cold molasses poured from a pitcher.

Reluctantly, Keturah left the brothers to eye each other like roosters in a barnyard.

As they strolled to the store, Delilah whispered, "Do you really believe he asked your father and he said yes?" Her keen eyes searched Keturah's face.

She gaped. "Of course."

"How do you know?"

Keturah paused. She said quietly, "I believe Henry."

Delilah gave a rueful smile. "I do, too. Why, I'm not sure."

"He is a good man." Keturah didn't know what else to say.

After a pause, Delilah opened the store's door. "All right. Let's ask. Though I do believe those two would rather I stayed on shore."

"Pshaw," Keturah said, though she feared Delilah spoke the truth.

Mr. Scott, who also knew Sol as trustworthy, agreed, and they ran back to the dock.

The boat was small, tapered at front and back, with a patched canvas awning at the stern. But Keturah pretended she had stepped into Papa's history book. She became the ancient queen Cleopatra, about to board her barge on the Nile.

"Afternoon, ladies." Sol gave them his friendly, toothless grin. "Little warmer than usual in November. Good day for a ride."

"I promise not to fall in." Keturah returned the grin.

"Henry here will keep a good hold on ya."

The remark made her blush. She couldn't look at Henry, so she looked at Charlie. Was he born with that smile, glittering like the water's surface in the sun? She pictured him in a dashing gentleman's garb, silk hat in hand.

"I'll assist the ladies." Charlie lifted her onto the boat as if she weighed no more than a milkweed seed, taking his time about releasing her.

Friends helped her down from wagons all the time. But Charlie's touch made her want to fly!

Henry, his face turning dull red, extended his hand to Delilah. He loosened the boat from the dock.

"Ladies, hold on to the tent, please." Sol took charge. "Get them settin' poles, boys, and give us a push out into the river."

Henry accepted a pole from the other oarsman, a big, silent man whose cheek bulged with a large tobacco chaw. Charlie manned his pole at the opposite side.

Keturah hoped the atmosphere would lighten as they sailed. The brothers dug their poles into the river bottom, and the boat nosed off the dock as if eager to be free.

Suddenly, Keturah floated down the Ohio, vast and blue. She felt as if they skimmed on sky. Wonderful. Frightening. She gripped the awning's splintery wooden frame, her knuckles whitening.

"Are you well?" Delilah gave her a quizzical look. "'Tis but water."

"Mama never even let me have a swimming hole—"

"You should have had more brothers." Delilah clicked her tongue. "But look yonder at our oarsmen. Perhaps their skill will ease your mind."

"Give the ladies a song, boys!" Sol called without a break in his rowing. *"En roulant ma boule,"* he sang in a booming voice.

Henry and Charlie, pulling on big oars, answered him in harmony.

"En roulant ma boule roulant, en roulant ma boule."

The spritely song tweaked frowns into smiles, fears into fun. Keturah would not allow her wayward feet to dance to the happy rhythm, but her fingers tapped against the awning's frame.

Henry grinned as he rowed, his rich, strong baritone weaving through Sol's solos and Charlie's higher tones. She'd heard Henry mouth a few notes, but now he sang full voice. What a gift God had given. If only he could sing at Meeting. Perhaps he would sing some French Christmas carols for her. Keturah hummed along, though singing was not her strong point.

"What does it mean?" Delilah asked when the singing boatmen paused for breath. "How did you learn it?"

"Henry and Charlie's grandpa taught it to me before you was born," Sol answered. "Good song to keep us rowin'."

"Grand-pére sang it to us when we were little." Henry's face softened as he pulled. "The chorus is about rolling a ball, and while he sang it, Grand-pére rolled a rag ball to Charlie and me."

Keturah smiled at the picture of an old man playing with two dark-haired little boys—until Charlie spoke.

"You were his favorite." His smile did not fade, but his lips tightened away from his white teeth like an animal's.

Keturah started. Delilah gave Charlie a sharp look. Henry pulled steadily at his oars, eyes straight ahead.

"Alouette, gentille alouette, alouette, je te plumerai," Charlie sang, giving Keturah a wink.

She couldn't help laughing, but judging from the look in his eye, she did not ask what this song meant. Instead, she swept her gaze over the river, an everlasting poem of liquid and light. Occasional grayish-white limestone cliffs jutted ancient chins above black leafless trees along the shore, raising their branches in salute to their Creator.

"'O Lord, our Lord, how excellent is thy name in all the earth.'" Keturah could no more keep the psalm from her lips than she could stop breathing. Her gaze caught Henry's. Though he said nothing, she knew his silent song matched hers word for word.

Charlie shook his head, chuckling.

"Slow that rowin', boys," Sol drawled. "Have to turn around soon and pole, so take a break."

Henry released his oars and unfolded his long frame, his gaze still intertwined with hers. "So, you like the water after all?"

"I like this view of it," she said softly. "I thank thee. No one could have told me how grand it is."

The glow on his face warmed her. "I think it even more beautiful in winter than summer."

"But never lovely as you." Charlie's glinting smile melted into a look of little-boy adoration.

Delilah yanked her arm. "Come, there is something on your face." She pulled Keturah under the awning and brushed at her cheek.

"Did I not wash the crumbs from my face before we left?" How annoying, in the midst of such poetry, such romance, to present a face like a dirty urchin.

"No crumbs," Delilah hissed in her ear. "But do not let him cast his spell on you."

"Whatever does thee mean?" Keturah pulled away.

"Charlie would turn any woman's head. He no doubt has turned many." Her friend's eyes bored into hers. "Would you encourage such boldness?"

Keturah wiped her cheek to continue the facade and tried to speak lightly. "Thee acts as if I have pledged marriage. A few pretty words mean little."

She brushed past Delilah to the deck, back to the sweet freedom of the river flowing on forever, the wind in her face, and Charlie's velvet gaze.

"Pole us home, boys." Sol swung the sweep to steer the boat back. Guiding it close to the shore where the current was not as strong, he sang new verses to "En roulant ma boule." Charlie almost danced along the gunwales of the boat as he sang and pushed his pole into the river bottom.

Though the water seemed gentle, all four men joined in poling the boat back to the Rock and Cave dock. Delilah stood at her elbow—silent, thank heaven—and Keturah savored the last stretch of her first boat ride. The afternoon sun, a rotund King Midas, turned everything in its path to gold. Charlie, bronzed like an Egyptian god, guided their river chariot away from danger. Keturah clapped her hands to the men's rollicking song, letting its magic pump through her veins.

Only later, after Papa's pleased grin at her ecstasy and their wagon ride home, did she realize Henry, while poling back, had not sung a note.

Chapter 6

enry knew the look all too well: the shining blankness in women's eyes when they looked at Charlie, as if they had turned into empty-headed china dolls in a store window. Why had he thought Keturah different?

He dove into his corn husk tick without undressing and pulled the ragged quilts over his head. Out of habit, his fingers sought the leather pouch hidden under his shirt and felt the coins he'd hoarded for her Christmas gift. A shudder of anger passed through him. Just let Charlie try sleeping in the loft tonight. He felt like flinging the little bag into the river. Instead, he tossed and rolled, his muscles reminding him of extra hours he had loaded and rowed to make the money. Would he let Charlie push him into throwing away something so valuable?

Try as he might, he could not forget Keturah's wonder at the river's beauty, the way she spoke of its Creator as he did. He pictured those soft red lips pressed against his. His hands cupped her face as he and the sun's rays played with stray wisps of her golden hair.

He sat up. *Stupid!* How could he, lanky, silent Henry, who long had played second fiddle to Charlie's charms, hope to kiss Keturah? She had forgotten his existence—almost didn't say good-bye when they landed at the dock. Not that he had lingered.

He buried his face in his hands. *Oh God, why did You ever let me see her, hear her voice?*

No angels answered. He did not expect any. Neither did he expect this odd Quiet to invade him. Its current felt strong as the Ohio's after a storm, yet it gently floated his wounded heart along like a leaf.

A door opened downstairs. Footsteps shuffled like milling cattle. Probably his uncle. A faint catlike tread of moccasins. Charlie. Henry felt as if someone had dumped hot coals into his clothes. His body tensed, his fists clenched, readying for the fight of his life. But the Quiet swirled through his rage like a river of peace, leaving him limp. He flopped onto his mattress and listened.

No more steps. No ladder creaks. Henry gave a silent, mirthless chuckle. Above all, Charlie protected himself. If he were smart, he would not come to the loft tonight, nor tomorrow, nor next week.

The Quiet continued flowing over Henry's seething insides. He wanted to tell it to go away. Yet he wanted to say, *Stay forever.* Finally he gave a weak shrug. *All right, God. I won't kill him. But if I don't, he'll hurt Keturah.*

Tears, like hot springs, welled in him. Keturah again in his mind's eye, the river behind her, the psalm on her lips. Keturah, her eyes locked with his in something bigger than an embrace.

Did God mean Charlie would not win her after all? Joy and caution collided like boulders, sapping the last of his strength. Finally he folded his hands in prayer. *Please take care of her.*

He dropped into a coma-like sleep.

◆　◆　◆

Henry no longer sat in the back at Meeting. When he moved behind one large Quaker family, they blocked his view of Keturah.

With his eyes off her shining hair, he regained his mind. Henry saw the plain truth: If he had indeed held Keturah, he had lost her. Of that he was certain. If, during their weekly get-togethers, Henry spoke to Keturah of village news or dared offer a fragment of his deeper thoughts, Charlie pickpocketed them as smoothly as he did his victims' money. Within seconds his gilded, counterfeit charm dazzled Keturah so that she saw no one but him. Henry wondered if he should stay away. Would Keturah notice?

The elderly man sitting in front of Henry turned and cast him a curious glance. Had he said her name aloud? He stared at his hands, chiding himself for thinking about her. Henry focused anew on the speaker's ministry about the Light of Christ who dwelled in His every follower, giving guidance and hope throughout one's life.

Henry had heard such claims since he first came to Meeting, but today he listened well to God and the Friends He inspired. The man's words filled Henry's empty heart until he thought he would burst, yet he longed for more. Keturah or no Keturah, he believed what he heard. Why nibble scraps of truth when a feast awaited? He wanted nothing more to do with the sin and pain of his pirate past. He would not face life any longer without the Light of Christ inside.

After Meeting he spoke to Friend Wilkes as he often did. Instead of discussing the latest pamphlet he'd borrowed, Henry expressed his desire.

"Thee has experienced convincement?" The man's kind eyes searched Henry's face and, he felt, his soul.

He answered steadily, "I have."

"Now is a hard time for thee." A statement, not a question.

So Keturah's father had sensed the growing gap between Keturah and him. The man's gentleness eroded Henry's resolve to appear strong. "It is."

His voice squeaked. He wanted to hide, but he lifted his chin. "In the midst of hardness, we learn true wisdom. Isn't that what the scriptures teach?"

"Indeed." Friend Wilkes laid a hand on his shoulder. "But I would that thee be sure. Will thee lay over several weeks before declaring thy intentions?"

"*Lay over?*"

"Ponder, pray, consider, so thee can make a solid decision."

He wanted to belong now. And never look back. Disappointment sucked the air from him. Why did Friend Wilkes suggest delay? Did Quakers try to discourage others from joining? Or only him?

"I will continue to hold thee in the Light and advise thee." Friend Wilkes clasped Henry's hand. His fatherly smile eased Henry's anxiety. "And I will rejoice when thee becomes a part of us."

He meant it. Henry had no idea why the man advised postponement, but he would do as Friend Wilkes said.

◆　◆　◆

"Delilah, I thank thee for rescuing us from the cold." Keturah threw her arms around her friend. The group sat on hide-seated chairs and stumpy logs around the crackling fireplace, warming blue hands in the Scotts' hospitable cabin.

"Pa said we can get together to talk in his store's back room from now on. But today, we have a party." Delilah's dark eyes sparkled. "After all, it soon will be Christmas."

"You saved our lives." Charlie made a gentlemanly bow. Zechariah, Delilah's new, very large beau, hovered nearby. Keturah noticed Charlie did not kiss Delilah's hand.

Henry nodded his thanks and drew closer to the fire. Thin as a lathe, he froze outdoors. Sometimes he coughed, worrying Keturah.

Delilah and her mother handed out hot cider and sweet buns. They all sang to Zechariah's fiddle and played Blindman's Buff and Who's Got the Thimble?

"No fair!" Keturah laughed when Charlie cornered her the fourth time. "Thee always finds me."

" 'Tis true." Delilah stared at Charlie's blindfold, but with her mother's warning glance, she began gathering mugs.

Henry, who had been laughing like a boy, grew quiet.

Keturah sighed. Henry said less and less. Although Charlie's face and gallantry thrilled her, she missed talking with Henry about God, about poetry, about everything. Perhaps when she gave him her Christmas gift, he would entrust her with his smile again and feel freer to share his mind.

Too soon it was time to go. As usual Caleb and Priscilla wandered off while they waited outside the store for Papa. Keturah handed each brother two small brown packages she had decorated with yew sprigs and their red berries. "Merry Christmas."

Henry's face lit up as he unwrapped the stockings she'd knitted. Although her sampler was progressing, the red shawl had performed no miracle to improve her poor attempts at other housewifely arts. At least the baggy stockings would keep his toes warm.

"Thank you, Keturah."

That measured, golden look. Henry could not begin to equal Charlie's charm, but his gaze, unchanged since the day he rescued her from the river, washed over her, warm as July.

"I will treasure them forever." Charlie kissed her hand, but he looked and sounded impatient.

She cringed as they opened their second packages. What had possessed her to experiment? "I tried a new honey cookie recipe—"

Henry munched a gluey "treat" with a determined smile. "Very, er, sweet." His words sounded muffled.

"I will cherish them." Charlie carefully rewrapped the cookies. "But now, dear Keturah, I have a gift for you."

He opened a blue velvet box. In the white satiny folds lay a gleaming silver locket, the likes of which she had never seen. Charlie pressed the locket open. Inside lay a curl of his shining black hair. His finger outlined her face with a featherlight touch that left a burning trail in its wake.

When she came to herself, Caleb was waving good-bye to Priscilla, and Papa was driving up. Her heart thumped loud as a churn, but she put the locket into her pocket and kept her face calm while Charlie helped her into the wagon.

Henry was nowhere to be seen.

Chapter 7

K eturah, I would speak with thee."

She almost dropped her needle. Since childhood, Caleb had teased her. But today his serious tone matched his face as he stood in their cabin's doorway. She stuck the needle into her Christmas sampler and drew the red shawl around her. "Close the door before we catch our deaths."

He thumped it shut then faced her. "Does Charlie have thy heart?"

Heat rose in her cheeks. She fingered the sampler's corner. What business was it of his? If only Mama and Papa had not gone visiting.

His blue eyes probed hers.

She tried to laugh. "Surely thee knows I would make no promise to him. He has not yet spoken to Papa about courting me—"

"Nor is he likely to." Caleb sat opposite her in Papa's big chair and scanned her face with a keen, very un-Caleb look. "I fear an unworthy man has stolen thy heart."

She glared. "Does thee judge a man by his cabin and livestock and money? Papa never taught us so."

"I do not." Caleb paused. "I did not when Henry pursued thee."

She looked down at her hands. "Thee art mistaken. Henry desired only my friendship." Apparently no longer. How she missed his odd but refreshing wisdom and slow, rich smile. He even missed Meeting two weeks straight—though Charlie now attended on First Day! She smiled, hopeful he would come to love God as she did.

Still, Caleb's stare disturbed her. "Thee is an intelligent woman, Keturah, with much learning. But thee knows little of men."

She did not know which bewildered her more, the compliment or the insult. But she would not swallow this outrage. "Certainly thee is an authority on women—"

"I am not. Or I would have persuaded Priscilla's mother to let me marry her." His head dropped.

Despite herself, sympathy softened her armor. "Perhaps thee would have been wise to avoid falling in love with an only child."

His eyes shot blue sparks. "Thee talks of wisdom! Surely thee knows Charlie's attendance at Meeting is only to win thee. He cares nothing for God or His ways."

"Like God, thee can read his heart?" She crossed her arms.

"I do not need to. Charlie is often mentioned as a thief. Some even link him to the vile happenings at Ford's Ferry and Potts' Inn."

Fury spurted through her veins. "Dare thee speak of whisperings with no evidence—"

"Thy locket is evidence enough." His face hardened. "How would a poor boatman come upon an expensive trinket?"

Tears boiled from her eyes. "It belonged to his mother. She wanted him to give it to the one he loves most."

"Mayhap, Charlie took it from her. Or she herself stole it." Caleb tried to capture her gaze. "Keturah, open thy eyes. Some say Charlie's father and grandfather were pirates who preyed on innocent folk."

She sprang from her rocker. She crossed the room and turned away. Silence, like an enormous ax, fell between her and Caleb, broken only by the fire's mutterings.

Finally she spoke. "Charlie's family has long lived in darkness. So the Light of Christ cannot dwell in him. Thee believes this?"

"Thee knows I do not. Henry lived with the same evils, yet spoke to Papa of convincement until—"

"Until Charlie came to Meeting, too." She whirled around and glared at him.

"Until thee made a fool of thyself over Charlie. Can thee not see?" Caleb's words exploded like live coals in a barrel of gunpowder.

"So I have neglected to use my influence on Henry, yet should not do so with Charlie." She lifted the latch and slammed the door behind her, clutching her red shawl like a best friend as she ran for the washhouse.

◆　◆　◆

Henry held his breath, motionless in the thicket. Early evening darkness cloaked Ford's Ferry Road, the only road to Potts' Inn. The few remaining leaves hanging from overhead branches gave their death rattle. He'd heard nothing more. So far.

For a moment Henry wished he'd brought whiskey. But a jugful did him no good after he lost Keturah. It would do him no good tonight. Charlie's life might depend on his keeping a clear head.

Charlie deserves what he gets.

True, but ever since Ma told him she'd overheard Charlie's plans to ride Ford's Ferry Road, he'd stuffed his mind's whisper into a bag and tried to drown it.

Ma taught her sons to be thieves. But she didn't want them to be murderers. If Charlie "guided" travelers from Ford's Ferry to their deaths at Potts' Inn, he might as well wear a noose around his neck. Ma had heard that the brash new constable planned to raid the inn.

Charlie had stayed away from home—wisely—after giving Keturah that locket. Yet now Henry was trying to save his neck. Charlie, who stole people, just as he stole valuables. Charlie, who stole Keturah.

He deserves what he gets.

Let Charlie destroy himself. It would be so easy to go home to his warm loft. No more of Charlie's lies. No more taunts.

You'd have Keturah to yourself.

A vision of her gleaming hair glowed in the shadows like a thousand candles;

her warm, laughing face and lips so close, she lit his. A rush of heat ran down him. Keturah might be his—if he let Charlie reap what he had sown, as he had read in the Bible.

A tiny star gleamed through the clouds above the road, capturing Henry's eye and sending it heavenward. Then the star fell, its showy path snuffed out in a moment. His inner flames died with it, leaving him dark and empty as the night. But another faint star escaped the murky clouds, refusing to be devoured. To his surprise, the yearning for God bubbled up inside him. The Quiet answered it, filling him till he thought he would explode from joy and anguish. Why would God want anything to do with him? Didn't He know about his drinking and returning to the old ways—about the hatred inside him, the rage at Charlie that could make him a murderer, too?

What do I do? He almost cried aloud. *Do I warn Charlie? Do I go home?*

A baby's soft cry nearly made him jump out of his moccasins. Down the road, Henry spied two horse-sized shadows and recognized his brother's stealthy gait. Horror clogged Henry's throat. Children as well as adults disappeared upon entering the inn's welcoming, deadly door. And Charlie was leading a family there.

Potts would never let a constable take him alive. Would these innocent people survive a gun battle? He heard another child's voice.

Henry whistled the redbird's call he and his brother had, since childhood, used to indicate danger.

He saw Charlie lift his head then raise his rifle. Henry stuck a leg out of the thicket and shuffled his moccasin through dead leaves. If Charlie was drunk and trigger-happy, he'd rather take it in the leg than the chest.

"What's this, Henry?"

He sounded annoyed but stone sober. Maybe Potts or Ford had threatened him to stay away from drink. A tall figure rode the horse behind Charlie, even taller because he wore a stovepipe hat. Henry addressed the man. "Sorry to bring you bad news, sir, but Mr. Potts sent me to tell you the inn is full."

A young woman's voice wailed from the other horse. "But Mr. Ford said the inn would accommodate us!"

"Are you sure?" The man spoke loudly because the baby now screamed at the top of its lungs. "The children are in need of shelter."

Sending up frantic silent prayers, Henry kept his voice calm. "It would be unwise to travel eight more miles, only to be turned away."

Finally Charlie spoke. "Perhaps a family in Rock and Cave will take you in."

Charlie understood! Giving thanks, Henry held his breath. Would the man believe him?

"If that is our only choice." The woman almost moaned.

The man swore at his horse as he turned him. "Take us there."

"We will do our best to find lodgings," Henry promised.

"You mean *you* will," Charlie hissed in his ear.

Henry nodded and pressed his thumb hard into Charlie's arm. Another signal he should lie low. Charlie slipped to the side of the road.

"Are you not going with us?" Anger filled the man's voice. "What about the money I paid? And why should we trust him?"

"He is my brother. You can trust him," Charlie said.

If things weren't so desperate, Henry might have laughed. Instead, he said, "I will guide you to the village free of charge."

The man gave a grudging assent, and Charlie disappeared into the underbrush.

Henry clasped the woman's bridle and began the slow, dark journey through the forest to Rock and Cave. Where would he ask? He dare not take them to those he knew, to be stripped of their belongings like a Christmas goose of its feathers.

If only the Wilkeses lived in this direction. Memories of Delilah's large cabin prodded his mind. If the Scotts could not help, he would check with Priscilla's family. He did not know them except for Meeting, but he could not imagine Quakers leaving a mother and children out in the winter darkness.

He wiggled stiff fingers. His weary legs felt like logs. As he led the horses back to Rock and Cave, the faint star brightened, reminding him of the Christmas story. How had Joseph felt, guiding a woman about to give birth along a dark, dangerous road? Keturah also showed him the terrible story of King Herod's attempts to kill baby Jesus. Tonight, as Henry guided the angry man and sniffling family to Rock and Cave, he prayed God would send angels to protect them all—and his scheming, conscienceless brother.

◆　◆　◆

"Mama?" Keturah, amazed as if the skeletal trees had budded green, stared at the stout figure walking toward Papa's wagon. "Is she going with us to town?"

Papa flicked the reins. He did not look at Keturah. "She has not seen her friends for many months."

A small circle of dismay spun in Keturah's middle. "But she hates the river—"

"Thy mama has been known to change her mind." Papa turned to meet his wife.

Mama knew the only way to make beds. To braid Keturah's hair. To stir soup. When had she changed her mind about anything?

Mama's black Meeting dress rustled as Papa helped her up beside Keturah. She cast a glance back at Caleb. He looked away.

What had transpired? Whatever it was, she liked it less and less.

Her mood did not lighten when they pulled up to Scott's store. Henry had absented himself from the group again. But Charlie's smile sent a thrill through her as if she had touched lightning.

Until Mama followed them into the store. Thankfully, she remained out front while Keturah, Charlie, and the others found seats in the back room. Oblivious to naught but each other, her friends murmured and giggled.

Charlie kissed her hand. "My love, I have waited all week—"

"Thank you, Friend Scott," Mama's words boomed like cannon shots. "I would like two bags of flour."

Keturah tried to ignore the conversation. "I wear thy locket close to my heart—"

"Thy hog butchering went well?" Mama continued. "I declare, we didn't get half enough liver or sweetbreads—"

Keturah almost gagged. Mama knew full well she despised both. Mama chattered on with the storekeeper, then with his wife, until tears of fury blinded Keturah. Were not she and Charlie adults? Had they not remained with the group as was proper? If only they could spend time alone—or at least without an accompanying hog-killing dialogue. She might even talk with him about God, as she did with Henry. A flash of brilliance lit her despair. She addressed Priscilla.

"We do not know when we will see the sun again. Why not walk by the river?"

Caleb's taut mouth told Keturah he knew exactly what she was doing. But Priscilla, delighted, pulled him to his feet. Delilah told her father where they were going. Once they left the store, the group would slowly, quietly separate into couples.

Mama, tying her bonnet, met them at the store's door. "Wonderful idea."

No. No. She wouldn't—

"We do not know when we shall see the sun again, do we?" Mama almost marched them toward the river, her steps firm and unswerving.

"Exactly what Keturah said," Zechariah said innocently.

Caleb grinned.

Even the brisk breeze could not cool Keturah's burning cheeks. Charlie wore a pained smile. Mama stuck to them until they returned to the store. While the group drank sassafras tea, she babbled on and on to anyone who would listen.

"Can I meet you alone?" Charlie whispered.

"I do not know!" Keturah gritted her teeth. She felt like a chastened, naughty child.

"At your house?" His warm breath caressed her cheek.

"Tomorrow, when my parents visit friends. But Caleb will be home." She thought quickly. "No one will be working in the washhouse on First Day."

"I will meet you there." He lowered his voice to a husky plea. "Do not disappoint me, my love."

Chapter 8

Henry glanced at Charlie, sitting next to him during Meeting, feigning attentiveness to the speakers. Did his brother hear even one word about the goodness of Christ? Henry, back at Meeting for the first time in weeks, listened. Despite his pain at seeing Keturah and the insanity of Charlie's presence there, he practically wallowed in the warmth of the Light of Christ. Never again would he allow anyone or anything to separate him from God.

Afterward the Friends did not quiz him on his absence or ask what brought him back. Instead, they welcomed him with smiles that made him feel as if they really were his friends. Friend Wilkes rested his big hand on his shoulder, eyes filled with gladness. "Would thee read a pamphlet on God's charity toward us?"

"I would." Henry could hardly wait to explore its depths.

Friend Wilkes's delight faded as he greeted Charlie. Other Friends spoke kindly to his brother, who was on his best behavior. But for the first time Henry could remember, Charlie did not overwhelm a group with his charm. Although the Friends did not know Charlie, they knew him.

"Thee has returned."

He had not noticed Keturah's approach. *God, do not let me falter.*

Her dazzling smile was genuine, but her brilliant eyes, ever forthright, did not meet his. They drifted with only glances at Charlie instead of the usual adoring gaze. Henry's breath quickened. Did she know the truth about his brother?

But the glances shared between them were still potent. The faint flutter of hope Henry harbored dissolved. Only a fool would not sense their attraction. But Keturah seemed uneasy. And her cold hand, extended in fellowship, clung to his shocked fingers an extra moment. "I am thankful to see thee."

Charlie edged her away. Henry felt almost grateful. He could hardly bear her troubled glance. Then a torrent of fear swept him away.

He had protected travelers on Ford's Ferry Road from Ford, from Potts, and from Charlie. What had he done to protect Keturah?

◆　◆　◆

She shivered despite the red shawl. Mama and Papa had left an hour ago. Caleb snored in the cabin by the fire. Surely Charlie would come soon.

The washhouse's rickety door opened. Charlie, sporting a dashing black cloak, clasped her cold hand to his warm lips. Could any girl wish for a more handsome beau?

"Ah, a smile." He tapped her lips with his finger. "Now you look like my Keturah, the most beautiful girl in Illinois. No, the most beautiful girl in the world!"

"Flatterer." But her pulse soared at his words, his touch.

"I only speak the truth." He drew her to him.

How she yearned to melt into his arms. But she could not dissolve the unease she felt at deceiving Mama and Papa. Even Caleb with his self-righteous sermonizing.

Not that she had lied about Charlie's visit. She simply had not mentioned it—

"The smile disappears again?" Charlie gently turned her chin up.

His luminous black eyes nearly undid her. But she needed to talk. "I—I do not like to mislead my parents." There. She finally said the words that pestered her like cawing crows.

"Nor do I." Charlie drew back. "But your ma would smother our love. And though I come to Meeting, I fear your pa does not accept me."

Indignation spurted through her. Why did they not believe a man could change? Surely the Light of Christ could accomplish all things.

"I understand their doubts, my love." Charlie looked at her gravely. "I have done many things I am not proud of."

"As have we all."

He patted her cheek. "But as time passes, God will help them understand."

She hugged him fiercely. He drew her eager lips to his in a long, tender kiss. Her heart stopped. Would the wonder of his kiss steal her very life? If it did, oh, dying was worth it.

Minutes passed by with Keturah in a happy daze. How amazing to laugh, talk, and hold Charlie, as a woman—without a parent's critical eye, Caleb's sermons, and the Friends' scrutiny. At the thought, her celebration dimmed a little.

"You need my help to smile again."

Charlie knew her feelings. She loved that about him.

"Next week we will talk about your special Christmas gift." He touched her hair.

"But thee already gave me my locket." She gently pulled it from beneath her dress's high neckline.

"But this is something you have wanted a long time." Charlie's eyes shone. "A steamboat ride!"

She felt her jaw drop. "How? When?"

He laughed until she cautioned him to take care. "I will tell you next First Day when we meet here again. But say nothing. It will be our secret."

Still stunned, she pressed her cheek against his broad chest. "Charlie, my first Christmas with thee will be the best ever."

◆　◆　◆

Henry watched from the underbrush at the village's edge. Was Keturah's mother trying to avoid Charlie? She and her daughter entered Scott's store alone, well ahead of their usual time.

He breathed a prayer of thanksgiving. He had had no idea how he would talk privately with Keturah. Now there was a chance—if God indeed was guiding his steps. *Lord, give me the right words.*

He pushed through the store's door before he talked himself out of it. Keturah looked like a storm cloud. But he dared not risk losing this opportunity. "Friend Wilkes, may I speak with Keturah? Alone? It will not be long."

Keturah's eyebrows shot up. Her mother's eyes scoured him. But she gave a slow nod. Henry hustled Keturah back by the shovels and hoes.

"Henry, what would thee say to me?" Keturah's eyes shifted behind her as though she were listening for her mother. Or Charlie?

Keturah's sweet, puzzled question nearly destroyed his resolve. Had she truly no idea of the warning he must give? "I would not upset you, Keturah. But I have prayed much about this. I can no longer keep quiet."

She paused. "Say on."

He stumbled on his words. "Charlie may have made you promises, but he's made them to many women."

Silence. Then, "He himself has told me of his past."

"But I do not speak of his past. I speak of now." Henry fought to keep his voice under control. "Charlie comes to Meeting. But he lives a true devil of a life. He knows nothing of the Light of Christ."

He thought his words would shrivel her. Instead, she gave him a piercing, sorrowful look that bled his heart. "Thee, Charlie's own brother, would join in the attack on him? I thought better of thee, Henry." Her snow-white front teeth bit down on her red lip.

"Do not think better of me." There. He finally said what he dreaded to tell her. "Although I hurt no one, I was his partner in theft. The Bible I now read I stole from a circuit rider." He hung his head. "But God's Light has changed me."

"Blessed be God's Light." Her voice softened.

To his amazement, she clasped his hand. "I would that we be good friends, Henry. I miss thee."

Paralyzed, he did not know what to say. What to do.

"I can only hope thee will see how God is changing Charlie as well."

With that she swept back to her mother, her head high—like a graceful, lovely doe with no inkling of the hunter who waited in the shadows, sharp arrows in hand.

◆　◆　◆

Why had Charlie wanted to ride the steamship at night?

Keturah knew the answer. Her parents, who now dogged her every move, would never consent, even if in broad daylight. An invitation to accompany her and Charlie would be rejected. Their stubborn refusal to open their hearts to him angered her. Still, creeping out of bed with the mantel clock's eleventh chime—two hours after the family retired—awakened niggling doubts. Waiting in the washhouse without a lit candle gave her the shivers. She snuggled into the red shawl, glad the night felt more like fall than almost Christmas.

The door gave a welcome creak. "Are you ready, my love?"

Relief swathed her like the shawl. She'd known Charlie would come. Her family—and Henry—would one day understand. She took his hand and stepped into the silvery world. The moon's friendly face smiled down on them as they slipped through the trees to Charlie's horse, tied a few hundred yards away.

His hands lifted her high to the saddle. Breathless, she felt as if she had grown wings. He vaulted to a place behind her, his brawny arms surrounding her. What would it be like with Charlie in her life every day, every moment?

Riding through the silent fairy-tale woods with him was better than any Christmas gift she could imagine. As they neared Rock and Cave, she realized they were not mounted on the old brown nag she'd seen Charlie ride but on a spirited black stallion. "When did thee buy a new horse? Or did thee borrow one?"

He gave an odd chuckle. "I borrowed it. But I will own a new one before long. Maybe two. Or three."

As if to celebrate, he pulled her to him and kissed her, hard and quick.

Her heartbeat sped up, but his kiss, which often left a spicy fragrance of horehound or sassafras, tasted as if he had consumed turpentine. "What on earth did thee drink?"

He gripped her shoulder. "How will I surprise you if you ask all these questions?"

What more could he do to make this night complete? "Thee already told me the Christmas surprise—the steamboat ride."

His white teeth flashed in the moonlight. "You misjudge me, my love." He pulled her face to his again. "You have no idea what wonderful plans I've made."

Chapter 9

Charlie had not mentioned walking to the big cave. Remembering Papa's refusal to take her as a child, she savored an additional moment of triumph. Along with riding the steamboat, she would visit the cave. Still, its giant stony mouth, facing the river's broad, silvery black water, gaped as if she were a choice victual.

Behind her Charlie gave a chittery birdcall. Startled, Keturah halted. Charlie nearly fell over her and swore. She turned to him, grieved he would use such language on their special night.

"You're not afraid, are you?" In his gentle tone, she heard a note of derision. "It's not that dark inside the cave. They've built a fire to keep you warm."

"They?" She frowned.

He took her arm. "Friends I invited to share the steamboat ride."

She found herself swallowed by gloom, her feet swishing and stumbling through stinking dead leaves in a surprisingly large passageway. A team of horses could drive through here.

A glower of firelight pocked aged limestone walls scabbed by fungi. In the semi-darkness, her ankle scraped against sharp rocks protruding from the cave floor. She stopped again. "Do I know thy friends?"

He almost pushed her forward. "More questions." He clicked his tongue, almost like Mama. "How disappointing. I thought you liked adventures."

Stung, she raised her chin. "If thee likens adventures to filthy caves, then no, I do not."

He laughed. "Now that's my Keturah. Full of fire."

Without warning, he swung her into his arms and whirled her into a large circular cavern as if they had entered a ballroom. She tingled at his embrace, but the echo of savage laughter, blended with Charlie's, pierced her.

Dusky light of the tiny campfire's coals carved three men into ogres. Shining eyes, reflecting its glow, burned her cheeks. The turpentine odor she smelled on Charlie's lips reeked from every nook. Whiskey. It had to be. She did not know what wretched trick Charlie was playing, but this had gone far enough. She turned to him and said in a low voice, "Please take me home."

"I would not think of it." His beautifully shaped lips met in a little-boy pout. "I promised you a steamboat ride. And I always keep my promises."

The men laughed again. So did Charlie. He poured whiskey from a jug into a gourd and turned to her. "Never too early for a Christmas toast. Drink to our health and happiness."

When she said nothing, he downed it in one gulp. She fought panic that soured her throat like bile. He swilled another.

"We better git movin'." One man slid a knife into a sheath hanging from his belt.

She thought she could not feel more frightened—until Charlie pulled an even larger blade from a poke lying on the cave floor. She could not breathe.

"True." He held the weapon up, smiling as red light glinted on the metal. "We will meet our steamship soon. You and Ned go ahead."

As the men left, Charlie turned and gestured carelessly at the shortest man. "Stay with him till I return."

Sudden fury poured from her. "If I choose not to?"

"You disappoint me again, my love." He sheathed his knife and reached for her cheek, his dark eyes molten.

When she shrank away, he yanked her to him, stripping her shawl from her shoulders, forcing his lips on hers.

Fight him. Scream. Someone must hear—

The other man chuckled. "Got a lively one, Charlie."

She bowed in pain, Charlie's iron hands jamming her wrists together behind her back. The short man bound them with rough rope and then tied her feet together and stuffed a greasy bandanna into her mouth. She choked, trying not to vomit.

"Why must you be so difficult?" Charlie chucked her on the chin. "I was hoping you would see the light."

She shuddered with outrage. How dare he use a sacred phrase?

Charlie laughed, threw her over his shoulder, and then dumped her into the darkness of a small side chamber. He kissed his fingers to her. "Farewell, love. I will see *thee* soon."

She lay bruised on the muddy floor, her stomach roiling.

"If you touch her, I'll cut your hands off." Charlie's deadly voice floated from the "ballroom" to her prison.

"Ye know I wouldn't," the man protested.

"Good." Charlie must have slapped his back. "Plenty of women when we land in New Orleans." He laughed again. "Plenty for all of us."

Chapter 10

Had she dozed a few minutes? A few hours? Did it matter?

She saw weeping shadows on the cave's ceiling and walls. Pointed rocks wounded her ribs, her shoulder. Gravel was embedded in her right cheek. She commanded her muscles to move so her pain would lessen. Helpless, they could not obey.

Would Charlie kill her before they left Rock and Cave?

His face was a cat's. She was his prey. How long would he toy with her? Would she live to celebrate Christmas Day? If so, what a merry time it would be. Keturah wept with the shadows. What a blind fool she had been.

God, I thought I knew Thy Light. Yet I did not listen to those Thee sent.

Mama. Papa. Even Caleb. The horrible gag muffled her yearning to a tiny moan. Was it only hours ago she'd sat by their fire, plotting wrong as Papa read the Bible?

Henry. His honest eyes as he tried to warn her. Her hot tears added to the dampness of the evil-smelling floor. Henry was a man of true faith and love. She chose what was false.

The chittering call again. Footsteps. Charlie.

God, forgive me, though I do not deserve it. Save me—if not in this life, in the next.

"Henry!" Her captor's voice sounded pleased. "You goin' with us to New Orleans?"

Henry? Gladness shot through her. Henry would help. He would rescue—

"Sure am. Told Charlie he can't have all the fun."

Henry's voice. But—but he talked like Charlie. *Oh God.*

"Good. I was afraid you got religion. Though Charlie said you saved his hide when that new constable caught wind of Ford's plans." The man chuckled knowingly. "Mebbe your brother'll thank you by sharing that pretty Quaker back there that's goin' with us."

"Maybe." Henry sounded as if they were speaking of hand-me-down horses. "She's a looker, but. . ."

She almost felt his shrug.

"In New Orleans, there'll be plenty of women to go round," the pirate finished.

Had it all been a ruse? Henry's supposed faith to impress her parents? His "warning" an effort to steal her from Charlie? She writhed, the rope's roughness skinning her limbs.

Henry, a pirate, too? *God, I cannot bear it.*

She heard the gurgle of whiskey pouring again. Her imagination already had painted ugly portraits of what she would suffer with Charlie. But Henry...

Numb, her mind and body turned to stone. Words, laughter. She heard but understood nothing. Deep inside, she pleaded with God to die, to sink into the cave's floor and become part of it forever.

A thump opened her eyes. Henry's tall silhouette held a knife. But instead of cold steel at her throat, ropes loosened. He set her, as if she were a doll, on her feet and wrapped her shawl around her. "I know you feel faint," he whispered. "But we must run. Now."

She moved her foot an inch. Two. Joy cascaded over her like a waterfall as he half guided, half carried her past the sprawled-out man.

"Smacked him with the whiskey jug," Henry answered her look.

Out, out, they hurried, into the blessed, clean December air. The glimmering wide ribbon of the river wrapped the night like a gift.

Henry lifted her off her feet and plunged into the thickest woods. She clung to him, ducking branches, feeling his long limbs eat up ground. Suddenly he skidded to a stop. "Keturah, I mean no disrespect. But I can run faster if I carry you over my shoulder."

The polite request almost broke her. She nodded, and he hoisted her carefully over his shoulder and ran like the wind through the night. A bumpy ride. She would be sore tomorrow as if she had ridden a pony in the Christmas race. But thanks to him, she dared hope she would see another day.

◆ ◆ ◆

Henry wound his way among bare-branched thickets, behind scraggly junipers, to a limestone cliff's wall. He slid Keturah from his shoulder. "Thank God, it's like an October night, rather than December. We'll hide here. In my prayer cave."

That she hung back did not surprise him. "I'll go in first."

He knelt and slipped through the narrow opening. A few bats flapped past him. He listened. Knife raised and shoulders hunched, he wound a path into the empty narrow room with moonlight leaking through the small opening in the top. It had never looked more beautiful. He returned to Keturah and coaxed her inside. He took his blanket from its oilskin packet and wrapped it around her. "Sorry. No food here. It would draw critters."

She stared past him, fascinated by the silvery lamp lit for them.

"Why, it shines like the Christmas star." Childlike, she stepped into its glory.

The star he'd seen the night he rescued Charlie had sent his mind heavenward as well. He longed to share a thousand treasures he'd crammed into his heart, but he gently pulled her back into the gray shadows. "We must keep quiet. We'll talk tomorrow. Tonight, I promise I will protect you. And I keep my promises."

Her eyes widened with new terror, and she shuddered uncontrollably.

What had he said? How could he take away her fear? He ached to hold her. But after her ordeal, she might scream, revealing their hiding place, or run away, an easy target for Charlie and his gang. In desperation Henry dropped the mask he'd worn all his life, putting every feeling he harbored for her on display. He prayed aloud.

"God, please protect us. Help Keturah not to be afraid."

Slowly she took his hand. "God keeps His promises, Henry." Her face mirrored the light. "I know thee will, too."

◆　◆　◆

She felt as if she had been beaten with a log. When one big hand shook her shoulder, she choked.

"Keturah. It's me."

Henry?

Her eyes opened to dim gray light. She leaned against hard, damp stone walls. A cave. She was in a cave. Spasms of panic shook her.

"There, there. You're safe." His long arm encircled her shoulders, and she remembered how they had agreed to share the blanket. The last thing she recalled was Henry sitting erect, his eyes like a hawk's, watching.

She clung to him. He touched her cheek. "Sorry I had to wake you so early. Surely Charlie wanted to hunt us down. But after stealing a steamship, the constable, not to mention James Ford, will chase after them. Ford doesn't like small potatoes like Charlie homing in on his territory."

She tried not to enjoy the picture of Charlie afraid, running for his life. Charlie captured and given what he deserved. Her head bowed. Not that she had been given what she deserved.

Henry went on, "If we go to the constable's now, perhaps we can take you home before your parents worry to find you gone."

Papa. Mama. She tried to scramble to her feet. She so hungered to see them. But how would she face them?

"I'll help you explain, if you want." Rising, Henry steadied her.

He risked his life to save her from her own folly. Now he offered to help her. "Henry, I do not know how thee came to rescue me—"

"When Charlie joined in James Ford's evil doings, I feared for you and for him. I followed him on his night prowlings and saw him take you into the cave."

How she wished she could disappear. Instead, she took his hands and forced herself to look him in the eye. "I have a world of apologies to make to thee, but we must go. I will begin, however, by offering my thanks."

He said nothing. But his tired face shone with such kindness. Last night she thought she would never kiss a man again. Today, how he drew her, but would he ever think of her in the same way? Tears dribbled down her cheeks. Weak and wounded, how could she make it through this day? Yet she must. Gently dropping his hands, she tried to brush dirt from her shawl and First Day dress, now in rags.

"Come, there will be time later to primp." For the first time, his voice held a note of amusement.

She stopped. "Thou art right. We must leave."

He hesitated. "Shall I carry you again?"

The thought brought a blush to her cheeks. "If I cannot keep up. But I will try."

"Perhaps we should pray?"

"Certainly. God has been so good to me." She took Henry's hand again. "If I needed God's help last night, I surely need Him today as I go home."

He squeezed her fingers. They bowed their heads in silence. *Lord Jesus, giver of undeserved mercy, I thank Thee for Thy protection of Henry and me. Please guide our hearts and words today.*

◆　◆　◆

"Mama! Papa!" God's timing, certainly. She dashed toward her parents, who had just pulled up to the constable's small cabin, their faces old and shriveled in the early morning grayness.

"Keturah!" Papa vaulted from the wagon and ran toward her, her stout mother not far behind. They devoured her in their arms, her mother weeping as if she could not stop. "We thought thee would never come home. We thought thee was dead."

Mama cupped her dirty, wounded face with trembling fingers. "Child, what happened to thee? What happened to my Keturah?"

"I am so, so sorry." She cried tears and tears. How freeing—to sorrow for the ignorance, the willfulness, the sheer stupidity of her actions.

"What goes on here?" The stocky constable, still wearing his nightcap, stuck his head out the cabin door. He glared at Henry, looking awkward and filthy, who said nothing. "What is the meaning of this?"

Sudden silence. Keturah felt the muscles in Papa's arms tighten like wire. He spoke very slowly as if digging the words out of hard places. "Henry, what is this about?"

She broke loose from him and ran to Henry then turned to her parents and the constable. "I tell thee truly, if Henry had not risked his life, I would not stand before thee alive." Her voice broke. She hugged Henry fiercely and then faced them. "Will thee hear our story?"

The constable's wife poked her head out. "Come in and get warm. He'll dress directly and then speak with you." She pulled her husband inside as if he were six.

Still distraught, Keturah hid a tiny grin. So like Papa and Mama. Her eyes returned to her parents. How she loved them. How she wished she had spared them such hurt. Would they forgive her?

They rushed to embrace her again. "Thee art our daughter, now and always," Papa said. He turned to Henry, his face working. "And if thee, young man, has indeed protected my child, I shall forever be in thy debt."

"We are Friends." For a moment Henry's calm faltered, and his eyes glistened.

What a world of meaning he put into few words. Keturah felt so proud of him and so ashamed of herself, she could not speak. But when he offered her his arm, she clung to him and followed Mama and Papa into the constable's home.

Chapter 11

Mama's First Day table outshone any Keturah could remember. Surely heroes did not die from gratitude, but if Mama had her way, urging seconds and thirds, Henry might be the first. She marveled he had room for both berry and apple pie.

Mama probably had not noticed today was Christmas. But Keturah, for the hundredth time since waking, gave silent thanks for life and for Immanuel, God with her always. Even in the cave.

Papa vigorously stirred honey into his hot cider in an attempt to hide his emotion. "Thee is such a blessing, Henry."

"And you have blessed me."

Keturah had not seen Henry's face glow like this in many days. Perhaps because Papa had told him at Meeting he would support his convincement. Perhaps because, though the ugly details of Keturah's ordeal were known only to weighty Friends, all quietly showed their appreciation for Henry's character and actions.

She found it harder to glow. True, everyday blessings, such as waking in her feather bed and hearing the *plop-plop* of Mama kneading bread, filled her with joy. Still, shame clouded her days. She had confessed her sins to God and to Friends, yet her past foolishness weighed her down. Going to Meeting took more courage than she possessed. Papa's gentle urging and Mama's inviting Henry to First Day dinner helped. But now dinner was done, and she almost hoped Henry would leave.

Instead, he lingered, talking with Papa and Caleb by the fire while she and Mama cleared up. Reluctantly, she sat in the rocker. Knitting, though it continued to try her patience, busied her hands and eyes.

"Friend Wilkes, may I speak with Keturah?"

Startled, she rocked on her foot.

"You may." Papa rose.

Mama stuck her needles into the ball of yarn as if this were normal. She followed Papa toward their room. "We would rest a little and read."

Caleb jauntily adjourned to saddle his horse. Priscilla's mother finally had consented to a weekly visit.

How Keturah would have treasured this moment, if only—

"Merry Christmas." Henry handed her two brown-papered packages from his poke and sat in Mama's chair beside her.

She did not know what to say. She did not know where to look. So she opened the first.

A Bible. A beautiful Bible that had cost him many, many hours of labor. Perhaps even many meals.

"Oh Henry." She ran her finger along its fine leather cover.

"I did not even steal this one."

She had never seen him look mischievous. Laughing and crying, she tried to thank him.

"It is I who thank thee." Henry's use of the word seemed natural. "I was drowning in darkness, trying to escape the thievery that came so naturally. If I had not met thee, would I have learned of the Light of Christ?"

She had not thought of it that way. "But I was such a terrible example—"

"Perhaps. And I would have preferred thee had not nearly drowned me in the river."

She giggled, but her mirth faded quickly. "I failed thee. I—I failed Charlie." She covered her face with her hands.

"Thee believed his lying heart." She felt Henry's long fingers gently pulling her hands away, his face only inches from hers. "I failed Charlie as well. If I had shared the Light instead of hating him for taking you away from me, he might not be running for his life. Sooner or later, I must try to find him." His sad face brightened. "But does not Christ light our darkness and take away our sin—all of it?"

She felt as if a summer sun bloomed inside. "I have another Christmas gift for thee."

She pulled it from her knitting basket and held it in front of his startled eyes. Carefully he undid the blue hair ribbon binding the brown package. He held the Christmas sampler she had stitched and framed, reading aloud: "'Therefore if any man be in Christ, he is a new creature: old things are passed away; behold, all things are become new.'"

He said nothing.

She winced. Her blind side had shown itself once more. While Henry might appreciate the Bible verse, what man wanted frippery with red roses?

Wait. Did his eyes look moist?

"How could thee have known? I—I read this verse the first time just before I began to attend Meeting, and I've read it many times since. In a way, I understood as I learned more about the inner Light. But not as I do now."

She nodded. "Sewing it, I believe, was Christ's gift to me as well."

"No better Christmas gift on earth." Henry clasped her hand.

Sitting beside him near the fire's cozy warmth, speaking of God's goodness—Keturah wanted to savor the moment forever.

Henry picked up his other gift. "This is nothing profound. But I thought thee might like it."

"I'm sure I will." Was it a picture? No, a poem printed on heavy paper with a scrolled border, called "A Visit from Saint Nicholas."

"It's a children's Christmas poem." Henry looked a little shy. "I bought it from a peddler from the East."

She had never read anything like it—Saint Nicholas, Christmas stockings, gifts, and reindeer. If the scripture made her feel brand-new, the story gave her the joy of a child! "Henry, it is a wonderful gift."

The look he gave her made her heart flutter. After all she'd put him through, could he still think of her as—as—

"I've heard flowers on ladies' samplers are symbolic." He ran his fingers over her imperfect embroidery. "What do roses stand for?"

"Love, usually." Quickly she added, "I wanted roses to remind those who view it of Christ's love."

"How wonderful." He touched her chin and gently turned her face to look at him. His golden-hazel eyes held hers as they had the moment he brought her up from the river. "Could they also stand for the love of Christ between a man and a woman?"

Her lips fumbled her breath. She finally squeaked out, "They could."

His lips rested, oh so lightly, on hers only a moment. "Perhaps, over time, they will."

Epilogue

Keturah donned her First Day bonnet and smoothed the silvery-gray silk dress Papa had insisted on providing. Mama justified the extravagance by pointing out that every married woman needed a nice dress for occasions of note throughout her life.

As they waited for Papa's wagon, however, her mother did not speak of practicalities nor guard against vanity. "My Keturah, thou art lovely, inside and out. God bless thee."

Keturah hugged her, feeling Mama's tears.

"Goodness, I'll stain thy dress." Mama dabbed at Keturah's neckline with a handkerchief, then at her eyes. She pulled a package from a cupboard. "I wanted to give this before thee leaves."

Keturah chuckled. "Mama, our cabin is almost next door." She opened the gift, and her knees nearly gave way.

"I knew this meant much to thee," Mama said.

Keturah's hands held the red shawl. She thought Mama had burned it. Instead, she'd washed and mended it. Now Keturah's tears threatened the new silk dress.

"If thee wears the shawl today, I will say nothing." Mama set her lips with heroic determination.

Keturah giggled, then cried, then giggled again. " 'Twould be a memorable wedding."

She hugged her mother tight. "I thank thee, Mama. I will wear it, as Henry loves the color on me. But not to Meeting."

Mama breathed a visible sigh of relief and then climbed into the wagon. They sat close together as they rode to the meetinghouse.

Keturah felt a little shy as she entered. But how handsome Henry looked in his black suit, his thick black hair shining in the candlelight. Mama had fattened him up, but he remained long and lean. Keturah knew the strength of those arms.

He saw her. His face lit up the world.

How fitting that on the Eve of Christ's birth they would celebrate their new life as one.

She and Mama sat by Henry's mother. After Henry's fruitless search for Charlie in New Orleans, she began to seek God, though she rarely came to Meeting. Keturah patted her hand.

One Friend delivered a short sermon, but the Spirit moved few. No doubt He understood they had waited long for this day, praying, studying, and counseling with her parents and other Friends. Now at Papa's nod, she joined Henry before the platform.

"Friends, I take Keturah Wilkes to be my wife, promising through divine assistance to be unto her a loving and faithful husband until it shall please the Lord, by death, to separate us." Henry's voice rose, warm and sure.

Hers wobbled as she repeated her vows, but with everything in her, she meant them. A Friends' wedding did not include a kiss. But seeing a lifetime of embraces in Henry's eyes, she figured she could wait.

◆　◆　◆

"I'm sure Henry here will keep a good hold on ya," Sol said.

Keturah smiled, remembering her first keelboat ride. Now Sol worked on this small steamboat. Not only had he arranged for their free ride together to McFarlan, but he had also helped Henry get a job on the vessel.

Meeting over, she reveled in the red shawl's warmth. She and Henry snuggled close as the boat chugged away from the dock, their families waving. Her first steamboat ride! How many dreams come true could one day hold?

Henry chuckled. "Thy mama does not like this."

"But she likes thee." Keturah gave him a coy look. "I like thee, too. But no stealing kisses until we are out of sight."

He shook his head at her. "Thee knows I'm a pirate."

How healing that such pain could be altered into laughter. "Thee did pirate me away from the pirates."

They chuckled again, but Henry's mirth quieted into thoughtfulness. For a while they stood in silence, watching the glistening river flow before them like the future.

"What are thy thoughts?" She learned each time she asked.

His grin surprised her. "I was thinking how God stole me from under the devil's very nose—through the birth of a Baby."

"As He did me. And through thy love." She gave the awaited kiss, long and sweet. Henry did not have to steal it.

Light of the World, Thee spirited us away from darkness. Every Christmas we will celebrate Thy birth together, giving thanks to Thee, blessed Pirate of our hearts.

Harrison Cake

Written by Rachel Macy, Quaker homemaker. From *Good Housekeeping*, Vol. 9 (1889).

"Now as this is centennial week, I will give thee a 'Harrison Cake' which I think was used in the days of President Harrison's grandfather."

    2 cups molasses
    1 cup butter
    3 to 4 cups flour
    1 cup sugar
    1 cup sour cream, divided
    1 teaspoonful baking soda
    1 teaspoonful powdered cloves
    2 cups currants

The butter should be cut small and put into a saucepan with the molasses. Melt them well and pour the mixture upon 3 or 4 cups of flour, then add the sugar and half the cream. The rest of the cream use to dissolve the soda in, and then add it. Add cloves. Take enough more flour to make about as thick as cupcake batter and stir it ten or fifteen minutes, add the currants. Bake in pans as cupcakes. Be careful it does not burn.

"Thee will notice this cake has no eggs."

Since winning a 2007 American Christian Fiction Writers Genesis award, **Rachael O. Phillips** has published seven novels, with contracts for six more, as well as three novellas and 700 articles. Rachael and her husband have three children and six perfect grandchildren. She would love to visit with you at http://rachaelophillips.com.

Equally Yoked

by Claire Sanders

Dedication

To my daughter, Grace, who lives up to her name every day

Be strong and of a good courage, fear not, nor be afraid of them: for the LORD thy God, he it is that doth go with thee; he will not fail thee, nor forsake thee.
DEUTERONOMY 31:6

Chapter 1

Southern Ohio, 1838

Susanna Griffith closed her eyes and burrowed deeper into the quilts. For a few moments, she'd been a girl again, picking blackberries from the brambles in her father's southern pasture and eating one sweet berry for every handful she dropped into the bucket. The summer sun had warmed her back as she searched for the ripest berries, while the blossoms' fragrance enveloped her. Perhaps she'd lie down in the soft grass and watch the pristine clouds float against the azure sky. It was so pleasant to be a girl again, free from responsibilities—and loneliness. Then the jarring crow of the rooster had woken her.

Weak rays of sunlight crept through the cabin's single window, reminding Susanna that it wasn't July but November. She reached across the bed for her husband.

Nathan wasn't there.

His pillow was as cold as a January frost, and their wedding quilt lay straight and unruffled on his side of the bed. The rooster bellowed another raucous greeting to the morning, and Susanna groaned as reality replaced her dream.

Why even get up? There was no husband who needed breakfast, no work to do that couldn't wait. Why not stay in bed? Perhaps she could recapture the pleasant dream the rooster had interrupted.

As if scolding her laziness, the rooster crowed a third time. The bird knew that morning meant breakfast, and Susanna's idleness was no excuse for neglecting her duties. It wasn't like her to be petulant. If she looked into the small mirror that hung over the washstand, she'd probably see her lower lip sticking out. But she was no longer a child afraid of being alone. She was a wife now. A wife whose husband had important work to do.

She pushed back the covers and dashed to the fireplace to stoke the fire. Then she crossed to the window. Above the trees she could see smoke curling from the chimney of her in-laws' farmhouse. Her sister-in-law was already up and preparing breakfast, though her newborn son had undoubtedly kept her awake most of the night. Miriam was truly a virtuous wife. Didn't she rise while it was yet night and provide food for her household?

And there she was, feeling sorry for herself because she was alone. The least she could do was take care of the livestock while her husband was away. It was bad enough she'd argued with Nathan before he left, had whined like a child instead of being a supportive helpmate. She had a lot of apologizing to do when he returned.

Nathan had built their cabin so well it warmed quickly. Susanna dressed, remembering her father's pronouncement when he'd inspected it a few days before her wedding. "Snug," he'd said. "It'll protect you from the coldest Ohio wind."

Nathan had chafed at what he'd considered to be faint praise, but Susanna had known better. Her father's words had been his way of agreeing to the marriage. "A man who cares for your physical welfare will surely care for the rest of you," he'd explained to her later. "I can go home and not worry about how well you're being looked after."

Had it really been only five months since Susanna became Mrs. Nathan Griffith? Making Nathan's cabin into a home had been her delight. The embroidered table scarves and bed linens she'd brought in her wedding chest had softened the cabin's rough edges, and the pewter candlesticks her parents had given her were still new enough to gleam on the mantel.

After tying a woolen cape over her shoulders to protect from the autumn chill, Susanna stepped outside and tended to her morning chores. When she finished, she changed her apron and reached for her bonnet. She fingered the stiff brim, a sigh escaping her lips. Before she married, she'd spent many an afternoon decorating her bonnets with ribbons and ruffles. When her mother-in-law had given her the plain white cap and black bonnet, Susanna had no doubt she was expected to wear it.

"Now thee looks like a proper Quaker wife," Nathan had said with an approving smile.

Susanna had grinned up at her husband. He'd taken a chance at marrying her, an outsider, but he'd reassured her that none of the Friends would doubt his choice of wives. "Thee is good and kind," he'd said, "and thy Light shines for all to see."

Susanna said a quick prayer for her husband's safe return then tied the bonnet over her linen cap. She gathered her basket of sewing and started down the wooded trail that led to her in-laws' farmhouse. Geese honked overhead, their arrow-shaped formation pointing due south.

"It's about time you were on your way," she said to the birds. "You're going to be late for the family reunion." Until that week, the autumn of 1838 had been mild. Couldn't blame the geese for tarrying while food was plentiful. But yesterday the north wind had brought a chill to the Ohio River Valley, signaling the birds that the scarcity of winter was near.

The Griffiths' dog, Jasper, bounded out of a thicket and bowed at Susanna's feet. "Well, good morning to you, too," she said, chuckling. Jasper barked and rolled onto his back, his tongue lolling out of his teeth. "I still think you're more wolf than dog." Susanna rubbed his belly with the sole of her walking boot. "But I'm not scared of you anymore."

Jasper scrambled to his feet and bounded down the trail, announcing her arrival. Susanna stepped into the clearing and caught sight of Miriam crouching near the door of the springhouse.

"Let me get that for you," Susanna called and hurried to Miriam's side.

Miriam straightened slowly, both hands on the small of her back. "I thank thee. Didn't think it would be so hard to bring in a crock of butter."

"It's too soon for you to be doing so much work. Your son is only two weeks old." Susanna handed her basket to Miriam and nestled the heavy crock of butter in the crook of her arm.

"How's Mother Griffith this morning?" Susanna followed Miriam along the stone path to the farmhouse door.

"Much better. Still coughing but no fever, thank the Lord."

"I'm sure the poultice you made helped. Have you heard from Father Griffith?"

"Not since his last letter. Although I did hear Reverend Mahan's trial has been set for the thirteenth. We'll know something soon enough."

"That poor man's been in jail for more than a month."

"And from what I hear, the mob's growing stronger each day. I know Father and Nathan want to be close enough to help Brother Mahan if the mob attacks. Still, their absence is hard on Mother."

And on me, Susanna thought. Her husband of five months had abandoned her and willingly put himself in harm's way, just so he could offer protection to another man.

A ripple of shame passed through Susanna. Nathan hadn't actually abandoned her. His family was close enough to help if she needed it. She should be proud of Nathan's commitment to the abolitionists' cause instead of complaining about her minor hardships.

Miriam placed a hand over her brow and scanned the bluff that formed the eastern boundary of the Griffith farm. "I see our watchman is still on duty."

Susanna followed Miriam's gaze. An icy hand squeezed her heart at the sight of the lone rider atop the bluff, his figure clearly silhouetted in the morning sun. "Where's your husband?"

"Eli's helping Brother Jackson bale hay this morning. Don't worry. Ever since Brother Mahan's arrest, we haven't had any special guests. That bounty hunter can sit up there until judgment day. He won't see anything worthwhile." Miriam opened the door and stepped aside, allowing Susanna to enter the kitchen. Then she hurried to the cradle near the fireplace.

"How's Samuel this morning?" Susanna removed her cape and bonnet.

"Fine as goose down and growing faster than a weed." Miriam patted the sleeping infant.

"Has Mother Griffith eaten?"

"Not yet. The biscuits are in the oven."

Susanna used the lifter to carefully remove the lid from the dutch oven. Although she was twenty years old, she could still hear her mother's stern voice, scolding her for spilling ashes in the food when she'd been a child. Six golden-brown biscuits smiled up at her. "Shall I take some tea and biscuits upstairs?"

"That would be so helpful, Susanna. And ask Mother if she's up to eating more this morning."

A short time later, Susanna climbed the stairs to her mother-in-law's bedroom. Martha Griffith, propped up by pillows, smiled when her daughter-in-law entered.

"Thank thee, daughter," Martha said as Susanna set the tray on the bed. "I hope thee brought two cups so we can visit for a while."

"Of course I did. Do you feel like eating more than biscuits this morning? How about some eggs?"

"Not yet, dear, but I am determined to get out of this bed and downstairs tomorrow. Now pull the chair closer and talk to me. Has thee heard anything from Mason County?"

"Not a word." Susanna moved the small rocking chair away from the fireplace and placed it beside the bed. "But Miriam says the trial date has been set. Surely Nathan and Father Griffith will be home shortly after that."

"I pray it may be so."

Susanna poured the tea then ran her finger around the rim of her cup. "I know the Bible tells us not to worry, yet it's hard to keep my mind from imagining the most horrible things."

Martha stretched out her hand, and Susanna clasped it with her own. "I know, daughter. I find much solace in the psalm 'Cast thy burden upon the Lord, and he shall sustain thee.'"

If only Susanna could, but stopping her worries was like trying to stop the rain from falling. They came of their own accord. "I try, Mother Griffith. Honest, I do. And yet I find worry creeping into my thoughts like weevils into grain."

"Then go to the Lord again and again. Every time thee finds thyself fretting over Nathan, picture our Lord walking beside him, guiding and protecting him."

Would she ever be as faithful as Mother Griffith? When it came to trusting in the Lord, Susanna was a caterpillar, and her mother-in-law a beautiful butterfly.

"Did thee bring thy sewing?" Martha asked, withdrawing her hand and sipping from her cup. "I cannot wait to see the little coat you are making for Samuel."

"I've only begun Samuel's coat. I wanted to finish the vest for Nathan before working on it. Do you think he'll be home by Christmas?"

"I pray they will be home long before the twenty-fifth. Susanna, has thee spoken to Nathan about celebrating Christmas?"

Susanna noted the concerned frown on her mother-in-law's brow. "Nathan told me the Friends don't observe Christmas, but I thought it would be all right to give him a small present. Do you object?"

"I do not object, but I fear our Quaker ways have been difficult for thee to accept. For us Friends, every day is a gift from God, none more special than the rest. How does thy family celebrate Christmas?"

"We go to church where we sing Christmas songs. Sometimes the children reenact the story of our Savior's birth. Then we share a meal with our friends and family and exchange gifts."

Martha's eyebrows drew together as she gave Susanna an assessing look. "As thee knows, we Friends do not believe in music at our Meetings. Our testimony of silence allows us to listen for the Lord's still, small voice. The expectant waiting is a powerful time."

"I've come to enjoy the weekly respite that quiet time with the Holy Spirit gives me."

Martha's knitted brow told Susanna that her mother-in-law was not appeased by her answer. "And where does thee stand on the issue of becoming one of the Friends?"

That was the question everyone wanted her to answer. Martha had made no secret of her disapproval of Nathan's choice of a non-Quaker to be his bride. Susanna had tried to win her approval, and Martha had been kind and loving in so many ways yet intractable on this one issue. "I–I'm still praying about it, Mother Griffith."

Martha sighed, a sound of long-suffering and strained patience.

Time to change the subject, Susanna thought. She removed a bundle of gray cloth from her basket and spread the vest on her mother-in-law's lap. "All that's left to do are the button holes. Friends don't have anything against buttons, do they?"

Martha inspected the garment. "The Lord has given thee a wonderful talent, daughter. My own mother despaired of ever teaching me to make stitches as small and straight as thine. And while it is true that we Friends believe in plain dress as a way to honor the beautiful spirits our Lord gave us, I have yet to hear anyone speak ill of an unassuming button."

◆　◆　◆

As night fell, Susanna sat in her chair in front of the cabin's fireplace. Shadows danced on Nathan's empty chair, and a new pang of longing passed through her heart. How much longer until she reunited with her husband? It wasn't fair to be a newlywed and yet be alone. If only the Griffiths hadn't thrown in their lots with the Mahans, Nathan and his father would be home where they belonged.

Brother John Mahan had preached at her home church a few years ago, urging her neighbors to stand together against slavery. Susanna's father had declined to join the abolitionists. "I have a family to provide for and children to protect," he'd said, "but I'll pledge a yearly sum to support you."

Why couldn't Nathan have done the same? He should be sitting in their cabin instead of a strange boardinghouse on the other side of the river, where pro-slavery mobs threatened to tear down the jail and lynch a godly man accused of helping runaways.

The logs shifted in the fireplace, and Susanna added another piece of wood. She really should bank the fire and go to bed, but emptiness awaited her there. Spending the day with Mother Griffith and Miriam had helped the daylight hours pass quickly, though the night stretched before her like a shadowy cave. Perhaps she should have accepted their invitation to spend the night at the farmhouse, but she had wanted to return to her cabin. At least here she could see Nathan's handiwork and feel his love for her in every carefully crafted mortise and tenon. She pulled her shawl around her shoulders, blew out the candle, and rested her head against the back of the chair, waiting for sleep to claim her.

A few hours later, a knock on the cabin's door startled her awake. She leaned forward, her fingers grasping the arms of her rocker, her pulse thundering in her ears. Who would dare to call so late at night? Should she pretend no one was home? The fire had burned down, sending the barest light into the cabin. Whoever was outside couldn't know for sure she was there.

"Griffith?" a man's voice called. "Nathan Griffith?"

Tension coiled in Susanna's shoulders. She didn't recognize the voice, but surely a thief would not call her husband's name.

The man knocked again. "My name is Simmons. I've come with a special guest."

A special guest. That meant only one thing. A fugitive slave sought Nathan's help. What should she do? If she didn't answer, would the man go to the next safe house? Where was the closest safe house?

Eli would know. She could send the man to the Griffiths' farmhouse. Perhaps the runaway could stay with her until Eli came. If the bounty hunters spotted Mr. Simmons, he could be introduced as a relative, traveling to visit family.

Struggling to settle her heartbeat, Susanna touched a piece of straw to the embers, relit the candle, and made her way to the door. Perhaps she should take down the flintlock from its place over the mantel—but Nathan had never answered the door with a gun in his hands. With one last look at the musket, she slid the bolt and opened the door.

The man, short and squat as a rain barrel, had a whiskered face and a patched coat. "Nathan Griffith?" he asked.

Susanna shook her head. "You'll have to go someplace else. My husband can't help."

The man frowned. "Got no place else to go. This guest has got to get to the Quaker settlement in Bear Valley right away."

It was wrong to invite a man into her house when her husband was gone, but the longer the man stood in the doorway, the more likely it was that someone would spot him.

"Come in," she said.

"My name's Andrew Simmons." The man removed his hat and stepped through the doorway. "This cabin was mighty hard to find. Whoever built it didn't want just anybody stumbling upon it. Where's your husband?"

Surely she shouldn't admit she was alone. "A trail leads through the woods to the farmhouse. Go there and ask for Eli Wilson. He'll know what to do."

He frowned. "Wilson, you say? I don't know anyone by that name. I was told to find Nathan Griffith, no one else."

"Eli is married to Nathan's sister. He'll know the best place for you to take your guest. Make sure you're not seen, because bounty hunters have been watching the road and our homes."

Mr. Simmons shook his head and made a sound like an angry dog. "I knew it was wrong to come to someone I didn't know. But with the hornet's nest that's brewing in Mason County, my usual contacts have disappeared."

An idea popped into Susanna's mind. "Perhaps you could take your guest back to your house. Come back in a few weeks."

"Not possible. This is a young woman searching for her husband. She got word he's with the Quakers, and she's got to get there. Tomorrow wouldn't be too soon."

Susanna didn't know how Nathan and the others managed their clandestine journeys, but surely the runaway could wait until a safer time. "Where is your guest?"

"I put her in your barn," he said with a jerk of his head.

"I'll go for Eli," Susanna said. "You can wait here."

Mr. Simmons slapped his hat against his leg and muttered under his breath. "No, I'll go. No need to send a woman out in the middle of the night. Where's this trail?"

"I'll show you."

Susanna lit candles inside two punched tin lanterns and closed the apertures before stepping outside. A bounty hunter would have a hard time seeing the faint light, though the lantern would be enough to help Mr. Simmons find his way. She gave one lantern to the man and led him to the trail. "It's a well-worn path," she said. "No roots or branches to slow you down. The Griffiths have a dog, but they let him sleep in the kitchen on cold nights. He won't bother you. What's your guest's name?"

"Phoebe," he said and started down the trail.

She hurried to the barn. The mare nickered a greeting as she closed the door and exposed the candle's light. "Phoebe?" she called softly. The mare stamped her front hooves. No other sound met Susanna's ears. "Phoebe, my name is Susanna Griffith. Mr. Simmons told me you were here. I've come to help."

A timid voice, soft as the spring breeze, answered. "Yes, ma'am."

Susanna turned toward the voice. The lantern light illuminated a figure huddled in the corner of the barn. "I want you to come inside, Phoebe, and get warm. Mr. Simmons will be back soon, and you'll be on your way. Are you hungry?"

"Yes, ma'am. Thank you kindly."

Susanna walked slowly toward the woman. She hadn't seen many slaves in her life, but Phoebe was a surprise in many ways. She was tiny, barely reaching five feet, and her thin clothing was little more than rags. As Susanna's gaze traveled down Phoebe's slight figure, she gasped.

Phoebe smiled. "Yes, ma'am. I'm going to have a baby. Granny said it's almost my time. That's why I had to leave."

Susanna couldn't begin to understand why the imminent birth of her baby had forced Phoebe to escape, but that didn't change the fact that the runaway was in her barn, asking for help. "Let's get you into the cabin," she said. "I'm sure I have an extra cloak you can use to keep you warm for the rest of your journey." After concealing the lantern's light, Susanna opened the barn door. "Stay close to me. I don't dare use more light."

Phoebe touched Susanna's skirt. "I'll just hold on to your dress, if it's all right. I won't lose hold of you."

Susanna smiled at the younger woman. There was something about the tiny dark woman that Susanna liked. Obviously, courage didn't come in proportion to size.

Once inside the cabin, Susanna rebuilt the fire and filled the kettle with water. After hanging it from a crane, she swung the kettle over the fire. "We'll have some tea in a few minutes. Now sit here by the fireplace so you can warm up."

Phoebe eased herself into Nathan's chair, and Susanna passed a woolen blanket to her. In the firelight, Susanna could see Phoebe clearly. Had the poor girl actually walked this far with bare feet? Her frayed cloth dress barely reached her ankles, and she wore a faded blue covering over her hair. "I don't have much to offer you in the way of food," Susanna said. "But I'll get started on some griddle cakes."

"Thank you, ma'am."

Susanna set the long-handled skillet on the gridiron and turned to the task of mixing the batter. "Where are you from?"

Phoebe didn't answer. Susanna glanced over her shoulder to find Phoebe sleeping quietly. How exhausted she must be to fall asleep so quickly. She looked at the wet batter in the bowl and wondered if she should complete the simple meal. Then realizing she could send the griddle cakes with Eli, she finished the job.

Susanna had just removed the last cake from the griddle when she heard Eli's voice.

"Susanna? May I come in?"

She crossed to the door and let Eli and Mr. Simmons into her cabin.

Eli's gaze fell on Phoebe, who continued to sleep soundly in Nathan's chair. "Is everything all right, Susanna? I hope thee is not scared."

"Not now," she said. "I confess Mr. Simmons gave me a start, but I'm all right."

"Are those griddle cakes?" asked Mr. Simmons.

"Yes, would you like some?"

"Don't mind if I do." He seated himself at the table.

Susanna set the wooden bowl of griddle cakes on the table and added a small crock of honey. She turned to get him a knife and fork, but when she turned back, Mr. Simmons was already devouring the cakes with his fingers. Her gaze connected with Eli's.

Eli smiled and shrugged then pointed to the door. "Let's talk outside."

Susanna took her shawl from the peg and followed Eli. "What have you decided?"

"It takes about four hours to get to the Quaker settlement at Bear Valley, and dawn's only an hour away. Phoebe will have to wait until tomorrow evening. I'll take her back to the farmhouse. She can rest up and eat before starting on the last part of her trip. How old does thee think she is?"

"Younger than I," Susanna answered. "My guess is sixteen or seventeen. Did Mr. Simmons tell you she's in the family way?"

"Yes, but that can't be helped now. She's here, and we'll do the best we can for her. Mother Griffith says for thee to come to the house as usual, because the bounty hunters have been watching us for so long, they know our routines. If they don't see thee making thy daily visit, they're likely to pay a call to find out why."

"I'll be there."

Eli touched Susanna's arm in a supportive gesture. "I'll see thee at breakfast, then?"

Susanna nodded. "I'd offer to bring griddle cakes, but I don't think there will be any left."

◆ ◆ ◆

Eli, Miriam, and Martha were gathered at the kitchen table when Susanna arrived. "Good morning," she said. But anxious silence met her greeting. "What is it? Has something else happened?" Susanna's hand went to her throat. "Did you receive word from Nathan or Father Griffith?"

"No, daughter," Martha said. "I am sure Nathan and Thomas are fine. Sit down, and we will tell thee what we have decided."

"Thee is not going, Mother," Miriam said. "Thee has barely recovered from a bad case of the grippe. The journey would put thee either back in bed or in thy grave."

Susanna looked at Eli. "I thought you were going to take Phoebe to Bear Valley."

Eli opened his mouth to respond, but his wife answered.

"Eli can't go either," Miriam said. "Those shameful bounty hunters have left the bluff and set up camp on our property. There are two of them now, watching Eli's every move. Brother Jackson came over at daybreak to tell us."

"Those scoundrels showed up at our back door shortly after Eli returned from thy cabin," Martha added. "They did not recognize Mr. Simmons and suspected he had information about a runaway. I have to give Brother Simmons credit. He was as calm as a pond at sunset. He did not give away a thing."

"They asked to search our house and barn," Miriam said. "Eli let them in, but they didn't come close to finding our secret room. Still, it's obvious they suspected something."

"Phoebe's still here?" Susanna asked.

"Of course she's still here," Miriam said. "I brought her breakfast and told her she'd be leaving today."

It was all happening too fast for Susanna. "If the house is being watched so closely, maybe she should stay until the bounty hunters move on."

"Too dangerous to let her stay," Eli said. "That's why I'm taking her tonight."

Miriam groaned. "Please don't risk it, Eli. There are others who can take Phoebe. Men who don't have newborn babies to watch over. If thee leaves, who will protect us the next time those rogues knock on our door?"

"It is not right to put our problems on our neighbors' shoulders," Martha said. "God sent Phoebe to us, and it is up to us to do what we have pledged. I will take the hay wagon to the Quaker settlement with Phoebe hidden in the secret compartment. I am able to drive a wagon."

"For four hours in the cold November weather?" Miriam asked. "Not to mention the clouds building in the north. They look like snow to me. Thee would be risking thy life just as much as Eli if thee did that."

369

Susanna's in-laws fell silent. There seemed to be no solution acceptable to all of them, but Susanna knew what needed to be done.

"I'll take her," she said.

All eyes turned to her. "What did thee say?" Martha asked.

Susanna could barely believe the words had come out of her mouth, but there was no better solution. "I'll take her. I know where the Quaker settlement is. My family's farm is east of there. I'll go tonight."

"No," Eli said. "I won't allow it. It's my place to take Phoebe. Thee never pledged thyself to this cause."

"It's too much to ask, Susanna," Miriam said. "Thee has never done anything like this."

"If you didn't have Samuel to care for, would you do it?" Susanna asked.

"Of course, but I'm older. And I've made the journey with my father."

"I've made the same journey with my father," Susanna reminded her. "I admit we didn't travel in the dark, but I'm sure I can find it."

The three were silent as the possibility of Susanna escorting Phoebe seemed to solidify in their minds.

"I don't think the bounty hunters have been watching Nathan's cabin," Eli said. "With him gone, there's no reason to watch it."

"Susanna *can't* go," Miriam repeated. "She's too young."

"Which is why she is beyond the bounty hunters' suspicion," Martha said. "Both Susanna and I will go."

"No," Susanna said. "You're not well yet, Mother Griffith. I agree with Miriam. You must get better."

"I won't let thee go by thyself," Miriam said.

Susanna almost smiled at her sister-in-law's forceful tone. Surely Miriam could see Susanna was the only choice. "If Eli accompanies me, he'll bring attention to us. And like Mother Griffith says, Phoebe is our responsibility."

Silent seconds passed. When each person met her gaze and smiled, Susanna knew they'd reached the same conclusion.

Martha reached across the table and took Susanna's hand. "Yet who knows whether thee has come to the kingdom for such a time as this?"

Yes, Susanna thought. Like Queen Esther, she was in a unique position to help her new family.

Eli ran his hands through his hair and shook his head. "Nathan will have my hide for this."

Susanna smiled in return. She was going.

Chapter 2

On the fourteenth of November, Nathan Griffith and his father, Thomas, stepped out of the boardinghouse and walked along the muddy main road in Washington, Kentucky. Everywhere he looked, Nathan saw evidence of fear. Windows were shuttered and barred, water barrels filled in case of fire, and men buying extra ammunition. Rumors of a slave revolt or of abolitionists riding into town to free their comrade floated through the town like cinders from a brush fire.

"It is a good thing we came," Thomas said. "Brother Mahan should not have to face this alone."

John Mahan had been in jail for nearly two months, shackled like a murderer and forced to endure hardships he didn't deserve. "The trial is set to begin at eleven o'clock," Nathan said. "As soon as it's over, we should return home."

"I agree, but we will have to see how things turn out. After that false start yesterday, who knows what today's proceedings will bring?"

"I hardly know which will fare better for him. If he's found guilty, the mob will surely hang him. But if the jury declares his innocence, the mob may still attack out of anger."

"I believe he will be cleared of the trumped-up charges. My hope is that we can help him get across the river and on his way home before the mob has time to form."

Nathan prayed for their success. As Quakers, he and his father believed that violence was a sin, but Nathan knew peaceful reconciliation would not be an option for a hate-crazed mob. They could do little else for Reverend Mahan except visit him in jail and offer their help.

At the small jailhouse, Nathan and Thomas checked in with the jailer, walked down the narrow stairs to the dirt-floor cellar, and stooped under a low-hanging doorframe to the cell. Brother Mahan stood to his full height as they entered.

"Good morning, Friends," Brother Mahan greeted them. "Blessed is the day that the Lord has made."

"We shall rejoice and be glad in it," Thomas said. "It is good to see thee smiling this morning, Brother Mahan."

"I have no fear of what's to come. I've known from the beginning this is a case that must be seen through to its end. Once I am acquitted, it will prevent future cases of a similar nature."

"Still," Nathan said, "it has been a hardship for thee and thy family. And all because of lies. Lies men told after swearing before God to tell the truth."

There was no answer for that. It was well known that Brother Mahan's accusers had lied about him crossing into Kentucky in order to incite slaves to leave. Thomas placed one hand on Brother Mahan's shoulder and the other on his son's. "Let us pray."

The men stood, heads bowed, while each spoke to the Lord in silent prayer. Nathan's mind wandered from the jail cell back to the cabin where his wife waited. Thank goodness Susanna was safe with his family. She was so young and unaware of the dangers the Griffiths faced whenever they helped runaway slaves.

Nathan's heart eased as he pictured Susanna in their cabin. By now she'd be feeding the chickens or turning the horses out to pasture. She'd written to him of her daily visits with his mother. Surely his mother had come to realize what a treasure Susanna was, despite that she'd not yet decided to become a member of the Society of Friends.

Susanna was warmth and gentleness and all things good and kind. Nathan asked the Lord to protect his dear wife and the rest of his family then hastened to the *Amen* when he heard voices outside the cell.

Chambers Baird, Mahan's attorney, was escorted into the room. "Morning, gentlemen," he said. The men exchanged handshakes. "Now if you will excuse us, I must prepare my client for today's proceedings."

"Of course," Thomas said. "We will be in the courtroom, Brother Mahan, and we will be waiting with a fresh horse to take thee home."

"I'll be ready," Mahan replied and smiled broadly.

◆　◆　◆

The cold had settled into the Ohio Valley like an unwanted houseguest. That afternoon Susanna dressed with extra care, layering bustling petticoats beneath her skirt, her jacket covering several blouses and sweaters. She would leave at three o'clock, driving a wagonload of hay. If stopped by the bounty hunters, she'd say she was taking the load to Friends. By saying that, she'd be spared from the sin of lying, just as Eli had sidestepped the issue when asked if he had a slave in his house.

"We consider every man free in God's eyes," Martha had explained. "Therefore we never consider our special guests to be slaves. Just as we did not lie when we introduced Mr. Simmons as our cousin, for we are all brothers and sisters in the family of our Lord."

Susanna walked the short distance to the Griffiths' house and found Phoebe seated at the kitchen table. One look at the petite girl, smothered in layers of clothing and wrapped in a wool blanket, made Susanna hide her smile behind her fingers.

Phoebe laughed with her. "I know, ma'am. I look like a pile of old clothes somebody threw in the rag pile. But Miss Miriam fixed me a special bed in the wagon, and while you're up top driving those horses in the cold, I'll be warm and snug."

Martha walked into the kitchen and took both of Susanna's hands in hers. "Now, daughter." Her brows drew together in a serious frown. "I have a hundred things to say. Is thee ready to listen?"

A hundred things? Perhaps Susanna should write them down.

"First," Martha said, "do not put thy life in danger. I know thee to be a smart girl. Use the intelligence God gave thee if difficulties arise. Second, it will be dark in just a few hours, but Eli has hitched our best horses for the job. They are reliable and steadfast and will keep going until thee has reached thy destination. Third, remember that the Lord sends angels with thee. Rely on them for protection. And fourth, take my cape and gloves. They are the warmest we have."

Susanna smiled at her mother-in-law. "That's only four, Mother Griffith. What about the other ninety-six?"

Martha squeezed Susanna's hands. "I will save them until thee returns. Now, is thee ready?"

Susanna had worried all day about her journey. What if the bounty hunters caught Phoebe? Susanna would undoubtedly be arrested for aiding a fugitive slave and perhaps thrown in jail. Although that possibility was remote, some women had been imprisoned as the slaveholders became more and more desperate to recover their lost property. Finally after a day spent chasing away the what-ifs as though they were pesky flies, it was time to set out. "Oh yes, I'm anxious to get started."

Eli entered the kitchen and stopped at the hearth long enough to warm his hands. "It's getting colder by the hour. I wish we didn't have to send thee right away."

Susanna flicked her gaze to Phoebe's abdomen. She wasn't one to judge, but surely Phoebe would deliver her child soon. "I'll be in the hands of Friends in a few hours. I'm sure we'll rest in warm beds tonight."

Martha gave Susanna's hands a final squeeze and picked up a large covered basket. "Everything is packed and ready for thee. I even put in some of the gingerbread thee loves so much."

"Thank you." Susanna took the basket. "Someday you'll have to teach me how to make it."

"When thee returns, daughter."

Eli turned from the fireplace and addressed their special guest. "Are you ready, Phoebe?"

"Oh yes," Phoebe answered, her eyes sparkling. "I've been praying for this day for many years, and now it's finally come. Just think, I'll be with my husband tonight, and we'll both be free."

Eli stooped to help Phoebe, who rose with difficulty from her chair. "Not yet, baby." She patted her middle. "You just stay in there a few more days. Soon you can come out and say hello to your daddy. Just a little while more."

Susanna gave Martha one last hug then trailed Eli and Phoebe to the barnyard. The wagon, piled with hay, looked as ordinary as every other hay wagon she'd seen. Eli crouched under the wagon, removed a wooden slat, and revealed the cramped space where Phoebe would lie amid blankets. *It's barely bigger than a coffin,* Susanna thought then whisked the image out of her mind. She was going to take Phoebe to safety. She was going to return to the Griffiths' farmhouse tomorrow. She wouldn't allow another doubt to slither into her mind.

Susanna watched the young girl step onto the mounting block Eli had supplied and slowly slide her body into the space.

Eli replaced the slat and redistributed the hay so that nothing looked out of place then threw the pitchfork on top of the load. After handing Susanna up to the driver's bench, he smiled warmly. "Good journey. We'll see thee tomorrow."

Susanna tried to fill her smile with confidence. "Tomorrow," she promised. She turned her gaze forward, snapped the reins, and the horses plodded forward.

◆ ◆ ◆

The first snow of the season came just as Susanna crossed the bridge over Red Oak Creek. She wasn't alarmed. The flakes fell like gentle feathers and melted as they touched the ground. Even though her toes were numb and her cheeks stung from the cold, this type of snow was no threat.

It reminded her of the day Nathan had asked her to marry him. He'd courted her for nearly a year, and everyone in her family knew his intentions, yet he'd taken his time getting around to the asking. That February day, he asked her to go for a walk in the snow. Her mother began to object but perhaps read something on Nathan's face and agreed to the outing. Susanna and Nathan walked down the lane, arm in arm, with only the whisper of snowflakes to disturb the winter silence.

They turned at the end of the lane to make their way back when he stopped and faced her. "Susanna?"

She waited for him to go on, but he only smiled down at her, his brown eyes shining with kindness and love.

"Susanna," he repeated.

"Yes, Nathan?"

"Thee knows I've been speaking with thy parents about my family's farm near Ripley," he said, his breath visible in the frosty air.

"Yes, Nathan. I know."

"And thee knows my family is Quaker."

"Yes, Nathan."

"Does thee object?"

"Object to your family being Quakers? Of course not. Why do you ask?"

He took her gloved hands in his and held them against his chest. "Because if thee agrees to be my wife, thee will live with me and my family. I don't require thee to become one of the Friends, Susanna. That decision is up to thee and thy soul. But it's my hope that thee will agree to become my wife and to raise our children in the Quaker way."

She laughed, but the look of confusion on Nathan's face quickly quelled her laughter. "Oh Nathan," she said, covering her mouth with one hand. "I'm not laughing at your proposal. I'm laughing with relief."

"Relief?"

"Yes! Thank goodness, you finally asked!"

His frown vanished as he pulled her close and tilted her chin toward his face. "Does thee agree to marry me, Susanna?"

"Of course, Nathan. I've been waiting and waiting for you to ask."

His nose was cold, but his lips were warm when he kissed her. The first of many kisses.

She ran back to her house, bursting with the news. Her parents set the date for the second Saturday in June. She floated through the next months, preparing her wedding chest and dreaming of becoming Nathan's wife.

Although Susanna's father had sold many horses to Nathan's father through the years, she'd never met the women in his family. When Martha and Miriam, dressed in plain gray dresses and black bonnets, arrived the day before her wedding, Susanna was unsure how they would receive her. She knew his mother had been concerned about her not being a Quaker, but Nathan was resolute. "Susanna is the woman of my heart," he said. "She's willing to learn more about the Society of Friends, and that's good enough for me."

How his words warmed her heart and calmed her apprehension. Concern about earning her mother-in-law's approval dwindled in the face of her husband's love, and she married Nathan with confidence and pride.

The horses stopped, stirring Susanna from her pleasant memories. A broken tree limb lay across the road, snow lining its bare branches. She hadn't realized how thick the snow had gotten. She tied the reins to the bench, climbed down the wagon, and pulled the branches out of the way. Thank goodness none of them were too heavy for her to move. Eli hadn't sent an ax or hatchet with her.

She reseated herself on the bench, a gust of wind swirling her skirts about her. It was getting colder as the sun moved closer to the horizon, but still Susanna wasn't alarmed. Two horses could easily pull the wagon as long as she stayed on the road. Perhaps she should check on Phoebe before she drove farther, but anyone who saw her might deduce the hay was a ruse.

Susanna snapped the reins and gave a silent prayer of thanksgiving as the horses began to move. Just as Mother Griffith had promised, the team pulled with resolute determination, needing almost no guidance from Susanna. Evening transformed into night, and the wind intensified, blowing the snow in horizontal sheets across the road.

A gust of wind struck her head-on, the snow clinging to the tendrils of hair that had escaped her cap. Susanna gathered the reins in one gloved hand and used the other to adjust a scarf around her bonnet. There was one good thing about the stiff brims of the Quaker bonnet—it kept most of the snow out of her face. If only all the Quaker ways were as easy as changing her bonnet style. She still hadn't adopted the Griffiths' way of speaking. Nathan used what he called plain speech whenever he spoke with the Friends, but never when he was conducting business in town. How odd it had been when Nathan first addressed her as *thee*. Now she yearned to hear his voice, telling her of his love and approval. When he finally came home, she'd cook his favorite meal and then simply sit and watch him eat. Her eyes were hungry for the sight of her husband. Especially the sight of him in their cabin, safe and warm.

Did Phoebe feel the same way? All of Susanna's troubles seemed insignificant compared to those of the young woman who lay hidden under the wagon. Not only was Phoebe a fugitive from the law, but she was also heavy with child. She'd risked her life, and her child's life, to be reunited with her husband.

If a woman was willing to risk everything in order to escape, then slavery must be worse than Susanna had ever imagined. The river that separated free Ohio from slave Kentucky had seen its share of drowned men and women, each one willing to die rather than live as a slave. But why did the sins of others have to endanger her husband?

Because Nathan couldn't sit and do nothing. At least that's how he'd explained it to her. "'Therefore all things whatsoever ye would that men should do to you, do ye even so to them,'" he'd quoted and then kissed her forehead as if to say *argument concluded.*

Susanna hadn't been able to stop herself from quarreling when Nathan announced his intentions to accompany his father to Kentucky. Wouldn't he be surprised to know she was helping a runaway? A few weeks earlier, she'd insisted that Brother Mahan's fight had nothing to do with the Griffiths. Now she would be counted among the abolitionists.

The wind changed direction and speed. It howled through the heavily laden evergreens and pummeled her body with frosty fists. When the frigid wind stung her face like tiny pins, she knew it could mean only one thing.

Ice.

If the snow mixed with ice, the road would quickly become too slick. She estimated she was still an hour away from the Quaker settlement, but in this weather, it might take longer. Would she make it there before ice turned the road into a frozen byway? She urged the horses to pick up speed, but they increased their pace for no more than a hundred yards before they returned to their slower gait. In the dark Susanna couldn't gauge the amount of ice collecting on the road, so perhaps it was wiser to let the horses set their own speed. They could feel the road beneath their hooves, and in the near-whiteout conditions of this storm, the horses were better judges than she.

If only she weren't out here alone. What had she been thinking, volunteering to take a runaway slave to safety? This had never been her fight. She should have waited for someone else to come for Phoebe. Someone who wouldn't have had to travel alone or someone who had a better hiding place for the runaway. Could she really withstand this storm for another hour? For more than an hour? As it was, someone would probably find her covered in ice, frozen to the bench like a human-sized icicle. But there was no place to stop. She'd never be able to build a fire in this wind, and surely Phoebe wouldn't survive a full night in that small compartment under the wagon.

Susanna took a deep breath and struggled to calm her fears. Yes, the weather was bad, but panic and fear wouldn't help. Her horses were still plodding forward, and as long as they continued to move, she and her charge would eventually get to their destination. The Quaker settlement was due north of her current position. All she had to do was keep going.

Just keep going.

The horses stopped again. One horse whinnied while the other looked back at her as if waiting for a decision. Susanna squinted at the road ahead but saw nothing except a wall of snow.

A thousand needles pricked her feet as she jumped the short distance from the wheel's hub to the ground, her limbs protesting the movement. She patted the withers of the horse on the left. "What is it?" she asked.

The horse swung its head toward the sound of her voice and shifted its weight from one hoof to the other. Susanna walked a few feet ahead and saw what had stopped the horses. The bridge over Washburn Run was gone.

She recalled the map Eli had drawn for her. "I don't need a map," she'd protested. "I know the road very well." But now she regretted her words. Although she'd made the trip with her father, she'd never thought to ask about alternate routes.

Going forward wasn't an option. Even if the horses could swim the icy water, Phoebe would likely drown. Going back wasn't an option. She'd come two-thirds of the way and returning to the Griffiths wouldn't solve anything. But staying put wasn't an option either. No one who might offer help was likely to be on the road in this weather, and Eli had cautioned her against trusting strangers.

Susanna absentmindedly stroked the horse and closed her eyes. A new level of weariness settled in her bones. If only she were in her warm cabin, safely tucked under quilts while the earth froze outside. If only she could snuggle under the hay until the weather quieted. If she could just rest for a little while, close her eyes, and let the worries dissolve into dreams of sunny summer days. . . .

A sudden gust of wind swirled her skirt and petticoats, sending a frigid tendril into the last warm spot on her body. This was madness. She couldn't simply stay on the road like a pile of stones. There was nothing wrong with the wagon, and she had to find shelter for the horses. What had Mother Griffith said to her? Rely on her intelligence and on the Lord's help. Susanna lifted her gaze. Her intelligence seemed to be as frozen as the rest of her. "What should I do, Lord?" she asked the dark sky. "Where should I go?"

No answer came.

Susanna sighed and rubbed her cold nose on the horse's warm neck. Then as if driven by an invisible hand, the horses pricked their ears and began to move. Was this like Balaam's donkey? Had they seen an angel Susanna could not see?

She stepped away from the wagon and watched the horses circle until they stopped, the wagon now headed in the opposite direction. "Fine with me," Susanna said to the animals. "If you've got an idea, I'm willing to go along with it."

She walked to the back of the wagon and raised her voice above the wind. "Everything's all right, Phoebe. We're just taking a different way." No response came from the secret compartment. Was Phoebe still alive? Had she frozen to death, despite the extra clothing and quilts?

Susanna's heart shuddered at the thought of little Phoebe lying dead in that cramped space. She lowered her face to the spot where she knew Phoebe's head was. "Phoebe?" she called again, unsuccessful at hiding the growing tension in her voice. No answer.

"Phoebe!" Susanna shouted, preparing to remove the wooden slat. Then she heard the faint knocking from beneath the hay, and relief warmed her frozen body. Phoebe was all right. Frightened perhaps, and undoubtedly cold, but still alive.

Susanna climbed up the wagon and resumed her perch on the bench. A quick flick of the reins was all the horses needed to resume their steady pace. But where were they going? Susanna knew that a tired horse would instinctively head for the barn, but they were too far from home. Then she saw a glimmer of hope.

A light shone through the blustering snow, a mere pinpoint of illumination that glowed in the frigid gloom. As the wagon drew nearer, two dark shapes formed—a farmhouse and a barn. So that's what the horses had sensed.

Somebody else's barn.

Chapter 3

Susanna tucked the quilts around Phoebe and rubbed the young girl's fingers. "You must have been freezing in that wagon."

"Don't worry about me, ma'am." Phoebe smiled. "All I had to do was lie quiet. You're the one with the red nose and white lips."

"Oh I'm sure I look a sight," Susanna said. "After I get you settled, I'll see to the horses and bring up the basket of food."

A frown crossed Phoebe's brow. "Do you think we'll be at your friends' farm tomorrow?"

Susanna wanted to comfort the girl, and an empty reassurance popped into her mind, though there was no use promising what she couldn't guarantee. "The Friends' settlement is only an hour or so away, Phoebe. But we can't travel on the roads until this storm passes."

Phoebe's gaze swept the loft. "We'll be warm enough in here, don't you think? If it's warm enough for the animals, it'll be warm enough for us."

As long as no one finds us, Susanna thought. The farmer who owned this barn seemed to be tucked in his warm house for the night. Susanna had simply opened the doors, and the horses had pulled the wagon into the barn. Now that she'd seen to Phoebe's safety, it was time to unhitch the horses and let them rest for the night.

"I'll be back in a few minutes," Susanna promised. "Do you like gingerbread?"

"I don't know, ma'am," Phoebe answered. "Don't think I've ever tasted it before."

"Well then, you're in for a treat." Susanna smiled in what she hoped was a reassuring manner and descended the ladder. When her feet touched the packed dirt of the barn's floor, she sagged against the rungs. "Thank You, Lord," she whispered. "Thank You for this shelter and for keeping Phoebe safe."

One horse nickered softly, and an involuntary smile crossed Susanna's lips. "And, oh yes, Lord. Thank You for the wisdom of horses."

The horse is probably laughing at that, Susanna thought. She pushed herself away from the ladder and went to unfasten the harnesses. The barn was large with stalls for two horses and one milk cow. Since there were no empty stalls for her horses, she let them walk freely in the barn. One animal went to the back of the wagon and began eating the hay, while the other drank deeply from the water trough.

Satisfied that she could do nothing else for them, Susanna took the basket of food from the wagon and returned to Phoebe. "Now," she said, and sat next to the girl, "let's see what Mother Griffith packed for us."

"Granny makes butter cookies for the master's family. Sometimes she brings home a few for us."

Susanna passed a plate of cold chicken to Phoebe. "Is your grandmother the cook?"

"The baker," Phoebe answered, her mouth full of meat. "Demetria is the cook. Master Hansen's so rich, he's got a big old kitchen that's always hopping. But Granny isn't my grandmother."

"She isn't?"

"No, ma'am. All I know is I was born in Tennessee. But Granny, she's been good to me. When Tom and me got married, Granny made me the prettiest little bouquet of white and blue flowers. I don't know where she got flowers in January, but I suspect the master's wife would've been mighty angry if she'd discovered some of her hothouse flowers were gone. What about you, ma'am? Did you have one of those big old weddings with a new dress and sweet cake?"

Susanna thought back to her wedding day. "I suppose I did. I got married last summer. My mother and I worked on my dress for a month."

"What color was it?"

"Yellow," Susanna said.

"Oh, I've always been partial to yellow. And did you put flowers in your hair?"

"Not in my hair but on my bonnet."

Phoebe frowned. "It's not for me to say, ma'am, but I'm not sure flowers would help much on that bonnet."

Susanna touched the brim of her Quaker bonnet. "Oh no, not this bonnet. This is my married bonnet. My wedding bonnet was yellow, just like my dress."

"They made you wear that black bonnet after you got married?"

"No. I mean, nobody made me wear it. I chose to wear it, to show I was part of a Quaker family."

As though sensing she was stepping into dangerous territory, Phoebe changed the subject. "What else is in that basket, ma'am?"

"What? Oh, sorry." Susanna's attention returned to the basket, where she found boiled potatoes. How could she have gone on and on about her wedding when Phoebe was probably starving?

"Tomorrow we'll have us a hot breakfast, I reckon," Phoebe said.

"If the storm blows itself out in time. Not even our know-it-all horses could find the road in this blizzard."

"Know-it-all horses?" Phoebe repeated. "What do you mean by—"

A man's voice stopped Phoebe's question. "Who's there?" he yelled.

The cold potato solidified in Susanna's mouth. She'd been talking so much she hadn't heard the door open. She glanced at Phoebe's round, frightened eyes and put a finger to her lips. Phoebe nodded her understanding.

"Who's there?" the man bellowed. "You didn't drive a hay wagon into my barn, unhitch your team, and leave. I know you're here."

Susanna covered Phoebe's face with a quilt. If the farmer found them, perhaps he'd believe Susanna was alone, that she'd been on the road, been caught by the storm, and had made a pallet in the shelter of his barn. It was the truth, after all. Just not the complete truth.

"This is the last time I'm asking before I get my new Kentucky rifle," he yelled menacingly. "Who's there?" He was losing whatever patience he had.

Susanna forced her voice out of her throat. "I am."

The sound of a woman's voice must have caught the farmer by surprise because her answer was met by silence. But a few seconds later, she heard footsteps on the rungs of the ladder. A flat-brimmed hat dusted with snow came into view, quickly followed by a white-bearded face.

The farmer lifted his lantern above his head, casting weak light on Susanna's seated form. He frowned at her for several tense seconds then lowered the lantern and descended the ladder.

When she heard the barn door close, Susanna let out the breath she'd been unconsciously holding. He'd seen she was alone, drawn the conclusion she'd hoped for, and had let her be. She laid a hand on top of the quilt. "It's all right," she whispered to the inert form. "I think he's going to let us stay. We won't have to face the snow until tomorrow morning."

Phoebe uncovered her face and struggled to sit up. "Granny said that after I make it to the Quaker settlement, the people there will help me and Tom move all the way to Canada. She said it's mighty cold in Canada. Colder even than Ohio. I guess I'd better get used to being cold."

"Canada can't be cold year round." Susanna searched the basket for the gingerbread. "I bet the spring and summer are beautiful there. I saw a drawing once of a giant waterfall in Canada. It was like a whole river falling off the side of a mountain, and at the bottom plumes of mist rose higher than the trees on the bank."

"That must be a sight to see." Phoebe bit into the sweet bread.

The two women ate in silence, allowing Susanna to hear clearly the sound of the barn door opening. Alarm shot through her heart. Why had the farmer come back? Susanna hastily re-covered Phoebe's head and turned to face the ladder.

It wasn't a scowling, bearded face that rose above the loft but rather an older woman's soft countenance. She placed a lantern on the floor and smiled at Susanna. "Now then," she said softly. "What's this all about?"

Susanna swallowed hard and blurted out her story. The woman listened intently, nodding her head while Susanna explained her journey to the Quaker settlement in Bear Valley, and clucking her tongue in sympathy as Susanna described the blinding storm.

"You poor thing," the woman said. "But what about your companion? My husband said two people needed our help."

Susanna tried to hide her surprise. How had that farmer made out Phoebe's form in the dark loft? "Two people?" she repeated.

The farmer's wife stepped off the ladder and into the loft. "Two plates," she explained, pointing to the pile of bones. "You may have eaten all that chicken by yourself, but you wouldn't have used two plates to do it."

Susanna felt her face redden with mortification. What if her oversight had ruined all of Phoebe's hopes? She got to her feet and forced herself to meet the older woman's eyes.

The farmer's wife touched Susanna's arm. "I see by your bonnet that you're a Quaker."

"My husband's family are Friends," Susanna answered. "I wear the bonnet out of respect for them."

The older woman's eyebrows drew together in a look of confusion. "You're not a Quaker? Is that what you're saying?"

"Yes, but. . .I mean, no. I'm. . ." No one had ever challenged Susanna in this manner. Only those who knew her and the Griffiths knew that Susanna had yet to petition the committee for membership in the Society of Friends.

The farmer's wife patted Susanna's arm. "No matter. I only ask because the fact that you're going to the settlement at Bear Valley with a person you want to keep hidden makes me wonder if you've got a runaway slave hidden beneath those quilts."

Susanna felt her stomach drop to her knees. Had she really made it this far, come so close to delivering Phoebe to safety, only to fail?

"And that bonnet says Quaker whether you deny it or not," the older woman continued. "We know the Quakers at Bear Valley have helped many a runaway before. Plus, a woman needing help would have come straight to the house, not tried to hide in our barn."

Susanna fisted her hands near her heart. She was at the mercy of this woman and her husband. "What are you going to do?"

"Help you inside and bed you down near the fireplace. If the storm has blown itself out by daybreak, my husband and I will put you back on the road."

Unbidden tears sprang into Susanna's eyes. "Oh, thank you," she whispered.

"We are Samuel and Elizabeth Miller, and you are safe with us tonight. Once morning comes, you and your companion will have to be on your way. Alone."

"Yes, thank you," Susanna agreed. A new surge of energy strengthened her legs as she turned to help Phoebe to her feet. Mrs. Miller might think she'd be alone, but Susanna had learned one thing in the last few hours. The Lord was most certainly with her.

◆　◆　◆

Daybreak found Susanna sitting across the kitchen table from Samuel Miller. She'd greeted him cheerfully, even offered to help prepare breakfast, but the farmer continued to glower at her under his white bushy eyebrows.

"There are quite a few snowdrifts on my fields," he said, "and I can't say if the road will be any better. But I dare not allow that runaway to remain on my property much longer."

"I understand," Susanna answered. "We'll be on our way. Can you direct me to another road that will take us to the Quaker settlement?"

"*Humph,*" he said. "It's not much of a road, but it's the only way. There's a network of trails the farmers around here use to drive livestock to market. That'll have to do." He pushed back from the table and reached for his hat and jacket. "Come to the barn when you're ready, and I'll show you the way. My wife and your companion are already there."

"Thank you," Susanna said, but the farmer was gone. *Strange man,* she thought. He'd been willing to let her and Phoebe stay in his house; now he wanted nothing to do with them.

Susanna put on the final layers of her clothing and stepped outside. Pristine snow lay on the ground, and deep drifts bordered the house and barn, but the wind had finally stilled. Glints of sunlight bounced off the crystalline flakes, filling Susanna with a renewed sense of purpose. At least there'd be no storm to fight.

In the barn she found the team hitched to the wagon. Phoebe sat on a nearby bench, smiling. "Today's the day," she announced. "Today I see my Tom. Are you rested and ready to go?"

Susanna's heart warmed at Phoebe's cheerfulness. "I'm ready. But sorry to say you'll have to go back into the hiding spot."

"I know," Phoebe replied. "That don't matter to me. Just give me a hand, and I'll squeeze myself right in."

"Let me help you," Mrs. Miller said, rounding the wagon. "Susanna, I refilled your basket with a few things to eat on the road."

Susanna reached for Mrs. Miller. "Thank you for everything." She squeezed the older woman's hands. "If ever I can repay you—"

"Just take care of yourself," Mrs. Miller interrupted. "There wasn't anyone on the road during last night's storm, but today will be different."

Susanna climbed up the wagon and took her place on the bench. Mr. Miller rode up on a large roan gelding. "I'll go ahead of you. Follow my tracks. If I see anyone who may give you trouble, I'll come back to make sure you're all right. Otherwise, it'd be better for me and Mrs. Miller if no one suspected we traveled together."

He was going to guide her? That was more than she'd expected. Perhaps his stern face masked a gentle heart. "Thank you, Mr. Miller. I appreciate all your kindness."

The farmer gave no response, only darkened his countenance and prodded his horse to move. Susanna looked back to where Mrs. Miller stood alone. The farmer's wife gave a nod, signaling that Phoebe was situated. After lifting her hand in farewell, Susanna drove the horses through the open barn door.

"Thank You for the Millers, Lord," she said as the wagon rumbled along the snow-covered ground. "Thank You for opening their hearts to us."

Chapter 4

Nathan and his father squeezed into the small courtroom on the second floor of the courthouse. Spectators spilled out onto the building's wide porch and to the lawn. Atop the courthouse, a bell tolled eleven times as the judge took his seat and called the court to order. Despite the crowd, the room was silent.

Witnesses and lawyers took turns giving evidence and arguing legal points, but Nathan's mind was on the other side of the Ohio River. If all went well, he'd go home to Susanna soon. How he missed her smile and her warm softness. He couldn't wait to sit by the evening fire and tell her about all he'd seen and done in Kentucky.

"Does thee see how calm Brother Mahan is?" Thomas whispered. "How strong he is in the Lord?"

Nathan refocused his attention on the lawyers. How eloquently they spoke against a citizen of Ohio being tried by a court in Kentucky. Yet their persuasive words did not hide the biggest threat to Nathan's family. If Brother Mahan were found guilty, the Griffiths and all the other abolitionists who helped runaway slaves could be identified and dragged out of the Free States for trials in the South.

Fraudulent trials no doubt, just like this one. Nathan thought of Brother Mahan's wife, Polly. She and the children had also suffered. What if Nathan had to make a decision between what his conscience told him was right and his duty as a husband to protect Susanna? Would he make the right choice?

As so often happened, a Bible verse floated into his mind. *Take therefore no thought for the morrow: for the morrow shall take thought for the things of itself.* Nathan gave silent thanks for the Holy Spirit's comfort. Yes, he'd see this trial through. He'd stand at his father's side, and then go home to his wife.

His lovely wife, safe at home.

◆ ◆ ◆

Susanna followed the gelding's tracks into the rising sun. Why had the Millers been so cautious about letting her and Phoebe stay with them? She knew runaways could sometimes bring huge bounties to the hunters who tracked them, but neither the farmer nor his wife had said a word about fear of discovery.

Of course when Susanna had asked about Phoebe's whereabouts, Mrs. Miller had indicated that the girl was "safe in an upstairs room." Maybe the Millers had a hiding place. That would mean they were part of the network of people who helped runaway slaves and, other than their kindness to two strangers caught in a blizzard, the Millers had given no hint of their involvement.

Susanna turned her face to warm in the winter sunlight. God's creation never ceased to amaze her. A few hours earlier, she'd been fighting freezing wind and biting snow. Now she crossed the placid landscape at an untroubled pace. The route wound through fenced fields that lay under untouched mantles of snow, and although there were high drifts against the fences, the snow on the trail was only a few inches deep. Scattered along the way, heavily laden evergreens huddled in tight groups. On any other day, when she wasn't worried about a runaway slave, Susanna would've enjoyed the drive.

Mr. Miller had ridden so far ahead of her she'd never actually seen him, but his tracks made the course easy to follow. She scanned the trail he'd set for her. His horse's tracks showed a clear route, but a few yards later she pulled her team to a stop.

There was a troubling disturbance in the immaculate snow. Hoofprints led from the tree line to the trail, stomping the snow into violet slush where Mr. Miller's horse had halted. Then what had happened? Susanna urged the horses on a few yards until she saw the single horse's tracks leading away from the slush.

"*Whoa,*" she called to the horses, pulling on the reins. The obedient team halted as Susanna pondered the situation. Evidently, Mr. Miller had been stopped on the road, perhaps hailed by other travelers. He'd gone on, apparently alone. But if that were the case, where were the other travelers?

There were no other tracks. Either the other horses had evaporated into the sky or returned to the tree line from whence they'd come. That meant they were probably still there. A sharp pain darted through Susanna's head, and she rubbed her gloved hand against her forehead. Hadn't Mr. Miller said he'd come back if she were in trouble? Did the fact that he'd ridden ahead mean there was no danger?

Susanna's head dropped to her chest. What should she do? Hadn't she been through enough already? She'd nearly frozen to death the night before, and now just when the way seemed clear, she was forced to make another decision. Go ahead into possible danger, or turn back?

Turn back to where? Not to the Millers' farm. They'd made it clear they weren't willing to risk anything more.

Perhaps she could unhitch one of the horses and ride it to the settlement. She'd be faster on horseback, perhaps fast enough to outrun whatever trouble pursued her. And once she was among the Friends, one or more of them could return with her to the wagon.

But that would mean leaving Phoebe alone. Besides, she had no saddle for the horse, and she hadn't ridden bareback since she'd been a little girl. Images of galloping past villainous bounty hunters faded as reality took hold. If Susanna tried to outrace any pursuers, she'd end up on her bottom in the snow.

Susanna examined the single horse's tracks that led away from the slushy mess. Her imagination was running away with her. Obviously, Mr. Miller had been stopped by someone and then ridden on alone. That he hadn't returned to warn her could mean only one thing: she had nothing to worry about.

Susanna flicked the reins across the horses' backs, and the wagon pulled ahead. They'd only traversed a few yards when two riders dashed from the tree line, their horses sending white plumes into the air as hooves crunched on snow. The lead rider blocked the trail, forcing Susanna's horses to stop while the other man paused beside the wagon.

He was a heavyset man dressed in a blue duster. He touched the brim of his hat in greeting. "Morning, ma'am. How are you this fine morning?"

His friendly tone didn't fool Susanna. While one hand held his horse's reins, the other rested on the rifle laid across his saddle.

The second rider, a lean man with a sweat-stained hat, moved to the opposite side of the wagon. "Seems as though she don't much want to talk to you, Baxter."

The first rider smiled again. "Is that right, ma'am? You don't want to talk to me?"

It was one thing to be stopped by these men, but another to be toyed with—like a cat with its prey. "What do you want?" Susanna asked.

"So you do have a voice," Baxter said, a tobacco-stained smile crossing his face. "See there, Jamison? She ain't scared of me."

Jamison moved his jacket so that Susanna could see the pistol he'd shoved into his waistband. "I guess she's not," he replied.

Were they thieves? Bounty hunters? Only men determined to cause trouble carried pistols. Susanna put iron into her voice. "I repeat. What do you want?"

Baxter stood in his stirrups and leaned toward her. "I'll tell you what we want." His words were ripe with menace. "We want to know what you've got in that wagon."

Susanna adopted a casual air and looked over her shoulder then frowned at Baxter in a pretense of confusion. "Hay, of course."

Jamison laughed loudly. "Guess she told you." He threw his voice into a falsetto and imitated her. "Hay, of course."

Baxter wasn't amused. "I see by your bonnet that you're a Quaker. Bet you're on your way to that Quaker settlement in Bear Valley."

Susanna bristled at his intimidation. "What business is it of yours?"

Jamison let out another bark of laughter. "You've got yourself a hot one there, Baxter. Maybe *you* should be scared of *her*."

Baxter ignored his partner's outburst. "It's what's under the hay that interests me, ma'am. You see, we know Quakers like to hide runaway slaves any way they can. And a wagon big as this one, loaded with all that hay. . . Why, I'm thinking there could be at least four or five grown men hidden in there."

Susanna straightened, preparing herself to take on whatever trouble these men hurled. "No men are hidden in that hay," she asserted.

Baxter scratched the back of his head, pushing his hat low across his forehead. "I've heard that Quakers consider it a sin to tell a lie, but I don't think I quite believe you. It's awfully strange for a woman to be driving a hay wagon all by herself. Where's your man?"

Although she'd been trying to deny her fear, dread settled in the pit of Susanna's stomach. These men were bounty hunters. If they found Phoebe, who knew where they'd stop in their desire to punish those who aided the runaways?

"No answer, eh?" Baxter sneered at her. "Jamison, you awake over there?"

"Yes, boss."

"Go to the back, and light that hay on fire. Then we'll just sit back and wait for the slaves to jump out."

Fire? Alarm joined the dread in Susanna's belly. The fire could easily destroy the wagon and the hay. The thought of Phoebe trapped in the smoke and flames, burned alive or suffocated by the smoke, gave rise to a new level of terror.

Jamison dismounted and walked to the back of the wagon. Although Susanna couldn't see him, she heard the flint striking steel and knew she had only seconds to act. What should she do?

Drive ahead? No. There was no way her heavy wagon could outrun these men's horses. Where was Mr. Miller? Why hadn't he come back to help?

Baxter moved his horse to the rear of the wagon. "What's wrong?" he asked the other bounty hunter. "Don't tell me you can't light a fire."

"You know I can," Jamison answered. "But it's not so easy with wet hay."

Baxter climbed off his horse. "Give me that," he ordered. "I'll do it."

This is my chance, Susanna thought. With both men on the ground, she'd have a few moments to act before they could remount and chase her. The sickening smell of smoke wafted from the back of the wagon. How could she protect Phoebe?

She scanned the trail, desperately seeking a solution.

Then she saw the answer.

Susanna yelled and snapped the reins hard, forcing the team to pull quickly. The horses whinnied and flattened their ears as smoke reached their noses, but they obeyed her command.

It would be difficult to convince the team to do what she wanted, but perhaps the smoke would confuse them enough to go against their natural instincts. She snapped the reins harder, and the animals picked up speed.

Behind her, she heard the men cursing and undoubtedly struggling to mount. She dared not look back. With another sharp snap of the reins, she drove the horses straight into a snowdrift.

The horses struggled to pull away but Susanna held the reins. "Whoa," she called. "Easy, now. Easy." She tied the reins to the bench and peered down the side of the wagon. *Yes!* She'd buried the secret compartment in the snow. That should protect Phoebe from both fire and smoke.

Without a second's hesitation, Susanna crawled over the bench to the top of the hay mound. She grabbed the pitchfork and tossed the burning clumps of hay onto the surrounding snow. *Hold on, Phoebe,* she pleaded silently. *Just hold on.*

Baxter and Jamison rode toward the wagon, the leaner man laughing and slapping his hat on his thigh. "What do you think you're doing, you crazy Quaker?" Baxter yelled. "You're going to get yourself burnt to a crisp."

Susanna ignored the men. From her spot on top of the load, she could see what the bounty hunters couldn't. The hay, still damp from the previous night's snow, was smoking more than burning, and the dry hay near the wagon's floor was packed too tightly to get enough air to burn. If she could remove the few patches of smoldering hay, she'd reduce the possibility of Phoebe taking in too much smoke.

Baxter used his rifle to nudge Jamison. "Get up there and help her."

Jamison stopped laughing. "What? Have you lost your mind, too?"

"You heard me," the heavyset man said. "Since the hay's too wet to burn good, get up there and help her throw it all out."

"I ain't no farmhand," Jamison argued. A look passed between the men. Then Jamison dismounted and, muttering beneath his breath, climbed to the top of the mound. He snatched the pitchfork from Susanna's hands. "Get down," he commanded. "Get out of here so I can find the runaways you're trying so hard to save."

She hesitated. Should she cooperate or stand up to the bounty hunter? If he emptied the wagon, he'd prove there were no slaves beneath the hay. Then perhaps the two men would let her go on her way.

Jamison lowered his head to within an inch of hers and snarled, "Get off this wagon right now, or I'll throw you off."

She should be frightened. Any woman who knew what was good for her would be trembling by now. But other than her fear for Phoebe's survival, the only thing Susanna felt was anger.

Gathering her dignity around her like an invisible cloak, Susanna turned her back on the scoundrel and climbed down the wagon. When she was out of the way, Baxter took her place and began throwing armfuls of hay onto the snow. What would the bounty hunters do when they discovered there were no runaways in her wagon? Would they simply leave, or would they take out their disappointment on her?

Susanna stood by the horses as hay spurted from the wagon like water from a spring. There was only one thing left to do.

She knelt in the snow, closed her eyes, and folded her hands in front of her chest. "Dear Lord," she prayed, "I've been taught that every man is illuminated by the divine Light of Christ. Use that Light, O Lord, to help Mr. Baxter and Mr. Jamison look into their consciences. Give them the strength to overcome the darkness that prods them to do these wicked deeds. Help them to know the grace of God, which can bring salvation to their lives, no matter the depth of their sins."

Susanna opened her eyes. Both men stared down at her.

Baxter removed his hat and scowled at her. "Are you praying?"

"I am," Susanna said firmly.

"Are you praying for us?"

"Yes," she said.

Baxter climbed down the wagon and yanked Susanna to her feet. "Stop it! I don't need nobody praying for me. Nobody!"

Susanna met his scowl with a patient gaze.

Baxter pivoted and called up to the other man. "Can you touch the bottom with that pitchfork?"

Jamison stuck the tool through the hay in several spots then repeated the action down the length of the wagon. "Seems as though she was telling the truth, boss. Nothing in this wagon but hay."

Baxter glared at Susanna. "Burn it. No Quaker's going to pray for me and get away with it." He strode to his horse.

Susanna returned to her knees.

"Did you hear me?" Baxter yelled. "Burn it!"

Jamison climbed down and mounted his horse. "No."

Baxter's face darkened. "Why, you worthless skunk. I knew you'd be no good when the going got tough. Get out of my way, and I'll burn it."

"No, boss. Nobody's going to burn this lady's wagon. And nobody's going to harm one hair on her head. What we've got here is a fine Christian lady who's done nothing wrong. She told us there weren't any slaves under the hay, and there aren't. So now we're going to go back to the tree where we tied that farmer then go on about our business."

Mr. Miller! The bounty hunters had ambushed him.

Baxter cursed loudly and spurred his horse. "This is quits for us," he yelled over his shoulder as he rode away.

"Good riddance!" Jamison shouted.

Susanna watched the bounty hunter's blue duster disappear into the dense forest.

Jamison walked toward Susanna, the pitchfork resting on his shoulder. "My mama used to pray for me. Course, it didn't do any good, but. . ."

Susanna stood. "If she could see you now, Mr. Jamison, I believe she'd be proud."

The man ducked his head, his face flooding with color. "I don't know about that, ma'am." He walked toward the wagon, stopped, and turned back to Susanna. "Let's get this wagon out of the snow and the hay reloaded. We've got a farmer to rescue. I don't imagine his horse went far without him. He'll probably need a ride."

◆　◆　◆

The sun was straight above Susanna's head by the time she arrived at the settlement. It didn't take long for her to identify the meetinghouse. Following Eli's instructions, she stopped the wagon in front of the building and waited for someone to come.

A trio of men approached. "Good day, Friend," they called.

"Good day, Friends," Susanna said. "I'm looking for Mr. Freeman. Can you help me?"

The men exchanged gazes, and the oldest of the three came closer. "If thee will allow me to join thee on the bench, I would be glad to drive thy wagon to Friend Freeman's barn."

This was the reply she'd been expecting. Eli had told her of the secret signal for communicating the presence of a runaway slave needing help. Once she'd uttered the name *Freeman*, the men of the settlement knew of her precious cargo. "Of course." She moved to allow room for the man to join her.

"I am Abner Larson." He took the reins and guided the horses away from the cluster of houses.

"My name is Susanna Griffith. My brother-in-law, Eli Wilson, sent me here."

Mr. Larson's shoulders visibly relaxed. "Oh yes. Eli. He has been here many times. Usually Brother Eli comes with Nathan Griffith. Be you Nathan's wife?"

Susanna felt her spirit lift at the mention of Nathan. "I am."

"How long has thee been on the road, sister?"

"One night. Do you know Samuel Miller, a farmer who lives about two hours west of here?"

"I know him. He used to help many a poor soul seeking shelter. His son was badly injured by those who would keep the slave in shackles, and the Millers declined to help any longer."

That explained it. When he'd seen the settlement buildings, Mr. Miller had bid her farewell and turned his horse toward home.

"Why does thee ask about the Millers?" Mr. Larson asked.

"They helped me last night when I was caught in the blizzard."

"Thee was out in that terrible storm? Many a good man has been lost in blinding snow like that. Thank the Lord the Millers helped thee. Was the rest of thy journey smooth?"

Susanna almost laughed. *Smooth* wasn't a word she'd use to describe her encounter with the bounty hunters.

Mr. Larson listened as she told of the scoundrels who had tried to burn the hay. "Sister Griffith!" he exclaimed when she finished. "That was certainly quick thinking on thy part. As it says in the book of James, the prayer of the righteous is powerful and effective. Seems as though the Lord used thee to remind the rogue of Christ's goodness that lives in us all. But why does thee travel alone? Could not Brother Eli or Brother Nathan make the trip?"

Susanna explained the circumstances of her solitary journey. When she told Mr. Larson about Phoebe's imminent delivery, he blanched and prodded the horses to move faster. Soon they arrived at a farmhouse surrounded by tall spruce trees. The wagon wheels had barely stopped moving when a group of men and women hurried from the house and nearby barn.

How good it was to be among Friends again. The women's white caps and the men's broad-brimmed black hats convinced Susanna she'd finally arrived safely. But what about Phoebe? Susanna hadn't dared to stop and check on the girl for fear that other bounty hunters could be spying on her.

A pair of strong arms lifted Susanna off the wagon, and she hurried to the back. Two men had removed the partition and were helping Phoebe slide out of the compartment. Susanna rushed to her side. "We made it, Phoebe. We're here at last. Are you all right?"

Tears streamed down Phoebe's face. "Am I free?" she whispered hoarsely. "Am I free?"

"Yes, Phoebe. You're free."

Phoebe wrapped her arms around her abdomen. "Oh, Lord! Thank You, Lord. Thank You, Jesus. My baby will never be a slave. Thank You, Lord."

Susanna's vision blurred as tears filled her eyes. She'd be willing to endure much more than a blizzard to feel the way she did at that moment.

"Where's my Tom?" Phoebe asked. "Do any of you know my husband, Tom? He came from the Hansen farm in Bracken County, Kentucky. Please, where's my Tom?"

Heads turned as the Friends muttered among themselves. When the conversation abated, Mr. Larson spoke for the group. "Is thy husband a tall man with a scar across his right cheek?"

"Yes," Phoebe answered. "Where is he? Where's my husband?"

"He is on a neighboring farm, only a few miles away. We will send for him." Mr. Larson gestured to a petite woman in a blue dress. "This is my wife. She will take care of thee."

Mrs. Larson came to Phoebe's side. "I fear that thy pains have already started. Am I right?"

Pains? Had Phoebe been in the first stages of delivering her child while she'd been stuffed in that stifling compartment?

"Yes, ma'am." Phoebe took a few steps and bent at the waist, her hands on her knees. "I didn't know the pains would be so strong. Granny told me the first hours of childbearing were the easiest."

"Come into the house," Mrs. Larson said, "and we will make thee comfortable. And do not worry about a thing. Many a baby has been born on this farm."

A look of uncertainty shadowed Phoebe's face, and she looked questioningly at Susanna. "It's all right," Susanna said reassuringly. "No one's going to hurt you or your baby. And your husband will be here soon."

Phoebe looked at the surrounding women then turned pleading eyes to Susanna. "Will you stay with me, ma'am? At least until my Tom comes?"

The Griffiths were expecting Susanna to return that very day. If she left within the hour, she'd be home by late afternoon. Phoebe's hand lightly touched Susanna's. "Please, ma'am?"

The poor girl. After what she'd been through the last few days, who could blame Phoebe for needing someone she knew to stay close? Susanna covered Phoebe's hand with her own. "Of course," she replied.

Chapter 5

Nathan and his father slowed their horses to a walk. "We'll be home soon," Thomas said. "No need to work the horses into a lather just to get there a few minutes earlier."

"I know thee is right, but I long to be home."

"Perhaps thee is missing thy wife." Thomas grinned teasingly.

"I find no shame in admitting it. Letters have been small comfort."

"I believe we were right to go to Mason County. Once again we have witnessed the truth behind the Lord's words: 'All things work together for good to them that love God.' I will never forget the silence of the courtroom when the jury pronounced Brother Mahan not guilty. Not even Judge Reid had the temerity to issue one of his lengthy philosophical statements."

"And the way Reverend Mahan stood motionless and stared silently at the judge. He was like a prophet of old, daring the nonbeliever to deny the power of the Lord."

"Brother Mahan will be home soon. His health is not good, but a few weeks at home will surely cure him."

They pulled their horses to a stop at the top of the hill. From that spot Nathan could see the Griffiths' farm and house.

"Smoke is coming out of the chimney," he said, "and the horses are in the pasture. Seems as though everything's right enough."

"Yes," Thomas said. "But does thee see that smoke rising from the woods to the west?"

Nathan squinted in the direction his father had indicated. "Someone's made camp."

"Someone who wants to keep an eye on us. It is just as Brother Jackson told us. Bounty hunters so brazen, they have trespassed onto our property."

Apprehension squeezed Nathan's heart. He'd been wrong to leave his wife alone with rascals camping two hundred yards away from their cabin. "I need to go on, Father. After I've checked on Susanna, I'll bring her to the house."

Thomas nodded, and Nathan turned his horse toward the sheltered spot where he'd built the cabin for his wife. The weeks he'd spent in Kentucky seemed like months. Now that Brother Mahan was finally free from the awful jail, perhaps Nathan's life could return to its normal routine.

Nathan spurred his horse into a trot, a pace that matched his own heartbeat. He'd done what he could to keep in touch with his family, but nothing could replace the feel of his wife in his arms. Once they were safely reunited, he'd hold Susanna until his arms ached from the pleasure of it.

When the cabin came into view, Nathan smiled broadly. One second later, the smile withered into a concerned frown. There was no smoke coming from the chimney. Even if Susanna had left for a few hours, he should be able to smell wood smoke from the banked coals. He scanned the meadow where his horses grazed during fair-weather days; it was empty. Even the barnyard was bare, devoid of the ever-present chickens that spent the day scratching for bugs and seeds.

The cabin was a lifeless shell. A pain shot through Nathan's jaw as he realized something was seriously wrong. He fought the dreadful images that besieged his mind, holding panic at bay while he dismounted and ran into the cabin.

The cabin's single room was neat. The bed linens were arranged perfectly, and clean dishes had been placed on the shelves. Susanna's clothes hung from the pegs he'd driven into the wall, but her jacket, cape, and bonnet were missing.

Nathan forced air into his lungs. The orderliness of the cabin told him no one had broken in, and the absence of Susanna's outer garments pointed to the fact that she'd simply left.

Where was she?

Gradually Nathan's breath slowed, and his heartbeat resumed a normal rate. As his body relaxed, logic reappeared in his troubled mind. Susanna had probably gone to stay with his mother and sister in his absence. It was too much to expect a young woman, married for only five months, to live alone for three weeks.

Nathan stepped outside and started down the trail that led to his parents' house. Halfway there, his mother met him.

"Praise the Lord, thee has returned safely." Martha threw her arms around his neck.

"It's good to see thee, Mother." Nathan stepped back from her embrace and scanned the trail. "Where's Susanna? Isn't she with thee?"

Martha squeezed Nathan's hand in hers. "I have something to tell thee, son."

◆ ◆ ◆

Nathan paced back and forth in front of the kitchen fireplace while his family watched. "I can't believe thee let her go," he said through clenched teeth. "Especially thee, Eli. Thee knows what could happen to Susanna if she's discovered."

Miriam stood to face her brother. "We've explained the circumstances of Susanna's journey. She was the only one of us who could go. Thee must not blame my husband."

When his wife was safely home, Nathan would apologize to whomever he'd offended. For the moment, he had no patience for politeness. "I'll be leaving within the hour. I need to change horses and pack provisions."

"Leaving?" Martha asked. "Where is thee going?"

"After Susanna of course. There's only one road to the Friends' settlement in Bear Valley. I'm sure to meet her on the way."

"That would not be wise," Thomas said.

Nathan spun on his heel, ready to dispute his father's words. "Now thee speaks of wisdom? No one considered what was wise when they sent my wife on a perilous journey."

Thomas's eyebrows rose, and Nathan knew his tone had been impertinent. His father answered with calm deliberation. "I agree that thee should go. Not only for Susanna's sake but for thy own. I advise thee to wait until darkness falls. If the bounty hunters see thee leave, they are likely to follow. And that would put Susanna in greater jeopardy. We cannot know for sure that Susanna has delivered her special guest."

Nathan's shoulders slumped. Although he was anxious to find his wife and bring her back to the safety of their cabin, he knew his father was right. His hands fisted at his side. "This is my fault." His jaw tightened.

"No, son. Susanna chose to make this trip, and we must honor the call she heard."

"I thought I could keep Susanna away from the danger. If anything happens to her—" Nathan covered his face with his hand and turned away from his family. He fought to maintain his composure, but his mother's gentle hand on his shoulder almost undid him.

"We have been in constant prayer for Susanna since she drove away," she said soothingly. "We will continue, without ceasing, until she returns."

Nathan's body longed to move, to mount a fresh horse and search for his wife. The muscles in his jaw clenched and unclenched as his good sense battled against his instincts. He'd pledged to protect Susanna. Was prayer really the only thing he could do? He looked at the earnest, placid faces of his sister and parents. They'd found comfort in the Lord, but Nathan's fretfulness would not allow him to be still.

"I'll pray," Nathan said. "But it will be outside where I can watch for the first sight of my wife."

◆　◆　◆

Susanna sat by Phoebe's bed, wiping beads of perspiration from the girl's face and counting the minutes until Tom arrived. Susanna couldn't listen anymore to Phoebe's moans. Susanna had helped with births before, but nothing in her experience had prepared her for Phoebe's screams.

The midwife took no heed of Phoebe's distress. "It's a big baby and a little mother," she explained. "But there's no need to worry. Everything's moving right on schedule."

Phoebe blew out a long breath and relaxed her grip on the bedclothes. "I guess it won't be much longer before I'll be seeing my son."

Realizing the girl must be in between pains, Susanna refilled a cup with cool water. "You think it's a boy?"

"Must be. The way he's been kicking, and the fight he's putting up just to get out and see the world. . . Why, it must be a boy."

"What will you name him?"

Phoebe drained the cup and returned it to Susanna. "Tom, of course, after his daddy."

"And if it's a girl?"

Phoebe raised her eyebrows. "A girl? I hadn't much thought about girl names."

"Children are often named after grandparents. What is your mother's name?"

"Oh ma'am, I don't know that. For as long as I can remember, there's just been Granny. She says my mama was sold shortly after I was weaned, and nobody knows who my daddy was. Granny took me in."

The image of a slave woman forced to abandon her child burned into Susanna's mind. That explained why Phoebe had risked her life and her baby's life to reach freedom. No one would separate Phoebe from her baby the way a cow was separated from a calf.

The midwife returned with clean linen. "There's someone here to see you," she said, smiling broadly.

For a second Susanna didn't know if the woman addressed her or Phoebe, but when a tall, dark man rushed into the room, Phoebe gave a shout of joy.

"Tom! Oh Tom!" They embraced, and tears of joy streamed down the young girl's cheeks. "I made it, Tom," Phoebe said, between chortles of laughter. "I made it just in time."

Tom did not respond, only tightened his hold on his wife.

Susanna took the opportunity to slip away and search for the Larsons. She found the farmer with another man, emptying the Griffiths' hay wagon. Mrs. Larson stood nearby.

"How fares our guest?" the man asked.

"The midwife says the baby will come soon. I didn't know you had need of the hay."

"Yes, Sister Griffith. That's the way thy husband and I have arranged the passage. Those who watch the roads see a load of hay headed north and an empty wagon headed south. I sell the hay for thy family. In fact, when thee returns tomorrow, I have a bag of coins to send with thee."

"Thank you, but I wish to begin my journey now. My responsibility to Phoebe has been discharged, and my husband's family expects me today."

"No, sister. Stay thee the night. Tomorrow morning Friend Jacobson and his son will escort thee to your home."

"I'd rather go while the good weather holds. It's only four hours to the Griffiths' farm. If I leave now, I'll be home just after dark."

Mrs. Larson spoke for the first time. "'Tis not wise to travel the roads at night, sister. I know thee undertook the journey in the dark, but that could not be helped. Thy way home will be much safer."

"Besides," Mr. Larson added, "Brother Jacobson and his son cannot leave until morning. Although we could not offer thee our protection yesterday, we most certainly will tomorrow."

There was no way they could force her to stay. If she had to, she could hitch the horses to the wagon by herself and make the journey on her own.

Mrs. Larson laid a hand on Susanna's arm, startling her from her thoughts. "Thy mind is easy to read, sister. Thy face shows quite clearly what thee is considering.

And thee is correct. My husband and I will not force thee to stay. But thee risked so much to come, why prolong that risk by returning tonight?"

"My husband's family will be worried if I don't return tonight."

"Better a sleepless night followed by a morning of rejoicing than months of grief, should any harm come to thee."

While Susanna paused to consider her options, Mrs. Larson guided her out of the barn and toward the house. Susanna tossed one last look over her shoulder at the Griffiths' hay wagon. Although the Larsons' persuasion had been gentle, they'd made the decision for her. She'd be going home the next morning.

◆　◆　◆

A band of pale peach light rose above the trees, changing the black sky to violet when Susanna knocked softly at Phoebe's door. She knew the girl must be exhausted, yet she craved one last look at the beautiful baby born in the wee hours of the morning.

"Come in," Phoebe said.

"I don't want to disturb you," Susanna said, entering the room. "I wanted to say good-bye."

Phoebe held out a hand, and Susanna sat on the edge of the bed. "Oh ma'am. How am I ever going to finish saying thank you? Because of you, my baby was born free. She'll never be a slave. I'll never have to watch her being carted away to another farm far away from me." Phoebe patted the child cradled in her arms.

Susanna used her finger to lift the baby's tiny, fisted hand. "She's so beautiful. Have you and Tom thought of a name yet?"

"We came up with the best name in the world for this little girl. We're going to call her Liberty Susanna."

Susanna felt the warmth as it rushed into her cheeks and knew she must be blushing. "Oh Phoebe. You didn't name her. . .I mean, you didn't call her Susanna because. . ."

"Of course we did, ma'am. My baby and I owe everything to you. Our lives, our freedom, our whole future. Tom says that once I'm able to travel, we'll be on the road to Canada. He says your friends have a town there where the freed slaves live and work. It'll just be wonderful, don't you think? Me and Tom and Libby?"

Susanna raised the baby's hand to her lips and kissed it. "Hello, Libby. You're a lucky little girl to have such a brave mama."

"I don't know about that, ma'am. From what you told me, sounds like you had to face some mighty big wolves along the way. All I had to do was lie quietly in the bottom of a wagon."

"But my adventure's over." Susanna tucked the baby's hand under its blanket. "I'll be back home in a few hours." The rumble of men's voices carried up the stairs. "In fact, that's probably my escort. Two Friends are going to accompany me this morning."

Phoebe squeezed Susanna's hand. "I hope I get to see you again someday, ma'am. I hope you'll get to see Libby when she's all grown up and beautiful. Won't that be the day? When my little girl can go anywhere she wants and not be afraid of slavers trying to catch her?"

"I pray that day comes soon."

Heavy footsteps trod up the stairs and stopped at Phoebe's door. "Susanna?" Mrs. Larson called. "Are you there?"

"Yes. Come in."

The door swung open, and Susanna's heart bounded for joy. There, in the doorway, stood her husband. "Nathan!" She shot off the bed and into his arms.

Nathan's arms tightened around her, and his lips brushed her hair. Tears filled Susanna's eyes as she lifted silent thanks for his safe return.

"*Shh.*" Nathan wiped away her tears with his thumb. "No need to cry. Everything's all right now."

"I know," Susanna whispered, her throat tight. "I know." She breathed deeply, inhaling the scent of her husband, and her worries evaporated. Nathan was safe and well.

His work-hardened hands cupped her face, lifting her gaze to his. "What's this I hear about a blizzard, two bounty hunters, a fire, and a runaway?"

Susanna ducked her head in embarrassment. Was Nathan angry? How did he know everything?

"Friend Larson told me all about thy trip when I found him at the meetinghouse," Nathan said. "I believe thee will have quite a story to tell on the way home."

Was that a smile Susanna heard in her husband's voice? Susanna glanced at Nathan's face and saw love and approval beaming from his eyes. She laid her head on his chest and rejoiced to feel his arms tighten around her once again.

The whimper of a baby caused Nathan to ease back from Susanna. "May I meet our special guest?"

Susanna took his hand and led him to the bed. "Nathan, this is Phoebe and her daughter, Liberty."

"Liberty Susanna." Phoebe moved the blanket away from the baby's face.

Nathan smiled down at his wife. "Good name."

◆　　◆　　◆

The piercing crow of the rooster woke Susanna, but she didn't have to wonder where her husband was. His arm held her tightly against him under the quilts. After an evening of celebrating her safe return with Nathan's family, the exhausted couple had returned to their cabin and stumbled into bed.

Nathan's lips on her head let Susanna know he no longer slept. "Good morning, Wife," he said, yawning. "Did thee sleep well?"

"Very well. It's good to have you home again."

"It's good to be home."

A noise caused Susanna to rise up on one elbow. "Someone's in the barnyard."

"Is there?" Nathan yawned again.

"You know there is." Susanna narrowed her eyes. "Why aren't you concerned?"

"It's only Eli. He agreed to tend the stock one more day so we could rest. Lie down again so I may talk to thee."

Susanna nestled her head on her husband's shoulder. "You were mighty quiet yesterday when I told you everything that happened on the way to Bear Valley. Now that you've had time to think about it, I'm afraid of what you have to say."

"Afraid, Susanna? Of me?"

"No, Nathan. Never. But I fear you will chastise me for the risk I took, and if truth be told, I can't wait to do it again."

Nathan's fingers stroked Susanna's hair, the seconds ticking away in silence. Susanna had pledged to obey her husband, and if he forbade her from helping the runaways, she'd have no choice but to abide by his decision. Yet her experience with Phoebe had given her a purpose she'd never imagined. She could no longer simply look the other way.

Nathan's fingers stilled. "Thee would risk thy life again to help another runaway?"

Susanna rose to one elbow and looked into her husband's dark eyes. "Don't you risk your life when you go?"

"Not as much as thee did. A woman traveling alone can be a lure for evil men. Does thee know what losing thee would mean to me? My heart would never heal from such a loss."

Susanna's heart warmed at her husband's words. "Nor would mine if I lost you. The weeks without you were the loneliest of my life. I've come to love your mother and sister as though they were my own family, but they were no substitute for you."

Nathan sat up and frowned at Susanna. "As your husband, I have the right to forbid thee from helping the runaways."

The very words Susanna had dreaded. But her husband's serious expression didn't deter her. "Don't the Friends believe that men and women are created equal in the eyes of God?"

"Thee speaks of the testimony of equality, and I do my best to be a witness to that belief. But how can I fulfill my pledge to protect thee if thee refuses to keep thyself away from danger?"

"It wouldn't always be as dangerous as it was with Phoebe. Eli and your father both said Phoebe's situation was unusual. And your sister told me runaways sometimes stay several days until suitable passage can be arranged."

"That's true."

"So it's unlikely that I'll ever be in such a dangerous circumstance again."

"Perhaps," Nathan muttered between clenched teeth.

Susanna rose to her knees and faced her husband. "I want to be your equal, Nathan. Knowing that I helped Phoebe and her baby made me feel as though I could fly. Don't ask me to give up such a wonderful mission. Until slavery is banished from this country, I want to be at your side, fighting it every step of the way."

Nathan took Susanna's hands in his and spoke in a soft tone. "Thee speaks more like a Friend every day. Has thee thought more about petitioning the committee for admittance?"

"I know your mother wants me to join. I've adopted the bonnet, and I enjoy going to First Day Meetings. But you said you'd give me all the time I needed."

"And I intend to keep my word. Now that thee wishes to enlist in the Quaker struggle against slavery, I thought that perhaps thee was ready to join."

"I love your family, Nathan, and I love you. But taking that last step. . .throwing off my family's traditions and taking up yours. . .oh, I don't know what's holding me back."

Susanna looked away from her husband's piercing gaze. He wanted her to join his faith. Was that so awful? If she did take that last step, if she did take up the title of Quaker, would he allow her to aid the runaways who came to the Griffiths for help?

"Nathan." Her words struggled past the lump in her throat. "Do you want me to become a Quaker?"

"That is a question that only thee and thy soul can answer, Susanna. If the Holy Spirit moves thee to join the Society, then I will be glad."

She swallowed and looked at her husband. "And if I never join?"

"Then we will continue as we are. Surely thee knows my love does not hinge on thee becoming a Friend."

Susanna blew out a breath. How good Nathan was. How blessed she was to have a husband who loved the Lord and who loved her. Yet the question remained unanswered. "If I petition the committee for admittance, then will you allow me to help you when the runaways come?"

Nathan laid his cheek in his hand and studied her. After a long silence, he finally spoke. "I will not prevent thee from helping, Susanna. If thee feels moved to do something to help the runaways or to put an end to the abomination of slavery, I will not forbid it. But Susanna, thee must allow me to guide thee in these matters. My family has helped in this cause for many years. Tread softly, Wife, and take the counsel of those who know the dangers."

Susanna threw her arms around her husband's neck, and he fell back on the pillows, his laughter ringing through the cabin. "Hold on there, Wife, or thee will send us both to the cold floor!"

Susanna snuggled against him, returning her head to his shoulder. "Thank you, Nathan."

Nathan's arms surrounded her. "I do not believe that thee is the same wife I left three weeks ago."

"Of course I am. Who else would I be?"

"'Tis true thy name is still Susanna Griffith, but thee is not the girl I left. I know thee chafed at being left alone. Yet I returned to find a woman prepared to take on the worst atrocity known to mankind. Mother says thee has grown up."

Susanna recalled her pouting and sulking. Had it been only a few days ago that she'd been tempted to brood in the mire of self-pity? She felt her face flush with embarrassment and covered her face with the sheet. "I hope Mother Griffith will forgive me."

"Worry not," Nathan said. "In fact, while thee was telling everyone about thy adventure last night, Mother told me that she and Father have decided they will celebrate Christmas."

Susanna's head popped back up. "Really? Won't they get in trouble?"

"Of course not. Our Meeting leaves matters such as these to each person's conscience. Mother says we will exchange gifts and have a family dinner. Is there more we should do?"

"No! I mean, that would be wonderful. My family goes to church on Christmas morning, and there are traditional songs—"

"I can't promise any singing, Susanna. Thee knows how the Friends feel about music. But if thee wants to sing. . ."

"No! I mean. . . It doesn't matter. If I feel a Christmas carol coming on, I'll go to the barn and sing to the animals. How about that?"

Nathan held her chin in his fingers. "Would thee sing to the animals and not to me? Let me know of thy intention, and I'll escort thee to the lucky animals that get to hear thy voice lifted in song."

Laughter bubbled up from her heart. Helping Phoebe had tested Susanna, and she'd passed the test. All of her fears and worries had been for naught. Phoebe was on her way to safety, Nathan was home, and she could continue to help the fugitive slaves. "Oh Nathan." Susanna flung her arms around his neck. "Thee is so good to me."

Gingerbread Cookies

(from Colonial Williamsburg, Virginia)

1 cup sugar
2 teaspoons ginger
1 teaspoon nutmeg
1 teaspoon cinnamon
1½ teaspoons baking soda
½ teaspoon salt
1 cup melted butter
½ cup evaporated milk
1 cup unsulfured molasses
¾ teaspoon vanilla
¾ teaspoon lemon extract
4 cups stone-ground or unbleached flour, unsifted

Combine sugar, ginger, nutmeg, cinnamon, baking soda, and salt. Mix well. Add melted butter, evaporated milk, and molasses. Add extracts. Mix well. Add flour 1 cup at a time, stirring constantly. Dough should be stiff enough to handle without sticking to fingers. Knead dough for a smoother texture. Add up to ½ cup additional flour if necessary to prevent sticking. When dough is smooth, roll out to ¼-inch thick on floured surface and cut into cookies. Bake on floured or greased cookie sheets in preheated 375 degree oven for 10 to 12 minutes. Gingerbread cookies are done when they spring back when touched.

After many years of writing and publishing in the nonfiction world of academia, **Claire Sanders** turned her energy, humor, and creativity toward the production of compelling romantic fiction. Claire lives in the greater Houston area with her daughter and two well-loved dogs. When she isn't writing, you'll find her cooking, gardening, and dreaming of places to travel.

Abigail's Christmas Candles

by Anna Schmidt

Chapter 1

I f you ask me, the elders made a poor choice for the teaching position. She may be the bishop's niece, still. . ."

Two local women who had just left the local butcher shop were speaking in low but audible tones as Abigail Yoder passed. Their starched white prayer caps were covered by felt bonnets anchored under their double chins with black fabric ties. Abigail nodded politely, although what she really wanted to do was let them know that they might as well have spoken in their normal voices. Since her arrival in the small Mennonite community of Hope, Wisconsin, she had grown used to the gossip that followed her everywhere. As someone from a similar, if larger, Mennonite community in the lake country of northern New York, she understood that she was viewed as different, and in the Mennonite world, different was not something to which one aspired. Conformity was the rule of the day. One did not stand out either by dress, by speech, or by deed. She had taken great care to wear the dresses her aunt had sewn for her to replace the three dresses she had brought with her. Her own clothes were plain by New York standards, but apparently in Wisconsin, they were viewed as tantamount to ball gowns. As her aunt had explained, the fabric was a finer weave, giving the garment a softer drape from the homespun dresses worn by their neighbors and therefore setting her apart.

She had moved to Wisconsin because her mother was convinced that Abigail's uncle Oscar, and his wife, Beulah, were getting "up in years," as she liked to say. And since the couple had not been blessed with children, her mother insisted that Abigail go to them and fulfill the role that a grown daughter might. "Just look at his last letter," her mother said. "The village is in need of a teacher—a position your Aunt Beulah is perfectly suited for. Yet according to this"—she waved the letter at Abigail—"Beulah does not wish to teach. That is my brother's way of saying she is in poor health."

"Nonsense," Uncle Oscar had roared when he and Aunt Beulah met Abigail at the train station and she repeated her mother's concerns about their health. "Indeed, I wrote your mother that we were in need of help. Now that the harvest is in, the time has come for the children to return to class. What we need is a teacher, not a nursemaid. Your last letter indicated a certain restlessness with your situation at home. I thought you might benefit from a change of scenery. I also believe that you are the person we need to fill the void."

"Is there no one here in town who might suit?" Abigail had been surprised at the heartiness of both her aunt and uncle. They certainly looked as if they were perfectly capable of managing without her.

"There was," Aunt Beulah replied, pursing her lips as if reluctant to speak further on the matter. "Unfortunately, she had other plans."

"She ran off with a peddler," Uncle Oscar announced with a shake of his head. He studied Abigail closely. "Do you think you can manage twelve students, Abigail? The older boys are sure to put you to the test."

Abigail smiled. "I have nine brothers and sisters, Uncle."

"And you have parents to help manage there. This will be different. How old are you?"

She realized that serving as the community's schoolmarm was certainly more appealing than helping her aunt with the daily housekeeping, which is what she had been doing back home in New York. She sat tall on the buggy seat. "I am nineteen."

Her uncle winked at her. "Good. Old enough to have the good sense the Lord endowed you with and still young and spry enough to manage a classroom. You'll do fine. Classes begin in two weeks."

But now, two weeks later, the women gossiping outside the butcher shop were not the only doubters in town. The first Sunday that Abigail had accompanied her uncle and aunt to services, she had taken her place, as was the custom, in the front pew on one side of the church with the other unmarried women and young girls. Once seated, she had the feeling she was being watched. Of course she had expected curiosity, but this feeling was different. She risked a sideways glance and saw a man seated across the aisle who was not much older than she was. His was not a gaze of natural curiosity. No, this man was scowling at her. More to the point when she met his eyes, he did not have the grace to look away. If anything, his frown deepened.

"That's Aaron Miller," the girl seated next to her whispered. "Is he not the most handsome man you've ever seen?" She did not wait for an answer. "He has the largest farm in the area, and he has not yet married, and—"

"Rebecca!" A woman two pews behind them hissed the girl's name, and she folded her hands in her lap and bowed her head. But she cast her eyes sideways at Abigail and smiled.

For her part Abigail could not seem to resist one last glance across the aisle that separated the men from the women. The man was still staring pointedly at her, his lips pressed into a hard, unyielding furrow of disapproval. Abigail turned her attention back to her uncle, who was speaking to the congregants, but her mind overflowed with protests. What right had this man to judge her in any way? They had not yet been introduced, and therefore he certainly had no grounds for disapproving of her. He could not possibly be more than three years her elder and— The girl, Rebecca, nudged her as the congregation joined in the first hymn of the morning.

Three hours later when the service ended and the women had filed out the side entrance and into the small kitchen to set out the noonday meal, Abigail did her best to melt into the activity. She made no effort to contribute to the buzz of chatter, having learned on her first such attempts to engage others in conversation that anything she might say about life back in New York would be met with silence. But Rebecca—who could not be more than fourteen—seemed determined to continue the exchange she'd begun during services.

"I cannot wait for our classes to begin," she said as she helped Abigail slice pies into eight even pieces. "Father says I am already too old for schooling and should by now know everything I need, but I made him a bargain. I told him that I would work doubly hard helping with the planting in spring if he would allow me one more year." She smiled shyly and lowered her voice. "My mother says that my father spoils me."

"I take it your father has agreed to your bargain?"

"He has."

"Well then, I shall be pleased to have you in the class." Abigail smiled at the girl as the two of them carried pies into the sanctuary that had been converted into a dining room. The benches they had sat on for the service had been placed around the room and in some cases stacked to form tables to hold the spread of food. As she placed the pies on one of the tables, Abigail looked up and into the eyes of the farmer Aaron Miller.

"*Guten Morgen,*" she said and was surprised that her voice faltered. She cleared her throat and tried again. "*Ich bin—*"

"I know who you are, Abigail Yoder," he replied, cutting off her words almost before she could speak them. It was the way of their faith to address people by full name rather than by title so as not to give the idea that one person was more important than another. On the other hand, it certainly appeared to Abigail that Aaron Miller might prefer a title such as *Mr.* or *Herr.* "What I do not yet know," he continued, "is whether or not you are up to the task of schooling our children."

No wonder the man had never married. What woman would put up with such rudeness? Abigail smiled, hoping to disarm him. It did not work. "Perhaps you would like to come to my class and observe my methods," she said.

"I fully intend to do just that," he replied then abruptly turned away.

◆ ◆ ◆

In Aaron Miller's opinion, Abigail Yoder was far too young, far too high-spirited, and above all, far too pretty to be effective as the town's teacher. The last woman in the role had also been pretty and high-spirited, and look how that had turned out. Aaron had been prepared to ask Sarah Detweiler to be his wife. The entire community had simply assumed their union would take place in the autumn. But that spring, Sarah shocked everyone by leaving in the middle of the night. A peddler had set up his wagon on the outskirts of their little community and hawked his wares to anyone who passed that way—including Sarah.

One evening just before dusk, Aaron had been on his way back to his farm, enjoying the scent of apple blossoms and the warm breeze of May, when he noticed Sarah laughing and talking to the peddler. Then she entered the living quarters of the man's colorful wagon, and Aaron had wrestled with whether or not he should confront her then and there. Instead, he had walked on, aware that he was far too upset to hold a rational conversation with her at the moment. He decided he would call on Sarah the following day when he would not have the presence of the peddler. Clearly, he and his intended needed to come to an understanding. But by morning, both the peddler and Sarah were gone. Sarah had left a note for her parents. Her father had declared her dead to the family. Her mother had fought to hide her tears, and the entire town had buzzed about the scandal for days. Aaron had chosen Sarah to be his wife, not because he loved her, but because she seemed the most likely candidate. Yes, she was immature, but he had been certain that hard work and the children they would have would soon temper that. She was bright and in excellent health. She came from a good and pious family.

And now here was yet another woman seemingly made in the mold of Sarah Detweiler. He had already heard the gossips and matchmakers in their midst speculating on whether or not Aaron might find Abigail Yoder a suitable candidate for wife and mother now that Sarah was gone. Little did they understand that over the months since Sarah's betrayal, he had deliberately turned his thoughts away from matrimony and instead was determined to focus on the welfare of the community in general and the children in particular. If the newly established Mennonite community of Hope, Wisconsin, was to thrive, it would be because the children stayed and took on the shops and farms of their parents. No, Aaron Miller was finished with thoughts of marriage and a family for himself. It appeared to him that God's will for him was that he place his energy into the building of the community—and he saw having the proper teacher in the classroom as the place to begin.

Of course there was the fact that Abigail Yoder was the niece of their bishop, Oscar Yoder, the patriarch of the community. Oscar and his wife, Beulah, had founded the community, drawing relatives and friends from the East to Wisconsin's rich farmland over the last decade. If anyone deserved credit for the growth of the community, it was Oscar. But he and Beulah had not been blessed with children, so Aaron wondered if they could possibly understand the problems that he saw in bringing their niece to Hope.

He scanned the spare and plain room that served as Hope's church and community hall as he stood in a corner and ate his pie. Surely among the women of the community there was someone who would make an excellent teacher. If he could only identify another candidate, perhaps he might convince the elders that it would be best to place the children's welfare in the hands of someone local— someone who knew their ways. But as if she were bathed in light, Abigail Yoder drew his gaze once again. The fact that he could not seem to stop looking at her irked him. He told himself that it was because of his concern regarding her suitability for the position. But the truth was that when he looked at her, he was not thinking of her possibility for failure—or worse for causing more harm than good. He was struck by the way her eyes seemed to sparkle with interest as she spoke to young Rebecca Janzen. He was unable to look away from the way her rose-colored lips formed the words she spoke. He saw a wisp of her white-blond hair that had escaped her bun and prayer cap and was tickling her cheek. He felt the ridiculous need to tuck that errant curl behind her ear.

With the determination of a man born to discipline, Aaron turned away and found himself facing her uncle.

"Aaron, the harvest is in?" For weeks the men of the community had helped each other harvest their fields, stock their haylofts for the winter, and take their crops to market. The women had worked equally hard canning the produce and preparing meals for the men.

"It is and bountiful, thanks be to God."

"You have met our niece?"

"We spoke. She brought the pies to the table."

"And you chose well, I see," Beulah said with a smile as she joined her husband. "Abigail made that pie."

"Pride does not become you, my dear," Oscar scolded his wife, but he was smiling. "On the other hand, that does look mighty good."

"I'll see if there is a slice left," Beulah said, patting her husband's arm before threading her way through the crowd to the serving table.

Aaron cleared his throat. "Elder Yoder, I was thinking that given recent events surrounding the school and the welfare of the children. . ."

The older man's face reflected sympathy—perhaps even pity. "Abigail is young, Aaron, but she is not Sarah."

"Still, perhaps if one of the elders had kept a closer eye. . ."

"I am quite certain that Abigail would welcome anyone who would like to visit the classroom and observe her teaching."

"I was thinking that now that the harvest is finished and I have some time, perhaps I might assume that responsibility on behalf of the community."

"Excellent idea." And then Oscar Yoder did the most astonishing thing. He winked at Aaron and said, "After all, my niece seems to have sparked the interest of at least two other eligible young men." He nodded to where Josef Hamm and Samuel Lemke were edging their way closer to Abigail. Aaron was shocked to feel a jolt of distress that seemed inordinately close to jealousy.

◆　◆　◆

Abigail understood that it was not wise to be the center of attention, especially when it came to the eligible men in the community. Once again she was aware of the older women gathered in small cliques, their mouths working and their eyes shifting in her direction. When she saw two of the younger men moving her way, she put her arm around Rebecca's shoulder and said, "Perhaps you could introduce me to some of the other students."

As she had suspected, Rebecca was only too happy to do so. In minutes Abigail found herself surrounded by eight small children—boys and girls, several of them Rebecca's siblings. An older girl and two older boys kept their distance but were clearly curious about their new teacher. Abigail focused on learning the names of the children and pairing them with their parents and siblings. Once she had greeted each child and said how much she looked forward to seeing them in class, she asked her aunt to introduce her to the parents. All the while, she felt the eyes of Aaron Miller following her.

The farmer stood in a corner of the room, eating his pie and speaking to no one. It seemed to Abigail that the others avoided approaching him or engaging him in any conversation. She could not deny how handsome he was—tall and broad shouldered with thick russet hair and the tanned skin of someone who spent much of his day outdoors. He wore a creamy white collarless homespun shirt, black trousers with black suspenders, and the traditional flat-brimmed black hat. He was clean-shaven as befitted his station as a single man, and she was fascinated by how clean his large hands were, down to the fingernails that for many working men were never entirely free of dirt. When she lifted her gaze back to his face, he had brought his fork almost to his lips, but stopped. And he was staring right back at her.

She felt the color rise to her cheeks and turned away.

"Have you met Aaron Miller," her aunt asked, knowing as well as anyone in the hall that Abigail and the farmer had spoken earlier.

"Not officially."

"Well, no time like the present given that your uncle tells me he has volunteered to oversee your work—at least in the beginning."

"I. . .why would anyone feel it necessary to—"

Aunt Beulah patted her arm. "Oh, that's right. You haven't heard." In low tones she relayed the story of Abigail's predecessor eloping with the peddler just before the start of spring planting the previous year. "It's common knowledge that Aaron had set his sights on her to be his wife."

So that explained the scowl and the doubt she saw in his pale blue eyes whenever he looked her way. She bristled at the unfairness that he might assume that, just because she was young and unmarried, she was no different from the former teacher. She hooked her hand through her aunt's elbow and steered her toward the farmer. "Let's get this settled once and for all," she said through gritted teeth.

Chapter 2

Aaron set his empty pie plate on one of the benches as he observed the new schoolmarm and her aunt advancing on him. Beulah Yoder was smiling uncertainly, as if she was unsure of what was about to happen. The schoolteacher's mouth was set in a thin, determined line, and her dark brown eyes were flashing with indignation. Aaron stood straight and tall as he would when facing any coming storm.

"Aaron Miller, I believe you have not yet officially met my niece Abigail," Beulah Yoder began when they were as yet three feet away. "May I introduce Abigail Yoder?"

"*Ja. Wilkommen, Fraulein.*" He nodded curtly as she stopped just short of standing toe to toe with him. She gazed up at him from her position several inches shorter than his own six feet, yet he could not help but feel she was meeting him eye to eye.

"It is my pleasure to make your acquaintance, and I wish to assure you, Aaron Miller, that I have no plans that should bring either you or the rest of the community cause for alarm. If you would like to hear my credentials for teaching the children, I would be more than happy—"

Aaron stiffened, shocked by the forthright impertinence of her speech. "Our children are our future, Fraulein. This is perhaps not what you have known in your village. This is a small farming community that is dedicated to making a haven for the families currently residing here and the generations yet to come."

She squinted her eyes at him, and for one short moment he thought he had succeeded in overcoming her objections. But then she smiled, and while her smile muddled his thoughts when it came to maintaining control of the situation, there was a quirk to that smile that suggested she might be about to laugh at him.

"I see," she said, her voice now soft and respectful. "Perhaps your presence in the classroom will work to the children's advantage, then, because we are but weeks away from Christmas. I understand that traditionally the children present a pageant on Christmas Eve. It had been my thought to present a very special pageant for the community."

Aaron was relieved to see that the woman's aunt seemed to grasp at least the fact that her niece might be a bit too freethinking for their little community. "The children have always—" Beulah began.

"Yes, Auntie, I know you told me what has happened in the past. But this would be very special—a telling of the Christmas story in such a way that the children

411

would never forget—in a way that would inspire them." She turned her attention back to Aaron.

He swallowed hard. "I have a farm to manage as well as my duties here in town, Abigail Yoder," he said.

"Precisely. It is your farm that is the key. I assume you have a menagerie of livestock? Sheep? Cows? I suppose it would be too much to ask for camels, but dare I hope for a donkey?" Her lips twitched. The woman was indeed laughing at him.

"What is it you are talking about?" he grumbled and was pleased to see that Beulah Yoder seemed equally dismayed.

"A pageant with all the trimmings—kings and shepherds and a manger in a stable with livestock as appropriate. No roosters, please. They do tend to speak out at the most inopportune times."

To his consternation, her aunt clasped her hands together. "Oh Abigail, that does sound quite wonderful. Do you really think we can manage?" This last she directed to Aaron.

In fact, both women were gazing up at him with hopeful smiles, and in the case of the teacher, twinkling eyes. "Is it also your plan to instruct our young people in the basics of reading, writing, and learning their sums?"

"Oh yes, of course. But we have the long months of winter for that. Christmas comes but once a year, and preparing for the pageant gives us a very special opportunity for instructing the children in the more spiritual aspects of their education, would you not agree?"

This had to stop. "I will come by once school is in session to observe on behalf of the elders. If at that time you wish to present me with a written description of your plans, I will take them before the elders for discussion." He almost smiled. He was well aware that the other elders would be as shocked as he was with her plan. "And now if you will excuse me, I believe we have conducted far more business than is warranted for a Sabbath."

"Of course," the teacher said, her smile gone. "I apologize for intruding on your day of rest, and I look forward to our meeting tomorrow."

Before Aaron could take his leave of her, she had picked up his pie plate and headed back to the kitchen. He watched her go, thinking this woman was nothing like Sarah—she was far more intelligent. And the truth was that Abigail Yoder was a good deal more beautiful.

◆　◆　◆

On her first day of teaching, Abigail arrived early, prepared to start a fire in the woodstove that sat in the center of the small, one-room building, but Aaron was there ahead of her.

"We're likely in for a stretch of frigid weather," he announced without the preamble of a proper greeting. "I'll see to it that there is enough wood split for today, but the older boys have traditionally taken responsibility for restocking the pile before they leave for the day."

"Do all the students have chores they are expected to perform?" Abigail was simply making conversation as she removed her cape and hung it on one of the hooks that lined the wall near the door.

"That's for you to determine," he grumbled. "Your aunt can guide you in the matter."

Abigail bristled. She did not need "guidance"—she was simply asking a question. Honestly, this man could be so...

"You may wish to set down rules from the beginning. Sarah Detweiler was far too easy on the children. I assume it was to cover her own lack of knowledge. In your case—"

"In my case, the children and I will find our way, Aaron Miller." She brushed past him on her way to her desk and realized to her chagrin that not all the warmth she felt came from the fire. "Will you be staying to observe?" she asked as she set the cloth satchel she'd filled with books from her uncle's library on the desk.

He ignored her question as he stared at the stack of books. "What is all that?"

"Books."

He picked the top volume from her stack, read the title on the spine—*A History of the World*—and set it down. "You have need of only one book aside from the McGuffy Readers the children already have." He pointed to a shelf on the wall above the hooks where Abigail saw a row of worn readers.

"I have a Bible," she said, pointing to the single book she had placed separate from the stack. "In fact, we shall begin today learning the story of Christ's birth and developing the pageant we will offer the parents and others in the community just two short weeks from today."

"Traditionally, the children have simply—"

Abigail sighed. "There is much to be said for tradition; however, it is my observation that children also learn from new experiences—from looking at familiar information in new ways." She might have suddenly taken to speaking in tongues, so horrified was his expression. "And now if you will excuse me, I believe I hear the children arriving."

She moved past him to the door and opened it to welcome her class. The younger ones scurried in, their voices suddenly stilled by her presence. The older children, including Rebecca, cowed by Aaron's presence filed past her, mumbling a greeting as they placed their outer garments on hooks and took seats at the four larger desks.

Having finished stoking the fire, Aaron closed the iron door of the stove and took up a position near the door. He was still wearing his coat and hat, and Abigail hoped this meant he would not be staying long. His presence had not only intimidated the children, but it had also made her distinctly uncomfortable.

"Good morning, class," she said, fixing a bright smile on her face. "Would you please rise and bow your heads for silent prayer?"

As one the students did as instructed—a good sign. Abigail glanced at Aaron, who whipped off his hat and lowered his head as well. After a moment, she prayed, *Lord, listen to Your children praying and have mercy on them as together we make our way through the wilderness. Amen.*

She raised her head and nodded to the children to be seated. In the back of the room, Aaron was watching her closely, but for once he was not scowling in disapproval. Indeed, his expression was more one of curiosity. She decided to view that as progress.

Thinking it best to prove that she would indeed honor many of the established traditions at least as long as Aaron was there to observe, she began by making chore assignments. The older boys would stock the woodpile. Rebecca and Louisa would wash the boards. The younger children would collect the readers and slates and chalk and make sure all the desks were properly aligned and ready for the next day. Once she had established the chore routine, she passed out the readers and asked each student to find a passage to read aloud. While she had reviewed each child's progress with her aunt the evening before, she needed to see their status for herself. Once the reading was completed, she collected the readers, handed out slates, and gave the children problems to solve that were in keeping with their age.

If her intent was to bore Aaron Miller, she was not succeeding. He watched her closely and paid strict attention as each student performed. Occasionally—especially with the younger students—he showed a hint of a smile. She had the surprising thought that he would be a good father—strict, no doubt, but loving and patient. *Now, where did that idea come from?* She had just met this man. Furthermore, she was not of a mind to marry, at least for another two years. She forced her attention back to the children, praising them when they excelled and coaching them when they stumbled. She became so involved with them that she did not hear Aaron leave, but rather looked up when she felt the wind circling the room and saw the door close behind him.

"At last," she murmured, resisting the urge to clap her hands. "So, class, you have performed well. Now have your lunches, then put on your coats and gloves for time outside. Later this afternoon, we will begin work on a very special assignment—this year's Christmas pageant."

The two older boys groaned, but Rebecca shushed them. "It will be quite special," she whispered. "Real live animals and everything."

"The elders will never agree to that," Rebecca's friend Louisa said. "My father will put up a fuss if we change anything."

Abigail considered the girl, who was dressed in clothing too small for her lanky frame and who had said barely a word since arriving. But her reading had been passionate and filled with expression, and Abigail had already been thinking that she would make an excellent narrator for the pageant. She would have to ask Aunt Beulah about the girl—and her father—later that evening.

◆　◆　◆

Aaron had been reluctant to leave the classroom. Abigail Yoder might have some ideas that were foreign to this community, but there was no denying her skill at teaching. As he went about his farm chores, he thought of the report he would deliver to the other elders. She had certainly done nothing that gave cause for concern on this first morning. In his opinion, she would make a fine addition to the community. On the other hand, she had failed to produce the written description of the pageant that he had requested. Of course, he had become so involved in watching her with the children that he had failed to ask for the plan. Perhaps on his way to the meeting with the other elders in two days, he could stop at the school and retrieve the report.

On Wednesday afternoon, he headed into town for the meeting with the intent of stopping at the school on his way. It did not escape his notice that he had taken special care in his personal grooming before setting out, taking the time to scrub a spot from his shirt and brush the dust from his coat. When he arrived at the school, he was surprised to see Abigail in the yard with the two older male students. The boys took turns chopping wood while Abigail stacked the rough logs. He could not help but notice that the boys were laughing and talking freely with her as they worked. As he approached the group, he heard one of the boys telling her that he hoped to one day set up a business in carpentry, making furniture—an idea that she enthusiastically encouraged.

Aaron frowned. That boy was the sole male child in his large family. His parents would rely upon him to take over the farm one day. Certainly there might be time for making furniture during the long winters, but his responsibility must be—

"Aaron Miller, greetings." Abigail paused in her work once she saw him. She was wearing a heavy wool coat, thick knitted mittens, and a felt bonnet that covered her prayer cap but not all of her hair. She was holding a stack of logs and waiting for him to come closer. "As you can see, Isaac and Thomas are performing their task admirably."

The two boys glanced at him then turned back to their work. Aaron took the logs from Abigail and set them on the pile outside the schoolhouse door. "And yet they need your help as well," he said.

Abigail laughed, and the sound of it was like bells in the cold brittle air. "I insisted." She pointed to the north sky where ominous gray clouds were gathering. "It will snow again before dark, and I want to be sure they are safely home." She opened the door to the school and indicated that he should precede her inside, while she lingered to speak to the boys. "Go along now," she called to them. "We have plenty for tomorrow." The two boys called something back to her that Aaron did not hear, but she was smiling as she stepped inside and closed the door.

"How can I be of help, Aaron Miller?"

Aaron cleared his throat. "We had agreed that you would provide a written plan for the changes you wish to make to the Christmas pageant, Fraulein. I have come to collect that before I meet with the others tonight."

She pursed her lips and looked up at him, her fingers continuing to work the buttons of her coat. "We did not agree, Aaron Miller. You requested the report."

"You do not have it?"

"Yes, I have it, but I appreciate accuracy in my dealings with others." She rubbed her hands briskly together as she made her way to her desk and the satchel he'd seen before. He remained standing near the door while she removed a folded paper and held it out to him. "I believe this will suffice," she said, and then instead of delivering the paper, she laid it on her desk and began writing the next day's assignments on the chalkboard that dominated one wall of the small room.

She left him no choice but to collect the report himself. *"Danke,"* he muttered as he unfolded the single sheet and read it. "This will not do, Fraulein."

She held the chalk poised for the next word but did not turn to face him. "The report or the entire plan?"

"Both. . .neither." The description included plans for converting the classroom into a hay-filled stable, for marching animals down the center aisle to the staged area, for costumes for kings and shepherds, for. . . He could barely find words to express his disbelief. "Under no circumstances. . ."

She dropped the chalk in the tray, dusted off her hands, and stalked back to the hook where she had left her coat. "Then I will attend the meeting and explain," she announced as she put on her coat, the bonnet, and her mittens. She opened the door and looked back at him. "Coming?"

Since she left him little choice, Aaron closed the door to the school and hurried to catch up with her. The church was just down the lane from the school, and he could see the other elders arriving on foot or by sled. Snow was falling in fat gentle flakes that belied the storm building in the north. As she neared the church, for the first time Abigail hesitated, and Aaron was sure she had come to her senses. He stood next to her as the others entered the church and snow covered her hair and bonnet. "I will represent you in this, Abigail Yoder. You will do yourself no favor by inserting your presence in the meeting."

To his surprise, when she looked up at him, he saw tears glistening on the rims of her eyes. Whether they were a product of the cold or her frustration, he could not guess. What he knew was that those tears gave her a vulnerability that he could not abide. "I will make your case, if you will agree to await the decision at your uncle's."

"You do not agree with my plan," she pointed out.

"Perhaps with some minor adjustments, there are parts we could try this one year. Should it fail, we will return to the old ways."

She glanced at the church where the last of the elders except for Aaron had entered. "Very well. But when you make your report, please do not think of me and differences. Think of the children and how from the eldest down to the youngest child, they are eagerly studying the scriptures, seeking ways they might more accurately present the story. They are learning. Furthermore, they are building on their faith."

She turned and followed the path made by his larger boots back to the school. Aaron watched her go, making sure she did not fall, before he entered the church to deliver his report.

The other elders were gathered around a table, talking loudly with animated gestures to make their point. When they noticed Aaron at the back of the church, placing his coat on a hook, the room went silent. Aaron took a deep breath and joined them.

"The bishop will not join us for this meeting," he told them. "He wanted each of us to be free to speak our minds and hearts."

"Well, my mind and heart tell me this woman is not the right person to be teaching our children," Jacob Koop announced, and most of the others nodded in agreement. "She is putting ideas in the children's heads that do not fit with our ways."

"Have you observed Abigail Yoder in the classroom?" Aaron asked. "Have any of you?"

"I don't need to observe her," Jacob snapped. "All I have to do is listen to Louisa when she comes home. The girl is changed—full of senseless babbling and new ideas and such. I'm telling you we are on the wrong path here, and that woman is the cause."

Aaron was surprised that he felt the need to defend Abigail. "She has some new ideas for the pageant—that is true. However, I have observed her teaching methods. She follows the traditional ways in that." He saw some of the men who had been quick to agree with Jacob wavering. "I asked that she provide this body with a full description of her plans for the pageant." He unfolded the paper Abigail had given him and read it aloud.

"She plans on bringing livestock right inside the school?" Jacob was clearly appalled at the very idea.

"She does," Aaron agreed. "She has also indicated that there will be hay bales and a manger to set the scene. However, according to her plan, the spoken words will be delivered by one reader and come directly from the scriptures. I believe, Jacob Koop, that she has selected Louisa to be that reader."

A low murmur of surprise circled the table, but Jacob was unmoved. "This proves my point. Louisa is acting in ways she never did before—prideful ways."

"I understand that Abigail Yoder plans to decorate the church with greens and candles," another elder said—and once again the debate was on.

"Showing off, she is."

"Showing off her fancy Eastern ways, and if we allow her to teach our children. . ."

"What does Bishop Yoder have to say?" another man asked, and everyone turned their attention to Aaron.

"What do you expect him to say?" Jacob practically spat the words before turning away.

Aaron glanced around the table. Everywhere he looked, the elders were whispering and frowning with concern. Several were shaking their heads. Others were more animated, gesturing with their hands, their voices rising. It was apparent that the peacemakers among the gathering were outnumbered and had decided to stay silent. Certainly no one was speaking in Abigail's defense.

"What is your genuine impression of her, Brother Miller?" Jacob Koop demanded. "She's got my Louisa all puffed up about being in this pageant. Downright giddy she was when she got home today. Said her teacher even offered to let her wear a dress of hers—costume, she called it. You ask me, we need to cancel the whole business and send that woman packing back to New York."

"Putting on airs," another voice chimed in.

"It is not our way," another said to a chorus of agreement.

Aaron held up his hands, calling for quiet, and gradually the elders settled down. He realized they were also waiting for him to speak. It was commonly thought that when the day came to elect a new leader, Aaron Miller would be the choice of most if not all. They respected him. They would hear him out.

"First, allow me to repeat that after observing Abigail Yoder in the classroom earlier this week, I can assure you that she is well grounded in the fundamentals and has a way of drawing out the best in our children. In my opinion, she just needs to understand our ways—and how they may differ from hers. We need a teacher, and with what promises to be a hard winter, we must not be hasty in abandoning the gift God has sent us when He brought this young woman to us."

"You will speak to her, then?" one man demanded.

"If that is the will of all," Aaron replied.

"There can be no candles or greenery lining the windows. It is not only gaudy," another man insisted, "it is downright tawdry."

"And there will be no changes to what our pageant has been for all these years. The scripture read and the carols sung like always."

Aaron thought of the agreement he had gotten from Abigail earlier—to try her way once and if it did not work to return to the old way. "Perhaps if all the elders were to—"

Walter Janzen raised his hands, calling for silence. "We do not wish to seem to be ganging up on her. She is Oscar and Beulah Yoder's kin, after all. Let us be mindful of how we go about this. This young woman does not yet know our ways and deserves our forgiveness for any mistaken ideas she may hold. Aaron, you go alone."

"But go tonight and get it done," Jacob Koop shouted. His words were met with a murmur of agreement.

"I have already spoken to her. She has agreed that—"

"*She* has agreed?" Jacob bellowed. "She has turned your head, Aaron Miller."

"Brethren, could we not lose sight of the matter at hand?" Aaron replied, casting about for one person to speak in favor of allowing the teacher to try things her way this once. "Perhaps we should pray on the matter." He bowed his head, and the others followed—Jacob Koop reluctantly.

After several moments during which the atmosphere in the room calmed noticeably, Walter Janzen raised his head. "I propose that tomorrow Aaron Miller and I go together to speak with Abigail Yoder. The hour is late, and I propose we speak with our teacher tomorrow."

The room was silent except for nods from the elders. After a few seconds to allow for further objections, Aaron held up his hands, calling once again for prayer. As noisy as the hall had been when he arrived, that was how silent it was when Aaron left. Outside, the sky was heavy with the promise of more snow and the night was dark. He saw a light in Oscar Yoder's house and started down the lane toward it. As he looked back at the school—now dark—he imagined the offending candles lit and flickering in the windows. He had failed to notice that detail in the list of plans for the pageant. Surely she would understand why no one would stand for that. Anything that smacked of frivolity, having no utilitarian purpose, would not be tolerated. He thought about her excitement the Sunday she had asked him about animals she might use in the pageant, and he knew that talking her out of that might be far more difficult. She might agree to a compromise—animals but no candles—but she could have neither, and he was quite sure she would not like that.

He knew he should wait for Walter to call on her, but he felt it only right to prepare her for what was to come. He opened the gate leading to the Yoders' front walk.

◆　　◆　　◆

Abigail was working on the script for the pageant when she heard the knock at the door. Her aunt and uncle had already retired, and her uncle's snores resonated through the small house. She hesitated but then reminded herself this was not the larger community she'd lived in all her life back in New York. This was Hope, Wisconsin. If someone had come at this hour, that person must have a very good reason for calling so late. She wrapped her shawl around her shoulders and opened the door.

Her nemesis stood silhouetted against the dark night, snow swirling around him. He started to speak, stopped, and finally said, "Is your uncle at home?"

Abigail was put off by his gruff tone. "He is sleeping, as is my aunt. Is there a problem, Aaron Miller?" She stepped out onto the small stoop, pulling the door closed behind her and tightening the shawl she wore.

"It can wait," he mumbled and turned to go.

"Was there some business at the meeting that. . ." Why keep him there? Why not let him go on his way so she could get back to her work?

He hesitated as if trying to come to some decision. Finally he turned to face her. "You cannot place candles in the windows."

"They are important to the pageant."

"Will there not be enough light from the lanterns and the setting sun for the children to perform?"

"Of course. The candles are—"

"The candles are purely decorative and as such go against our beliefs in plain living. I will do what I can to honor the agreement you and I made regarding the pageant, but that agreement did not include the addition of candles and greenery."

She allowed him to get two steps away from the house before answering. "And if I refuse?"

She saw his large frame stiffen and knew it wasn't caused by the blast of cold wind that swept over them both. Slowly he turned to face her. "Are you determined to have us reject you, Abigail?" She was struck by his use of her Christian name without the surname attached. He was making a gesture of friendship—one she was tempted to accept since she had made few friends in the weeks she'd been in Hope. "Are you so anxious to return East," he continued, "that you would do so at the expense of embarrassing your uncle?"

"I have given my uncle my reasons for placing the candles and greenery in the windows. He has agreed to consider my purpose and pray for guidance. Perhaps you and the others who object might wish to be as charitable in hearing me out."

"We are not finished with this discussion. Tomorrow Walter Janzen and I will come to the school before classes begin to speak with you about the pageant. The elders have—"

She did not wait for him to complete his statement. Her fingers were numb and stiff as she clutched her shawl, opened the door, and slipped back inside the house. Once inside, she hurried to the stove to warm her hands, but she could not seem to stop shivering. It was more than the cold. It was also her fear that she had made a terrible mistake. Aaron Miller had offered her something she had failed to consider. Her aunt and uncle were dear to her, and she would not cause them grief. Perhaps he was right in demanding she not include the candles and greenery. On the other hand, if only he and the others would allow her to explain that each candle carried the name of one of the students and would be lighted only at the close of the pageant as a symbol of their light shining out to guide the Christ child.

◆ ◆ ◆

Impossible woman!

Aaron crossed the snow-covered fields on his way back to his dark farmhouse. After he'd left Abigail—or rather after she had dismissed him by going inside and closing the door—he had started for home. But Jacob Koop and three other men had been waiting for him. Among them was Samuel Lemke.

"Did you set her straight?" Samuel demanded.

"She has discussed the matter with the bishop, and he is praying on it and will give her his answer tomorrow."

"The bishop is her uncle," Koop reminded the group. "How much praying will it take to turn that around?"

Samuel appeared to be wavering. "Maybe it is only right that—"

"You speak from your heart, Samuel," the third man said. "Your feelings for this woman are no secret."

"My feelings have changed. I do not like her ways," Samuel replied.

Jacob Koop cleared his throat loudly. "You may court her or not, Samuel. That is hardly the issue. She is leading our children down wrongful paths and must be stopped. And if the bishop has not the will to do so, then we must. She returns the pageant to its original form, or there will be no pageant and she will be barred from the school."

He stalked off.

Aaron knew that in spite of Jacob's bad temper, many in the community would agree with him. After all, the community had been founded by people leaving a larger Mennonite settlement just over the border in Illinois, and the leaving had been for a similar cause. The citizens that had established the community of Hope had been alarmed at the increasingly liberal ways of their Illinois brethren.

"Will you refuse her the livestock, then?" Samuel asked.

Aaron had forgotten all about the idea of having live animals as part of the pageant. He should have told her that live animals were out of the question. He turned back toward the Yoder house but saw that the light he'd seen in the sitting room was no longer there. "We'll wait for the bishop's decision on the matter," he told the two men still waiting with him.

"And the livestock?"

Aaron ignored the question. "Godspeed, my friends."

As he reached his farm and stepped inside the barn to check on the stock, Aaron decided he had no need to either deny or agree to Abigail's request for a cow, a sheep, and a donkey. Surely her uncle would see the folly in all of this and put a stop to it. In the meantime, a storm was brewing and there would be several more inches of snow come morning. Perhaps God was the one squelching Abigail's newfangled ideas. For the first time all evening, Aaron felt a smile tugging at his lips. If the storm were the blizzard it promised to be, there would be no pageant, for everyone would be confined to their homes for the next several days.

Chapter 3

The following day dawned under a sky leaden with gray clouds. The snow everyone had expected had not materialized, but the threat was present. Abigail did not know whether to be pleased or apprehensive. She fingered the wax of the candles she had gathered for the pageant's ending—two for each window of the school. One for each child. As she waited for Aaron and Walter Janzen to come, she printed a card with each child's name and set the finished cards with the candles. The two elders who had been charged with meeting with her were reasonable men. Surely once they heard why the candles were important...

The meeting lasted less than fifteen minutes. Clearly the two men had reached their decision before entering the schoolhouse. There were to be no animals and definitely no candles and greenery. Beyond that, having studied the script, they saw no harm in delivering the good news of Christ's birth in the way Abigail had proposed. When she started to protest, Walter stopped her with one raised hand.

"We are offering a fair compromise, Abigail Yoder—one that has elements to satisfy all concerned. Consider that if you insist on your way, you will be labeled—and rightly so—as prideful, and it is my opinion that parents will not allow their children to attend, much less participate in this program."

"Very well," Abigail said softly. "Thank you." She could hear the children arriving for their final day of class before the pageant. "If you will excuse me, I need a few moments to pray for guidance in telling the children this news—for they will be disappointed."

"They would not be disappointed, Abigail Yoder, had you not filled their heads with ideas you must have known would be challenged." Walter pressed his point. "We have agreed to the idea of a manger and single narrator. We have agreed that the children may take the parts of shepherds and kings and Mary and Joseph. These are gifts, Abigail Yoder, that you would be wise to accept with grace and gratitude."

She nodded and felt tears welling. The elder was right. She had once again simply assumed that others would be as enthusiastic about her ideas as she was. Her parents had warned her that one day her willfulness would get her into trouble. "I understand," she whispered and turned away so the men would not see her tears.

As if the day were not bad enough already, Louisa Koop did not come to school that morning, nor was she present for the class's last rehearsal of the pageant the following day, and it seemed to Abigail that the wooden box holding the candles loomed larger than life on the bookshelf at the back of the classroom. That afternoon as she rehearsed the children and took the reader's part herself, her gaze kept wandering to that box. She could accept that, in the view of others, placing the candles in the windows would serve no useful purpose and the greenery was indeed purely decorative. But what if the children carried the candles as they came to visit the manger? It would be dusk by the time the pageant reached its end. Of course there would be lanterns in the school, but what if the light increased as the story unfolded so that by the end of it, the entire church was alive with light almost as if the star itself had entered the space?

Abigail watched as her students halfheartedly went through the motions of their parts. As she had predicted, they had been terribly disappointed when she'd reported there would be no livestock or candles. But they knew better than to protest openly. Instead, their protest took the form of apathy. She wanted to tell them her new idea, but she would not risk disappointing them again, and certainly if any one of them reported her idea to their parents, the news would spread and the pageant would be canceled.

No, Abigail would pray on the matter between now and the hour for the pageant and seek God's guidance to do the right thing. After all, was her fixation with the candles the work of the devil or the work of God? Sometimes it was so very difficult to decide.

◆　◆　◆

The day of the pageant, there was still no sign of Louisa as the clock ticked on toward four—the hour for the pageant to be presented. The citizens of Hope took their places on benches moved from the church for the occasion. The children were nervous and excited, aware of the objections of their parents and others even if they did not understand the reasons behind those concerns. The stage was set with Rebecca in place as Mary and one of the two older boys standing next to her as Joseph. A wooden manger stuffed to overflowing with hay to hide the absence of an actual baby sat center stage. Abigail briefly considered asking the other older boy to replace Louisa as narrator, but he was a slow reader and his voice skipped comically from low to high registers without warning. She decided she would take the role herself.

Just as she was settling the younger children into their places as shepherds, kings, and angels, she heard a rustle of surprise among those gathered in the audience. She looked up to see Aaron herding a calf and lamb up the aisle. Outside the open door, she saw a donkey.

"Best make this quick," he muttered when he reached her. He handed off the staff for herding the animals to the older boy playing the role of shepherd and took his seat in the front row.

Abigail's heart was beating so fast she thought it might be heard by others. "Thank you," she whispered, following Mary and Joseph up the aisle and outside so they could make their entrance, arriving at the inn. Several people were whispering, and she realized the tone had changed from one of disapproval to one of excitement. It was all going to work out after all. Oh, how she wished Louisa could be part of this!

◆ ◆ ◆

Aaron had had no intention of bringing the animals. He'd had little intention of attending the pageant, but when he had awakened that morning and realized the storm had still not come, he was mystified. He had been so sure that by dawn several more inches of new snow would lie on top of the foot or so already covering the ground. He'd further expected that a strong north wind would be whipping the fresh snow into dangerous drifts that would make travel by foot or animal impossible. Aaron was rarely wrong about weather—a man simply had to read the signs that God laid out for him.

As he went about his chores, he found himself wondering if the unexpected break in the weather were indeed a sign. He also thought a good deal about Abigail Yoder. To his consternation, it wasn't her penchant for changing the ways of the community that was uppermost in his mind. No, when he thought of Abigail, it was the way her eyes twinkled when she smiled, or the way he was tempted to smooth out the tiny lines that marred her forehead when she disagreed with something. Most recently he had found himself imagining what she might look like with her hair undone and spilling down her back like a waterfall lit by the sun.

Enough.

He sat alone at the small kitchen table, eating his noonday meal, the clock on the mantel ticking off the minutes, all the while picturing her with the children—surely every bit as excited as they were about the pageant. It was ridiculous of her to consider using livestock in the performance. Animals were as unpredictable as small children—perhaps even more so. And yet although she had agreed to the elders' terms to cut them from the pageant, he saw her point. Making the animals part of the story would not only enhance the children's understanding of the miracle, but it might also bring some much-needed hope for better times to come for the adults.

That was when he decided to bring the calf and lamb. He was on his way down the path when he heard the donkey bray and turned back. Just as he reached the church, it started to snow—soft gentle flakes that to him felt like approval.

Now he sat with the other adults and watched as the children played out their roles and Abigail read straight from the scripture. If anyone had thought she intended to rewrite the holy words, they were proved wrong. She read of the journey to Bethlehem and no room at the inn, of shepherds in the fields, and of kings following a star. With each change of scene, the children took their parts—each carrying a lighted candle—until the tableau at the front of the classroom was almost like a painting that Aaron had once seen of the Nativity. Mary seated, Joseph standing by, the shepherds to one side, the kings bowing before the manger, and everything cast in the soft glow of a dozen candles. The room was as still as the dying day outside the small building, and as he looked around, he saw some of the adults wipe tears from their eyes.

Abigail had just stepped to the front of the room when the door to the schoolroom banged open and Jacob Koop strode in—his beard and shoulders covered in snow. "Where is she?" he demanded as he advanced on Abigail. "What have you done with my girl?"

Oscar Yoder rose immediately and started toward Jacob, his hands raised in a gesture of conciliation. Abigail stood her ground, neither backing away nor showing any sign of fear at Koop's menacing posture. "Louisa is not here, Jacob Koop," she said in the same calm voice she had used for reading the scripture.

Koop snorted. "A likely story. You put all these worldly ideas in her head, and now you try to hide her as well?"

"No one is hiding anyone, Jacob," the bishop said, stepping between his niece and the outraged man. He turned to the audience. "Has anyone here seen Louisa today?"

There was a murmur of dissent followed by a buzz of growing concern. Aaron stood and placed his hand gently on Jacob's shoulder. "When did you last see her and where?"

He felt all the fight go out of his friend as Jacob collapsed onto a bench and buried his face in his hands. "This morning. She did her chores as usual then said she was coming to the school. I forbid it, and she went inside the house. She's a good girl. I thought. . . I never thought. . ."

"And when did you realize she was not at the farm?" Aaron asked. It was imperative that they gather as much information as possible. Through the open door at the back of the room, he could see that the snow had started to accumulate as the wind whistled and moaned through any opening it could find.

Jacob shook his head.

Aaron mentally calculated how long it would have taken the man to reach town from his farm and how long before that Louisa would have left, hoping to make it in time to play her part in the pageant.

"We have to find her," Abigail said, and Aaron realized she was speaking directly to him.

"I'll go," he said, and when he saw several others prepared to join him, he held up his hands to stop them. "Get your families safely home. She cannot have gotten far from the farm—perhaps she fell or—"

"I'll come with you," Abigail announced as she handed her uncle the Bible from which she'd read. "Now, listen to me, children. We will find Louisa, and you must pray for her safety. Happy Christmas to you all," she added as she touched each child's face and blew out their candle. One by one the children nodded as their parents gathered coats and mittens and began dressing the children for the trek home. Thankfully, most of the families had relatives living in town, and those that didn't were soon invited to take shelter for the night by shopkeepers and others.

"Jacob Koop," Abigail said softly, turning her attention to the distraught father. "We will find Louisa."

Once again rage filled the man with a strength that would have frightened most women. He stood and glared at Abigail. "This is your fault—all your fault, Abigail Yoder. And know now that if harm has come to my child, you will pay dearly." He spat the words at her, and Aaron watched as Abigail accepted them.

"Believe me when I tell you that if something dire has befallen Louisa, no one could possibly punish me more than I will punish myself." She slipped past her uncle and Jacob and hurried to the back of the room, where she collected her cloak and bonnet and shawl. "We should get started," she said to Aaron as she tied her shawl over her bonnet to keep it in place and protect her face from the wind and blowing snow. "It is already dark."

To Aaron's astonishment, neither her aunt nor her uncle made a move to stop her from this folly. "Do something," he hissed at Beulah Yoder, who ignored his plea as she took down a lantern from a hook and handed it to Abigail.

"Your uncle and I will wait here with Jacob. Go on now, and may God be with you and that dear child." She walked her niece to the door then looked back at Aaron. "Time is of the essence, Aaron Miller," she said impatiently.

Aaron collected his outer garments and followed Abigail out into the night. Now he was charged not only with finding Jacob's daughter but also with keeping Abigail safe. He hurried to catch up with her, hoping that she might listen to reason.

"Wait," he shouted, holding his bent arm over his face to shield his eyes from the icy sting of the driven snow. She marched doggedly on. Was she ignoring him? Or perhaps—giving her the benefit of the doubt—she could not hear him calling.

◆ ◆ ◆

Abigail heard Aaron call out to her, but nothing and no one would stop her from finding Louisa. Her guilt at encouraging the girl in spite of Jacob Koop's objections was prideful and wrong. She should have respected his views whether or not she agreed with them. That was the problem with her—had always been her problem. She had this habit of questioning her elders and their ways. She was quite sure this was the root cause behind her mother wanting her to come to Wisconsin. In effect, her mother had hoped her brother—the bishop—would have more success in tempering Abigail's penchant for wanting to try new things than she and Abigail's father had managed.

Abigail whispered a prayer as she fought her way through the drifts and blowing snow. She assumed Aaron was coming after her but gave that little thought until she felt his large hand close around her upper arm like a vise, pulling her to a halt.

"Go back to the school," he yelled as the wind howled through the bare trees. "I'll find her."

"No." The cold filled her lungs, making it difficult to breathe much less hold a conversation. When he continued to hold her arm, she looked up at him. "We are wasting time," she shouted, even as she tugged to free herself and move on. To her surprise he did not release her, but neither did he try and stop her from going on the search. Instead, he loosened his hold enough to guide her over a patch of black ice that was covered over with blowing snow.

"This way." He pointed toward a lane that was barely distinguishable between the piles of snow to either side. "It's the shortest distance to the Koop farm."

Abigail followed the trail he broke through the snow, but within minutes her skirts were soaked and heavy, and she knew she was slowing him down. When she saw a dilapidated shed just off the beaten path, she pointed. He nodded, and the two of them headed for the outbuilding.

Aaron pulled back the door and waited for her to enter before following and pulling the door closed again. Inside there were only slits of waning daylight finding their way through the cracks in the walls and the hole in the ceiling, but at least they could talk without shouting and they were out of the wind and stinging snow.

"Your dress is soaked," he said.

"Yes. It hinders my ability to keep up, so why don't you go ahead?"

"And you will return to the school to wait?"

"You are certain that this is the way that Louisa would come from her father's farm?"

"It is."

Abigail was trying hard to think like the girl would. "She knew she was late, so she would have taken this way. Perhaps the trail was blocked—a fallen tree or some other obstacle—and she had to leave the trail and could not find her way back." Her teeth chattered as she tried to work through the details, and she had wrapped her arms around her upper body to try and stop the shivering. "If I wait here, perhaps Louisa will find her way here."

"You cannot stay here without a fire to warm yourself. Look at you. You're shaking with cold."

Before she could protest, he removed his heavy coat and wrapped her in its warmth. Next he began gathering wood and kindling for a fire. Blessedly, there was a shallow pit in the earthen floor. Using a stick and the heel of his boot, Aaron scraped at the dirt to make the hole deeper then piled the kindling and wood in the pit. But Abigail could see he was at a loss for how to start the fire. She rustled through the layers of her outer garments until she found her apron pocket and produced three wooden matches.

"I brought them from home to light the candles at the school," she explained when he looked at her as if she had just performed a miracle. "Hopefully, they are dry enough."

He struck the first match, and it flamed to life. For the first time since she'd met him, Aaron Miller favored her with a genuine smile. And that smile, she decided, had been well worth the wait. He was a handsome man in any case, but when he smiled, his entire face changed. His expression softened and his eyes sparkled. Or perhaps that was the light of the flame reflected in his eyes. What she knew for certain was that they were standing close to each other, and they were staring at each other, and her heart was hammering—and she was no longer cold.

As the match burned down almost to his fingertips, he bent and lit the kindling—dry leaves he'd collected from under the eaves of the shed's roof. He cupped his hands around his mouth to form a sort of bellows as he blew the smoldering leaves and dried pine branches to life. "There," he said as he stood. "You'll be all right here as long as you keep the fire going."

"Yes," she said softly.

She removed his coat from her shoulders and handed it to him. He hesitated. "Take it," she urged. "I have the fire."

"Do not try and go out searching on your own," he ordered, his tone more the one he had taken with her from that first day.

"I won't stay here indefinitely," she replied, jutting out her chin to show him he could not order her around.

To her shock he cupped her chin in his hand. "None of this is your fault, Abigail, and it will not help for you to be lost in the storm as well." He ran the pad of his thumb over her skin and then released her. When he pushed the door open, the wind filled the shed, threatening to extinguish the fire. But within seconds, Aaron had closed the door. He was gone.

"Please lead him to her," Abigail prayed as she settled herself on the floor near the fire and spread out the skirt of her dress around her to allow it to dry.

◆　◆　◆

The storm continued to worsen. The snow flew through the air, blinding Aaron as he made his way forward. He tried calling the girl's name but soon realized the wind was simply throwing his words back in his face. Normally, he would have searched with a torch in hand to light his way, but no torch could have survived this storm. He pressed on, pausing now and then to place markers—a stack of fallen tree branches or large rocks—so that he could find his way back.

At least he had persuaded Abigail to stay behind by the fire. As he trudged on, he thought about the whiff of her that had clung to his coat when she returned it. He thought about the way she had looked at him when the match flared to life. He thought about the way his heart had pounded, echoing in his temples, his throat, his chest. He thought about the way she had challenged him and he had touched her face, cradling that impudent chin in his palm. He thought what it might be like to kiss her and knew the way his breathing was becoming more difficult had more to do with her than with the battle he was waging against the blizzard.

"Louisa Koop," he bellowed, forcing himself to focus on the situation at hand. A child was missing—had been missing now for hours. He should have joined those who had demanded that the pageant be canceled. He should have insisted that the children all remain safely in their homes with their parents. He should not have been blinded by his attraction to the bishop's niece. Yet he had to admit that in spite of their objections to the changes Abigail had made in the traditional pageant, in the end it had brought everyone together in a way that Aaron had not seen before. The atmosphere in the school packed with people had been one of community—people coming together. If this child were lost, all of that would be lost as well.

As he slogged on, he turned his thoughts to prayer that he would find the girl soon—and that she would be alive.

◆　◆　◆

There was no way for Abigail to know how long she sat by the fire—long enough that her dress was nearly dry and she had piled on more wood to keep the flame going. Through the hole in the roof, she could see the sky as black as the ink her older students used for their lessons. She pictured the way Louisa sat bent over her work, determined to get everything perfect. She thought of how the girl had at first resisted efforts to have her take on the larger role in the pageant and how, when she received the support of Rebecca Janzen, she had blossomed into a gifted reader. She closed her eyes and saw Louisa's shy smile when Abigail had brought her a dress to wear for the pageant. Was she wearing that dress now? Most likely.

Abigail began to pace the confines of the shed, pausing now and again to listen because outside something had changed. The wind had died, and when she looked up, she saw a star twinkling down at her—a sign that the storm was waning. Would it be foolhardy for her to venture out? Louisa might be nearby, and if so, Aaron might have passed by her without knowing. Surely it would be wise for her to check the immediate area.

She banked the fire, hoping it would stay lit, for she realized Aaron had kept the remaining two matches. After wrapping her shawl around her head and shoulders, she pushed against the door. It did not budge. She tried again, putting her entire weight into the action. It moved a couple of inches—enough for her to realize that the snow had piled up outside the door. Given the time of night and falling temperatures, that snow was probably more like ice. She grabbed a small log and wedged it between the door and the frame. Using it as a lever, she pried the door open enough that she was able to squeeze through. Once outside she used the log to push and scrape as much snow as possible away from the door. Then to protect the fire, she jammed the log into the snow and up against the door to hold it shut.

Breathless from the exertion and cold, she took a moment to get her bearings. The wind whistled through the trees surrounding the shed, and snow whirled around her, stinging her cheeks.

"Louisa!" She might as well have whispered the missing girl's name for all the good shouting it did. "Oh Louisa, where are you?" she sighed as she tried to think what to do.

To one side of the shed was a thick forest of evergreens—their boughs so heavy with snow that they were bent almost to the ground. Still, she saw that they had formed a kind of barrier to the drifting snow, and she could just make out a path that was deep with snow but that looked passable. She headed for it, praying every step of the way that this path would lead her to Louisa. Clutching her skirts tight with one hand, she slowly made her way deeper into the woods. The laden trees dropped snowballs on her head and shoulders, and she had not gotten very far when she was almost covered by an avalanche of snow falling from a cluster of trees. In that instant, she imagined Louisa experiencing something similar. But Louisa was small and thin, and the outer garments she wore to school were no match for the weight of that cascade of snow.

She pushed herself forward, trying to see the way ahead and always watching for places where the snow might have plunged onto the path without warning. Once again she was soaked and chilled to the bone, but she would not give up the search.

With nothing to keep her going but her thoughts and her determination to find Louisa, she reviewed her actions over the last weeks. Had she unwittingly contributed to this tragedy? Had there been no good in what she had done? Had her zeal for showing the children a new way of presenting the pageant indeed been born of her own vanity? And if they did not find the girl in time—what then?

Either way, she decided she would resign her position and return to New York. Even if her insistence on change had come from innocent and virtuous motives, she had failed to consider the consequences. She had certainly not allowed herself to see what consequences might result from encouraging Louisa. No, she had wronged these children and their parents, caused them unnecessary worry and possibly—in the case of Jacob Koop—heartbreak. She would beg forgiveness and then leave them in peace.

Knowing that Louisa had now been missing for hours, she pressed on. Her eyes burned from the strain of trying to see in the dark, but then she realized that seeing was becoming easier. She looked up and saw a break in the clouds as they moved like a river across a nearly full moon. In seconds the light was once again extinguished by clouds, but a few minutes later, it reappeared and she thanked God for calming the storm. Then she saw a dark shape some yards ahead—another outbuilding. *Please let her have taken cover there,* she prayed as she stumbled along, dragging each foot and her sopping wet skirt from the deep snow in order to take the next step.

This shed had no door, and wide gaps had opened between the boards, giving the wind and snow access to the interior. She stopped to catch her breath before entering. The wind had calmed, and all she could hear around her was her own labored breathing—and someone singing.

◆　◆　◆

Aaron blew on his fingers through the wool of his gloves—anything to feel a wisp of warmth. He had followed the path all the way back to the Koop farm. The house was dark, and he could hear the livestock moving around in the barn. He took a chance and entered the back door of the house.

"Louisa?"

The silence was as oppressive as the cold. There was no fire banked in the stove in the kitchen—a room that even in the dark he could see was pristine. Jacob's wife had died several years earlier. Louisa was his only child, and Aaron assumed she had taken over the keeping of the house in her late mother's stead. He moved on to the front of the small house, checking the single bedroom and the front sitting room. In the bedroom, he saw men's clothing on the hooks—Jacob's. He wondered where the girl slept and had her clothes.

"Louisa Koop," he shouted. When there was no answer, he knew she was not there. On his way out he spotted a quilt neatly folded at the foot of the single bed and took it. When he found the girl, he was certain she would need all the warmth he could offer. As an afterthought he retraced his steps and took a woolen shirt and a jacket from the hooks in Jacob's room and left the house.

Outside he paused. The sky was beginning to clear some, and the wind had died down to a breeze light enough to flurry the snow but not so strong as to throw it in his face. With the wind now at his back, the return trek would be easier. He considered his next move. Go back the way he had come, or try a different route? In the end he chose the latter, striding off into the deep woods that lay to the south of the property. Unlike the trail between the Koop farm and the village, where the path was beaten down, this way was deep with snow, making his journey slow and tedious, but Aaron used the time to pray silently—pray for Louisa to be found and pray that Abigail was all right.

It was ridiculous how often his thoughts turned to Abigail. What did he know of her other than that she was Oscar Yoder's niece. He had great respect for the Yoders, but Abigail was a stranger to their community—to their ways. Look how she had already upset people with her newfangled ideas. Still, she sometimes looked at him in a way that made his breath quicken. But he hardly had to remind himself that she was strong-willed, and in a woman of their faith, that could be a dangerous thing.

On the other hand, whenever he had touched her, he could not deny the effect even a simple brush of her hand had on him. In those few instances, his heartbeat had an unfamiliar drumming pattern, and he had felt heat rise to his face. More often than not, he had found some excuse to look away. But while it was simple enough to avoid being in Abigail's physical presence, it seemed impossible to avoid the image and thought of her invading his thoughts and dreams. Lately he had found himself wondering if she might make a proper wife for him and mother for his children—their children.

That idea stopped him in his tracks. It must be the cold. It must be his fear that Louisa would not be found. He needed to clear his head. He pressed on, calling out Louisa's name from time to time now that the wind had lessened.

◆　◆　◆

"Louisa!" Abigail could not believe her eyes when she saw the girl huddled in a corner of the shed. At first she thought the cold and fear had rattled her brain, making her imagine the face she had so hoped to see was now staring up at her. "You're shaking," she whispered as she stepped closer, opened her cloak, and held out her arms to the girl.

Louisa scrambled to her feet and staggered forward to accept the haven offered. "I was so scared," she whispered, "but I prayed hard, and then I thought maybe God would hear my song, and here you are." Her voice was a weak hoarse whisper, and Abigail could feel the cold of the girl seeping into her. She held her close as she guided her to the place in the shed that seemed the most protected from the elements.

"We've been searching everywhere for you," she said as she cast about for the possibility of something with which she might light a fire, both to warm them and to lead Aaron to them. Seeing nothing and realizing anew that she had given Aaron the matches, she tightened her grip on Louisa's shoulders. "We have to try and get back to the village," she said. "Your father is there, and he is very worried."

To her surprise, the girl resisted any attempt to move her toward the opening.

"He will be angry," Louisa protested.

"No, Louisa. He was angry with me for encouraging you. And rightly so. Your father blames me for your disobedience—not you."

"He will beat me," she whispered.

Abigail shuddered. "You must take responsibility for your part in this, Louisa—apologize for disobeying and for causing him worry." She was about to assure the girl that no father would strike a contrite child, although she had no way of knowing whether or not that was true, when suddenly Louisa went limp against her and slid to the ground.

"No," she whispered as she knelt next to the child, trying without success to revive her and noticing that in spite of her chills, she was burning up with fever. *What now?* She could not carry the girl, who, though small, was nearly Abigail's size. She searched the shed for something she might use as a litter so that she might drag the girl to safety. *Oh, where is Aaron?*

Chapter 4

Aaron had made it all the way back to the shed where he had left Abigail. The fire was cold, and he saw no sign of her anywhere. He shouted her name and Louisa's repeatedly, making quarter turns, hoping his voice would carry, and then listening in case there was an answering call.

Silence.

He looked for tracks, the sweep of her skirt on the snow, but the wind had covered everything over. He stared at the way he had come and instinctively knew that she would not have replicated his search. No, she would have chosen a different way. He saw the narrow trail that passed under the canopy of snow-laden evergreens and headed for it. A few steps in, he realized that because of the protective cover, any signs of someone passing that way had been at least partially preserved. He knelt and removed his glove as he ran his bare fingers over the ground.

There! An indentation. . .and another. He stood and hurried along the narrow trail, and by the time he spotted the half-demolished shed, he was running. He cupped his hands around his mouth and bellowed her name. "Abigail!"

"In here," came the answering shout.

He burst through what was left of the shed's door and stopped, his heart hammering with disbelief that at last he had found her—found them both—for once his eyes adjusted to the dark interior, he saw that Abigail was cradling the lifeless girl. "No," he whispered, even as he opened the quilt he had brought from the farmhouse and wrapped it around her and the girl, adding the woolen jacket he'd pulled from the hook in Koop's bedroom to further protect the child. "Is she. . ."

"She fainted. She is so very thin, and look at this coat. It's practically threadbare. We need to get her out of here and back to someplace warm as soon as possible. Are we nearer the farm or the village?"

"The village." He lifted the girl high in his arms and waited for Abigail to get to her feet. "The storm has passed—at least for a time."

"There's the moon to light our way," Abigail said, and he wondered if she always saw the good in even the direst of circumstances.

As they pushed forward, he was relieved to realize that the wind had calmed, but the moon dodged in and out of clouds—sometimes making the way clear and other times leaving them once again in darkness. "Follow my steps," he instructed when she fell behind and he saw that she was struggling to keep up with his longer strides.

"You go ahead," she insisted. "I'll be able to follow your steps, but it is vital that we get Louisa to warmth and care as quickly as possible. Go," she urged.

"No," he replied. "Come here and climb onto my back. Louisa is no more weight than a sack of flour." When she hesitated, he added, "I will not leave you here, Abigail."

"You are quite stubborn, aren't you?"

He bent so that she could wrap her arms around his neck and cling to his sides with her knees. "No more than you," he muttered as he stood, adjusted to the added weight, and moved on.

They said nothing more, but he was inordinately aware of her body pressed to his and her breath warming his ear. He kept his eyes on the ground, concentrating on each step so as not to fall and take Abigail and Louisa with him.

"I will resign of course," she said so softly that he thought perhaps he had imagined the words.

"Louisa will be all right. Already she is starting to come around."

"Still, I was wrong to try and make changes without seeking the approval of all. It was prideful."

Aaron realized he found this entire conversation unsettling. What was she saying? If she resigned, what would she do? "Are you thinking of returning to New York?"

"Yes. I mean, surely that is best."

Everything in Aaron's mind and body screamed no. But what did he care where she went? Yes, it would be upsetting for the children to have to adjust to yet another teacher, but other than that—

"Aaron, look." Abigail was pointing ahead.

Aaron lifted his eyes from the trail and focused on the distance where a strange light glowed on the horizon.

"Listen," Abigail whispered as she unclasped her hands from around his neck and slid to stand next to him. "I hear singing. It was what led me to Louisa, and now it is what will lead us to safety."

Before he could stop her, she plunged forward, waving her arms above her head and crying out, "We found her!"

In his arms Louisa stirred and opened her eyes. "Papa?"

"Soon," Aaron promised and lengthened his strides as he reached the packed snow of the road that led to the church.

◆　◆　◆

Abigail could not believe her eyes. In the distance she saw the silhouettes of people gathered on the horizon, some of them holding torches. She blinked and swiped at her eyes, certain that this was a mirage—something she had prayed for but still did not seem possible. Yet the vision remained, and once again she heard singing—carols—the old favorites sung every year.

She began to run—or stumble forward—as fast as her soaked shoes and heavy wet clothing would allow. "We found her," she shouted, the words catching in her throat on the wave of tears that threatened to overcome her. "Over here," she called, waving her arms above her head as she passed Aaron and took the lead.

One of the men had hitched up a cart on runners to a team of large Percheron horses. Riding in back she saw an older woman and recognized Lizzie Bontrager who served the community as midwife—as close to a doctor as would be available until the snow melted.

"Here," Abigail cried, still trying to slog through the deep snow to reach their rescuers. She felt Aaron's hand close around her shoulder.

"They are nearly here, Abigail." He shifted Louisa in his arms and pointed. "Look, Louisa, your father is driving that cart."

Sure enough, it was Jacob Koop who pulled the horses to a halt.

"We found her," Abigail said, but Jacob looked past her to Aaron.

"Is my daughter alive?" he demanded.

"I am all right, Papa—truly. I am so sorry for disobeying you, and—" Anything more she might have said was lost in a fit of coughing.

Aaron laid her in the back of the cart on the pile of hay covered in quilts. The midwife knelt beside her, examining her as best she could in the dark and cold. Without another word, Jacob Koop snapped the reins and turned back toward town, leaving Abigail and Aaron standing in the field. In the act of laying Louisa on the cart bed, the jacket Aaron had covered her with fell to the ground. He picked it up and placed it around Abigail's shoulders.

She pulled it closer, but it did little to alleviate the chill that had worked its way deep inside her. She started forward but stumbled and fell into the snow. She was so very tired and unsure of how she could take the steps necessary to make it back to the village.

Aaron lifted her in his arms.

"No," she protested.

"Yes," he insisted. "We are both half frozen, and the sooner we are before a warm fire, the less likely that one or both of us will be spending Christmas sick in bed."

"But—"

"Abigail Yoder, you have had your way, and now it is time for you to adhere to what I—what others deem best."

She could find no words. She wanted to remind him that she was perfectly capable of walking—although the last several steps had been pure agony. Even so, to arrive back in town being carried by him when the whole populace was likely to be there. . . If she hadn't been the object of gossip and speculation in the past, she would surely be that now. She clamped her lips closed and stared off toward the fire of the torches that reminded her anew of the candles the children had carried as part of the pageant.

Tears leaked down her cheeks, and she used the corner of her shawl to wipe them away.

"Do not let them see you crying, Abigail Yoder." His voice was soft and comforting. "You have done nothing wrong."

Oh, but she had—and that was why she must resign her position and return to New York at the first opportunity.

♦ ♦ ♦

Traditionally, after services in the morning, Christmas Day was spent in prayer, meditation, and scripture reading—either silently if alone or aloud if there were others in the household. The day after or "Second Christmas" was a time for visiting, sharing meals, and exchanging simple handmade gifts. Aaron usually went into the village on Christmas Day for church and then returned to the farm to spend the day alone. He had no relations in the area. Others had offered to look after his livestock if he wanted to travel back to Ohio to spend time with his brothers and their families, but he had declined. Usually, he joined the Yoders for the noon meal on Second Christmas—Beulah and Oscar were like parents to him and he enjoyed their company. But this year Abigail would be there, and for reasons he could not yet fully grasp, that made a difference.

So on Christmas morning as he dressed for the trip to the village to attend services, he decided that he would tell Beulah not to plan on him for the meal. He would stop by for a short visit later in the day—as would many others—but he would not share their meal. *What reason will you give?* Every excuse that came to mind had all the elements of a lie—and he would not lie, but neither could he envision himself sitting across from or next to Abigail without imagining the two of them sharing meals for years to come. With the dilemma that was Abigail swirling through his brain, he clamped on his black broad-brimmed hat and started the walk to town, hoping the cold, crisp air would clear his mind and give him resolution.

By the time he reached the church, most of the townspeople had already gathered. They milled around outside, greeting one another in low respectful voices while their children ran about the churchyard, throwing snowballs or playing tag as they dodged along the row of parked black carriages belonging to those whose farms were too distant for walking. Some spoke in low murmurs of the miracle of Louisa's rescue as they waited for services to begin. Others hailed the latest arrivals before corralling their offspring and entering the church—men through one door and women through another.

The first person Aaron saw when he entered the side door was Abigail. She was seated by herself in the first row of benches reserved for the women and girls. She was still dressed in the clothes she had been wearing for the pageant—the clothes that had been wet and frozen stiff by the time they returned with Louisa. They were dry now, no doubt thanks to the fire in the stove that had clearly been kept going through the night, but nettles and burrs clung to the fabric, and her hair was in some disarray with her prayer cap at a cockeyed angle.

"She has been there through the night," Oscar Yoder whispered. "We came to tell her that Louisa would fully recover, but still she stayed." He frowned. "My wife is quite worried. . .as am I."

"She blames herself that Louisa disobeyed her father and was lost."

"I have tried to remind her that God has brought Louisa safely back to us, but she says nothing. Perhaps you. . . ?"

The villagers were filing in, and Aaron saw Rebecca Janzen take her place on the bench next to Abigail. Abigail did not move a muscle, and something about her stillness apparently kept the usually talkative Rebecca from trying to engage her in conversation. The service began, and three hours later everyone filed out in silence and made their way back to their homes. There would be no community meal on this day—it was a day for fasting.

Aaron remained seated, his head bowed but his eyes on Abigail.

The church emptied, and he heard the last of the wagons leave the yard. But still she did not move. Aaron rose and stoked the fire in the iron stove at the center of the room, and when she still did not stir, he sat next to her, careful to leave a proper space between. Words failed him, but prayer never had, so he bowed his head and prayed for Abigail, who was clearly in pain.

They sat there until the church filled with the shadows of dusk. Twice Beulah Yoder came to the side door and looked in. When she made a move toward Abigail, Aaron waved her away. Whatever Abigail was wrestling with, he felt certain that she had made a leap from praying for forgiveness to punishing herself. He needed to get back to the farm and tend to his stock and chores, but how could he leave her?

"Abigail?"

It was the first sound either of them had made in all the time they had sat there, and his voice in the empty sanctuary sounded loud and intrusive. He reached over and took her hand, prying it lose from the grip she had on her soiled skirt. He laced his fingers through hers, noting how cold hers were.

"Let me walk you home," he said. "The fire is almost out, and it is wasteful to keep it going through the night." She made no move to show she agreed or disagreed. "It will be dark soon," he added.

She looked up for the first time and took in her surroundings. She released a long sigh as if she had been holding her breath for a very long time. He stood and drew her to her feet, and when she faltered, he released her hand and wrapped his arm around her shoulders to steady her.

"Come on," he said, wondering how this woman who had always seemed so strong and prepared to deal with him or anyone who crossed her could now seem so small and frail. "Can you walk?"

This elicited a slight flash of indignation that he recognized—that gave him hope. She straightened but did not move away from the harbor of his support.

"I must leave," she said, her voice raspy from lack of use.

"Yes," he agreed. "It's time to go home to your uncle and aunt for they are—"

She shook off his words. "Leave here—leave Hope," she said.

"And abandon the children who have come to rely on you—who have come to love you?" He tried and failed to contain his frustration. He had the urge to shake her until she saw the obvious. "We need you, Abigail Yoder."

He stopped short of adding, "I need you." But he could not deny that it was true.

◆　◆　◆

Abigail allowed Aaron to walk with her back to her uncle's house. When she opened the door, her aunt fell upon her and hugged her close.

"I am sorry for worrying you, Aunt Beulah," she said, her voice muffled by the woman's embrace. Over her aunt's shoulder, she saw her uncle thanking Aaron and bidding him a good night. Aaron moved back toward the door, his eyes on her, a worried frown creasing his high forehead. She realized the frown was not the one she'd first known—the scowl of disapproval. No, the lines etched into his brow now were those of concern—and caring. She pulled free of her aunt and faced her uncle and Aaron. "I apologize for worrying all of you, but I am all right and relieved to hear that Louisa Koop is also recovering."

"You need to eat something and then get some rest. Let's get you out of those clothes and into something clean and warm, and then I'll bring you some tea and toast," Beulah fussed. She guided Abigail toward the hall that led to the small bedrooms, passing Aaron along the way. "You'll be here for Christmas dinner tomorrow," she said, pausing to look up at the farmer. Abigail smiled because it was not a request but an instruction.

"I. . . Perhaps it might be best if. . . Ja. I will come for dinner," Aaron replied, delivering his answer not to Beulah but to Abigail.

She felt the corners of her mouth lift slightly and knew by the way he smothered a smile that he had seen it—and that it had pleased him.

While her aunt left her to make the promised tea and toast, Abigail washed herself, brushed the tangles from her hair, braided it, and put on her nightgown. She sat on the side of the narrow bed and sipped the hot tea and nibbled at a corner of the toast her aunt brought her. "Louisa?" she asked, her throat raw from the hours spent searching for the girl.

"She will be fine. She spent the night at Lizzie Bontrager's."

"And her father?"

"Jacob Koop stayed with the Janzens."

"I need to apologize to him," Louisa murmured as she put the cup to her lips and allowed the steam to warm her face. "Although he will not offer forgiveness—and he will be right to withhold it."

"Nonsense. Your uncle and I have asked him to come for dinner tomorrow. Perhaps once he has prayed on the matter and sees that Louisa will be just fine, he will open his heart—and mind." She took the empty cup from Abigail and then pulled back the covers. "To bed with you, child."

Abigail did as her aunt asked. "I have prayed on the matter, Aunt Beulah, and I am convinced that God is leading me to leave Hope and return to New York."

Beulah chewed on her lower lip. "You are so certain that this is what you are being led to do?"

"As certain as I can be," Abigail replied with a yawn. And convinced that the matter was settled finally, she drifted to sleep.

◆　◆　◆

It was midmorning before she woke. She dressed quickly, embarrassed to have left her aunt with all the preparations for the large gathering of friends that would share the day's meal. But when she went to the kitchen, she realized she needn't have worried. The small room was filled with women working in unison to produce the pies, cookies, and side dishes that would be offered along with roast chicken to those gathered for the celebration.

"Ah, at last," Aunt Beulah said. "We've been wondering when you might join us. Come help Rose make the *Pfeffernüsse*."

Shyly, Abigail tied on an apron and took her place next to Rebecca's mother. Rose Janzen smiled at her. "You gave us all a bit of a fright, Abigail," Rose said, and Abigail was well aware that conversation among the other women had come to a halt as they all focused on her—including some women who she had overheard state outright that she was not the right choice for teaching the children. Rose slid a bowl filled with golden batter across the table to her.

"It is ready for the flour and spices," she said.

Abigail added flour to the mix of butter, buttermilk, sugar, and eggs and grated the cinnamon, cloves, ginger, and anise to add to the dough. Last she ground pepper—the spice that gave the cookie its name and unique taste. The repetitive rhythm of mixing and adding more ingredients calmed her, and she found that she was enjoying listening to the women, who had returned to bantering about this or that. When Rose inquired how Abigail's mother made the traditional cookie, she replied, "She uses molasses in the place of corn syrup." And when that started an entirely new round of conversation about the diversity of recipes for the treat, she felt a kinship with these women for the first time since coming to Hope.

For the rest of the morning, she worked in concert with the other women. After she and Rose rolled the dough into long ropes and set them out in the cold, she set the table, allowing time for the dough to chill enough that it could be easily cut into the bite-size cookies. The house was filled with the fragrance of baking and chickens roasting, and before Abigail knew it, the men began to arrive, bringing with them the children and helping to set up extra tables and benches for the meal. When they saw her, the younger children squealed with delight and ran to her, and she had to fight the tears that threatened to fall at the thought of leaving these dear ones. Rebecca Janzen, as usual, came directly to the point.

"Are you recovered?"

"I am," Abigail assured her, and the two older boys who stood nearby, pretending not to listen, grinned when she answered Rebecca.

Then she saw Aaron Miller standing just inside the front door, his eyes on her, and as he threaded his way through the other guests, her heart began to thrum in a beat that left her quite breathless. Behind her she could hear the women whispering and knew they had noticed the way Aaron looked at her—and she looked at him. To her surprise, the women seemed to approve, but they did not understand that in spite of her feelings for Aaron, she had decided leaving was the only way to show Jacob Koop that she fully understood and accepted responsibility for her arrogance.

"Walk with me, Abigail Yoder," Aaron said when he was close enough to speak only to her.

Intending to explain her decision to him—feeling she owed him that—she did not hesitate but took down her shawl from a hook near the back door and walked outside. The day was pleasant, with no sign of the blizzard other than piles of pristine snow and trees hung with icicles. The sky was clear blue, and the air was cold but bracing. She turned her face to the sun and closed her eyes, praying God would give her the words she would need today—for Aaron, for Jacob Koop, and for the children, who were sure to protest her decision.

Aaron cleared his throat. "Abigail Yoder, we have not known one another for very long," he began. "And yet. . ."

Behind them they heard muffled giggles and turned to see some of the children watching them from the back stoop. Aaron frowned and took hold of her elbow, leading her toward the row of carriages parked outside the barn. She had to stop him before he said something he would regret.

"Aaron, this is unseemly," she protested. "The entire village is inside my uncle's house, and—"

"Then say that you will not leave us. Say that you will stay—for the children."

Her heart sank. Once again her pride had misled her. She had been so certain that he was about to ask her to stay for his sake—because he needed her, because he cared. But instead, she saw now that he was speaking to her in his role as elder—perhaps speaking for others who were unwilling to have her leave. "I cannot stay," she said and hurried away from him, back to the kitchen and the puzzled frowns of the other women.

◆ ◆ ◆

Aaron was at a loss. He had arrived early enough that he had seen her with the other women in the kitchen, laughing and jabbering the way women did. And then when the children ran to her, grasping her skirts with hugs, had that meant nothing to her? How could she allow Jacob Koop to dictate her decision? He saw the farmer pull his wagon to a halt next to the Yoder house and help Louisa down from the high seat.

"Jacob Koop," he called.

Jacob paused, said something to Louisa, and watched as the girl walked on to the house. "I know what you want to say, Brother Miller, but surely you understand that I cannot forgive Abigail Yoder for her transgressions—only God can do that."

"She will leave us." Aaron saw that this was news to Jacob—unsettling news.

"Louisa could have frozen to death. She could have died of pneumonia."

"And yet, God be thanked, she did not. Nor did Abigail, who thought nothing of her own safety as she searched for Louisa. Abigail Yoder did nothing to influence Louisa's decision to disobey you. Indeed, she would have told your daughter that your wishes must come before her own."

"That young woman taught her to—"

"Abigail Yoder gave these children—including Louisa—a new appreciation for the scriptures. You would fault her for that?"

Jacob rubbed his bare hand over his beard as he considered Aaron's question. He was not a vindictive man. He was a father who had lost his wife and then had to face the possibility of losing his only child as well. "I am doing the best I can for Louisa," he argued.

"Then as you have forgiven her for her disobedience, let her see you forgive Abigail."

Aaron thought the man would refuse—would stalk off toward the house, collect Louisa, and leave. To his surprise, Jacob glanced toward the house. "She is there—the teacher?"

"Ja."

Jacob started across the yard, and Aaron followed him. When they reached the house, those standing in the doorway parted to allow them to pass. There in the center of the kitchen, they saw Abigail and Louisa hugging each other, as all around them the other women wiped away tears with the hems of their aprons. Aaron held his breath, prepared for an ugly scene. But instead of approaching Abigail, Jacob turned away from the kitchen and greeted Oscar Yoder, thanking him for including them in the day's festivities.

Abigail continued talking to Louisa and the women in the kitchen, but her eyes followed Jacob Koop. When Aaron saw her wipe her hands on her apron and excuse herself from the others, he moved to intercept her. "Leave it, Abigail," he said softly.

She smiled at him. "Do not be concerned, Aaron. I have to speak with Jacob Koop sometime." She placed her hand on his forearm. "It will be all right," she assured him as she stepped around him and approached Louisa's father, who was still talking with her uncle.

Aaron saw Oscar Yoder notice Abigail's approach and saw that he was as worried as Aaron.

"Excuse me, Uncle Oscar, but I need to speak with Jacob Koop—if he will allow me to do so. I want to apologize and assure him that I have seen the error of my ways."

The room went silent as word spread and others moved closer to listen.

"Louisa could have been taken sick or worse," Jacob grumbled, not quite looking at Abigail.

"I will not dispute that," Abigail replied. "I have prayed on the matter, and I believe that the answer to the situation is for me to resign my post with the school and return to my family in New York. I will stay until a substitute or replacement can be found, but after that. . ."

Throughout the crowded house, word spread of Abigail's resignation. Aaron heard Rebecca Janzen pleading with her parents to do something. "Please, Mama—Papa. Abigail Yoder is the best teacher we have ever had. We cannot let her leave just because—"

The Janzens bade the child to be quiet, and once again the room fell silent as everyone waited to see what Jacob Koop would say. "If that is your decision," he said with a shrug as if it did not matter to him one way or another. He turned away from her and joined some of the other men.

Immediately Abigail was surrounded by several of the women and all of the older children—including Louisa—all talking at once and insisting that she reconsider. But Abigail simply smiled and repeated her belief that this was all for the best.

"Do something, Aaron Miller," Rose Janzen hissed. He hadn't even realized she was standing next to him. "Make her understand that we need her to stay."

"Why would she listen to me?"

Rose rolled her eyes. "Maybe because she is in love with you. And I may be a bit past my prime, but I'm not too old to miss the fact that you are in love with her. Now do something."

He was about to protest that he and Abigail had known each other only a few weeks, but Rose had already headed back to the kitchen, where the women were busy setting out the dinner. Besides, she was right—at least about his feelings for Abigail. Apparently, love did not follow a timetable. All through the meal, he tried to think of what he could possibly do or say that would change Abigail's mind, and it was only as the afternoon shadows lengthened and the bishop lit a lantern that he found his answer.

◆　◆　◆

The minute the words were out of her mouth, Abigail felt relieved. She had not only made her plans known to Jacob Koop but to the entire community as well. She was touched by the protests of the children and some of the women, but her mind was made up. She joined the other women to help serve the dinner, which had to be done in shifts because so many people had come to the bishop's house for the feast. By the time everyone had eaten, the dishes had been cleared and washed, and the families had started for their respective homes, she was at peace with her decision. Oh, she would miss the children of course—and Aaron—but she had promised the older children that she would write to them and they could share her letters with the younger ones.

She and three of the women who lived in the village were wiping the last of the dishes when Aaron entered the kitchen and came straight to her. "Will you take a sleigh ride with me, Abigail Yoder?"

She was aware of the looks the other women exchanged. She was also aware that a man and woman did not go out together without others unless they had announced their intent to begin a courtship that would lead to marriage. She also knew that agreeing to take a sleigh ride with Aaron after dark would raise eyebrows and set tongues wagging. But oh, how she wanted this one last opportunity to be with him.

"I will, Aaron Miller," she replied and handed the dish towel she held to Rose Janzen, who was absolutely beaming at Aaron. She took down her coat from a hook, tied on her bonnet, and followed him out the back door. He walked toward the barn, where she saw a carriage on runners hitched to a team of horses, and she hesitated. But the moon was rising, and stars were shining in the clear sky. She knew she would remember this night forever.

He helped her climb into the carriage, covered her with a lap robe, and then got in and took the reins. As soon as they hit clear land, he snapped the reins and the horses took off. Abigail couldn't help it—she squealed with excitement and grabbed hold of his arm. He grinned at her, and taking the reins in one hand, he put his free arm around her and pulled her close.

After a while, he slowed the team to a stop on a hill that overlooked a frozen creek and his property.

"This is your farm?"

He nodded and then pointed out the various landmarks to her—the barn, the chicken coop, the fields he would plant that spring and those he would leave fallow to recover for the following season. "And there is the house," he said.

The dwelling was large—two stories that glowed white in the moonlight, the many windows reflecting the snow. "It is a good house, Aaron," she whispered.

"It needs something more," he said. He cupped her chin and turned her face to his. The brim of his hat shadowed his face and she could not see his expression, but she prayed that his face reflected her own feelings. "It needs a woman. . .and children. It needs you, Abigail. I need you," he whispered just before their lips met.

Abigail had kissed two boys in her life, but those kisses had been child's play compared to the kiss she now shared with Aaron. This was a kiss that had not been born of youthful curiosity. This was a kiss shared by two adults who had each come to a crossroads in their lives and found the other standing there—waiting.

"Say you will stay," he said.

She laughed. "And why would I do that, Aaron Miller?"

"Because I am not only asking you to stay for the sake of the children—I am asking you to be my wife."

She started to protest that they barely knew one another, yet she felt she had known this man her whole life. "I will stay," she said softly, "for you."

"And the children."

"No, Aaron, I have given my word, and while some of the parents and towns-people have shown me friendship and welcome, that does not extend to everyone."

"You are wrong," he said, pulling away from her and taking up the reins once more. "And I will prove it."

Once again he set the horses dashing across the snow-covered fields back toward the village. When the first houses came into view, he slowed the sleigh and once again wrapped his arm around her. "Look, Abigail," he said softly, pointing to a row of small cottages. In every house a candle glowed. "And there," he whispered, turning so that they were passing the church and the school, where a candle glowed in every window. "Abigail's Christmas candles," he said as he pulled the sleigh to a stop in front of the school. "You wanted them to guide the Christ child, but tonight they shine for you. Welcome home, Abigail."

Her heart was full as Aaron helped her down and walked with her into the schoolhouse. There, her aunt and uncle, half the village, and all the children waited. "Surprise!" the children shouted and then ran to her, hugging her and pleading with her to change her mind about leaving.

"All right," she finally agreed, laughing. "I will stay." And then she saw Louisa

Koop. "Louisa, should you be here? Your father—"

"The bishop has convinced him that if we are to find a replacement for you, I am the most likely candidate. When he heard that the position pays a salary, he agreed. I'm to board with your aunt and uncle while you train me. He wasn't happy about that, but—"

"He'll come around," Aunt Beulah assured the girl, shooing her back to where the other children were enjoying the last of the Pfeffernüsse cookies and cups of hot cocoa. "Well?" she demanded, looking from Abigail to Aaron and back again. "We did our part, Aaron Miller, have you done yours?"

Abigail felt a blush creep up her neck. "Auntie!"

Instead of answering Beulah, Aaron clapped his hands to gain the attention of all those assembled. "I have an announcement," he shouted. The room went still. "Abigail Yoder has agreed to stay on as our teacher." The room exploded with cheers, but Aaron was not finished. Once again he called for quiet and then turned and faced Abigail, taking her hands in his. "I am doubly blessed, for Abigail Yoder has not only agreed to stay on as teacher, but she has also agreed to become my wife," he said in a voice that broke with emotion.

Without taking her eyes from Aaron's beloved face, Abigail said, "After we found Louisa, I sat for hours in prayer and meditation. I was seeking answers, and I thought the only possible solution was to leave. But now I understand that God's answer for me was not in the mistakes of the past but in the promise of the future."

"Kiss her, Aaron Miller," Josef Hamm shouted from his position near the front of the gathering. Others took up the chant.

And as Aaron bent his head to hers and she wrapped her arms around his neck, the last thing she saw before closing her eyes to receive that kiss was the glow of candlelight.

Christmas Brown Jam Cookies
GLUTEN-FREE COOKIES

¾ cup maple syrup
½ cup sugar
¼ cup sour cream
¼ cup lard (Tenderflake)
½ teaspoon vanilla
2 teaspoons cocoa powder
½ teaspoon baking soda
½ teaspoon ground star aniseed (a must ingredient)
1 cup rice flour
½ cup white bean flour
½ cup tapioca starch
¼ cup coconut flour
1 rounded teaspoon xanthan gum

Beat syrup, sugar, sour cream, lard, and vanilla until well blended. Add the well-mixed-together dry ingredients. Mix well, then add more rice flour with your hands a little at a time until you have a soft, nonsticky dough. Cover and let stand in refrigerator for a few hours or overnight.

Roll out on surface sprinkled with sweet rice flour as needed to keep dough from sticking. I found rolling out the dough in smaller amounts easier to handle. Cut with round cookie cutter and drop your favorite jam on each round. Traditionally, half the cookies were made with yellow jam (apricot or gooseberry) and the other half with red (plum), and when they were served, you never knew which color you would get. Fold the circles in half and pinch the edges firmly together. Place on baking sheets and bake at 375 degrees for about 15 minutes or until edges turn brown. These cookies are hard when they cool, then they are stored in a sealed container and by the next day are soft and delicious. The cookies may be either left plain or frosted with the following frosting.

FROSTING
Boil 1 cup sugar and 4 tablespoons water until string stage (takes a few minutes). Then pour syrup over one stiffly beaten egg white, continuing to beat until stiff and smooth. The Mennonite women would then put the cookies in a large bowl and pour the frosting over top, using their hands to coat them. I find it easier to put a rack over waxed paper, put the cookies on the rack, and pour the frosting over them. Let the frosting dry before you put the cookies in containers.

Anna Schmidt is the author of over twenty works of fiction. Among her many honors, Anna is the recipient of *Romantic Times'* Reviewer's Choice Award and a finalist for the RITA award for romantic fiction. She enjoys gardening and collecting seashells at her winter home in Florida.

JOIN US ONLINE!

Christian Fiction for Women

Christian Fiction for Women is your online home for the latest in Christian fiction.

Check us out online for:

- Giveaways
- Recipes
- Info about Upcoming Releases
- Book Trailers
- News and More!

Find Christian Fiction for Women at Your Favorite Social Media Site:

 Search "Christian Fiction for Women"

 @fictionforwomen